Praise for Robert Ludlum and
The Scorpio Illusion

"VINTAGE LUDLUM at his devious best . . . THE QUINTESSENTIAL THRILLER . . . *The Scorpio Illusion* promises to be one of the hits of summer and a must for beach reading!"
—*News–Free Press*, Chattanooga

"*The Scorpio Illusion* proves o⬛⬛⬛ that ROBERT LUDLUM IS THE MA⬛⬛⬛IPPING, FAST-MOVING INTRIGU⬛⬛⬛ed at weaving a tapestry of stu⬛⬛⬛s, then assembling them in ⬛⬛⬛ping the reader's attention ne⬛⬛⬛W BOOKS PROCLAIMED T⬛⬛⬛IPPERS REALLY ARE. TH⬛⬛⬛ *Daily Oklahoman*

"FULL OF SUSP⬛⬛⬛IGUE AND SURPRISES."
—*Des Moines Sunday Register*

"Gripping, unpretentious excitement . . . THE SCORPIO ILLUSION MEASURES UP TO EVERY EXPECTATION . . . firmly entrenches Robert Ludlum as the master of large-scale intrigue and will stimulate his diehard readers to obtain a passport for any future adventure."
—*Richmond Times-Dispatch*

"PAGE-TURNING ACTION."
—*Abilene Reporter–News*

"THE OBI-WAN KENOBI OF SPY NOVELISTS."
—*USA Weekend*

ALSO BY ROBERT LUDLUM

The Road to Omaha
The Bourne Ultimatum
The Icarus Agenda
The Bourne Supremacy
The Aquitaine Progression
The Parsifal Mosaic
The Bourne Identity
The Matarese Circle
The Gemini Contenders
The Holcroft Covenant
The Chancellor Manuscript
The Road to Gandolfo
The Rhinemann Exchange
Trevayne
The Matlock Paper
The Osterman Weekend
The Scarlatti Inheritance

THE
SCORPIO
ILLUSION

ROBERT LUDLUM

BANTAM BOOKS

New York   Toronto   London   Sydney   Auckland

THE SCORPIO ILLUSION

A Bantam Book
Hardcover edition/June 1993
International edition/September 1993
Bantam paperback edition/June 1994

ISBN: 0-553-56603-2 (Bantam)
ISBN: 0-553-56838-8 (Canada)

Published simultaneously in the United States and Canada

Bantam Books are published by Bantam Books, a division of
Bantam Doubleday Dell Publishing Group, Inc. Its trademark,
consisting of the words "Bantam Books" and the portrayal of a
rooster, is Registered in U.S. Patent and Trademark Office and in
other countries. Marca Registrada. Bantam Books, 1540
Broadway, New York, New York 10036.

PRINTED IN THE UNITED STATES OF AMERICA

OPM   0 9 8 7 6 5 4 3 2

For Jeffrey, Shannon, and James
Ever a joy!

— PROLOGUE —

Ashkelon, Israel, 2:47 a.m.

The night rain came down like sheets of silver knives, the dark sky filled with darker masses of swirling black clouds, the swells of the sea and the whipping winds murderous for the two rubber rafts lashed to each other as they approached the shoreline.

The raiding party was drenched, their blackened faces streaked with anxious sweat and rain, their eyes blinking continuously, straining to catch glimpses of the beach. The unit consisted of eight Palestinian men from the Baaka Valley, and one woman, not of their birthright, but committed to their cause, for it was an integral part of her own, inseparable from the commitment she had made years before. *Muerte a toda autoridad!* She was the wife of the raiding party's leader.

"Only minutes now!" cried the large man as he knelt beside the woman. Like the others, his weapons were tightly strapped to his dark clothes; a black waterproof knapsack high on his back contained explosives. "Remember, when we get off, throw the anchor over between the boats, that's important."

"I understand, my husband, but I'd feel better going with you—"

"And leave us no means of getting away to fight again?" he asked. "The electrical power grids are less than three kilometers from the coast; they feed Tel Aviv, and once we blow them up, there'll be chaos. We'll steal

1

a vehicle and be back within the hour, but our equipment must be here!"

"I understand."

"Do you, my wife? Can you imagine what it will be like? Most, if not all, of Tel Aviv in darkness! And Ashkelon itself, of course. It's perfect . . . and you, my love, you were the one who found the vulnerability, the perfect target!"

"I merely suggested it." Her hand caressed his cheek. "Just come back to me, my love, for you *are* my love."

"There's no doubt of it, my Amaya of the fires. . . . We're close enough. . . . *Now!*" The leader of the raiding party signaled his men on both rafts. All slipped over the sides into the heavy surf, their weapons held high, their bodies assaulted by the crashing waves as they lurched through the soft sand to the beach. On shore, the leader pressed his flashlight once, a single, short illumination that meant the entire unit was on enemy ground, prepared to penetrate and do its work. The wife threw the heavy anchor over the side between the two lashed rubber boats, keeping them in concert in the waves. She pulled her hand-held radio to ear and mouth; it would be used only in an emergency, as the Jews were too smart not to have the coastal frequencies monitored.

Then, suddenly, with terrible finality, all dreams of glory exploded with the savage bursts of gunfire on the flanks of the raiding party. It was a massacre, soldiers racing down in the sand, firing their weapons into the pulsating bodies of the Ashkelon Brigade, blowing heads apart, showing no mercy for the invading enemies. *No prisoners! Only death!*

The woman-wife in the outlying raft moved swiftly despite her torment, despite the shock that paralyzed her mind, her rapid movements failing to lessen the agony that swept through her, merely blurring it with action born of survival. She plunged her long-bladed knife into the sides and bottoms of both PVC boats, grabbed her waterproof pouch containing weapons and forged documents, and slipped over the side into the heavy sea. Fighting the surf and the undertow with all her considerable strength, she made her way south along the shore about fifty meters, where she swam diagonally over the waves into the beach. Prone in the shallow water, the harsh rain nearly blinding her, she crawled back to the killing ground. Then she heard the shouts of Israeli soldiers yelling in Hebrew; every muscle and fiber in her body froze in ice-hot fury.

"We should have taken prisoners."

"Why, to kill our children later, as they slaughtered my two sons in the school bus?"

"We'll be criticized—they're all dead."

"So are my mother and father. The bastards gunned them down in a vineyard, two old people among the grapes."

"Let them rot in hell! The Hezbollah tortured my brother to death!"

"Take out their weapons and fire off rounds . . . graze our arms and our legs!"

"Jacob's right! They fought back; we might all have been killed!"

"Then one of us should run back to the compound for reenforcements!"

"Where are their boats?"

"They're gone now, nowhere to be seen! There were probably dozens! That's the reason we killed the ones we saw!"

"Hurry, Jacob! We can't give the goddamn liberal press any ammunition!"

"Wait! This one's still alive!"

"Let him die. Remove their weapons and commence firing."

The staccato fusillade filled the night and the rain. Then the soldiers threw the raiding party's guns down beside the corpses and raced back up into the sand dunes filled with wild sea grass. In moments there were erratic flashes of cupped matches and cigarette lighters; the savage massacre was over, the cover-up begun.

Still, the woman moved cautiously forward on her stomach in the shallow water, the ringing echoes of the gunfire fueling the loathing that filled her—loathing and great loss. They had slaughtered the one man on earth she could love, the only man she could commit to as an equal, for none other had her strengths, her determination. He was gone, and there would never be another like him, a godlike firebrand with fierce eyes, whose voice could move crowds to both tears and laughter. And she was always there beside him, guiding him, adoring him. Their world of violence would never see a team like the two of them again.

She heard a moan, a quiet cry that pierced the rain and the surf. A body was rolling down the slope of sand to the water's edge—only feet ahead of her. She crawled rapidly to the figure and grabbed him; his head was facedown in the sand. She turned him over, the rain washing over the blood-soaked features. It was her husband, a large part of his throat and skull a mass of scarlet-red tissue. She held him fiercely; he opened his eyes once, then closed them for the final time.

The wife looked up at the sand dunes and the cupped flares of matches and the glows of lighted cigarettes through the rain. With money and her false papers, she would cut a path through the despised Israel, leaving death in her wake. She would return to the Baaka Valley and reach the High Councils. She knew exactly what she was going to do.

Muerte a toda autoridad!

BAAKA VALLEY, LEBANON, 12:17 P.M.

The scorching noonday sun caked the dirt roads of the refugee camp, an enclave of a displaced people, many beaten into submission by events they could neither fathom nor control. Their gaits were slow, trudging, their faces set, and in their dark, downcast eyes a hollowness that bespoke the pain of fading memories, of images that would never be real again. Others, however, were defiant, submission to be reviled, acceptance of the status quo unthinkable, something to be scorned. These were the *muquateen,* the soldiers of Allah, the avengers of God. They walked rapidly, with purpose, their ever-present weapons strapped to their shoulders, their heads moving sharply, constantly aware, their eyes focused and filled with hatred.

It was four days since the massacre at Ashkelon. The woman clad in a green khaki uniform, its sleeves rolled up, walked out of her modest three-room structure; "house" would be misleading. Its door was covered with black cloth, the universal sign of death; passersby stared at it and raised their eyes to the sky, mumbling prayers for the departed; every now and then a wail emerged, asking Allah to avenge the dreadful death. For this was the home of the Ashkelon Brigade's leader, and the woman striding down the dirt road had been his wife. But more than a woman, more than a wife, she was among the great *muquateen* in this convoluted valley of submission and rebellion, she and her husband symbols of hope for a cause all but lost.

As she strode down the caked street past an open market, the crowd dispersed for her, many touching her gently, worshipfully, uttering continuous prayers, until all, as one, began chanting *"Baj, Baj, Baj . . . Baj!"*

The woman acknowledged no one, instead pressing forward to a wooden, barracklike meeting hall at the end of the road. Inside, waiting for her, were the leaders of the Baaka Valley's High Councils. She walked inside; a guard closed the door and she faced nine men seated behind a long table. The greetings were brief, solemn condolences offered. The chairman of the committee, an elderly Arab, spoke from the central chair.

"Your communication reached us. To say that it was astonishing would be a grave understatement."

"Grave, in a word, says it," said a middle-aged man dressed in one of the many uniforms of the *muquateen*. "For that's what you'll be buying, I hope you know that."

"If that's so, I'll join my husband quicker, won't I?"

"I wasn't aware that you subscribed to our beliefs," said another.

"Whether I do or not is irrelevant. I ask only that you support me financially. I believe that over the years I've earned that support."

"Unquestionably," agreed yet another. "You've been a remarkable force, and with your husband, may he rest with Allah in His gardens, even extraordinary. Yet, I see a difficulty—"

"I, and those few I choose to go with me, will be acting alone, solely in revenge for Ashkelon. We will be a provisional wing accountable to no one but ourselves. Does that answer your 'difficulty'?"

"If you can do it," replied another leader.

"I've already proved that I can. Do I have to refer you to the records?"

"No, it's not necessary," said the chairman. "On numerous occasions you've sent our enemies searching in such outrageous directions that several brother governments were penalized for acts they knew nothing about."

"If it's necessary, I shall continue that practice. We—you—have enemies and traitors everywhere, even among your '*brother* governments.' Authority everywhere corrupts itself."

"You don't trust anyone, do you?" asked the middle-aged Arab.

"I resent that statement. I married one of you for life. I gave you his life."

"I apologize."

"You should. My answer, please?"

"You shall have whatever you need," said the chairman of the committee. "Coordinate with Bahrain, as you have done in the past."

"Thank you."

"Finally, when you reach the United States, you will operate through another network. They will watch you, test you, and when they are convinced that you are truly a stealth weapon of your own making and no threat to them, they will reach you and you will become one of them."

"Who are they?"

"They are known in the deepest channels of secrecy as the Scorpions—*Scorpios*, to be precise."

S undown. The distressed sloop, its mainmast shattered by lightning, its sails ripped by the winds of
the open sea, drifted into the small, quiet beach of
a private island in the Lesser Antilles. During the past
three days, before the dead calm descended, this section
of the Caribbean had suffered not only a hurricane with
the force of the infamous Hugo, but sixteen hours later
a tropical storm whose bolts of lightning and earth-
shaking thunder had set fire to a thousand palms and
caused a hundred thousand residents of the island chain
to look to their gods for deliverance.

The Great House on this island, however, had survived both catastrophes. It was made of iron-bolted
stone and steel and built into the huge rising hill on the
north side, impenetrable, indestructible, a fortress. That
the nearly destroyed sloop had managed to survive and
find its way into the sweeping rock-hewn cove and the
small beach was a miracle, but it was an ominous miracle, not of her God's making, that caused the tall black
maid in a white uniform to rush down the stone steps
to the water's edge and fire four shots into the air from
the gun in her hand.

"*Ganja!*" she yelled. "No lousy *ganja* here! You go
'way!"

The lone figure, kneeling on the deck of the boat, was
a woman in her mid-thirties. Her features were sharp,
her long hair stringy and unkempt, her shorts and halter
abused by the weather she had endured . . . and her eyes
were enigmatically cold as she rested her powerful rifle

on the gunwale and peered through the telescopic sight; she squeezed the trigger. The loud report shattered the stillness of the island cove, echoing off the rocks and the hill beyond. Instantly, the uniformed maid fell facedown into the gently lapping waves.

"There's shooting, *gunshots*!" A shirtless, strapping young man, well over six feet in height and seventeen years of age, burst out of the cabin below. He was well-muscled and handsome, with cleanly chiseled, even classic Roman features. "What's happening? What have you done?"

"No more than had to be done," said the woman calmly. "Please get to the bow and jump over when you see the sand; it's still light enough. Then pull us into shore."

He did not move to obey, but stared at the slain white-uniformed figure on the beach, rubbing his hands nervously over his cutoff jeans. "My God, she's just a servant!" he cried, his English accented with his native Italian. "You are a monster!"

"It is ever so, my child. Am I not in bed? And was I not when I killed those three men who bound your hands, whipped a rope around your neck, and were about to throw you off the pier, hanging you for murdering the dock *suprèmo*?"

"I didn't kill him. I've told you that over and over again!"

"They thought you did and that was enough."

"I wanted to go to the police. You wouldn't let me!"

"Foolish child. Do you think you would ever have reached a courtroom? Never. You would have been shot in the streets, a piece of garbage blown away, for the *suprèmo* benefited the dockworkers with his thefts and corruption."

"I had angry words with him, nothing more! I went away and drank wine."

"Oh, you certainly did, a great deal of wine by yourself. When they found you in the alley, you were incoherent until you realized that a rope was around your throat, your feet at the edge of the pier. . . . And for how many weeks did I hide you, racing from one place to another while the scum of the waterfronts were hunting you, sworn to kill you on sight?"

"I never understood why you were so good to me."

"I had my reasons . . . I still have them."

"As God is my witness, Cabi," the young man said, still staring at the white-uniformed corpse on the beach. "I owe you my life, but I never . . . never expected anything like this!"

"Would you rather return to Italy, to Portici and your family, and face certain death?"

"No, no, of course not, Signora Cabrini."

"Then welcome to our world, my darling toy," said the woman, smiling. "And believe me, you'll want whatever I care to give you. You're so perfect; I cannot tell you how perfect you are. . . . Over the side, my adorable Nico. . . . *Now!*"

The young man did as he was told.

DEUXIÈME BUREAU, PARIS

"It is she," said the man behind the desk in the darkened office. On the right wall was projected a detailed map of the Caribbean, specifically of the Lesser Antilles, a flickering blue dot centered on the island of Saba. "We can presume she sailed through the Anegada Passage between Dog Island and Virgin Gorda—that's the only way she could survive the weather. If she survived."

"Perhaps she didn't," said an aide, sitting in front of the desk and staring at the map. "It would certainly make our lives easier."

"Of course it would." The head of the Deuxième lit a cigarette. "But for a she-wolf who has lived through the worst of Beirut and the Baaka Valley, I want irrefutable proof before I call off the hunt."

"I know those waters," said a second man, who stood to the left of the desk. "I was posted to Martinique during the Soviet-Cuban threat, and I can tell you the winds can be vicious. From what I understand of the battering those seas took, my guess is that she did not survive, not with what she was sailing."

"My assumption is that she did." The Deuxième chief spoke sharply. "I cannot afford to guess. I know those waters only by the maps, but I see scores of natural recesses and small harbors she could have gone into. I've studied them."

"Not so, Henri. In those islands the storms blow first one minute clockwise, the next counterclockwise. If such inlets existed, they'd be marked, inhabited. I *know* them; studying them on a map is merely a distant exercise, not seeking them out, looking for Soviet submarines. I tell you, she did not survive."

"I hope you're right, Ardisonne. This world cannot afford Amaya Bajaratt."

CENTRAL INTELLIGENCE AGENCY, LANGLEY, VIRGINIA

In the white-walled subcellar communications complex of the CIA, a single locked room was reserved for a unit of twelve analysts, nine men and three women, who worked in shifts of four around the clock. They were multilingual specialists in international radio traffic, including two of the Agency's most experienced cryptographers, and all were ordered not to discuss their activities with anyone, spouses no exception.

A fortyish man in shirt-sleeves wheeled back his cushioned swivel chair and glanced at his colleagues on the midnight shift, a woman and two other men; it was nearing four o'clock in the morning, half their tour over. "I may have something," he said to no one specifically.

"What?" asked the woman. "It's a dull night as far as I'm concerned."

"Break it up for us, Ron," the man nearest the speaker said. "Radio Baghdad is lulling me to sleep with its bilge."

"Try Bahrain, not Baghdad," said Ron, picking up a printout discharged from his word processor into a wire basket.

"What's with the rich folks?" The third man looked up from his electronic console.

"That's just it, rich. Our source in Manamah passed the word that a half a million, U.S., had been transferred to a coded account in Zurich destined for—"

"Half a million?" interrupted the second man. "In their league that's chickenshit!"

"I haven't told you its destination or the method of transfer. The Bank of Abu Dhabi to Zurich's Crédit Suisse—"

"That's the Baaka Valley routing." The woman spoke with instant recognition. "Destination?"

"The Caribbean, the precise location unknown."

"*Find* it!"

"At the moment, that's impossible."

"Why?" asked the third man. "Because it can't be confirmed?"

"It's confirmed all right, the worst way possible. Our source was killed an hour after he made contact with our embassy point man, a protocol officer who's being pulled out posthaste."

"The Baaka," said the woman quietly. "The Caribbean. *Bajaratt*."

"I'll secure-fax this up to O'Ryan. We need his brains."

"If it's half a million today," said the third man, "it could be five tomorrow, once the D-route proves out."

"I knew our source in Bahrain." The woman spoke sadly. "He was a good guy with a lovely wife and kids—goddamn it. *Bajaratt!*"

MI-6, LONDON

"Our field man in Dominica flew north and confirms the information the French sent us." The chairman of Britain's foreign service intelligence approached a square table in the center of the conference room. Covering the surface was a large, thick volume, one of hundreds in the bookshelves, that held detailed cloth maps of specific areas of the world. The gold lettering across the black cover of the volume on the table read: *The Caribbean—Windward and Leeward Islands. The Antilles. British and U.S. Virgin Territories.* "Index someplace called the Anegada Passage, would you please?" he asked his associate.

"Of course." The other man in the strategy room moved quickly as he noticed the frustration of his superior; it was not due to the situation but instead to his rigid right hand that would not obey his commands. The associate flipped the heavy cloth pages to the map in question. "Here it is. . . . Good God, no one could have traveled so far in those storms, not with a craft that size."

"Perhaps she didn't make it."

"Make what?"

"Wherever she was going."

"From Basse-Terre to the Anegada during *those* three days? I'd think not. She'd have to have been in open water more than half the time to reach it so quickly."

"That's why I asked you here. You know the area quite well, don't you? You were posted there."

"If there's such a thing as an expert, I suspect I qualify. I was the Sixer control for nine years, based on Tortola, and flew all over the damned place—rather a pleasant life, actually. I still stay in touch with old friends; they all thought I was a fairly well situated runaway with a penchant for flying my plane from island to island."

"Yes, I've read your file. You did outstanding work."

"The cold war was on my side and I was fourteen years younger—and I wasn't a young man then. I wouldn't get behind the controls of a dual engine over those waters now on a heavy bet."

"Yes, I understand," said the chairman, bending over the map. "So it's your expert opinion that she couldn't have survived."

"*Couldn't* is an absolute. Let's say it's highly unlikely, damn near impossible."

"That's what your counterpart at the Deuxième thinks."

"Ardisonne?"

"You know him?"

"Code name Richelieu. Yes, of course. Good man, if rather opinionated. Operated out of Martinique."

"He's adamant. He's convinced she went down at sea."

"In this case, his opinion is probably justified. But, if I may, since you've asked me up here for whatever I can offer, might I ask a question or two?"

"Go ahead, Officer Cooke."

"This Bajaratt woman is obviously somewhat of a legend in the Baaka Valley, but I've been poring over those lists for the past several years and I don't recall ever having seen the name. Why is that?"

"Because it's not her own, not the Bajaratt part," interrupted the head of MI-6. "It's the name she gave herself years ago, the name she thinks preserves her secrets, since she believes no one has any idea where it came from or who she really is. On the assumption that we might be infiltrated, and in the projection that she could be on to larger things, we've kept that information in our black files."

"Oh, yes, yes, I see. If you know a false name and its origins, meaning the real one, you can trace a background, build a personality, even a pattern of predictability. But who exactly is she, what is she?"

"One of the most accomplished terrorists alive."

"Arab?"

"No."

"Israeli?"

"No, and I wouldn't broach that speculation too broadly."

"Nonsense. The Mossad has a broad spectrum of activities. . . . But, if you will, please answer my question. Remember, I've spent most of my service on the other side of the world. Just why is this woman such a priority-red?"

"She's for sale."

"She's what . . . ?"

"She goes wherever there's unrest, rebellion, insurgency, and sells her talents to the highest bidder—with remarkable results, I might add."

"Forgive me, but that sounds balmy. A lone woman walks into caldrons of revolt and sells *advice*? What does she do, take out advertisements in the newspapers?"

"She doesn't have to, Geoff," replied the chairman of MI-6, returning to the conference table and sitting down somewhat awkwardly as he adjusted the chair with his left hand. "She's a scholar where destabilization's concerned. She knows the strengths and weaknesses of all the warring factions, as well as the leaders and how to reach them. She has no lasting allegiances, moral or political. Her profession is death. It's as simple as that."

"I don't think that's simple at all."

"The result is, not the beginning, of course, not where she came from. . . . Sit down, Geoffrey, and let me tell you a brief story as we've pieced it together." The chairman opened a large manila envelope in front of him and removed three photographs, enlargements of rapidly taken candid shots of a woman in motion. The face in each, however, was clearly in focus, the sunlight bright. "This is Amaya Bajaratt."

"They're three different people!" exclaimed Geoffrey Cooke.

"Which one is she?" posed the chairman. "Or is she all three?"

"I see what you mean . . ." said the foreign service officer hesitantly. "The hair is different in each—blond, black, and, I assume, light brown; short, long, and midlength—but the features are different . . . yet not markedly so. Still, they *are* different."

"Flesh toned plastic? Wax? Control of facial muscles? None is difficult."

"Spectrographs would tell you, I should think. At least with respect to the additives, the plastics, and the wax."

"They should, but they don't. Our experts say that there are chemical compounds that can fool photoelectric scans, or even a refraction of bright light that can do the same—which means, of course, they don't know and won't risk a judgment call."

"All right," said Cooke. "She's presumably one or all three of these women, but how the devil can you be sure?"

"Reliability, I suppose."

"Reliability?"

"We and the French paid a great deal of money for these photographs, each from covert assets we've used for years. None of them cares to cut off a valuable financial source by providing us with a fake. Each believes he's captured Bajaratt on film."

"But where was she going? From Basse-Terre to the Anegada, if it is the Anegada, is well over two hundred kilometers—during a couple of raging storms. And why the Anegada Passage?"

"Because the sloop was spotted off the coast of Marigot—it couldn't make it into the shore for the rocks, and the small harbor was being whipped to smithereens."

"Spotted by whom?"

"Fishermen who service the hotels on Anguilla. The sighting was also confirmed by our man in Dominica." Noting Cooke's bewilderment, the chairman continued. "Our man flew to Basse-Terre, following our lead from Paris, and ascertained that a woman of the approximate age of the Bajaratt in these pictures chartered a boat with a tall, muscular young man. A very young man. That corresponded to Paris's information that a female of her general age and description—presumably using a false passport—flew out of Marseilles in the company of such a youngster to the island of Guadeloupe, two islands, actually, as you well know, Grande- and Basse-Terre."

"How did Marseilles customs make the connection between the boy and the woman?"

"He couldn't speak French; she said he was a distant relative from Latvia placed in her charge after his parents died."

"Damned improbable."

"But perfectly acceptable to our friends across the Channel. They disregard anything north of the Rhône."

"Why would she travel with a teenager?"

"You tell me. I haven't the vaguest idea."

"And to repeat, where was she going?"

"A larger conundrum. She's obviously an experienced sailor. She'd know enough to get into shore before it struck, especially since the sloop had a radio, and alerts were being broadcast all over the area in four languages."

"Unless she had a rendevous that had to be met on time."

"Naturally, it's the only plausible answer, but at the all too conceivable loss of her life?"

"Again, improbable," agreed the former MI-6 control. "Unless there were circumstances we know nothing about. . . . Go on; you've obviously built something."

"Something, not a great deal, I'm afraid. On the prem-isc that a terrorist is rarely born a terrorist but becomes one through events, and on the strength of reports that although multilingual, she was heard speaking a language that was damn near impossible to understand—"

"For most Europeans that language would be Basque," interrupted Cooke quietly.

"Precisely. We sent a deep-cover unit into the provinces of Vizcaya and Alva to see what they could dig up. They traced down the story of a particularly nasty incident that took place a number of years ago at a small rebel village in the western Pyrenees. The sort of thing that's memorialized in mountain legends, passed down through generations."

"Something like My Lai or the Babi Yar?" asked Cooke. "Wholesale slaughter?"

"Worse, if possible. In a raid against the rebels, the entire adult population of the village was executed by an unsanctioned rogue unit—*adult* being twelve years and older. The younger children were forced to watch and left to die in the mountains."

"This Bajaratt is one of those children?"

"Let me try to explain. The Basques living in those mountains are very isolated. Their custom is to bury their records among the northernmost cypress trees in their territory, and attached to our unit was an anthropologist, an expert in the mountain people of the Pyrenees who could speak and read the language; he found those records. The last few pages were written by a young female child who described the horror, which included the beheading of her parents in front of her eyes by bayonets, sharpened as her father and mother watched their executioners honing their blades against the rocks."

"How horrible! And that child is this woman Bajaratt?"

"She signed her name *Amaya el Baj . . . Yovamanaree,* which is the closest thing in Basque to the Spanish *'jovena mujer,'* young woman. There followed a single phrase in perfect Spanish. *'Muerte a toda autoridad'*—"

" 'Death to all authority,' " Cooke translated. "Is that it?"

"No, two things more. She added a final note, and, mind you, a child of ten wrote it. *'Shirharrá Baj.'* "

"What the hell is that?"

"Roughly, a young woman soon to be ready for conception but who will never bring a child into this world."

"Certainly macabre, yet quite understandable, I suppose."

"The mountain legends talk of a child-woman who led the other village children out of the hills, avoiding scores of patrols, who even killed soldiers with their own bayonets by luring them into traps all by herself."

"A girl of ten . . . it's incredible!" Geoffrey Cooke frowned. "You said there were two things more. What's the other?"

"The last piece of evidence that for us confirmed her identity. Among the buried records were family histories—certain more isolated branches of the Basques live in fear of inbreeding, which is why so many young men and women are sent away. At any rate, there was the family 'Aquirre, first child a female baptized Amaya,' a common name. The surname Aquirre was scratched out—furiously scratched out as if by an angry child, the name Bajaratt replacing it."

"Good heavens, why? Or did you ever find out?"

"We did, and it was a nasty business. Without going into the messier parts, our lads leaned hard on our counterparts in Madrid, going so far as to threaten them with our total withdrawal where they needed us most unless they opened certain sealed records pertaining to the Basque raids. You used the word macabre; you don't know how apt that is. We found the name Bajaratt, a sergeant—mother Spanish, father border French, accounting for the name—who had been part of the outrageous, buried assault on that mountain village. In short

words, he was the soldier who cut off the head of Amaya
Aquirre's mother. She took that name for all it repre-
sented to her in horror, certainly not in honor, but for
a dedicated purpose—she would never forget for a moment as long as she lived. She would become a killer as
loathsome as the man she watched pulling the bayonet
through her mother's neck.''

"It's warped in the extreme," said Cooke, barely audible, "but so very understandable. A child assumes the
mantle of a monster, fantasizing vengeance through
identification. It's not unlike the Stockholm syndrome,
when prisoners of war in brutal circumstances identify
with their captors. How much more so with a child. . . .
So Amaya Aquirre is Amaya Bajaratt. Yet, although
denying her true surname, she never spelled out the Bajaratt.''

"We brought in a psychiatrist who specializes in children's disorders,'' added the chairman of MI-6. "He
told us that a young female of ten is somewhat more
advanced than her male counterpart—and since I have
numerous grandchildren, I must reluctantly agree. He
said that a girl of that age who'd gone through such
ultimate stress and pain would have a tendency to reveal
only part of herself, not all.''

"I'm not sure I follow you.''

"He put it this way, the testosterone syndrome, he
called it. A male child in like circumstances might easily
write 'Death to all authority' and sign his full name, a
mark of vengeance for everyone to see, whereas the
young female will behave differently, withholding complete information, for she must think ahead to the real
vengeance. She must outsmart, not out-muscle her enemies. . . . Still, she can't help but put part of herself into
the ledger.''

"I suppose that makes sense," said Cooke, nodding.
"But good God—records buried in the ground, cypress
trees and backwoods rites of passage through blood-
shed . . . mass executions, beheadings with bayonets,

and a child of ten living through it all! *Christ*, you're dealing with a totally committed psychopath! She wants only to see heads severed from their bodies and plummeting to the ground, as happened to her parents."

"*Muerte a toda autoridad*," said the chief of MI-6. "The heads of authority—everywhere."

"Yes, I understood the phrase—"

"I'm afraid you can't possibly understand the gravity of its relevance."

"I beg your pardon?"

"For the past several years Bajaratt has lived in the Baaka Valley with the leader of a particularly violent Palestinian faction whose cause she fanatically identified with. Apparently she and her lover were married sometime last spring in one of those under-the-fruit-tree ceremonies. He was killed nine weeks ago in a raid on the beaches of Ashkelon, south of Tel Aviv."

"Oh, yes, I remember reading about that," said Cooke. "Killed to a man, no prisoners."

"Do you remember the statement issued worldwide by the remaining members of the faction, namely its new leader?"

"Something about weapons, I believe."

"Exactly. The statement read in part that the Israeli weapons that killed the 'avenging freedom fighters' were manufactured in America, England, and France, and that the people whose lands were stolen from them would never forget or forgive the beasts who provided those weapons."

"We hear that rot all the time. So what?"

"So Amaya Bajaratt, adding the nom de guerre The Unforgiving, passed a message to the High Councils in the Baaka Valley; your friends or ex-friends in the Mossad picked it up, thank God. She and her comrades have dedicated their lives to taking the 'heads of the four great beasts.' She herself will be the 'lightning rod that sends out the signal.' "

"What signal?"

"As near as the Mossad can determine, it will be the sign for her hidden killers in London, Paris, and Jerusalem to strike. The Israelis believe it's implicit in the part of the message that says 'As the vilest of these beasts falls across the great sea, so must the others follow quickly.' "

"The vilest . . . ? Across . . . ? Good Lord, America?"

"Yes, Officer Cooke, Amaya Bajaratt is on her way to assassinate the President of the United States. That's her signal."

"That's preposterous!"

"Her record suggests that it may not be. Professionally, she's rarely if ever failed. She's a pathological genius, and these are her final kills, her revenge against all 'brutal' authority, but now with the added dimension of a deeply personal motive—the death of her husband. She must be stopped, Geoffrey. Which is why the Foreign Office, with this organization's full compliance, has decided that you should immediately return to your former post in the Caribbean. In your own words, there's no one with more expertise."

"My God, you're talking to a sixty-four-year-old man who's about to retire!"

"You still have contacts throughout the islands. Where they've been altered, we'll provide an entrée. Frankly, we believe you can make swifter headway than anyone else we know. We've got to find her and take her out."

"Has it occurred to you, old boy, that even if I left today, by the time I got there she could have skipped to heaven knows where? Forgive me, but the word *balmy* comes back to me."

"As to her 'skipping,' " said the chairman, briefly smiling, "neither the French nor we believe she'll be going anywhere for a number of days, perhaps a week, even two."

"Your crystal balls tell you that?"

"No, our collective common sense. The enormity of

her task, as she sees it, will require a fair degree of planning, involving human, financial, and technical resources, including aircraft. She may be a psychopath, but she's no fool; she won't attempt to mount her quest on the U.S. mainland."

"So where better than beyond the immediate scrutiny of the federal authorities," said Cooke grudgingly. "Yet near enough to have access to the offshore banks and onshore personnel."

"That's the way we read it," agreed the head of MI-6.

"Why did she pass that message to the Baaka councils, I wonder?"

"Her Götterdämmerung, perhaps. She wants the glory of her kills. It's psychologically consistent."

"Yes, well, you've presented me with a rather irresistible assignment, haven't you?"

"I had hoped to."

"Took me right through the proper stages, didn't you? From a distant enigma with a horrible yet fascinating dossier to an immediate crisis. All the right buttons pushed."

"Is there another way to do it?"

"Not if you're a pro, and you wouldn't be sitting in that chair if you weren't." Cooke rose to his feet, his eyes locked with those of his superior. "And now that you may assume my commitment, I'd like to make a suggestion."

"Be my guest, old chap."

"I wasn't entirely candid with you a few minutes ago. I said I still stay in touch with old friends, implying a social correspondence. By and large that's true, but it's not complete. Actually, I've spent most of my annual holidays in the islands—they do draw you back, you know. And, naturally," he continued, "former colleagues and new acquaintances of similar backgrounds will get together and reminisce."

"Oh, quite naturally."

"Yes, well, two years ago I met an American fellow who knows more about the islands than I ever did or ever will. He charters his two yachts out of various marinas from Charlotte Amalie to Antigua. He knows every harbor, every cove and inlet throughout the chain; he has to."

"Those are fine credentials, Geoffrey, but hardly the sort—"

"Please," interrupted Cooke. "I haven't finished. To anticipate your objection, he's a retired officer of U.S. Naval Intelligence. He's relatively young, early to mid-forties, I'd say, and I've no real knowledge of why he left the service, but I gather the circumstances weren't very pleasant. Still, he could be an asset on this assignment."

The chairman of MI-6 leaned forward over his desk, his rigid right hand lagging behind his left. "His name is Tyrell Nathaniel Hawthorne the Third. He's the son of a professor of American literature at the University of Oregon, and the circumstances of his separation from naval intelligence were very unpleasant, indeed. And, yes, he'd be an enormous asset, but no one in Washington's intelligence circles can recruit him. They've tried strenuously, giving him a lot of background, hoping to change his mind; they can't move him. He has very little regard for such people, believing as he does that they don't know the difference between the truth and a lie. He's told them all to go to hell."

"Good Lord!" cried Geoffrey Cooke. "You knew about my holidays, you knew all along. You even knew I'd met him."

"A pleasant three-day sail through the Leewards, along with your friend Ardisonne, code name Richelieu."

"You *bastard*."

"Come now, Officer Cooke, how can you? Incidentally, former Lieutenant Commander Hawthorne is on his way to the marina in British Gorda, where I suspect he'll have trouble with his auxiliary engine. Your plane leaves for Anguilla at five o'clock, plenty of time to pack. From there, you and your friend Ardisonne will take a small private aircraft to Virgin Gorda." The chairman of MI-6, Special Branch, flashed a brilliant smile. "It should be a splendid reunion."

DEPARTMENT OF STATE, WASHINGTON, D.C.

Seated around the table in the continuously swept conference room were the secretaries of state and defense, the directors of the Central Intelligence Agency and the Federal Bureau of Investigation, the chiefs of Army and Navy Intelligence, and the chairman of the Joint Chiefs of Staff. To the left of each man was his selected aide, a high-level subordinate beyond security reproach. Chairing the meeting was the secretary of state. He spoke.

"You've all gotten the same information I have, so we can dispense with extraneous introductions. There'll be some of you here who think we're overreacting, and until this morning, I must admit I would have been counted among you. A lone female terrorist with an obsession to assassinate the President, and thereby trigger the assassinations of the political leaders of Great Britain, France, and Israel, seemed just too farfetched. However, at six o'clock this morning I received a call from our director of the CIA, and then at eleven he called me again, and I began to change my mind. Would you please clarify, Mr. Gillette?"

"I'll do my best, Mr. Secretary," said the portly DCI. "Yesterday our source in Bahrain who monitors the financial transactions from the Baaka Valley was killed an hour after he alerted our undercover contact that a half million dollars had been transferred to Zurich's Crédit Suisse. The amount wasn't startling, but when our asset in Zurich tried to reach his own source at the bank, an off-the-books, highly paid source, he couldn't get anywhere. When later he pressed—anonymously, of course, merely an old friend—he was told that the man had flown to London on business. Later still, our asset returned to his apartment, where there was a message on his answering machine. It was from his source, who certainly wasn't in London, because he asked, apparently rather desperately, that our man meet him at a café in Dudendorf, a city twenty-odd miles north of Zurich. Our asset drove there but his source never showed up."

"What do you make of it?" asked the chief of Army G-2.

"He was taken out to eliminate the money trail," answered a burly man with thinning red hair who was seated at the DCI's left. "That's a projection, not confirmed," he added.

"Based on what?" questioned the secretary of defense.

"On logic," the Agency aide continued curtly. "First Bahrain's killed for passing the initial information, then Zurich builds a London cover so he can get to our asset in Dudendorf away from his usual environs. The Baaka found him and wants to cut off the trail, which it did."

"Over a six-figure transfer?" asked the chief of naval intelligence. "That's a lot of trouble over a minor amount, isn't it?"

"Because the amount doesn't mean doodly," said the heavyset aide with the puffed face. "It's who's on the receiving end, and the whereabouts of whoever that person is; that's what they're covering. Also, once the transfer is established as clean, the money could escalate a hundred times over."

"*Bajaratt*," said the secretary of state. "So she's begun her journey. . . . All right, this is the way we're going to operate, and maximum security is the key. With the exception of the Agency's radio traffic people, we at this table, and *only* we, will exchange information as our departments pick it up. Put all your personal office faxes into confidential modes, all telephone calls between ourselves on secure lines. Nothing goes out beyond this circle unless approved by me or the DCI. Even the rumors of such an operation could backfire and create a confusion we don't need." There was a hum; it came from the red telephone in front of the secretary of state. He picked it up. "Yes? . . . It's for you," he said, looking at the Agency's director. Gillette rose from his chair and went to the head of the table; he took the phone and identified himself.

"I understand," he said after listening for nearly a minute. He replaced the telephone and stared at his heavyset aide with the thinning red hair. "You've got your confirmation, O'Ryan. Our man in Zurich was found in the Spitzplatz, shot twice through the head."

"They're making sure that bitch's ass is covered," said the CIA analyst named O'Ryan.

2

The tall, unshaven man in white sailing shorts and black tank shirt, his skin burned to a deep bronze by the tropic sun, raced across the walkway and up the pier containing slips for the powerboats. He reached the end of the wooden planks and shouted at the two men on an incoming skiff.

"What the hell do you mean, I've got a leak in the auxiliary? I used it in dead air and it was perfectly fine!"

"Look, mate," replied a British mechanic, his voice weary as Tyrell Hawthorne grabbed the rope thrown at him. "I don't give a shit if it's a newborn babe of a motor. You ain't got an ounce of oil in your crankcase; it's all soiling our lovely little refuge here. Now, if you want to take that mother out, and you hit some more deaders, go right ahead and blow the engine. But I'm sure as hell gonna make my report. I ain't gonna be responsible for your stupidity."

"All right, all right," said Hawthorne, grabbing the man's hand as he climbed up the ladder to the dock. "What do you figure?"

"Rotted gaskets and two ruined cylinders, Tye." The mechanic turned and secured the second line around a pylon so his companion could climb up on the dock. "How many times have I told you, laddie, you're too good with the clouds and the windies. You've got to use your metals more; they dry out in this fuckin' sun! Now, haven't I told you that a couple of dozen times?"

"Yes, Marty, you have. I can't deny it."

"You couldn't! And with the prices you charge, you

29

sure ain't worried about fuel costs, that even I can figure."

"It's not the money," protested the skipper. "Except for prolonged dead spots, the charters like to sail, you know that. When can you have it fixed—a couple of hours?"

"Over your life, Tye-Boy. Try tomorrow noon—if I get the proper bore grinders flown in from Saint T. in the morning."

"Damn it! I've got some good repeats on board, and they expect to hit Tortola tonight."

"Get 'em a few rum-punchies, Gordie style, and get 'em rooms at the club. They'll never know the difference."

"I don't have a choice," said Hawthorne, turning and starting down the pier. "A hundred-and-ten-proof Overton coming up." The charter captain hastened his pace past the slips.

"Sorry, mate," Martin the mechanic said to himself as he watched his friend turn left on the walkway. "I hate to do this to you, but I've got my orders."

Darkness enveloped the Caribbean. The hour was late as Captain Tyrell Hawthorne, sole owner of Olympic Charters, Ltd., U.S. Virgin Islands Registry, led his clients, first one couple and then the other, to their accommodations at the yacht club's beach hotel. Their rooms were not what either twosome expected to wake up in, but going to sleep was no problem; the bartender had made certain of that. So Tye Hawthorne returned to the deserted open-air bar on the beach and rendered his thanks to the man behind it in more concrete terms. He gave the black bartender fifty American dollars.

"Hey, Tye-Boy, you don't have to do this."

"Then why are you gripping it so tightly in your fist?"

"Instinct, *mon*. You can have it back."

They both laughed; it was a ritual.

"How's business, Captain?" asked the bartender, pouring Hawthorne a glass of his customary white wine.

"Not bad, Roger. Both our boats are chartered, and if my idiot brother can find his way back to Red Hook in Saint T., we could even make a profit this year."

"Hey, *mon,* I like your brother. He's a funny guy."

"Oh, he's a real cartoon, Roge. Did you know that kid is a doctor?"

"What, *mon?* Alla times he comes here, I got aches and pains all over me, and I coulda asked him?"

"No, not that kind of doctor," broke in Tyrell. "He has a doctorate degree in literature, just like our dad."

"He don' fix bones and aches? So what good is it?"

"That's what he said. He said he broke his ass for eight years to get the damn thing and ended up making less money than a garbage collector in San Francisco. He was fed up, you know what I mean?"

"Sure," replied the bartender. "Five years ago I hauled fish off the charters and cleaned the throw-ups of the tourists an' put 'em to bed when they drunk. No life, *mon!* So I bettered myself and learned how to *get* 'em drunk."

"Good move."

"*Bad* move, Tye-Boy," said Roger, suddenly whispering and reaching below the counter. "Two *mon* walkin' down from the path. They lookin' fer somebody, and you are the only somebody here. Also, I got a feeling— I don' like 'em; they keep checkin' their jackets, their sleeves, an' they walk too slow. But don' worry, I got my gun."

"Hey, come on, Roge, what are you talking about?" Hawthorne turned on the barstool. "Geoff!" he cried. "Is that you, Cooke? . . . And Jacques, you too? What the hell are you guys doing here? . . . Put away the hardware, Roger, these are old friends of mine."

"I'll put it away when I learn they got no hardware of their own."

"Hey, fellas, this is another old friend—and the islands have been a little rough lately. Just hold out your hands and tell him you haven't got any weapons, okay?"

"How could we possibly have any weapons?" said Geoffrey Cooke contemptuously. "We both flew over on international flights where metal detectors are very much in evidence."

"*Mais oui!*" added Ardisonne, code name Richelieu.

"They're okay," said Hawthorne, leaping off the barstool and shaking hands with both older men. "Remember our sail through the—oh, oh, why *are* you here? I thought you were both retired."

"We have to talk, Tyrell," said Cooke.

"Immediately," said Ardisonne. "There is no time to waste."

"Hey, wait a minute. Suddenly my perfectly okay engine doesn't work; *suddenly,* out of a quiet night on the beach Cookie arrives with our old pal Richelieu from Martinique. What's going on, gentlemen?"

"I said we had to talk, Tyrell," insisted Geoffrey Cooke, MI-6.

"I'm not sure we do," replied former Lieutenant Commander Hawthorne, U.S. Naval Intelligence. "Because if what you want to talk about has anything to do with the crap Washington is laying on me, forget it."

"You have every right to abhor Washington," said Ardisonne in his heavily accented English, "but you have no reason not to listen to us. Can you think of a reason? You are correct when you say we should be retired, but 'suddenly,' to use your own word, we are not. Why is that? Is it not reason enough to listen to us?"

"Hear me, and hear me well, fellas. . . . What you represent cost me the woman I wanted to spend the rest of my life with. The goddamned games killed her in Amsterdam, so I trust you can understand when I say I don't care to talk to you. . . . Give these 'secret agents' a drink, Roge, and put it on my tab. I'm heading out to the boat."

"I submit, Tyrell, that neither I nor Ardisonne had

anything to do with Amsterdam," said Cooke. "You know that."

"The fucking games did, and you know *that*."

"Far removed, *mon ami*," said code name Richelieu. "Could we have sailed together otherwise?"

"Listen to me, Tye." Geoffrey Cooke clamped his hand with a great deal of force on Hawthorne's shoulder. "We were good friends, and we really must talk."

"Holy *shit*!" Tyrell grabbed his arm. "He used a needle on me—it was a *needle*! It went through my shirt! Get your gun, Roge . . . !"

Before the bartender could retrieve his weapon, Richelieu raised his arm and leveled it at his target. He snapped his index finger; a narcotizing dart flew out of his sleeve into the neck of the man behind the outdoor bar.

Sunrise. The images came into focus but they were not what Hawthorne's flashes of recollection projected. Neither face hovering above him belonged to Geoffrey Cooke or Jacques Ardisonne. Instead, they were the familiar features of Marty and his sidekick, Mickey, the cockney dock mechanics of Virgin Gorda.

"How're you doin', bloke?" asked Marty.

"You want a touch of gin, mate?" said Mickey. "Sometimes it clears the head."

"What the hell happened?" Tyrell blinked his eyes, trying to adjust to the bright sunlight that streamed through the windows. "Where's Roger?"

"In the next bed," Martin replied. "We kinda commandeered this villa—we tol' the front desk we found a nest of snakes crawlin' into the place."

"There are no snakes on Gorda."

"They don't know that," said Mickey. "They're mostly loser ninnies from London."

"Then where are Cooke and Ardisonne—the guys who freezed us?"

"Right over there, Tye-Boy." Martin pointed at two straight-backed chairs across the room. Strapped into them with towels wrapped and tied around their mouths were Geoffrey Cooke and Jacques Ardisonne. "I tol' the Mick here that I had to do what I did 'cause they said the bloody crown demanded it, but nobody said nuthin' 'bout what I do *after* that. You ain't been out of our sight. And if those bahstards had done you any real damage, they'd be floatin' bait without a hook on Shark Island."

"Then there was nothing wrong with the engine?"

"Not a thing, chappie. The head boy at Government House called me personally and said it was for your own good. Some fuckin' good, huh, mate?"

"Some fucking good," agreed Hawthorne, elbowing himself off the pillow and looking at his former friends.

"Hey, *mon!*" came the throated cry from Roger, on the next bed, his head thrashing back and forth.

"Check him out, Marty," ordered Tyrell, pulling his legs over the mattress to the floor.

"He's okay, Tye," said Mickey, kneeling beside the black man. "I made that old Frenchie tell us what he did to you two—it was that or his balls in a cylinder—and he said the whatever-it-was would wear off in five or six hours."

"The six hours are up, Mick. Another six, or however long it takes, are about to begin."

The woman helped the young man to secure the hull of the sloop in the sand by looping the bow line over a protruding rock in the breakwall beyond the short beach, a breakwall concealed behind a profusion of vines and creeping foliage. "It won't move now, Nicolo," she said, studying what was left of the boat. "Not that it matters. We might as well use the damn thing for firewood."

"You are mad!" The muscular adolescent started to

yank a few supplies, including the rifle, from the deck of the beached sloop. "But for the grace of Christ we would be dead, our bodies at the bottom of the sea."

"Keep the rifle but leave the rest," ordered Bajaratt. "We won't need any of it."

"How do you know? Where are we? . . . Why did you *do* it?"

"Because I had to."

"You don't give me an answer!"

"Very well, my lovely child, I suppose you're entitled to one."

"*Entitled?* Three days of not knowing whether I'd live or die, frightened out of my mind? Yes, I think I'm entitled."

"Oh, come now, it was never that bad. What you didn't realize was that we were never more than two or three hundred meters offshore and always to the leeward of the winds; it's why we came about so frequently. Of course, I could not control the lightning."

"Insane, you're insane!"

"Not really. Not too long ago I sailed these waters for nearly two years. I know them very well."

"Why did you *do* it?" he repeated. "You nearly killed us! And why did you shoot the black woman?"

Bajaratt gestured at the corpse. "Take her weapon; the water rises halfway up to the top of that hidden breakwall. She'll be carried out to sea during the night."

"You tell me nothing!"

"Let's be clear about that, Nicolo. You have a right to know only what I care to tell you. I saved your life, young man, and at great expense hid you for days on end from waterfront scum who would have killed you on sight. Further, I have deposited many millions of lira for you in the Banco di Napoli, and for these acts I have the privilege of withholding whatever I care not to discuss. . . . Pick up the weapon."

"Oh, my God," whispered the young man, bending over the uniformed body of the dead woman and wincing as he removed the gun from her hand; the small waves lapped over her face. "There's no one else *here*?"

"No one who counts." The woman's eyes strayed up to the island fortress as the memories swept through her mind. "Only a retarded gardener who controls a pack of mastiff attack dogs, and he himself is easily controlled. The owner of this island is an old friend, an old man who needs medical care. He's in Miami, Florida, for radiation treatments. He goes there on the first of every month for five days. That's all you have to know. Come, we'll go up the steps."

"Who is this man?" asked the boy, staring at Bajaratt in the sand.

"My only real father," answered Amaya Aquirre-Bajaratt softly, dreamily, as they slogged across the beach, her abrupt silence signaling Nicolo not to interrupt her thoughts. And such thoughts they were! The happiest two years of a life consigned to hell. The *padrone*, the *vizioso elegante*, was the man she admired most. At twenty-four years of age he had controlled the casinos in Havana, the tall, blond golden boy of Cuba with the ice-blue eyes, chosen by the dons from Palermo, New York, and Miami. He had been afraid of no one, instilling fear in everyone who opposed his decisions. Few had dared, and those who did disappeared. The Baj had heard the stories—in the Baaka, Bahrain, and Cairo.

The *capo dei capi* of the Mafia had chosen him, believing he was their most talented acolyte since Capone, who had ruled the American city of Chicago by the time he was a mere twenty-seven. But it all had collapsed for the young *padrone* when the crazy Fidel came down from the hills and ruined everything, including the Cuba he vowed to save.

Nothing, however, stopped the golden *vizioso elegante*, the man some called the "Mars of the Caribbean." He went first to Buenos Aires, where he built an organization second to none, working with the generals, of course. Then he moved to Rio de Janeiro, building further, exceeding his superiors' wildest dreams. Consolidating his efforts from an estate exceeding a hidden ten thousand acres, he brokered death throughout the world, recruiting an army of former soldiers, experts in the killing skills, outcasts from the militaries of many countries, and sold those skills for unheard of sums of money. Assassination was his product, and there was no end of buyers in a politically turbulent world. *La nostra Legione Straniero* the dons called it, roaring with laughter as they drank their *vino* in Palermo, New York, Miami, and Dallas, accepting their percentages of each expensive kill. Indeed, the *padrone*'s silent, unseen army was their own Foreign Legion.

Until age and illness forced the *padrone* to retreat to his impregnable island. And then, suddenly, a woman came into his life. Across the globe, Bajaratt had been severely wounded in the Cyprus port of Vasilikos while hunting down an execution unit sent out by the Mossad to kill a Palestinian hero who had been spotted there, the firebrand who later became her husband. Leading the counterstrike, the Baj had trapped the executioners offshore, and like a pirate queen, flanking and outflanking them in a fast boat at night, had forced them into the shoals under floodlights, while continuously firing murderous rounds into the cornered Israelis. She had caught four bullets in her stomach, tearing apart her intestines, her life all but given up for lost.

An underground doctor on Cyprus made it plain that he could only patch her up, partially stemming the internal bleeding. Heavily iced, she might last a day or two, but that was all without advanced surgery. And there was another consideration: No hospital or surgical team with the required technology—either in the civilized Mediterranean or Europe itself—would accept an obviously wounded terrorist without alerting the authorities . . . and the Soviet Union was no longer a refuge.

However, repeated urgent calls to the Baaka Valley revealed a possible solution, certainly no guarantee that she would live, but at least an attempt—if she could last two days, or, better, three. There was a man in the Caribbean, a powerful broker of all things, from narcotics to industrial espionage to military secrets and extraordinary arms shipments. He had worked frequently with and for the Baaka, realizing well over two billion American dollars for his endeavors throughout the Middle East. He could not refuse the High Councils; even he dared not do so.

For several hours he had tried, but the notorious freedom fighter whose life the woman had saved would not be denied. Should the man in the Caribbean refuse, he swore to bring down all the knives in the Baaka Valley, first and foremost his own, across the throats of the ungrateful broker and his allies everywhere.

Half dead, the Baj had been flown to Ankara, and from there on a military cargo jet to Martinique, where she was transferred to a dual-engine seaplane. Eleven hours after leaving Cyprus, she arrived at the dock on the *padrone*'s uncharted island. A team of surgeons from Miami who had been in consultation with the doctor on Cyprus were waiting for her; her life had been saved, no expense spared by the reluctant *padrone*.

As Bajaratt and Nicolo approached the stone staircase that led up to the fortress-estate, the Baj could not help but suddenly laugh out loud.

"What is it?" asked Nicolo sharply. "I don't find anything to be happy about."

"It's nothing, my adorable Adonis. I was just remembering my first days here. You wouldn't find it interesting. . . . Come now, the steps are a trial, but they are splendid to run up and down to regain one's strength."

"I need no such exercise."

"I once did." As they began the climb, the memories of those early weeks with the *padrone* came back to her, and recalling them, there was a great deal to laugh about. At first, when she became mobile, they were like two circling, suspicious cats, she outraged by the luxury he permitted himself, he frustrated by her interference with his opulent way of life. Then, quite accidentally, she invaded his kitchen when he was displeased with the cook's cannelloni Sambuca Florentine—the same cook who now lay dead thirty feet behind them at the water's edge. With great apologies to the servant, Bajaratt prepared her own; it pleased the unpleasant owner of the island. Next came chess. The *padrone* claimed he was a master; the young mistress beat him twice, then quite obviously let him win the third time. He roared with laughter, knowing what she had done and appreciating her charity.

"You are a lovely woman," he had said, "but never do that again."

"Then I shall beat you every time, and you'll be angry."

"No, my child, I will learn from you. It's the story of my life. I learn from everyone. . . . I once wanted to be a big movie star, believing my height and my body and my shining yellow hair would be loved by the camera. Do you know what happened? Never mind, I'll tell you. Rossellini saw a test I made for Cinecittà in Rome; guess what he said? . . . Never mind, I'll tell you. He said there was an ugliness in my blue eyes, an evil he could not explain. He was right, I went elsewhere."

From that night on they spent hours together, the two on equal footing, each recognizing the obsessions of the other, each accepting the other's genius. Finally, one late afternoon, sitting on the veranda, looking at a magenta sun, the *padrone* said, "You are the daughter I could never have."

"You are my only real father," Bajaratt had replied.

Nicolo, a step ahead of the Baj, held out his arm as they reached the top step. A flagstone path in front of them led to a huge, wide engraved door at least three inches thick. "I think it's open, Cabi."

"It is," agreed Bajaratt. "Hectra must have been in a hurry and forgot to close it."

"Who?"

"It's not important. Give me the rifle in case a dog is loose." They approached the half-closed door. "Kick it open, Nicolo," she said.

Suddenly, as they walked inside, from nowhere and everywhere explosions filled the great hall. The blasts of powerful, short-barreled shotguns echoed off the stone walls as Bajaratt and the boy sprang to the marble floor, Amaya firing indiscriminately—again nowhere and everywhere—until she was out of shells. Then, as the billows of smoke began to rise to the high ceiling, there was silence, a sudden quiet that found both intruders without harm. And both raised their heads as the smoke disappeared through the shafts of the setting sun, streaking through the small windows; each was alive and neither knew why. Then, revealed through the rising smoke was the figure of an old man in a wheelchair propelling himself forward from a recess at the far end of the hall. On the semicircular balcony above the curving staircase stood two men holding the Sicilian weapon of choice—the short-barreled *lupo* shotgun. They were smiling; their ammunition had been false, shells without lethal contents—blanks.

"Oh, *my*, Annie!" cried the frail voice from the wheelchair, the language English but with the rasp of an accent. "I never thought you would do it."

"You're in Miami—you're always in Miami! For your treatments!"

"Come now, Baj, how much more good can they do for me? ... But to kill your old friend Hectra, who nursed you back to health five years ago, that killing was an act of commitment. ... Incidentally, you owe me a woman of like loyalty. Shall it be you?"

Bajaratt got slowly to her feet. "I needed this place for only a few days and no one, *no* one, could know where I was or what I was doing, or whom I was going to meet, not even Hectra. You have the radios, the satellites—you showed me them yourself!"

"You say no one knows what you're doing, or, more precisely, what you intend to do? Do you think this decrepit figure before you has lost his mind before his body? . . . I assure you, I have not. Any more than I have lost my familiars from the Baaka to the French Deuxième to the brilliant MI-6 and their less than admirable American colleagues. I know exactly what your intentions are. . . . *'Muerte a toda autoridad,'* is it not true?"

"It is my life—the end of my life, no doubt, but I shall do it, *padrone.*"

"Yes, I understand. No matter how much we inflict, each of us can take only so much pain. I'm sorry for your loss, Annie, your newest loss, the death in Ashkelon, of course. I'm told he was an outstanding man, truly a leader, decisive and fearless."

"I saw in him a great deal of you, *padrone,* of what you were at his age."

"He was somewhat more idealistic, I imagine."

"He could have been so many things, anything he wanted to be, but the world would not let him. Any more than it would me. The things we can't control control us."

"Quite true, my daughter. I wanted to be a movie star, did I ever tell you that?"

"You would have been brilliant, my only real father," said Bajaratt. "But will you let me fulfill my final mission in life?"

"Only with my help, my only real daughter. I, too, want all the controllers dead—for they have made both of us what we are. . . . Come and embrace me, as you used to do. You are home."

As Bajaratt knelt and extended her arms to the old invalid, he gestured toward the young man, who still crouched on the marble floor, taking in the scene with fascinated, frightened eyes.

"Who the hell is he?" he asked.

"His name is Nicolo Montavi, and he's the essential core of my plan," whispered the Baj. "He knows me as Signora Cabrini and he calls me Cabi."

"Cabrini? As in the beloved American saint?"

"*Naturalmente*. For through my actions I will become the second American saint, won't I?"

"Delusions call for a great deal of rum and a very large meal. I'll see to it."

"You'll let me go on, won't you, *padrone*?"

"Of course I will, my daughter, but only with my help. The killing of such men—the world will be gripped by fear and panic. It will be our ultimate statement before we die!"

3

The Caribbean sun burned the earth and the rocks and the sand on the island of Virgin Gorda. It was eleven o'clock in the morning, prelude to the scorching hour of noon, and Tyrell Hawthorne's "charters" protected themselves under the thatched roof of the outdoor beach bar, doing whatever they could possibly do to alleviate their nausea. When told by their captain that due to a mechanical emergency they could not sail until midafternoon at the earliest, four sighs of relief accompanied three one-hundred dollar bills pressed into his hand by a banker from Greenwich, Connecticut, who pleaded, "For Christ's sake, make it tomorrow."

Tyrell returned to the villa, where Mickey stood guard over Cooke and Ardisonne while his colleague, Marty, attended to the docks. By now the two intruders had been stripped to their shorts, their clothes deposited at the hotel laundry. Hawthorne slammed the door and turned to the mechanic. "Mick, do me a favor. Go to the chickee and bring me two bottles of Montrachet Grand Cru—forget it, two bottles of white wine and I don't care if it's Thunderbird."

"What year?" asked Ardisonne.

"Last week," replied Tyrell. Mickey left quickly and Hawthorne continued. "All right, you secret agents you, let's 'carry on,' as the English say."

"You're not funny," said Cooke.

"Oh, it's great when you Euros come up with your fog-bound narrow streets and your trench coats lurking

43

around waterfronts, but why don't you face it? High tech has replaced you, just as it replaced me. Amsterdam taught me that, unless they all lied on their own, which they couldn't have. They were programmed by the numbers, do and say what the machines tell you, that's all you know!"

"Not true, *mon ami*. Put simply, we are not equipped to deal with that technology. We are of the old school, and believe me when I tell you, it is coming back in ways you cannot imagine. The computers and their modems, the satellites and their high-altitude photographs, borders crossed by television and radio signals—all are *magnifique*, but they do not and cannot deal with the human condition. We did that . . . *you* did that. We meet a man or a woman face-to-face, our eyes and our instincts tell us whether he or she is the enemy. Machines cannot do the same."

"Is that lecture by way of telling me our combined medieval practices can find this dragon lady, Bajaratt, quicker than faxing her photograph, description, and whatever else you've got to your secure sources on roughly fifty habitable islands? If so, I can only presume you should immediately be forced back into retirement."

"I believe what Jacques is suggesting," broke in Cooke, "is that our expertise, combined with available technology, can be more effective than one without the other."

"Well said, *mon ami*. This psychopathic female, this killer, is not without brains or resources."

"According to Washington, she's also not without a lot of hate rattling around in that brain of hers."

"Certainly no justification for what she's done, or God help us, what she intends to do," the man from MI-6 said emphatically.

"No, it isn't," agreed Hawthorne. "But I wonder who and what she might be now if there'd been someone to help her years ago. . . . Christ almighty, the heads of your mother and father cut off in front of your eyes! I think if that had happened to my brother and me, we'd both be every bit the killer she is."

"You lost a wife you loved very much, Tyrell," said Cooke. "You didn't become a killer."

"No, I didn't," replied Hawthorne. "But I'd be a liar if I didn't tell you I thought about killing a number of people—not only thought about it, but in several cases planned it."

"But you didn't carry out those plans."

"Only because I had help . . . believe me, *only* because there was someone to stop me." Tyrell glanced out the window at the sea, the constant movement briefly mesmerizing him. There had been someone, and, oh, God, how he missed her! In drunken moments he would tell her of his plans to take out *this* one and *that* one, even going so far as to open locked drawers on his boat and, in a stupor, show her his plans, diagrams of streets and buildings, his strategies for ending the lives that caused the death of his wife. Dominique would hold him as he swayed in an alcoholic daze, whispering into his ear that causing death would not bring back the dead, only create pain for many others who had no connection with Ingrid Johansen Hawthorne. In the mornings she would still be there beside him, dismissing his hung-over guilt with gentle laughter, yet reminding him how foolish and how dangerous were his fantasies; she wanted him alive. Christ, he loved her! And when she disappeared, the whiskey went with her. Perhaps it was another fantasy, but he often wondered: If he had stopped his heavy drinking before, might she have stayed?

"I apologize for intruding," said Ardisonne, both he and Cooke disturbed by Hawthorne's sudden silence.

"You didn't intrude; it's just private."

"So what is your answer, Commander? We've told you everything, even apologized for our actions last night, which at the time seemed appropriate. When a bartender stares at you with great hostility and lowers his body below the counter at a deserted chickee at night, well, both Jacques and I know the islands."

"You have a point, but you used overkill. You said we had to talk right away; it was urgent. Yet you put me out for damn near six hours. Some urgency, pal."

"Our measures were not designed for you or your friend the bartender," said Ardisonne. "To be frank, they were designed for other people."

"What other people?"

"Oh, come on, Tyrell, you're not naive. The Baaka Valley is not without connections everywhere, and only the most innocent believe our services do not have corrupted personnel in one department or another. Twenty thousand pounds can turn a bureaucrat's head."

"You thought you might be intercepted?"

"We couldn't dismiss the possibility, old boy, therefore we've carried only what's in our heads, nothing in writing about Bajaratt, no photographs, no dossiers, no background material whatsoever. However, should anyone have been tipped off and tried to stop us, either in Paris, London, or Antigua, we could stop them."

"So you're back in your trench coats, prowling the dark alleys."

"Why dismiss secrecy and hidden weapons? They saved your life more than once during the cold war, is it not so?"

"Maybe once or twice, no more than that, and I tried like hell not to become paranoid. Until Amsterdam it was pretty cut-and-dried. Who can you turn and how much will it cost?"

"It's a different world now, Commander, we no longer have the luxury of known enemies. There's another breed, and they're neither agents nor double agents, or moles on one side or the other to be unearthed—those times are gone. Someday we may look back on them and realize how simple they were, for our root mentalities were not that different. It's all changed now; we're no longer dealing with people who think anything like the way we used to think. We're dealing with hate, not power or geopolitical influence, but pure, raw hatred. The whipped of the world are turning, their age-old frustrations exploding, blind vengeance paramount."

"That's dramatic, Geoff, but I think you're blowing it out of proportion. Washington knows about the woman, and until she's taken out, the President won't be put in vulnerable situations. I assume it'll be the same in London, Paris, and Jerusalem."

"Who is truly invulnerable, Tyrell?"

"No one, of course, but she'd have to be a goddamned illusionist to get by armies of guards and the most sophisticated security equipment in the world. From what I've been told by Washington, the Oval Office's every move is controlled. No exteriors, no crowds, everything in-house and totally isolated. So, I repeat for the umpteenth time, what the hell do you need me for?"

"Because she is an *illusionniste!*" said Ardisonne. "She has eluded the Deuxième, MI-6, the Mossad, Interpol, and every special branch of intelligence and counterintelligence you can name. But, at last, we know she is in a specific area, a sector we can cross and crisscross with all the technological devices we can employ, along with the most vital component we have at our disposal. The human equation: a dragnet, the search led by experienced hunters who know the quarry's current territory, back alleys, waterfronts, and all."

Hawthorne studied both men in silence, his eyes roving from one to the other. "Suppose under certain conditions I agreed to help you," he said finally. "Where would we begin?"

"With the technology you hold in such exalted esteem," answered Cooke. "Every NATO intelligence station and all police authorities throughout the Caribbean are being wired composite descriptions of Bajaratt and the young man she's traveling with."

"Oh, that's bright!" said Tyrell, laughing sarcastically. "You send out a blanket alert all over the islands and expect responses? You shock me, gentlemen, I thought you knew all the back alleys and waterfronts."

"What is your point?" asked Ardisonne, not amused.

"My point is that you've got barely a thirty percent chance of hearing anything from anyone who spots them, official or otherwise. If somebody does, he won't come running back to you, he'll come *on* to the lady and a few thousand dollars will close his mouth. You've been away too long, fellas, this isn't the land of Oz. Except for places like this, it's poverty row from island to island."

"How would you have done it?" said Cooke.

"The way you should have," replied Hawthorne. "You say she has to have access to the offshore banks, that's your key; nobody down here provides large amounts of money to strangers except face-to-face. Concentrate on the islands with those facilities, which cuts you down to twenty or twenty-five. Between the two of you, you've covered most if not all of them during your tours here. Reach your blinds with a great deal of cash and have *them* make their own arrangements with the authorities. The back door down here is far more effective than the front entrance. I'm surprised I have to tell you that."

"I can't fault your reasoning, chap, but I'm afraid we don't have time. Paris estimates that she'll be here for a minimum of a fortnight; London believes far less, say five to eight days maximum."

"Then you've thrown your jockey at the starting gate. You've lost the race down here; she'll stay out of your net."

"Not necessarily," said code name Richelieu.

"London was responsible for the strategy," Cooke explained. "And we didn't overlook the corruption to which you refer. Accompanying the alert is an addendum that can scarcely be ignored. The governments of England, France, and the U.S. have pledged a million American dollars apiece for information that leads to the capture of the two fugitives. Conversely, should it be learned that such information was withheld, punishment in the extreme will be administered."

Hawthorne whistled. "Wow," he said softly. "The hardball is made of concrete. It's open up for three million dollars or close out with a bullet in your head in one of those dark alleys."

"Precisely," agreed the veteran of MI-6.

"You stole it from the old NKVD—even the KGB was prettier."

"Hardly. It goes back to Beowulf. Very effective."

"*Time*, Tyrell!" said Ardisonne. "We must move quickly."

"When was the alert sent out? The descriptions?"

Cooke looked at his watch. "Approximately six hours ago, five A.M., Greenwich time."

"Where's the base of operations?"

"Temporarily Tower Street, London."

"MI-6," said Hawthorne.

"You mentioned 'certain conditions,' Tyrell," said Cooke. "May we assume that in the interests of global stability, you'll join us?"

"You can't assume a thing. I have no affection for the assholes who run this planet. You want me in, you'll pay, whether or not they get blown away, and you'll pay up front."

"That's hardly cricket, chap—"

"I don't play cricket. For my brother and me to really make a go of this business we need two more boats— used, but good, class-A boats. That's seven fifty apiece, a total of one million five. In my bank on Saint T. by tomorrow morning. Early."

"Isn't that rather excessive?"

"*Excessive?* When you're willing to pay three million dollars to some informer who may accidentally stumble on this Bajaratt and the kid? Come off it, Geoffrey. Pay up or I'm off to Tortola at ten A.M. tomorrow."

"You're a self-important son of a bitch, Hawthorne."

"Then drop out and I'll sail for Tortola."

"You know I can't do that. However, I wonder if you're worth the money."

"You won't know that until I'm paid, will you?"

CENTRAL INTELLIGENCE AGENCY, LANGLEY, VIRGINIA

The gray-haired Raymond Gillette, director of the CIA, stared at the uniformed naval officer sitting in front of his desk, his gaze an admixture of reluctant respect and disgust. "MI-6, with some help from the Deuxième, did what you couldn't do, Captain," he said quietly. "They recruited Hawthorne."

"We tried," said Captain Henry Stevens, chief of naval intelligence. There was no apology in his sharp reply as he braced his lean fifty-year-old body in the chair as if conveying a sense of physical superiority over the obese DCI. "Hawthorne was a dupe of the first rank and never accepted the fact. In plain words, he was a goddamned fool and wouldn't believe us when we presented him with irrefutable proof."

"That his Swedish wife was an agent, or at least a paid informer, for the Soviets?"

"Precisely."

"Whose proof?"

"Ours. Meticulously documented."

"By whom?"

"On-scene sources; they confirmed it to a man."

"In Amsterdam," said Gillette, no question in his statement.

"Yes."

"I read your file."

"Then you saw how indisputable the data was. The woman was under constant surveillance—Christ, married two months after their meeting to a ranking undercover officer of naval intelligence—and seen, *photographed,* going into the rear entrance of the Soviet embassy at night on eleven different occasions! What else do you need?"

"Cross-checking comes to mind. With us, perhaps."

"Covert operations computers do that."

"Not always, and if you don't know that, you should be demoted to seaman."

"I don't have to take that from you, civilian."

"You'd better take it from me—from someone who has a regard for your other accomplishments—or you might find yourself in a courtroom, both civilian and military. That is, if you survived twenty-four hours after Hawthorne learned the truth."

"What the hell are you talking about?"

"I've read *our* file on Hawthorne's wife."

"So?"

"You spread the word and had every asset in your Amsterdam orbit swear under N.I. Code Twelve—severe anonymity—that Hawthorne's wife, an interpreter with full clearance, was working for Moscow. Each was instilled with the exact words right down the line. 'Ingrid Hawthorne is a traitor to NATO; she makes constant contact with the Soviets.' It was all like a broken record playing the same phrase over and over again."

"It was true!"

"It was false, Captain. She was working for us."

"You're out of your mind—I don't believe you!"

"Read our file. . . . As I piece it together, so your hands would appear clean, you passed another lie that happened to be the truth, a fatal truth. You sent word through a selected asset with KGB internals that Mrs. Hawthorne was a double agent, that her marriage was real, not a ceremony of convenience, as the Soviets believed it was. They eliminated her and dumped her body in the Heren Canal. We lost an extraordinary penetration and Hawthorne lost a wife."

"Oh, my God!" Stevens writhed in his chair, his body jerking nervously back and forth between the arms.

"Why the hell didn't anyone tell us?" Then abruptly, he stopped, his eyes riveted on the director. "Wait a minute! If what you say is true, why didn't she ever tell Hawthorne?"

"We can only speculate. They were in the same business; she knew about him, but he didn't know about her. If he had, he would have forced her to stop, obviously knowing the risks."

"How could she *not* tell him?"

"Scandinavian sangfroid, perhaps. Watch their tennis players. She couldn't stop, you see. Her father died in a Siberian gulag as an anti-Soviet activist captured in Riga when she was quite young. She changed her name, built her own dossier, learned fluent Russian as well as French and English, and went to work for us in The Hague."

"We had none of that in our records!"

"You could have had it if you'd picked up a telephone before making decisions. She was logged out of the system."

"Bullshit! Who the hell can trust *anybody*?"

"Maybe that's why I'm here, young man," said Gillette, his narrow, flesh-encased eyes conveying equal parts contempt and understanding. "I'm a pretty old geezer out of G-2, Vietnam, where things were really screwed up, so messy that I emerged with a terrific reputation that I didn't deserve—to the contrary, I probably should have been court-martialed. So I know where you're coming from, Captain, which doesn't excuse you *or* me, but I think you should know the truth."

"If you felt that way, why did you take this job?"

"You called me a civilian, and you're right on the mark, a very rich civilian. I made a great deal of money, in part due to that undeserved reputation, so when I was tapped for this job, I decided it was payback time. I'd like to try to make things a little better in this very necessary area of the government . . . to make up for past mistakes, maybe."

"Considering your mistakes, what made you think you're qualified?"

"Because of those mistakes. We're so panic-prone over secrets, we all too frequently fail to communicate essentials—or seek them out. For instance, I don't think you'll repeat the error of Ingrid Hawthorne."

"It wasn't my error! You just said it: She wasn't logged in the system!"

"Neither are eighty to a hundred others, what do you think of that?"

"I think it smells!"

"Including several dozen assets of your own."

"That was before I came on board," said the naval officer curtly. "A system doesn't work if it's disregarded. There are fail-safe procedures in those computers."

"Don't tell that to the hackers who broke into the Pentagon machines. They might not believe you."

"One in a million chances!"

"Roughly the same as a specific sperm fertilizing an egg, yet nine months later a life is there. And you took one of those lives, Captain."

"Goddamn you—"

"Spare me," said the CIA director, holding up his hands, his elbows on the arms of the chair. "That information remains in the confines of this room. For your edification, I made a similar mistake on the Ho Chi Minh trail—and that, too, will remain in this room."

"Are we finished?"

"Not yet. I can't order you, but I'd suggest you reach Hawthorne and give him whatever oceangoing help he needs. You're all over the Caribbean, and we're stretched thin down there."

"He won't talk to me," said the captain slowly, quietly. "I tried several times. As soon as he realized who it was, he hung up without a word."

"He's talked to someone on your staff, MI-6 confirmed it. He told their man, Cooke, in Virgin Gorda, that Hawthorne knew about the Bajaratt woman, that the Oval Office was under max-security, the President in a jacket. If you didn't tell him, who did?"

"I put it up for grabs," replied Stevens reluctantly. "After I couldn't get anywhere with that bastard, I told a few men who knew him that if anyone felt he could make any progress with him, to go ahead and give Tye the scenario."

"Tye?"

"We knew each other, not well, but we'd have drinks now and then. My wife worked at the embassy in Amsterdam; they were friends."

"He suspected you in his wife's murder?"

"Hell, I showed him the photographs but swore we had nothing to do with her death—which actually we didn't."

"But you did."

"There's no way he could have known that; besides, the Soviets left their mark as a warning to others."

"But we all develop instincts, don't we?"

"What do you want from me, Mr. Director? I'm out of conversation."

"Since the British recruited him, hold an immediate staff meeting and figure out what you can do to help." The DCI leaned over his desk and wrote on a memo pad. "Coordinate with MI-6 and the Deuxième; here are the two men you should contact, and only them and only on scrambler." The director held out the paper.

"Right to the top," remarked the officer from naval intelligence, reading the names. "What's the code?"

"Little Girl Blood. That's when you go on scrambler."

"You know," said Stevens, getting up from the chair and putting the note in his pocket, "I have an idea that we all may really be overreacting. We've lived through dozens of alerts like this—hit teams being sent out from the Middle East, psychos waiting to take a shot at the big man in airports, nuts rounded up who've written crazy letters—and ninety-nine percent of the time they

turned out to be vapors. Suddenly, a lone woman traveling with a kid shows up on our subcellar screens, and
the alarms rattle cages from Jerusalem to D.C. with loud
bells in Paris and London. Doesn't that strike you as a
little heavy?"

"How thoroughly did you read the information I got
from London and forwarded to you?" asked the DCI.

"Very. She's a psychotic for all the reasons the Freudi-
ans expound on, and, without doubt, obsession-ori-
ented. That doesn't make her super Amazon."

"Because she isn't. A larger-than-life subject is an
easier target; he or she stands out. Bajaratt could be the
girl next door in Centerville, U.S.A., or the vacuous
fashion model on Paris's Saint-Honoré, or a shy sabra
private in the Israeli Army. She doesn't lead charges,
Captain, she orchestrates them, that's her genius. She
creates events, then moves the principals within them
toward the predetermined objectives. If she were an
American and of a different mentality, she'd probably
be sitting where I am."

"May I ask . . . ?" The naval officer shifted his feet,
breathing deeply, his face growing red as the blood rose
to his head. "What I did—oh, *God*, what I *did*—you
said it would remain in this room."

"It will."

"*Christ*, why did I *do* it?" The officer's eyes were
clouded as his body shook. "I killed Tye's wife . . . !"

"It's over, Captain Stevens. Unfortunately, you'll live
with it for the rest of your life—as I have for over thirty
years since the Ho Chi Minh. That's our punishment."

Tyrell's brother, Marc Anthony Hawthorne—"Marc-
Boy" in the Caribbean's lingua franca—had flown to
Virgin Gorda to take over his sibling's charter. Marc
Hawthorne was in several respects the eternal younger
brother, slightly taller than the tall Tyrell, quite a bit
more slender—very thin to be precise—and with a face

similar in appearance but without the crow's-feet or the neutral eyes of his older, more experienced brother. He was seven years younger, and although it was apparent that he held the first Hawthorne son in great affection, it was also obvious that he frequently questioned his brother's intellect.

"Come on, Tye!" he said emphatically as they stood on the deserted dock at sundown. "You quit all that crap! You can't go back, I won't let you!"

"I wish you could stop me, bro, but you can't."

"What the hell is this?" Marc lowered his voice to a guttural incantation. "*Once a navy man, always navy!* Is that what you're saying?"

"Not at all. It's just that I can do what they can't do. Cooke and Ardisonne flew around these islands; I've sailed them. I know every inlet, every land mass, mapped and unmapped, and there aren't too many 'autoritees' I haven't bribed with a dollar or fifty."

"But why, for Christ's sake?"

"I'm not sure, Marc, but maybe it's something Cooke said. He said they were the 'whipped of the world,' not the enemies we knew before, but a new breed, raging fanatics who just want to destroy everything they believe has kept them in the garbage dumps."

"That's probably socioeconomically true. But, I repeat, why are you getting involved?"

"I just told you, I can do what they can't do."

"That's not a *why*, that's an egotistical quasi-justification."

"All right, brother-academic, I'll try to explain. Ingrid was killed—for one reason or another, perhaps I'll never find out which—but you can't live with a woman like her without knowing that she wanted the violence to stop—one way or another. At this point I honestly don't know which side she was on, but I do know she wanted peace. I'd hold her in my arms and out of nowhere she'd cry, 'Why can't it stop? Why can't the *brutality* stop?' . . . Later, when they told me she was a Soviet mole . . .

well, I still can't believe it, but if she was, it was for the right reasons. She *did* want peace; she was my wife, and I loved her, and she couldn't lie to me when she was in my arms."

Silence. Finally Marc spoke softly. "I won't even pretend to understand that world you lived in. God knows, I couldn't handle it. Still, I have to ask you again, why are you really going back?"

"Because there's someone out there who represents something more powerful than we can understand that has to be stopped, and if I can help stop that psychopath because I know a few dirty games, maybe someday I'll feel better about Ingrid. It was the filthy games that killed her."

"You're persuasive, Tye," Marc said.

"I'm glad you agree." Hawthorne looked at his younger brother and flicked his hand against Marc's shoulder. "Because for the next week or so you're running the business, which includes looking around for two new sloops, class A, large sail, fore and aft. If you find one suddenly on the market at a good price and I'm not available, put a binder on it."

"With what? Paper we can't back up?"

"The money will be at our bank in Saint T. tomorrow morning, courtesy of my temporary employers."

"I'm glad you mix idealism with reality."

"They owe me, more than they could ever pay."

"In the meantime, what do I do about another charter captain? We've got two bookings next Monday."

"I called Barbie in Red Hook; she'll come on board. Her boat still isn't repaired from the hurricane."

"Tye, you know charters don't feel comfortable with women skippers!"

"Just tell her to do what she does with her own charters when they find out that B. Pace isn't Bruce or Ben but Barbara. She punches out her steward as soon as everyone's on board."

"She also pays him for taking the shot."

"So pay, we're rich."

Suddenly, the roar of an automobile engine, followed by screeching tires, filled the twilight from the nearby parking area beyond the dock. Within seconds the muffled voices of Cooke and Ardisonne were heard shouting at Marty and Mickey in the yacht club's repair shop. Moments later the Englishman and the Frenchman came rushing across the walkway.

"Something's happened," said Tyrell quietly.

"Something's *happened*!" exclaimed Geoffrey Cooke as both men turned and ran up the pier, breathless. "We've just come from Government House. . . . Hello, Marc, I'm afraid we have to talk to your brother privately." The MI-Sixer pulled Hawthorne to the far left of the pier, code name Richelieu following.

"Take it easy," said Hawthorne. "Catch your breath and slow down."

"There's no time!" Ardisonne said. "We've received four reports, each claiming to have seen the woman and the young man."

"Same island?"

"No, three, damn it!" said Cooke. "But each has an international bank."

"That means two reports came from one—"

"St. Croix, Christiansted. A plane's waiting for us at the airfield. I'll take St. Croix."

"Why?" countered Hawthorne angrily. "I don't want to hurt you, Geoff, but I'm younger and pretty obviously in better shape than you. Give me St. Croix."

"You haven't seen the photographs!"

"From what you told me, they're three different people, so what good are they?"

"You forget so easily, Tyrell. It's a far chance, but one of them may be the right one. We certainly can't dismiss them."

"Get them to me."

"They have to come by courier; Virgin Gorda's out of our secure routing. The Deuxième is flying them in from Martinique by diplomatic pouch first thing tomorrow."

"We cannot waste the time," insisted Ardisonne.

"I'll give you the names of our sources, Tyrell," said Cooke. "You'll take St. Barthélemy. Jacques will cover Anguilla."

Hawthorne woke up on the narrow bed in the hotel on the island of St. Barts, still angry at Geoffrey Cooke for having sent him into a no-win situation. The native source he had reached through the chief of island security was a known drug informant, a hustler overreaching himself for the prize of three million American dollars. He had seen an elderly German lady, escorted by her adolescent grandson, disembark from the St. Martin hydrofoil. With that flimsy evidence, he had gone for the prize. The grandmother in question, however, proved to be an overly made-up, very Germanic mother who disapproved of her daughter's plebeian life-style, and had offered to take her grandson on a grand tour of the islands.

"*Goddamn it!*" exploded Hawthorne, reaching for the telephone to order whatever breakfast the hotel had available.

Tyrell walked the streets of St. Barts, passing the time until he flagged a taxi to the airport, where a plane would take him back to British Gorda. There was nothing else to do but walk around; he hated being in hotel rooms alone. They were like solitary prison cells, where a person rapidly became angry with his own company.

And then it happened. Fifty feet away, walking across the street toward the entrance of the Bank of Scotland, was the woman who had saved his sanity, if not his life. She was, if possible, even more beautiful. Her long, dark hair framing the lovely features of her suntanned face, the way she walked, the sure glide of the cosmopolitan Parisienne who was never above being courteous to strangers. It all came back to him, the glorious sight of her almost more than he could bear.

"*Dominique!*" he shouted, parting the bodies in front of him and racing into the street toward the woman he had not seen for so long, *too* long. She turned on the curb, her face lighting up, her smile filled with joy. He pulled her across the pavement to a storefront, and they embraced, holding one another in quickly remembered warmth and affection. "They told me you went back to Paris!"

"I did, my darling. I had to get my life together."

"Not a word, not a letter, even a call. I went out of my *mind*!"

"I could never replace Ingrid, I knew that."

"Didn't you know how much I wanted you to try?"

"We come from different worlds, my dearest. Your life is here; mine is in Europe. I have responsibilities you don't have, Tye, I tried to tell you that."

"I remember only too well. Save the Children, Relief for Somalia—two or three other initials I could never figure out."

"I'd been away too long, far longer than I would have been without you. Organizationally, things were a mess, and several interfering government regimes weren't helping. But now that the Quai d'Orsay is firmly behind us, things are easier."

"How so?"

"For example, one time last year in Ethiopia . . ."

As she spoke of the triumphs of her several charities— over bureaucratic barriers or far worse—her natural ebullience lent a kind of lovely electricity to everything about her. Her wide, soft eyes were so alive, her face so expressive, revealing that well of infinite hope she drew from and which sustained her. Her capacity for compassion was almost unreal, made infinitely credible by a sincerity that bordered on naiveté, in itself denied by a soft-spoken intelligence and worldliness.

". . . so you see, we got through with twenty-eight trucks! You can't imagine what it was like to see the villagers, especially the children whose hunger was in their faces, and the older ones who had nearly given up hope! I don't think I ever cried with so much happiness. . . . And now the supplies get through regularly, and we're branching out everywhere, as long as we keep up the pressure!"

"Keep up . . . ?"

"You know, my darling, harass the harassers with our own threats, presented gently, of course, with our very official documents. The Republic of France is not to be toyed with!" Dominique smiled triumphantly, her eyes bright.

He loved her so. She could not leave him again!

"Let's go get a drink," said Hawthorne.

"Oh, yes, please! I do so want to talk to you, Tye. I missed you so. I have an appointment with my uncle's lawyer at the bank, but he can wait."

"It's called island charm. Nobody gets anywhere on time."

"I'll call him from wherever we are."

— 4 —

T hey sat at a sidewalk café, their hands clasped across the table as a waiter brought Dominique an iced tea and Hawthorne a carafe of chilled white wine. Tyrell spoke.

"Why did you disappear?"

"I told you. I had other commitments."

"We might have become one, a commitment, I mean."

"That's what frightened me. Quite simply, you were becoming too important."

"For what? I thought you felt the way I did."

"Your confusion and your guilt about Ingrid were overwhelming, Tye. You didn't drink because you were an alcoholic, your charters proved that. You simply had to go a little wild when you weren't responsible for anyone but yourself. You couldn't forgive yourself for what happened."

"That was it, wasn't it?"

"What was?"

"You wanted to be more than a nursemaid, and I was so wrapped up in myself, I couldn't see it. I'm so sorry."

"Tye, you were deeply hurt and bewildered, I understood that. If I'd felt the way you say, we wouldn't have had the time we did together. Almost two years, my darling."

"It wasn't long enough."

"No, it wasn't."

"Remember how we first met?" asked Hawthorne warmly, his eyes locked with hers.

"How could I forget?" she replied, laughing softly and squeezing his hand. "I'd leased a boat and was sailing it into the marina on St. Thomas when I had some difficulty pulling into the slip I was told to use."

"*Difficulty?* You came in under full sail as though you were tacking toward a racing marker. You scared the hell out of me."

"I don't know how afraid you were, but you were certainly angry."

"Dominique, my sloop was moored in your direct line of attack."

"Oh, yes, you stood on your deck, waving your arms and swearing at me—but then I did manage to miss you, didn't I?"

"I still don't know how you did it."

"You couldn't see, my darling. You were so angry, you'd fallen into the water." They both laughed, leaning toward each other over the table. "I felt so ashamed," continued Dominique softly. "But I did apologize to you when you came on shore."

"Yes, you did, at Fishbait's Whisky Shack. Your coming over to me made me the envy of all the charters . . . and it was the beginning of some of the happiest months of my life. What I remember best were the sails we took alone to so many tiny islands, sleeping on the beaches—making love there."

"And *loving,* my darling."

"Can we start again? The past recedes, and I'm a lot less screwed up now. I'm even known to laugh a lot and tell dumb jokes, and you'd like my brother. . . . Can we start again, Dominique?"

"I'm married, Tye."

It was as though Hawthorne had been struck by the bow of an ocean liner while in a fog-bound sea. For several moments he could not speak, speech was beyond him; he was capable only of lowering his eyes and doing his best to simulate normal breathing. He began to release Dominique's hand; she abruptly stopped him, covering both with her free one. "Please don't, my darling."

"He's a lucky fellow," said Tyrell, staring at their hands. "Is he also a nice guy?"

"He's sweet and devoted and very, very rich."

"He's got two out of three more than I do. But devoted I would be."

"The rich helped, I won't deny that. I don't have particularly expensive tastes, but my causes aren't cheap. And the modeling profession, which certainly afforded me a lovely apartment and glorious clothes, doesn't care to hire crazy crusaders. I was glad to leave it behind me. I was never comfortable showing off designs barely an iota of the buying public could afford."

"You're in another world, lady. You're also a happily married woman, then?"

"I didn't say that," said Dominique quietly, firmly, her eyes now focused on their entwined hands.

"I missed something."

"We are a marriage of convenience, as La Rochefoucauld phrased it."

"I beg your pardon?" Hawthorne raised his eyes, studying her passive face.

"My husband is a closet homosexual."

"Thank God for favors, large and small."

"He'd find that amusing. . . . We lead a strange life, Tye. He's quite influential and extremely generous, not only in helping me raise funds but in the area of government assistance, which we frequently need."

"As in those official documents you mentioned?" said Tyrell.

"Right to the top of the Quai d'Orsay." Dominique smiled her engaging smile. "He says it's little enough he can do, for he insists I'm an enormous asset to him."

"Obviously. No one could possibly ignore him with you at his side."

"Oh, he goes further than that. He insists I attract a better class of clients, for only the wealthiest could afford me, if I were available. It's a joke, of course." With what appeared to be warm regret, Dominique disengaged her hands from his.

"Of course." Hawthorne poured the rest of the wine into his glass and leaned back in his chair. "You're out here visiting your uncle on Saba?" he asked.

"Good Lord, I completely forgot! I really must call the bank and reach his lawyer. . . . Now you know what happens to me when I see you again."

"I'd like to believe that——"

"You can, Tyrell," interrupted Dominique softly, leaning forward, her wide brown eyes riveted on his. "You really can, my darling. . . . Where's the phone, I'm sure I saw one."

"It's in the lobby."

"I'll be back in a few minutes. Dear old Uncle is thinking of moving again; his neighbors have become too considerate."

"Saba's recluse of recluses, as I recall," said Tyrell, smiling. "No phones, no mail, and, where possible, no visitors."

"I insisted on a satellite dish." Dominique moved back her chair and stood up. "He loves to watch international soccer; he thinks it's black magic, but he watches it constantly. . . . I'll hurry."

"I'll be here." Hawthorne gazed at the receding figure of the woman he had thought was gone from his life. The rush of contradictory information was not much different from being buffeted by strong winds. The marriage had nearly drowned him; the marriage that was not a marriage at all had restored his breath, the new buoyancy exhilarating. . . . He could not lose her again; he *would* not lose her again.

He wondered if she would think to call her uncle on Saba and tell him she'd be late returning. There were interisland planes usually every hour until the early evening, an aerial network throughout the chain. Theirs could not be a brief hello and good-bye, it was unthinkable, and he knew her well enough to realize she understood that. He smiled to himself at the thought of the eccentric uncle he had never met, the Parisian attorney who had spent more than thirty years in the swirling, back-stabbing world of arbitrage, racing from boardrooms to courtrooms, millions in the balance with every decision he made, and even then wary of panicking clients who too frequently put money before principle, voiding his hours of concentration.

All of this for a quiet, gentle man who wanted only to get away from the energy-sapping insanity and paint flowers and sunsets, a self-proclaimed latter-day Gauguin. Upon his retirement, Dominique said, he had packed his elderly maid, left a cold, impervious wife with more than enough to continue her extravagant ways, not bothered to contact two insufferable daughters, both infected with their mother's disease of greed, and flown off to the Caribbean "in search of my Tahiti."

Saba had been an accident brought about by a conversation with a stranger at the airport bar in Martinique. The man was a runaway who had decided to run back and spend his final years in the lights of Paris, and he had a modest but well-built house to sell on an island called Saba. Intrigued, Dominique's uncle had inquired further and was shown several billfold snapshots of the house in question. Sight unseen, except for the snapshots, the retired attorney bought it instantly, drawing up the papers himself on a nearby table while his maid looked on in astonishment and not a little trepidation. He then proceeded to place a call to his Paris firm, instructing his former vice president, now president, to pay the owner in full upon the man's arrival in Paris. His former subordinate was to deduct the purchase price from his former superior's generous pension. There was only one proviso—delivered to the owner in the airport's bar. The man was to reach the local telephone company on Saba and have every phone in the house removed immediately. The perplexed returning expatriate, his good fortune beyond his dreams, got in touch with the island phone office on an airport pay phone, fairly screaming his instructions.

The Caribbean was filled with such stories, for the islands were a haven for the disaffected, the burnt out, and the progressively dissolute. It took someone with compassion to understand them, someone of substance to care. And Dominique, one of the world's original do-gooders, cared enough for her runaway uncle to pay attention.

"Would you believe it?" Dominique interrupted Tyrell's reverie as she approached her chair. "The lawyer left a message for me that he was tied up and could we make it tomorrow! He made it abundantly clear that he would have phoned me on the island *if* there were a telephone."

"Logic's on his side."

"Then I made another call, Commander—it was Commander, wasn't it?" Dominique sat down.

"Long ago," replied Tyrell, shaking his head, "and I've since upgraded myself. I'm a captain now, because it's my own ship—boat."

"That's upgrading?"

"Take my word for it, a full promotion. Whom did you call?"

"My uncle's neighbors, the couple are so considerate, he wants to move again. They keep coming over with fresh vegetables from their garden, bypass the maid, and interrupt his painting—or his soccer."

"They sound like nice people."

"They are; he isn't, bless his cantankerous heart. Nevertheless, I gave them a chance to legitimately break in on him. I asked them to go over and tell him that there were problems with off-island ownership of property, that his lawyer, the bank, and I were trying to resolve them. I'd be quite late getting back."

"Wonder of wonders," said Hawthorne, grinning, his full buoyancy returned. "I was hoping you'd manage to reach him."

"Could I do anything else, my darling? I wasn't being polite, Tye. I've missed you so."

"I just checked out of a room down the street," Tyrell said hesitantly. "I'm sure I can get it back."

"Please. Do so, *please*. What's the name of the hotel?"

"*Hotel*'s a little grand for what it is. It's called the Flamboyant, also a touch out of its class."

"Go there, my darling, and I'll join you in ten or fifteen minutes. Tell the desk I'm expected and to give me the room number."

"Why?"

"I want to bring you—us—a present. This is a celebration!" she said.

They held each other in the confines of the small hotel room, Dominique trembling in Hawthorne's arms. The gift she had brought them was three bottles of chilled champagne, all carried upstairs in ice buckets by an overtipped desk clerk.

"At least it's white wine," said Tyrell, releasing her and going to the trays on the bureau, opening the first bottle. "Do you realize I haven't had any whiskey since four days after you disappeared? Of course, I drank up the entire island's supply in those four days and lost two charters, but that's when the bourbon bottles went into the drink."

"Then my leaving you had one positive result. Whiskey was only a crutch for you, not a necessity." Dominique sat at the small round table that overlooked the harbor of St. Barts.

"Spare me, I'm not the same guy." Hawthorne carried their glasses and the bottle to the table, then pulled back the chair opposite her. "What's that corny phrase?" he said, sitting down. " 'Here's looking at you, kid'?"

"Here's to both of us, my darling." They drank, and Hawthorne refilled their glasses.

"So you have a charter here?" asked Dominique.

"No," Tyrell thought quickly, looking briefly out the window. "I'm checking out Barts for a Florida hotel syndicate; they're counting on the fact that gambling will be here soon and want my input. It's happening all over the islands, the economies are screaming for it."

"Yes, I've heard that. It's sad, in a way."

"Very sad, and probably unavoidable. Casinos make for jobs. . . . I don't want to talk about the islands, I want to talk about us."

"What's there to talk about, Tye? Your life is here, mine is in Europe, or Africa, or the refugee camps in the besieged countries, where people need our help. Pour me another; you and the wine are intoxicating."

"What about you, a life for *you*?" Hawthorne filled their glasses.

"It will come soon enough, my darling. One day I'll come back, and, if you're not entangled, I'll sit on your Olympic Charters doorstep and say, 'Hello there, Commander, take me or throw me to the sharks.' "

"How soon is soon enough?"

"Not much longer; even my strength is wearing out. . . . But let's not talk about the inevitable, Tye. We must talk about now."

"What?"

"Courtesy of my uncle's neighbors, I spoke to my husband this morning. I must fly back to Paris tonight. He has business with the royal family in Monaco and wants me with him."

"Tonight?"

"I can't deny him, Tye, he's done so much for me and demands only my presence. He's sending a company jet to Martinique for me. I'll be in Paris in several hours, do a flurry of packing and shopping in the morning, and meet him in Nice later in the day."

"You'll disappear again," said Hawthorne, the long-absent champagne suddenly slurring his speech. "You won't come back!"

"You're so terribly wrong, my darling . . . my love. I'll return in two or three weeks, *believe* me. But for now, for these few hours, *be* with me, stay with me, make *love* to me!" Dominique rose from the chair, removed the jacket of her white pantsuit, and began unbuttoning her blouse. Tyrell got up and removed his clothes, pausing to refill their glasses. "For God's sake, *love* me!" cried Dominique, pulling them both to the bed.

The smoke of their cigarettes floated up to the ceiling in the glow of the outside afternoon sun, their bodies exhausted, Hawthorne's brain relaxed by the intensity of their lovemaking, along with long swallows from the bottle of champagne. "How is my love?" whispered Dominique as she rolled over on his prone, naked body, her generous breasts encompassing his face.

"If there's a heaven beyond this, I don't have to know it," answered Tyrell, smiling crookedly.

"That's such a terrible remark, I'm forced to pour you another glass. Me too."

"It's the last bottle, and we're overdoing the booze, lady."

"I don't care, it's our last hour—until I see you again." Dominique reached over the bed and poured the last of the champagne in their glasses, pools of liquid in circles on her side of the floor. "Here you are, my darling," she said, holding the glass to Tyrell's lips. She raised her right breast and placed it next to his cheek. "I must remember every moment with you."

"You look and feel only outstanding . . . I think that's a military term."

"I'll accept it, Commander—oh, I forgot, you don't like that title."

"I told you about Amsterdam," said Hawthorne, barely coherent. "I hate the title. . . . Oh, Christ, I'm

drunk, and I can't remember when—I've been drunk
before—"

"You're not anything of the sort, my darling, we're
just celebrating. Didn't we agree to that?"

"Yes . . . yeah, sure."

"Make love to me again, my dearest love."

"*What*. . . ?" Tyrell's head fell to the side; he had
passed out, the long, unfamiliar heavy intake of alcohol
too much for his blood.

Dominique rose quietly from the bed, went to her
clothes draped over the chair by the window, and
dressed quickly. Suddenly, she noticed Hawthorne's tan
cotton jacket on the floor where he had dropped it; it
was the common island uniform, a lightweight guayabera with four outside pockets worn over bare flesh in
the hot tropic sun. However, it was not the jacket itself
that caught her attention; instead, it was a folded, half-
crumpled envelope bordered by blue and red stripes, the
sort frequently used by governments or private clubs
wishing to appear official. She knelt down, pulled it out
of the pocket, and withdrew the contents, a concise and
precise handwritten note. She moved to the window to
read it clearly; it was written on a yacht club's stationery:

Subjects: Mature woman traveling with a young
man approximately half her age.

Details: Descriptions incomplete but could be Bajaratt and youthful escort as spotted in Marseilles.
Names on St. Martin's hydrofoil manifest: Frau
Marlene Richter and Hans Bauer, grandchild. Bajaratt has no record of employing German names
previously, nor has it been established that she
speaks German, but it's entirely possible that she
does.

Contact: Inspector Lawrence Major, chief of Island Security, St. Barts.

Intermediary: Name withheld on demand.

Method/Operation: Approach subjects from behind, weapons drawn. Shout out the name Bajaratt and be prepared to fire.

Dominique squinted in the window's afternoon sunlight as she replaced the note in the envelope, crossed back to the cotton jacket, and restored the paper to the pocket. Straightening up, she stared at the naked figure on the bed. Her magnificent lover had lied. Captain Tyrell Hawthorne, Olympic Charters, U.S. Virgin Islands, was once again Commander Hawthorne, naval intelligence, Amsterdam, recruited to hunt down a terrorist from the Baaka Valley whose journey from Marseilles had been tracked to the Caribbean. How tragic and how tragically ironic, thought Dominique as she walked to the desk and picked up her purse. She then crossed to the bedside table, snapped on the radio, gradually turning up the volume until the harsh, violent beat of the island music filled the room. Hawthorne did not stir.

So terrible, so unnecessary . . . so full of a pain she dared not acknowledge, yet by denying it increasing the hurt. She had fantasized an existence that in another life she would have killed to live. An inconsequential husband who supported her causes unfailingly, leaving her to find what happiness she could without interference in a world of treachery and deceit. Would that it were all so simple, so unencumbered, but it was not! She loved the naked man on the bed, loved his mind, his body, even his suffering, for she understood them all. But this was the real world, not a fantasy.

She opened her purse and slowly, carefully, withdrew a small automatic, placing it against the pillow which she folded against Hawthorne's left temple, her index finger curved around the trigger, millimeters from the pull, as the reggae-calypso music reached successive crescendos. . . . *She could not do it!* She loathed herself but she *could not do it*! This was a man she loved, as fully as she had loved the firebrand of Ashkelon!

Amaya Bajaratt returned the weapon to her purse and raced out of the room.

Hawthorne woke up, his head splintered, his eyes unfocused, abruptly aware that Dominique was not beside him in the bed. Where was she? He leapt to his feet, instantly steadying himself, and looked for the antiquated phone. He saw it on the opposite bedside table and threw himself across the sheets, lifting the receiver and dialing the operator. "The woman who was here!" he shouted. "When did she leave?"

"Over an hour ago, *mon*," said the desk clerk. "A nice lady."

Tyrell slammed down the phone, walked into the small, inadequate bathroom, and filled the inadequate sink with cold water. He plunged his face into it, his thoughts on the island of Saba. Surely she would not return to Paris without seeing her uncle once more. . . . Before that he had to reach Geoffrey Cooke in Virgin Gorda, if only to tell him that his sighting was a bust.

"Christiansted was a toilet too, old boy, and so was Anguilla," said Cooke from Virgin Gorda. "I guess we were all chasing feathers. Are you coming back this afternoon?"

"No, I'm following up something else."

"You found something?"

"Found and lost, Geoff. It's important to me, not to you. I'll check in later."

"Please do. We've got two more reports which Jacques and I will cover."

"Leave word with Marty where I can reach you."

"The mechanic fellow?"

"And then some."

The pontoons of the seaplane crunched down into the calm waters and taxied in a semicircle into the rock-hewn cove of the private island. The pilot maneuvered the aircraft toward the short dock, where one of the *lupo*-armed guards stood waiting. The capo caught the overhanging wing, steadying the seaplane as Bajaratt stepped down on a pontoon, gripped the attendant's briefly freed hands, and climbed onto the dock.

"The *padrone* has had a good day, signora," the man said in heavily accented English, shouting to be heard over the sound of the propellers. "Seeing you again is better than all the treatments in Miami. He sang opera while I bathed him."

"Can you manage things here?" asked the Baj quickly. "I have to go to him right away."

"What is there to manage, signora? I push the wing away and our *amico silenzioso* does the rest."

"*Va bene!*" Amaya raced up the stone steps, catching her breath as she reached the top. It was better not to show anxiety. The *padrone* dismissed anyone who displayed signs of losing control, which she had not, but the fact that her presence was known in the intelligence circles that covered the islands was a shock. She could accept the *padrone*'s knowing, for he had debts owed to him throughout the world of the Baaka Valley, but for a hunt to have been mounted that reached the point of recruiting the retired Hawthorne was not acceptable. Breathing deeply, Bajaratt walked up the flagstone path and yanked down the bronze handle of the door. She pushed it open, holding her place in the frame, only to see the frail figure in the wheelchair waving childishly at her from halfway across the huge stone foyer.

"*Ciao,* Annie!" said the *padrone,* smiling weakly, and with what minor enthusiasm he could muster. "Did you have a fine day, my only daughter?"

"I never got to the bank," replied Bajaratt curtly, walking inside.

"That's regrettable. Why not? Adore you as I do, my child, I will not permit any funds to be transferred to you from my accounts. It's far too dangerous, and my familiars in the Mediterranean can well afford to send you anything you need."

"I'm not concerned with the money," said Amaya. "I can return tomorrow and get it, but what does concern me is that the Americans, the British, and the French know I'm in the islands!"

"But of course they do, Annie! *I* knew you were coming; where do you think I learned that?"

"I assumed through the Baaka financial establishment."

"Did I not mention the Deuxième, MI-6, even the Americans?"

"Forgive me, *padrone,* but the brilliant film star in you often leads to exaggeration."

"*Molto bene!*" laughed the invalid, rasping with constricted vocal cords. "Yet not entirely true. I have Americans on a distant payroll; they informed me that there was an alert out for you down here. But what area, what island? *Impossibile!* No one knows what you look like, and you are a master—perhaps I should say a mistress—of different appearances. Where is the danger?"

"Do you remember a man named Hawthorne?"

"Oh, yes, yes, of course. A discredited officer of U.S. intelligence, navy, I believe, once married to a Soviet double agent. You found out who he was and engineered a meeting, then enjoyed him for a number of months while you were recovering from your wounds. You thought you might learn something from his expertise."

"What I learned was of little value, but he's now back in business, hunting for Bajaratt. I ran into him this afternoon, I was with him this afternoon."

"How extraordinary, my daughter," said the *padrone,* his watery blue eyes studying Bajaratt's face. "And how fortunate for you. You were a very happy woman during those months, as I recall."

"One takes minor pleasures where one can find them, my father. He was merely an unknowing instrument of instruction should there be anything I might use."

"An instrument that produced music in you, perhaps?"

"Rubbish!"

"You sang and pranced about like the child you never were."

"Your cinematic memories warp your observations. My wounds were simply healing, that's all. . . . He's here, don't you understand? He'll go to Saba and look for me there!"

"Oh, yes, I recall. An imaginary old French uncle, wasn't it?"

"He must be killed, *padrone*!"

"Why didn't you kill him this afternoon?"

"There was no opportunity. I was seen with him, I'd have been caught."

"Even more extraordinary," said the old Italian quietly. "The Baj of high regard always created her own opportunities."

"Stop it, my only father! *Kill* him!"

"Very well, my daughter. The heart is not always resolute. . . . Saba, you say? It's less than an hour in our cigarette boat." The *padrone* raised his head. "*Scozzi!*" he cried, summoning one of his attendants.

Speed was everything, for memories were short in the islands, almost always intentionally. Saba was not a usual charter stop, but Hawthorne knew it from the few times he had sailed there. Everyone on the docks in the immediate islands of Saint T. and Tortola accommodated the charter captains. It paid to do so, and Tyrell counted on that native trait.

He hired a seaplane out of Barts and flew into the island's modest harbor; he wanted all the cooperation he could engender. He appeared to get it, yet nothing made sense.

No one in the marina knew an old man with a French maid. Nor had anyone seen a woman fitting the description of Dominique. How could they *not* know her, a tall, striking white woman who came so often to visit her uncle? It was strange; the dock boys generally knew everything that took place in the small out islands, especially on the waterfronts. Boats came in with supplies, and supplies had to be delivered, and deliveries were paid for; it was the custom of the trade to know all the roads that led to every house on such a place as Saba. On the other hand, as he and Dominique had agreed, her uncle was the "recluse of recluses," and there was an airstrip as well as a few unpretentious stores whose fare could be augmented by provisions flown in by air. Perhaps it was enough for a frail old man and his maid.

Tyrell walked in the blistering heat to the island's shanty post office, only to be told by an arrogant postal clerk that "you make no sense, *mon*! No box for such a person or a woman who talk like a French mama."

That information was stranger than what he had heard at the marina. Dominique had explained years earlier that her uncle had a "rather decent" pension from his firm; the payments were sent to him every month. Again, there was the airstrip, which could provide another explanation. Mail was erratic in the minor islands; perhaps Paris sent their retired attorney his stipend by air from Martinique. It was certainly both safer and more efficient.

Tyrell learned quickly from the postal clerk where he could hire a motorbike, Saba's favored means of transport. It was simple; the man had several in the back for rent. All he had to do was leave a large deposit along with his driver's license and sign a paper stating he was responsible for all repairs, to be deducted from his deposit.

Hawthorne spent nearly three hours bouncing over the roads and through the hills, going from house to cottage to shack, invariably met by sullen residents wearing holstered firearms and protected by snarling island dogs. The exception was his last stop, a retired Anglican priest with a swollen nose and a blotched, red-veined face, his affliction obvious. Rum was immediately offered along with the opportunity to freshen up and remove the dust from his clothes and body. Both were gently declined due to the visitor's haste, and as Tyrell questioned the disheveled elderly prelate, his anxiety was apparent.

"I'm truly sorry to say there are no such persons on this island, young man."

"Are you sure?"

"Oh, yes, oh, yes," the priest had replied dreamily, yet not without subtle amusement. "Knowing my weaknesses, there are times of clarity when I feel the need to do God's work as I used to do. Like the wandering Peter, I go from place to place, bearing the Word of God the Father. I realize that I am quite rightfully treated like an old fool, but for a while I feel somewhat cleansed, and I can assure you my wits are about me. Over the past two years since I've been here, I've visited every residence—rich and poor, black and white—once, twice, three times. . . . There's no one on Saba such as you've described. Are you sure you won't have a rum? It's all I can offer, all I can afford, but I grow limes and mangoes; their mingled juices go well with the Cruzan."

"No, thank you, Father. I'm in a hurry."

"I don't think you want to thank me at all. It's in your very strained voice."

"Sorry. I'm just confused."

"Who isn't, young man?"

Hawthorne returned the motorbike to the post office, received his license and one half of his deposit without arguing, and walked back down the road to the marina and his chartered seaplane.

It was not there.

He hastened his pace, finally breaking into a run. He had to get back to Gorda . . . where the hell was the plane! It had been secured to the pier; the pilot and the dock boys had assured him that it would remain in place until he returned.

Then he saw the signs, hastily painted and nailed to posts, several spelled correctly, most not. DANGER. PYLON REPAIRS IN PROGRESS. BOATERS STAY WAY TILL DAMAGE FIXED.

For God's sake, it was nearly six o'clock in the evening, the waters darkening, the visibility underneath as opaque as night because of the lengthening shadows of the Caribbean sun. No one repaired pylons under those conditions; a pier could collapse, burying a scuba metalman under its weight without the light filtering down from above to warn him. Tyrell ran through the demarcation line to the single machine shop far to the right of the extended dock, its conveyor rail and heavy winches leading down to the water. There was no one inside. It was crazy! Men working underwater at this hour without backups, without oxygen and medical equipment in case of an accident? He raced out of the shop and down to the beach that led to the steps of the pier, aware that a cloud cover blurred the rays of the setting sun. How could anyone work this way? He had repaired hulls under similar conditions, but only with backups and lines held by those above, prepared to yank him up in an emergency. He climbed the steps and cautiously walked out on the pier. The clouds intercepted the sun, darker clouds now, rain clouds.

His first instinct was to raise the metal-men, and with the authority of the military officer he had been, to yell at everyone and tell them how stupid they were, then dismiss them for the night.

His authority diminished with each step he took; there were no lines, no bubbles in the darkened water. There was no one on the pier or beneath it. The marina was deserted.

Suddenly, the dock's floodlights atop aluminum poles switched on, the beams blinding. Then an ice-cold slice in his left shoulder was accompanied by a loud gunshot; he gripped the wound and plunged over the pier into the water, hearing a staccato volley of gunfire as he dove beneath the surface. For reasons he could never explain, he let his panic guide him. He swam underwater as long as his breath would permit to the nearest yacht he could recall. He surfaced twice, only his face, to inflate his lungs, and proceeded until he felt the hard wood of a boat's hull. He surfaced again in its deepest water line, breathed again, and swam under to the other side. He raised himself on the gunwale and looked over at the pier, now half in blurred, streaked sunlight, half under the glare of floodlights. His two would-be killers were crouching at the end of the dock, peering into the water.

"Suo sangue!" yelled one.

"Non basta!" roared the other, leaping into a motor-driven skiff and starting the engine, instructing his associate to release the line and jump in, his *lupo* at the ready. They crisscrossed the small harbor, an AK-47 and the shotgun of the wolf in their hands.

Hawthorne slithered over the gunwale of the yacht he had reached and found what he expected to find in nylon straps near the fishing tender—a simple scaling knife. He slipped back over the side and into the water; his shoes having disappeared, he removed his trousers, trying to remember where they sank, should he survive. He then wriggled his tan guayabera jacket loose, oddly thinking that Geoffrey Cooke would have to pay for his money, his papers, and his lost apparel. He swam into the darker waters, again suddenly aware that the driver of the small boat held a powerful flashlight which he kept roving over the sundown waters. Tyrell dove deep in the path of the skiff until he heard the motor above him.

Timing his moves, Hawthorne lunged to the surface directly behind the skiff and grabbed the pivoting metal casing of the engine, his head to the side, his hand in shadows, preventing the rudder from turning. Furious, and confused by the fact that the motor did not respond to his commands, the skipper leaned over the stern less than a foot above the wake. His eyes bulged at the sight of Tyrell's hand as if it were some monstrous tentacle from the deep. Before he could scream, Hawthorne plunged the blade of the scaling knife into the killer's neck, Tye's left hand surging up, gripping his would-be assassin's throat so that no sound emerged that carried above the engine. He yanked the corpse over the stern into the water, and carefully moving the propeller to far starboard, climbed into the killer's seat as the man in front obsessively moved his flashlight back and forth, scouring the watery path ahead. Hawthorne grabbed the AK-47 and spoke clearly.

"The waves splash a lot at this hour and the motor's pretty loud. I suggest you put down your weapon or join your friend. You, too, would make a nice tenderloin for our sharks. They're really benevolent creatures; they prefer what's already dead."

"*Che còsa? Impossibile!*"

"That's what we're going to talk about," said Tyrell, heading out to sea.

5

Darkness descended; the water was calm, the moon barely visible through the cloud cover as the small skiff bobbed up and down with the rhythm of the gentle ocean swells. The remaining killer sat nervously on the tiny seat at the bow, blinking his eyes and pulling up his hands under the glare of the powerful flashlight.

"Put your hands down," ordered Hawthorne.

"The light is blinding me. Take it away!"

"Actually, that could be a blessing, blindness, I mean, if you force me only to wound you before shoving you over the side."

"Che còsa?"

"We all have to die. Sometimes I think it's the quality of death, not the event that counts."

"What are you saying, signore . . . ?"

"You're going to tell me what I want to know or you're shark meat. If you're blind, you won't see the great white's row of pointed teeth before it chops you in half. The big fish are luminous, you know, seen clearly in dark water. Look! Over there, the dorsal fin! He must be an eighteen-footer; this is the season, you realize that, don't you? Why do you think there are shark-fishing contests throughout the islands at this time of year?"

"I know nothing of such things!"

"Then you don't get the local papers, but then, why should you? They don't carry much news from Sicily."

"Sicilia?"

"Somehow you don't strike me as a papal nuncio; they probably shoot better. . . . Come on, *paisan,* get in the real world—or get in the water with blood oozing out of your shoulder, as some is coming out of mine, and play games with our circling big fish whose jaws are larger than a third of its body."

The capo's head spun from side to side, his blinking eyes wide, his hands again trying to shield the light as he studied the water on both sides of the small boat. "I cannot *see!*"

"He's right behind you. Turn around and you'll spot it."

"In the name of Christ, do not do this!"

"Why did you try to kill me?"

"Orders!"

"From whom?" The assassin did not answer. "It's your death, not mine," said Tyrell, cocking the AK-47. "I'll chop off your left shoulder; the blood will spread quicker that way, like bleeding chum. Of course, the great whites like to nibble—hors d'oeuvres before the main meal." Hawthorne squeezed the trigger, the explosions filling the night as he sprayed the water to the right of the Mafia capo.

"Stop! . . . . Stop in the holy name of *Jesus!*"

"Wow, you guys get religion quickly." Hawthorne fired again, the volley ear-shattering, several bullets grazing the left shoulder of the mafioso.

"*Per piacere!* Please, I beg you!"

"My dorsal-finned friend down there is hungry. Why should I deny him?"

"You . . . you have heard of a valley. . . ?" the killer choked, searching for words, obviously, in panic, recalling other words he had heard before. "From far away, across the sea!"

"I've heard of the Baaka Valley," said Tyrell in a monotone. "It's across the Mediterranean. So?"

"That's where the orders come from, signore."

"Who's the relay? Who gave you those orders?"

"They come from Miami, what else can I tell you? I don't know the *capi*!"

"Why me?"

"I don't know, signore."

"*Bajaratt!*" roared Hawthorne, seeing what he wanted to see in the capo's wide eyes. "It is Bajaratt, isn't it?"

"*Sì, sì,* I have heard the name. Nothing more."

"From the Baaka?"

"Please, signore! I am merely a *soldato*, what do you want from me?"

"How did you find me? Did you follow a woman named Dominique Montaigne?"

"*Non capisco,* I do not know that name."

"Liar!" Again Tyrell fired the AK-47, but no longer penetrating the capo's shoulder, experience dictating his strategy with a terrified underling.

"I *swear!*" screamed the *capo subordinato*. "Others, also, have been looking for you."

"Because they know I'm looking for this Bajaratt."

"Whatever leads to you leads to you, signore."

"Apparently it does," said Tye, turning the boat around.

"I will not be killed. . . ?" The would-be assassin closed his eyes in prayer as Hawthorne swung the beam of the powerful flashlight away from his face. "I will not be fed to the sharks?"

"Can you swim?" asked Tye, ignoring the question.

"*Naturalmente,*" answered the capo, "but not in these waters, especially as I am bleeding."

"How good a swimmer are you?"

"I am a *Siciliano* from Messina. As a boy I dove for coins thrown by the tourists from the ships."

"That's good. Because I'm going to leave you a half mile offshore. You can handle the rest."

"With the sharks?"

"There hasn't been a shark in these waters for over twenty years. The coral odors repel them."

*   *   *

The Sicilian killer was lying, Hawthorne knew it. Whoever was behind the attempt on his life had bought the whole marina and closed it down. The Baaka Valley couldn't do that, Mafia or no Mafia. There was someone else who knew the islands and which buttons to press. Whoever that was was protecting the psychopath Bajaratt. Hawthorne, having stolen a pair of soiled coveralls, watched from the outside corner of the machine shop as the exhausted capo stumbled out of the mild surf onto the beach, so spent he lay prone on the sand, his body heaving, catching his breath. He had discarded his jacket and his shoes, but his bulging right trouser pocket indicated that he had put whatever possessions he felt necessary into it. Tyrell counted on him having them; a carrier pigeon without a capsule was a useless bird.

Two minutes passed and the mafioso raised his head in the glare of the floodlights. He awkwardly, painfully, got to his feet, looking swiftly to his right and his left, obviously trying to orient himself. The capo's head stopped swiveling, his eyes centered on the machine shop. That was the place where he and his dead colleague had initiated their operation; there was no other. The switch for the floodlights was there, the money passed inside. And there was a telephone on a counter. . . . At this point, thought Hawthorne, remembering a dozen such entrapments in Amsterdam, Brussels, and Munich, the mark was a programmed robot. He had to follow his instincts to survive. He did.

Breathless, the mafioso ran down the beach to the steps to the shop. Gripping the rail, he climbed them, every now and then grabbing his shoulder and grimacing at his minor wound. Tyrell smiled; his own shoulder had been cleansed by the sea and only trickled. Band-Aids would take care of them both, but psychologically the capo was singing melodramatic opera.

The killer reached the machine shop, kicked open the door with unnecessary force, and burst inside. Seconds later the floodlights were extinguished and a lamp was turned on. Hawthorne crept to the open door and listened as the mafioso argued with a Caribbean operator over the telephone.

"*Sì!* Yes, *yes,* it is a Miami *numero*—number!" The capo repeated the digits and Hawthorne printed them indelibly in his memory—my God, the games! "*Emergènza!*" yelled the mafioso, having reached Miami. "*Cerca il padrone via satellite! Presto!*" Moments passed before the panicked man, now holding his groin, spoke again, screamed again. "*Padrone, esso incredible! Scozzi è morto! Un diavolo da inferno . . . !*"

Tyrell could not understand all the frenzied Italian shouted by the capo into the phone, but he had picked up enough. He had a number in Miami, and the existence of someone called *padrone,* who was reached by an access-satellite relay—someone here in the islands who was aiding and abetting the terrorist Bajaratt.

"*Ho capito! Nuova York. Va bene!*"

Those last words, too, were not difficult to understand, thought Hawthorne as the mafioso hung up the phone and started anxiously toward the door. The capo was being ordered to New York, where he could disappear until summoned. Tyrell picked up one of the discarded rust-encrusted anchors that lay on the machine shop's platform, and as the killer walked through the door, he swung the heavy dual-pronged object into the mafioso's lower legs, fracturing both knees.

The capo screamed, collapsing to the wooden-planked floor, unconscious.

"*Ciao,*" said Hawthorne, bending over the body and plunging his hand into the right trouser pocket, pulling out everything inside. He studied the objects, disgusted with the owner. There was a thick black prayer book written in Italian, rosary beads, and a money clip with nine hundred French francs—approximately a hundred and eighty dollars. There was no billfold or wallet, no other papers—*Omertà*.

Tyrell took the money, rose to his feet, and raced away. Somewhere, somehow, he had to find a plane and a pilot.

The frail figure in the wheelchair rolled himself out of his study into his marbled aviary, where Bajaratt waited.

"Baj, you must leave immediately," he said firmly. "*Now*. The plane will be here within the hour, and Miami is sending two men to attend me."

"*Padrone*, you're crazy! I've made the contacts—your contacts—they're flying here to see me during the next three days. You've confirmed the Baaka deposits in St. Barts; there will be no paper trail."

"There is a far worse trail, my only daughter. Scozzi is dead, killed by your Hawthorne. Maggio is in hysterics on Saba, claiming your lover is a man from hell!"

"He is only a man," said Bajaratt coldly. "Why didn't they kill him?"

"I wish I knew, but you must leave. Immediately!"

"*Padrone*, how can you possibly think that Hawthorne could ever connect you with me, or even more impossibly think that Dominique Montaigne has any connection with Bajaratt? My *God*, we made love this afternoon and he believes I'm on my way back to Paris! He loves me, the fool!"

"Is he more clever than we believe?"

"Absolutely not! He's a wounded animal, ripe for succoring, therefore a perfect tunnel."

"How about you, my only daughter? Four years ago, I remember well your filling these halls with songs of delight. How you obviously cared for that man."

"Don't be ridiculous! I was within an instant of killing him only hours ago, when I realized that the front desk knew I was in his room. . . . You approved of my decision, *padrone,* even praised my caution. What can I *say?*"

"You don't say, Baj. *I* say. We'll fly you to St. Barts; you get your money in the morning and then you'll be taken to Miami or wherever you choose to go."

"What about my contacts? They expect to find me here."

"I'll take care of them. I'll give you a telephone number. Until you're reached by a higher authority, they'll do your bidding. . . . You are still my only daughter, Annie."

"*Padrone,* the telephone! I know exactly what to do."

"I trust you'll inform me first."

"We both have friends in Paris?"

"*Naturalmente.*"

"*Molto bene!*"

Hawthorne desperately needed to find a plane and a pilot, but they were not the first priorities. There was another: an unmitigated rat named Captain Henry Stevens, United States Naval Intelligence. The specter of Amsterdam suddenly rose like a fiery bird from the black ashes of a shattered dream. St. Barts and the disappearance of Dominique felt too similar to the horrible events that had led to the death of his wife. Nothing made sense! If Stevens was even remotely involved, Tye had to know! After giving a hundred French francs and spelling out his name and resumed rank to the sole uninterested radio operator in the control tower, which was neither a tower nor had much control over anything except for the strip lights, he had the use of Saba airfield's telephone. He had committed the Miami number to memory; Washington's was reflex.

"Department of the Navy," said the voice fifteen hundred miles north.

"Division One, Intelligence, please. Security code four-zero."

"An emergency, sir?"

"You've got it, sailor."

"I-One," said a second voice moments later. "Did I understand that this is a four-zero?"

"You did."

"Of what nature?"

"That can be relayed by me only to Captain Stevens. Track him down. Now."

"They're working overtime upstairs. Who's this?"

"*Amsterdam* will get you through. He'd want you to hurry."

"We'll see." The aloof intelligence officer obviously saw within seconds, as Stevens's voice came forcefully on the line.

"Hawthorne?"

"I thought you'd catch the connection, you son of a bitch."

"What's that mean?"

"You know damned well what it means! Your robots found me, and because your little egos couldn't handle MI-6 recruiting me, you took her to find out what you could, because you knew I wouldn't tell you a goddamned thing! I'm going to put your ass in a military court-martial, Henry."

"*Whoa,* back up. I don't have a clue as to where you're coming from or who the *her* is! I spent two lousy hours with the DCI yesterday, getting this ass reamed out because you wouldn't even talk to me, and now you're sounding off about our 'finding' you—wherever the hell you are—and kidnapping a woman we never heard of. Get off it!"

"You're a fucking liar! You lied in Amsterdam."

"I had my evidence, you saw it."

"You built it!"

"I didn't build anything, Hawthorne, it was built *for* me."

"This is Ingrid all over again!"

"*Bullshit!* And I repeat, we have no one in the islands who knows anything about you or any woman!"

"Really, Captain? A couple of your clowns phoned me down here and tried to sell me a tale of D.C. panic. They knew where I was; the rest would be easy, even for them."

"Then they know something I don't! And since I'm meeting with all of my so-called clowns this morning, maybe they'll tell me."

"They must have followed me to St. Barts, seen her with me, and grabbed her when she went out."

"Tye, for God's sake, you've got it all wrong! Of course I admit we tried like hell to pull you back in— we'd be damn fools if we didn't. But in point of fact we didn't succeed, did we? The Brits and the French did, but *we didn't*! We have no one down there who knows you from a—what was it you used to say?—oh, yeah, a baked potato."

"I'm not difficult to find; I even take out ads."

"And considering the fact that we want your help, the last thing we'd do is to take into custody a friend of yours for questioning. That's just too dumb. . . . Tye, are you back on the sauce?"

"A momentary lapse. It's irrelevant."

"Maybe it isn't."

"It is. I couldn't sail my charters if I were, and you know that."

"You've got a point."

"We both do," said Hawthorne quietly. "She was on her way back to Paris today, then down to Nice. She didn't want to go."

"Hell, that's probably it. She also probably didn't want any long good-byes."

"I won't accept that!"

"Maybe your temporary lapse won't let you. . . . Is it possible?"

"You know," replied Hawthorne reluctantly, the fight suddenly out of him, "she did it before, she just disappeared."

"I'll bet my pension she did it again. Call her in Paris tonight; my guess is you'll find her there."

"I can't. I don't know her husband's name."

"No comment, Commander."

"You don't understand—"

"I don't care to try—"

"We go back four . . . five years."

"Now I really tune out. That's when you left us."

"Yes, I left you. I left because I *sensed* something, sensed that something was really fouled up in Amsterdam, and it'll stay with me for the rest of my life."

"I can't help you there," said the head of naval intelligence after several moments of silence.

"I don't expect you to." Again there was silence.

"Are you making any progress with MI-6 and the Deuxième?" asked Stevens finally.

"Yes, as of less than an hour ago."

"I spoke with London and Paris at the suggestion of Gillette at Central Intelligence. I'm sure you'll want to confirm it, but since I'm closest, I'm to supply you with whatever you need."

"I don't have to confirm it. You'd be hanging yourself if you lied in a situation you can't control, Captain. You're not prone to doing that."

"You know, Hawthorne," said Stevens quietly, "I can put up with your shit only just so far—"

"You'll put up with whatever I care to dish out, Henry, let's get that straight! You're a cog and I'm an independent contract, and don't you forget it. I give the orders to you, you don't give them to me, because if you try, I'll walk away. Understood?"

A third and prolonged silence ensued before the naval intelligence chief spoke. "Do you want to give me a progress report?"

"You're damn right I do, and I want immediate activity. I've got a number in Miami that has an access satellite relay to a phone here in the islands. I need the location as soon as you can get it."

"Bajaratt?"

"It's got to be. Here's the number." Tyrell recited it, requested confirmation for accuracy, gave him the airstrip number on Saba, and was about to hang up the telephone when Stevens broke in.

"Tyrell!" he said. "Our differences aside—and I mean that—can you give me any background, any fill?"

"No."

"For Christ's sake, why not? I'm your official liaison now, cleared, incidentally, by all your governments, and you know what that means—'a cog' says it very well. I'll be making heavy demands and people will want explanations."

"Which means the inner sanctum reports are circulated, right?"

"On a maximum security basis. It's standard, you know that."

"Then my answer's emphatically no. The Baaka Valley could be a ski resort as far as you're concerned, but not to me. I've seen their goddamned tentacles reach out from Lebanon to Bahrain, from Geneva to Marseilles, from Stuttgart to Lockerbie. Your crowd is riddled, Henry, but you just don't see it. . . . If you get anything soon, call me here on Saba; if later, reach me at the yacht club in Virgin Gorda."

During the next hour and a half, three private aircraft flew into the Saba strip but none would consider the disheveled Hawthorne's pleas of urgency and promises of money to fly him to Gorda. According to the radio operator, a fourth and last plane was due in approximately thirty-five minutes. After its arrival, the strip was shut down for the night.

"Does he make contact before landing?"

"Sure, *mon*, it's dark up in the approach. If there's any wind, I give him direction and velocity."

"When the pilot checks in, I want to talk to him."

"Sure, *mon*, anyt'in' for the gov'mint."

Forty-one anxiety-filled minutes later, the tower radio erupted. "Saba, this is incoming flight from Oranjestad, F-O-four-six-five, as scheduled. Are conditions normal?"

"Another ten minutes, *mon*, and you got *no* conditions 'cause we got rules. You're late, F-O-five."

"Come off it, boy, my people are good customers."

"Not in that plane, *mon*. I don't know you—"

"We're a new run. I can see your lights. Repeat, is everything normal? There's been a hell of a lot of dicey weather recently."

"Normal, *mon*, except there's someone here who wants to speak to you, *honkie*."

"Who the fuck do you think you're talking to—"

"This is Commander T. Hawthorne, U.S. Navy," said Tyrell, grabbing the outdated microphone. "We have an emergency here on Saba and must appropriate your aircraft to fly me to British Virgin Gorda. The flight plan has been approved and you will be generously compensated for your time and inconvenience. How's your fuel? We'll get out a truck if necessary."

"Aye, aye, sailor!" came the excited response over the loudspeaker as Hawthorne stared out the large window that reached to the ceiling and overlooked the airstrip. Then to his astonishment, the lights of the descending plane swung upward, banking to the right, getting away from Saba as fast as possible.

"What the hell is he doing?" yelled Tyrell. "What are you doing, pilot?" he repeated into the microphone. "I just told you, this is an emergency!"

There was no reply over the speaker, only silence.

"He don' wanna land here, *mon*," said the radio operator.

"Why not?"

"Maybe 'cause you talked to him. He say he out of Oranjestad—maybe yes, maybe no, *mon*. Maybe he fly out of Vieques, which maybe mean he fly from Cuba."

"Son of a bitch!" Hawthorne slammed his hand on the back of a chair. "What are you people running here?"

"Don' yell at me, *mon*. I make my reports every day but no gov'mint people ever listen. Bad planes come in here alla' time, but nobody listen."

"I'm sorry," said Tye, looking at the concerned face of the black radioman. "I've also got another call to make. The navy will pay." He dialed interisland to Gorda.

"Tye-Boy, where the hell are ya?" shouted Marty. "Yer supposed to be here."

"I couldn't—I can't—get a plane out of Saba. I've been trying for damn near three hours."

"Those minnow islands close up early."

"I'll survive until morning, but if I can't get a flight then, I'll call you to send one over."

"No sweat. . . . But you got a message, Tye—"

"From a man named Stevens?"

"If he's from Paris. The front desk called me a couple of hours ago askin' if your charter was still here and, naturally, having talked to yer friend Cooke, I said I was takin' all yer messages. I got it right here. It's from Dominique, with a telephone number in Paris."

"Give it to me!" Hawthorne grabbed a pencil from the tower desk. The mechanic from Gorda spelled out the number slowly. "One last thing," said Hawthorne. "Hold on a minute." Tye turned to the radio operator. "I obviously can't get a flight out tonight, so where can I stay? It's important."

"If it's that important, *mon,* you can stay here—there's a bed in a room over there, but you won't get no food, except plenty of coffee. My superiors will bill the navy and take the money themselves, but you can stay here when I shut down. I'll bring you something to eat in the morning. I arrive at six."

"And you'll get enough money from me to tell your superiors to pound sand!"

"That is attractive."

"What's the number here?" The radio operator gave it to him, and Hawthorne returned to the phone, repeating it to Marty. "If a man named Stevens—hell, if anyone calls me—give him that number, okay? And thanks."

"Tye-Boy," said the mechanic cautiously, "yer not into somethin' over yer head, are you, lad?"

"I hope not," replied Hawthorne, cutting off the line and immediately dialing the number for Paris.

"*Âllo, la maison de Couvier,*" a female voice said.

"*S'il vous plaît, la madame,*" replied Tyrell, his fluency in French adequate for the moment. "Madame Dominique, please."

"I'm sorry, monsieur, Madame Dominique barely arrived when her husband called from Monte Carlo, insisting that she join him immediately. . . . As I am a confidante of the madame, may I ask if you are the man from the islands?"

"I am."

"She instructed me to tell you that all is well, and that she will return to you as soon as she can. I praise God, monsieur. You are what she needs, what she *deserves*. I am Pauline, and you must never talk to anyone in this house but me. Shall we have a code between us in the event the madame cannot be reached?"

"I know just the one. I'll say, 'Saba calling.' And tell her I don't understand. She wasn't *there!*"

"I'm sure there is a reason, monsieur, and I'm certain madame will explain."

"I consider you a friend, Pauline."

"Forever, monsieur."

* * *

On his private island, the *padrone* hissed and giggled as he wheeled himself to the telephone and dialed the hotel in St. Barts, his new assistants racing behind him. "You were right, my only daughter!" he shouted into the phone after reaching the room. "He bought it! Hook, line, and sinker, as the banal Americans say. He now has a confidante in Paris by the name of Pauline!"

"Of course, my only father," said Bajaratt over the telephone. "But I can conceive of another problem, and it disturbs me greatly."

"What's that, Annie? Your intuitions have proved too accurate to dismiss."

"Their headquarters are temporarily at the yacht club in British Virgin Gorda—what have they received from MI-6? Or even American intelligence?"

"What do you want me to do?"

"Send an *animale* from Miami or Puerto Rico. Find out who they have there—and what they have there."

"It is done, my child."

It was four o'clock in the morning when the telephone pierced the silence of the deserted control tower. Hawthorne rolled off the short bed in panic, blinking his eyes, trying to orient himself, and rushed through the open door to the telephone on the desk.

"Yes?" he cried. "Who is it?" he said rapidly, shaking his head to throw off the sleep.

"Stevens, you bastard," said the intelligence officer from Washington. "I've been at this for damn near six hours, and someday you'd better explain to my wife—who for reasons I'll never understand happens to like you—that I've been working for you and not out tripping the light fantastic with a nonexistent girlfriend."

"Anyone who uses the phrase tripping the light fantastic hasn't a thing to worry about. What have you got?"

"To begin with, everything's so buried, it would take an archaeologist to sort it out. That number in Miami is unlisted, naturally—"

"I hope that wasn't a problem for you," broke in Tyrell sarcastically.

Stevens ignored him. "It's billed to a popular restaurant on Collins Avenue called Wellington's, only the owner doesn't know a thing about it because he's never gotten a bill. He offered up the accounting firm that does his bookkeeping and pays his bills for verification."

"The line can be traced; it's called installation."

"Oh, it was traced all right. To a voice-activated machine on a yacht in Miami harbor. The owner's a Brazilian, currently unreachable in Brazil."

"That *lupo* wasn't talking to a machine!" insisted Hawthorne. "There was someone at the other end."

"I don't doubt it. How often have you and I monitored a drop or a pay phone during an operational time span? That someone on the yacht was told to be there when your *lupo* called."

"So you didn't get anything."

"I didn't say that," Stevens corrected him. "We called in the electronic whiz kids with their voodoo equipment. I'm told they tore that machine apart like Swiss watchmakers, factoring it with several hundred programs, and came up with what they call a satellite laser search."

"What does all that mean?"

"It means they came up with map coordinates based on probable satellite transmissions. They've narrowed down the reception areas to roughly a hundred-plus square miles between the Anegada Passage and Nevis."

"That's meaningless!"

"Not exactly. Number one, that yacht is now under

constant surveillance. Whoever goes near it will be taken in and broken—chemically or otherwise."

"What's number two?"

"Less effective, I'm afraid," answered Stevens. "We've got a smaller version of an AWAC at Patrick Air Force Base in Cocoa, Florida. It can pick up satellite transmissions, but the transmissions have to be active in order to pinpoint the reception dishes. We're sending it out."

"So they'll shut down on both sides, all transmissions!"

"That's what we're counting on. *Somebody's* going to check on that yacht, that machine. They *have* to. We've short-circuited it, so someone's got to come down and find out what's wrong and retrieve any messages received. It's foolproof, Tye. They don't know we found it, and the second anybody approaches that boat, we've got him."

"Something's wrong," said Hawthorne. "Something's wrong, but I don't know what it is."

The last light of the descending moon passed over the Miami skyline as dawn broke over the eastern horizon. A telescopic video camera was trained on the yacht in the marina, every image projected on a screen in a warehouse two hundred yards away on the waterfront. Three agents of the Federal Bureau of Investigation successively kept their eyes open, taking turns at a table where a red telephone with a single black button would instantly connect them to both the CIA and naval intelligence in Washington.

"This is bullshit," said the agent on watch as he got up from his chair to answer the door. "The pizza's here and I'm not picking up the whole tab." His two companions opened their eyes in their chairs, yawning as the door was opened.

The gunfire from the single automatic weapon was

absolute and lethal. In less than four seconds the three agents were slaughtered, sprawled across the floor, their blood-soaked bodies riddled. And on the television screen the yacht in the harbor exploded, the sharp, jagged flames drawn to the Miami skies.

6

"Jesus Christ!" roared Stevens over the phone to Hawthorne on Saba. "Miami was a massacre! They know *everything*! Everything we do!"

"Which means you've got a leak."

"I can't believe it!"

"Believe it, it's real. I'll be back in Gorda in an hour or so—"

"To hell with Gorda, we're picking you up in Saba. Our mappers say it's near the target area."

"Your plane can't land on this strip, Henry."

"The hell it can't. I've checked with our aircraft controls, you've got almost three thousand feet; with reverse thrust at max, they can make it. I want you to check out those coordinates—it's all we've got left! If anything turns up, take whatever action you deem necessary. The plane's under your command."

"A hundred square miles between the Anegada and Nevis? Are you out of your goddamned mind?"

"Have you got a better suggestion? We're dealing with a psychopathic female who could blow governments apart. Frankly, with what I've learned about her, I'm scared, Tye, really scared!"

"I don't have a better suggestion," Hawthorne conceded quietly. "I'll cancel Gorda and wait here. I hope Patrick's got an outstanding pilot."

The AWAC II appeared in the western sky, a fat, snub-nosed, unattractive aircraft with its huge disk protruding

100

above the fuselage. The super-secret plane descended, but instead of landing, swept up toward the end of the runway, circled, and repeated the procedure a second time. Watching, Tyrell had come to the conclusion that the pilot was radioing Patrick Air Force Base and telling them they were out of their minds, when, on the third approach, the bulky aircraft seemed to float down precariously close to the edge of the strip like a feathered pillow, its jet engines instantly roaring in reverse thrust.

"Hey, *mon*!" cried the tower controller, his eyes wide, his breathing momentarily suspended as the plane came to a stop several hundred feet from the end of the runway, then turned and taxied back. "That pilot, he *good*! I never seen nothin' like that here on Saba. He flyin' a pregnant cow!"

"I'm off, Calvin," said Hawthorne, heading for the door. "You'll hear from me or my associates. Take the money."

"Like I said last night, *mon*, that would be attractive."

Tyrell raced out onto the field as the side door of the AWAC II opened and an officer, followed by a master sergeant, descended the extended metal steps and stretched their bodies. "Damn fine flying, Lieutenant," said Hawthorne, approaching and spotting the silver bar on the officer's collar.

"We try to deliver the electronic mail, friend." He was hatless, with light brown hair, and a pronounced southern accent. "You the mech-man here?" he asked, eyeing Tyrell's grease-laden coveralls.

"No, I'm the package you're picking up."

"No kiddin'?"

"Ask for an ID," said the older master sergeant, his right hand ominously inside his flight jacket.

"I'm Hawthorne!"

"Prove it, buddy," continued the sergeant quietly. "You don't look like any commander to me."

"I'm not a commander—well, I was once, but not

now. *Christ,* didn't Washington explain? Whatever identification I had is at the bottom of the harbor here."

"Now, isn't that convenient?" said the enlisted man, slowly withdrawing a general issue Colt .45 from his jacket. "My colleague, the lieutenant here, operates all that fancy equipment, but I'm on board to look after other interests. Like, shall we say, security?"

"Put it away, Charlie," a female voice said as a slender figure in uniform emerged from the hatch door and descended the steps to the ground. The woman approached Hawthorne and extended her hand. "Major Catherine Neilsen, Commander. Sorry for the two passes over the field, but the doubts you expressed to Captain Stevens were on the mark. That was a chancy touchdown. . . . It's okay, Charlie, Washington faxed down his photograph. This is the man."

"You're the pilot?"

"Does that shock the commander?"

"I'm not a commander—"

"The navy says you are. Sergeant, perhaps you should keep your sidearm out in the open."

"With pleasure, Major."

"Will you people cut the . . . the . . . nonsense!"

"You mean cut the shit?" asked the pilot.

"That's just what I mean."

"And maybe that's just what we object to. We accept the premise that the services cooperate with one another, but we find it difficult to be told that a former naval officer with absolutely no knowledge of our operations is in command of our aircraft."

"Look, lady . . . miss . . . *Major,* I didn't ask for anything! I got roped into this mess like you did."

"We don't know what the 'mess' is, *Mr.* Hawthorne. We only know that we're to traverse the given parameters of an area, scanning for satellite transmissions, intercept whatever we find, and deliver the data to you. Then *you,* and *only* you, tell us what to do."

"That's . . . that's *crap.*"

"That's pure shit, Commander."

"Exactly."

"I'm glad we understand each other." The major took off her visored officer's cap, removed several barrettes, and shook her blond hair loose. "Now, I don't care to breach security, but I'd like an overall view of what you expect of us, Commander."

"Look, *Major*, I'm just a charter man in the islands. I gave up the military Sturm und Drang four, nearly five years ago, and I suddenly got recruited by three governments, three different countries, who mistakenly think I can help in what they call a crisis. Now, if you think otherwise, take this pregnant cow of a plane out of here and leave me alone!"

"I can't do that."

"Why not?"

"Orders."

"You're one tough lady, Major."

"You're one outspoken former naval officer, *mister*."

"So what do we do now? Stand here and insult each other?"

"I suggest we get on with the operation. Climb on board."

"Is that an order?"

"You know I can't do that," said the pilot, brushing her hair back with her left hand. "We're on the ground, where you're my superior officer; upstairs we're more equal. . . . Still, you're in command of the aircraft."

"*Good*. Get your asses back inside and let's get airborne."

The muffled roar of the jet engines became a constant irritant as the AWAC II crisscrossed the skies, forever banking to reenter the surveillance pattern from yet another point of the compass. The first lieutenant in charge of the complex electronic equipment kept pressing esoteric buttons and twirling mysterious dials while erratic beeps were heard in greater and lesser degrees of volume. With each burst of activity he touched a brief sequence of letters on a computer that produced a printout of his efforts into a wire basket attached to his processor.

"For God's sake, what's happening?" said Hawthorne, who was sitting across from the young officer in a strapped swivel seat.

"Don't let the hogs rattle ya, Commander," replied the lieutenant. "They git a mite loud at lunchtime."

"What the hell does *that* mean?"

"It means please shut up, sir, 'cause I gotta concentrate—if the navy will let me—sir."

Tyrell unbuckled his strap, got to his feet, and walked forward into the open flight deck, where Major Catherine Neilsen was at the controls. "May I sit down?" he asked, gesturing at the vacant seat beside hers.

"You don't have to ask, Commander. You're in charge of this bird except where airborne safety and regulations are involved."

"Can we get by the military horseshit, Major?" said Hawthorne, sitting down and strapping himself in, relieved that the numbing rush of the jets was reduced. "I told you, I'm not navy anymore, and I need your help, not your hostility."

"Okay, how can I help—*hold* it!" The pilot adjusted her earphone. "*What,* Jackson? . . . Reenter the last trajectory from the SP? . . . Will do, genius." Neilsen again banked the plane in a semicircle. "I'm sorry, Commander, where were we? . . . Oh, yes, how can I help?"

"You can start by explaining: What is the last trajectory and why are you reentering it, and what the hell is the 'genius' doing back there?"

The major laughed; it was a nice laugh, devoid of ridicule or pretentious authority; it was a grown-up girl laughing because the situation was funny. "To begin with, Jackson *is* a genius, sir—"

"Cut the 'sir,' please. I'm not a lieutenant commander

anymore, and even if I were, that's not superior to a major."

"Okay, Mr. Hawthorne—"

"Try Tye. Short for Tyrell. That's my name."

"Tyrell? What a dreadful name! He killed the two young princes in the Tower of London; it's right there in Shakespeare's *Richard III*."

"My father had a warped sense of humor. If my brother had been a girl, he swore he'd have called her Medea. As it happened, he was a boy, so Dad settled for Marcus Antonius Hawthorne; our mother switched it to Marc Anthony."

"I think I'd like your father. Mine, who barely made the farm work in Minnesota, was an education-starved son of Swedish immigrants. It was either studying like hell to get into West Point and a free college education or slopping cowshit for the rest of my life. He was very clear about that."

"I think I'd like your father too."

"Back to your questions, please," said Neilsen, suddenly distancing herself. "Jackson Poole—of the Louisiana Pooles, mind you," she allowed, permitting a slight smile to crease her lips, "is a genius with that equipment, as well as a damn fine pilot; he's my relief, but if I touch his machinery, I get yelled at."

"That's two tough talents. Sounds like he's an interesting guy."

"He really is. He went into the army because that's where all the real money was going for computer science, but without too many qualified takers. He's pretty much been able to write his own ticket. Merit counts in the services; they can't afford to overlook ability. . . . Incidentally, he just told me to reenter this trajectory from SP. In simple language, that means we sweep back and retrace our current path across the target area from the parameter starting point."

"And *that* means?"

"He's trying to find you a pattern—not of the traffic he can identify, which has to be at least fifty to seventy-five, discounting scrambled military and diplomatic—but by factoring in the aberrations, the unusual, the relatively untraceable."

"He can do that with those buttons and dials and squeaks?"

"Oh, yes, he can do that."

"I hate Renaissance men."

"Did I mention he's also one of Patrick's top karate instructors?"

"If he picks a fight with you, Major," said Tyrell, smiling, "I'm on *his* side. A crippled midget could knock me out of the ring."

"Not according to your dossier."

"My dossier? Is nothing sacred?"

"Not when you're assuming even limited control over an equally ranking commanding officer from another branch. Military courtesy as well as regulations require that the replacing officer be convinced of the validity of the command replacement. I was convinced."

"You sure as hell didn't show it back on Saba."

"I was angry, as angry as you would have been if a stranger had walked into your sphere of operations and said he was taking over."

"I never said that."

"Of course you did. You made it abundantly clear when you said 'get your asses' on board. That's when I knew you were still Lieutenant Commander Hawthorne."

"*Hold it!*" came the cry from the AWAC II's huge hull, so loud it was heard over the engines, while sending shock waves through the earphones. "It's *crazy!*" Jackson Poole was standing up over his elongated Formica desk and waving his arms.

"Cool it, my darling!" ordered Major Neilsen, steadying the aircraft. "Sit down and tell us calmly what you've got. . . . Commander, please put on the earphones so you can hear everything."

" 'My *darling*'?" Tyrell interrupted involuntarily, his voice carrying harshly over the intercom.

"It's aircraft slang, Commander. Don't read anything into it," said Major Neilsen.

"Not a thing, Navy," added the master sergeant of security called Charlie. "You may have the brass, *sir,* but you're still a guest here."

"You know, Sergeant, you're becoming a large pain in the ass!"

"Put a lid on it, Hawthorne," said the blond-haired pilot. "What did you find, Lieutenant?"

"What doesn't *exist,* Cathy! It's not on any of the charts—the area maps—and I've checked every detailed program on the screen!"

"Be clearer, please."

"The signal bounces off a Japanese satellite and beams down to *nothing,* at least nothing on our maps. But it has to *be* there! The transmission's clear."

"Lieutenant," Tyrell broke in, "can your machines tell us where the transmission's coming from?"

"Not specifically; our big brothers probably could, but we're limited. All I can do is give you a computerized laser projection."

"What the hell is that?"

"You know, like those indoor golf games where you hit a ball off a tee into an electronic screen and you get an instant picture where it goes down the fairway."

"I'm not a golfer, but I'll take your word for it. How long will it take you?"

"I'm working on it while we're talkin'. . . . I can almost guarantee this one."

"This one what?"

"The transmission to our nowhere downstairs. It's from someplace in the Mediterranean, by way of the Japanese satellite Noguma."

"Italy? Southern Italy?"

"Could be. Or northern Africa. That's the general area."

"That's our target!" said Hawthorne.

"You're sure?" asked Neilsen.

"I've got a raw shoulder to prove it, three strips of tape and all. Lieutenant, can you give me precise, and I mean *precise*, navigational coordinates to that nowhere downstairs?"

"Hell, yes, Yankee, I punched 'em in. Small land masses about thirty miles due north of Anguilla."

"I'm pretty sure I know them! Poole, you *are* a genius."

"Not me, sir. It's the equipment."

"We can do better than coordinates," said Catherine Neilsen, inching her wheel forward into a descent. "We'll find that 'nowhere downstairs' so clearly that you'll know every inch of the terrain."

"*No*. . . . Please don't do that."

"Are you nuts? We're here, we're above it, and we can do it!"

"And whoever's down there will know you're doing it."

"You're damn right."

"And that's damn wrong. What's the nearest place where you can land this cow?"

"This *aircraft*, which I'm very fond of—admittedly an awkward cow—may not land on foreign territory; that's strict military regulations."

"I didn't ask you whether you *may*, Major, I simply asked you where you *can*. Where?"

"My charts say St. Martin. It's French and Dutch."

"I know that, I'm a charter man, remember? . . . Is there anything in this panoply of exotic equipment in front of me that can operate as a perfectly normal telephone?"

"Certainly. It's called a telephone and it's right there below your armrest."

"You're kidding." Hawthorne found it, pulled it out of its cradle, and asked, "How do I use it?"

"As you would a normal telephone, but with the knowledge that your conversation is recorded by Patrick Air Force Base and immediately forwarded to the Pentagon."

"I love it," said Tyrell, dialing furiously. In seconds he continued. "I-One and make it quick, sailor! The code is four-zero and my main man is Captain Henry Stevens, and do me a favor and bypass the asshole who wants my life history. The name Tye—spelled T-Y-E—will get you through."

"*Hawthorne,* where are you? What have you got?" Stevens was on the line barely three seconds later, his words running over one another.

"Our conversation's being taped and forwarded to Arlington—"

"Not from that plane it isn't; I've got a black drape on it. You can assume you're in a confessional with the high priest of secrets. What's the news?"

"This fat, ugly aircraft you spun out of Patrick is a wonder. We found the transmission target, and I want a lieutenant named Poole made immediately a colonel or a general!"

"Tye, are you drinking?"

"I wish to hell I were. Also, while you're at your Pentagon games, there's a pilot named Neilsen, first name Catherine, who I insist be made head of the air force. How does *that* grab you, Hank?"

"You *are* back on the sauce," said Stevens angrily.

"No way, Henry." Tyrell spoke softly, his sobriety apparent. "I just want you to know how good they are."

"Okay, I accept that, and commendations will follow, okay? Now, what about the target?"

"It's unlisted, unmapped, but I know that cluster of so-called uninhabited islands—there must be five or six—and thanks to this plane here, I have the exact coordinates."

"That's terrific. Bajaratt's got to be there! We'll send in a strike!"

"Not yet. Let me go in first to make sure she *is* there. And if she is, who her conduits are. They're the link to the terrorist network working our side."

"Tye, I've got to ask you, you were very effective years ago at this sort of thing, but it's been a while. . . . Can you hack it, Commander? I don't want . . . your life on my slate."

"I assume you're alluding to my deceased wife, *Captain*."

"I refuse to go into that again. We had nothing to do with her death."

"Then why do I keep wondering?"

"That's your problem, Tye, not ours. I just want to make sure you're not biting off more than you can chew."

"You don't have anybody else, so let's bypass the horseshit. I want this plane to land in St. Martin, the French side. So you reach the Deuxième in the Quai d'Orsay and clear it with Patrick Air Force Base in Florida. We land, and I'm given whatever equipment I need. Over and out, Henry. *Move*."

Hawthorne replaced the phone, closed his eyes briefly, then turned to the pilot. "Head for St. Martin, Major," he said wearily. "We'll be cleared, I assure you."

"I was on the telephone channel," said Neilsen with quiet authority. "Actually it's a captain's responsibility to monitor all conversations from such aircraft as this. I'm sure you understand that."

"I'm sure I have to."

"You mentioned your wife—the death of your wife."

"I guess I did. Stevens and I go back a long way, and sometimes I bring up things I shouldn't."

"I'm sorry. About your wife, I mean."

"Thank you," said Tyrell, falling silent. *It was those two simple words "my darling" that had so unnerved*

*him, making him behave like a fool. It was as though
the endearment belonged to him and no one else, certainly not to an arrogant American female air force officer speaking to a subordinate. It was so essentially a
European expression, to be said quietly, either with feeling or so casually that deep and abiding warmth was
implicit. Only two women in his life had ever used those
words with any regularity. Ingrid and Dominique—the
only women he had ever loved, one a wife he adored,
the other a gossamer creature of loveliness as elusive as
she was real, who had nurtured him back to sanity.
Those words belonged to them, and addressed only to
him. Still, he had behaved like an idiot; expressions were
not the single property of anyone, he knew that. Still,
again, they should not be abused, trivialized. Oh, Christ!
He had to snap out of it. There was work to do. The
target!*

"St. Martin dead ahead . . . Tye," said Major Neilsen
softly.

"What? . . . Oh, sorry, what did you say?"

"You were either in a trance or you dozed with your
eyes open for a few minutes. I've been given clearance
to land in St. Martin—both by Patrick and the French
authorities. We'll park at the end of the field and a guard
detail will surround the aircraft, which Charlie will secure. . . . I asked that you be professional, but I never
expected anything like this."

"You called me Tye."

"You ordered me to, Commander. Don't read any
thing into it, sir."

"I promise not to."

"According to Patrick *and* the French, we're assigned
to you until you release us. They said that could be all
day and perhaps tomorrow. . . . What the hell is going
on, Hawthorne? You talk about terrorists and links to
terrorists, and we find unmapped islands that the goddamned navy is prepared to blow out of the water! I'd
say that's a little out of the ordinary, even for our work."

"It's all out of the ordinary, even the extraordinary, Major . . . Cathy—don't read anything into that, Madame Pilot."

"Be serious; we have a right to know. You call the shots as to where we go. You just proved that. But I *am* the pilot and I'm responsible for this very expensive aircraft and its crew."

"You're right, you are the pilot. So why don't you tell me, where's your first flight officer, your copilot, as we land-based civilians call it?"

"I told you, Poole's qualified," answered Neilsen, her voice dropping.

"Gee whiz, Major Neilsen, why does it strike me that someone's missing on this bird?"

"All right," said Catherine, embarrassed. "Your Captain Stevens was emphatic that we leave Patrick on the dot of zero-minus this morning, but we couldn't reach Sal, who usually sits in your seat. We all know there've been some marriage problems, so we didn't look too hard—as I say, Lieutenant Poole's as good a pilot as I am, and that's going some."

"It certainly is. And this Sal is another extremely qualified female officer?"

"Sal is short for Salvatore. He's a terrific guy, but he's got a flaky wife, very heavy into booze. Since we were covered, we took off to accommodate the navy's request—request, hell, *demand*."

"Isn't that against regulations?"

"Look, don't tell me you've never covered for a friend. We thought this was a two- to four-hour sky search—we'd get back and no one would be the wiser, and maybe Mancini could solve some of his problems. Is that such a crime, for a *friend*?"

"No, it isn't," replied Hawthorne, his mind racing, going back over a score of gaps that had nullified a hundred covert operations in his other life. "Can Patrick monitor communications from this plane?"

"Of course, but you heard Stevens. Nothing's logged or sent to the Pentagon. It's a black drape."

"Yes, I understand that, but the air base in Florida can listen in."

"A select few, yes."

"Radio the base and ask to speak to your friend Mancini."

"What? And louse him up?"

"Just do it, Major. Please, remember, I'm in control of this aircraft except for airborne contingencies."

"You bastard!"

"Just do it. Now."

Neilsen got on the Patrick frequency and, with deeply felt reluctance, spoke. "My subflight officer would like to speak with Captain Mancini. Is he there?"

"Hi, Major," said the female voice over the loudspeaker. "I'm sorry, Sal left for home about ten minutes ago, but since we're not logged or anything, I gotta tell you, Cathy, he really appreciates what you did."

"This is Lieutenant Commander Hawthorne, naval intelligence," Tyrell broke in, the microphone at his lips. "Did Captain Mancini overhear our communications?"

"Sure, he's select—who's the navy spook, Cathy?"

"Just answer his questions, Alice," said Neilsen, staring at Tyrell.

"When did Captain Mancini arrive at your commcenter?"

"Oh, I don't know, about three or four hours ago, roughly two hours after the AWAC II was airborne."

"Wasn't his appearance awkward for him? He was scheduled to be on board, but he wasn't."

"Hey, Commander, we're all human, not robots. They couldn't reach him in time, and we all know that plane is covered pilot-wise."

"I still want to know why he was in your select commcenter under these circumstances. It seems to me he'd be better off to remain unreachable."

"How do *I* know . . . sir? Captain Sal's a very concerned person. I guess he felt guilty, or something. He took notes on everything you guys said."

"Put out an order for his arrest," said Hawthorne.

"What?"

"You heard me. Immediate arrest and total isolation until you hear from a man named Stevens at naval intelligence. He'll instruct you what to do."

"I don't believe this!"

"Believe it, or you're not only out of a job, Alice, you may be in a penitentiary." Hawthorne replaced the microphone.

"What the hell have you *done*?" cried Catherine Neilsen.

"You know exactly what I did. A man on constant security alert, reachable by whatever number he gives to his base, including a government-provided vehicle telephone, doesn't get any message but suddenly turns up at his base's comm-center? . . . How did he know to be there? He supposedly hadn't received any call, and even if he did, it's the last place he'd want to be seen."

"I don't want to believe what you're thinking."

"Then give me a logical answer."

"I can't."

"Then let me give *you* one, and let me quote verbatim from a man you've talked to who's on top of this operation. . . . 'They're everywhere, they know everything we do.' Does that make a little bit of sense to you?"

"Sal wouldn't do that!"

"He left ten minutes ago for his home. Call back your base and tell them to patch you through to his car."

The pilot did as she was ordered, switching the radio connection to the flight desk's loudspeakers. They heard the steady ringing on Captain Mancini's car telephone. There was no answer. "Oh, God!"

"How far is his house from Patrick?"

"About forty minutes," said Neilsen softly. "He has

to live away from the base. I told you, he has serious problems with his wife."

"Have you ever been there? To his house?"

"No."

"Have you ever met his wife?"

"No. All of us know when to butt out."

"Then how do you know he's even married?"

"It's on his record! Also, we're very close here; he talks."

"That's a joke, lady. How often do you cross the Caribbean?"

"Two or three times a week. It's routine."

"Who coordinates your routings?"

"My flight officer, naturally. . . . Sal."

"My order to Patrick stands. Take us into St. Martin, Major."

Captain Salvatore Mancini, out of uniform and dressed in casual clothes, a white guayabera, dark trousers, and leather sandals, walked into Wellington's on Miami Beach's Collins Avenue. He approached the crowded, raucous bar and exchanged glances with the bartender, who proceeded to nod his head twice, so subtly that none of the customers noticed.

The captain continued toward a wide corridor that held the rest rooms with a pay telephone at the far end. He inserted a coin and dialed collect to a number in Washington, D.C., giving his name as "Wellington" to the operator.

"Scorpio Nine," said Mancini into the phone when the line was picked up. "You have a message?"

"You're finished, get out of there," replied the voice on the other end.

"You've got to be kidding!"

"Your associates are sorrier than you are, believe me," said the voice. "You're to hire a rental car under your third driver's license and go to the West Palm airport, where there's a reservation for you under that name to the Bahamas on Sunburst Jetlines. It's the four P.M. flight to Freeport. You'll be met there and flown to wherever they say."

"Who the hell's going to be the watchman for the old man's island? Who keeps us away from there?"

"Not you. I myself picked up the order on our secure line from Patrick, Scorpio Nine. The order has gone out for your arrest. They found you."

"Who . . . *who*?"

"A man named Hawthorne. He was part of this outfit five years ago."

"He's a dead man!"

"You're not alone in that projection."

7

Nicolo Montavi of Portici leaned against the wall by a window overlooking the hotel's courtyard café on the island of St. Barts. Muted voices floated up, mingled with the soft sounds of clinking glasses and quiet laughter. It was late afternoon, the natives and the tourists about to enter the evening hours where pleasures could be had and profits made. It was not so different from the shoreline cafés in Naples, not so grand perhaps, but grander than those in Portici. . . . Portici? Would he ever see his home again?

Certainly not in any normal way, he understood that. He had been condemned by the waterfront, *un traditore ai compagni*, a traitor to all the work crews on the piers. He would be dead now were it not for the strange, rich signora who had saved him from being thrown off a dock with a rope around his neck. And the weeks when she hid him, running from town to town, city to city, constantly aware that he was being pursued, afraid to go outside, even at night, especially at night, when the hunters roamed the streets—crate hooks, knives, and guns their weapons of vengeance. Vengeance for a crime he did not commit!

"Even I cannot save you," his older brother had said during one of their furtive telephone calls. "If I see you, I'll have to kill you myself, or I'll be killed, along with our mother and our sisters. Our house is always watched, men waiting for you to return. If our father— may he sleep with Christ—had not been so strong and well liked, we might all be dead by now."

"But I didn't kill the *capogruppo!*"

"Then who did, my foolish brother? You were the last to see him; you threatened to tear his heart out."

"It was only an expression. He stole from me!"

"He stole from *everyone,* mainly from the holds of the cargo ships, and his death cost all of us millions of lire, for he needed our cooperation, our silence."

"What am I to do?"

"Your signora spoke with Mama. She told her you would be safer out of the country, that she would look after you like a son."

"Not like any son we know—"

"Go with her! In two or three years maybe things will change, who knows?"

Nothing would change, thought Nicolo, turning partially away from the window, his head angled down as if he were still observing the scene below. From the corner of his eye he saw his *bella signora* sitting across the large room in front of a dressing table. Her hands and fingers were moving quickly, doing odd things with her hair. He watched her, even more bewildered as she wrapped a wide, stuffed corset around her waist, pulled an outsized undergarment down over it, and stood up, studying herself in the mirror. So absorbed was she that she was oblivious of him, not realizing that he was staring at her. She turned in circles, her eyes constantly angled toward her image in the glass. Suddenly, Nicolo was astonished; she was a different *woman.* Her long, dark hair was no longer attractive; it was knotted at the nape of her neck, straight back and stern. And her *face,* it was almost pale, or gray, but nothing like it had been—it was actually ugly, with dark shadows under her eyes, the flesh somehow lined and weary, an aging mask of her former self. . . . Her body was disgusting, a plump pig with no breasts or any indication of the exciting woman it had replaced.

Instinctively, Nicolo turned back to the window,

somehow—he did not know how—realizing that he should not have seen what he saw. Confirmation of his judgment came moments later. Signora Cabrini moved quickly, noisily, across the room and announced:

"My darling, I'm going to take a shower if this god-forsaken place can send the water up three flights."

"Certainly, Cabi," said Nicolo, his eyes on the court-yard café below.

"And when I'm finished, we must have a long talk, for you're about to experience the adventure of your life."

"*Cèrto, signora.*"

"That's one of the things we're going to talk about, my beautiful boy. From now on, you speak only Italian."

"My father would rise out of his grave, Cabi. He taught all of his children to speak English. He said it was the way to progress oneself. He would whip us at the supper table if we spoke Italian."

"Your father was a relic of the war, Nico, when he sold *vino* and women to the American soldiers. These are entirely different circumstances. I'll be out in a few minutes."

"When you're finished, may we go down to the res-taurant? I'm very hungry."

"You're always hungry, Nico, but I'm afraid we can't. We have a lot to discuss. However, I've made arrange-ments with the hotel. You'll have everything you choose from the menu downstairs. You like room service, don't you, my darling?"

"*Cèrto,*" repeated Nicolo, now turning around as Ba-jaratt abruptly did the same; she had *not* wanted him to see her performing in front of the faraway mirror.

"*Va bene,*" said the Baj, heading into the bathroom. "*Solo italiano. Grazie!*"

She treated him like a *fool*! thought Nicolo angrily. This wealthy bitch who claimed to find so many de-lights with his body—as he did with hers, he had to admit—had not treated him so well, so generously, and for so long without a purpose. It had to be, for a handsome dock boy could make thousands of lire bedding an amorous tourist, first carrying her luggage for a tip that was nothing compared to what she paid him later. *Benissimo!* But this was not the way of Signora Cabrini; she had done too much, constantly talking to him about his honest desires to get an education and leave the piers of Portici, going so far as to deposit funds for him in the Banco di Napoli so he could later better his life—if he accompanied her on a trip. What choice did he have? Left to be hunted by the killers from the waterfront? She kept telling him how perfect he was . . . for what?

They had gone to the police in Rome, special police, men who saw them only at night and in darkened rooms, where he had been fingerprinted for documents he signed, but which she kept. Then there were two embassies, again at night, only one or two officials present, and more documents, more papers, and photographs. For *what*? . . . She was about to tell him, he knew it, he felt it. ". . . You're about to experience the adventure of your life." What else could it be? And whatever it was, again he had no choice but to accept. For now. There was a saying on the docks that never left him, as eager as he was to leave the docks. "Kiss the boot of the tourist until you can steal it." For a woman who killed as casually as he had seen her kill, he would do no less. She called him her toy, and he would be her toy. Until he could steal, perhaps.

Nicolo took another look at the bustling courtyard below, feeling as he had felt during their last weeks in Italy—a prisoner. Throughout those suffocating days he could not leave the confines of wherever they were, whether it was a hotel room, or on board a boat owned by an acquaintance of Cabrini's, or even in a motor home that the signora would rent so they could move swiftly from place to place. It was all necessary, she had explained, because they had to be in the Neapolitan area, for one day a freighter would sail into port and she had to be there at the first dawn to receive a package sent to her. And, indeed, on a Tuesday evening, while poring over the shipping news in the area's papers, the freighter in question was listed as arriving shortly past midnight. Long before the sun came up, the signora was gone from their hotel room; when she returned later that morning, without a package, she had announced: "We fly to Marseilles this afternoon, my beautiful young lover. Our journey begins."

"To *where*, Cabi?" She had suggested the shortened name in respect to Nicolo's deep religious feelings, although, in truth, Cabrini was simply the name of a wealthy estate outside Portofino.

"Trust me, Nico," she had replied. "Think of the funds I've deposited for your future, and trust me."

"You carry no package."

"Ah, but I do." The signora had opened her large purse and removed a thick white envelope. "This is our itinerary—our transportation is confirmed, my darling."

"That had to come to you on a ship?"

"Oh, yes, Nico, some things must be delivered by hand. . . . Now, no more questions, we must pack—as little as possible, only what we can carry."

The dock boy moved away from the window, thinking that the conversation he recalled had occurred less than a week ago, and what a week it had been! From near death in storms at sea to real death on a strange, unbelievable island owned by the strangest old man he had ever encountered. Even this morning, when the seaplane was late due to bad weather, it angered the ancient, sick *padrone*, who kept screaming that they had to leave. And here, on this other, civilized island, where Cabi went from shop to shop, buying so many articles they filled two bags, along with a cheap suit for him that did not fit.

"Later, we'll throw it away," she had said.

Nicolo walked aimlessly over to the signora's dressing table, bewildered by the assortment of creams and powders and small bottles that reminded him of his three sisters in Portici. They were the *trucco* their papa yelled about so often, even when he was dying and the girls were paraded in to say good-bye to him on his deathbed.

"What are you doing, Nico?" Bajaratt walked out of the bathroom, draped in towels, her sudden appearance startling the dock boy.

"Nothing, Cabi, just thinking of my sisters—all these things on your table."

"Surely you know that women are vain."

"You don't need any of those—"

"You're a love," interrupted the Baj, waving him aside and sitting down. "There's a bottle of passable wine in one of the bags on the table in front of the couch. Open it and pour us some, less for you, for you have a long night of study before you."

"Oh?"

"You may call it part of the education you seek that will permit you to leave the docks of Portici."

"*Oh?*"

"Bring us our wine, darling." The wine poured, the glasses in their hands, Bajaratt gave her young charge the white envelope she had received from the freighter in Naples; she told him to sit on the couch and open it. "You read very well, don't you, Nico?"

"You know I do," he replied. "I've nearly completed my *scuola media*."

"Then start reading these pages, and as you read, I'll begin to explain to you."

"*Signora?*" Nicolo's eyes were riveted on the first page. "What *is* this?"

"Your adventure, sweet Apollo. I'm going to turn you into a young *barone*."

"*Che pazzía!* I wouldn't know how to behave like a baron."

"Just be yourself, as shy and courteous as you are. Americans love modest nobility. They think it's so democratic, so appealing."

"Cabi, these people—"

"Your lineage, my dearest. They are a noble family from the hills of Ravello who a year or so ago came upon difficult times. They were barely able to pay their bills, their lands and their grand estate were draining them—poor vineyards, overindulgence, wastrel children, all the normal afflictions of the rich. But suddenly, wondrously, they are wealthy again. Isn't that astonishing?"

"It's very good for them, but what has it to do with me—"

"Read on, Nico," Bajaratt interrupted. "They have millions now; once more they have great respect, and all Italy worships them. The vicissitudes of the rich run in cycles—long-ago investments rise to the skies, vineyards suddenly become *classico,* foreign real estate turns to gold—do you follow me, Nico?"

"I'm reading as fast as I can, listening as hard as—"

"*Look* at me, Nicolo," the Baj broke in firmly. "There was a son. He died of drugs eighteen months ago in the infamous Wädenschwill ghetto. His body was cremated on the orders of the family, no ceremony, no announcements; they were too ashamed."

"What are you saying to me, Signora Cabrini?" asked the dock boy quietly.

"Your age is within a year of his, your appearance quite similar until he was wasted by narcotics. . . . You are now *he*, Nicolo, it's as simple as that."

"You're not making sense, Cabi," said the boy from Portici, frightened and barely audible.

"You don't know how many days I looked for you along the waterfronts, my child-man. Someone who had the modest but imposing presence of everyone's image of nobility, especially the Americans'. Everything you must learn is written on those pages: your life, your parents, your schooling, your hobbies and accomplishments, even the names of certain family friends and former estate employees, all beyond reach, incidentally. . . . Oh, don't look so terrified. Just familiarize yourself, you won't have to be specific, as I am your aunt as well as your interpreter and I'll never leave your side. Remember, however, you speak only *italiano*."

"Please . . . *per piacere*, signora!" stammered Nicolo. "I'm confused."

"Then, as I've said before, think of the money in your bank account and do as you're told. I'm going to introduce you to many important Americans. Very rich, very powerful. They will like you very much."

"Because I am this someone I am not?"

"Because your family in Ravello is investing heavily in American enterprise. You will promise to make contributions to many causes—museums, symphonies, charities—even to certain political men who wish to accommodate your family."

"I will?"

"Yes, but only and always through me. Can you imagine, you may one day be invited to the White House to meet the President of the United States?"

"*Il presidente?*" cried the adolescent, his eyes wide, his joyous grin genuine. "It's all so *fantastico*, I am in a dream, no?"

"A dream well thought out, my excitable child. Tomorrow I will buy you a wardrobe fit for one of the wealthiest young men on earth. Tomorrow we start our journey into this dream of yours, this dream of mine."

"What is the dream, signora? What does it mean?"

"Why not tell you, you won't understand anyway? When certain people hunt for certain other people, they look for the secretive, for the hidden, for the obscure. Not for what's in front of their eyes."

"You're right, Cabi, I don't understand."

"That's just fine," said Bajaratt.

But Nicolo understood only too well as he hungrily returned to the pages in front of him. On the docks it was called *estorsione,* the selling back of a kissed, stolen boot for many times its value because its mere presence could bring about the destruction of the owner. His time would come, thought the dock boy from Portici, but until it did, he would enter into the signora's game with enthusiasm, always remembering that she killed too easily.

It was 6:45 in the evening when the stranger walked into the lobby of the Virgin Gorda Yacht Club. He was a short, stout, balding man dressed in sharply creased white trousers and a navy blue blazer with the gold and black crest of the San Diego Yachting Association on his breast pocket. It was an impressive emblem, so closely connected as it was to the Americas Cup and all the racing glory that went with it.

He signed his name on the register. Ralph W. Grimshaw, attorney and yachtsman. Coronado, California.

"We, of course, have a courtesy exchange with San Diego," said the tuxedoed clerk behind the counter, nervously checking his files. "I'm rather new on the job, so it may take me a while to figure the discount."

"It's not important, young man," said Grimshaw, smiling. "The discount isn't vital, and if your club, like ours, has troubles in these difficult times, why not forget the courtesy? I'd be happy to pay full price—as a matter of fact, I insist upon it."

"That's very kind of you, sir."

"You're British, aren't you, fella?"

"Yes, sir, sent over by the Savoy Group . . . for training, you understand."

"I sure do. You couldn't get any better training than in a place like this. I own a couple of hotels in southern Cal, and let me tell you, you send your best young people to the toughest spots to learn how rough it can be."

"You really think so, sir? I rather thought otherwise."

"Then you don't know how hotel management works. It's the way we determine who our most promising up-and-comers are—put 'em into the worst situations and see how they perform."

"I hadn't even considered that—"

"Don't tell your bosses I let you in on the secret, 'cause I know the Savoy Group and they know me. Just keep your whistle clean and spot the heavy hitters when they come into town, that's another secret, the most important one."

"Yes, sir. Thank you, sir. How long will your stay be, Mr. Grimshaw?"

"Short, very short, a day, perhaps two. I'm checking out a boat we may purchase for our club, then it's off to London."

"Yes, sir. The boy will take your luggage to the room, sir," said the clerk, glancing around the fairly crowded lobby for a bellhop.

"That's okay, son, I've only got an overnighter; the rest of my stuff is back in P.R. for the London flight. Just give me the key, I'll find it. Actually, I'm kind of in a hurry."

"A hurry, sir?"

"Yes, I'm to meet our appraiser down at the marina and I'm an hour late. Man named Hawthorne. Know him?"

"Captain Tyrell Hawthorne?" asked the young Englishman, slightly surprised.

"Yes, that's the one."

"I'm afraid he's not here, sir."

"What?"

"His charter left early this afternoon, I believe."

"He can't *do* that!"

"The circumstances would appear to be odd, sir," said the clerk, leaning forward, obviously impressed by the "heavy hitter" familiar with the Savoy Group. "We've received several calls for Captain Hawthorne, all of which were transferred to our head of dock maintenance, a man named Martin Caine, who's taking his messages."

"That's odd, all right. We paid the guy! Except the name Caine was somewhere in the basket."

"Not only that, sir," continued the clerk, warming up to his new association with the wealthy attorney-yachtsman who had such enviable connections in London. "Captain Hawthorne's associate—Mr. Cooke, Mr. Geoffrey Cooke—left a large envelope in our safe for the captain."

"Cooke? . . . Of course, he's our money man. That envelope's meant for me, young fella. It's got the breakdown of the replacement cost specifications."

"The what, Mr. Grimshaw?"

"You don't buy a yacht for two million dollars if the cost of replacing worn-out equipment tallies up to another five hundred thousand or more."

"Two *million* . . . ?"

"It's only a medium-size boat, son. If you'll get me the envelope, I'll unwind for the evening, then catch the first flight to Puerto Rico and be off to London. . . . Incidentally, let me have your name. One of our Anglo merger litigants is on the Savoy Group's board—Bascomb. Surely you know him."

"I'm afraid I don't, sir."

"Well, he's going to know who *you* are. The envelope, please."

"Well, Mr. Grimshaw, our instructions are to give it only to Captain Hawthorne."

"Yes, of course, but he's not here and I am, and I've fully identified both the captain and Mr. Cooke as our—well, basically our employees—haven't I?"

"Yes, you have, sir, no question about it."

"Good. You'll go far with my London friends. Now, let me have your card, young fella."

"Actually, I don't have a card—it hasn't been printed yet."

"Then spell out your name on one of those registration slips, that'll catch old Bascomb's attention." The clerk did so with alacrity. The stranger named Grimshaw took it and smiled. "Someday, son, when I'm staying at the Savoy and you're the manager, you might send me a dozen of those great oysters."

"With great pleasure, sir!"

"The envelope, please."

"Of course, Mr. Grimshaw!"

The man named Grimshaw sat in his room, the telephone in his gloved hand. "I have everything they've got," he said into the phone to Miami, "the whole enchilada, including three photographs of the Baj, presumably unseen since they were sealed in an official Brit envelope. I'll burn them and then I've got to get out of here. I've no idea when this Hawthorne or the Sixer named Cooke will show up, but I can't be here. . . . Yes, I understand the seven-thirty curfew on planes; what's your suggestion? . . . A seaplane dead south on Sebastian's Point? . . . No, I'll find it. I'll be there. Nine o'clock. If I'm late, don't panic, I'll get there. . . . There's something I have to take care of first, a matter of communications. Hawthorne's message center has to go."

Tyrell stood with Major Catherine Neilsen and Lieutenant Jackson Poole in the holding room of the St. Martin's airport, waiting for word from Master Sergeant Charles O'Brian, chief of security for the AWAC II.

Suddenly, the sergeant stormed through the double doors, his head turned, his eyes on the field outside, and announced, "I'm staying on board, Major! No one in that detail speaks English, and I don't like anybody who can't understand me."

"Charlie, they're our allies," said Neilsen. "Patrick cleared them, and we're going to be here for the rest of the day and probably overnight. Let the bird go, nobody's going to touch it."

"Can't do that, Cathy—*Major*."

"Damn it, Charlie, loosen up."

"Can't do that either. I don't like it here."

Sundown. Then darkness, and Hawthorne studied the computerized printouts expunged from Lieutenant Poole's airborne printer, the junior officer at his side in the hotel room. "It's got to be one of these four islands, then," said Tyrell, holding the lamp over the printouts.

"If we could have gotten low enough, like Cathy wanted to do, we'd have verified which one."

"But if we had, they'd have known we were doing just that, correct?"

"So what? . . . My major was right, you're pig-headed."

"She really doesn't like me, does she?"

"Oh, hell, it's not you. She's what we call in *Loosiana* a real *feminyne* firster, brass balls and all."

"But you seem to get along with her."

" 'Cause she's the best there is, why not?"

"Then you don't object to the *feminyne*-first routine."

"The hell I don't, I sure do! She's my boss, but I'd be a damn liar if I didn't say I couldn't get a letch for her— I mean look at her, man, that's a *woman*. But like I say, she's my superior. She's air force to the core. Don't mess."

"She thinks the world of you, Lieutenant."

"Yeah, sure, like an idiot kid brother who happens to know how to tune in a VCR."

"You really do like her, don't you, Jackson?"

"Let me tell you something, I'd kill for that lady, but I'm not in her class. I'm a techno-nerd, and I know it. Maybe sometime—"

The rapping on the hotel door was frantic. "Goddamn it, open *up!*" screamed Major Catherine Neilsen.

Hawthorne reached the door first and unlatched the lock as the major burst inside. "They blew up our aircraft! Charlie's *dead!*"

The *padrone* hung up the phone, the features of his gaunt, withered face rigid, resigned. Once again a coward had come through for him, for the luxuries he provided. A coward in the French Deuxième who was afraid to face life without the "inheritance" that the unknown force in the Caribbean could eliminate in the morning. The man was a weakling, forever succumbing to his elegant and elegantly carnal appetites, yet forever pretending to be above the corruption that both sustained him and potentially destroyed him. One always looked for an influential coward, puffed him up, and let his inflated carcass hang out to dry, his perpetual sweat keeping him functional. Now it was outrage piled upon outrage, from Miami to St. Martin, with an important theft on British Gorda they would soon learn about. The Baj's hunters would be in panic, searching in all the wrong disparate places, peering into shadows when they should look toward the light. There would be no fancy American planes flying over the area for at least three hours or more, after which all transmission receivers would be shut down, all beams deflected back into nothing.

The infirm old man picked up the phone, leaned forward in his wheelchair, and carefully pressed a series of numbers on his electronic console. The ringing on the other end of the line stopped, interrupted by a flat, metallic voice. "At the signal, enter your access code." The long beep ceased and the *padrone* touched five additional digits; the ringing continued until another voice spoke. "Hello, Caribe, you're taking a chance with this transmission, I hope you know that."

"Not as of eight minutes ago, Scorpio Two. The flying intruder is no longer."

"What?"

"It was just eliminated at its temporary resting place; there'll be nothing in the air for at least three hours or so."

"The news hasn't reached us."

"Stay by your phone, *amico*, it will soon."

"You may have longer than you think," said the man in Washington, D.C. "The nearest thing to that aircraft is at Andrews."

"That's good news," the *padrone* said. "Now, Scorpio Two, I have a request, a necessity which I'd rather not discuss in depth."

"I've never asked you to discuss anything, *padrone*. Thanks to my 'inheritance,' my children are getting fine educations. They certainly wouldn't be where they are on my government salary."

"And your wife, *amico*?"

"Every day is Christmas for that bitch, and every Sunday she offers prayers at Mass for a nonexistent horse-breeding uncle in Ireland."

"*Molto bene*. Your life is in order, then."

"In ways the government should have paid for long ago. I've been the brains here for twenty-one years, but they don't think I dress right or walk right or look right, so the announcements are made to the press by idiots who use *my* findings, and my name is never even mentioned!"

"*Calma, amico*. As they say, you have the last laugh, the silent one, is it not so?"

"I sure do, and I'm grateful."

"Then you must accommodate me now; it should not be a difficult task."

"Name it."

"In your official capacity you can order immigration and customs personnel to pass private aircraft flying into the country without examining those on board, am I correct?"

"Certainly. National security. I need the name of the company that owns the plane, its identification, the international airport of entry, and the number of passengers."

"The name is Sunburst Jetlines, Florida. The number, NC twenty-one BFN; the port of entry, Fort Lauderdale. There's a pilot, his copilot, and a single male passenger."

"Anyone I ought to know?"

"Why not? We have no intention of withholding his name or bringing him into your country illegally—quite the contrary; within days his presence will be known in all the wealthy circles and he'll be much sought after. However, he wants those few days to move about freely and see old friends."

"Who the hell is he, the Pope?"

"No, but there are hostesses from Palm Beach to Park Avenue who will treat him as though he were."

"Which means I probably never heard of him."

"You probably haven't and I assure you it's no disgrace. Naturally, all his proper papers will be furnished your officials in Fort Lauderdale, who undoubtedly never heard of him either. We only prefer that he remain on board until he reaches the private field in West Palm Beach, where his limousine will meet him."

"Since it doesn't matter, what's his name?"

"Dante Paolo, son of the baron of Ravello, the Ravello both his surname and the province which his family settled several centuries ago." The *padrone* lowered his voice. "Confidentially, he's being trained to assume extraordinary responsibilities. He's the son of one of Italy's wealthiest noble families. The barony of Ravello, to be precise."

"Top-grade Fortune 500, is that it?"

"Enviably so. Their vineyards produce the finest Greco di Tufo, and their industrial investments rival those of Giovanni Agnelli. Dante Paolo will be studying potential acquisitions in your country and report back to his father. All very legitimate, I might add, and if we can do a great Italian family an incidental favor, perhaps at a later time we may be remembered kindly. Is it not the way of our world?"

"You don't even need me for this one. The Department of Commerce would break their asses to accommodate your megabucks traveler."

"Of course, but to remove such grand *nobiltà* from seeking such accommodations eliminates a degree of inconvenience, doesn't it? . . . And they know who did it for them, no? So you do it for me, *capisci*?"

"It's done. Cleared on arrival, no jerking chains. What's the ETA and the equipment?"

"Seven o'clock tomorrow morning, and the plane is a Lear 25."

"Check, I've got it. . . . *Hold* it, my red phone's blowing off the hook. Stay there, Caribe." A minute and forty-six seconds later, the *padrone*'s contact came back on the line. "You were right, we just got the word! Patrick's AWAC II was blown up in St. Martin with a crewman on board! We're on full alert. Do you want to discuss the situation?"

"There's nothing to discuss, Scorpio Two. There *is* no situation, the crisis is over. As of this call, I am shut down, incommunicado. I have disappeared."

Eighteen hundred miles northwest of the fortress island, a heavyset man with thinning red hair above a puffed, freckled face sat in his office at the Central Intelligence Agency in Langley, Virginia. The cigar in his mouth had lobbed ashes on his blue polyester tie; he blew them off,

the spittle forming circles on the water-resistant fabric.
He replaced the ultrasecure telephone in the steel drawer
on the lower base of his desk. To the casual—even the
attentive eye—it was no drawer at all, merely part of
the desk next to the rug. He relit his cigar; life was good,
really good. So who gave a shit.

8

The body was covered by a hospital sheet and driven away in an ambulance under the airport's floodlights. Hawthorne had made the formal identification from what was left of the remains, insisting that Major Neilsen and Lieutenant Poole stay away while he did so. In the near distance, the smoldering hulk of the surveillance aircraft had been reduced to an ugly skeleton, twisted black struts protruding above the charred, smoking ruins of the disembodied fuselage, the metal sheets of its walls peeled back like the dismembered chest cavity of a huge, burning, upturned insect.

Jackson Poole wept openly, collapsing to the ground and vomiting in whatever shadows he could find. Tyrell knelt beside him; there was nothing else to do but put his arm around the lieutenant's shoulders and hold him; words from a stranger about a dead friend held no meaning, only unwarranted intrusion. Tye looked over at Catherine Neilsen, Major, air-force-to-the-core, and saw that she was standing rigid, her features strained, holding back her tears. He slowly released Poole, got to his feet, and approached her.

"You know, it's okay to cry," he said gently, standing in front of her but offering no contact, his arms at his sides. "There's nothing in the officer's manual that says it's prohibited. You lost someone close to you."

"I know—both," said the major, swallowing, tears appearing in her eyes, obviously reluctantly, as she began to tremble. "I feel so helpless, so inadequate," she added. "Why?"

135

"I'm not sure. I'm trained not to be."

"No, you're trained not to appear that way in the presence of your subordinates during moments of indecision, which everyone has. There's a difference."

"I . . . I've never been in combat."

"You are now, Major. Maybe not ever again, but now you've seen it."

"Seen it? Oh, my God, I've never even seen anyone killed . . . much less anyone I cared deeply for."

"It's not a requirement for flight training."

"I should be stronger, *feel* stronger."

"Then you'd be a fraud as well as a goddamned fool, and both make lousy officers. This isn't a dumb movie, Cathy, it's real. No one trusts a military superior who has no emotions in the face of personal loss. Do you know why?"

"I don't know anything right now—"

"Let me tell you: He'll get you killed."

"I got Charlie killed."

"No, you didn't, I was there. He insisted on staying in that aircraft."

"I should have ordered him not to."

"You did, Major, I heard you. You went by the book, but he refused to obey your order."

"What?" said Neilsen, her eyes barely focused as she stared at Hawthorne. "You're trying to comfort me somehow, aren't you?"

"Only in the most reasonable way, Major. If my purpose was to lessen your grief, I'd probably hold you and let you cry your eyes out, but I won't do that. Number one, you'd despise me for it later; and number two, you've got to face the American consul general and several of his staff. They've been held at the gate, but they're now screaming diplomatic privilege and will be allowed out here in about five minutes."

"*You* did that?"

"So cry now, lady, let it out for Charlie now, then go

back to your rule book. It's okay, I've been where you are and no one ever demoted me for it."

"Oh, God, *Charlie*!" sobbed Neilsen, her head falling into Hawthorne's chest. He held her, his arms soft, encompassing.

The minutes passed; her tears subsided and Tye tilted her chin up with an unobtrusive hand. "That's all the time you've got, that's another thing I learned. Dry your eyes as best you can, but in no way think you have to deny what you feel. . . . You can use the sleeve of my coveralls."

"What . . . what are you talking about?"

"The consul and his men are driving out. I'm going over to see Poole; he's on his feet now. I'll be right back." Hawthorne started away, stopped by Neilsen's hand on his shoulder. "What is it?" he asked, turning.

"I don't know," she replied, shaking her head as the flag-bearing official car of the American consulate raced across the field toward them. "Thank you, I guess. . . . It's government time," she added. "I'll deal with them. It's up to Washington now."

"Then shape up, Major . . . and you're very welcome." Tyrell reached Jackson Poole, who held on to the rail of a fire engine's hose track, a handkerchief at his lips, his head sunken, his face conveying a terrible sadness. "How are you doing, Lieutenant?"

Poole suddenly lurched from the rail and grabbed Hawthorne by the front of his coveralls. "What the hell is this all *about*, goddamn you to *hell*," he shouted. "You killed Charlie, you fucker!"

"No, Poole, I didn't kill Charlie," said Tye, making no attempt to interfere with the lieutenant's hands. "Others did, but I didn't."

"You called my buddy a large pain in the ass!"

"That had nothing to do with his death or with the plane having been blown up, and you know that."

"Yeah, I guess I do," said Poole quietly, releasing the

bunched cloth of Hawthorne's coveralls. "It's just that before you came along it was Cathy, Sal, Charlie, and me, and we had a good thing goin'. Now we've got no Charlie, and Sal's disappeared, and Big Lady's a pile of Beirut garbage."

"Big Lady?"

"Our AWAC. We named it for Cathy. . . . Why the hell did you come into our lives?"

"It wasn't my option, Jackson. Actually, you came into mine. I didn't even know you existed."

"Yeah, well, everything's just so screwed up, I can't figure anymore, and let me tell ya', I figure things out better than most anybody I know!"

"With computers and laser beams and access codes and squeaks the rest of us don't understand," said Hawthorne sharply, harshly. "But let me tell *you* something, Lieutenant. There's another world out there, and you haven't got a clue about it. It's called the human quotient, and it hasn't a goddamned thing to do with your machines and your electronic wizardry. It's what people like me have had to deal with on a day-to-day basis for years—not blips on a printout but men and women who may be our friends or may want to kill us. Try factoring those equations into your steel whirligigs!"

"Christ, you're really pissed off."

"You're goddamned right I am. I heard what I just said to you a couple of days ago from one of the best undercover men I ever knew, and I told him he was crazy. Oh, boy, do I take it back!"

"Maybe we both should cool it," said the subdued lieutenant as the consulate vehicle sped back across the field. "Cathy just got finished with the government boys and looks a tad unhappy."

Neilsen approached, frowning, uncertainty mixed with bewilderment and sadness. "They're heading back to their scramblers and some specific instructions," she said. Then she looked hard at the former officer of naval intelligence. "What have you really gotten us into, Hawthorne?"

"I wish I could give you an answer, Major. All I know is that it's a hell of a lot more than I bargained for. Tonight proved it. Charlie proved it."

"Oh, God, *Charlie* . . . !"

"Stop it, Cathy," said Jackson Poole suddenly, firmly. "We've got work to do, and by the Lord Jesus I want to do it. For Charlie!"

It was not an easy decision, but it was reluctantly made by the furious command at the air force base in Cocoa, Florida, beaten into submission by the combined powers of the Department of the Navy, the Central Intelligence Agency, and finally, irrevocably, the subterranean strategy rooms at the White House. The sabotage of the AWAC II was to be kept under wraps, a cover story put out to the effect that a faulty fuel line caused the explosion of a Patrick training aircraft that had landed in the French territory for emergency repairs. Fortunately, there were no casualties. Relatives of the unmarried Master Sergeant Charles O'Brian were brought to Washington and briefed separately by the director of the Central Intelligence Agency, whose orders to the team of investigators were to "run silent but run deep."

"Little Girl Blood," as the search was labeled in the most secret circles, was red line, the ultimate concern of the combined services. Every international flight from all points of the compass was scrutinized, passengers detained, some for hours as each targeted traveler or travelers, together or apart, were placed in isolation, their papers put under computer scans, checked, and rechecked for flaws of origin. The number of detainees reached hundreds, then more than a thousand. *The New York Times* called it "excessive harassment without foundation," while the *International Herald Tribune* reported it as "American paranoia, not a single weapon or illegal substance found." Yet no answers, much less explanations, came from London, Paris, or Washington. The name Bajaratt was never to be mentioned, the scenario never revealed. . . . Look for a woman traveling with a young man, a teenager, nationality unknown.

And while they searched, the Lear 25 flew into Fort Lauderdale, the pilot a man who had flown the route several hundred times, the copilot a heavyset woman, formerly of the Israeli Air Command, her dark hair swept up under her visored cap; in the rear seat was a tall young man. Among the customs personnel recruited for the occasion was a pleasant official who greeted them in Italian and swiftly processed their immigration papers. Amaya Bajaratt and Nicolo Montavi of Portici had landed on American soil.

"I swear to God I don't know how come you can reach so high," said Jackson Poole as he entered the hotel room on St. Martin where Hawthorne and Catherine Neilsen were studying the lieutenant's printouts, "but it sure as hell doesn't exceed your grasp."

"In a Minnesota farm girl's vocabulary, does that mean we're cleared?" asked Cathy.

"Hell, Major, this Yankee charter pirate just adopted us, with or without our consent."

"I also run a slave ship," said Tyrell softly, returning to the computerized charts, employing a hastily supplied magnified micro-ruler under the glare of a table lamp.

"Clarification, please, Lieutenant?"

"He owns us, Cath."

"I can assure you not totally," Major Neilsen said.

"Well, we kinda volunteered too. The orders are not to use any pilot here because someone *here* blew up Big Lady and everything stays in a blackout. Since you're checked out in seagoing props, you elected yourself, Cath. And since I'm a lot younger than he is, probably stronger too, Patrick kinda threw up its hands and said 'whatever he needs.' "

"Is there anything else you'd like to add?" said Hawthorne, bending over the table. "Like how you take me for walks and make sure I get my Geritol?"

"Hey, come on," Catherine Neilsen broke in. "You made it clear that you wanted to use us, but you couldn't ask us, much less order us, to help. We told you we *wanted* to. For Charlie."

"I don't know what's out there, and I put limits on my authority."

"Cut the bullshit, Tye," demanded Cathy. "Where do we go from here?"

"I know these islands. They're like a short volcanic atoll not worth pulling into because there's nothing there, just rocks and beaches that can slice through your Dock-sides. They're garbage."

"One of 'em isn't," countered Poole. "Take my equipment's word for it."

"I do," agreed Hawthorne. "So we've got to get close up. The French are giving us a seaplane—muffled dual engines—and we'll coordinate tonight five miles south of the southernmost island with a two-man minisub hauled by a British P.T. hovercraft out of Gorda."

"Two-man?" cried Neilsen. "What about *me?*"

"You're staying with the plane and the hover."

"The hell I will. You tell the Brits to send along a pilot without any explanations; it's done all the time. . . . Forget rank, Charlie was like my older brother, if I had one. I go where you and Jackson go. Anyway, you need me."

"May I ask why?"

"Certainly. While you two *men* are on your scouting patrol, what do you intend to do with the sub? Let it sink into the mud?"

"No, we'll beach it under camouflage, which I happen to know something about."

"Considering an obvious alternative, that's a poor

decision where survival tactics are concerned, which *I* happen to know something about. Should you find the island you hope is there—"

"It's there," said Poole, interrupting. "My machines don't lie."

"Then say you do," Cathy conceded. "I submit that such a place would be extremely well protected both in manpower and technology, especially the latter. It would be a relatively simple matter to ring a small coastline with electronic detectors. Do you agree, Jackson?"

"Hell, yes, Cath."

"I further submit that it would be a lot smarter to surface offshore, eject you, and let you swim to your point of entry, which we can determine on-scene."

"Try slipping over the side, no ejections, no bodies flying in the air, and I still don't like it. You're exaggerating a primitive, minimally inhabited small island's technical resources."

"I don't know about that, Tye," the lieutenant countered. "I could set up a computerized scanner system like Cathy described with a P.C., a three-hundred-dollar generator, and a couple of dozen sensor disks, and I'm *not* exaggeratin'."

"Are you serious?" Tyrell looked hard at Poole.

"I'm not sure how I can explain this to you," Poole continued, "but ten or twelve years ago, when I was a teenager, my daddy bought a VCR with a remote control. It was the worst damn thing he could have done to us short of buyin' a desktop computer. He never got it right, especially when he tried to tape a Saints game or a program he couldn't see at the time but wanted to watch later. I mean, he got real *angry*, screamin' and hollerin' and finally throwin' that nemesis of his out with the trash. And my daddy's smart, one hell of a lawyer, but the numbers and the symbols and all those buttons you gotta press to get what you want became his personal enemies."

"Is there a point to this?" Hawthorne asked.

"There surely is," Poole answered. "He hated what he wasn't brought up with because he couldn't get used to it, not in mech-tech terms—"

"In what . . . ?"

"He's a generous man in human terms, like when the blacks ran for government positions; he thought that was just fine, and it was about time. But he couldn't adjust to the high-tech advances because they came too fast and they weren't human. He was afraid of them."

"Lieutenant, what the hell are you trying to tell me?"

"That it's really all so simple once you get used to it. My little sister and I were brought up on P.C.s, school computers, and video games—Daddy never objected, he just refused to watch us—and we got used to all those buttons and the symbols, even chip production."

"What's your goddamned point?"

"My kid sister's a programmer in Silicon Valley and already makin' more money than I ever will, but I'm using equipment she would kill for."

"So?"

"So Cathy's right and I'm right. Her projections and my expertise coincide. She's theorized what could be on that island and my provable concept of a simple P.C., a three-hundred-dollar generator, and a couple of dozen disks confirms it. No big deal technically, but it could be big trouble for us."

"What you're really saying after all this horseshit is that I should go along with her, right?"

"Listen, Tye, this lady is very important to me, and I don't like what she's doing any more than you do, but I know her. When she's right, she's damned right, especially where tactics and procedures are concerned; she's read all the books."

"How about skippering a minisubmarine?"

"Anything that goes forward or backward in the sky, on the ground, or in the water, I can handle," said the major, answering for herself. "Give me an hour with the controls and a set of diagrams, and I'll get you from A to Z with twenty-five stops in between."

"I like your modesty. I also don't trust it."

"I also know that underwater demolition teams can be taught to drive them in twenty minutes."

"It took me a half hour," said Hawthorne futilely.

"You're slow, as I expected. Look, Tye, I'm not an idiot. If anyone suggested that I go on a scout-and-search with you, I'd have to refuse. Not because I'm a coward, but because I'm neither physically suited nor mentally trained for such work and I could be a detriment to you. But in a machine that I can handle, I can be an asset. We'll be in radio contact, and I'll be wherever you want me at any given time. I'm your backup if you get into trouble."

"Is she always so logical, Jackson?"

Before a grinning Poole could reply, the telephone rang, and as he was nearest, he walked to the bedside table and picked it up. "Yes?" he answered cautiously, then, after listening, turned to Hawthorne, his hand over the phone. "Someone named Cooke is calling you."

"It's about time!" Tyrell took the receiver from the lieutenant. "Where the hell have you been?" he demanded.

"I might ask the same of you," said the voice from Virgin Gorda. "We just got back here, found absolutely no messages from you, and discovered that we've been raped!"

"What are you talking about?"

"I had to call that ass Stevens to learn where you were."

"Didn't you check with Marty?"

"Marty's gone, as well as his friend Mickey. They've simply vanished, old boy."

"Son of a bitch!" roared Hawthorne. "What's the rape?"

"The envelope I left for you in the vault is also gone. *Everything*—our whole agenda to date."

"Jesus Christ!"

"In the wrong hands, that material—"

"I don't give a damn about wrong hands or right hands, I want to know where Marty is, and Mickey! They wouldn't take off like birds, that's not like them. They'd leave a note, a reason! . . . Doesn't anybody know *anything*?"

"Apparently not. They say a fellow they call Old Ridgeley went down to the shop where the boys were supposed to be working on his engines, and he found both the bloody motors apart and no one there."

"It smells!" yelled Hawthorne. "They're friends of mine—what the hell have I done?"

"If that bothers you, perhaps you should know the worst," Cooke said. "The clerk who gave the envelope away claims he correctly delivered it to a 'gentleman' of great reputation in London named Grimshaw, who identified all of us, and made it clear that it was his rightful property, as he had paid us for the information."

"What information?"

"Inspection of a yacht his club in San Diego was buying, cost specifications of equipment that had to be replaced, and general seaworthy evaluation. I must say it was a convincing story. Unfortunately the young man bought it."

"Have the son of a bitch shot or at least fired."

"He's already left, old boy, terminated his employment when he was first soundly criticized. He said he was assured of a position at the Savoy in London, and was altogether sick of this backwater bog island. He took the last flight out of here for Puerto Rico, arrogantly stating that he rather hoped he'd be on the same plane to London as this Grimshaw. He actually told the manager here that the poor fellow might not have his job in a day or so."

"Check the P.R. passenger manifests for all flights to—" Tyrell stopped, audibly sighing. "Hell, you've already done it."

"Naturally."

"No Grimshaw," said Hawthorne.

"No Grimshaw," confirmed Cooke.

"And he sure as hell isn't there at the club."

"His room is spotless, the telephone wiped clean, both doorknobs as well."

"A professional. . . . Goddamn it!"

"It's done; we can't dwell on it, Tye."

"I can dwell on Marty and Mickey, and you can bet your ass on that!"

"We've sent out the British Navy P.T.'s, and the authorities are searching the island. . . . Wait a minute, Tyrell, Jacques just came in; he has something to tell me. Stay on the line."

"Will do," said Hawthorne, capping the mouthpiece and turning to Catherine Neilsen and Jackson Poole. "We've been deep-sixed in Gorda," he explained. "A good friend of mine who was acting as my conduit, and his sidekick, also a friend, have disappeared. Also, all the material we had on that *bitch*."

Neilsen and Poole looked at each other. The lieutenant shrugged, conveying the fact that he did not understand Tyrell's words. The major agreed by way of arched eyebrows and a shrug, followed instantly by a shake of her head, telegraphing the order *not to inquire*.

"Geoff, where are you?" Hawthorne shouted into the phone, the prolonged silence over the line not only irritating but ominous. Finally, the voice was there.

"I'm so terribly sorry, Tyrell," Cooke began quietly. "I wish I didn't have to tell you this. A patrol boat picked up the body of Michael Simms about nine hundred meters offshore. He'd been shot in the head."

"Oh, my God," said Hawthorne quietly. "How did he get out there?"

"Based on preliminary evaluation, essentially flakes

of paint on his clothing, the authorities believe he was shot, placed in a small motorized boat, and sent on automatic speed into open water. They think he was probably hanging over the side and the chop sent him overboard."

"Which means we'll never find Marty, or if someone does, he'll be deep dead in a skiff with an empty gas tank."

"I'm afraid the British Navy agrees with that assessment. The orders from London and Washington are to keep everything quiet."

"Damn it! I put both those guys into this bullshit. They were heroes in war, and they were killed for bullshit!"

"Forgive me, Tye, but I truly believe it's not bullshit. If anything, this coupled with the massacre in Miami, your own experience on Saba, and that plane in St. Martin proves we're dealing with a problem of enormous severity. This woman—these *people*—have resources beyond any previous estimates."

"I know," said Hawthorne, barely audible. "I also know how a couple of new associates of mine feel about Charlie."

"Who?"

"Nothing, never mind, Geoff. Did Stevens fill you in on our plans over here?"

"Yes, he did, and frankly, Tyrell, I must ask you, do you honestly think you're up to it? I mean, you've been away from this sort of thing for a few years—"

"What the hell did you and Stevens have, an old maid's sewing circle?" Hawthorne interrupted angrily. "Let me explain something to you, Cooke, I'm forty years of age—"

"Forty-two," whispered Catherine Neilsen from across the room. "The dossier—"

"*Shut* up! . . . No, not you, Geoff. The answer to your question is yes. We're leaving in an hour and we've got a lot to do. I'll contact you later. Name your conduit."

"The manager?" offered the man from MI-6 over the line.

"No, not him. He's too busy running the place. . . . Use Roger, the chickee bartender, he's perfect."

"Oh, yes, the black fellow with the gun. Good choice."

"Be in touch," said Tyrell, hanging up and turning to Major Neilsen. "My age being an inconsequential oversight, I was accurate when I said we'll be in a two-man submarine, because that's what it is. Not three or four, but two. I hope you and your 'darling' are pretty damned familiar, because since you insist on being on board, you'll either be on top of him or below him!"

"There's a minor amendment to the minisub's nomenclature, Commander Hawthorne," the major interjected. "In back of—or perhaps I should say aft of—the rear seat is a lateral storage compartment equal to if not larger in size than the personnel stations. It holds an inflatable PVC life raft, basic provisions for five days, as well as weapons and flares. I suggest we dispense with the provisions, you store whatever equipment you need, and there'll be no problem with space for me."

"How do you know so much about minisubs?"

"She used to go out with a navy sky jock from Pensacola who was heavy into the underwater world," replied the lieutenant. "Sal and Charlie and I were happy as hogs in a mud hole when she told him to go fly to Saturn; he was one miserable arrogant stiff."

"Please, Jackson, some things are not for discussion."

"You mean like dossiers?" asked Hawthorne.

"That was military protocol."

"Dug up from the War of 1812. . . . All right, forget it." Hawthorne walked to the table and the papers. "We can take the P.T. to within, say, a mile or so south of the first island, all lights out, of course, going only by Loran. Now, over here." Tyrell pointed his ruler to the data faxed down from Washington that spelled out everything that was known about the atoll. Fortunately included were charts prepared by such men as Hawthorne going back sixty years. Reefs that had to be marked, unseen volcanic rocks noted so that sailors would not be smashed into them or drowned in the angry waters. "There's a break in the outer reef here," he said, touching a spot on a sailing chart.

"Won't our sonar pick it up?" asked Poole.

"If we're submersed, it probably will," answered Tye. "But if we surface, it won't, and we could land up on a pile of coral below the beams."

"Then we stay submerged," said Catherine.

"Then we reach the inner reef for which there's no definition and we're sailing blind," replied Hawthorne. "And this is only the first island. Shit!"

"May I make a suggestion?" asked Neilsen.

"Be my guest."

"In combat flight training, when we hit massive cloud cover we go as low as possible, just above the carpeting clouds, where our instruments are at sighting maximum. Why don't we reverse the procedure? We go as high in the water as possible, utilizing the wide-angle periscope, and at minimum speed we'd merely bounce off the reefs or rocks if we made contact."

"Stripped of the fancy lingo," said Poole, "it's really very simple. Like computers, you go gradual. Half into 'em and half out of 'em; part eyes-on-the-objective, ten fingers on the buttons."

"What buttons?"

"Can you get me a simple laptop and a dozen sensor disks I can instant glue to this sub's exterior?"

"Of course not, there's no time."

"Then strike the buttons. Cathy's theory still holds."

"I hope to hell it does."

9

The run-down motel in West Palm Beach was merely a temporary stopover for the *barone-cadetto di Ravello*, who was registered as a construction worker, in the company of his middle-aged aunt, a domestic from Lake Worth, who was sponsoring her nephew in these "greata United States, you know watta I mean? A fine boy who works hard!"

However, by nine-thirty in the morning, both "aunt" and "nephew" were on Palm Beach's Worth Avenue, selecting and paying in cash for the finest clothes in the most exclusive shops on that very exclusive strip. And the rumors began to fly: He's an Italian baron, from Ravello they say, but *shhh*! Nobody must know! He's called a *barone-cadetto*, that's a first son in training for the title, and his aunt is a *contessa*, a real countess. I tell you, they're buying up the street, everything the finest! All his luggage was lost on Alitalia, can you believe that?

Naturally, everyone on Worth Avenue believed it as their cash registers rang and the owners called their favorite newspaper columnists in Palm Beach and Miami, willing to break their silence as long as their establishments were prominently mentioned.

At nine o'clock in the evening the motel room filled with boxes of clothing and Louis Vuitton luggage, Bajaratt removed the slightly padded dress from her body, exhaled audibly, and fell into the double bed. "I'm exhausted!" she cried.

150

"*I'm* not!" Nicolo was exuberant. "I've never been treated like this. It is *magnifico!*"

"Save it, Nico. Tomorrow we move into a grand hotel across the bridge; everything's been arranged. Now, leave me alone, no impetuous adolescent advances, if you please. I must think, then sleep."

"You think, signora. I'm going to have a glass of wine."

"Don't overdo it. We have a busy day tomorrow."

"*Naturalmente,*" agreed the dock boy. "Then I shall study some more. *Il barone-cadetto di Ravello* must be prepared, no?"

"Yes."

Ten minutes later the Baj was asleep, and across the room, under the spill of a floor lamp beside the sofa, Nicolo raised his glass above the pages of his new identity. "To you, Saint Cabrini," he said silently, mouthing the words. "And to me, the baron-to-be."

It was eleven-fifteen, the night sky clear, the Caribbean moon bright, its rays bouncing off the dark waters. The seaplane had rendezvoused with the hovercraft from Virgin Gorda at 10:05. In the time since, the three Americans had exchanged their clothes for the black wet suits provided by the British, along with small, silenced pistols holstered to their belts and Velcroed waterproof pouches for flares, night vision binoculars and their hand-held radios. Also, as it was essential to the scouting mission, they had instructed Major Neilsen in the operation of the miniature submarine; she would assume the controls once her companions left the craft to search the islands. This instruction was left to a recalcitrant young British commando who felt strongly that he should be part of the scouting patrol and not—definitely not—an American female pilot. His opposition weakened after the major took him aside at the stern of the ship and held a very private conversation. Although a certain reluctance remained, he became a formidable teacher; within the hour he was proud of his student.

"I hate to think what you promised him," said Tyrell as the pilot climbed up on deck after completing her final maneuvering exercises over a square mile of ocean.

"Is this pig time?"

"Come on, I'm trying to lighten the moment; we're going to have a long night."

"I told him the truth—about Charlie. That I really felt I owed it to him. I guess I was convincing."

"Of that I'm sure."

"I also made it clear that if I couldn't hack it, I'd bow out. I wouldn't risk two other lives. . . . That Brit really wants to go with you, and he could have loused me up, but he didn't. He knows where I'm at and he put me through the paces."

"I believe you, Major," said Hawthorne sincerely. "We're weighing anchor for the first island in a few minutes. Anything you want to tell the pilot from Gorda who's going to take over the seaplane you flew here? About the plane itself, I mean."

"He's quarantined below. He's not supposed to see us or we him. I was going to leave him a short note."

"That's what I meant. Write it now."

"Actually, it's so short, the skipper can tell him. It's the left rudder; there's a drag on it, so he's got to compensate. He'd find out in a couple of minutes anyway."

"I'll relay it. If you've got any plumbing to take care of, do it now. You may not get another chance until morning."

"Everything's taken care of, thank you, but I don't thank the people who designed these damned suits. To say the least, they're male chauvinists."

"No problems from where I stand," said Tyrell, glancing briefly at the black-encased figure in front of him in the moonlight.

"That's the problem. You stand."

"We're on!" Jackson Poole approached the two of

them on the aft deck. "The captain says they're hauling up the sub and we're supposed to practice positioning ourselves in case of any storage adjustments."

"So soon?" asked Neilsen.

"It's not so soon, Cathy. The man says that the way this thing travels, we'll reach our jump point in twenty minutes or less."

"Sir!" Major Neilsen's instructor rushed forward out of the shadows, standing rigid, and rendering Hawthorne a British flat-handed salute.

"Yes, we just got the word, Sergeant. The sub's being hoisted; we're ready."

"Not that, sir," barked the soldier. "May I ask how long it's been since you've operated this equipment, sir?"

"Oh, hell, five or six years."

"British manufactured?"

"Predominantly ours, but I've used yours. There's very little difference."

"Not adequate, sir."

"I beg your pardon?"

"I cannot permit you to get behind the controls of our equipment."

"You *what*?"

"The lady here has demonstrated excellent capability with regard to its operation, quite remarkable, actually."

"Well, I had some experience in Pensacola, Sergeant," said Neilsen demurely.

"Extremely well absorbed, ma'am."

"You mean she's driving when we first leash off?"

"That's correct, sir."

"Cut the *sir* crap. I know those islands, she doesn't!"

"Then you're not aware of the technological developments. There is a television screen that clearly shows the driver whatever is seen by the periscope in the second personnel seat. If you're not aware of that, you may not be aware of other advances. No, I'm sorry, sir, but I cannot permit you the first position."

"This is crazy . . . !"

"No, sir. This machine cost the British government a minimum of four hundred thousand pounds, and I cannot permit first position to someone who hasn't skippered one in years. Now, if you'll step to the bow, the pilot is waiting to come up here and be transferred to the plane."

"Inform him that there's a drag on the left rudder," said Catherine. "Everything else is normal."

"Very well, ma'am. I'll summon you as soon as we pull the aircraft alongside and the pilot is cast off." The sergeant stood erect, nodded at no one specifically, avoiding Hawthorne's stare, and walked away.

"I've been sandbagged!" said Tyrell angrily as they walked forward on the deck.

"You'll see, Tye," said Catherine when they reached the bow of the strangely contoured patrol boat. "It'll be better this way. I wouldn't have tried to do it if I thought otherwise, and I meant what I said: If I couldn't do it, I'd have bowed out."

"*Why* is it better this way?" asked Hawthorne.

"Because you can concentrate on what you're looking for and not worry about driving."

Tyrell looked at her, seeing in the moonlight the guarded plea in her large gray-green eyes, a little girl's eyes in the attractive face of a very accomplished woman. "You may be right, Major, I won't deny that. I just wish you'd done it another way."

"I couldn't because I didn't know whether I *could*."

Hawthorne smiled, his anger receding. "Do you always have an answer for everything?"

"Does the bayou get wet?" said the tall, slender Poole, who had been leaning over the gunwale, pretending not to hear the conversation.

"Don't say it," ordered Tyrell, holding up his hands in front of Neilsen's face. "Don't say 'Be quiet, my darling'!"

"Oh, that," said Catherine, laughing. "Someday we'll tell you how it happened, and you may just start calling him that yourself." Suddenly Neilsen's eyes grew distant and sad. "It was Sal's and Charlie's idea, they came up with it."

"With what?"

"Forget it," replied Cathy, blinking, her eyes bright again. "If you haven't got a patent on the phrase."

"*Sir!*" announced the sergeant-commando as he emerged from the shadows of the starboard rail. "We've secured the submarine for immersible procedures."

"Let's go."

The first island was volcanic garbage, nothing more and nothing less. They had penetrated the inner reef, surfaced, and saw nothing but jagged rock and rotted foliage barely kept alive by the intermittent rains absorbed by the sun-dried ground of earth and sand.

"Forget it," Tyrell ordered his skipper in the forward seat. "Head out for number two, it's less than a mile from here, due east-southeast, as I remember."

"You remember correctly," Catherine said from behind the controls. "I've got the chart and I've programmed our reentry out. Close hatches and prepare to submerge."

The second island, less than a mile northeast, was, if possible, a lesser candidate for Poole's electronic alarms. It was a barren rock formation devoid of greenery or sand-filled beaches, a volcanic aberration that held no worth for human or animal habitation. The three-man minisub headed for the third island, four miles directly north of the second. There was erratic greenery, but it had been whipped by the recent storms, untended by man. What palm trees there were had been battered, bent, many broken to the ground, an isolated land mass left to the elements. They were about to proceed to the east to the next island when Hawthorne, studying the television screen in front of Neilsen, spoke.

"Hold it, Cathy," he said quietly. "Reverse engines and then turn ninety degrees from your position."

"Why?"

"Something's wrong. The topside radar's beaming back. *Submerge.*"

"Why?"

"Do as I say."

"Sure, but I'd like to know why."

"So would I," said Poole from the rear compartment.

"Be quiet." Hawthorne stared alternately at the television screen and the radar grid in front of him. "Keep the periscope above water."

"It's there," said Neilsen.

"That's *it,*" said Tyrell. "Your machines were right, Basin Street. We've got it."

"What have we got?" asked Neilsen.

"A wall. A goddamned man-made *wall* that bounces back the radar. Steel-encased is my guess; it's concealed but it repulses the beams."

"What do we do now?"

"Circle the island, then come back here if we don't find any surprises."

They slowly rounded the small island, barely breaking the surface, the undetectable radar beams scanning every foot of the coastline. For visual sighting, Poole squeezed up into Tyrell's open hatch, a pair of night-vision binoculars at his eyes.

"Oh, boy," said the lieutenant, angling his head down to be heard. "They've got detectors all over the place, every twenty or thirty feet, I figure, and definitely in series sequence."

"Describe what you see," said Hawthorne.

"They look like small glass reflectors, some on the palms, others on poles deep in the ground. Those on the tree trunks have single black or green wires going up through the leaves, the ones on the poles—lucite or plastic sticks—don't seem to have any wires, not that I can tell."

"They're threaded," explained Hawthorne, "buried four to six feet under; you couldn't see them unless you were ten inches in front of them in broad daylight, and maybe not even then."

"How come?"

"They're clear blank veins, the contact colors at each end to connect the series. You were right about that part, the series."

"Christmas tree lights?"

"Yes, but with backups. You can't short one and knock out the series. The wires lead to batteries, above or below, that override the shorts and maintain contact."

"Well, listen to the tech man! What are they?"

"Trip beams, and your computer mumbo jumbo is part of the mechanism. The beams can measure density—mass, if you like—so as to prevent small animals and birds from setting off the alarms."

"You impress me, Tye."

"They've been around since you were playing video games."

"How do we get through 'em?"

"We crawl on our stomachs. It's no big deal, Lieutenant. In the old days—five or six years ago—the boys from the KGB and we pure fellows on our side would drink up a storm in Amsterdam, telling one another how stupid we all were."

"You did that?"

"We all did that, Jackson. Don't ponder it. But don't push it either."

"You know, Commander, you really do puzzle me."

"Like somebody once wrote, it's all a puzzlement, young man. . . . *Hold* it, Major!" Catherine Neilsen looked up from the controls. "There's the cove, the same one where we got the repelled beams before. From the wall."

"Should I head in?"

"Hell, no. Proceed straight west, about a quarter of a mile, no more than that."

"Then what?"

"Then your 'darling' and I are going to jump ship. . . . Get down from there, Poole. Check your weapon and zip-lock your equipment."

"I'm on your side, Commander. You sound real purposeful," replied Poole.

The telephone rang, its harsh bell startling Bajaratt out of her sleep, causing her instinctively to plunge her hand beneath the pillow for her automatic. Then, sitting up, blinking, her breath suspended, she imposed a control over her reactions that in no way diminished her astonishment. No one knew where she was—*they* were! From the airport, only fifteen minutes away, she had taken three different taxis to get to the motel, the first two in her disguise as a middle-aged former Israeli Air Force pilot, the third as an unmade-up harridan who spoke only broken English. Such motels as the one they were in did not require references, much less authentic names. The ringing started again; she instantly picked up the phone to cut it off, glancing at Nicolo beside her. He was fast asleep, his breathing steady, his breath reeking of stale wine.

"Yes?" she said quietly into the telephone, looking at the red numbers of the screwed-down clock radio on the bedside table. It was 1:35 A.M.

"Sorry to wake you," said the pleasant male voice on the line, "but our orders are to assist you, and I have information you may want to think about."

"Who are you?"

"Names aren't part of our instructions. Suffice it to say that our group holds a sick old man in the Caribbean in great esteem."

"How did you find me?"

"Because I knew who and what to look for, and there weren't that many places where you could be. . . . We met briefly at Fort Lauderdale customs, but that's not important, my information could be. Come on, lady, don't give me a hard time. I'm taking a risk some people would say I'm out of my mind to take."

"I apologize. Frankly, you surprised me—"

"No, I didn't," the pleasant voice interrupted. "I shocked you."

"Very well, I'll accept that. What is your information?"

"You did a hell of a job this afternoon; the Palm Beach barracudas are in a social feeding frenzy, as I'm sure you expected."

"It was merely an introduction."

"It was a lot more than that. You've got a small press conference tomorrow."

"*What?*"

"You heard me. This isn't the New York–Washington orbit by a long shot, but we've got some decent newspeople down here, especially where the Beach society is concerned. It wasn't difficult to figure where you'd be staying, so a few of them descended on The Breakers. We just felt you ought to know. You can refuse, of course, but we didn't think you'd want to be . . . surprised."

"Thank you. Is there a number where I can reach you?"

"Are you crazy?" The line went dead, replaced by a dial tone.

Bajaratt hung up the phone; she got out of bed and for several minutes paced back and forth in front of the pile of luggage and boxes from the shops on Worth Avenue. It was a minor thing, she thought, looking at the packages and complimenting herself on her foresight, but she had requested that all price tags and marks of the newly-purchased be removed from the clothing. Packing everything would be far easier in the morning. That was minor; something else was not.

"Nicolo!" she said loudly, slapping his bare feet that extended beyond the lifted sheets. "Wake up!"

"What . . . ? What is it, Cabi? It's dark."

"It isn't now." The Baj walked to the floor lamp next to the sofa and turned it on. The dock boy sat up, rubbing his eyes and yawning. "How much did you drink?" asked Bajaratt.

"Two or three glasses of wine," he answered angrily. "Is that a crime, signora?"

"No, but did you study the information in those pages as you said you would?"

"Of course. I studied them last night for hours, then this morning on the plane, and in the taxis and before we went to the elegant stores. Tonight I read for at least an hour; you were asleep."

"Can you remember everything?"

"I remember what I can remember, what do you want from me?"

"Where did you go to school?" asked the Baj harshly, standing at the foot of the bed.

"I was tutored at our estate in Ravello for ten years," replied the young man, the answer an emphatic robotic reflex.

"And then?"

"L'École du Noblesse in Lausanne," Nicolo shot back. "In preparation for—for—"

"Quickly! In preparation for *what*?"

"For the Université de Genève, that's it! . . . And then my ailing father called me back to Ravello to absorb the family business . . . yes, he called me back, the family business."

"Don't hesitate! They'll think you're lying."

"Who?"

"After your father called you back?"

"I employed my own tutors—" Nicolo paused, squinting, then the memorized words came rushing from his mouth. ". . . for two years to make up for my lack of university training—five hours every day! I'm told that my scores on the *esami di stato* in Milano placed me in the highest levels."

"Also documented," said Bajaratt, nodding. "You did that very well, Nico."

"I will do it better, but it's all false, isn't it, signora? Suppose someone who speaks Italian asks me questions I cannot answer?"

"We've gone over that. You simply change the subject, which I will change for you."

"Why did you wake me up and go through all this?"

"It was necessary. You didn't hear it, the wine blocked your ears, but I had a telephone call. When we arrive at the hotel tomorrow, there will be newspaper people who want to interview you."

"No, Cabi. Who would care to interview a dock boy from Portici? They don't want to interview me, they want to interview the *barone-cadetto di Ravello*, is it not so?"

"Listen to me, Nico." The Baj, hearing the discontent in his voice, sat at the edge of the bed next to Nicolo. "You can really *be* that *barone-cadetto*, you know. The family has seen photographs of you, and they have learned of your sincere aspirations to become an educated man, a fine *nobile italiano*. They're prepared to welcome you as the son they never had."

"Once more you speak crazy words, signora. Who among the nobility wants their bloodlines tainted by the docks?"

"This family does, for it has nothing left but someone like you. They trust me, as you must trust me. Exchange your miserable life for another, far better, far richer."

"But until that time comes, if it ever comes, it's you who wants me to be the *barone-cadetto*, is that not so?"

"Yes, of course."

"It's very important to you, for reasons you say I must not inquire about."

"Considering everything I've done for you, including saving your life, I think I deserve that respect."

"Oh, yes, you do, Cabi. And I deserve to be rewarded for all the studying I've done on your behalf, not mine." Nicolo raised his arms, placing his hands on her shoulders, and pulled her slowly across the bed. She did not resist the boy-man.

10

I t was shortly past two A.M. when Hawthorne and Poole, in their black wet suits, crawled over the sharp rocks that were their point of entry on the unmapped island, the third of the volcanic atoll.

"Stay on your stomach," said Tyrell into his radio. "Up ahead hug the ground like you were part of the dirt, have you got that?"

"Hell, yes, don't you worry about it" was the whispered reply.

"Once we're past the first trips, stay low for another fifty to sixty feet, okay? The trip beams will recede at various heights for about thirty feet on the premise that humans will stand up before then once on shore, but snakes and rabbits can't, now do you read me?"

"There are snakes here?"

"No, there are *not* snakes here, I'm simply trying to explain how these systems work," Tye said sharply. "Just stay down until I get up."

"Whatever you say," said Poole.

Sixty-eight seconds later, they had reached a flat stretch of the sun scorched grass so common to the islands, a barren field incapable of nurturing palms or flamboyant trees. "*Now,*" said Hawthorne, getting to his feet. "We're clear." They raced across the acre of wasteland, suddenly stopping at strange, muffled sounds in the distance, animal sounds, high-pitched and erratic. "Dogs," whispered Tyrell into the radio. "They've picked up our scent."

"Oh, my God!"

"It's the wind—it's from the northwest."

"What does that mean?"

"It means we run like hell southeast. Follow me." Hawthorne and Poole ran diagonally to their left toward the shoreline, entering a grove of traveler's-palms. Breathless and standing next to each other under the cover of the spreading foliage, Tyrell spoke. "This doesn't make sense."

"Why? The dogs aren't yipping."

"We're out of their wind scent, but that's not what I mean." Tye looked around, angling his eyes up and around. "These palms are traveler's; they grow out like fans, the kind you wave in front of your face."

"So?"

"They're the first to crack in heavy winds—see, a few have broken from the storms, but a lot of them haven't."

"*So?*"

"What we saw from the sub, directly in front of the cove. Most everything had been leveled, uprooted, flat on the ground."

"I don't know what you're talkin' about. Some trees survive, some don't. So what?"

"These are on fairly high ground, the cove's lower."

"Freaks of nature," explained Poole. "When Lake Pontchartrain blows, all kinds of crazy things happen. One time the whole left side of our summer place was ripped off, but a doghouse right in front of it wasn't touched. No accountin' for nature."

"Maybe, maybe not. Come on." They threaded their way through the thick fan-shaped trees until they came to a small promontory that overlooked the cove. Tyrell removed the pair of night-vision binoculars from his belted pouch and brought them to his eyes. "Come here, Jackson. Look through these—directly across, near the top of the hill over there—and tell me what you see." Tyrell gave the younger man the binoculars and watched him as Poole scanned the ground above the cove.

"Hey, it's weird, Tye," said the air force officer.

"'There's a few blurred lines of light through the trees, goin' straight across a long way and angled down, but no source.'"

"Deep green hurricane shutters, camouflaged. No one's ever designed the perfect machinery for exterior 'hurricanes'; the slats haven't been invented that close perfectly every time, every inch. Your beeping machines were on the mark, Lieutenant. That's one big mother of a house over there, and inside is someone very important to this insanity, maybe the bitch herself."

"Y'know, Commander, don't you think it's about time you told the major and me what this whole god-damned thing's about? We hear things like 'that bitch' and 'terrorists' and 'disappearin' secret papers' and 'international chaos,' and we've been damn well *ordered* not to ask questions. Well, Cath won't say it 'cause she's by-the-book Neilsen, and like me she's doin' what she's doin' because of Charlie, but here I part company with her. I don't give a fiddler's fart about orders. If I'm goin' to get my precious body blown away, I want to know why."

"Good heavens, Lieutenant, I didn't know you had so many words in you."

"I'm one bright son of a bitch, Commander. Now, what the fuck is this all about?"

"Insubordinate too. All right, Poole, I'll level. It's about the assassination of the President of the United States."

"*What . . . ?*"

"And the terrorist is a woman who might just pull it off."

"You're out of your mind! That's plain crazy!"

"So were Dallas and Ford's Theatre . . . The word we've received from the Baaka Valley is that if this assassination takes place, there are three other targets—the Prime Minister of England, the President of France, and the head of the Israeli government. All to follow quickly. The signal is the killing of the President."

"It couldn't happen!"

"You saw what happened on St. Martin's, what happened to Charlie and your plane despite guaranteed maximum security on one of our most classified tech-weapons. What you don't know is that a team of deep-cover FBI agents was massacred in Miami while on surveillance relative to this operation, and I was nearly killed on Saba tracking down an unrelated situation because somebody learned I'd been recruited. There are leaks in Paris and Washington that we know about; London is still an enigma. In the words of a friend of mine, who I hate to admit is a terrific intelligence officer with MI-6, this woman and her people have resources no one ever dreamed of. Does that answer your question, Lieutenant Poole?"

"Oh, my God!" came the scratchy voice of Major Catherine Neilsen over Poole's radio.

"Yeah," said the lieutenant, glancing down at the pouch that held the radio. "I had it on, hope you don't mind. Saves you from repeating it all."

"I could break you both down to privates for that!" exploded Hawthorne. "Did it occur to you that whoever's in that house might have a frequency scanner?"

"Correction," said Neilsen's voice over the radio. "This is military-direct, off frequency within two thousand meters. We're secure. . . . Thank you, Jackson, I think we can proceed now. And thank *you, Mister* Hawthorne. Sometimes the troops have to have a clue, I'm sure you understand that."

"I understand that you two are impossible! The end of tolerance. . . . Where are you, Cathy?"

"About four hundred feet west of the cove. I figured you'd be going back there."

"Head into it, but stay submerged at least forty feet from shore. We don't know the capability of the trip beams."

"Right on. Out."

"Out," said Poole, reaching down into his pouch and snapping off the radio.

"That was a dirty trick, Jackson."

"Surely was, but look how much we got cleared up. Before we had Charlie, now we got even more."

"Don't forget Mancini, your ersatz pal, Sal. He would have had you blown out of the sky without thinking twice."

"I don't want to think about him. I can't handle it."

"Then don't." Tyrell pointed below to the cove. "Let's go." The two black-suited figures moved like roving silhouettes, zigzagging down the incline to the cove. "On your stomach," Hawthorne whispered into the radio as they reached the beach. "We'll crawl up to that stretch of flat bush. If I'm not mistaken, it's a wall."

"Well, I'll be a shorn possum!" exclaimed Poole when they had crept to the sheer vine-laden embankment and he thrust his hand through the foliage. "It *is* a wall, pure concrete."

"With more steel struts than an airport runway," added Tyrell. "This was made for bombs, not little typhoons or mere hurricanes. Stay low! . . . Come on, I have an idea we'll find a few more surprises."

They did. The first was a layer of green Astroturf that covered an ascending row of stone steps leading to a break in the hill just below the top. "We'd never spot this airborne," said the lieutenant.

"That's the point, Jackson. Whoever it is doesn't roll out a red carpet, he rolls down a green one."

"Must be a very private kind of individual."

"I'd say you're right. Stay to the left and slither up like a snake." The two men made their way up on their stomachs step by covered step, slowly, silently, until they came to a break in the stone staircase that seemed to lead to the outlines of a palm-covered structure beyond. Hawthorne lifted the carpet of green, revealing a flagstone path. "My God, it's so simple," he whispered to

Poole. "You could do it with any house in the country-side or at the shore and never spot it from the air or the water."

"Sure could," agreed the air force officer, impressed. "This grass stuff is a snap, but those palm trees, they're a whole whale of a lot of difference."

"What?"

"They're fake."

"They *are*?"

"You're no country boy, Commander, at least not one from Louisiana. Palms sweat in the early morning hours; it's the change in temperature 'cause they're alive. Look, there's not a glisten of moisture on those big leaves. They're nothin' more than big dead cotton flowers, also too big for the trunks, which are probably plastic."

"Which means they're mechanized cover—camouflage."

"Probably computerized, easy to do if you access-code your radar to your machinery."

"*Huh?*"

"Come on, Tye, it's simple. Like garage doors that open when headlights hit the receptors; this is just the reverse. The sky and sea sensors pick up the unfamiliar, and the equipment goes to work. They close up the shop."

"Just like that?"

"Sure. A plane or a boat that comes too close, say three or four thousand feet up or a couple of miles out on the water, the disks send the information to a computer and the machines are activated, like garage doors closin' down by remote. I could design a system like that for a few thousand bucks, but the Pentagon doesn't want to hear my figures."

"You'd bankrupt the economy," Hawthorne whispered.

"That's what my daddy says, but my little sister agrees with me."

"The young shall inherit the earth and all its buttons."

"What do we do now? Walk through those big cotton leaves and announce ourselves?"

"No, we don't walk, we crawl very silently around those big cotton leaves and do our best not to be announced."

"What are we lookin' for?"

"Whatever we can see."

"What then?"

"Depends on what we see."

"You're filled with all kinds of plans."

"Some things you can't put into a computer, young man. Come on."

They crept over the hard, sharp zoysia grass, a favored ground cover in the Caribbean, and swept around the uprooted false palms, both men peering down into the machinery and touching the "bark" of the first "trunk." Poole nodded in the moonlight, as if to confirm his previous guesswork that it was a thick tube of mottled plastic, indistinguishable from the real thing but a far lighter load on the mechanism. Hawthorne gestured at a low break in the greenery, indicating that the lieutenant should follow him.

One behind the other they crawled through the tunnel of dyed cloth to a point directly below a line of light from a parted slat. Both quietly stood up and looked inside; there was no activity to be seen, so Tyrell separated the shutter strip an additional inch for a better view. What they saw was astonishing.

The interior of the house had the appearance of some doge's Renaissance villa, huge arches leading from one area to another, gold-flaked marble everywhere, and on the white walls tapestries of a quality usually inherited or on loan to museums. A figure came into sight, an old man in a motorized wheelchair. He was crossing under the archways from one room to another. He disappeared from view, but following him was a blond-haired giant, his massive shoulders stretching the cloth of his guayabera jacket. Hawthorne touched Poole's shoulder, point-ing out the length of the house, and by his gesture telling the air force officer again to follow him. The lieutenant did so, each man sidestepping his way, silently pushing the huge cloth palms away as he progressed, until Tyrell reached what he estimated to be the area where the old man in the wheelchair had gone. The hurricane shutters emitted no light in this stretch of the wall, so Hawthorne grabbed Poole's arm, pulled the lieutenant beside him, and parted a slat at eye level.

Inside was the unbelievable, a fantasy created by a gambling maniac. It was a miniature casino designed for an emperor, an emperor racked with insomnia. There were slot machines, a pool table, a very low, curved blackjack table, and a wheel of fortune, all waist level for the wheelchair, the flat surfaces covered with stacks of paper money at the edges. Whoever the old man was, he was betting both for and against the house. He couldn't lose.

The blond bodyguard—he couldn't be anything else—stood beside the gaunt, balding white-haired man in the wheelchair, yawning as the old man put coins into a slot and laughed or grimaced at the results. Then a second man appeared, wheeling in a cart of food with a carafe of red wine and placing it alongside the invalid. The old cripple scowled, then shouted at his second guard-cum-chef, who instantly bowed and removed a dish, apparently stating it would be replaced immedi-ately.

"Come on!" whispered Tyrell. "There won't be a better time. We've got to find a way in while that other gorilla is gone!"

"Where?"

"How do *I* know? Let's go!"

"Wait a minute!" whispered Poole. "I know this glass, this window. It's a dual pane with a vacuum in between, and once the vacuum is filled with air, you can break it with a heavy elbow."

"How do we do that?"

"Our guns have silencers, right?"

"Yes."

"And when a slot machine pays off, bells ring, right?"

"Sure."

"We wait till we see he hits a big one, then poke two holes on either side and break the damn thing in."

"Lieutenant, you may be a genius after all."

"I've been tryin' to tell you that but you won't listen. You hit the low right corner, I hit the low left. We give the glass a couple of seconds to fog up, then smash it in. Actually, with a cushion of air it should make less noise than a regular window."

"Whatever you say, General."

Both men stripped open their Velcroed holsters and whipped out their weapons.

"He's hit one, Tye!" cried Poole as the old man inside began waving his arms in front of the blinding lights of the blinking, glittering slot machine.

Both fired their weapons and pushed up the exterior shutters as the mistlike vapor filled the glass, then crashed through the window while the slot machine was still blinking and spewing out coins, its bells clamoring, echoing off the marble walls. Amid the shattered glass they crouched on the floor as the stunned guard spun around and reached into his belt.

"Don't even try it!" Hawthorne said in a strident whisper as the deafening slot machine grew silent. "If either one of you raises your voice, it'll be the last sound you make. Trust me, I really don't like you."

"*Impossible!*" screamed the old man in the wheel-chair, in shock at the sight of the two invaders in their black wet suits.

"Oh, it's real possible," said Poole, getting to his feet first and leveling his gun at the invalid. "I speak a little Italian, courtesy of a guy I thought was my friend, but if you and he had Charlie killed, you're not gonna need that wheelchair a second more."

"We want him alive, not dead," broke in Tyrell. "Cool it, Lieutenant, that's an order."

"It's a tough one to obey, Commander."

"Cover me," said Hawthorne. He approached the blond guard, yanked up his guayabera, and slipped the revolver out of his belt. "Get by the side of the archway, Jackson, and hug the wall," Tyrell continued, his concentration on the now furious, agitated guard. "If you're thinking what I think you're thinking," he snapped at the man, "reevaluate. I said I wanted Methuselah here alive. You I couldn't possibly care less about. Move between those two slot machines, *now*. And don't figure you can risk jumping me. Thugs don't interest me; they're expendable. *Move!*"

The huge guard squeezed between the lowered machines, sweat rolling down his forehead, his eyes on fire. "You don't get outta here," he mumbled in broken English.

"You don't think so?" Hawthorne walked rapidly to the side of the adjacent slot machine, switching his weapon to his left hand and removing the radio from his pouch. He snapped on the transmitter, brought the instrument to his lips, and spoke quietly. "Can you hear me, Major?"

"Every syllable, Commander." The female voice that issued out of the miniaturized speaker astonished the guard, and for an instant infuriated the helpless old man in the wheelchair, whose whole body suddenly trembled with anger and fear. Then, as quickly as his fury had been summoned, it disappeared. Instead, he stared at Hawthorne and grinned; it was the most malevolent smile Tye had ever seen, for a moment transfixing him. "What's your status?" asked Neilsen over the radio.

"A home run, Cathy," replied Hawthorne, taking his eyes off the disturbing face of evil incarnate below. "We're inside the first cousin to Hadrian's villa. We've got two of the residents and we're waiting for a third. Who else is here, if anyone, we don't know."

"Should I radio the Brit P.T. with your findings?" Hearing the words, the old man bolted forward in the wheelchair, his hand clutching an instrument in the padded arm, his fury returning. He was stopped by Poole's foot, his hand fell away, grabbing a spoke.

"It's beyond your military-direct, isn't it?"

"True."

"Then wait until Jackson has studied whatever equipment is here. I wouldn't want specifics picked up from the ether. But if by some chance we go out of contact, then make that call quickly."

"Keep your radio on."

"I intend to. It'll be muffled in the pouch, but you'll hear enough." Footsteps! From an outer area, heels against hard marble. "I'm off, Major," whispered Tye. Hawthorne replaced the radio, switched his weapon, and pointed it at the head of the blond giant three feet away above the next slot machine.

"*Arresto!*" shrieked the old Italian, suddenly propelling his chair forward toward the archway. As he did so, the blond guard crashed his immense bulk into the slot machine on his left, hurling it into Tyrell's body with such force that it sent Hawthorne to the marble floor, machine and man instantly on top of him, his right arm pinned, his weapon useless. Simultaneously, there was the smashing of china plates beyond the arch. As the blond giant's fingers dug into the flesh of Tyrell's throat, choking off all air, a silenced gunshot pierced the space above Hawthorne, blowing apart half the guard's head. He fell away as Tye wrenched his arm from under the massive, blinking, silent slot machine, and sprang to his feet only to observe Andrew Jackson Poole V subdue the third man with a series of punishing blows, delivered by flying feet and flat hands until the second guard staggered out of control. The lieutenant grabbed him and threw the man's dead weight across the frail back of the invalid, stopping the patriarch in mid-flight.

"*Hawthorne? . . . Jackson?*" Catherine Neilsen's

voice shot out from the pouch-encased radio. "What happened? I heard a lot of noise!"

"Hold on," said Tyrell, breathless, walking to the nonproductive one-armed bandit, leaning down and pulling the plug out of the wall. The maniacal blinking stopped; it was both calming and ominous. The old man struggled under the weight of his guard's unconscious body until Poole removed it, letting it crash to the floor, the skull thumping onto the marble. "We're back in control," Hawthorne continued into the radio. "And I'll insist on nothing less than the rank of general for an under-thirty lieutenant named Andrew Jackson Poole. *Christ,* he saved my life!"

"He does small favors. What now?"

"We'll check out the premises and then the equipment. Stay on."

Tye and Jackson gagged and tightly strapped the guard and the old Italian, hands and feet, into the chairs, lashed them to the upturned slot machine with clothesline they found in a kitchen cabinet, and proceeded to search the house, then the estate itself. They crawled around the grounds southeast of the fenced kennels, which were barely forty yards from the main house, until they spotted a small all-green cabin, large palms surrounding it, with a dim pulsating light from a very small window. They crept up to the sheltered glass; inside was a figure on a reclining chair, large flowering plants all around him, staring at a television screen and punching the air with his fists at a sequence of cartoons.

"That boy isn't playin' with a full deck," whispered Poole.

"No, he's not," Hawthorne said, "but he's still another body capable of being ordered to do something we wouldn't like."

"What do you want to do?"

"The door's on the other side. We'll break in, tie him up, and you do one of your things that puts him out for a couple of hours so he can't interfere."

"A simple spinal chop," the lieutenant said.

"Right. . . . Be quiet! He hears something; he's going for a red box on a table across the room. Let's *go!*"

The two black-suited figures raced around the camouflaged cabin, broke through the door, and confronted a bewildered man who did nothing but smile at them as he turned off the screeching machine on the table. "That's my signal to release the dogs," he said hesitantly. "It's always the signal," he added, reaching for a lever against the wall. "I must do it immediately."

"No!" shouted Hawthorne. "The signal was wrong!"

"Oh, it's never wrong," said the gardener dreamily. "Never, never wrong." He pulled the lever. Within seconds the vicious howling, screaming sounds of attack dogs were heard racing past the cabin to the main house. "There they go," said the half-witted man, smiling. "They're my good boys."

"How did you get that signal?" demanded Tyrell. "*How?*"

"It's on the *padrone*'s chair. We practice a lot, but, you see, the *padrone* will now and then set it off when he has wine and his hand touches the button. I heard it a few minutes ago, but it stopped very quickly, so I believed the great *padrone* made a mistake and his guard corrected it. But not now, not a second time. He means it, and I must go and be with my friends. It's very important."

"One of his oars is out of the water," said Poole.

"Maybe both, Lieutenant, but we have to get back there. . . . *Flares.*"

"What?"

"Next to scent, dogs will go after light—explosions of light. Take out a couple of flares, stick one of them under your wet suit, and rub it back and forth through your armpit. Rub it thoroughly, and trust that your not having a bath in two or three days will do it!"

"This is most embarrassin'," said Poole, following orders.

"Do it!"

"I'm doing it!"

"Light the other one and throw it out the door to the left as far as you can. Then the second unlit one."

"Here they go." Within seconds the dogs raced by the cabin after the arcing flare in search of the sudden light. The barking was maniacal as the dogs huddled around the sizzling tube, picking up the human scent from the unlit one and snapping at one another in frustration.

"Listen to me, sir," said Hawthorne, turning to the mentally enfeebled guardian of the dogs. "This is all a game—the *padrone* likes games, doesn't he?"

"Oh, yes, yes, he does! Sometimes he plays all night in his parlor."

"Well, this is just another game, and we're all having fun. You can go back to your television."

"Oh, thank you. Thank you very much." The man sat down, laughing at the cartoons on the screen.

"Thanks, Tye. I don't relish choppin' old guys like that—"

With an impatient shake of his head Tyrell signaled the lieutenant to follow him as he raced back to the mansion, shutting the doors and confronting the withered old man in the wheelchair beside his unconscious guard. "All right, you bastard!" shouted Tyrell. "I want to know what you know."

"I know nothing," rasped the elderly Italian. The malevolent grin returned. "You kill me, you have nothing."

"That could be a wrong assessment, *padrone*—it is *padrone*, isn't it? That's what the poor half-wit in the cabin called you. What did you do, have a lobotomy done on him?"

"God made him the perfect servant, not I."

"I have an idea that in your vocabulary, you and God are pretty closely related."

"Blasphemy, Commander—"

"Commander?"

"It's what your colleague and the woman over the radio called you, is it not?"

Hawthorne stared at the satanic cripple; why did he think he should *know* him? "Lieutenant, check out the room with all that electronic equipment you know so much about. It's over there by—"

"I know exactly where it is," interrupted Poole. "I can't wait to program a few memory banks. That stuff is top of the charts!" The air force officer moved rapidly toward the *padrone*'s study.

"Perhaps I should tell you," said Hawthorne, standing in front of the old man. "My colleague is our government's secret weapon. There isn't a computer made he can't break into. He's the one who found you, found this place. From a beam in the Mediterranean bounced off a Japanese satellite."

"He'll find nothing—*nothing*!"

"Then why do I detect a pinch of doubt in your voice? . . . Oh, I think I know. You're not sure, and that scares the hell out of you."

"This is a meaningless conversation."

"Not really," said Tyrell, taking out his gun from the Velcroed holster. "I just want you to know where you stand. What I'm going to say now is very meaningful. How do we get the dogs back into the kennels?"

"I have no idea—" Hawthorne squeezed the trigger of his weapon, the spit electric, the bullet grazing the *padrone*'s right earlobe, the blood coursing down his neck. "You kill me, you have *nothing*!" shouted the old man.

"But if I don't kill you, I still have nothing, isn't that right?" Tyrell fired again, this time creasing the *padrone*'s left cheek. The blood splashed over his face and across his throat. "You've got one more chance," Hawthorne said. "I had a lot of practice in Europe. . . . Dogs that can be released on command from a kennel can be returned to a kennel by a second command. Do it, or my next bullet goes right into your left eye. *Il sinistro*, isn't that the term?"

Without speaking, the invalid awkwardly, strenuously, moved his strapped right arm, manipulating his trembling fingers over the side of the wheelchair, where there was a panel of five buttons in a semicircle. He pressed the fifth. Instantly, there was an animal chorus of wild howls and harsh barking, the sounds receding until there was silence. "They're back in the kennels," said the *padrone*, his eyes hard, contempt in his voice. "The gate closes automatically."

"What are the other buttons for?"

"They're of no concern to you now. The first three are for my personal maid and my two attendants; the maid is no longer with us, and you killed my head attendant. The last two are for the dogs."

"You're lying. One of those signals reached that quasi-vegetable in the cabin. *He* released the dogs."

"He receives the signal wherever he is, and if there are guests or new personnel on the island, he must be with the dogs, for he can control them. Frequently, men with lesser intellect speak to the animals far better than we of higher intelligence. I believe it's a matter of more mutual trust."

"We're not guests here, so who's new?"

"My two attendants, including the one you murdered. They've been here less than a week, and the dogs are not yet accustomed to them."

Hawthorne leaned over and unstrapped the old man's arms, then crossed to a low marble table where there was a gold receptacle for facial tissues. He picked it up and carried it back to the *padrone.* "Dry your cuts."

"Does the sight of the blood you drew disturb you?"

"Not one bit. When I think what you're into—when I think of Miami and Saba and St. Martin and that psychopathic bitch—the sight of your corpse would be a distinct pleasure."

"You do not know that I am involved in anything but

prolonging the life of this wretched body," said the old Italian as he blotted his right ear, then held a wad of tissue against his left cheek. "I am an invalid living out my final years in the isolated luxury I so richly deserve. I have done nothing remotely illegal, I have merely entertained a few cherished friends who reach me by satellite telephone or fly in to visit me."

"Let's start with your name."

"I have no name, I am only the *padrone*."

"Yes, I heard that in the cabin—and once before on Saba, where two mafiosi bribed the crews on the waterfront and tried to kill me."

"*Mafiosi?* What do I know of such things as the Mafia?"

"One of those two hit men, the one who survived, had a lot to say when he was faced with the prospect of swimming among sharks with a bleeding shoulder. I have an idea that when we circulate your fingerprints, including a set to Interpol, we'll learn who you are, and I doubt that it'll be a sweet old grandfather who likes to play slot machines."

"Really?" The *padrone* put down the tissues, smiling his ugly, arrogant smile at Hawthorne as he turned over both hands, exposing the palms. Tyrell was both repelled and stunned. The ends of each finger were pure white; the flesh had long ago been burnt off, replaced by a smooth, flat substitute, the fused shavings of human or animal skin perhaps. "My hands were scorched by a burning German tank in the Second World War. I've always been grateful to the American army doctors who took pity on a young partisan who fought with their troops."

"Oh, that's beautiful," said Tye. "I suppose you were also decorated."

"Unfortunately, none of us could permit that. The more fanatical of the *fascisti* were known to take reprisals. All our records were destroyed to protect us and our families. You should have done the same in Vietnam."

"*Really* beautiful."

"So you see . . . nothing."

Neither Hawthorne nor the old man was aware of Poole's lean, black-suited figure standing in the archway. He had approached quietly and was watching, listening. "You're almost right," said the lieutenant. "There was almost nothin', but not all the way to zero. Your system's terrific, I'll say that, but any system's only as good as the person using it."

"What are you saying?" asked Tyrell.

"This equipment can do everything but make moonshine, and it's been used by someone who knows how to erase the memories on the first and second recalls and did just that. There's zilch on every disk except for three printouts near the end of the last one. Whoever used it then must have been someone else, because the delete-memory wasn't touched."

"Would you mind speaking English, not computerese?"

"I pulled up three telephone numbers, area codes and all, then checked the destinations. One was to Switzerland, and I'll bet my hush puppies it's to a bank; the second was to Paris; and the third to Palm Beach, Florida."

11

The white limousine drew up to the canopied entrance of The Breakers hotel in Palm Beach and was immediately surrounded by the gold-braided doorman, the assistant doorman, and three red-uniformed bellhops. It was a scene reminiscent of a modernized Belle Époque, masters and servants knowing their places, content with their privileges and enthusiastic in their servitudes. The first to emerge was a full-figured, middle-aged grande dame dressed in the finery of the Via Condotti, Rome's avenue of high fashion. Her wide-brimmed hat above the flowered silk dress cast shadows across a tanned face that bespoke generations of aristocracy. The features were sharp and harmonious, the skin smooth, what lines there were more imagined than seen. Amaya Bajaratt was no longer a wild, unkempt terrorist on a raft or a boat at sea, or a uniformed fighter from the Baaka Valley, or a frumpish ex-pilot for the Israeli Air Force. She was now the Countess Cabrini, reputed to be one of the wealthiest women in Europe, with an industrialist brother in Ravello who was even richer. She threw her head back gracefully and smiled as the tall, extremely handsome young man stepped out of the limousine, resplendent in a crested navy blue blazer, gray flannels, and patent leather Imperiale loafers.

The morning-coated manager of the elegant hotel rushed out with two assistants, one of them obviously an Italian, more obviously a translator. Greetings were exchanged in both languages until the guardian aunt of the *barone-cadetto* held up her hand and announced:

"The young *barone* has many things to do in this great country of yours, and he would prefer that you address him in English so he might absorb the language. He will not at first understand much of what you say, but he insists—and, naturally, I'm at his side to translate for him."

"Madame," said the manager quietly, standing beside Bajaratt as the considerable luggage was gathered by the bellhops. "There's no reason for you to put up with the inconvenience should you not care to, but there are reporters from several local newspapers as well as their photographers in one of our larger conference rooms. They'd like to meet the young baron, naturally. How they were alerted to his presence, I have no idea, but I can assure you it was not through this hotel. Our reputation for confidentiality is unparalleled."

"Oh, someone was naughty!" exclaimed the *contessa* Cabrini, breaking into a resigned smile. "Don't worry, *Signor Amministratore,* it happens whenever he goes to Rome or London. Not Paris, however, for France abounds with false nobility, and the socialist press no longer cares."

"You may avoid these, of course. It's why I had our security place them in the conference room."

"No, that's all right. I'll speak to the *barone-cadetto;* we'll give the journalists a few minutes. After all, he's here to make friends, not antagonize your newspapers."

"I'll go ahead then and tell them, and also make it clear it can't be a long session. Jet lag's a universal fatigue."

"No, signore, I shouldn't say that. He arrived yesterday and actually bought clothes not five minutes away from here. We wouldn't care to give false information so easily contradicted."

"But the reservation was for today, madame."

"Come now, we were both his age once, weren't we, signore?"

"I never looked like he does, I can assure you of that."

"Very few young men do, but neither his looks nor his title alter his perfectly normal youthful appetites, do you see what I mean?"

"It's not difficult, madame. A close personal friend for the evening."

"Even I do not know her name."

"I understand. My assistant will see you inside and I'll take care of everything."

"You are a wonderful man, *Signor Amministratore*."

"*Grazie,* Countess."

The manager nodded and walked up the carpeted steps as Bajaratt turned and approached Nicolo, who was talking to the assistant manager and the interpreter. "What are you three conspiring about, Dante?" asked the *contessa* in Italian.

"*Ma niente*," replied Nicolo, smiling at the interpreter. "My new friend and I were discussing the beautiful surroundings and the fine weather," he continued in Italian. "I told him my studies and my father's business have taken up all my time, so I have not learned to play the golf."

"*Va bene.*"

"He says he will find me an instructor."

"You have too much work to do for such things," said the Baj, taking Nicolo by the arm and leading him to the carpeted steps as the young man nodded pleasantly to the two men behind him. "Nico, do not be so *familiar*," whispered Amaya. "It's not becoming for a man of your station. Be cordial, but keep in mind that he is beneath you."

"Beneath me?" asked the assumed *barone-cadetto* as the doors of the lobby were held open for them. "Sometimes you talk in circles, signora. You want me to be somebody else, which I have learned by memory, yet you also want me to be myself."

"That's exactly what I want," said Bajaratt in a harsh

whisper, still in Italian. "The one thing I do *not* want is for you to think for yourself. I think *for* you, is that understood?"

"Of course, Cabi. I'm sorry."

"That's better. We'll have a grand time tonight, Nico, for my body aches for you, you're so beautiful, as I knew you would be!" As the dock boy started to put his arm affectionately around her shoulder, she suddenly moved away. "*Stop.* The assistant manager is rushing up to take us to the reporters and the photographers."

"The what?"

"I told you last night. You are going to meet the press. It's nothing grand, merely the society pages."

"Oh, yes, and I understand very little English. I turn to you with the questions, is that right?"

"*All* the questions."

"This way, please," said the manager's first assistant, "it's just a short walk to the Regal Room."

The press conference lasted exactly twenty-three minutes. The small crowd of journalists and photographers had their ingrained hostility toward enormously wealthy European nobility rapidly diffused by the tall, shy, ingratiating *barone-cadetto*. The questions came with staccato regularity, initially negative, and repelled by the Contessa Cabrini, an aunt of the *barone-cadetto di Ravello*, who, as was agreed to in the ground rules, would be referred to only as the "interpreter." Then an Italian-speaking reporter from *The Miami Herald* asked in the young baron's language: "Why do you think you're accorded all this attention? Do you think you deserve it? What have you really done outside of being born?"

"I really don't believe I deserve anything until I can prove what I can do, which will take a long time. . . . On the other hand, signore, would you care to accompany me on a dive into the Mediterranean waters to the depth of a hundred or so meters on behalf of oceanographic science? Or perhaps you might join me on the search-and-rescue teams in the Maritime Alps, where we have scaled down the rocks several thousand feet to bring the presumed dead back to life. . . . *My* life, signore, may be one of privilege, but it has not been without its modest contributions."

The Contessa Cabrini instantly translated for the audience of journalists as flashbulbs snapped, streaks of light illuminating the handsome face of the unpretentious young baron as his "interpreter" stepped away, out of the photographs.

"Hey, *Dante!*" yelled a female correspondent. "Why don't you give up the nobility bit and get yourself a television series? You're a hunk, kid!"

"*Non capisco, signora.*"

"I agree with the girls," an elderly male reporter in the front row broke in above the laughter. "You're a good-looking young fella, but I don't think you're here to bowl over our young ladies."

Upon the instant, unnecessary translation, the young baron replied, "Please, Mr. Journalist, if I understand you, I should very much like to meet American girls, whom I would treat with great respect. On the television they are so alive and attractive—so *Italian,* if you'll forgive me."

"Are you running for political office?" asked another reporter. "If you are, you've got the women's vote."

"I only run in the mornings, signore. Ten or twelve miles. It is very good for the body."

"What's your agenda here, baron?" continued the reporter in the front row. "I checked with your family in Ravello, your father, in fact, and he made it clear that you were to bring back a number of recommendations based on your observations of American investments, their viability, their projections. Is that correct, sir?"

The translation was complex and quiet, several points repeated several times, instructions as to his reply contained therein. "My father has schooled me well, signore, and we will speak each day on the telephone. I am his eyes and his ears, and he trusts me."

"Will you be traveling a lot?"

"I believe a great many entrepreneurs will be coming to him," interrupted the *contessa* without translating. "Firms are only as good as the executives who run them. The *barone-cadetto* is trained in economics, for his responsibilities are great. He will look for conviction and integrity and match them against the figures."

"Outside of profit-and-loss statements," said an intense female reporter, her short, dark hair framing an angry face, "has any thought been given to the socioeconomic conditions prevalent in those areas targeted for investment, or is it just business as usual—go where the profits are?"

"I suggest that is—how do you say it?—a prejudiced question," replied the *contessa*.

"A loaded question," a male voice at the rear corrected her.

"But I should be happy to answer it," the *contessa* continued. "Perhaps the lady might place a telephone call to any journalist of her choosing in or around Ravello, even Rome. She will learn for herself the high esteem accorded the family in the *provincia*. In good times and not so good they have been most generous in the areas of medicine, shelter, and employment. They treat their wealth as a gift that requires responsibility as well as authority. They have a social conscience and it will not change over here."

"The kid can't answer for himself?" pressed the querulous reporter.

"This *kid,* as you call him, is far too modest to extol his family's virtues in public. As you may notice, he cannot understand everything you say, but the look in his eyes will tell you that he is much offended, particularly since he cannot comprehend the reason for your hostility."

"*Mi scusi,*" said the reporter from *The Miami Herald* in fluent Italian. "I also spoke with your father, the baron in Ravello—on background, naturally—and I apologize for my colleague," he added, aiming a nasty grin at the woman. "She's a pain in the ass."

"*Grazie.*"

"*Prego.*"

"If we may revert to English," said a heavyset journalist in the front on the right. "I certainly don't subscribe to our colleague's innuendos, but the young baron's spokeswoman has raised a point. As you know, there are deep pockets of unemployment in this country. Would the family's social conscience conceivably extend to those areas?"

"If the proper situation were presented, I'm sure they'd be among the first, sir. The *barone di Ravello* is an astute international businessman who recognizes the value of loyalty as clearly as he does the satisfaction of charity."

"You're going to get a hell of a lot of phone calls," said the heavyset reporter. "It's not hard news by a long shot, but it could be."

"I'm afraid that will be all, ladies and gentlemen. It's been a trying morning and we have the rest of the day to go through." Smiling and nodding graciously to the reporters, Bajaratt led her handsome charge from the room, delighted with the flattering comments about him. There would, indeed, be many phone calls, just as she had planned.

The Palm Beach social network operated with frightening efficiency. By four o'clock that afternoon they had received sixteen firm invitations and eleven inquiries as to when various hostesses might plan luncheons or dinner parties in honor of Dante Paolo, *barone-cadetto di Ravello*.

With equal efficiency Bajaratt went through her notebooks and selected five of the most prestigious invitations to accept, houses where the elite of politics and industry were most likely to attend the functions. She then called the rejects and with profound apologies demurred, hoping with all her heart that they would meet at so-and-so's and so-and-so's, who had reached the young baron first. Cats stalk, considered the Baj, striking out with their claws only when a piece of the mouse is withheld from them. They would *all* be wherever she and Nicolo went.

Muerte a toda autoridad!

It was only the beginning, but the journey would be swift. It was time to check London, Paris, and Jerusalem. *Death to the merchants of death at Ashkelon.*

"Ashkelon," said the quiet male voice in London.

"It's Bajaratt. Are you progressing?"

"Within a week we'll have Downing Street covered. Men in police uniforms, refuse details in lovely garbage-spotted white overalls. *Vengeance* for Ashkelon!"

"It may take me more than a week, you understand that."

"No matter," said London. "We'll be all the more entrenched, all the more familiar. We cannot fail!"

"Forever Ashkelon."

"Ashkelon," said the female voice in Paris.

"Bajaratt. How are things?"

"Sometimes I think too simple. The man comes and goes flanked by such nonchalant guards we would have them executed in the Baaka. The French are so arrogant, so careless of danger, it's ludicrous. We've checked out the rooftops—they're not even covered!"

"Beware the nonchalant French dandies, they can turn and strike like cobras. Remember the *Résistance*."

"That's *merde,* as they say. If they know about us, they're not taking us seriously. Don't they understand that we're willing to *die*? Vengeance for *Ashkelon*!"

"Forever Ashkelon."

*   *   *

"*Ashkelon*," whispered the guttural voice in Jerusalem.

"You know who I am."

"Of course. I led the prayers for you and your husband under the orange trees. He will be avenged, our cause avenged, believe me."

"I'd rather hear about your progress."

"Oh, you're so cold, Baj, so cold."

"My husband never thought so. Your *progress*?"

"Shit, we're more Jew-like than the odious Jews! Our black hats and our black braids and our stupid white shawls all move rhythmically as we peck our heads at that fucking wall. We can blow that bastard away when he walks out of the Knesset. A few of us may even escape to fight again. We only wait for the news, for your signal."

"It will take a while."

"Take all the time you like, Baj. During the evenings we put on I.D.F. uniforms and climb upon hungry sabra women, each of us praying to Allah that an Arab will grow in their bellies."

"Stick to business, my friend."

"We *stick* it to the Jew whores!"

"Not at the expense of your mission!"

"Never. Vengeance for Ashkelon!"

"Forever Ashkelon."

Amaya Bajaratt left the bank of public phones in the hotel lobby, having replaced in her purse the various credit cards supplied her by Bahrain. She took the elevator upstairs and walked down the elegant corridor to their suite. Inside, the dimly lit sitting room was empty, lonely. She crossed to the open door of the darkened bedroom. Young Nicolo was, as usual, naked and supine on the large bed; he was fast asleep, his magnificent body inviting. As she studied him, she could not help but think of her husband, her so-brief husband. Both men had long, slender, muscular bodies, one far younger than the other, of course, but the similarity was there. She was drawn to such bodies, as she had been drawn to the naked Hawthorne barely two days earlier. Suddenly, she heard and felt her own breathing; she touched the swelling nipples of her breasts and was aware of the aching urgency of her groin. It made up for so much she could never have. Years before, a doctor in Madrid had performed a simple operation that would forever preclude conception—*this* was all she had.

She walked to the foot of the bed and undressed, now as naked as the body in front of her, below her.

"Nico," she said gently. "Wake up, Nicolo."

"What . . . ?" stuttered the young man, blinking open his eyes.

"I am here for you . . . my darling." *You must,* she thought. *It's all I have left!*

"What's the number in Paris?" asked Hawthorne, standing over the *padrone* but addressing Poole in the doorway.

"That I checked out," answered the lieutenant. "It's around ten o'clock in the morning there, so I figured I wasn't going to put anybody into shock."

"*And?*"

"It doesn't make sense, Tye. It's a travel agency on the Champs-Élysées."

"What happened when you called?"

"Sure as possumshit it was a private number. The lady said something in French, and when I said in English that I hoped I had the right number, she asked me in English if I was calling a French-sounding travel agency, and I said I sure as hell was and it was urgent. . . . That's when she asked me what my color was, and naturally I said white, and she said 'and,' and I didn't know what to say, so she hung up."

"You didn't have the code, Jackson; there's no way you could have."

"I guess I didn't."

"I'll put Stevens on it, unless I can convince our *padrone* here to be more cooperative."

"I know nothing of such things!" shouted the invalid.

"No, you probably don't," agreed Tyrell. "Those last calls, the undeleted calls, weren't made by you, but by someone who didn't know how to erase them. Shades of Rosemary Woods, *padrone*."

"Nothing, I know nothing!"

"What about Palm Beach, Lieutenant?"

"Just as crazy, Commander. It's the number of a very ritzy restaurant on Worth Avenue. They said I had to make a reservation two weeks in advance unless I was on their preferred list."

"That's not crazy at all, Jackson, it's part of the mosaic, part of the pay dirt. The preferred list is just that, preferred by way of a name you couldn't invent and followed by words you couldn't know. I'll turn that over to Stevens with the Paris conduit." Tyrell looked down at the old man; the bleeding in his left cheek had ebbed, blotted by a wad of tissue that hung from his flesh. "You're going on a trip, *paisan*," said Hawthorne.

"I cannot leave this house."

"Oh, you're leaving, scungilli—"

"Then put a bullet in my head now, you might as well."

"It's tempting, but I don't think so. I want you to meet some former associates of mine, from another life, you might say—"

"Everything is here to keep me alive! You want a dead man on your hands?"

"Not really, although it's a moot point in your case," replied Tyrell. "So I'd suggest you point out the specific equipment you need for a short flight, just the basic stuff. You'll be in a mainland hospital in a few hours, and guess what? I'll bet you'll have a private room."

"I cannot be moved!"

"Would you care to place a bet?" asked Hawthorne, reaching into his pouch as static erupted from the radio.

Neilsen's words were spoken in a monotone, control imposed over anxiety. "We have a problem."

"What *happened*?" barked Poole. "Are you in trouble?"

"What's wrong?" asked Tyrell.

"The pilot of the seaplane radioed the Brit patrol boat—his left rudder snapped, then flew off! He went down roughly a hundred and twenty kilometers north of the hover's fix. They're going after him, assuming the poor guy survives."

"Cathy, answer me as honestly as you can," said Hawthorne. "From what you know about that aircraft, could it have been sabotage?"

"What do you think's been busting my head for the last couple of minutes? I hadn't even considered it and I should have! Good God, our AWAC was blown up— *Charlie!*"

"All right, calm down. Stay the course. *How* could it have been sabotage?"

"The cables, damn it to hell!" Rapidly, Cathy explained that every movable part of the plane was operated by dual steel cables. That both sets of cables could shard at once was inconceivable.

"Sabotage," Tyrell concluded quietly.

"Both were shortened together so they'd snap at the same time," said Neilsen, more controlled now. "And I never even considered the possibility. *Shit!*"

"Will you please stop whipping yourself, Major? *I* didn't consider it either. Someone in St. Martin slipped by the Deuxième, and if he or she could do that, we were stationary ducks."

"The mechs!" yelled the pilot over the radio. "Bring in every goddamned mechanic on that island and burn his feet. It's one of them!"

"Believe me, Cathy, whoever it was is gone. That's the way it is."

"I can't stand it! The Brit flying that plane may be dead!"

"That's the way it is," repeated Hawthorne. "Maybe now you'll understand why a lot of people in Washington, London, Paris, and Jerusalem are afraid to leave their desks, their phones. We're not dealing with a single psychopathic terrorist, we're dealing with an obsessed zealot who's running a network of raging fanatics perfectly willing to die to make their kills."

"Christ, what do we do?"

"Right now you beach the sub in the cove and come up to the house. We'll raise the shutters so you can see it clearly."

"I should stay in touch with the hovercraft—"

"Things won't change whether you do or not," interrupted Tyrell curtly. "I want you up here—"

"Where's Poole?"

"Right now he's wheeling our patient out into the hall. Beach the sub, Major, nothing's going to happen here. That's an order!"

But suddenly, without a decibel of noise, without a hint of impending devastation, everything happened. The explosions were everywhere, walls collapsing, marble columns breaking, crashing into the marble floors below; beyond the archway to the communications complex, the equipment began bursting apart, wires splattering against each other in shattering electric contact, short bolts of lightning shooting into the air. Tyrell raced into the foyer, rolling on the floor over and over to avoid the falling debris, his eyes focused on Poole, whose leg was caught beneath a shelving unit beyond another collapsing archway. Hawthorne sprang to his feet and ran to the lieutenant, pulling him out from under the attached shelves and dragging him toward the arch. It fell apart, heavy slabs of marble plummeting to the floor;

Tye yanked Poole back until there was a break in the collapse, then rushed through, hauling the lieutenant behind him as the arch fell, leaving a jagged wall of marble that would have crushed them both. Hawthorne looked above it, seeing only the *padrone,* laughing hysterically in his wheelchair as his entire surroundings crashed down upon him. With a final effort Tyrell looped his right arm around Poole's chest, and angling his shoulder, burst through the heavy glass door and the hurricane shutters beyond. Together, they hit the trunk of an ersatz palm as the lieutenant screamed.

"Stop! My leg! I can't *move!*"

"You damn well better. These palms are going to go up next!" With those words Hawthorne dragged Poole, zigzagging through the real and false foliage until they reached the dry grass.

"Lemme go, fer Christ's sake! We're flat and I'm hurting real bad!"

"I'll tell you when you're hurting enough," cried Tyrell, his voice carrying over the fires and the continuous conflagrations within the once-châteaulike estate. The moment came barely thirty seconds later. The entire ring of ersatz palm trees exploded with the force of twenty tons of dynamite.

"I don't believe it!" whispered Poole, nearly comatose as he and Hawthorne lay beside each other, prone in the dark, harsh, sun-parched field. "He blew the whole fuckin' thing up!"

"He didn't have a choice, Lieutenant," Tye said grimly.

Poole, however, was not listening. "Oh, my God— Cathy!" he screamed. "Where's Cathy?"

Across the field, a black-suited figure appeared, racing around the towering flames and screaming incoherently. Hawthorne got to his feet and ran forward, shouting at the top of his voice. "Cathy, we're here! We're okay!"

In the mountainous light of the fires, Major Catherine Neilsen raced into the dark, harsh field and fell into the arms of Lieutenant Commander Tyrell Hawthorne (Retired). "Thank God, you're all right! Where's Jackson?"

"Over here, Cath!" Poole cried from the shadows beyond. "That Yankee son of a bitch and me are even now. He pulled me out of there!"

"Oh, my *darling!*" shouted the major in a most unmilitary fashion as she released the commander and ran to the lieutenant, falling down and embracing him.

"I'm really, *really* missing something," said Hawthorne quietly to himself as he walked toward the two figures on the ground.

12

The subdued string quartet played gracefully on a balcony above the outside terrace that overlooked the pool, sparkling blue from the underwater lights; altogether, it was an appropriate mise-en-scène for an early evening on Palm Beach's Gold Coast. Three bars and twice as many buffet tables were placed around the large, manicured lawn, lighted by torches and manned by servants in yellow jackets who courteously dispensed food and drink to the resort's elite, resplendent in their summer formal wear. It was a splendid picture of the good life, richly deserved by the privileged. And the center of attraction was a tall, bewildered, extremely handsome young man with a crested scarlet sash replacing his tuxedo's cummerbund. He was not entirely sure what was happening to him, but it was far better than any attention he had ever received on the docks of Portici.

Following the reception line, during which his aunt, the *contessa*, acted as his interpreter, he was paraded around the large gathering by a possessive hostess with very white teeth too large for her mouth, and bluish-white hair. Amaya Bajaratt followed, never more than several steps behind her "nephew."

"The one she's bringing you to—you met him in the line—is a senator, and very powerful," she whispered, hastening forward, as their hostess steered them toward a short fat man. "When you meet him now, rattle off whatever you like in Italian, and when he speaks, turn to me. That's *all*."

"All right, all *right*, signora."

Reintroductions were made by the enthusiastic hostess. "Senator Nesbitt, the *barone di Ravello*—"

"*Scusi, signora,*" broke in Nicolo gently. "*Il barone-cadetto di Ravello.*"

"Oh, yes, of course—I think. My Italian's quite rusty."

"If it was ever shiny, Sylvia." The senator smiled good-naturedly at Nico and bowed his head at the *contessa*. "A pleasure, young man," he continued, shaking hands. "You're not your father yet, and I trust not for many years."

"*Si?*" replied the impostor, instinctively turning to Bajaratt, who translated in Italian. "*Non, per centi anni, Senatore!*" exclaimed Nicolo.

"He says he hopes not for a hundred years," explained the Baj. "He is a devoted son."

"Nice to hear that these days," said Nesbitt, his eyes leveled at the presumed *contessa*. "Perhaps you might ask the young baron—forgive me, that's probably not correct—"

"*Barone-cadetto,*" rejoined Bajaratt, smiling. "It simply means the next-in-line. The more common term is *baroncino*, but his father is of the old school, and believes '*barone-cadetto*' is less diminutive, with more authority. Dante Paolo was simply clarifying his title, which is far less meaningful to him than learning whatever he can from such an experienced man as yourself, Senator. . . . You wished me to ask him what?"

"I read the newspaper account of his press conference yesterday—to be frank, my secretary pointed it out, as I'm not an avid reader of the society pages—and I was struck by his statement about loyalty and charity. How his family values the benefits of loyalty as highly as it values the satisfaction of charity."

"Quite true, Senator Nesbitt. Both have served the family well."

"I'm not from this state, madame—excuse me, *contessa*—"

"Irrelevant, believe me."

"Thank you . . . I suppose you could call me a country lawyer who went higher than he ever expected."

"The 'country,' as I understand you, is the true spine of any nation, signore."

"That's nicely phrased, nicely phrased indeed. I'm the senior senator from the state of Michigan, where in all honesty there are many problems, but in my judgment, an equal number of investment opportunities, especially at today's prices. The future is in growth with a dedicated, skilled work force, and we have a great deal of both."

"*Please,* Senator, reach us tomorrow. I'll clear your call through the front desk and explain to Dante Paolo how impressed I am by your credentials and your expertise."

"Actually, I'm on vacation," said the gray-haired man, a diamond-encrusted Rolex his personal symbol of achievement as he raised it for a third time in four minutes to check the hour. "Have to get near a phone pretty soon—a call from those sleepless gnomes in Geneva, you do understand?"

"By all means, signore," replied the Baj. "The *barone-cadetto* and I are most impressed by your suggestions—really remarkable investments."

"I tell you, Countess, the Ravello family could realize sizable profits. My companies in California are literally supplying seven percent of the Pentagon's allocations, and it can only grow. We're high tech; all the rest are low tech by comparison, if you catch my meaning. Others will fall, but not us; we've got twelve former generals and eight admirals on our payroll."

"Please, reach us tomorrow. I'll clear your call."

* * *

"You understand, ma'am, that I'm not at liberty to give you or the young royal fella here all the details, but *space* is where it's at and we are *there*. We've got the ears of all the future-thinkin' members of Congress—not a few of whom have invested heavily in our stock for research and development in Texas, Oklahoma, and Missouri— and the payoffs are goin' to be stratospheric! I can put you in touch, kinda quietly, you understand, with a corral full of congressmen and senators."

"Please, reach us tomorrow. I'll clear your call."

"Party politics are a national game," said a grinning, red-haired man in his early thirties after shaking hands with the *barone-cadetto* and bowing lower than necessary to the *contessa*. "You'll find that out if you've circulated without your hostess, our Madame Defarge with an overbite."

"The evening's getting late, and I think Sylvia gave up," said the Baj, laughing. "She began to leave us several guests ago, having assured herself that Dante had met everyone of importance."

"Oh, then she forgot about me," countered the redhead. "She should know better; after all, I got a hurry-up invitation."

"And who are you?"

"Only one of the brightest political campaign strategists in the country, but unfortunately my reputation hasn't spread much beyond the state level—a number of states, however."

"Then you are not really important," concluded the *contessa*. "Except insofar as you received an invitation. How so?"

"Because my unique talents persuaded *The New York Times* to run my op-ed opinions on a fairly regular basis.

It's lousy pay, but in my business, if you get your name in print enough times in the Big Mother, you've got a bigger paycheck down the road. Simple as that."

"Yes, well, this has been a most charming and enlightening conversation, but I'm afraid the *barone-cadetto* and I are exhausted. We shall say good night, *Signor Giornalista*."

"Please wait, Countess. You may not believe it, but I'm on your side, if you're for real, if *he's* for real."

"Why would you think otherwise?"

"He's right over there." The young op-ed columnist nodded his head through the crowds at a medium-size, swarthy-faced man who stared at them through the passing figures. It was the reporter from *The Miami Herald* who spoke fluent Italian. "Talk to him, lady, not me. He thinks you're both fakes."

Hawthorne, his whole body aching from the furious activity on the smoldering hill, sat with Poole on the dark moonlit beach, both men stripped to their shorts, the wet suits discarded. They waited for Catherine Neilsen to emerge from the minisubmarine, secured by its weight in shallow water.

"How's the leg?" asked Tyrell, his speech slowed by exhaustion.

"Nothing broken, just a bunch of damned painful bruises," replied the lieutenant. "What about your shoulder? You got a mess of blood still oozing under Cathy's bandage."

"It's stopping. She didn't butterfly the tape, that's all."

"Are you criticizing my superior officer?" asked Poole, smiling.

"I wouldn't dare—not in front of you, my *darling*."

"Hey, that really grabs you, doesn't it?"

"No, Jackson, it doesn't grab me anywhere. Only I find it a touch mystifying in light of our previous conversation, in which you made reference to unrequited affection."

"I think I said 'letch,' Commander, nothin' permanent."

"Do I hear another Poole?"

"No, you hear a Louisiana husband-to-be whose bride didn't get to the church on time."

"I beg your pardon?" said Hawthorne, opening his sagging eyelids and staring at the half-grinning air force officer in the moonlight.

"Oh, I had to beg more pardons than you ever will—so many it became a joke, like 'my darlin'.' "

"Would you care to fill me in?"

"Sure." Poole smiled, then chuckled at the memory. "I got pissed and went bayou wild, that's what happened. My intended and I lined up the finest Baptist church in Miami, which ain't easy to locate in the better parts of that fair city, and my family and her family were there, and after two hours of waitin', her maid of honor came screamin' into the fuckin' place with a note for me. . . . My bride had run off with a guitar player."

"Good Lord, I'm sorry—"

"Don't be. Better then than after a couple of kids—but that's when I went bayou."

"Bayou?" Despite the crying need for sleep, Tyrell could not keep his eyes off Poole.

"I ran out of that place like a laser, got myself a couple of bottles of bourbon—and drove my honeymoon car, danglin' cans and spray-painted windows and all, into downtown Miami and the roughest strip joints I could find. The more I drank, the more I figured I should at least get laid—oh, the pity."

"For God's sake, don't stop there."

"Well, Cathy, Sal, and Charlie figured I was goin' bayou, so they came after me. They weren't so goddamned smart like they thought they were; hell, that car was kinda outstandin', you know what I mean?"

"It's a given. What happened?"

"A riot, Commander, that's what happened. They found me in a joint where I was slightly misbehavin', like with the Cubano owner's favorite chick-of-the-week. Now, Sal and Charlie were pretty proficient in hand-to-hand—not in my class, but adequate—and they convinced a number of the enemy to leave me alone, but the problem was to get me out of there."

"Christ, *why*?"

"I still wanted to get laid."

"Oh, my *God*." Hawthorne dropped his chin, half in astonishment, half in fatigue.

"So Cathy wrapped her arms around my head and kept whispering into my ear, sorta loud, 'my *darlin'*, my *darlin'*, my *darlin'*,' as she dragged me out of there. That's how it happened."

"That's it?"

"That's it."

Silence. Finally, Tyrell spoke wearily. "You know, you really *are* lunatics."

"Hey, Commander, who found you this place?"

"All right, you're not dumb lunatics—"

"Listen up!" shouted Major Neilsen, climbing out of the tiny sub into the waist-high waves in her wet suit. "We've got our orders through the Brit hover, confirmed by Washington and Paris. A flyboat from Patrick will be here by dawn, in about three to four hours, and we get on board. Oh, and the pilot survived; a broken leg and half drowned, but he'll make it."

"Where are they taking us?" asked Hawthorne.

"They didn't tell me. Just out of here."

"What about the pups?" demanded Poole. In the distance the confused baying of the guard dogs could still be heard. "I ain't leavin' until they're looked after."

"A K-9 trainer will be on the aircraft to take care of the animals, as well as the gardener; he'll accompany the investigating unit. They'll stay here for a day or so."

"I repeat, where is your plane from Patrick taking us?"

"I don't know. Probably back to the base."

"No way! I'm being dropped off on Gorda if I have to 'chute out. I've done it before."

"Why?"

"Because two of my friends were killed there, and I want to know why and by whom! That's the trail I intend to follow; it's the only one that makes sense. That bitch psycho is operating from the islands."

"Once we're on board the aircraft, you can get in touch with anybody you like. You've already proven you can reach the people who make decisions."

"You're right," Hawthorne agreed, lowering his voice. "I'm sorry, I've no right blowing up at you."

"No, you don't. You lost two friends, and in our own way so did we. I thought we were on the same side. You made a pretty good case for it a few hours ago."

"I think what the major's trying to say is that if you hop off in Virgin Gorda, we're going with you," said Poole. "We distinctly remember our orders. We were assigned to you, and we want to help," he added, wincing as he raised his back against the concealed breakwall.

"You're not going to be much help in your condition, Lieutenant."

"That'll change in a day with a couple of hot tubs and maybe some cortisone," Jackson said. "Remember, I've got experience in the physical areas. I know when I'm hurt and when I'm *hurt*. I ain't."

"All right," said Tye, fatigue overwhelming his resistance, "suppose I don't send you back to your base, will you both accept the fact that I'm running the show? You do as I say?"

"Naturally," said the major. "You're in command."

"That hasn't made much impact so far."

"What she means, Commander—"

"Will you *stop* telling him what I mean," said the major, sinking cross-legged to the sand as she stared at Poole menacingly.

"Okay, okay," Tye interrupted. "You're on board. For what, God knows."

"Talking about being on board," said Neilsen, looking at Tyrell. "You don't get along with Captain Stevens, do you?"

"It doesn't matter. I'm not accountable to him."

"He's your superior officer—"

"The hell he is. I was hired by MI-6, London."

"*Hired?*" exclaimed Poole.

"That's right. They met my price, Lieutenant." Hawthorne arched his neck; he was exhausted.

"But everything you said about this incredible terrorist and the army of fanatics behind her, all ready to commit mass assassinations—you joined up for a *price?*"

"That's the way it was, yes."

"You're one strange guy, Commander Hawthorne. I'm not sure I understand you at all."

"Your understanding me, Major, isn't germane to this operation."

"Of course not . . . sir."

"It isn't germane, Cath, 'cause you're cuttin' around the nerve endings," said Poole, his back against the vine-laden breakwall.

"What the hell are you talking about?" asked Hawthorne. His eyes half closed, he kept blinking back the exhaustion but with each blink was nodding closer to sleep.

"I was on the Patrick phone too. Your wife was killed for what you figure were the wrong reasons, that much I got, and that's why you wouldn't go back to your old crowd even if they offered you half the real estate in Washington."

"You're very observant," said Hawthorne softly, his chin sinking into his chest. "Even if you don't know what you're talking about."

"Then something else happened," continued Poole. "When we picked you up on Saba, you made like you didn't give a shit, but you did. You were like a man on fire when my equipment began deliverin'. You began to see something you didn't see before, and you got real sharp. You even nailed Sal Mancini like a rattlesnake strikin' out at a rat."

"What are you driving at, Jackson?" asked Cathy.

"Somethin' he knows and won't tell us," replied Poole.

". . . The *bastards*," whispered Tyrell, his head nodding up and down, his eyes closed now.

"How long has it been since you slept?" asked Catherine, moving over in the sand next to Hawthorne.

"I'm fine. . . ."

"The hell you are," said the pilot, her hand steadying Tyrell's weaving shoulder. "You're spiraling out of action, Commander."

"*Dominique?*" murmured Hawthorne suddenly, his body arching back, as if in slow motion, held by Neilsen's arm.

"Who?"

"Hold it, Cath," said Poole, extending his right hand in the moonlight. "Is Dominique your wife?"

"No!" rasped Tye, only half conscious. "Ingrid . . ."

"She was the one who was killed?"

"*Lies!* They said she was on a . . . Soviet payroll."

"Was she?" asked Neilsen, now cradling the failing Hawthorne.

"I don't know," said Tyrell, barely able to be heard. "She wanted everything to stop."

"Everything what?" pressed the lieutenant.

"I don't know—everything."

"Go to sleep, Tye," said Cathy.

"*No!*" objected Poole. "Who's Dominique?" But Hawthorne had lapsed into unconsciousness on the beach. "That man's got problems."

"Shut up and build a fire," ordered the major.

Eighteen minutes later, the flames of the fire casting shadows over the beach, the limping Poole sat down on the sand and looked over at Cathy, who was staring down at the sleeping Tyrell. "He *does* have problems, doesn't he?" said the major.

"More than we ever had, including Pensacola and Miami."

"He's a good guy, Jackson."

"Tell me something I don't know, Cath. I've been watchin' you, your bullshit and all, and like the commander said, I'm pretty observant. You and he could make one hell of a couple."

"Don't be ridiculous."

"Look at him. He's clouds above Pensacola. I mean, he's a man, not some prick who keeps lookin' into mirrors."

"He's not too terrible," said the air force pilot, holding Tyrell's head as she piled a pillow of sand below it. "Let's say he's not unqualified."

"Go for it, Cath. I'm the genius, remember?"

"He's not ready, Jackson. Neither am I."

"Do me a favor."

"What?"

"Do what comes naturally."

The major looked over at the lieutenant, then down at the reposed face of Tyrell Nathaniel Hawthorne partially on her lap. She leaned down and kissed his parted lips.

"*Dominique?*"

"No, Commander. Somebody else."

"*Buona sera, signore,*" said Bajaratt, leading her reluctant *barone-cadetto* to the reporter from *The Miami Herald* who spoke fluent Italian. "The red-haired young man suggested that we come and speak with you. Your account of the press conference yesterday was most flattering indeed. We thank you."

"Sorry we only made the beachfront pages, but he's a hell of a kid, Countess," said the journalist pleasantly.

"You're both pretty awesome, in fact. By the way, my name's Del Rossi."

"Yet something troubles you?"

"You could say that, but I'm not ready to go into print with it."

"And what exactly is that?"

"What's your game, lady?"

"I don't understand you—"

"But *he* does. He understands every word we're saying in English."

"Why do you think that?"

"Because I'm bilingual. It's always in the eyes, isn't it? A flash of understanding, a glint of resentment or humor having nothing to do with a tone of voice or an expression."

"Or partial comprehension, perhaps strengthened by previously translated conversation—is that not possible, fellow linguist?"

"Anything's possible, Countess, but he *does* speak and understand English—isn't that *right*, young *fella*?"

"What—*che còsa?*"

"Case closed, lady." Del Rossi smiled under Bajaratt's glare. "But, hey, I don't fault you for it, Countess. Actually, it's pretty damned smart."

"And what do you mean by *that*?" asked the Baj icily.

"It's called deniability by way of misinterpretation. The old Soviets, the Chinese, and the White House are experts at it. He can say anything he likes, then retract it and claim he didn't understand."

"But *why*?" pressed Bajaratt.

"I haven't figured that out yet, which accounts for my not going into print."

"But were you not one of the journalists who spoke to the *barone* himself in Ravello?"

"That's right, and to be frank, he wasn't the best source I've ever had. He kept saying '*tutto quello che dice è vero*' and '*qualsiasi cosa dica.*' Essentially, 'whatever he says is the truth.' What truth, Countess?"

"The family's investments, of course."

"Maybe, but why did I get the feeling that talking to the great baron was about as helpful as talking to an answering machine?"

"An overactive imagination, signore. It is late and we must leave. *Buona nòtte.*"

"I'm going too," said the reporter. "It's a pretty long drive to Miami."

"We must find our host and hostess." The Baj took Nicolo's arm, leading him away.

"I'll stay a proper twenty paces behind," added Del Rossi, obviously enjoying the moment.

Bajaratt turned, suddenly looking at the reporter warmly, the ice gone from her eyes. "Why, *Signor Giornalista*? That would be very undemocratic of you. It would appear that you disapprove of us, disapprove of our positions."

"Oh, no, Countess, I neither approve nor disapprove. In my business we don't make judgments, we just tell it like it is."

"Then do so, but now you walk on my other side and I shall be between two handsome *italiani* as we say our farewells."

"You're something else, lady." Del Rossi stepped forward, politely offering his arm.

"And you're too elliptical for me, signore," said the Baj as all three began across the lawn. Then, without warning, the Countess Cabrini lurched downward, her body twisting, her heel apparently caught in a patch of soft grass or a sprinkler head. She cried out as Nicolo and Del Rossi instantly sprang down to her, both on their knees, their hands reaching for her. "My foot! Free it, *please,* or remove my shoe!"

"I've got it," said the reporter, lifting her ankle gently off the grass.

"Oh, thank you!" exclaimed Bajaratt, grabbing Del Rossi's leg for support as guests raced over, surrounding them.

"*Ouch!*" sputtered the reporter as a trickle of blood appeared on his trousers while he and Nicolo lifted the countess to her feet.

"Thank you—thank you *all*. I'm fine, really I'm *fine*. I'm simply mortified at my awkwardness!" A chorus of sympathy and understanding greeted her, so the *contessa* and her escorts proceeded to their hosts, who were on the patio, saying good night to departing guests. "Good heavens!" said Bajaratt, seeing the thin rivulet of blood on Del Rossi's right pant leg. "When I grabbed you, that damned bracelet of mine ripped your trousers. Worse, it cut you! I'm so dreadfully sorry!"

"It's nothing, Countess, just a scratch."

"You must send me the bill for your trousers! . . . I adore this bracelet, but those gold points are frightening. I shall *never* wear it again!"

"Hey, the pants are off the rack at a discount place. Don't worry about any bill. . . . Just remember, lady, you're nice and I'm nice, but I haven't stopped digging."

" 'Digging' what, signore? Dirt?"

"I don't touch dirt, Countess, I leave that to others. But earth that's been made toxic, that's something else."

"Then dig, please," said the Baj, glancing at the gold bracelet firmly in place around her right wrist, the point of a golden thorn red with blood, its tiny orifice dark . . . open. "There will be nothing."

The Miami Herald

Herald Reporter Killed in Accident

WEST PALM BEACH, Tuesday, Aug. 12—Pulitzer Prize winner Angelo Del Rossi, an outstanding reporter for this newspaper, was killed last night on Route 95 when his car swerved off the road and crashed into the concrete housing of an electrical relay station. It was presumed that Del Rossi fell asleep at the wheel. Several of his bereaved colleagues expressed not only sorrow but reluctant understanding. "He was a tiger, a real news-hound," said one. "He'd go for days without sleep for a story." Last evening Del Rossi was returning from a buffet dinner honoring the recently arrived *barone-cadetto* of Ravello, one Dante Paolo. The young baron-to-be expressed both shock and horror, saying through his interpreter that he had struck up an immediate friendship with the Italian-speaking Del Rossi, who had promised to teach him how to play golf.

Mr. Del Rossi is survived by his wife, Ruth, and two daughters.

Il Progresso Ravello
(translated)

Baron on Mediterranean Cruise

RAVELLO, 13 Aug.—Carlo Vittorio, of Ravello, the much-decorated baron, citing a recurrence of poor health, will embark on an extended cruise aboard his yacht, *Il Nicolo*, throughout the Mediterranean. "The islands of our great sea will restore me so I may return to my responsibilities," he said at a farewell party on the dock at Napoli.

13

The early orange sun pulsated across the blue-green waters as foraging birds whistled and cawed in the upper palms and the hanging tropical foliage. Tyrell snapped open his eyes, startled, unsure, then astonished to realize that his head was touching Cathy's shoulder, her sleeping face only inches away from his. Slowly, he rolled away and got to his hands and knees, blinking at the brilliant light, suddenly whipping around at the popping sounds of a fire and the sight of a limping Poole dragging debris which he threw over the flames. The rising dark smoke was the only obstruction in a clear, cloudless sky.

"What's that for?" asked Hawthorne, instantly repeating the question in a whisper as the lieutenant brought his index finger to his lips. "What's it for?"

"I figured if the pilot of the aircraft got a wrong number in the coordinates, he'd spot the fire. Just a backup, that's all."

"You're walking . . . ?"

"I told you it wasn't more than a couple of bruises. I spent a half hour in the water soakin' 'em and movin' 'em; they're tolerable now."

"When's the plane due?"

"Six o'clock, give or take, weather permitting," answered Catherine Neilsen, her eyes still closed. "And you can both stop whispering." The pilot raised herself on her elbows, pulled up the sleeve of her unzipped wet suit, and looked at her watch. "My God, it's a quarter to!"

"So?" said Poole. "You got an appointment at the beauty parlor?"

"Not too distant a relative, Jackson. This girl has to head up into the vines and pull a contortionist's act. . . . Speaking of which, would you two gentlemen please return to your suits? Two men in their shorts—one revealingly wet, I might add—and a lone female officer on a proverbial desert island isn't the image I want carried back to Patrick."

"To Patrick?" objected Hawthorne sharply. "Who said anything about your air force base?"

"We've been over that, Tye, and if you don't remember, nobody can blame you. Three hours ago you were just about the most exhausted man I've ever seen. You could still use a week's sleep."

"You're right, not about the sleep, but I remember. Regardless of the orders, I'll reach Stevens in D.C. and get off at Gorda."

"Wrong," protested Poole. "You don't get off at Gorda, *we* get off. You may have a score or six to settle, but we have one that's damned important to Cath and me. The name's Charlie—you do remember him?"

"I do," said Tyrell, studying the lieutenant. "We'll get off at Gorda."

"There's the plane!" cried Cathy, jumping to her feet. "I've got to hurry!"

"Believe me," said the lieutenant. "They'll wait until you have your permanent."

"Get into your suits!" snapped the major, hurrying up the embankment and into the shoreline woods.

"Ashkelon," whispered the voice in London.

"Forever," replied the Baj. "I may not be able to contact you at the assigned times and telephones for the next several days. We're flying to New York and things will be hectic."

"It doesn't matter. We're doing splendidly. One of our people has just been hired for the security detail at Downing Street's transport pool."

"That *is* splendid."

"About you, Baj?"

"The same. The circles are widening, yet growing more selective. Vengeance will be ours, my friend."

"I've never doubted it."

"Reach Paris and Jerusalem with my news, but tell them to adhere to our schedule of times and locations in case of an emergency."

"I spoke to Jerusalem this morning; the hot-headed bastard's ecstatic."

"How so?"

"He fell in with a group of senior staff officers from the I.D.F. at a restaurant in Tel Aviv. It was a drunken night and they loved his singing. He's been invited to several parties."

"Tell him to be careful. His papers are as false as his uniform."

"There's no one better under cover, Baj. Besides, he recognized two of the officers; suckling pigs of the butcher Sharon."

"Interesting," said Bajaratt after a moment of silence. "Sharon could be a welcome bonus."

"That was Jerusalem's thinking."

"But not at the expense of the prize, tell him that."

"He understands."

"Anything new in Paris?"

"Well, you know she's sleeping with a ranking member of the Chamber of Deputies, a close friend of the President. She's a foxy girl, very clever."

"It would be better if she were sleeping with the President."

"It could happen."

"Ashkelon," said the Baj, signing off the call.

"Forever," said the voice in London.

* * *

British Virgin Gorda was still asleep when the U.S. Air Force seaplane, cleared by Government House, glided into the water two miles south of the yacht club. Hawthorne had requested no assistance insofar as the aircraft's standard equipment included several PVC inflatable boats, and he wanted their entry to the island to be as secure as possible. When he had replaced the radio phone on the bulkhead cradle, Catherine Neilsen called out from a nearby seat, her voice loud enough to be heard over the outside engines.

"Just a minute, profound leader, haven't you forgotten something?"

"What? I got us to Gorda, what else do you want?"

"Clothes, perhaps? Ours are on a British hovercraft a couple of hundred miles from here, and it strikes me that we'd be noticed in these black Spider-Man outfits. If you think I'm going to walk around in a bra and panties alongside two unshaven gorillas in white shorts, think again, Commander."

"I guess we gotta take wearin' apparel out of your expertise, huh, Tye?" said Poole, grinning. " 'Course, you like greasy coveralls, but we come from a better class of folk."

So Hawthorne got back on the phone and was patched into the yacht club's switchboard. "Mr. Geoffrey Cooke, please." Tyrell waited while the incessant, erratic ringing went unanswered. Finally, the clerk came back on the line.

"I'm sorry, sir, there's no answer."

"Try Monsieur Ardisonne, Jacques Ardisonne."

"Very well, sir." Again the ringing continued to no avail, and again the clerk returned to the phone. "I'm afraid it's the same, sir."

"Look, this is Tyrell Hawthorne and I've got a problem—"

"Captain Hawthorne? I thought it sounded like you, but there's so much noise on your end."

"Who's this?"

"Beckwith, sir, the night clerk, *mon*. Did I sound reasonably English, sir?"

"Right out of Buckingham Palace," said Tye, relieved that he remembered the man. "Listen, Beck, I've got to reach Roger, and I left his home number on my boat. Can you get it for me?"

"Don't have to, Cap'n. He fillin' in for the day boy who got himself in jail for a fight. I'll connect you."

"Where you been all night, Tye-Boy?" Roger, the chickee bartender, said. "You lizard-scamp from one place to 'nother and don't tell nobody!"

"Where are Cooke and Ardisonne?" Hawthorne cut in.

"We all tried to call you in St. Martin—you disappeared, *mon*."

"Where are they?"

"Off-island, Tye-Boy. They got a call from Puerto Rico around ten-thirty, a very crazy call, *mon*, so crazy they reached Government House an' all kinda crazy things happen! The police drive 'em to Sebastian's Point, and the coast patrol take 'em out to a seaplane and a pilot who's gonna take 'em back to P.R., that's what they told me to tell you!"

"That's all?"

"No, *mon*, I save the best for last . . . I think. They said to tell you they had someone named Grimshaw—"

"*Breakthrough!*" shouted Hawthorne, his voice carrying through the fuselage of the plane.

"What happened?" cried Neilsen.

"What is it, Tye?" yelled Poole.

"We've *got* one of them! . . . Anything else, Roge?"

"Not actually, 'cept those two white *cocoruroos* stuck me with a tab I already run up."

"You'll be paid off fifty times over, pal!"

"Just half'd be enough. I can steal the rest."

"One last thing, Roge. I'm flying in with two friends, but we need some clothes. . . ."

Chickee-Roge met them on the isolated east beach, a hundred-plus yards away from the yacht club's docks, and pulled the heavy rubber boat up into the sand. "It's still too early for the tourists to come down, and the pot skippers can't see you, so follow me. I got an empty villa where you can change; the clothes are up there. . . . Wait a minute. What am I supposed to do with the inflatable? That's a two-thousand-dollar piece of equipment."

"Deflate it and sell it," said Hawthorne. "Just make sure you block out the various initials. If you don't know how, I'll teach you. Let's get up to the villa."

The clothes were perfectly adequate, and in Major Neilsen's case, more than acceptable.

"Hey, Cathy, you look gorgeous!" Poole gave a low whistle as the pilot emerged from a bedroom in a flowing muumuu embossed with hot tropical colors, all in the abstract patterns of peacock and parrot feathers, and designed to emphasize the upper and lower swells of a woman's form.

Girlishly, Cathy pivoted around. "Why, Lieutenant, I've never heard you say anything like that. . . . Except maybe once, in a Miami strip joint."

"Miami doesn't count, and you know it, but except for that wedding—which I don't much remember—I've never seen you in a dress, surely not one like that. What do you say, Tye? Does she pass muster-plus, or what?"

"You look lovely, Catherine," Hawthorne said simply.

"Thank you, Tyrell. I'm not used to all this flattery. I think I'm blushing, would you believe that?"

"I would like to," replied Tye softly, suddenly seeing on his inner screen the face of the sleeping Cathy next to him—or was it Dominique?—but no matter, both images touched him . . . the last with a stabbing pang of loss. Why had she left him again? "We should hear soon from Cooke and Ardisonne in Puerto Rico," said Hawthorne abruptly, breaking the interlude of admiration and turning to a window. "I want this Grimshaw, I want to break him myself and make him tell me how they found Marty and Mickey."

"And Charlie," added Poole. "Don't forget Charlie—"

"Who the hell *are* these people who can do what they do?" cried Tyrell, hammering his fist on the nearest piece of furniture.

"You said they came from the Middle East," offered Cathy.

"That's true, but it's too broad. You don't know the Baaka Valley. I do. There are a dozen factions fighting one another for supremacy, each claiming to be the terrible sword of Allah. This group is different; they may be fanatics, but they go way beyond Allah or Jesus or Mohammed or Moses. Their sources are too diverse, the infrastructure too widespread—good Lord, leaks in Washington and Paris that we know about, Mafia connections, an island fortress, Japanese satellites, Swiss accounts, drops in Miami and Palm Beach, and who knows what else! Those contacts aren't the result of fanatical appeals to the believers of selected gods and prophets. No, they may be zealots, but they're also mercenaries, capitalists of terrorism engaged in a worldwide business."

"They must have one hell of a big client list," said Poole. "Where do they get them?"

"It's a two-way street, Jackson. They sell and they buy."

"Buy what?"

"For lack of a better word, destabilization. The means *to* it and the execution *of* it."

"I guess the next question is why," said Neilsen,

frowning. "I can understand the fanaticism, but why would people not even remotely interested in their causes—the Mafia, for example—cooperate, much less pay for it?"

"Because such people *are* interested and it hasn't a damn thing to do with religious or philosophical convictions. It has to do with power. And money. Wherever there's destabilization, there's a power vacuum, and millions, hell, *billions,* can be made. In the panic, governments can be infiltrated, men put where others want them to be for future use, whole countries brought under the control of vested interests who aren't discovered until they've milked their territories dry, by which time they disappear, or their political asylums are guaranteed."

"Things can really happen that way?"

"Lady, I've *seen* it. From Greece to Uganda, Haiti to Argentina, Chile to Panama, and most of the former Eastern bloc—their ruling bureaucrats were as Communist as the Rockefellers."

"Well, I'll be dipped in muleshit!" exclaimed Lieutenant Poole. "I just never thought in those terms. I'm ashamed of myself, 'cause I see what you mean."

"Don't whip yourself. It was my business, Jackson. Projection is the bottom line where intelligence is concerned."

"What do we do now, Tye?" said Cathy.

"We wait to hear from Cooke and Ardisonne. If it's what I think, we'll fly to Puerto Rico under military security."

There was a knock on the villa's door, an unnecessary knock, as the voice that followed belonged to the chickee bartender. "It's me. I've gotta talk to you, Tye-Boy."

"For God's sake, Roge, the door's not locked!"

"Maybe I don' want to come in," said Roger, slouching inside and closing the door, a newspaper in his hand. He crossed to Hawthorne and held out the paper for him. "It's the early edition of *The San Juan Star;* it was flown in a half hour ago and the front desk is cacklin' like chickens. The small story, *mon,* is on page three, I folded it for you."

Two Dead Men Washed Up on Morro Castle Rocks

SAN JUAN, Saturday—The bodies of two middle-aged men were discovered early this morning pinned between the rocks on this area of the coast, west of the water shacks. The two were identified by means of their passports as Geoffrey Alan Cooke, a British citizen, and Jacques René Ardisonne of France. The cause of death was established as drowning prior to being smashed into the rocks. The authorities will be making further inquiries in the U.K. and France.

Tyrell Hawthorne threw the newspaper on the floor, spun around, and raced to the window, smashing his fist through the glass, leaving his hand covered with blood.

The Manhattan penthouse, high above Fifth Avenue, overlooked the lights of Central Park and was properly aglow with subdued crystal chandeliers and glass-enclosed floral candles on damask-draped tables. Among the guests were the movers and shakers of the city: politicians, real estate tycoons, bankers and prominent newspaper columnists, plus several instantly recognizable stars of films and television, as well as a smattering of established authors, all of whom had been published in Italy. They had been summoned by their host, a flamboyant entrepreneur whose questionable manipulations in the bond market had gone unnoticed while a great many of his associates had gone to jail. His Agincourt, however, was on the horizon, his outstanding debts soon to be called in, and his favors to the movers and the shakers reluctantly acknowledged, so all were there. The object of their attention was a young man whose recommendations to his immensely wealthy father, the baron of Ravello, could considerably lessen the host's difficulties.

The evening progressed with oily smoothness, the *barone-cadetto* and his aunt, the *contessa*, receiving the guests as though they were a czar's favored son and sister in old St. Petersburg. To the Baj's annoyance, one of the young television actresses spoke Italian and engaged "Dante Paolo" in prolonged conversation once the introductions were over and everyone mingled with cocktails. It was hardly jealousy that disturbed Bajaratt, it was the specter of danger. A sophisticated, multilingual young woman might easily spot flaws in Nicolo's "noble" upbringing. The danger, however, blew away like an overinflated sausage casing when Nico turned to the Baj, the dark-haired actress at his side.

"*Cara Zia,* my new friend speaks a fine Italian," he cried in that language.

"I gathered that," said Bajaratt, also in Italian and without much enthusiasm. "Were you educated in Rome, my child, or perhaps Switzerland?"

"Gosh, no, Countess. After high school, the only teachers I had were some method weirdos in acting class until I got the TV series."

"You've seen her, my dear aunt, *I've* seen her! In our country it's called *Vendetta delle Selle,* everybody watches it! She plays the sweet girl who cares for her younger brother and sister after the bandits killed their parents."

"The translation's not too hot, Dante. *Revenge of the Saddles* doesn't really say it. But look, who cares? They watch."

"Then your fluency in our language . . . ?"

"My father owns an Italian deli in Brooklyn. Where they live, not too many people over forty speak English."

"Her father hangs whole provolones and cheeses

from Portofino and the best *prichute* from the south. Oh, I would love to go to this Brooklyn!"

"I'm afraid there's no time, Dante. I'm flying back to the coast tomorrow morning," the actress said.

"My dear child," the Baj said quickly in Italian, her coolness receding rapidly as she smiled at the actress, a new warmth in the tone of her voice, an idea forming. "Is it so necessary that you return to . . . to—"

"The coast, we call it," completed the young woman. "That's California. I have to be back on the set in four days, and I need at least a couple to run on the beach and work off my family's cooking. The *Saddles* big sister has to look the part."

"If you stayed just one more day, it would still leave you two for your beach, not so?"

"Sure, but why?"

"My nephew is very taken with you—"

"Wait a minute, lady!" the actress burst out in English, obviously offended.

"No, *please*," broke in Bajaratt, also in English. "You misunderstand me. *Rispetto, rispetto totale*. Always in public and I would be with you—a proper chaperone. It's just that all these business conferences with people so much older, I thought perhaps a day off, sightseeing with someone nearer his own age who speaks his language, would be a welcome relief. He must get tired of his old aunt."

"If you're 'old,' Countess," said the young woman, relieved and reverting to Italian, "then I'm still in the first grade."

"Then you'll stay?"

"Oh, well . . . why not?" the young actress said, gazing at Nicolo's handsome face and breaking into a smile.

"Since we should start early in the morning," said Bajaratt, "may we get you a room at our hotel after dinner?"

"You don't know Papa. When I'm in New York I

sleep at home, Countess. My uncle Ruggio owns his own taxicab and he's waiting for me."

"We can see you home to this Brooklyn," insisted Nicolo excitedly. "We have a limousine!"

"Then I can show you Papa's store! The cheese, the salamis, the prosciutto."

"Please, *cara Zia*?"

"Uncle Ruggio can follow us, that way Papa can't get angry."

"Your father protects you, doesn't he?" said Bajaratt.

"Tell me about it! Since I've been in L.A., one unmarried female relative after another shares my apartment. One leaves and twenty minutes later another shows up!"

"A good Italian father who instructs his family in the proper traditions."

"Angelo Capelli, father of Angel Capell—that's what my agent shortened it to; he thought Angelina Capelli belonged in a New Jersey diner. He's the toughest papa in Brooklyn. But if I tell him that I'm bringing home a real baron to meet Mama and him . . ."

"Zia Cabrini," said Nicolo, in his words an edge of authority. "We've met everybody, can't we leave? I can smell the cheeses, taste the *prichute*!"

"I'll see what I can do, my nephew—but may I have a word with you privately? . . . It's nothing at all, young lady, just a few words about a man he will meet before we leave. Business, of course."

"Oh, sure. There's a critic from the *Times* who gave me a terrific review for a small part I played in the Village; it led to the series. I sent him a letter, but I've never thanked him personally. See you in a few minutes." The young actress, carrying a champagne glass filled with ginger ale, walked toward an obese, gray-bearded man with the eyes of a leopard and the lips of an orangutan.

"What is it, signora? Have I done something wrong?"

"Not at all, my darling, you are having fun with someone your own age and that's fine. But remember, you do not speak English! Do not even betray an inkling in your eyes that you understand English!"

"Cabi, we speak only Italian together. . . . You're not angry that I find her attractive, are you?"

"You'd be a fool not to, Nicolo. Middle-class morality is irrelevant to you or to me, but something tells me you should not treat her as you might a woman from the docks of Portici anxious for your body."

"Never! She may be famous but she is a pure Italian girl whom I respect in the family traditions as I do my sisters. She is not part of the world you brought me into."

"Are you dissatisfied with that world, Nico?"

"How could I be? I've never lived like this—never dreamed I would."

"Good. Go to your *bellissima ragazza*, I'll join you soon." The Baj turned and glided gracefully toward their host, who was in a deep, even contentious, discussion with two bankers. Suddenly a hand touched her elbow, gently yet firmly. She snapped her head around only to stare at the attractive face of an aging, white-haired man who might have stepped out of an English magazine advertisement extolling the virtues of a Rolls-Royce. "Have we met, sir?" asked Bajaratt.

"We have now, Countess," replied the man, lifting her left hand, his lips touching the flesh. "I was a late arrival, but I see that all goes well with you."

"It is a charming evening, of course."

"Oh, this is the crowd for it, take my word. Charm lathering over the room like barrels of shaving cream. Power and wealth combine to turn maggots into butterflies—monarch butterflies."

"Are you a writer . . . a novelist, perhaps? I've met several here tonight."

"Good heavens, no, I can barely get through a letter without a secretary. Piquant observations are merely part of my stock-in-trade."

"And what do you trade, signore?"

"A certain aristocratic legacy, one might say, pur-
veyed primarily among the diplomatic corps—the corps
of many countries—generally at the behest of the State
Department."

"How intriguing."

"It's that, of course," agreed the stranger, smiling.
"However, since I'm neither an alcoholic nor politically
ambitious, and have a rather splendid estate that I truly
enjoy displaying, the State Department finds my environs
an attractive neutral ground for visiting dignitaries. You
can't ride horses with a man or a woman, then play
tennis, or swim in a pool with a cascading waterfall,
have an attractive meal, and subsequently behave like
a boor in negotiations. . . . Naturally, there are other
inducements, both male and female."

"Why are you telling me all this, signore?" asked
Bajaratt, studying the self-proclaimed aristocrat.

"Because everything I own, everything I learned, came
to me years ago in Havana, my dear," the man replied,
his eyes locked with those of the Baj. "Does that tell you
anything, Countess?"

"Why should it?" said Amaya, her expression totally
neutral, her breathing, however, suspended.

"Then I'll be quick, for we have only moments before
some sycophant interrupts us. You have several numbers, but you don't have the telephone codes over here,
and now you must. I left a waxed envelope for you
at your hotel; if there are cracks in the wax, call me
immediately at the Plaza and everything will be changed.
The name is Van Nostrand, Suite Nine B."

"And if the seal is intact?"

"Then from tomorrow on, use those three numbers
to reach me. I'll be at one of them night and day. You
now have a friend you need."

"A 'friend I need'? You talk in circles, really, you do."

"Stop it, Baj," whispered the Rolls-Royce advertisement, again smiling. "The *padrone* is dead!"

Bajaratt gasped. "What are you saying?"

"He's gone. . . . For God's sake, look pleasant."

"The disease won, then. He lost."

"It was not the disease. He blew up the entire compound, himself in it. He had no alternative."

"But why?"

"They found him; it was always a possibility. Among his last instructions were to befriend you and offer you whatever assistance I could should anything happen to him—naturally or unnaturally. Within limits, I'm your obedient servant . . . *Contessa.*"

"But what happened? You tell me nothing!"

"Not now. Later."

"My true father—"

"No longer. He's gone. You turn to me now, and through me to my considerable resources." Van Nostrand arched his head as if responding with laughter at a remark made by the countess.

"Who are you?"

"I told you, a friend whom you need."

"You are the *padrone*'s contact here in America?"

"His and others', but mainly his. In every other sense, I was *solely* his. . . . Havana, I did mention Havana."

"What did he tell you—about me?"

"He adored you and admired you enormously. You were a great comfort to him, and he therefore demanded that I help you in any way that I can."

"Help me in what way?"

"Using my assets to get you from one place to another, one person to another, with as little or as much attention as you wish. And to obey your orders as long as they are not in conflict with mine—ours."

"Ours?"

"I am the leader of the Scorpios."

"*Scorpiones!*" The Baj kept her voice barely above a whisper, muted and mingling with the hum of the guests, her control absolute. "The head of the High Councils spoke of you. He said I would be watched, tested, and if I were accepted, someone would reach me and I would become one of you."

"I shouldn't go that far, *Contessa,* but you may well be given extraordinary assistance—"

"I simply never associated the Scorpios with the *padrone,*" Bajaratt said.

"Genuine credit is elusive, isn't it? . . . The *padrone* created us, with my invaluable assistance, of course. As to your being tested, what you accomplished in Palm Beach eliminates any further examination. It was simply outrageous—and outrageously marvelous!"

"Who are the Scorpios, can you tell me?"

"In a general way, yes, nothing specific. We are twenty-five in number, that's our limit." Again Van Nostrand laughed heartily at another nonexistent remark. "We're in various professions and occupations, selected very carefully for maximum advantage—I made those decisions with an eye toward profiting our many clients. The *padrone* always felt that if a day passed without realizing at least a million dollars, it was a day wasted."

"I never knew that side of—of . . . my only father. Can all the Scorpions be trusted?"

"They're terrified into being so, and that's all I'll tell you. They obey orders, or death is a preferable option."

"Do you know why I'm here, Signor Van Nostrand?"

"I didn't need our mutual friend to explain it to me. I have very close ties with rarefied government officials."

"And?" said the Baj, staring at Van Nostrand.

"It's madness!" he whispered. "But I can see where the *padrone* would find it exhilarating."

"And you?"

"In death as in life, I am beholden only to him. I was and am nothing without the *padrone.* I did mention that, didn't I?"

"Yes, you did. He was everything they say in Havana, no?"

"He was the fierce, golden-haired Mars of the Caribbean, so young, so magnificent. Had Fidel enlisted his genius rather than banishing it, Cuba today would be an island paradise, wealthy beyond imagination."

"And the *padrone*'s island, how was it found?"

"A man named Hawthorne, a former officer in naval intelligence."

The color drained from Bajaratt's face. "He will die," she said quietly.

The interlude in Brooklyn was endurable for the Baj only because the strategy was sound. Angelo Capelli and his wife, Rosa, a strikingly handsome couple, for none but such a union could produce the young actress Angel Capell, were delighted by the modest *barone-cadetto*, who in turn was overwhelmed by the Salumeria Capelli, a delicatessen in the old tradition, where more and more was better and better, and small round tables were placed about for those caring to eat the Casa Capelli on the premises. Photographs of the family's daughter were everywhere, the majority scenes from the television series, and Angel's younger brother, a sixteen-year-old, shorter but nearly as handsome as Nicolo, rapidly became friends with the *barone-cadetto*. Provolone was cut, prosciutto and salami sliced, and a cold pasta with Rosa's own tomato sauce presented, along with several bottles of Chianti Classico. The tables were clustered and a full-fledged *antipasto misto* was had by all.

"See, *cara Zia*, I told you!" cried Dante Paolo in Italian. "Isn't this better than eating with all those stuffed shirts?"

"Our host was mortified, my nephew."

"Why? Whose ass was I supposed to kiss next? There weren't any left!"

The roar of laughter was punctuated by Bajaratt's humorous admonition. "*Really*, Dante—but I suspect you're right."

"You kiss *nobody's* ass!" roared Angelo Capelli.

"Please, Papa, your language—"

"You please, daughter. He is the cadet-baron of Ravello! Anyway, he said it first."

"He's right, Angelina—Angel—I did."

"Such a nice young man," said Rosa. "So natural and down-to-earth."

"Why shouldn't I be, Signora Capelli?" asked an exuberant Nicolo. "I did not demand to be born with a title. I just arrived—oh, Mother mine, did I just arrive!"

Again there was an explosion of laughter, the democratization of nobility complete. And then there was a knocking at the delicatessen's locked door. The Baj spoke in English. "Forgive me, *famiglia Capelli*, but my nephew wished so much to have memories of this evening that he asked me to have a photographer come around to take some pictures. If it offends you, I'll send him away."

"Offend us?" cried the father. "It is an honor beyond our expectations. My son, let the man in, quickly!"

Having secured a limousine for the next morning at the concierge's desk, Bajaratt walked across the hotel lobby to the bank of pay phones. Taking a scrap of paper from her purse, she dialed the Plaza, asking for Suite 9B.

"Yes?" answered the male voice.

"Van Nostrand, it is I."

"You're not calling from your room, are you?"

"I shouldn't dignify that question, but of course not. I'm in the lobby."

"Give me the number, I'll go downstairs."

The Baj did so, and seven minutes later the public telephone rang. "Was that necessary?" she asked, lifting the receiver before the first ring was completed.

"I shouldn't dignify the question," replied Van Nostrand, chuckling, "but yes, it was. I'm a known confidant of the State Department, and there are numerous people vitally interested in my communications. Hotel switchboards can be bribed; the cost is minimal and those paying are frequently quite impressive."

"Espionage?"

"Rarely beyond our shores these days, rather in Washington itself. It's called turf sniping. But enough of my perhaps overly cautious procedures. Was my envelope intact?"

"It was, I studied it under a glass in the harshest light."

"Good. I don't have to tell you that where possible, the calls should be made from public phones. It's not altogether necessary, but preferable when there is more than one call. We don't like patterns."

"No, you don't have to tell me that," Bajaratt broke in. "However, since you have close ties, as you put it, with government officials, where is this former naval intelligence officer named Hawthorne now?"

"I would prefer that you leave him to me. As I understand your objective, hunting him would only impede your progress—and that of your associates."

"He's too clever for you, old man."

"You sound as if you know him—"

"I know his reputation. He was the best in Amsterdam . . . he and his wife."

"How interesting. I happen to know that information is off the books."

"I, too, have my sources, Signor Van Nostrand."

"Even the *padrone* did not know, and I had no chance to tell him. Extremely interesting. . . . As to my being old, my dear Baj, may I remind you that I have at my disposal over here a *thousand* times your resources in the dark arts."

"You don't understand—"

"Oh, yes, I do!" interrupted the State Department liaison in sudden fury. "You may call him your only true father, but he was my *life!*"

"I beg your pardon?"

"You heard me," said Van Nostrand coldly. "For

thirty years we shared everything—*everything*. Havana, Rio, Buenos Aires—two lives as one, he the master, of course. Until he was diagnosed ten years ago, and he sent me away to serve him in other endeavors."

"I had no idea—"

"Then let me ask you a question, young lady. In the two years you spent on that island, did you ever see another woman except for Hectra, the black Amazon?"

"Oh, my God."

"Does it shock you?"

"Not sexually, that's immaterial. I just never even considered it."

"None ever did. 'Mars and Neptune' he called the two of us, one ruling for all the Caribbean to see, the other underneath, guiding him, instructing him in the courtesies and subtleties an education brings. . . . Now, you understand me, Baj! This Hawthorne is *mine* to kill, no one else's!"

The limousine crisscrossed Manhattan, east and west, north and south, from the United Nations to the television studios by the Hudson River, from Battery Park to the Museum of Natural History, each new sight enthralling the excited "Dante Paolo" to the delight of Angel Capell, whose celebrated presence instantly opened doors and gave rise to special tours. And somehow, some way, there were photographers everywhere. It was no surprise to Angel, who was used to the attention, and who kept telling Nicolo, "*Anche i paparazzi devono vivere*"—they, too, had to make a living. However, what neither the young television star nor her escort noticed was that not one photograph was taken of Amaya Bajaratt. It was a preordained condition, negotiated by the "*contessa*" in return for access to the limousine's schedule.

Lunch at the Four Seasons on 52nd Street was capped by the two ingratiating owners presenting the young couple with the establishment's Chocolate Velvet Cake, the white lettering on the top welcoming the handsome *barone-cadetto* and his beautiful companion, who was an American treasure.

As the youngsters lingered over second helpings of cake and coffee, the countess interrupted. "Perhaps we should return to our limousine," said Bajaratt. "We have four other places I promised Dante we'd see."

"Then I'll ask the waiter to put the cake in a container for the driver."

"You are very considerate, Angelina."

On the way out, the Baj slowed her pace on the staircase, for below by the hatcheck counter were three photographers. They did their jobs as the privileged young couple smiled graciously at each other.

Perfect.

The New York Times
(Business Section)

BROOKLYN, Aug. 28—Dante Paolo, the *barone-cadetto* of Ravello, who is representing his father, the immensely wealthy baron, has struck up a friendship with one of America's favorite young television stars, Angel Capell, of the TV series *Saddles Ride for Revenge.* The accompanying photograph shows Miss Capell, born Angelina Capelli and who speaks fluent Italian, with the baron-to-be and her family in Brooklyn. It is reported that numerous corporations in the tri-state area have put out interoffice memoranda seeking executives who speak Italian.

The New York Daily News

Italian Royal and America's Sweetheart
an Item?

Other photos inside. Is it a whirlwind courtship?

The National Enquirer

Is the Angel of America Pregnant?

Who knows? But they're more than "friends"!

"This is disgusting!" shouted Nicolo. The newspapers in his hand, he paced the hotel room. "I'm so embarrassed! What can I say to her?"

"Nothing at the moment, Nico, she's on a plane to California. She gave you her telephone number, so call her later."

"She'll think I'm a monster!"

"I don't believe so. I suspect she's had more experience in these matters than to take such articles seriously."

"But where did all those photographers come from? How did they know where to be?"

"She told you herself, my handsome young man. The *paparazzi* also must make a living; she understands that. What perhaps she did not modestly make clear was just how famous she is. . . . I should have known better, of course."

The Baj walked out of the elevator into the hotel lobby and crossed to the bank of public telephones. The numbers memorized, she dialed them and reached Van Nostrand.

"Well, the young man and his girlfriend are certainly all over the papers," he said. "Good heavens, what publicity—nearly on a par with Grace and Rainier! Of course, the American public laps it up, it's their fantasies, naturally."

"Then I have accomplished my purpose. The coverage in Washington was adequate?"

"Adequate? From the *Post* to the *Times* to every rag in the supermarkets, the two of them are prime copy! And I should tell you, since it was mentioned in several society columns that I was there in New York, I've had numerous calls from the elite of the Beltway asking if I knew the young baron—more to the point, if I knew his father."

"What did you say?"

"No comment, which is naturally comment enough, since close friendships are never commented upon in this city unless there are reasons to do so. So far, the price in terms of influence is not high enough, but it will get there. Not that it matters, frankly."

"Then it's time we move on to Washington—without publicity."

"As you wish."

"You can accommodate us?"

"What do you mean? I can send a plane for you, of course."

"I mean at your grand estate, the estate you own because of Havana."

"It's out of the question," said Van Nostrand curtly.

"Why is that?"

"I have my own agenda. I expect to have former Commander Tyrell Hawthorne as my guest within forty-eight hours. Twelve hours later, you and the boy can have the run of the whole goddamned place, for I'll be gone."

14

T yrell Hawthorne, dressed in a lightweight, many-pocketed safari jacket and khakis he had purchased at the airport, looked at his bandaged hand in the moonlight. It had been wrapped by Major Catherine Neilsen the day before on the island of Virgin Gorda. They were now in the open candlelit courtyard of the San Juan Hotel in Isla Verde, Puerto Rico, both waiting for Lieutenant A. J. Poole to return from a conference with U.S. Naval Intelligence, a conference Tyrell had refused to attend. "If I'm not there, I'm not committed to their stupidities" was the way he had phrased it. "Let Jackson be the conduit. I can always shoot him and say I never heard a word." A third glass of Chablis arrived at the table. The air force major was still nursing her large iced tea.

"Why do I think you're used to harder stuff?" said Cathy, nodding at the wine.

"Because I was until I found out it wasn't to my benefit. Is that sufficient?"

"I wasn't trying to pry—"

"Where the hell is he? That goddamned meeting couldn't have lasted more than ten minutes if he told them what I wanted him to!"

"You need them, Tye. You can't act alone, you know that."

"I got the name of Cooke and Ardisonne's pilot from a general aviation mechanic, and for the moment that's all I need. Alfred Simon, scum-plus!"

"Come on, you yourself said he was a hired hand—

an X-outside you called him, although I haven't the vaguest idea what it means."

"It's simple. Someone who's hired to do a job but he's outside the circle—he doesn't actually know who hired him."

"Then what good is the name?"

"Because if what minor skills I once had haven't completely deserted me, there's a chance I can penetrate that circle."

"By yourself?"

"I'm not an idiot, Cathy, and the category of dead heroes has never appealed to me. That's when I call in all the firepower I can muster. Until then I can move faster alone, in or out of sanction."

"What does that mean?"

"No one to tell me that I should or shouldn't do this or that because it will have an effect on something else they can't tell me about."

"You sound like you're excluding me and Jackson."

"Oh, no, Major, you're in till things get hairy, and your bayou genius is in for the duration, unless he quits on me. I need a base camp manned by people I can trust."

"Thank you for that, and while I'm at it, thanks for the clothes. They have nice shops here."

"That's one thing our Henry Stevens is good for. He wires money as if he has the codes to the Fort Knox vaults, which he probably has."

"I kept all the receipts—"

"Burn 'em, they're traceable paper and undesirable in the extreme. Don't you know *anything*, Major Neilsen? You'd make a lousy field officer. You must never leave an excess of contingency funds, it just isn't ethical."

"I'll try to remember that, Commander."

"As Poole would say, you do look gorgeous."

"Why, thank you, sir. Jackson chose this outfit."

"You know that kid could become obsessive instant hate. We should put him in a cell with my younger brother; those two Mensa brats would refry each other's brains with their intense intellectuality."

"Speaking of which, a very intense Lieutenant Poole has just arrived. He's scanning the tables for us."

Andrew Jackson Poole V pulled back a chair and sat down, his spine rigid. "The next time you got a conference with those muleshoes, you go yourself, big guy!" he whispered harshly. "Those assholes can't speak a simple declarative sentence."

"It's called obfuscation, Lieutenant," said Hawthorne, smiling. "As in they didn't really say what you heard, but you drew your own conclusions which they can reject at a later date. Therefore, whatever goes wrong is your fault, not theirs. . . . Did you give them my message?"

"Oh, they've got no problem with that. You can go after your X-rated pilot, or whatever he is, but there's a new wrinkle that could make him obsolete."

"What is it?"

"Some big-shot dude who must be pretty high in Washington has information for you, and as sure as 'gators eat meat, it's got something to do with the current situation."

"Let's have it."

"This wrinkle has a wrinkle on it, Tye. He passed over your old buddy Stevens and came directly down here by way of the secretary of defense, who had you traced. Stevens is out in the cold on this."

"What?"

"He'll talk only to you."

"Why? Who is he?"

Poole reached into his recently purchased, very expensive navy blue blazer and took out an official-looking envelope with thick red security tape bonded to the center of the paper. "You tell us, if you've a mind to," said the lieutenant. "This is for you, and I gotta explain that the head intelligence honcho at the base—some wide-eyed cat who took me into his office and told me he was ordered to keep his mouth shut—was scared shitless. He said he expected only you, and when I said you weren't available, he said he wouldn't give it to me, so I said, 'That's fine, he'll never get it,' so he said he'd send me back to wherever we were under escort, and that escort would observe me delivering the envelope to you personally, probably with a high-speed camera."

"Goddamned kindergarten games," said Hawthorne.

"He's the ensign looking over the flower box on our left," said Cathy. Tye and Jackson turned around; the head behind a row of orchids ducked, the epauleted white shirt dashing to the right toward the entrance. "The ball's in your court, Commander."

"Let's see if it is," said Tyrell, ripping the tape and opening the envelope. He extracted the one-page note and, reading it, closed his eyes. "What's left?" he said, his voice barely audible. He dropped the paper on the table, his eyes staring into nothing across the room.

"May I?" asked Catherine, slowly picking up the note, but not turning it over to read until she understood there would be no objection from Hawthorne.

> A terrible thing was done and it should be rectified. I refer to Amsterdam, of course. What you do not know is that there was a connection between your wife and the Baaka Valley. She was sacrificed for an aborted strategy that may well be in operation currently. What I have to tell you is solely between the two of us, for you may know more than you think, and despite the potential crisis, only you can decide whether to act on that information. You are entitled to the decision.
>
> As scheduled, you will receive this while I am away, but I shall return tomorrow afternoon by three o'clock. Please reach me at the telephone

*number below and arrangements will be made for
your transportation to my house in the country.*

> *Very truly yours,*
> *NVN*

A telephone number was in the lower left corner;
other than that there was no identification whatsoever
on the handwritten note. However, there was a post-
script below the initials.

*I loathe being melodramatic, but please destroy
this communication after extracting the number of
my private phone.*

"What does he know?" said Hawthorne, finding a faint,
frightened voice, asking the question of himself as much
as of his two companions. "Who *is* he?"

"If the base honcho knows, he's not saying, which
means he doesn't because he would have said it."

"How can you be sure of that?" asked Cathy.

"I told him my leader wasn't in the market for unso-
licited communiqués that weren't cleared by the navy
spooks in D.C. That's when he dumped on me about the
secretary of defense and all the secrecy that went with
the trace."

"You do have balls, Jackson," said Tyrell sincerely.

"I'm also just army enough to get a mite jumpy when
strict chains of command are skirted by civilian hush-
hush bullshit. That's when I smell rodents goin' around
secure channels to nail another military. I can give you
chapter and verse going back to Pearl Harbor."

"In this case, there could be a very good reason, Lieutenant. My wife was murdered in Amsterdam."

"I know that, but why has this dude kept his mouth
shut for five years if he's got something to tell you? Why
now?"

"He made that clear, and you said it yourself. He believes there's a connection to the present situation; he spelled it out. My wife was *sacrificed*."

"And I'm truly sorry about that, but we've seen what these scumbuckets can do, what they've *done*, and the contacts they've got in D.C. and Paris and London . . . and you tell Cath and me that it's all just a little tip of the iceberg, right?"

"Yes, that's right."

"So this world we know could be in a real goddamned international mess, wouldn't you say?"

"I think I tried to make that clear."

"Then who are you to stand between whoever this big shot is and his goin' directly to the President of the United States and all the national security agencies that man's got wired into his console?"

"I don't know."

"So think about it! He even gives you an option whether or not to act on the information he *thinks* you know. Considerin' everything involved, what kind of reasonin' is that? One ex-lieutenant commander in the navy who's not exactly held in high esteem against the life of the most powerful leader in the world? Think, Tye!"

"I can't," mumbled Hawthorne, a tremble developing in his hands, his eyes wavering. "I just can't. . . . She was my wife."

"Cut it out, Commander, no tears from you."

"Stop it, Jackson!"

"The hell I will, Cath. This whole thing smells!"

"I have to *know*—" Tyrell's voice broke off, then, as suddenly as his painful introspection had arrived, it vanished, replaced by a blinking, very controlled Hawthorne. "We'll find out tomorrow, won't we?" he said, sitting up as straight as Lieutenant Poole. "Until then, I'm going after that pilot. He's in Old San Juan."

"This has to be very difficult for you." Neilsen covered Tyrell's extended left hand with her own. "You're a strong guy."

"You've got it wrong," said Hawthorne, his tired eyes locked with Catherine's. "Until I talk with the man who wrote this 'communication,' I'm the biggest coward you ever met."

"So let's go after the X-rated pilot," Poole broke in, his voice steady.

"Jackson, please—"

"I know what I'm doing, Cath. It's no good stewin' while you wait for the moonshine to drip. C'mon, Commander, let's roll into San Juan."

"No, you stay here with Cathy, I'll go alone."

"Negative, *sir*." Poole rose from his chair, standing at attention above Hawthorne.

"What did you say?" Tyrell blinked his eyes and looked up at the young air force officer, his expression strained, angry. "I said I'm going alone, didn't you hear me?"

"Affirmative, sir," replied Poole in a military monotone. "However, I'm exercisin' a junior officer's prerogative when, in his best judgment, his superior is in need of assistance, and that assistance in no way compromises his current duties. It's clearly spelled out in the Air Force Manual of Regulations in Article Seven, Section—"

"Oh, shut up!"

"Don't argue with him," said Catherine softly, squeezing Hawthorne's hand as she removed hers. "He'll quote every regulation to counter you from page one on if you do. He's done it with me more times than I can count."

"Okay, you win, Lieutenant." Tyrell rose from his chair. "Let's roll. Into Old San Juan."

"May I suggest, sir, that we stop in the men's room first?"

"I'm fine. I'll wait outside."

"I further suggest, sir, that you join me."

"Why?"

"My answer will explain why the meeting with your friends at naval intelligence took so long. Bein' stationed in Florida, I'm familiar with San Juan. It took a little time to locate the shops I needed to find, especially one which would cooperate. The ensign was too scared to argue."

"What the hell are you talking about?"

"Since we left those outsize guns we had in Gorda, I took the liberty of buying us a couple of weapons— figuring you had that pilot in mind, and knowing something about Old San Juan. Walther P.K.—autos, eight rounds, three clips apiece, and with a two-and-one-half-inch barrel, very unobtrusive in coat pockets."

"He knows guns too?" asked Hawthorne quietly, looking down at Catherine.

"I don't think he's ever fired one in anger," answered the major, "but he's got a master's equivalent in weapons analysis."

"How are you in brain surgery?"

"I got as far as lobotomy procedures, but it was too messy. . . . Look, I don't think it's too smart to hand you a gun and three clips of ammunition right out in the open. Frankly, I'm too tall and good-lookin' for people not to notice, you know what I mean?"

"You're the essence of modesty, Lieutenant."

"Oh, hell, you're not so bad yourself, even if you're kind of maturelike."

"Stay in the suite, Cathy," said Tyrell.

"Check in with me every half hour, I insist on it."

"If we can, Major."

"*Ashkelon!*" cried the voice over the public telephone in the Hay-Adams hotel in Washington.

"I'm here, Jerusalem," said Bajaratt. "What happened?"

"The Mossad picked up our lead man!"

"How?"

"There was a party at the kibbutz Irshun outside of Tel Aviv. Several were less drunk than the others, and they found him raping a sabra in the field."

"The *idiot*!"

"They've got him in chains inside the kibbutz jailhouse, awaiting their superiors from Tel Aviv."

"Can you get to him?"

"There's a Jew we can bribe, we're sure of it."

"Then do it. Kill him. We can't allow him to be put under drugs."

"It is done. Ashkelon forever."

"Forever," said Bajaratt, hanging up the phone.

Nils Van Nostrand walked into the study at his immense estate in Fairfax, Virginia. The huge room was devoid of its usual accoutrements, for they were all packed in cartons, all designated by shipping labels to a freight depot in Lisbon, Portugal, ultimately, secretly, to be delivered to a mansion on the shores of Lake Geneva, Switzerland. The rest of the house, its interiors and all its grounds, stables, horses, and various livestock—domestic and wild—had been sold confidentially to a Saudi sheikh who would legally take possession in thirty days. It was all Van Nostrand needed, far more, in fact. He went to his desk, picked up the secure red telephone, and dialed.

"Scorpio Three," said the voice on the line.

"This is S-One and I'll be brief. My time has come. I'm retiring."

"My God, that's a shock! You've been a rock for all of us."

"These things happen. I know when to leave. Tonight, before I disappear, I'll program this phone to you and send word to our Providers. One day they'll summon you, for you are now accountable to them. Incidentally, if a woman calls, identifying herself as the Baj, give her whatever she needs. That's an order from the *padrone*."

"Understood. Will we hear from you again?"

"Frankly, I doubt it. I have a last assignment to complete, and then it's absolute retirement. Scorpio Two is adequate and has extensive expertise, but he doesn't possess your background or sophistication. He'd be out of his depth."

"I think you mean he doesn't have my law firm in Washington."

"Regardless, tomorrow morning you will be Scorpio One."

"It's an honor I shall take to my grave."

"Not too quickly, I trust."

Bajaratt climbed out of the taxi, beckoning Nicolo to hurry. The young man followed as the Baj paid the driver through the window.

"Thanks, lady, that's very nice of you. Hey, isn't that the young fella we've all been reading about? From Italy?"

"I'm afraid he is, signore."

"Wait'll I tell my wife, she's Italian. She brought home one of those papers from Shoppers World with pictures of that actress, Angel Capell, and his royal highness there."

"They're just good friends—"

"Hey, I don't make no judgments, lady. She's a terrific kid, everybody loves her, and those tabloids are garbage!"

"She's a delightful girl. Thank you, signore."

"Hey, it's my pleasure."

"Come, Dante." Bajaratt took Nicolo's arm, propelling him into the fashionable café-of-the-moment in Georgetown. The luncheon crowd was a mix of matrons in silks, younger women in Armani blouses and Calvin Klein denims, along with the usual parade of wealthy, would-be young Turks—recent appointees whose faces reflected their own images of the best-and-the-brightest—and lastly, a few working members of Congress who impatiently kept glancing at their wristwatches. "Remember, Nico," said the Baj as the maître d' made obsequious gestures amid more obsequious welcomes. "He is the senator you met in Palm Beach, the lawyer from the state of Michigan. His name is Nesbitt."

Effusive reintroductions accomplished and iced coffee ordered for all three, the senator from Michigan spoke. "I've never been here before," he said, "but one of my aides knew it immediately. Apparently it's very popular."

"It was merely a whim, signore. Our hostess the other night in Palm Beach mentioned it, therefore I suggested it."

"Yes, she would." The senator glanced around, amusement in his eyes. "Did you get the material I sent to your hotel last evening?"

"Indeed, yes, and I went over it for several hours with Dante Paolo—*Vero, Dante? Le carte di ieri sera, ti ricordi?*"

"*Certo, Zia, altro che.*"

"He and his father, the baron, are most interested, but certain questions have arisen."

"Naturally. The study was a relatively detailed overview of the industrial opportunities, not an in-depth analysis of each possibility. If there's interest, my staff can work up additional data."

"That, of course, would be required prior to any serious negotiations, but perhaps we can speak of—as you say—an 'overview.' "

"Anything you wish. Specifically in what areas?"

"*Incentivi,* signore . . . as you say, 'incentives.' We could be talking about hundreds of millions of dollars. Acceptable risk is one thing, and the baron has never shied away from it, but certain controls might be necessary to assure that fairness, is it not so?"

"Again, in what specific areas, Countess? *Controls* is a pretty tough term in our economy."

"*Pockets of unemployment,* I suspect, is even tougher. But perhaps *controls* is too inhibiting; shall we say *documents of mutual understanding*?"

"Such as?"

"Frankly, at the first sign of financial health, it would be troublesome in the extreme should whatever labor organizations that might be involved make excessive demands—"

"That's an easy one to dispose of," Nesbitt interrupted. "The staffs both here and in Lansing did some missionary work in that area, and I myself made a number of phone calls. The unions have grown considerably more sophisticated where economics are concerned. Many of their members have been out of work for two and three years; they're not going to hammer the golden egg from a risk-taking goose. Ask the Japanese, who've got plants in Pennsylvania, the Carolinas, and God knows where else."

"You relieve us greatly, signore."

"And you'll get that sort of thing in writing, everything relative to productivity and investment return. What else?"

"Is it not always forever the same, whether in this country or our own, wherever industrialists deal with governments?"

"Taxes?" asked the legislator, the start of a frown creasing his forehead, disapproval in the offing. "They're equitably levied, Countess—"

"No, no, no, signore! You misunderstand me. As you Americans say, death and taxes are both inevitable. . . . No, I refer to what appears to much of Italian business as your extraordinary, even intemperate, government interference in the business community. Safety and integrity notwithstanding, we've heard horror stories about delays costing millions over one bureaucratic procedure or another—*local, state, and federal* is the phrase I myself have heard, as has the baron."

"Safety—and as much integrity as the marketplace

demands, notwithstanding," said the senator, smiling.
"The powers of my state, as constitutionally spelled out,
will make damn sure there'll be no unwarranted interference of any kind. We can't afford to do otherwise, and
in service to my constituents, I'll put that in writing."

"Excellent, that's wonderful. . . . There is one last
thing, *Signore Senatore*, and it is a personal request that
you may refuse with no lack of respect on my part."

"What's that, Countess?"

"Like all great and worldly men, my brother the
baron carries about him a certain justifiable pride, not
only for his accomplishments, but also for his family,
especially his son, who has sacrificed a normal, privileged adolescence to come to his father's aid."

"He's a very fine young man. Like everyone else, I've
read the papers, the articles about his friendship with
that lovely television actress, Angel Capell—"

"Ah, *Angelina*," said Nicolo softly, accentuating each
syllable of the name. "*Una bellissima ragazza!*"

"*Basta, mio Dante.*"

"I was especially taken with the photographs of the
two of them with her family in the delicatessen in Brooklyn. The highest-paid campaign manager couldn't have
come up with that photo op."

"It was all quite accidental—but to the request I wish
to make of you."

"Of course. The baron's pride, his family, especially
this fine son of his. What can I do?"

"Would it be possible to arrange a brief private meeting between the *barone-cadetto* and the President—only
a minute or two, so I might send back a photograph of
them together? It would bring such happiness to the
baron, and I would certainly tell my brother how it came
about."

"I think that can be arranged, although in all honesty,
there's been a considerable backlash about foreign investment—"

"Oh, I understand that, signore, I, too, read the papers! It's why I said brief and private, just Dante Paolo and myself, and only for the baron of Ravello, no newspaper publicity whatsoever. . . . Naturally, if it is too much to ask, I withdraw my request and apologize for bringing it up."

"Now, just a minute, Countess," said Nesbitt quietly, pensively. "It'll take a few days, but I think I can work it out. Our state's junior senator is of the President's party, and I backed a bill of his because I thought it was right, but it could cost me votes—"

"I don't understand."

"He's a close friend of the President's and he appreciated my support—he also knows damn well what the baron's infusion of money could do for the state—and what I could do to him if he even marginally interfered. . . . Yes, Countess, I can work it out."

"You all sound so Italian."

"Machiavelli had his points, my dear Countess."

Hawthorne and Poole walked cautiously down the cobblestone street in the lowest-rent district of Old San Juan. The section was devoid of tourist traps except for those devoted to sailors', soldiers', and addicts' more carnal appetites. The streetlamps were only partially operational, say one out of four, so there were far more shadows falling across the decrepit buildings than there was illumination. The two men approached the address of the pilot who had flown the murdered Cooke and Ardisonne from Gorda to Puerto Rico, both abruptly surprised by the loud, boisterous voices coming from within the ancient three-story stone structure.

"This cat's pad beats anything on Bourbon Street, Commander. What the hell's goin' on in there?"

"Apparently a party, Lieutenant, and we're about to crash the gate, since we weren't invited."

"Would you mind if I did that, sir?"

"Do what?"

"Crash the gate. My good leg is one of the strongest in a situation like this."

"Let's knock first and see what happens." Tyrell did, and they found out quickly. A slat was opened in the center of the door, a pair of wide, mascaraed eyes peering through it. "We were told to come here," said Hawthorne pleasantly.

"What chu name?"

"Smith and Jones, that's what we were supposed to say."

"Get the fuck outta here, gringos!" The slat was slammed shut.

"I believe your experienced leg is in order, Poole."

"Your weapon at-the-ready, Tye?"

"Execute, Lieutenant."

"Here we go, Commander!" Poole smashed the door with his left foot, shattering it everywhere as the two of them crashed through the splintered wood, their weapons leveled. "Don't one of you move a bayou-straw inch or I'll pull my trigger!" screamed the lieutenant. "Holy *shit*!"

The threat was not necessary. Someone in panic had fallen across the tape machine, breaking the wires to the speaker. The subsequent silence was broken by a number of males pulling up their trousers, racing down the staircase and out the door. The lack of modesty was observable only in the dimly lit, smoke-layered, downstairs living room, where the majority of young, and not so young, ladies were barebreasted, their lower coverings making a joke of the thinnest bikinis. There was one extension of this professional exhibitionism, singularly revealed by a light-haired, late-middle-aged man who seemed oblivious of the chaos. He kept pounding his hips in the heat of intercourse on a pillowed couch in the corner with a dark-haired woman who screamed, trying frantically to tell him to cease his endeavors.

"What . . . what? Shut your mouth and stay *with* me!"

"Maybe you should shut off your engine and listen up, Simon," said Hawthorne, approaching the gaudy velveteen couch in the shadowed corner of the room.

"Yo, grunt!" roared the man as he spun around, shock but no fear in his cold eyes at the sight of the weapons.

"All you girls!" Poole yelled, addressing not only the women in the living room but also those who came running down the stairs. "I figure you should get outta here. We got personal things to talk about, and they don't concern you. . . . You, too, lady, if you can get away from that bastard."

"¡Gracias, señor! ¡Muchas gracias!"

"Tell your friends to find other jobs!" shouted the young air force officer as the prostitutes raced out the door into the street. "They can get *dead* this way!"

The room was deserted except for the half-drunken pilot who pulled part of the shiny dark-red cover over his naked waist. "Who the hell are you?" he asked. "What do you want from me?"

"For starters, I want to know where you come from," said Tyrell. "You're not normal, Simon."

"It's none of your fucking business, baby."

"This gun at your head says it is, *baby*."

"You think that's a threat? Squeeze it, babe, do me a favor."

"Definitely not normal. 'Yo, *grunt*.' . . . You're military, aren't you?"

"Once, a hundred years ago."

"I was military too. Who blew you out of the sky?"

"Why do you care?"

"Because I'm tracking some very bad people. Tell me or you're dead, *babe*."

"Okay, okay, who gives a shit? I was a drop pilot out of Vientiane flying under Royal Lao Air—"

"A CIA subsidiary," broke in Hawthorne.

"You got it, pal. The Panmunjom talks started and the Senate began asking questions, so the spy boys had to dump the whole fucking mess on somebody's lap. They sold all six planes to me for a hundred thousand, which they advanced me, then buried. To *me*, an underage sharecrop pilot who got into service by signing my old lady's name because my old man was long gone— for Christ's sake, I was only eighteen! I lost all but one aircraft to mech failure and cannibalizing, but they were still there and all registered to me under highly questionable circumstances."

"You had one plane left, equipment worth at least two million. What did you do, sell it so you could set up this little operation to supplement your airborne income?"

"Hell, I stole enough to buy this place years ago," replied Alfred Simon, sneering.

"What happened to the jet? It was a major asset."

"Was, and is. I flew it in hops over the down-under routes cleared with bribes. It's here but I never use it. I keep it greased and operational and hidden. I won't fly it until I'm ready to buy my own farm, diving straight into that fucking Pentagon, and blow those sons of bitches to hell who've kept me on the string for thirty-four years! Those bastards claim I stole ten million dollars' worth of aircraft from the U.S. government—read that as forty years in Leavenworth! . . . Hell, I haven't got a quarter of that long to live."

"But that string around your neck was sufficiently tight to have you pick up those two men at Sebastian's Point in Gorda."

"Hell, yes, but I wasn't the one who shoved 'em out of the plane during the final approach! I had nothing to do with that!"

"Who did?" roared Poole, slapping away Hawthorne's gun, and pressing his own into the pilot's forehead. "You're with those bastards who killed *Charlie*, man, and you're dead if you don't tell me!"

"Hey, come on!" cried the pilot, his body writhing under the deep-red cover. "The spook showed me his identification and said I'd never be called on the operation if I mentioned his name!"

"What was it?"

"*Hawthorne*. Somebody named Tyrone Hawthorne, or something like that."

15

T he manicured lawns of his estate glistened with
   morning dew as Nils Van Nostrand sat at his
   desk and stared out the window of his study,
deep in thought. Time was short and he needed the entire
day to make his arrangements, for his disappearance had
to be complete, his new identity initiated, all lines to
his past obliterated—his ultimate "death" incontestable.
Yet what remained of his natural life had to be civilized;
he could accept anonymity, even welcome it, but he
could not accept living without grace and comfort, and
he would not.

So many years ago, too many to count, he and his
partner for life, *il vizioso elegante*—Mars and Neptune!—had purchased a walled, secluded lakefront estate in Geneva for their elder years. The deed was
recorded in the name of an Argentine colonel, a bisexual
bachelor who was only too pleased to serve the younger,
all-powerful *padrone* and his confidant. Since that time,
an obscure rental agency in Lausanne had secured an
annual stipend that by itself could pay for the firm's
existence with but a few additional clients. There were,
however, several absolutes that, if broken, would result
in a dissolution of the contract. Number one: Never to
attempt to explore the ownership of the estate; two: No
lease could be for less than two years nor longer than
five; three: All payments were to be made to a numbered
account in Bern, subtracting an additional twenty percent over and above the firm's commission for service

and silence. The fourth year was up for the current residents, the unexpired six months of the fifth compensated for by returning the half year's rent along with an additional sixty days' notice of vacancy. Van Nostrand would put those two months to splendid use; they were his timetable for oblivion. The odyssey would begin with the death of the *padrone*'s killer, one former Lieutenant Commander Tyrell Hawthorne. Tonight.

The day, however, was the prelude to his journey. People he had helped throughout his years in Washington now had to accede to his courteous, if strange, requests. It was vital none know that the others were also lending him assistance. Nevertheless, as the capital was a font of misinformation, rumor, diversion, and self-protection, it was necessary that there be a common thread in his appeals, so that if, like the disintegrating web of a spider, one strand after another broke from the weight of truth, there would be a common core all could retreat to. Van Nostrand could even hear the words.

You too? My God, after all he did for the country, at his own expense, it's little enough we could do! Don't you agree?

Of course everyone would agree, for self-protection was the quintessential law of survival in Washington. Inquiries would die quickly with the presumption of his death.

The common thread? Obscure, incomplete, but heartbreaking, especially from a selfless, patriotic man who seemed to have everything—immense wealth, influence, respect, and withal, uncommon modesty. A child, perhaps; a child had universal appeal. What kind of child . . . ? A girl, obviously; look how people everywhere slobbered over that little actress, Angel whatever her name was. Circumstances? Again obvious. The blood of his blood, lost to him for years due to a tragic situation. The event? Marriage? Death? . . . Death; it was the chord of finality. Van Nostrand was ready; the words would come, they always did. Mars used to say to his Neptune: "Your thoughts are so serpentine. You think beyond the thoughts of others. I like that, I need that."

The aristocrat picked up the red telephone and dialed the direct, private secure number of the secretary of state. "Yes?" said the voice in Washington.

"Bruce, it's Nils. I really hate to bother you, especially on this phone, but I'm not sure where else to turn."

"Anytime, my friend. You've certainly earned a minor convenience in light of your major contributions. What is it?"

"Have you got a minute or two?"

"Certainly. To tell you the truth, I just finished an irritating meeting with the Philippine ambassador, and I've got my shoes off. What can I do for you?"

"It's extremely personal, Bruce, and, of course, confidential."

"This line is secure, you know that," interrupted the secretary of state gently.

"Yes, I know that. It's why I used it."

"Go ahead, my friend."

"Good Lord, I *need* a friend right now."

"I'm here."

"I've never discussed this publicly, and rarely in private, but years ago, when I was living in Europe, my marriage was falling apart—we were both at fault; she was an intemperate German and I was an unresponsive husband who disliked confrontations. She opted for more exciting fields and I fell in love with a married woman, deeply in love, as she did with me. The circumstances prohibited her getting a divorce—her husband was a politician running on a vociferously Catholic ticket and wouldn't permit it—but we had a child together, a girl. She was, naturally, passed off as his, but he knew the truth, and forbade his wife ever to see me again, and I was never to see the child."

"How dreadful! Couldn't she have revolted, forced the issue?"

"He told her that if she did, he would have both mother and child killed before he was ruined politically. An accident, of course."

"The son of a bitch!"

"Oh, yes, that he was; that he is."

"Is? Do you want me to arrange State emergency transport to get"—here the secretary paused—"mother and daughter brought over here under diplomatic immunity? Just say the word, Nils. I'll coordinate with Central Intelligence and it's done."

"I'm afraid it's too late, Bruce. My daughter is twenty-four years of age and dying."

"Oh, my God . . . !"

"What I want, what I beg of you, is to fly me with diplomatic clearance to Brussels, no immigration procedures, no computerized passport entry—that man has eyes and ears everywhere, I'm an obsession with him. I must get to Europe without anyone knowing I'm there. I must see my child before she's gone from us, and once she is, live somewhere with my love in our last years, to make up for the time we've lost."

"Oh, Christ, Nils, what you're going through, what you've *been* through!"

"Can you do this for me, Bruce?"

"Of course. An airport away from Washington—less chance of your being recognized. Military escort here and in Brussels; first on board, last to get off, and with a curtained seat in front of the bulkhead. When do you want to leave?"

"This evening, if you can arrange it. Naturally, I insist on paying for everything."

"After all you've done for us? Never mind payment. I'll call you back within the hour."

How easily the words came, thought Van Nostrand as he hung up the phone. *The essence of pure evil, Mars always said, was to dress the archangel of Satan in the pure white robes of goodness and mercy.* Of course, Neptune had taught him that.

The next call was to the director of the Central Intelligence Agency, whose organization frequently used one of Van Nostrand's guest cottages as a safe house for defectors and stressed-out field agents under medical debriefing.

". . . Jesus, Nils, that's a terrible thing! Give me the bastard's name. I've got dark assets all over Europe who'll remove him. And I don't say that lightly—I avoid last extremities as if they were my own—but that scum doesn't deserve to live another day! My God, your own daughter!"

"No, my good friend, I don't believe in violence."

"Neither do I, but the most violent thing on earth was done against you and the mother of your child. Years of living under the threat of both being killed? An infant and her mother?"

"There's another way, and I ask you only to listen to me."

"What is it?"

"I can get them out and into a safe situation, but it will take a great deal of money, which I certainly have. However, if I use the normal transfer procedures, they will be picked up by the European banking community and he'll know I'm over there."

"You're really going?"

"How many years have I got left to spend with my lost love, my dearest love?"

"I'm not sure I understand."

"He'll find out and he'll kill her. He's sworn to do it."

"That bastard. Give me his name!"

"My religious beliefs do not permit me to do that."

"So what the hell does? What have you got left?"

"Complete secrecy. My money's all here, and, naturally, I intend to pay every dollar of tax I owe my country, but I need the rest to be transferred confidentially, legitimately, to any bank of your choosing in Switzerland. Frankly, I've sold my estate for twenty million dollars. The papers are all signed, but nothing will be processed or made public until a month after I'm gone."

"So little? You should get at least twice that. I'm a businessman, remember?"

"The problem is I don't have the time to negotiate. My child is dying and my love is withering in despair and absolute terror. Can you help me?"

"Send me a power of attorney for our records—buried records—and call me when you get to Europe. I'll have everything for you."

"Don't forget the taxes—"

"After all you've done for us? We'll discuss that later. Stay well and find what happiness you can, Nils. God knows you deserve it."

How easily the words came. Van Nostrand leafed once again through his personal telephone directory, which he always kept in a locked steel drawer of his desk when not in use; he would take it with him when he disappeared. He found the name and private number of his next appeal, the chief of Special Forces, Clandestine Operations, United States Army. The man was a quasi-psychotic who took as much pride in confusing his superiors as he did in obtaining his objectives, which he did with such alarming consistency that even the adversarial Central Intelligence Agency granted him grudging respect. His people had infiltrated not only the KGB, MI-6, and the Deuxième, but the holy, impenetrable Mossad. He had done so with highly selected, multilingual personnel who carried extraordinarily well-produced false papers that passed electronic scans . . . and with a great deal of input from the widely traveled, immensely informed Van Nostrand. They were friends, and the lieutenant general had enjoyed many a pleasant weekend at the Fairfax estate with well-endowed and most willing young women, while his wife thought he was in Bangkok or Kuala Lumpur.

"I've never heard anything so rotten, Nils! Who does that fucker think he is? I'll fly over myself and take him out! Christ almighty, your daughter dying, and her mother under a death threat for twenty-some years! He's *history,* buddy!"

"It's not the way, General, believe me when I tell you that. Once our beloved child is gone, there is only disappearance. Killing him would make him a martyr in the eyes of his devoted followers—fanatics, really. They would immediately suspect his wife, for it's rumored that she both loathes and fears him. She would instantly have that 'accident' he's planned for her all these many years."

"Has it occurred to you that if he thinks she's run away with you, and he *will,* he'll hunt you both down?"

"I sincerely doubt it, my friend. Our child will die, the public damage to him removed. A wife may quietly leave a powerful political figure and it's not actually news. However, such a man living for over twenty years with a child he thought was his but wasn't, that *is* news. If he was cuckolded once with concrete results, how many other times were there? That's the damage. Embarrassment."

"Okay, so termination is out. What can I do?"

"I need a rather unique passport by late this afternoon, a false passport of non-American origin."

"No kidding?" said the lieutenant general, his voice pleasantly warming to the subject. "How come?"

"Partially because of what you suggested. He could trace us through computerized international traffic, although I don't think he will, but basically I intend to purchase property. Since I'm not unknown, I don't care to have my name picked up by the press. That *would* be an invitation."

"Gotcha! What did you have in mind?"

"Well, as I spent several years in Argentina, building my international markets, and I speak fluent Spanish, I thought it should be Argentine."

"No sweat. As with twenty-eight other countries, we've duplicated their plates and I've got the best graphics anywhere. Have you figured out a name, a date of birth?"

"Yes, I have. I knew a man who disappeared, as so many did in those days. Colonel Alejandro Schrieber-Cortez."

"Spell it, Nils."

Van Nostrand did, providing also a date and place of birth from memory—such memories. "What else do you need?"

"Eye and hair color and a passport photo taken within the last five years."

"I'll have all that hand-delivered to you by noon. . . . You understand, General, I could go to Bruce at State, but this really isn't in his realm of expertise—"

"That asshole couldn't mount this kind of thing any more than he could handle the best-looking hooker in town. And that *civilian* at the Agency would fuck it up with a brushed photograph! . . . You want to come in here and have my boys work up a new picture? Hair color, contacts in the eyes?"

"Forgive me, my friend, but you and I have discussed these procedures many times. You even gave me the names of several specialists off your books, remember?"

"*Remember?*" The general laughed. "At *your* place? Those visits are out of my memory bank."

"One is coming over within the hour. A man named Crowe."

"The Bird? He's got magic in his lenses. . . . Tell him to bring his stuff directly to me and I'll take care of everything. It's the least I can do, old buddy."

The last call was to the secretary of defense, a highly intelligent, civilized man who was in the wrong job, a fact he was beginning to realize after five months in office. He had been a brilliant executive in the private sector, rising to the position of chief executive officer of the third largest corporation in America, but he was no match for the competitive, gluttonous generals and admirals of the Pentagon. In a world where profit-and-loss sheets were not only meaningless but nonexistent, and massive purchase of product the difference between survival and Armageddon, he was out of his depth. In the acknowledged Darwinian environs of corporate ascendancy he was a master of calm reasoning, leaving the hatchets to rewarded subordinates; but in the brutal competition between the services for military procurement he was at a loss because it had nothing to do with profits. The Pentagon had applauded his appointment.

"They want it *all*!" the secretary had said confidentially to his friend Van Nostrand, an unpaid public servant of like heritage, money, family, and brains. "And most of the time when I raise the subject of increasing budgetary constraints, they force-feed me a hundred scenarios, half of which I can't understand, spelling out a military doomsday if they don't get what they want."

"You must be far tougher with them, Mr. Secretary. Certainly, you've had to deal with reduced budgets before—"

"Of course I have," the secretary, Van Nostrand's guest over brandy that evening, had said. "But implicit in those orders was always the possibility that one or another of my executives might lose his position if my demands weren't carried out. . . . You can't fire these sons of bitches! Besides, confrontations aren't my style."

"So have your civilian aides do it."

"That's what's so stupid! Men like me come and go, but the bureaucratic staffs, those government G-7s or 8s, or whatever they are, are here to stay. And where do they get their perks, their flights on military aircraft to Caribbean resorts beholden to army engineers or naval coastal surveys? Don't bother to answer, I've learned that much."

"A conundrum, then?"

"An impossible situation, at least for someone like me—or even you, I suspect. I'll give it another three or four months, then invent some personal reason to resign."

"Health? One of the most celebrated halfbacks in Yale's football history, a leading spokesman for the President's fitness program? No one will believe it, you jog incessantly in all those government-sponsored television commercials."

"The sixty-six-year-old athlete." The secretary laughed. "My wife loathes Washington. She'll be delighted to be the object of my profound concern, and I'm not above bribing her doctor."

Fortunately for Van Nostrand, the secretary of defense had not yet announced his resignation. Therefore, quite naturally, the secretary was brought into the Little Girl Blood circle, and when Van Nostrand had called, stating that he believed there could be a connection between the current assassination conspiracy and an obscure former officer in naval intelligence named Hawthorne, the secretary had jumped into the breach at the financier's request. What Van Nostrand had told him was both simple and alarming, and necessitated going around normal channels, namely bypassing Captain Henry Stevens, who would interfere. This Hawthorne had to be found, an inflammatory letter sent to him. . . . The world of the terrorist Bajaratt was an international netherworld, a world someone like Van Nostrand had to be aware of; and if through his scores of intermediaries and informants he had heard something, learned something, for God's sake give him all the help one could!

"Hello, Howard?"

"My God, Nils, I was so tempted to call you, but you specifically said I shouldn't. I don't think I could have held out much longer."

"My deepest apologies, my friend, but there's been a

confluence of emergencies: the first, our geopolitical crisis; and the other so personally painful that I can barely speak of it. . . . Did Hawthorne receive my message?"

"They processed the film last night and flew up the negatives—we won't accept faxes—and it's confirmed. Tyrell N. Hawthorne was handed your envelope at 9:12 P.M. in the courtyard café of the San Juan Hotel. We matched the photos under spectrographs and it's him."

"Good. Then I'll hear from the former commander and he'll come to see me. I pray to God that our meeting will produce something of value for you."

"You won't tell me what it is?"

"I can't, Howard, for the specific details could be inaccurate and cast disrepute on an honorable man. I can tell you only that my information speculates on the possibility that this Hawthorne may be a member of the international Alpha market. Of course, it may be totally untrue."

"*Alpha* market? What's that?"

"Assassination, my friend. They kill for the highest bidder, but most, as veterans of deep cover, black operations, they've eluded all traps. However, there's no concrete proof regarding Hawthorne."

"Jesus Christ! Do you mean he could be working with the Bajaratt woman instead of hunting her down?"

"It's a theory based on logical assumptions, and could be terribly wrong or tragically right, we'll know this evening. If all goes according to schedule, he'll be here between six and seven tonight. Soon thereafter, we'll learn the truth."

"How?"

"I'll confront him with what I know, and he'll have to respond."

"I can't permit it! I'll have your place surrounded!"

"Absolutely not. Because if he is who he's reputed to be, he'll send out scouts to survey the grounds; if your men are spotted, he'll never arrive."

"You could be killed!"

"Unlikely. My security personnel are everywhere, and they're acutely thorough."

"That's not good enough!"

"It's more than sufficient, my friend. However if it will ease your mind, send a single car to my entrance road after seven o'clock. If Hawthorne is driven away by my limousine, you'll know my information was wrong, and you must never mention that I brought it up. If it's not wrong, my own people will be on top of the situation and will reach you instantly, for I won't have time to call you myself. My schedule's extraordinarily tight. It will be a last act of patriotism by an old man who loves this land as no other. . . . I'm leaving the country, Howard."

"I don't understand . . . !"

"I mentioned to you a few moments ago about my facing two emergencies, and I know of no other way to say it. Two catastrophic events coming together at the same time, and although I am a deeply religious man, I have to ask where is my God?"

"What happened, Nils . . . ?"

"It began years ago when I was in Europe. My marriage was falling apart—" Van Nostrand replayed his litany of sorrow, love, illegitimacy, and subsequent horror to the same effect he had evoked in his previous appeals. "I must leave, Howard, never, perhaps, to return."

"Nils, I'm so sorry! God, that's terrible!"

"We'll find a life, my love and I. I am a fortunate man in many ways, and I ask nothing of anyone. My affairs are in order, my transportation arranged."

"What a loss for all of us."

"What a gain for me, my friend, the greatest prize in my long years of modest accomplishments. Good-bye, my dear Howard."

Van Nostrand replaced the phone, his mind instantly shutting out the saddened, self-pitying image of the boring secretary of defense, except for the lingering knowledge that Howard Davenport was the only person to whom he had mentioned Hawthorne's name. He would think about that later. Now, however, Van Nostrand considered his *pièce du combat,* the death of Tyrell Hawthorne. It would be brutal and quick, but surgically precise, producing the greatest pain. The first bullets would be fired into the most sensitive organs. Then a pistol-whipped face, finally a long-bladed knife in the left eye, *l'occhio sinistro.* He would watch it all, avenging the death of his lover, the *padrone.* And, at the last, from far away, he would hear the whispered accolades accorded him in the corridors of power.... *"A true patriot." "A finer American there never was!" "What he must have gone through! With all his other problems." "He never would have permitted it had that scum Hawthorne not made extraordinary threats!" "Keep it quiet! We can't allow questions!"*

Mars undoubtedly would have screamed: *"Ècco! Perchè? We buy these kills from the families! Why do you do it this way?"*

"La mente di un serpente," would undoubtedly have been Neptune's reply. "The cunning of a snake, *padrone.* I strike, then I must vanish into the underbrush, never to be seen again. But there must be those who know the snake was there, even if he was in the skin of a saint. Besides, your families talk too much, negotiate, ponder too long. The quickest way is to call in debts from men in high office, above suspicion, so that when my 'death' occurs, they can mourn together, confirming the loss of a saint. *Finito! Basta!"*

After the death of Tyrell Hawthorne.

"His name was *Hawthorne?"* Tyrell asked in astonishment of the half-drunken pilot and owner of a whorehouse in Old San Juan. "What the hell are you saying?"

"I'm telling you what the spook told me," answered Alfred Simon. He was slowly sobering up at the sight of the two weapons leveled at his head. "Also, what I could read in the flight deck's light. The name on the ID was Hawthorne."

"Who's your contact?"

"What contact . . . ?"

"Who hires you?"

"How the hell do I know?"

"You have to get messages, your instructions!"

"One of my girls. Somebody comes in to check out the merchandise and leaves a note with the broad and passes her a few extra dollars. I get the note an hour or so later. It's standard, and I don't even press for the extra bread, which, incidentally, because I treat my girls right, they've told me about."

"I don't follow you."

"On a good night, which of these *putas* can remember who had her last, or next to last, or even next to last after that?"

"He's really an 'X-rated outside,' Commander," said Poole.

" 'Commander'?" The pilot had sat forward on the couch. "You a big gun?"

"Big enough for you, *babe*. . . . Which of your girls gave you the instructions for Gorda?"

"The one I was porking—she's one hell of a kid, only seventeen—"

"You son of a bitch!" roared Poole, smashing his fist into the pimp's face, sending the pilot back into the pillows, his mouth bleeding. "My sister was that age once, and I ripped the bastard to pieces who tried that shit on her!"

"Stop it, Lieutenant! We're interested in information, not reformation."

"I get goddamned pissed off at people like this scum."

"I understand that, but right now we're looking for something else. . . . You asked if I was a commander,

Simon, and the answer is yes, I am. I'm also wired into D.C. intelligence, way high up. Does that answer your question?"

"Can you get them off my back?"

"Can you give me something to make me try?"

"Okay . . . okay. Most of my dark-flannel missions are made at night, between seven o'clock and eight, and always from the same runway. The same air controller gives me the green light for takeoff; it never varies, he's always the same one."

"What's his name?"

"They don't give names, but he's bright, and he's got a high-pitched voice and he coughs a lot, but he's always the one assigned to my equipment. For a long time I thought it was just coincidence, then I began to think it was weird-plus."

"I want to talk to the girl who gave you the message for Gorda."

"Man, are you kidding? You boys blew 'em away! They won't come back until the front door is fixed and everything looks normal."

"Where does she live?"

"Where does she live—where do they *all* live? Right here, with maids to clean their rooms, do their laundry, and fix them damn good meals. Let's get something straight, big gun. I was an officer too, and I know how to keep my mechs in top form."

"You mean if your front door isn't replaced—"

"They'll stay away. Wouldn't you?"

"Hey, Jackson—"

"Don't bother," the lieutenant said. "You got tools somewhere, whoremaster?"

"Downstairs, in the cellar."

"I'll go look." Poole disappeared through the basement door.

"How long are those air controllers on duty during the seven to eight o'clock shift?"

"They come on at six and leave at one, which means

you've got an hour and twenty minutes to reach him—
say an hour-minus, since you're at least fifteen to twenty-
five minutes to the airport, if you've got a fast car."

"We don't have a car."

"Mine's for rent. A thousand dollars an hour."

"Give me the keys," said Hawthorne, "or you've got
a tunnel between your ears."

"Be my guest," the pilot replied, reaching to the side
table and retrieving a ring of keys. "It's in the back lot,
a white Caddy convertible."

"Lieutenant!" shouted Hawthorne, ripping out the
only telephone in the room and backing toward the cellar door, his gun in his hand. "We're moving, let's go!"

"Hell, man. I found a couple of old doors down here
that I could—"

"Stow it, and get up here. We're going to the airport
and we've got to get there in less time than we've got."

"I'm on your side, Commander." Poole raced up the
steps. "What about him?" said the lieutenant, staring at
Simon.

"Oh, I'll be here, yo-yo," the pilot replied. "Where
the hell am I going?"

The aircraft controller was nowhere in the tower, although the others easily identified him by the description
of his high-pitched voice. His name was Cornwall, and
his colleagues had been erratically, dangerously, covering for him for the past forty-five minutes. So perilous
was his absence that a controller who was taking a stress-
relief break was called in to replace him.

The missing man was found by a cook in the galley,
a bleeding red spot in the center of his forehead. The
airport police were summoned and the questioning began, interrogations that lasted nearly three hours. Tyrell's replies were those of a professional, an admixture
of ignorance, innocence, and concern for a friend of a
friend he had never met.

Finally released, Hawthorne and Poole raced back to the whorehouse in Old San Juan.

"Now I'll fix the door," said the confused, angry lieutenant, heading down to the basement as an exhausted Tyrell fell into a soft chair. The owner of the establishment had passed out on the couch. In moments, Hawthorne was asleep.

Sunlight burst through the room as Tyrell and the pilot sat up, rubbing their eyes, trying to adjust to the reality of day. Across the room, on a green chaise longue, lay Poole, his soft, winsome snoring somehow reflecting the essentially gentle man that he was. Where the shattered front door had been was a perfectly acceptable substitute; it was all intact, including a slat in the upper panel.

"Who the hell is he?" asked the severely hung-over Alfred Simon.

"My military chargé d'affaires," answered Hawthorne, getting unsteadily to his feet. "Don't make a move against me or he'll smash you to smithereens with one foot."

"The way I feel, Minnie Mouse could do that."

"I gather you're not flying today."

"Oh, no, I've got too much respect for reflexes to get near a plane."

"Glad to hear it. You haven't got a hell of a lot of respect for much else."

"I don't need a lecture from you, sailor, I just need to know you can help me."

"Why should I? The man was dead."

"*What?*"

"You heard me, that air controller was shot, a bullet in the middle of his forehead."

"Jesus Christ!"

"Maybe you tipped someone off that we were going after him."

"How? You tore out the phone!"

"I'm sure there are others—"

"One other, and it's in my room on the third floor, and if you think I could have managed those steps last night, then I'm in the wrong business. I should have been an actor. Also, why would I? I want your help."

"A certain logic's on your side. . . . Then we must have been followed here. Whoever it was knew we'd found you but figured we were looking for someone else beyond you."

"You know what you're saying, don't you?" Simon's cold eyes were riveted on Hawthorne. "You're saying that since I'm part of the chain, I could be next—with a bullet in *my* forehead!"

"The thought crossed my mind—"

"Well, for Christ's sake, do something!"

"What do you suggest? . . . Incidentally, after three o'clock this afternoon I'm occupied with another matter. I'll be gone."

"And leave me in this fucking mess?"

"Let's put it this way," said Tyrell, glancing at his watch. "It's six-fifteen, so we've got roughly nine hours to figure something out."

"You could get me protection in nine goddamned minutes!"

"It's not that easy. Taxpayers' money used to harbor a rogue U.S. pilot who happens to own a whorehouse? Think of the congressional hearings."

"Think of my life!"

"Last night you challenged me to pull the trigger—"

"I was drunk, for God's sake! You're so fucking pure, you never got pissed and found out that you didn't particularly like the way things were?"

"I'll let that pass. We've still got nine hours, so let's start thinking. And the better you think, the closer I am to getting you protection. . . . How did they first recruit you?"

"Hell, it was years ago, I can hardly remember—"

"Remember now!"

"A big guy, like you, but with gray hair, very high-class; good-looking face—y'know, like those advertisements for fancy men's clothes. He came to me and said that all the bad bullshit about me could be stricken from the records if I did what he wanted."

"Did you?"

"Sure, why not? I started running Cuban cigars—can you believe that, Cuban *cigars*—they came wrapped, waterproof cartons dropped by instant chutes into the fishing grounds forty miles off the Keys in Florida."

"Drugs," said Hawthorne, no question in his reply.

"They sure as hell weren't cigars."

"And you kept doing this?"

"Let me tell you something, Commander. I got a couple of kids in Milwaukee I've never even seen, but they're mine. I don't push drugs, and when I put two and two together and came up with four, I told them I was out. That's when the big fancy man, who walked like a swish, made it clear that the government would come down on me like a meat ax. I either did what they said or I was in Leavenworth. I wouldn't be able to send any more money to Milwaukee. For my two kids I've never seen."

"You're a very complicated man, Mr. Pilot."

"Tell me about it. I need a drink."

"Your bar's within lurching distance. Get one. And then start thinking further."

"Well," said the damaged whoremaster, weaving toward the bar. "There's always, like maybe once, twice, or three times a year, an uptight son of a bitch with a jacket and a tie who comes here and asks for the best toaster—"

"Toaster?"

"Oral sex, what can I say?"

"And?"

"He has a good time, but he never touches the girl, you know what I mean?"

"It's not exactly in my frame of reference."

"He never takes his clothes off."

"So?"

"So that's not exactly natural. So, naturally, I got curious and had one of my girls give him a rocket—"

"A rocket?"

"A little powder in his drink that sends him into space."

"Thank you."

"And guess what we found? In his wallet are a dozen IDs, business cards, country club memberships, the whole ball of wax. He's a lawyer, a real high-class attorney from one of those megabucks firms in Washington."

"What was your conclusion?"

"I don't know, but it's not normal, you know what I mean?"

"I'm not sure I do."

"A zipper-jock like that can get whatever he wants in the uptown joints—why does he come downtown? To a place like this?"

"Because it *is* 'downtown.' Anonymity, that's understandable."

"Maybe, but maybe not. The girls tell me he's always asking questions. Like who are my customers; who looks maybe Arab or light-skinned African—what the hell has that got to do with good old plain sex?"

"You think he's a conduit?"

"I don't know what that means."

"Someone who carries information, but doesn't necessarily know from whom to whom."

"You got me."

"Could you identify him? In case his IDs were garbage."

"Sure. Class acts stand out down here." The pilot poured himself a half glass of Canadian whiskey, downing it with several swallows. *"Similis similibus curantor,"* he intoned while closing his eyes and belching.

"I beg your pardon?"

"It's an old medieval prayer. Translated, it means 'the hair of the dog.' "

"Okay, we've got two 'class acts': The man who recruited you, and a lawyer from D.C. who doesn't take off his clothes in a whorehouse. What're their names?"

"The recruiter called himself Mr. Neptune, but I haven't seen him or talked to him in years. The legal beagle's name is Ingersol, David Ingersol, but like I said, he may be just a weird cipher."

"We'll check him out. . . . Before Gorda, what was your last job?"

"My bread and butter, besides this place, is legit tourist stuff—"

"I mean related to your recruiter," Tyrell interrupted.

"Seaplane runs, usually once a week, sometimes twice, to a crummy little island you can barely find on the charts."

"With a cove, a short dock, and a house built into the hill."

"Yeah! How did you know?"

"It's gone."

"The island?"

"The house. What did you fly there? Or who?"

"Supplies, mainly. Lots of fruit and vegetables and fresh meat—whoever lived there didn't like frozen junk. And visitors, guests for the day who I'd pick up late in the afternoon; they never stayed overnight. Except one."

"What do you mean? Who was it?"

"No names were ever used. She was a woman and one hell of a looker."

"A woman?"

"And then some, pal. French, Spanish, or Italian, I don't know which, but a long-legged broad, maybe in her thirties."

"*Bajaratt!*" whispered Hawthorne to himself.

"What did you say?"

"Nothing. When did you last see her? Where?"

"A couple of days ago. I dropped her off at the island after picking her up in St. Barts."

Tyrell gasped, his breath suspended, no air permitted into his lungs. *Madness! . . . Dominique?*

16

"**Y**ou're *lying*!" Hawthorne gripped the pilot by his soiled shirt, causing the man to drop his glass, which shattered on the floor. "Who the hell *are* you? First you use my name for a killer on your fucking plane from Gorda, now you're telling me a close friend, a very close friend, is the psycho bitch half the world is looking for! You're a goddamned *liar*! Who put you up to it?"

"What's all this caterwaulin' about?" A startled Jackson Poole, awakened by the noise, swung his legs over the chaise longue.

"Let go of me, you fruitcake!" The pilot clutched at the bar to steady himself. "You got shoes on; I don't and there's broken glass all over the place!"

"And in ten seconds I'll scrape your face across it! Who told you to do this?"

"What the fuck are you talking about?"

"It's Amsterdam all over again! What do you know about Amsterdam?"

"For Christ's sake, I've never been there! . . . Lemme *go*!"

"The woman on St. Barts! Light or dark hair?"

"Dark. I told you, Italian or Spanish—"

"How tall?"

"With heels, about my size, and I'm five nine—"

"Face . . . complexion?"

"She was tan, like from the sun—"

"What was she wearing?"

"I don't know—"

"Think!"

"White, it was white—a dress or a pantsuit—kinda businesslike."

"Son of a bitch, you're *lying*!" shouted Tyrell, forcing the man's back over the bar.

"Why the hell would I do that?"

"He's not lyin', Tye," said Poole. "He hasn't got the strength or the stomach for it; he's washed out."

"Oh, my *God*!" Hawthorne dropped his hands and turned away from both men, half whispering, half pleading. "Oh, my God, oh, God, oh, God!" He walked slowly toward the thick window that overlooked the filthy cobblestone street, his eyes glazed, a throated cry coming from deep inside him. ". . . Saba, Paris . . . Barts—all *lies*. Amsterdam, *Amsterdam!*"

"Amsterdam?" the pilot asked innocently as he lurched from the bar and carefully moved away, his bare feet avoiding the broken glass.

"Shut up," said Jackson quietly, staring at the trembling figure of Tyrell Hawthorne by the window. "The man's hurtin', sky pig."

"What's it got to do with me? What did I do?"

"Told him something he didn't want to hear, I guess."

"I just told him the truth."

Suddenly, furiously, Hawthorne whipped around, his eyes now glaring, focused, and filled with horror. "A phone!" he bellowed. "Where's your other telephone?"

"Three flights up, but the door's locked. The key's somewhere over—" It was as far as the pilot got. Tyrell was taking the steps three at a time, his pounding feet echoing throughout the old whorehouse. "Your commander's a maniac," said the owner. "What did he mean when he said I used his name before? That crazy spook on the plane was as clear as a compass fix. 'My name's Hawthorne.' He must have repeated it three or four times."

"He was lying. *That's* Hawthorne."

"*Holy—*"

"Nothin's holy about this whole damn thing," Poole said quietly.

Hawthorne repeatedly crashed his shoulder against the door of the pilot's private quarters on the third floor; the lock sprang on the fifth attempt. He rushed inside, momentarily bewildered by the neatness of the open, connecting rooms. He had expected a slovenly mess; instead, the suite might have been designed for an article in *Town and Country,* the furniture masculine, a mixture of expensive leather and dark wood, the walls paneled in light oak, the paintings costly reproductions of the Impressionists—diffused light, bright colors, gentle figures and gentler gardens. A man was denying himself in these rooms.

Where was the telephone? Tyrell raced through an arch into the bedroom; all around, on the bureau, the desk, the bedside tables, were framed photographs of two children, the same children pictured at varying ages. *There was the phone*—on the table at the right side of the bed. He ran to it, taking a piece of paper out of his jacket pocket—a number in Paris. Again he was momentarily stopped by the sight of another photograph. It was a picture of two young adults, a boy and a girl, both attractive and who looked remarkably alike. Good Lord, they're *twins*! thought Hawthorne. They were dressed in collegiate attire, a pleated plaid skirt and white blouse for the girl; a dark blazer and a striped tie for the boy. They were standing, smiling, beside a sign that read:

University of Wisconsin
Admissions Office

Then Tyrell saw the writing at the bottom of the photograph. The lettering was small but precise, the date a few years earlier.

They're still inseparable, Al, and in spite of the quarrels, they look after each other. You'd be proud, as they are of their father who died serving his country. Herb sends his best, as do I, and we thank you for your help.

A very, very complicated man, the pilot.
No time!
Hawthorne picked up the phone, waited for the dial tone, then pressed the numbers for Paris, reading them carefully from the scrap of paper.

"*La maison de Couvier,*" said the female voice three thousand miles away.

"Pauline?"

"Ah, monsieur, it is you, *n'est-ce pas*? Saba?"

"That's one of the things I have to ask her about. Why wasn't she there?"

"Oh, *I* asked her, monsieur, and madame said she never mentioned this Saba to you—you must have assumed it. Her uncle moved to a nearby island more than a year ago. His previous neighbors became too curious, too intrusive, and she saw no reason to—how do you say it?—take the time to explain, as she was flying immediately back to Paris and knew where to reach you when she returned."

"That's a very convenient explanation, Pauline."

"*Monsieur,* you are not filled with the jealousy—no, it cannot be, for there is no reason! You are always in her heart, I alone know that."

"I want to talk to her. Now!"

"She is not here, you know that."

"What's the hotel?"

"No hotel. Madame and monsieur are on a Monegasque yacht in the Mediterranean."

"Yachts have telephones. What's the oceangoing number?"

"I do not know, believe me. *Maintenant,* the madame is telephoning me in an hour or so, as we are to prepare a dinner party next week for the Swiss from Zurich. They dine quite differently—so German, you understand."

"I've got to talk to her!"

"Then you will, monsieur. Leave a number for me and I shall have her call you. Or call me back and I shall have a number for you. It is no problem."

"I'll do that." *A yacht in the Mediterranean, its telephone number not left in Paris in case of emergencies? Who was the woman who had gotten on Simon's plane in St. Barts? To what lengths would those who knew about Amsterdam go to drive him out of his mind? Someone dressed like Dominique inserted into the crazy mosaic! . . . Or was he lying to himself? Had he lied to himself in Amsterdam? If so, the lying had to stop.*

Tyrell hung up the phone, his trembling hand still on it, determined yet reluctant to call Henry Stevens in Washington. The fact that NVN, whoever he was, had gone around the chief of naval intelligence to reach the widower from NATO carried a message, but Hawthorne could not know what it was until three o'clock in the afternoon. He could wait until Stevens called him at the hotel in Isla Verde, which the captain surely would, or perhaps had—oh, Jesus, *Cathy!* He had forgotten about her; worse, Poole had also. Tyrell dialed immediately.

"Where have you two been?" cried Nielsen. "I've been worried sick. I've come very close to calling the consulate, the naval base—even your friend Stevens in D.C."

"You didn't call him, did you?"

"I didn't have to. He's called here three times since four o'clock this morning."

"You talked to him?"

"We're in the same suite of rooms, remember? He and I are practically on a first-name basis."

"You didn't say anything about the message I got last night—"

"Come on, Tye," protested Cathy. "I used to keep

our heifers' secrets too, and they only slept around a lot. Of course I didn't."

"What did he say—what did you say?"

"He wanted to know where you were, naturally, and naturally I told him I didn't know; and then he wanted to know when you'd be back, and I gave him the same answer. That's when he blew up and asked me if I knew *anything*. I told him I'd learned something about 'contingency funds' . . . he didn't think it was funny."

"Nothing's funny any longer."

"What happened?" asked the major quietly.

"We found the pilot and he led us to someone else."

"That's progress."

"Not much. The man was dead before we got there."

"Oh, my *God*! Are you all right? When are you coming back?"

"As soon as we can."

Hawthorne depressed the lever, cutting off the line; he waited several seconds, collecting his thoughts, one overriding everything else, consuming him. A tall woman in white with an attractive face tanned by the sun—taken from St. Barts and flown to the *padrone*'s island fortress. . . . Coincidence was nonexistent in the world he had left and was now propelled back into; manipulated insertion, one person for another with split-second timing, too inconceivable! . . . Oh, Christ, he was falling apart! *Stop it! Bring yourself back, block out the pain!* There was another insertion all too real, a note from an unknown NVN who would call him at three o'clock in the afternoon. *Concentrate!* . . . Dominique . . . ? *Concentrate!*

He lifted the phone and dialed Washington. Moments later Henry Stevens was on the line. "That A.F. major said she didn't know when you left, where you were, or when you'd be back. What the hell's going on?"

"You'll get a full report later, Henry. Right now I'm going to feed you four names, and I need whatever backgrounds you can dig up on them."

"How soon?"

"Try an hour."

"You're nuts."

"They could be close to Bajaratt—"

"You've got it. Who are they?"

"First is someone who calls himself Neptune, Mr. Neptune. Basic description is tall, distinguished, gray hair, say in his sixties."

"That's half the male population in Georgetown. The next?"

"A Washington lawyer named Ingersol—"

"As in Ingersol and White?" Stevens interrupted.

"Probably. Do you know him?"

"I know of him, most people do. David Ingersol, son of a highly respected former Supreme Court justice, Burning Tree and Chevy Chase golfer, friend to the powers that be and something of a power himself. Christ, you're not suggesting that Ingersol is part of—"

"I'm not suggesting anything, Henry," broke in Hawthorne.

"The hell you're not! And let me tell you, Tye, you're as far off base as you can get. I happen to know that Ingersol has done more than a few favors for Central Intelligence during his Euro-business trips."

"That makes me off base?"

"He's very well thought of over at Langley. The Agency isn't my favorite organization around here, they step on too many toes, as you damn well know, but their background checks beat anything in town, I can vouch for it. I can't believe they'd use someone like Ingersol without putting his head under a microscope."

"Then they missed the lower parts."

"What?"

"Look, as my source said, he may be just a weird cipher, but he was seen on the premises of someone who is involved—peripherally, blind on blind—but he was there."

"Okay, I've got a new relationship with the DCI. I'll go right to him. Who else?"

"An air controller at San Juan named Cornwall. He's dead."

"Dead?"

"Shot in the head shortly before we reached him at one o'clock this morning."

"How did you uncover him?"

"That's the fourth name, and with this one you've got to go subterranean."

"He's that close?"

"No, he's an X-outside. He's the source I just mentioned and deals only with blinds, but someone in your town has him on a leash. Whoever's on the other end of that leash could be a breakthrough."

"You're telling me that this Bajaratt has accomplices in the upper-level bureaucracy? Not just isolated bribes but honest-to-Christ accessories in the D.C. establishment?"

"Believe it."

"What's the name?"

"Simon, Alfred Simon. He was an underage drop pilot out of Vientiane, A.I.D., flying Royal Lao."

"CIA," said Stevens. "Those good, bad old days. Pouches filled with bribe money dropped to the tribes in the hills of Laos and Cambodia. The Montagnards took the worst beating; they were paid the most so the pilots stole the most from them. . . . How could anyone in Washington put a leash around somebody like that? You'd think it'd be the other way around."

"They unloaded their subsidiary aircraft on him, getting a young kid fly-boy to sign highly questionable papers of transfer when he was probably drunk. That way he's stigmatized as a mercenary and a thief, a soldier of fortune in it for the big money with no affiliation with our pure U.S. personnel."

"Then they pull the rug out and build a corruption

case against him, reversing the scam. He's got his dirty hand in the Washington cookie jar while our brave boys are dying."

"It's one hell of a rotten scenario."

"It is and it's classic, and he wouldn't have to be drunk, just greedy. He thinks he's been given merchandise worth a few million, especially if he's young, but doesn't realize he's on the hook for life while the spy junkies are off it. . . . I know just who to reach to find out what's buried on one Alfred Simon, pilot, A.I.D., Vientiane."

"Can you make sure no one will know you're looking?"

"All the way to the max," affirmed the head of naval intelligence. "Our source was an overseas case officer who moved up into the rarefied ranks of the analysts, but who also had her hand in a cookie jar, the Agency's, and we caught her dead to rights. Naturally, nothing was ever said, but you might say she's one of our stringers."

"Get back to me at the hotel," said Hawthorne. "If I'm delayed or not there, give everything you've got to Major Neilsen. She's now certified four-zero, unless you idiots have changed the classification."

"The way she sounds, is she certified for anything else?"

"Get off my back, Captain. Without her we'd be dead."

"Sorry, just trying to bring a touch of levity into a very trying situation."

"You're solid lead, Henry. Go to work, call me, and then go home to your wife and 'trip the light fantastic.' " Hawthorne slammed down the phone, aware that beads of sweat had formed at his hairline. What next? He had to keep moving! He had to stay in motion—he could not think of things that he . . . dared not think about. Yet he had to! He could lie to others, but not to himself, not any longer. Saba, a reclusive uncle, a confidante in Paris, benevolent causes—protestations of love. All lies.

Dominique! Dominique Montaigne was Bajaratt!

He would hunt her down or be killed in the attempt. Nothing on earth could stop him now. *Betrayal!*

At Central Headquarters, San Juan, Homicide Division, the murdered air controller's wife, one Rose Cornwall, had put on a superb performance for the Puerto Rico police. She was stoic and courageous despite the tragic loss that was obviously tearing her apart. . . . No, no, she could not help. Her loving husband hadn't an enemy in the world, for he was the kindest, most gentle man the good Lord ever gave life to, ask their parish priest. Debts, no; they lived well but always within their budget. Habits such as gambling in the casinos? Infrequently, and only at the slot machines, usually the twenty-five-cent variety where they limited themselves to twenty dollars apiece. Drugs? *Never;* he could barely take an aspirin, and he had cut down his cigarettes to just one after meals. Why had they come to Puerto Rico from Chicago five years ago? It was a far more comfortable life-style; the climate, the beaches, the Rain Forest—he loved to wander for hours in the Rain Forest—and without the terrible pressures of Chicago's O'Hare Airport.

"May I go home now? I'd like to be alone for a while until I call our priest. He's a wonderful man and will make the arrangements."

Rose Cornwall was escorted to her condominium in Isla Verde, but she did not telephone her priest. Instead, she called a number in Mayagüez.

"Listen, you son of a bitch, I covered for you shit-heads and now I want mine," the widow Cornwall said.

*   *   *

The telephone rang in the El San Juan suite as Catherine Neilsen sat at the desk, reading the newspaper account of the airport murder. She reached over quickly and picked up the bellowing, shrill instrument.

"Yes?"

"It's Stevens, Major."

"Call number five, if I can count."

"You can, and I presume he's there. I talked to him an hour and a half ago."

"Yes, he told me. He's in the shower, both of them are in showers, and let me tell you, they should stay in them for a long time. This place smells like a sickening flower spray."

"A what . . . ?"

"A whorehouse, Captain. Which is where they were, so I suppose it makes sense."

"What?"

"You do repeat yourself, don't you, sir?"

"Get him out of there! He's the one who put a priority-red on this data."

"I hope I don't shock him. Hold on, please." Neilsen walked into Hawthorne's bedroom, then to the bathroom door. Listening, she hesitated, then opened it, only to find a naked Tyrell drying himself with a huge towel. "Sorry to intrude, Commander. D.C. on the phone."

"Did you ever hear of knocking?"

"Not when a shower's on."

"Oh. . . . I forgot."

Wrapped in the towel, Hawthorne walked rapidly past the major to the bedroom phone. "What have you got, Henry?"

"On 'Neptune,' almost nothing—"

"What do you mean almost?"

"The southern hemisphere computers came up with a single entry. Apparently, years ago, there was a Neptune in Argentina, part of the generals' coup down there, but it was only a rumored nickname for some foreigner close to the big boys. No other information except for a Mr. Mars, same classification."

"Ingersol?"

"Whistle-clean, Tye, but you got Puerto Rico right. He flies down four or five times a year to service clients, all checked out, all legitimate."

"Only he's the client," said Hawthorne.

"How do you mean?"

"Never mind. A weird cipher. What about the controller, Cornwall?"

"A little more interesting. He was head of his section at O'Hare Airport, a bright guy making decent money but no threat to the country-club set by a long shot. However, a little digging turned up his wife's owning a piece of an old Chicago steak house. It's no Delmonico's, but it's one of the most popular in that section of the city, and she— read 'they'— sold her piece for a lot less than it's worth when they moved to Puerto Rico. It was a decent annual dividend."

"Which raises a question," interrupted Tyrell. "Where did they get the money to buy that kind of annuity?"

"There's another question that might be the answer to that," said Stevens. "How does an air controller in San Juan, where the pay doesn't compare to O'Hare, buy a six-hundred-thousand-dollar condominium on the beach in Isla Verde? Her restaurant share could barely cover a third of it."

"Isla Verde . . . ?"

"The beachfront there is the better part of town."

"I know, it's where we're staying. Anything else on our mobile Cornwalls?"

"Opinion time, nothing in concrete."

"Translation, please?"

"They put air controllers through a battery of tests to see if they can handle the job. Cornwall passed among the elite—cold as ice, quick and methodical—but it seems he preferred night duty, in fact, insisted upon it, which is pretty unusual."

"He did the same down here, that's how my source fingered him. What was the opinion in Chicago?"

"That his marriage was on the rocks, maybe beyond repair."

"It obviously wasn't, since they came down here together and bought a condo for six hundred thousand."

"I said it was opinion time, not fact."

"Unless it's based on information that had him chasing women."

"The tests don't go that far. They need controllers. It just appeared that he didn't care to stay home nights."

"I'll follow up," said Hawthorne. "What about the subterranean, our pilot, Alfred Simon?"

"He's either lying to you or he's the sickest joker I've ever heard of."

"What?"

"He's pure Clorox with a couple of medals waiting for him if he ever surfaces. There's no mention of his taking over any Lao aircraft, illegitimately or otherwise. He was a very young air force second lieutenant who volunteered for hazardous operations out of Vientiane, and if he ever stole anything, no one ever reported it. If he walked into the Pentagon tomorrow, they'd hold a ceremony, hand him a few clusters for his air medals, and give him some hundred and eighty thousand-plus dollars in hazardous pay and pension accruals that he's never picked up."

"Jesus Christ. I'll tell you straight, Henry, he doesn't know anything about this!"

"How do you know?"

"Because I'm damn sure where he'd send the money."

"You're beyond me."

"I hope so. The bummer is that he's traded a lie that's strangled him for years for a reality that could kill him today."

"Still beyond me—"

"He's been blackmailed into working for the wrong people. Bajaratt's crowd."

"What are you going to do?" asked Stevens.

"I'm not, you are. I'm sending Second Lieutenant Alfred Simon to the naval base here, and you're going to fly him up to Washington and put him under a blanket until it's safe for him to come out and become a quiet hero with a few extra dollars."

"Why now?"

"Because if we delay, it could be too late, and we need him."

"To identify Neptune?"

"Among others we may not know about yet."

"One Simon, first-class military to D.C.," said the head of naval intelligence. "What's next?"

"Air Controller Cornwall's wife. What's her first name?"

"Rose."

"Somehow I think her petals have withered." Hawthorne hung up the phone and looked over at Cathy, leaning against the door frame. "I want you and Jackson to go back to Old San Juan and get Simon over to the naval base. Quickly."

"I hope he doesn't misinterpret and try to recruit me."

"You're not the type." Tyrell lifted a telephone directory out of the bedside table shelf and leafed through the Cs.

"I'm not sure whether that's a compliment or an insult."

"Whores don't wear guns, the bulge spoils the curves, so make damn sure yours is in evidence."

"I don't have a gun."

"Take mine, it's on the bureau. . . . Here it is, *Cornwall,* the only one in Verde."

"What do you know?" said the major, taking the Walther P.K. automatic from the top of the bureau. "It's so small, it can fit into my purse."

"You've got a purse?" Hawthorne glanced up as

he scribbled the Cornwall address on the hotel memo pad.

"Well, normally I suppose I should wear a knapsack strapped to my back, but I've been carrying this lovely pearl-beaded handbag for the past twenty-four hours. It goes with the dress—Jackson approved."

"Hate the bastard. . . . Will you two get going?"

"He's just out of the shower, I can tell. He's still singing country, but it's too loud to be underwater."

"Then go dress the kid and get out of here. I really don't want another corpse on my hands, this one named Simon."

"Aye, aye, Commander."

Tyrell drove Alfred Simon's white Cadillac convertible into the parking lot of the Cornwalls' condominium complex. As Stevens had projected, it was the high-rent district of Isla Verde, not only on the beach, but with each apartment possessing its own wide, screened-in balcony overlooking the ocean and a huge, terraced pool below on either side.

Hawthorne got out of the car, walked up the path to the entrance, and gestured to the man on duty. As in all such buildings in the area, there was a uniformed doorman seated at a desk in a walled-off cubicle behind a sheet of thick glass; he pressed a button in front of him and spoke. "*Español* or *Ingles*, señor?"

"English," replied Tyrell. "I must see Mrs. Rose Cornwall, it's most urgent."

"Are you with the police, señor?"

"The police?" Hawthorne froze, but with the presence of mind to say casually but firmly, "Of course I am. United States Consulate, called by the police."

"Go right in, señor." The heavy door's buzzer released the lock and Tyrell went inside, turning instantly to the security guard beyond the open counter of the cubicle. "The Cornwalls' apartment number, please."

"Nine-oh-one, señor. Everyone is up there."

Everyone? What the *hell* . . . ? Hawthorne crossed rapidly to the bank of elevators and repeatedly stabbed the button until a door opened. The floors passed slowly, interminably, until he finally reached the ninth. He rushed out into the corridor, stopping abruptly at the sight of the crowd and the reflections in the hallway of repeated flashbulbs from inside the door twenty feet to his right. He strolled toward the gathering, noting that the majority of men and women were in police uniforms. Suddenly, a short, heavyset man in a gray suit and blue tie came out of the apartment, parting the bodies in front of him, flipping the pages of his notebook. He glanced up at Tyrell, then abruptly looked again, his dark eyes steady, disturbed. It was the police detective who had been at the airport barely eight hours before.

"Ah, señor, I see neither of us has gotten much sleep between tragedies. Her husband was killed last night and she this morning—and you, a stranger to both— unaccountably show up at both places."

"Cut it out, Lieutenant, I haven't got time for your bullshit. What happened?"

"You seem to have an extraordinary interest in this couple. Perhaps to deny your own involvement."

"Oh, sure, I dispatch each of them, then conveniently show up at the scenes of dispatch. *Boy*, am I smart. Now, come on, what happened?"

"Oh, be my guest, señor," said the detective, leading Hawthorne through the crowd into the living room of the condominium. It was a mess, furniture upturned everywhere, and everywhere shattered glass and china. However, there was no blood, no corpse. "This is the scene of your 'dispatch,' exactly as you expected to find it, am I right, señor?"

"Where's the body?"

"You do not know?"

"How could I?"

"Perhaps only you can answer that. You were at the

airport galley last night where we found the body of the air controller, the husband."

"Because someone kept screaming that he was in there!"

"And now you are here. Why is that?"

"That's confidential. . . . We can't have it all over your newspapers—we can't allow it."

"You cannot? Who are you, may I ask?"

"Tell me what happened, then maybe I'll answer."

"So the *americano* gives me orders?"

"It's a request, sir. I have to know."

"We will play your clever game, señor." The detective led Tyrell through the kneeling and bent-over fingerprint personnel to the balcony. The sliding doors were apart, the floor-to-ceiling screen split, as if by a heavy, sharp knife, the screen itself bent outward. "That is where the woman was pushed to her death nine stories below. Is it not familiar to you, señor?"

"What are you talking about?"

"Put the handcuffs on him!" the detective ordered the police officers behind Hawthorne.

"What?"

"You are my primary suspect, señor, and I have my reputation to think of."

Three hours and twenty-two minutes later, after vociferous arguing with a stubborn, self-important detective, Tyrell was permitted to make his very private telephone call. It was to Washington, and thirty-eight seconds after he hung up, a lower-echelon subordinate in the police department signed him out of jail with cursory apologies from his superiors. Hawthorne had no idea where Alfred Simon's Cadillac was being held, so he took a taxi back to the hotel.

"Where have you been for the past five hours?" Catherine asked.

"I rented a car downstairs and was about to slam a few knockers around this town!" added Poole.

"I was in jail," Hawthorne replied quietly, lying down on the couch. "Did you get Simon out?"

"With some difficulty," answered Neilsen. "To begin with, a somewhat snockered Mr. Simon did, indeed, think I'd be a nice addition to his stable—which was more of a compliment than I got from you."

"*Mea culpa.*"

"So we drove Simon to the base and poured a bucketful of coffee into him," Cathy continued. "Frankly, I don't think it helped much, he propositioned me twice in the wheelchair on the way to the aircraft."

"He's entitled. He's a bona fide hero."

"Entitled to *me*?"

"I didn't say that, I only said he was entitled to ask."

"Where do we go now?" asked Poole.

"What time is it?"

"Twelve minutes to three," answered Neilsen, watching Tyrell closely.

"Then we've got twelve minutes until we find out," said Hawthorne, sitting up, suddenly aware that he was perspiring . . . and the room was cool.

With each minute that passed, Tyrell's anxiety grew, uncontrollable images of Dominique/Bajaratt adding fury to his anxiety. He knew it would happen—he wasn't *doing* anything. Instead, he just kept moving, pacing aimlessly, almost grateful for the wasted hours at police headquarters, where the arguments and the pointless shouting had occupied him.

"It's three o'clock, Tye," said Cathy, "Would you rather we leave?"

Hawthorne stopped his erratic pacing; he studied both air force officers, his eyes shifting back and forth. "No," he said. "I want you here because I trust you."

"We care for you, Commander," added the major. "That's equally important."

"Thank you." Tyrell walked to the telephone and picked it up. He dialed.

"Yes?" The voice from Fairfax, Virginia, was cold, the single greeting drawn out as if the man speaking were reluctant to talk.

"It's Hawthorne."

"Please wait." There followed a series of short beeps before NVN returned. "Now we may speak freely, Commander," continued the voice, considerably more pleasant, "although our conversation would hardly be incriminating to either of us."

"Are we on tape? Is that what the noises were for?"

"Quite the opposite, we're on scrambler. A tape would only record garbled sounds. For both our sakes."

"Then you can say what you want to tell me. About Amsterdam."

"Not fully, for I need your eyes to complete the story."

"What do you mean?"

"Photographs. From Amsterdam. They show your wife, Ingrid Johansen Hawthorne, in the company of three men at four separate locations—the Zuiderkerk Zoo, the Rembrandt House, aboard a tourist canal boat, and at a café in Brussels. Each photograph indicates a confidential and highly intense conference. I am convinced that one, if not all three, were responsible for your wife's death, either by compromising her, or by the act itself."

"Who are they?"

"Not even on scrambler, Commander. I said one *if* not all three, and in truth I've identified only one. However, I'm certain you can identify the other two, but I can't. The files are closed, beyond my reach."

"Why are you so certain I can do that?"

"Because I've learned that they were among your covert assets in Amsterdam."

"That's more than thirty, perhaps forty, people. . . . You write that there was a Baaka connection."

"In the sense that the Baaka spreads its largess through Amsterdam as well as Washington."

"Washington?"

"Most definitely."

"And the 'aborted strategy' that may have come back? If two plus two is four, you're relating it to a current situation."

"I certainly am. Do you recall that five years ago, approximately three weeks before your wife was killed, the President of the United States was to attend a NATO conference in The Hague?"

"Sure, the whole thing was called off and moved to Toronto a month later."

"Do you remember why?"

"Of course. We'd picked up word that a dozen hit teams had been sent out of the Baaka to assassinate the President . . . and others."

"Precisely. The Prime Minister of Great Britain and the President of France among them."

"But where's the relationship, the connection?"

"I will explain it to you when you get here—after you identify the two unknown men, which I'm sure you can do. My plane will be at the General Aviation area at the San Juan Airport by four thirty; the counter will direct you. . . . Incidentally, my name is Van Nostrand, Nils Van Nostrand. And should you have any doubts about me, feel free to have your naval contacts put you in touch with the secretary of state, the director of the Central Intelligence Agency, and the secretary of defense. For God's sake, don't mention a word of what I've told you, but I believe they'll vouch for me."

"Those people are heavy cannons—"

"Also close friends and associates for many years," Van Nostrand interrupted. "If you simply say, in effect, that in your current professional status I've asked to meet with you, I'm quite sure they'll encourage you to do so."

"Which eliminates the need to make the calls," observed Hawthorne. "I'm traveling with two associates, Mr. Van Nostrand."

"Yes, I know. A Major Neilsen and a Lieutenant Poole, presently assigned to you by Patrick Air Force Base. I'm delighted to have them accompany you, but I'm afraid I cannot permit them to be at our meeting. There's a fine motel several miles down the road. I'll make reservations, billed to me, of course, and after you land, my car will take them there."

"*Christ!*" exploded Hawthorne suddenly. "If you had this information, why the hell did you wait so long to reach me?"

"It hasn't really been that long, Commander, and for obvious reasons, the time is right."

"Goddamn it, who's the man in the photographs you *did* identify? I'm a professional, Van Nostrand, and I've carried around in my head the names of more doubles and triples than you can count—while having pleasant dinners with all of them!"

"You insist?"

"I insist!"

"Very well. The man you've suspected for five years. Captain Henry Stevens, currently head of naval intelligence." Van Nostrand paused, then said, "He had no choice. It was either you killing him or the Soviets killing your wife. Stevens and she were lovers; they had been for several years. He couldn't let her go."

17

The figure moved in and out of the shadows along the path in Washington's Rock Creek Park, the intermittent streetlamps no match for the summer foliage. He heard the rushing waters from the ravine below and knew he was near the meeting ground; there was a bench equidistant from two lights on the dirt path. Half darkness, mostly darkness, for neither man could ever be seen with the other, it was a commandment never to be broken. Each was a Scorpio.

Seeing his colleague already seated on the bench, the glow of a cigar in his hand, David Ingersol approached, glancing back and forth, making sure they were alone. They were; he joined the man.

"Hello, David," said Scorpio Two, a heavyset, balding man with red hair, a pulled face, and a blunt nose.

"Good evening, Pat. Humid night, isn't it?"

"They say it isn't going to rain, but those assholes are usually wrong. I even brought an umbrella, one of that stupid kind that telescopes so short you can put it in your pocket, which is about all the damn thing's good for."

"I forgot one. I have a lot on my mind."

"That's pretty clear. The last time we met was over three years ago."

"This is far worse."

"Is it?"

"It's insane, you must know that," said Scorpio Three.

"I don't make such judgments. I'm a pretty wealthy man for following orders, not questioning them."

"To the point of your own self-destruction?"

"Hey, come on, Davey, we left the acolytes' brigade years ago when we sold our souls to the Providers."

"That sort of philosophical abstraction doesn't interest me. What does is protecting the assets we've accrued, what we've earned. That twisted, sick old man is dead, and with him went the senile insanity that produced this madness. . . . Ask yourself, O'Ryan, what possible benefit can we expect from an assassination—multiple assassinations?"

"None, except for the fact that we didn't stand in the way, which could be one hell of a benefit. Say, between our living or our being killed."

"Good God, by whom?"

"By the maniacs who are obsessed with this operation. She's not acting alone; she has her followers just as Abu Nidal and his types do. Maybe it's a smaller circle, but it's no less committed and no less resourceful. No, David, we do what Scorpio One tells us to do, and should anything happen to derail this crazy locomotive, he can report that we fulfilled our obligations. No blame can be directed at us."

"Report . . . ?"

"Jesus, Counselor, don't undermine my regard for your legal abilities by telling me you haven't thought through the Scorpios' place in the scheme of things. Well, maybe the law doesn't require such devious analysis, which I don't believe for a minute, but I've been an intelligence officer for twenty-six years, and I can spot a pyramid when a goddamn triangular quadrilateral mass is in front of my goddamned eyes. We may be three-quarters up; Scorpio One, seven-eighths, but there's a higher level and we're not it."

"I'm fully aware of the hierarchy, O'Ryan. I'm also aware of something you know nothing about."

"I find that hard to believe, since outside of Scorpio One I was the main man between the *padrone* and our small but important faction here. Frankly, as number two, I was the last person he spoke with before shutting down. He made that clear to me."

"I suspect he made one more call."

"Oh?"

"For all intents and purposes, by tomorrow morning, *I* will be Scorpio One. I'm afraid they saw fit to place me over you. All you have to do is call his secure number and you'll find it reaches me. That's your proof."

The Central Intelligence Agency analyst stared in the dim light at the lean, hard features of David Ingersol's face. Finally, he spoke. "I won't try to hide my disappointment, because I've been a hell of a lot more valuable than you, and I've got a far less advertised profile. On the other hand, you have your firm and the cars of certain people, and, I suppose, on that level it was inevitable. However, in my professional capacity, I've got to warn you, Davey. Be careful, very, *very* careful. You're too apparent."

"You don't understand, O'Ryan, that's my shroud. I'm respectability personified."

"Then don't ever go back to Puerto Rico."

"What?" It was as though Ingersol had been struck stark naked on the Beltway by a huge truck. "What are you . . . ?"

"You know what I'm talking about. Let's say I anticipated the news you just gave me. The fat Irish clown who eats too much and has a hot temper, and sometimes even wears white socks . . . passed over in favor of the fucking distinguished attorney with all the correct connections. Oh, you gotta believe he's got the impeccable Ivy League background, a Supreme Court justice for a father, a fine family belonging to all the right clubs— that makes you Scorpio One? You really think I can take that? . . . The *padrone* knew I was his head conduit here, and I can't believe he gave those instructions. You have nowhere near the access I have to international intelligence."

"Why Puerto Rico?" Ingersol asked in a terrified monotone, oblivious of Scorpio Two's diatribe.

"I have affidavits—only *I* have them, no one else— from the whores in a house on the Calle del Ocho in Old San Juan."

"I went there because Scorpio One instructed me to! I was checking up on the pilot!"

"To put it bluntly, S-Three, you went too far. One evening you even passed out—"

"Only briefly, barely a minute, and nothing happened! My money, my wallet, everything was intact! I was simply exhausted!"

"That doesn't matter, does it? I have the photographs, courtesy of my own sources in the Calle del Ocho, having nothing to do with our small fraternity here."

Ingersol repeatedly shook his head in slow, lateral movements, breathing deeply, his intensity lessening as he settled for a lawyer's reality, his own defeat. "What do you want, Patrick?"

"Control. I'm far more equipped than you. Everything you know you've learned from me. I'm in the Little Girl Blood circle, you're not."

"I can't change things, my name's been sent up."

"Oh, for Christ's sake, keep the title, I wouldn't think of taking it away from you. If I did, you'd have to disappear and that would raise too many questions. No, you're Scorpio One and you'll stay that way until your time comes, only I call the shots; it's better for everybody. You won't find it difficult; you'll be informed of everything."

"That's generous of you," said the attorney sarcastically.

"No, necessary. I'm not a generous man, but I can be amenable, isn't that the classy word? For instance, I agree with you, this craziness has to be aborted. It can only lead to the kind of chaos that hurts everyone. Every rock would be turned over and examined. We can't afford that."

"But in your words, we don't dare stand in the way. If anything happens to derail it, the Scorpios will be the first to be suspected, and I don't relish a Baaka Valley knife across my throat."

"Then we can't be in evidence; the credit has to go to our incredibly efficient intelligence service."

"They could find you, you know."

"A discovery I don't think you'd cry over, Davey-boyo, but actually they won't. I'll be on record as sending the troops in another direction with loud apologies afterward. Where's the woman now, do you know?"

"No one does. She and the young Latvian went underground, they could be anywhere."

"I cleared him through Lauderdale immigration, where they both went on to West Palm Beach. According to S-Twenty-two, they were last registered at a fleabag motel, then they disappeared."

"Anywhere," repeated Ingersol. "We don't know what they look like or where they are—no descriptions, no photographs—"

"MI-6 and the Deuxième sent us purported photographs of her; frankly, they're useless. It could be one person or three separate women, and considering her talent for changing appearances, no help at all."

"As you say, they've disappeared; we don't even know if they're traveling together or apart, or even what the young man's function is."

"He's a combination strong arm—a dull-witted bodyguard who does what he's told—and a necessary companion."

"I don't understand."

"From what the customs personnel in Marseilles can recall, he's a large, awkward Slovak kid they doubt can either read or write, but would probably break a man in half if ordered to."

"What is a 'necessary companion'?"

"The shrinks worked up a psychiatric profile based on everything they were fed by Israel's Mossad, and by Paris and London. A lot of it's psychobabble, but there's also some good common sense. . . . Like most fanatics, this Bajaratt does everything to excess, the extremes supposedly justifying what the head boys call the 'emotional intemperance' of her commitments. The profile suggests that she may be sexually active to the edge of nymphomania, but too careful to hop into strange beds, unless she does it on purpose. So, as a result, she needs a dumb stud whom she can control."

"They've vanished; they really could be anybody, anywhere, and always getting closer. What can we do? They could be simple tourists going through the White House, or protesters in front of it or on any side driveway with a bag full of grenades."

"All tours through the White House have been suspended—due to renovations, of course—and presidential motorcades into Washington have been eliminated. Both are unnecessary, frankly, because what you suggest isn't Bajaratt's style. Her tactics are to outwit and strike, not outgun and get slaughtered. It goes back to her childhood."

"Her childhood?"

"That's part of the access I have and you don't, Davey-boyo. It's why I'll be Scorpio One in all but the name."

"But what can we do?" Ingersol repeated.

"We wait. Before she strikes, she'll have to reach you, Scorpio One, if for no other reason than to facilitate her escape—that's assuming she survives."

"Suppose she's made her own arrangements?"

"Nobody in the field of black operations relies on one set of circumstances to get the hell out of ground-zero. That's another thing you don't know, S-Three. I've had covert field agents who've made out-of-sanction deals with three other departments, figuring I might not come through for them. It's standard. Loyalty's bullshit, survival is everything."

"Then you think she'll call me?"

"If she's got a brain in her head, she will, and I understand she's got a big one. . . . She'll call."

Amaya Bajaratt casually walked through the lobby of the hotel, very much the fortyish *contessa,* when she stopped, her whole body paralyzed. The blond-haired man at the front desk—the blond hair new, bleached—was a Mossad undercover agent, previously with dark brown hair, she had known in Haifa, slept with in Haifa! Gathering her thoughts, she hurried toward the elevators, instantly deciding the obvious. She and Nicolo had to move immediately—but *where*? And with what explanation? So many calls were coming to her at the hotel, calls from important men in the Senate and the House, politicians she was keeping on the Ravello string, not the least of whom was Nesbitt, the senator from Michigan, the man who could bring her to the ultimate confrontation, the final confrontation with the President of the United States. It was Wolfsschantze revisited, but she would be far more successful than the cadre of desperate generals who had opposed Adolf Hitler. . . . *Enough!* Now she had to get away from the hotel! She ran into an open elevator and pressed the button for the floor of her suite.

"Isn't she *beautiful,* Cabi?" cried Nicolo. He was sitting in front of the television set in the living room, watching a 6:30 rerun of Angel Capell's western series. "I spoke with her an hour ago, can you *believe* it? And there she *is!*"

"*Basta,* Nico! Remember, she is attracted to the *barone-cadetto* of Ravello, not an impoverished scum from the docks of Portici!"

"Why do you hurt me, signora?" asked Nicolo, his angry eyes locked with hers. "You said it was all right if I felt certain things about Angelina."

"Not any longer. We're moving!"

"Why?"

"Because I say so, you stupid boy," replied the Baj, going to the desk and the telephone. "Pack us, both of us. Now!" Bajaratt dialed the number that had been indelibly printed on her extraordinary memory. It was a single call, no pattern to be established, so she could use the hotel phone.

"Yes?" said the voice in Fairfax, Virginia.

"It is I, and I must have shelter, not at this hotel, not in Washington."

"Impossible. Not here, not tonight."

"I order you in the name of the *padrone,* and all his sources from the Baaka, through Palermo and Rome! They will hunt you down and kill you if you refuse me!"

Silence. Finally.

"I'll send a car for you, but we will not meet, not tonight."

"That doesn't matter. I need a telephone number. I have calls coming."

"You'll be in the farthest guest house on the compound, and each phone is on a dedicated line. When you're escorted there, you may call the hotel and give them the number. It's routed through the state of Utah and transmitted by satellite back here, so you have nothing to be concerned about."

"*Grazie.*"

"*Per cento anni, signora.* But I must warn you, tomorrow you are on your own."

"*Perchè?*"

"I will be gone, and you will know nothing. You are simply a friend from Europe who expects to hear from me soon, any hour, any day. However, you may use this number to reach my successor."

"I understand. Will I hear from you?"

"No. Never."

The Gulfstream jet entered the coastline of the United States east of Chesapeake Bay, over Cape Charles, Maryland. "Another fifteen minutes," said the pilot.

"Add a few," the copilot interrupted, studying the computerized map on the dashboard. "There's a rough front coming in, and we're circling north above it."

"Can you really land this bullet on someone's private property?" asked Poole. "You've got to have a three-thousand-plus strip."

The copilot glanced around at Poole in his civilian clothes. "You a pilot, mister?"

"Well, I've accumulated a few hours, nothin' like you fellas, but enough to know that you can't put this thing down in a cabbage patch."

"It's no patch, sir, it's a four-thousand-plus rug of asphalt with its own tower, which isn't exactly a tower 'cause it's like a glass cottage on the ground. We did a couple of practice runs this morning, and let me tell you, Mr. Van Nostrand goes first class."

"Apparently," said a visibly disturbed Hawthorne from the rear seat.

"You okay, Tye?" asked the major.

"I'm fine. I just want to get there."

Twenty-one minutes later the jet circled the vast, dark Virginia countryside. Below, cut out of the fields, was an airstrip bordered by amber lights; it was nearly a mile long. The pilot set the plane down, then taxied back to a waiting limousine; a golf cart was beside it.

Climbing out of the aircraft, the three passengers were met by two men, one in a black suit and a visored black hat, the other hatless, wearing a sport coat and tan slacks. Both were standing in the darkness in front of the amber lights.

"Commander Hawthorne?" said the hatless, jacketed man on the right, addressing Tyrell. "May I drive you in our cart to the main house? It's only a few hundred yards."

"Sure. Thanks."

"And the lady and the gentleman," said the chauffeur on the left. "Your rooms are ready for you at the Shenandoah Lodge, courtesy of Mr. Van Nostrand, of course. It's only ten minutes from here. Would you step into the limousine, please?"

"Certainly," replied Cathy.

"Nice wheels," said Poole.

"I'll join you later," added Hawthorne.

The driver of the golf cart stopped and looked at Tyrell. "Your accommodations are in the main house, sir. Everything's prepared for you."

"That's kind of Mr. Van Nostrand, but I have other plans after our meeting."

"He'll be very disappointed and I'm sure he'll persuade you to stay, Commander," added the chauffeur, opening the door of the limousine for Neilsen and Poole. "The chef has prepared a terrific dinner. I know, she's my wife."

"My apologies to her—"

"My Lawd, I forgot mah manners!" exclaimed Poole, turning from the huge Cadillac and looking over at the plane.

"What manners?" asked Cathy, leaning forward from inside the limousine.

"You and the commander said good-bye to those two pilots, but Ah didn't, and they were very nice showin' me how all those instruments work."

"What . . . ?"

"Be right back, y'all!" The lieutenant ran to the jet; he could be seen speaking briefly to the pilots, who were still in the flight deck, their lights on. Poole shook hands and walked rapidly back to the car as Hawthorne climbed into the golf cart, watching the young air force officer with curiosity. Poole had not only said good-bye to the pilots, he had done so effusively. "*There,* Ah feel better now. Mah daddy always says one should show courtesy and true gratitude to strangers who treat you kindly. Let's go, mister, Ah can't wait to have a hot shower; Ah haven't had one in days! My momma would strap me good for gettin' so mildewed. . . . See you later, Commander!" The lieutenant climbed into the limousine. Tyrell frowned as the golf cart drove between the amber lights and across a huge lawn toward the house.

The large Cadillac spun off the airstrip and entered a winding road that abruptly straightened; in the distance the headlights revealed a large iron gate with a guardhouse on the left side. There was another limousine as well; it had just been admitted and passed them in seconds, too rapidly for the occupants to be seen. Suddenly, Jackson Poole lurched from the rear seat onto the jump seat, and to Catherine's astonishment, he had the Walther automatic in his hand.

"Mah word, Mr. Driver, we gotta stop right now! Would you believe I forgot somethin'?"

"What was that, sir?" asked the startled chauffeur.

"Commander Hawthorne, you mudhog!" The lieutenant pressed the barrel of the automatic into the terrified driver's right temple. "Swing this mother around and shut off the headlights!"

"Jackson!" shouted Neilsen. "What are you *doing?*"

"This whole goddamned thing is rotten, Cathy. I said it before and I'll say it again—turn, you bastard, or your brains'll be all over the window!" The limousine made a swift, uncertain U-turn, careening into the grass as the chauffeur lunged to his right—a red alarm button! His hand never reached it. Poole hammered the gun into the man's neck, the crack sickening. The driver was instantly immobilized as the lieutenant yanked him away from his seat and plunged over the glassless partition, grabbing the wheel and steering the limousine into darkness; his foot found the brake. They slammed to a stop under the spreading limbs of a pine tree, less than seven feet head-on from the trunk. Poole arched his head back, breathing deeply.

"I think it's time for an explanation," said a shaken Neilsen from the back seat. "*Jackson,* you're implying that a man who told Tye openly to check him out with the secretaries of state and defense, along with the director of Central Intelligence, is not only a liar but something more than that!"

"If I'm wrong, I'll apologize, and quit the military, and join my little sister in California and get rich like she is."

"That's not an explanation, Lieutenant! Let's have it!"

"I went back to those two pilots—"

"Yes, you certainly did, telling us you hadn't said good-bye, which you most definitely had, and then announcing that you hadn't had a hot shower in days, when you spent forty-five minutes in one five hours ago in San Juan."

"I hope Tye got the message—"

"What message?"

"That things were rotten. Those two pilots aren't Van Nostrand's regulars," he explained. "The permanent airborne help is on vacation. Remember, they said they'd made a couple of practice runs this morning?"

"So? It's summer. People take vacations in summer!"

"What do we do when we want to keep a segment of an ongoing operation quiet?"

"We replace the personnel in relays, naturally. Usually from other bases. Again, so?"

"No contact, right?"

"Of course."

"Then put this together in your head, Cathy. Those

two sky jocks were clearing a civil flight plan to Douglass International in Charlotte, North Carolina, overseas departures, government escort to meet the plane in a secure area. There's supposed to be a single male passenger with diplomatic clearance authorized by the State Department. I tell you, those two pilots have never dealt on this level. They're a little nervous, and my guess is it's because they're not too clean."

"What aren't you telling me, Jackson?"

"They've been told the passenger is Van Nostrand himself, and they're scheduled to take off in one hour."

"In an hour?"

"Not much time for a fancy dinner and a damned important meeting, is it? The way I figure, those two jocks are sky vagrants, dishonorables or drug droppers who move from one job to another through the underground network."

"They seemed so nice—"

"You're a country girl, Cath, I'm from N'Orleans. We play a sweet trumpet while you get fleeced—not that *Ah* ever did such a thing—"

"What do we do now?"

"I hate bein' an alarmist, but do you still have Tye's weapon?"

"No. He strapped it to his leg."

"I'm checking our driver—*Christ,* he's got *two*! A big one and a little bitty thing. . . . Here, you take the big one and stay in the car; I'll put the other in my fancy jacket here. If anyone approaches the car, don't ask questions, just shoot; and if this son of a bitch moves, crack him good in the head."

"Bullshit, Lieutenant. I'm going with you!"

"I don't think you should, Major."

"I just gave you an order, Poole."

"There's an article in the Air Force Regulations that clearly states—"

"*Forget* it! Where you go, I go! What about the driver?"

"Give me a hand." Jackson pulled the chauffeur out of the limousine and started dragging him over the ground under the wide pine tree. "Take off his clothes, his shoes first," he continued as Cathy scurried alongside, yanking the driver's loafers off his feet. "Now the trousers," added Poole, reaching a tall hedgerow, where he stopped. "I'll take off his jacket and shirt . . . leave his shorts on, I'll get them last."

A minute later the stark-naked figure of the chauffeur was bound and gagged with strips of fabric torn from his clothing—none wide enough to service his dignity. The lieutenant delivered a final chop to the man's neck; the body shivered spastically, then once again was immobile.

"You didn't kill him, did you?" asked Neilsen, grimacing.

"If I stay here another five seconds, I may just do that. This bastard was gonna kill *us*, Cath, and I'm going to prove it to you."

"What are you talking about?"

"Let's go back to the limo, it's got a telephone. I'm damn sure I'm right."

Poole started the engine, activating the cellular phone, then yanked it out of its cradle and dialed information for the number of the Shenandoah Lodge. "This is an urgent call from Patrick Air Force Base," he said in monotonal officialese. "Please connect me with either Major Catherine Neilsen or a Lieutenant A. J. Poole. I repeat, this is an emergency."

"Yes, sir—*yes*, sir!" the flustered operator replied. "I'll check our room computers immediately." The line went silent; thirty-one seconds later a relieved operator came back on the phone. "There's no one by either name registered at the Shenandoah, sir."

"You need anything more, Major?" The lieutenant replaced the phone. "The bastard was going to kill us before we ever got to that place. Then maybe ten years from now our decomposed bodies are found in one of these 'Ginia swamps."

"We've got to get to Hawthorne!"

"You've got that right," Poole said.

Hawthorne was escorted into the enormous book-lined library of his host, Nils Van Nostrand. He declined a drink offered by the golf-cart driver, who stood in front of an elaborate glass-paneled bar.

"I drink only white wine, thanks," said Tyrell. "The cheaper the better and in small quantities."

"There's some excellent Pouilly-Fumé, sir."

"My stomach would revolt. It's used to lesser bouquets."

"As you wish, Commander, but I'm afraid I must ask you to remove the weapon attached to your right leg."

"My right *what* . . . ?"

"Please, sir," said the golf-cart chauffeur, taking a tiny plug out of his ear. "You've passed by four X-ray machines, from the front entrance through the hallway to this room. It was revealed on each camera. Remove it, please."

"It's just an old habit," said Hawthorne lamely, sitting down in the nearest chair and raising his trouser leg. "I'd do the same if I were meeting the Pope." He tore apart the Velcro, releasing the automatic, and kicked it across the floor. "Satisfied?"

"Thank you, sir. Mr. Van Nostrand will be here presently."

"You were the advance security, then?"

"My employer is a cautious man."

"He must have a lot of enemies."

"On the contrary, I couldn't possibly name one. He is, however, extremely wealthy, and as his chief of grounds security, I insist on certain procedures when people he does not know come to visit him. As a former intelligence officer, I'm sure you can approve."

"I obviously can't object. What were you, Army G-2?"

"No, Secret Service, assigned to the White House. The President was reluctant to see me go, but he understood the financial responsibilities of a married man with four children to put through college."

"You do your job well."

"I know. I'll be right outside the door when Mr. Van Nostrand arrives."

"Let's get something straight, Mr. Secret Service. I was brought here by your boss, I didn't invite myself."

"What kind of guest is it who straps a Walther P.K. to his leg? If I'm not mistaken, it's a favorite weapon of dangerous men."

"I told you, habit."

"Not here, Commander." He bent down and picked up the gun.

The door opened and the imposing figure of Nils Van Nostrand came into the room, his expression one of conviviality itself. "Good evening, Mr. Hawthorne," he said, approaching Tyrell and offering his hand as his visitor rose from the chair. "Forgive me for not greeting you when you arrived, but I was on the phone with a man I suggested you reach, the secretary of state. . . . I believe I recognize your jacket. Safarics, Johannesburg. Top grade."

"Sorry. Tony's Tropic Shop, San Juan Airport."

"Damn fine imitation. I dabbled for a while in fabrics. It's the pockets that make a bush jacket; all men like lots of pockets. At any rate, I do apologize for not meeting you at the airstrip."

"The time was put to good use," said Hawthorne, studying his host, almost mesmerized by Van Nostrand's appearance. *A big guy . . . with gray hair and very high-class . . . like those advertisements for fancy men's clothes.* "You've got terrific security."

"Oh, Brian here?" Van Nostrand laughed softly, gracefully, glancing kindly at his chief of grounds security. "Sometimes my good friend takes his job too seriously. I trust there was no inconvenience."

"None, sir." The man named Brian unobtrusively slipped the automatic into his pocket. "I offered the commander a drink, your Pouilly-Fumé, but he refused."

"Really? It's an excellent year, but then, perhaps Mr. Hawthorne prefers bourbon, sour mash to be precise."

"You've done your homework," said Tyrell, "but I'm afraid that's history."

"Yes, so I've been told. Would you please leave us, Brian? Our man in Amsterdam and I have confidential matters to discuss."

"Certainly, sir." The former Secret Service agent crossed to the door and let himself out.

"Now we're alone, Commander."

"We're alone, and you made an extraordinary statement concerning my wife and Captain Henry Stevens. I want to know what you've got to back it up."

"We'll get to that in time. Please, sit down, we'll chat for a few minutes."

"I don't care to chat! Why did you say what you did about my wife? You answer that and we may talk about other things, but it'll be a damn short conference."

"Yes, I was told you couldn't stay for dinner or even accept my hospitality for the night."

"I didn't come for dinner or to be your guest. I came to hear what you have to say about my wife's murder in Amsterdam and one Captain Henry Stevens. He may know something I don't, but you brought in another equation. Explain it!"

"I don't have to. You're here. And as eager as you are to learn of those circumstances, I'm equally filled with curiosity to know what happened on a certain obscure island in the Caribbean."

Silence. They stood only several feet apart, their eyes intensely on each other. Finally, Hawthorne spoke.

"You're Neptune, aren't you?"

"Indeed, I am, Commander. However, that information will never leave this room."

"You're sure of that?"

"Definitely. You are about to die, Mr. Hawthorne. *Now*, Brian!"

18

The gunfire shattered the silence of the immense compound as Poole and Catherine Neilsen repeatedly, in panic, pulled the triggers of their weapons, causing the library windows to collapse, shards of glass falling both inside and outside. The young lieutenant crashed through the remnants, rolling on the floor and propelling himself to his feet, his automatic leveled at the fallen bodies.

"You *okay?*" he shouted at the stunned Hawthorne, who had lurched into a corner behind a chair.

"Where the hell did you come from?" asked a breathless Tyrell, unsteadily getting to his knees. "I was finished, gone!"

"I figured something like that—"

"Those excessive good-byes to the pilots?" Hawthorne interrupted, gasping for breath, sweat breaking out on his forehead, "and the hot shower you hadn't had in days?"

"I'll catch you up later, but our driver's in the bushes and isn't goin' anywhere. Cathy and I walked around the house, saw you in here, and when that smooth-talkin' gorilla ran in with a gun in his hand, we figured we didn't have time to think."

"Thanks for not thinking. He told me I was dead."

"We've got to get out of here!"

"Will somebody help me through this goddamned window without slicing my flesh apart?" Cathy complained. "Incidentally, there are men racing up the road from the gate."

"We'll turn them around," said Hawthorne, joining Poole, lifting the major through the window, then running to the library door and locking it. When the knocking began, Tyrell did his best to imitate Van Nostrand's voice, mid-deep, mid-Atlantic. "Everything's fine, Brian was showing me a new automatic—return to your posts."

"Yes, sir," came the single reply. Automatically they reacted to a familiar name uttered by unquestioned authority. The footsteps receded.

"We're clean," said Tyrell.

"And you're out of your mind!" Cathy said in a harsh whisper. "There are two dead bodies here!"

"I didn't say forever, just for now."

"That jet's scheduled to take off in thirty-five minutes," said Poole. "I say we should be on it."

"Thirty-five minutes?" exclaimed Hawthorne.

"That's only part of it. Their passenger is supposed to be Van Nostrand, destination the international airport in Charlotte, North Carolina; accommodations, diplomatic cover. Not much time for a leisurely dinner or a pleasant overnight stay, unless you consider a lye pit in the woods a nice place to rest."

"My God, it was timed down to minutes!"

"Let's soar up to that lovely, safe, wild blue yonder."

"Not yet, Jackson," persisted Tye. "There are answers here. Van Nostrand was Alfred Simon's Mr. Neptune, and that puts him on a passenger list to the *padrone*'s island . . . and *that* makes him central to Bajaratt."

"You're sure you got it right?"

"I certainly am, Lieutenant. He admitted being Neptune, making it clear that the information wouldn't survive my execution."

"*Wow!*"

"A car came in when we were leaving," said Neilsen. "Could there be a connection with tonight?"

"Let's find out," said Tyrell.

"There are cottages all around the place, guesthouses probably, four or five at least," said Poole as he and Tyrell helped Catherine out the window. "I spotted 'em from the limo."

"There are no lights on anywhere," said Hawthorne, rounding the east end of the house, the expanse of lawn and foliage in darkness.

"There were before, I saw 'em only a few minutes ago."

"He's right," said Cathy. "Over there, in that direction." She pointed southwest; again, there was only darkness.

"Maybe I should go back to the strip and tell the pilots everything's okay. Those fellas were nervous, and that was before the shooting."

"Good idea," agreed Tyrell. "Tell them Van Nostrand was showing off his gun collection, that he's got a private gallery in the house."

"Nobody would buy that!" said Cathy.

"They'll buy anything as long as it's an explanation. They expect to be out of here in half an hour with a large paycheck, and that's all they care about. . . . As a matter of fact, seeing you will reassure them. Go with Jackson, will you?"

"What are you going to do?"

"Scout around. If you and Poole saw lights just a little while ago, why aren't they there now? We can assume no one else is in the house except the cook—not considering what Van Nostrand planned for me—and he sure as hell wasn't receiving other guests since he was flying out of here right away."

"Here's your gun," said the lieutenant, reaching into his belt and removing the automatic. "I took it from that bastard's pocket along with the Magnum in his hand. You can have that one too. I feel like an ammo depot 'cause I found two more on the limo driver."

"You gave one to me, Jackson," said Neilsen.

"Won't do you much good, Cath. By my count, you've got one shell left."

"Which I sincerely hope I never use—"

"You two get over to the airstrip. Make sure those pilots think that so far everything's on schedule, but if there's a delay, it'll be short. Van Nostrand's making calls to God and/or several ranking members of the administration who've got some explaining to do. Go on, hurry!"

"I had an idea, Tye," said Poole.

"What?"

"Both Cathy and I can fly that bird—"

"Forget it," Hawthorne interrupted. "I want those pilots to disappear. I don't want them here to be questioned when the bodies are found. My death was set up on a closed circuit; the only people who could identify us are the two drivers, and from what I gather, one's unconscious and the other's dead. It gives us space."

"Good thinking, Commander."

"That's what I used to get paid for, Major. Go on now."

The air force officers walked rapidly across the lawn toward the airstrip while Tyrell studied the southwest terrain. There was a profusion of pine trees symmetrically positioned, as if to lend a degree of privacy to each guest cottage beyond, barely seen in the erratic moonlight. Two were vaguely visible across a narrow dirt road, separated by several hundred feet. One of them had had its lights on less than ten minutes ago; which one was it? Guessing would not help; getting closer might. And getting closer meant moving very carefully while studying the rushing cloud cover that intermittently blocked the brighter moonlight, then deciding when to crawl or when to scramble during those moments of comparative darkness. Once more, memories of his other life flashed across his inner screen. Incidents when an outwardly perfectly normal, dull, bureaucratic

protocol officer became another person, running assets
during night rendezvous, meeting men and women in
fields and cathedrals, in alleyways and across border
checkpoints that had been penetrated by unrecon-
structed rebels. Where a single foolish indiscretion could
mean a bullet in the head from one side or the other.
The enemy or one's own. *Madness.*

Hawthorne looked up at the sky; a large cumulus was
drifting south; it would intercept the light of the moon
in a matter of seconds. The moment came and Tyrell
raced across the road, diving to the grass. He pounded
the earth on his hands and knees toward the nearer
guesthouse on the right, stopping instantly as the cloud
passed. Lying motionless on the lawn, he gripped his
automatic at his side.

Voices! Low, carried on the Virginia breezes as the
winds high above carried the clouds. *Two* voices. They
were similar but not the same, the pitches were different;
one was only slightly deeper, perhaps harsher, yet both
were excited, speaking rapidly—but not in English.
What *was* it? Hawthorne slowly raised his head. . . .
Silence. Then the two quiet voices were there again, but
they did not come from the nearest cottage, they came
from farther in the distance, from the guesthouse on the
left, several hundred feet away.

A light! Small, tiny, no more than a spot, a penlight
perhaps, but not a match, for it was steady, unflickering.
Someone was moving around inside, the beam swinging
rapidly back and forth—someone in a hurry, looking
for something. Somehow, some way, they were involved!
Then, as if to confirm his judgment, headlights suddenly
appeared, rushing up the narrow dirt road that bisected
the grounds between the main house and the cottages
on the south side of the estate. It was another limousine,
undoubtedly the one Poole and Neilsen had seen entering
the gate as they were approaching it. The car was now
returning to pick up its alarmed passengers from barely
a half hour ago; two people had heard gunshots; they

were not seeking any explanation but, instead, getting away from Van Nostrand's compound as quickly as possible!

The second Cadillac swung around a circle in the road, a U-turn that was the end of a quaint, countrified cul-de-sac, eliminating the need for reversing the vehicle on its way back to the front gate. It came to a sudden stop, the tires screeching as two figures raced out of the guesthouse, the larger one carrying two suitcases. Tye could not let them escape, he had to stop them.

He fired his automatic in the air. "Stay where you are!" he shouted, getting to his feet and rushing forward. "Don't get in that car!"

Out of the darkness there was a blinding spotlight centered on Hawthorne, its wash illuminating two men climbing into the limousine too briefly for him to see anything clearly. . . . Spotlights at night and racing figures were a part of his past; he stopped, spun to his right, then pivoted and lunged to his left, rolling violently over and over, out of the beam's periphery, lurching behind a clump of shrubbery as a staccato volley of gunfire ripped up the dark lawn where he was presumed to have sought safety. The car sped away, its tires spinning crazily on the dirt road, swirls of dust hovering over the surface. Tye closed his eyes in fury and attacked the earth with the handle of his gun.

"Hawthorne, where *are* you?" It was Cathy's voice, calling frantically as she ran across the road below his position.

"Jesus Christ, Cath, that was a regular *fusillade*!" joined in Poole, not far behind her. "Tye, say something! Oh, my God, he may have been shot—"

"No, *no* . . . !"

"I'm not sure," said Hawthorne, raising his voice, and slowly, painfully, getting to his feet, momentarily pausing, his hands on his knees.

"Where are you . . . ?"

"Over here," Tyrell answered, the rushing clouds in

the sky permitting a few moments of the moon, its light revealing him as he walked haltingly around the shrubs.

"There he is!" cried Neilsen, racing ahead.

"Are you hurt?" the lieutenant asked as he and the major converged breathless on Hawthorne. "Are you?" pressed Poole, holding Tye's arm. "Hurt?"

"Not from the fire," Hawthorne answered, grimacing and arching his neck.

"What from?" asked Cathy. "Those were machine guns!"

"One weapon," Jackson broke in, "and by its lower register a MAC, not an Uzi."

"Can a MAC-10 be fired by a man driving a large car on a narrow dirt road?" posed Tyrell.

"Not too easily, I wouldn't think."

"Then I might be struck dead, but you could be wrong, Lieutenant."

"What goddamned *difference* does it make?" protested Neilsen.

"None at all," admitted Hawthorne. "I was just pointing out the possible fallibility of the pope from Pontchartrain. . . . No, I'm not wounded, only bruised by an evasive action I haven't practiced lately. How are Van Nostrand's pilots?"

"Only out of their minds," replied Cathy, "and I'm sure it's got something to do with Jackson's opinion that they're not up for good-conduct medals. They want out of here!"

"You left them before this happened—the gunfire?"

"Three minutes ago, no more," said Neilsen.

"Then there's nothing to stop them, and maybe that's for the best."

"Oh, there's somethin' to stop 'em, Commander."

"What are you talking about? They can just take off."

"You hear anything like a plane goin' airborne?" Poole grinned. "Ah played a kid's game with them. It's called Watch-the-Possum."

"Poole, I may just have you before a firing squad—"

"Oh, hell, it's a simple game and it always works—simple things usually do. While we're standin' around outside debatin' with these two kinda' hysterical vagrants, I pull back and look beyond the tail of the aircraft and sort of yell, 'Who the hell is that?' Naturally, they whip their heads around, probably expecting a group of vigilantes on motorcycles, so I lean inside the plane and take the door key out of the recessed shelf. 'Course they don't notice after I tell 'em it's a stray deer; they just breathe deep and lower their blood pressure as I shut the only open door, which locks automatically. . . . They're not goin' anywhere, Tye. And when they do, if they do, we can be with them."

"I was right about you, Lieutenant," Hawthorne observed, his eyes locked with Poole's. "Your instincts are terrific and your various capabilities match them—how's that for a service report?"

"Well, damn, Commander. Ah *thank* you, sir!"

"Not so fast. Those same attributes could put us in a hairy mess."

"How?" asked Cathy defensively.

"Since that plane didn't take off, it depends on what's happening at the front gate after the guards heard the machine gun firing, and what will happen when the cook can't reach Van Nostrand or her husband. They'll know we're still here because the plane *didn't* take off."

"If I remember," said Neilsen, "her husband was our driver."

"And the limousine has a telephone," added Tyrell.

"Holy shit, he's right!" exclaimed Poole. "Suppose the front gate tries the limo, then calls the police? Suppose they've already called 'em? They'll be here any minute, huntin' for us!"

"My instincts tell me they won't," countered Hawthorne, "but then, I don't have the confidence I once had. I've been away too long."

"It comes down to the gate," said Poole.

"Exactly," agreed Hawthorne. "If I'm right, there

should be cars or golf carts or at least men with flashlights racing down to this area of the compound, but there's nothing. Why not?"

"Maybe we should find out," said Jackson. "Maybe I should sort of stroll up there and see what's goin' on."

"And get shot, you idiot?"

"Come on, Cathy, I'm not carryin' a drum and a bugle."

"She's right," said Tyrell. "I may be an antique in some areas, but not this one. I'll go, and we'll meet at the plane."

"What happened here?" asked Neilsen. "What did you see?"

"Two men, one pretty tall and carrying suitcases, the other shorter and thinner and wearing a hat. They jumped into the car when the spotlight centered in on me."

"Who thinks about a hat at a time like that?" said Poole.

"Bald men, Jackson," answered Hawthorne. "It's a mark of identification. Standard procedure. . . . Take Cathy back to the plane and try to control the pilots—"

"He doesn't have to take me, I'm perfectly capable of—"

"Oh, shut up, Cath," Poole interrupted. "He only means that if those two creeps decide to mutiny, it's better I stop 'em than you shootin' them. Okay."

"All right."

"And listen to me," continued Tyrell, his voice firm. "If I run into trouble, I'll fire three rapid shots. That's your signal to fly out of here."

"And leave you behind?" asked Neilsen, astonished.

"That's right, Major. I think I told you that I'm no hero—I don't like heroes because too many die, and the prospect has no appeal for me. If there's trouble, I'm better off getting out of here alone, without any baggage."

"Thanks a lot!"

"It's what I was trained for, paid for."

"Hey, suppose I went with you?" said Poole.

"You answered that yourself, Lieutenant. Suppose the pilots decide to revolt?"

"Come on, Cath!"

The pale gray Defense Department Buick was parked off the road, out of sight, branches from the surrounding trees covering its hood and the windshield. It stood diagonally across the half-mile wooded drive that led to Van Nostrand's estate, the four men inside bored, irritated, and resentful that they had been given an after-hours assignment without either the authority to take action or an explanation as to why they were there. They were simply to observe, and not, under any circumstances, to be observed.

"There it goes!" said the driver, instantly reaching for his cigarettes on top of the dashboard as a limousine emerged from Van Nostrand's entrance and swung right. "If a stretch comes out of there after twenty-one hundred hours, we're home free."

"Then let's *go* home," said a Defense security officer in the back seat. "This was bullshit."

"Someone upstairs probably wanted to know who was humping who," added a second voice from the back.

"Pure bullshit," the man beside the driver said, reaching for the vehicle's radio. "I'll call it in, and let's get out of here. God love the pinstripe crowd."

Bajaratt sat back in the limousine, stunned, unable to formulate her thoughts. The man in the spotlight was *Hawthorne*! How could it be? It was impossible, yet he was there! Was it coincidence? Ridiculous. There had to be a pattern that permitted the impermissible—what was it? The *padrone*? Was that it? My God, it *was*. . . . The *padrone*, Mars and Neptune! The passions of remembered flesh intertwined with a coequal passion for power and supremacy. One taken from the other, killed by another. Oh, the goddamned fool! Van Nostrand could not let it go; he had summoned Hawthorne in order to kill him—*he's mine, no one else's*—and the Baj would never hear from him again after tonight.

It was a chess game invented in hell, the kings and the pawns irrevocably at odds, unable to eliminate one another without a breakthrough that could destroy them both. . . . But it could not happen. She was so close—a few days, and Ashkelon would be avenged—her whole wretched life mean something! *Muerte a toda autoridad!* She could not be stopped, it was unthinkable!

Paris. She had to find out.

"What is happening?" asked Nicolo, whispering, still breathing hard, erratically, from the gunfire and their swift escape. "I think you had better tell me."

"Nothing that concerns us," replied the Baj, reaching for the limousine's telephone.

Bajaratt dialed the overseas codes to Paris, then the number on the rue du Corniche. "Pauline?" she said emphatically. "I will speak to no other."

"It is I," confirmed the woman in Paris. "And you are—"

"The *padrone's* only daughter."

"It is enough. What can I do for you?"

"Has Saba called again?"

"*Certainement, madame.* And quite excited. He asked about your not being on the island of Saba, and I believe I assuaged him. He is satisfied."

"How satisfied?"

"He accepted the fact that your uncle left for another island and that you knew where to reach him when you returned to the Caribbean."

"Good. His Olympic Charters, Charlotte Amalie, right?"

"I would not know, madame."

"Then forget I told you. I'll leave him a message."

"Of course, madame. *Adieu*."

Bajaratt pressed the End button, discontinuing the call, then dialed the 809 number in St. Thomas for Olympic Charters. What she heard was precisely what she expected to hear at this hour of the night.

"*You have reached Olympic Charters, Charlotte Amalie. The office is closed and will open at 6 A.M. tomorrow. If this is an emergency, please press one, which will connect you to the Coast Guard patrol. Otherwise, you may leave a message.*"

"My darling, it's Dominique! I'm calling from a boring cruise off the coast of Portofino and, my darling, it is, as you Americans say, the *pits*! But the good news is that I'll be back in three weeks. I've convinced my husband that I must return to my uncle—he's on Dog Island now. I'm sorry I didn't mention it, but I did tell you he keeps moving, didn't I? Good heavens, Pauline scolded me so for not being clearer. It doesn't matter, we'll be together soon. I love you!"

The Baj replaced the phone, annoyed by Nicolo's stare. "Why did you say those things, Cabi?" asked the young man. "Are we flying back to the Caribbean? Where are we going? . . . Tonight, the gunfire, our racing away like this! What is happening, signora? You must tell me!"

"I cannot tell you what I don't know, Nico. You heard the driver, he said there was a robbery in progress. The owner of that estate is wealthy beyond our imaginations, and these are bad times in America. There is crime everywhere. That's why there's a gatehouse and guards and high fences. They must always be prepared for such terrible things. It has nothing to do with us, believe me."

"It is difficult for me to do that. If there are guards and so much protection, why are we running away?"

"The police, Nicolo! The police have been summoned, and we certainly don't want to be questioned by the police. We are visitors to this country; it would be embarrassing, humiliating. . . . What would Angelina think?"

"Oh. . . ." The dock boy's unrelenting gaze briefly softened. "Why did we come here?"

"Because, through a friend, I was told we'd have our own quarters, and servants . . . and our host would provide me with a secretary, for I have dozens of letters to write."

"You have so many words, and you are so many people." The young Italian continued to stare in the flashing shadows at the woman who had saved his life on the docks of Portici.

"Reflect on your lire in Napoli, my dear boy. I have to sort things out."

"Perhaps you should sort out where we will stay tonight."

"Ah, now you are thinking." The Baj pressed the intercom button for the driver. "Are there acceptable accommodations around here that you might suggest, my friend?"

"Yes, madame, I've called ahead and they are prepared for you. Guests of Mr. Van Nostrand, of course. It's the Shenandoah Lodge; you'll find it quite acceptable."

"Thank you."

Tyrell crept along the edge of the grass in the shadows of the bordering pine trees. The stone gatehouse with the forbidding barriers across the dual-lane road was no more than a hundred feet away, the last thirty or forty, however, without the cover of the pines. It was open space, a manicured lawn between the road and a ten-foot-high stockade fence with ominous-looking metal points atop each rounded shaft; it took no expertise to know that a powerful electric current flowed from tip to tip. Nor did it take years of experience to realize that the two barriers that fell across the wide entrance road were no mere wooden planks; their thickness indicated plates of laminated steel. Only a tank could crash through them, an automobile of whatever size would impact and be shattered as if it had crashed into a wall of iron. They were lowered now.

Hawthorne studied the gatehouse itself. The stone structure was square; the windows were of thick glass on the two sides that he could see, and a decorative turret reminiscent of a medieval castle completed the roof. The late Van Nostrand, a.k.a. Neptune, was a cautious man; the entrance to his extraordinary estate was break-proof, bulletproof, and heaven help the misguided penetrator who scaled the stockade fence. He'd be nuked until he was charred black flesh.

There was no one to be seen in either window, so Tye raced across the open space, hugging the stone of the gatehouse once he reached it. Slowly, very slowly, he inched his head to the left side of the impenetrable thick glass. What he saw not only stunned him—it made no sense! Seated in a chair, his body slumped over a Formica desk perhaps ten feet from the entrance, was a uniformed guard, his head covered with blood. He had been shot not once but several times in the skull.

Hawthorne circled the building to the door; it was open. He rushed inside and tried to assimilate everything there was to see. It was a kaleidoscope of high technology: three tiers of television screens, all in continuous motion, covering every area of the compound, even to the extent of picking up sound. The chirps and caws of birds mingled with the flapping of windblown leaves and the rustle of the tall grass in the outer perimeters of the enormous estate.

Why had the guard been killed? *Why?* Where was the benefit? And where were his backups? A man like Neptune, much less his paranoid chief of security, would never assign a main gate to one individual alone; it was crazy, and neither Van Nostrand nor the coldly efficient

Brian was crazy—warped, perhaps, but not stupid. Tye studied the equipment, wishing that Poole were in the gatehouse with him; various markings on different machines indicated that audio as well as visual tapes were in operation. Answers might be found if the right buttons were pressed, but conversely, everything could be erased if the wrong ones were activated.

The most mystifying fact was that the place was deserted. What did they know that caused them to run away? The gunfire? That did not make sense; the patrols were armed, as witnessed by the dead man in the chair, his holster still housing a .38 revolver. And Van Nostrand obviously hired and paid for complete loyalty; why hadn't his overpaid, loyal troops rushed to protect their benevolent employer? On cursory observation, it was doubtful they would find better jobs.

The gatehouse telephone rang, not simply startling Hawthorne, but shocking him into inaction. . . . *Impose a freeze control on yourself, Lieutenant. Ice cold, and in neutral. If the unexpected happens, make fucking sure you convey the fact that it's perfectly natural.*

Words from an early trainer in deep-cover naval intelligence, words Tyrell himself had passed on to so many others behind him . . . in Amsterdam.

Tyrell picked up the phone and coughed several times before speaking. " 'N'eahh?" he said, his voice indistinct, in the tone of a hostile greeting.

"What's happening out there?" a woman shouted over the line. "I can't reach anybody, not Mr. Van or Brian or my husband in the car—*nobody*! . . . And where have you been for the last five minutes? I keep ringing—nothing!"

"Lookin' around," replied Hawthorne gruffly.

"Those were gunshots, lots of 'em!"

"Huntin' deer maybe," said Tyrell, recalling Poole's game of Watch-the-Possum with the two pilots.

"With a machine gun? At night?"

"Different strokes, different folks."

"Crazy people, everybody's crazy here!"

"Yeah—"

"Well, if you reach Mr. Van or any of the others, you tell 'em I'm staying right here in the kitchen with all these heavy doors locked up tight. If they want dinner, they can call me!" With that declaration, the estate's chef slammed down the phone.

The status quo was even more bewildering if only because the woman confirmed it—everyone had fled, perhaps killing the one man who would not join them, who might implicate the others. It was as though the specter of some Armageddon had spread through the compound in whispers. *The time has come. It's tonight. Save ourselves!* What else could it be? . . . Still, there were answers here, but the only true answer, the sole connection to Bajaratt, was in the dead cells of the dead Van Nostrand's brain.

Hawthorne removed the blood-splattered .38 from the slain guard's holster; he held it between his thumb and forefinger, carrying it into the small open bathroom, where he wiped it with paper towels and shoved it into his belt. He walked back out to the gatehouse's equipment and once again studied it, concentrating on the panel above the counter nearest the entrance, presuming it would operate the road barriers. There were six outsize colored buttons forming two triangles, side by side, each identical. The buttons on the lower left were green; to their right, brown; and above, somewhat larger than those below, they were bright red. Beneath each was a yellow plaque with black lettering; in sequence, they read: OPEN, CLOSE, and under the red button above, the letters larger, ALARM.

Tyrell chose the triangle on the left and pressed the green OPEN; the nearest barrier rose slowly. He pressed the brown; it returned to its lateral position. The left triangle was obviously for vehicles entering the estate, the right for those departing. To be certain, he repeated the procedure on the second triangle; the far barrier rose and fell. So much for high tech; there was no point in activating the alarm and every reason not to.

He had made up his mind, assuming the risk was minimal, at least temporarily. He would rendezvous with Neilsen and Poole at the airstrip and announce his decision. They could either fly out with the pilots and follow up the Charlotte, North Carolina, connection— find out who specifically came out to escort Van Nostrand to his international departure gate—or they could stay with him and tear apart Van Nostrand's study. The option was theirs, either alternative a positive step. The airport "clearance" could come from any number of people, its origin bureaucratically buried or falsely attributed, but a specific escort could be traced upward. On the other hand, Tyrell could use two additional pairs of eyes to scrutinize whatever they might find in Van Nostrand's study, as well as in his living quarters. A man leaving his home under the stressful conditions self-imposed by this lord of the manor could easily become careless, forgetful.

Hawthorne pulled the dead guard off the blood-drenched desk, gripped him under the armpits, and dragged the corpse into the small bathroom. He had stopped to wash his hands in the tiny sink when he heard the sudden roar of a car's engine—loud, even furious, screeching to an abrupt stop. . . . Was he wrong? Were the police answering an emergency? Barely thinking, he raced out of the bathroom, grabbing the guard's cap off the floor, and stood facing the thick window; he was instantly relieved. The blue Chevrolet was civilian, and it was not entering the compound, it was leaving. He looked at the counter, at the buttons, instinctively knowing he would choose the one to the right, the exit triangle.

"Yes?" he said, flipping the toggle switch next to the built-in microphone.

"What the hell d'ya mean, yes, you dumb ninny?" came the excited voice over the gatehouse speakers. "Let me out of here! And when that jackass husband of mine comes back in the limo, tell him I went to my sister's; he can reach me there. . . . Hey, wait a minute! Who are you?"

"I'm new, ma'am," said Tyrell, pressing the green button on the second triangle. "Have a pleasant night, ma'am."

"Loonies, you're all lunatics! Planes flyin' in, guns goin' off, what next?" The Chevrolet raced out into the darkness as Hawthorne lowered the far barrier. Glancing around, he wondered if there was anything he should do, anything he should take. . . . Yes, there probably was; on the Formica desk, wet with glistening blood, was a large ringed notebook. He opened it and turned the loose-leaf pages; they held the names, dates, and times of Van Nostrand's guests going back to the first of the month, some eighteen days. In his haste, or anxiety, Neptune may have made his first mistake. Tyrell closed the notebook, put it under his arm—then suddenly, the obvious striking him, he slammed it back down on the desk and quickly flipped through the pages to that night's entry. The limousine that had sped away with two escaping passengers from the farthest guesthouse. Only one name was listed, but it was enough to set Hawthorne's brain on fire! For within it was part of a name the visitor had no idea her hunters were aware of, yet her maniacal ego demanded that it be there, a trail for official commissions and scholars of history to follow. She would not be denied that ultimate recognition.
    Madame Lebajerône, Paris.
    Lebajerône.
    The Baj.
    Dominique.
    Bajaratt!

19

T yrell left the gatehouse door ajar and ran up the road toward the break in the enormous lawn where he would cut across to reach the airstrip. Once on the grass, however, he slowed down, bewildered but not at first sure why; then he understood. He instinctively expected to see a wash of amber light the nearer he came to the runway. It was not there; there was only darkness. He resumed running, faster than before, racing through a narrow space in the tall hedgerow that bordered the edge of the field.

He had presumed that Neilsen and Poole would be waiting for him in plain sight on the strip with the two pilots. There was no one; something was wrong. He shoved the gatehouse log book under a bush, covering it with dirt, and looked up, studying the airfield.

Silence. Nothing. Only the yellowish-white outlines of the Gulfstream jet.

The *something* . . . movement! Where? It had come from the corner of his eye—to the right, obliquely across the tarmac, beyond it. He focused on the area, the shafts of moonlight now helping him, for the beams were reflected as if by mirrors. It was the control tower, inaccurately named, for it was not a tower but a one-story structure, mostly glass, with a dish antenna rising far above and anchored by wires to the roof. Someone had moved behind one of the large windows, caught in a refracted instant of a cloudless moon.

The darkened sky returned and Hawthorne lowered himself to the grass, scrambling back to the tall hedgerow, where he stood and began running from broken space to broken space, around the end of the strip. In less than a minute he was within a hundred yards of the ground-level "tower," gasping for breath, the sweat rolling down his face and neck, drenching his shirt. Had the two pilots overpowered Cathy and the armed, young air force lieutenant? Considering Poole's skills, it did not seem likely without gunfire, and there had been none.

Movement again! An opaque figure, or the shadow of a figure, had swiftly approached the huge glass window, then just as quickly receded from view. . . . They had seen him when he had run through the break in the hedgerow, and were watching for him now. Suddenly a recent memory came back to Hawthorne, the memory of three days ago—three nights ago—on an unnamed island north of the Anegada Passage. . . . *Fire.* One of the most potent images for man or animal, confirmed by the racing, snarling attack dogs on the *padrone*'s fortress in the sea.

Remaining behind the hedgerow, Tyrell scraped the ground for dried twigs and fallen brush burned by the summer sun, then reached up, feeling within the thick foliage for brittle, breakable branches; the farther up he went, the more plentiful they were. In roughly four perspiring minutes, he had built a mound nearly a foot in height and two feet wide; it was a "starter" that could ignite wet charcoal. He reached into his trouser pocket for his ever-present book of matches—ever-present from his heavy smoking days; he tore one off, cupped his hands, and struck it. He lit the base, shoving the matchbook into the pyre, then scrambled away on his hands and knees, circling deep to his right, behind the next section of the broken hedgerow, to the next after that. He was now parallel to the mostly glass structure, its metal door less than eighty feet away.

The burning bushes spread far more rapidly than Hawthorne thought possible, and he thanked whatever gods there were for the scorching Virginia sun. The moist night breezes from the hills had not yet arrived; the tops of the hedges were dry and the middle greenery permitted the flames to surge upward, quickly spreading in both directions. In moments the fires became an ominous succession of erupting flames, surging to the right and to the left like bright dual fuses. Then two—no, three figures—appeared at the large rear glass window; they were excited; heads nodded and shook; hands shot out and retracted, the shadowed bodies lurching one way and the other, indecisive, panicked. The metal door opened and the three figures were in the frame, one in front, two behind. Tyrell could not see their faces, but he knew that none was Neilsen or Poole. He withdrew the .38 from his belt and waited, asking himself three questions: Where were Cathy and Jackson? Who were these people, and what did they have to do with the disappearance of the two air force officers?

"Oh, my God, the fuel tanks!" shouted the man in front.

"Where are they?" The voice of the second man was familiar to Hawthorne—the copilot of the Gulfstream jet.

"Over there!" Tye could see the figure, gesturing wildly at some point on the airstrip. "It could blow the whole fucking place to the moon! They hold a hundred thousand gallons. High test, the highest!"

"It's all underground!" protested the pilot.

"Sure, pal, and what keeps it there are iron screw plates! Those tanks are only half full; the gas fumes are on top and they can blow with red hot metal. Let's get out of here!"

"We can't leave them!" cried the copilot. "That's murder, mister, and we don't want anything to do with it."

"Do what you want, you assholes, I'm leaving!" The man in front ran out on the grass, his racing silhouette passing the flames of the hedgerow behind him. The two pilots disappeared from view, running inside the building as Hawthorne lurched forward, lowering himself and scrambling, until he was at the corner of the glass-squared structure. He peered around the edge of the building. The hedgerow fires were moving steadily, rising to the sky. Suddenly, Poole and Neilsen, their hands bound behind them, their mouths strapped with gray pipe tape, were shoved out the door, Cathy falling as Jackson plummeted on top of her, covering her with his own body as if he expected gunfire. The pilots of the Gulfstream jet came out next, apparently frightened, unsure of themselves.

"Come on, both of you!" the copilot demanded. "Get up, let's go!"

"You're not going anywhere!" Tyrell was on his feet, the .38 swinging back and forth between the heads of the two pilots. "You lousy scum, help them up! Untie them, and remove those tapes!"

"Hey, man, we didn't do this 'cause we wanted to!" the copilot protested as he and his colleague quickly pulled Neilsen and Poole to their feet, untying them, and letting each remove the thick tape. "That lousy radioman had his gun on all of us."

"He told us to tie 'em up and gag 'em," broke in the pilot. "Then he figured that since we were working for Van Nostrand—he ran the practice turns this morning—we were okay."

"More than okay," the copilot interrupted, looking at the burning hedgerow. "He said we were cleared by 'Mr. Van's security,' but he didn't know these guys and he wasn't taking chances. . . . Let's get the hell out of here. You heard what he said, the fuel tanks!"

"Where are they?" asked Hawthorne.

"About four hundred feet west of this glass radio barn," answered Poole. "I saw the pumps while Cath and I were waiting for you."

"I don't care where they are!" the copilot shouted. "That bastard said they could blow us to the moon!"

"They could," said the lieutenant, "but it's not likely.

Those pumps have backup insulators, and the screw plates would have to be hit with a blowtorch to reach a combustible temperature."

"Could it happen?"

"Sure, Tye, one chance out of maybe a couple of hundred. Hell, the No Smoking signs in gas stations make sense."

Hawthorne turned to the frightened pilots. "The odds are way in your favor, fellas," he said. "Give me your wallets, your IDs. Also your passports."

"What is this, a goddamned bust?"

"It won't be if you do what I tell you to do. Come on, hand them over! I'll give them back."

"Who are you, some kind of federal?" The pilot reluctantly reached into his pockets and handed Tyrell his wallet and passport. "I hope you realize that we were legitimately employed and carry no firearms or illegal substances. Search us and the aircraft if you want to. You won't find a thing."

"Sounds like you've been through this sort of routine before . . . you, too, sky jock! That is the proper term, isn't it?"

"I'm a licensed pilot who free-lances his services, mister," said the copilot, also handing Hawthorne the demanded items.

"Get the names and pertinent information, Major," Tyrell continued, giving the wallets and passports to Neilsen. "Go inside and turn on a light."

"Right away, Commander." Cathy walked rapidly into the glass house.

"Major . . . Commander?" cried the pilot. "What the hell *is* this? Gunshots, a burning airstrip on a fancy estate, and the military? What did those sons of bitches get us into, Ben?"

"*Ah'm* a lieutenant," said Poole.

"Damned if I know, Sonny, but if we get out of here, we're taking our names off their list!"

"And just what list is that?" asked Hawthorne.

The flyers looked at each other. "Go on, tell him," said the pilot. "They haven't a fucking thing on us!"

"Sky Transport International," said the copilot. "It's a placement service, sort of a class-act employment agency."

"I'll bet it is. Where's it located?"

"Nashville."

"Even better. All those country millionaires."

"We've never knowingly flown a felon or any individual or individuals carrying illegal substances—"

"Yes, you've said that, Mr. Pilot. Outside of your legal expertise, where were you trained? The military?"

"Absolutely not," replied the copilot angrily. "The finest civilian schools, top graded by the FAA with a combined five thousand hours logged."

"You got somethin' against the military?" asked Poole.

"The rigidity of the chain of command excludes individual initiative. We're better pilots."

"Now, just wait a hog-damned minute . . . !"

"Hold it, Lieutenant." Catherine Neilsen came out of the radio house. "Any surprises?" asked Hawthorne, gesturing for the major to return the wallets and passports.

"One or two," replied Cathy, handing their property over to the pilots. "Our fly-boys are named Benjamin and Ezekiel Jones. They're brothers. They've been traveling extensively during the past twenty months or so. Interesting places like Cartagena, Caracas, Port-au-Prince, and Estero, Florida."

"The lopsided rectangle," said Tyrell. "The last leg over the Everglades."

"Drop zones alpha through omega," commented Poole, disgust in his voice. "Pin-point releases the order of the day—like in OD, you bastards. Boy, did Ezekiel get the wheel!"

"That's Sonny!" said the pilot.

"Can we get the hell out of here?" Sweat poured

down the copilot's face as he kept glancing at the hedge-row fires.

"Oh, you're going to leave right away," answered Hawthorne, "and you're going to leave the way I tell you and *do* what I tell you. The lieutenant informs me that you've been cleared for Charlotte, North Caro-lina—"

"The departure time's passed and we haven't con-firmed a new one!" Benjamin Jones objected. "We'd never get clearance for that routing—there's traffic up there!"

"You boys better go back to one of those top-rated schools," said Jackson. "By the time you circle at a few hundred feet, I'll either have you a new routing or con-firm the old one."

"You can do that, Poole?"

"Certainly, he can," replied Cathy. "So can I. That equipment reaches towers from Dulles to Atlanta. As Ben here said on the way up, Van Nostrand goes first class."

"You expect us to fly right into a crowd of federals waiting for a passenger we haven't got?" shouted Sonny-Ezekiel Jones. "You're out of your fucking mind!"

"You're out of yours if you don't," said Tyrell calmly, reaching into his pocket for a small telephone pad and pencil, courtesy of the hotel in San Juan. "Here's the number you're to call when you get to Charlotte. Use a credit card, because it's in the Virgin Islands, and you'll reach an answering machine."

"You're crazy!" yelled Benjamin Jones.

"I really believe you should. You see, you'll never fly a remotely legitimate plane again in this country if you refuse. On the other hand, if you do what I tell you to do, you're home free—with one proviso, which I'll get to in a moment."

"What proviso? What are we supposed to do?"

"To begin with, you won't be met by a crowd, but by Van Nostrand's diplomatic escort—at best, one or two people. I want their names—you refuse even to speak to them until they sign a release."

"What release?"

"The date, time, and signatures that match their identifications, and the name of the specific individual who cleared your passenger and authorized the escort. They won't like it, but they'll understand; it goes with the territory."

"So we get the information, then what?" asked the brighter Ben Jones. "We don't have Van Nostrand to deliver! . . . Where is he anyway?"

"Indisposed."

"So what the hell do we say?"

"That it was a dry run; Van Nostrand's orders. They may even understand that better. Then get to a phone and call this number." Hawthorne shoved the small piece of paper into the copilot's shirt pocket.

"Hey, wait a fucking minute!" Sonny-Ezekiel said. "What about our bread?"

"How much are you owed?"

"Ten thousand—five apiece."

"For a day's work? That's really inflated, Zeke. I'll bet it's nearer two apiece."

"We'll settle for four, that's eight, and it's Sonny!"

"Tell you what, Sonny. I'll okay four thousand if you deliver the information in Charlotte. If you don't, it's zip-zero."

"Words, Commander," said Benjamin Jones. "They sound pretty, but how do we get paid?"

"Easiest thing in the world. Give me twelve hours after your call from Charlotte. Then name a time and a place on that answering machine in St. Thomas, and a messenger will show up with the money."

"Words."

"Do I look or sound like a damn fool who'd give you a telephone drop you could trace?"

"Suppose no one answers," pressed the younger brother.

"Someone will. Look, we're wasting time and you don't have a choice! I assume you've got the ignition key or whatever you call it."

"First thing I did," replied Sonny. "Only it's a key to the pilot's door; the plane operates with switches, groundhog."

"Then get going."

"Don't even consider screwing us," said Benjamin. "We don't know what happened here, but if you think we bought that shooting-gallery bullshit, think again, and the fact that our employer isn't on the plane makes us wonder. I've read about this Van Nostrand—he's news, if you understand me. We could go public for a price."

"Are you threatening an officer of the United States Navy—naval intelligence, to be precise?"

"Are you bribing us, Commander? With United States taxpayers' money?"

"You're pretty sharp, Jones, but then, I've learned that younger brothers often are—usually to their detriment. . . . Get out of here. I'll check St. Thomas in a couple of hours."

"Circle and radio me at three hundred feet," said Poole. "Keep your equipment tight to the area."

The brothers looked at each other. Sonny-Ezekiel shrugged, then glanced back at Hawthorne. "Reach that machine of yours, Commander. Then reach it again for our paycheck, only no check, hard cash."

"Ben," said Tyrell firmly, looking hard at the younger Jones. "Deliver Charlotte to me, or I'll track that Gulfstream to wherever you think you might sell it. And lastly, my proviso: Get out of the drug trade."

"Son of a bitch!" muttered the copilot as both men turned and raced toward the lower hedgerow which had begun to burn itself out, now more smoke than flames.

"The fires are dying," said Cathy.

"The dry tops flare quickly," observed Jackson. "More light than heat so the green won't take."

"It's still got a way to travel," said Hawthorne.

"No, it doesn't," Poole corrected him, heading toward the door of the radio house. "There's at least a hundred feet of space between the bushes and the pumps."

"That's why they wouldn't blow," observed Neilsen.

"I didn't care to be so specific, Cath. . . . I've got work to do. I know the tower at Andrews, and they'll reach National for F.P. clearance before a computer can burp. That Gulfstream's on its way to Charlotte."

"Meet us at the house, in the library," Hawthorne said to Poole as the lieutenant disappeared into the tower. "Come on," he added, turning to the major. "I want to tear that place apart. We've got to find a way to contact that other limousine. Bajaratt's in it."

"My God! Are you *sure*?"

"I'll prove it. I hid the gatehouse's entry log across the field. That limo you saw was the last car to enter; the proof is in the name, come on, I'll show you." Together they ran below and around the smoking, smoldering hedgerow to the area where Tyrell had concealed the thick, ringed ledger. Out of breath, Hawthorne knelt down to retrieve it.

It was not there.

Like a starving man searching for edible roots, Tye ripped up the earth, lurching from one side to the other, controlling his panic. He stopped, his eyes blazing. "It's gone!" he whispered, blinking, as rivulets of sweat rolled down his face.

"Gone . . . ?" Neilsen frowned, bewildered. "Could you have dropped it in the excitement?"

"I put it right there!" Hawthorne lunged to his feet like an angry cobra, whipping the .38 out of his belt. "And I don't drop things in excitement, Major."

"Sorry."

"So am I . . . I probably have dozens of times, but not this time. To begin with, it's too big and too important. . . . Christ, someone else is here, someone we can't see who's watching us!"

"The cook? Guards from the gatehouse?"

"You don't understand, Cathy. Everyone's left, they've disappeared, even the cook—I let her out myself. Nobody can be reached by phone, she told me that."

"Everyone?"

"Except for a guard who was killed, shot through the head at his desk."

"But if that entry log isn't here—"

"Exactly. Someone stayed behind, someone who knows Van Nostrand's dead and wants to pick up whatever he can from an estate filled with high-priced goodies."

"Then why the gatehouse log? It's not silver or crystal or an art object."

Tyrell squinted, staring at Neilsen in the moonlight. "Thank you, Major, you just told me something I should have realized. Our illusive stranger is further up the totem than I considered. That log is worthless, except to somebody who knows how important it is. I've *really* been away too long."

"What do you want to do?"

"Whatever it is, very carefully. You've got a gun, don't you?"

"Jackson gave me the one he took from the radioman. I think it's bigger."

"That's better. Hold it out so it's obvious and follow me. Do as I do—circle every few steps, countering my turns, if you can. I'll circle left, you circle right; that way all points are covered. Can you do that?"

"Can I handle a minisub I never saw before?"

"It's not the same, Major. You're not handling a machine now, you *are* the machine. This is firing into a shadow that may or may not be human, and there can't be any excuse for not doing so. Our lives could be over in a moment of indecision."

"I read, speak, and understand English, Tye, and if you're trying to frighten me, you've succeeded."

"Good. Bravery frightens *me;* you can die from it." Moving carefully, the two circling figures crossed the vast lawn toward the great house; they reached the shattered library window, the subdued lighting inside emphasizing the jagged shards of glass within the frame. Tyrell hammered the barrel of his weapon along the bottom ledge to reduce the risk of cutting themselves when they climbed through. "Okay, I'll go first and pull you up," said Hawthorne as a nervous Catherine Neilsen stood behind him, facing the darkness, her automatic sweeping back and forth.

"I'm not sure I even want to turn around," said Cathy. "I really don't like guns, but right now I feel very user-friendly with this ugly thing."

"I approve of your attitude, Major." Tyrell leapt up, vaulting through the frame with his left hand, the .38 in his right. "All right," he continued, standing inside the window. "Put the gun—wherever you can put it—and grab my arm."

"My God, it scratches like hell!" cried Neilsen, slipping the automatic into the top of her belted dress, and grabbing Hawthorne's extended left arm. "Now what?"

"Put your feet against the side of the building and do what comes naturally as I pull you up. It's only a couple of steps, you'll make it . . . but don't put your feet on the ledge, if you can help it. You don't have shoes."

"I was wearing high heels, remember? They don't go with running for your life." The major did as she was told, her dress raised to her hips as she scaled the four feet to the window. "And modesty can go down the tube," she added, muttering, "if my underwear turns you on, that's your problem."

The bodies of Van Nostrand and his security chief lay where they fell; there was no sign that anything had changed, that anyone had been in the library since the gunfire that ended their lives. To make sure, Hawthorne crossed rapidly to the heavy paneled door; it was still locked.

"I'll cover us from the window," said Tye. "Check the telephone console; there should be a memory bank describing what numbers reach whom. See if there are speed dials to the limousines."

His back against the wall, Hawthorne stood by the shattered glass frame as Neilsen went to the desk. "There's a large plastic square that must have covered an index on the front of the phone," said Cathy. "It's been ripped out; there are pieces of thick paper around the edges, as if someone had trouble removing it."

"Look in the drawers, the wastebaskets, anyplace it might have been thrown."

Drawers were rapidly pulled open and slammed shut. "They're empty," she said, picking up a brass wastebasket and putting it on the desk chair. "Not much here—oh, wait a minute."

"What?"

"It's a receipt from a shipping company, Sea Lane Containers. I know that firm; the high brass use it when they're being transferred to an overseas post for a couple of years."

"What does it say?"

" 'N. Van Nostrand, thirty-day storage, Lisbon, Portugal.' Then, below under Items: 'Twenty-seven cartons, personal effects, resealable tapes for customs inspection.' It's signed by a G. Alvarado, secretary to N.V.N."

"That's all?"

"Only other thing is a line after Instructions. It says: 'Sender will claim at S.L.C. Lisbon depot.' That's it. . . . Why would anybody discard a receipt for twenty-seven cartons of personal possessions when a great many of them have to be terribly valuable?"

"The first thing that comes to mind is that if you're a Van Nostrand, you don't need a receipt to claim your shipment. What else is in the wastebasket?"

"Nothing, really. . . . Three candy wrappers, a couple

of crumpled-up memo pages with nothing on them, and a stock market computer printout dated today."

"Useless," said Tyrell, his eyes on the grounds outside. "Or maybe not," he added. "Why *would* Van Nostrand throw away that receipt? Or, put another way, why would he even bother to throw it away?"

"Are you taking lessons from Poole? You've lost me."

"He had a secretary; why didn't he simply give it to her? She was obviously handling everything, so why did he keep it?"

"To claim the shipment in Lisbon—oh, oh, forget it, as you would say. He threw it away."

"Why?"

"Damned if I know, Commander. I'm a pilot, not a psychiatrist."

"Neither am I, but I know a plant when a cactus is shoved down my throat."

"That sounds clever, but I don't know what you mean."

"I'm not clever, just experienced. Van Nostrand, for reasons I can't understand, wanted that receipt to be found."

"After his death?"

"Of course not. He had no idea he was going to die; he was on his way to Charlotte, North Carolina, but he wanted it to be found."

"By whom?"

"By someone who would make a connection with something that hasn't happened—maybe. Call it warped intuition, but it's pretty strong. . . . Look around. Everywhere. Pull what books are left out of the shelves, check the cabinets, the bar, everything."

"What am I looking for?"

"Anything that's hidden—" He stopped abruptly, then said, "Hold it! Turn off the lights!"

Neilsen switched off an upright lamp and then the

light on the desk. The room went dark. "What is it, Tye?"

"Someone with a penlight—a tiny circle on the grass—our undeparted stranger."

"What's he doing?"

"Walking straight toward this window—"

"With the lights off?"

"Good question. He didn't stop or even pause when you put them out. He just keeps walking forward like some kind of robot."

"I found a flashlight!" Neilsen whispered from behind the desk. "I thought I saw one in the bottom drawer; I was right."

"Crawl around and roll it to me."

Cathy did so and Tyrell flagged it with his left hand, pulling it to his side as the zombielike figure kept marching toward the house. In seconds it had reached the window. Suddenly a hysterical scream pierced the silence.

"Get out of there! You have no *right* in his *private* quarters! I'll tell *Mr. Van.* He'll have you *killed!*"

Hawthorne snapped on the flashlight, the .38 aimed at the figure's head. To his amazement, the figure was an old woman, her face deeply lined, with perfectly coiffed white hair and wearing an expensive dark print dress. She clutched the blood-stained gatehouse log under her left arm. She held no weapon, only a drugstore penlight in her right hand. She was pathetic, her eyes wild with unfocused fury.

"Why would Mr. Van Nostrand want to kill us?" asked Tyrell calmly, softly. "We're here at his request; in fact, his plane brought us here. As you can see by this broken window, he had every reason to ask for our assistance."

"You're from his army, then?" the old woman asked, her voice lower, more controlled, yet still harsh and slightly accented.

"His army?" Tye moved the flashlight beam above the old woman's head, away from her eyes.

"His and Mars's, of course." The woman paused, as if gasping for elusive breath.

"Of course. . . . Neptune and Mars, isn't that right?"

"Certainly. He said he would call you one day; we both knew it was coming, you see."

"What was coming?"

"The uprising, naturally." Again the woman breathed deeply, her eyes eerily straying. "We must protect ourselves as well as our own—everyone who's with us!"

"From the rebels, of course." Hawthorne studied the intense face. Though she was clearly unbalanced, her appearance and demeanor, even in anger and fear, bespoke an aristocracy . . . in South America? That was the accent, Hispanic or Portuguese. . . . Portuguese, Rio de Janeiro? Mars and Neptune—*Rio*!

"From the human *garbage,* that's who!" Her voice was as close to a shriek as her breeding would permit. "Nils has worked all his life to improve their lot, to make things better, when all they want is more and more and more! And they deserve nothing! They're lazy, indulgent; they only make babies, they don't work!"

"Nils . . . ?"

"Mr. Van to you!" The woman coughed, the rattle hoarse, vibrating in her throat.

"But not to you . . . naturally."

"My dear young man, I've been with the boys for years, from the beginning. In the early days I was their hostess . . . all those glorious parties and banquets, even their own *carnavales*! Marvelous!"

"They must have been great," agreed Tyrell, nodding. "Still, we have to protect our own, everyone who's with us. That's why you took the gatehouse register, isn't it? I hid it in the dirt, under the bushes."

"It was you? Then you are a fool! Nothing of consequence must be left behind, don't you realize that? I've a mind to tell Nils about your negligence."

"Left behind . . . ?"

"We're leaving in the morning!" whispered the former hostess of Mars and Neptune, once again coughing. "Hasn't he told you that?"

"Yes, he has. We're making preparations."

"They've all been made, you ass! Brian just flew out in our plane to make the final arrangements. Portugal! Isn't it wonderful? Our belongings have already been sent. . . . Where is Nils—Mr. Van? I must tell him I'm finished."

"He's upstairs, checking on . . . his personal effects."

"That's ridiculous. Brian and I cleaned everything out this morning, and we don't miss a thing. I laid out his clothing, a pair of pajamas, and his toiletries, which can be left behind for those Arabs!"

"Arabs? Forget it! What did you just finish for him— Miss Alvarado . . . that is your name, isn't it?"

"Of course it is, Madame Gretchen Alvarado. My mother's first husband was a great hero in the war, a member of the High Command."

"You're the whole ball of wax, lady," said Tyrell quietly.

"*Madre de Dios,*" continued G. Alvarado dreamily. "Those early days with Mars and Neptune were truly magnificent, but naturally we never talk about them."

"What did you just finish for Mr. Van?"

"Praying, naturally. He asked me to go to our stone chapel on the hill and pray to our Savior for safe deliverance. As I'm sure you're aware, Mr. Van Nostrand is as devout as any priest you or I have ever known. . . . In truth, young man, my prayers were somewhat shortened, as there's apparently a malfunction in the air circulation machinery. My eyes teared and I could hardly breathe. Don't tell him, but there's still a terrible pain in my chest. Say nothing. He'd worry so about me."

"You left the chapel . . . ?"

"I walked down the road and saw you running—I thought it was Brian—so I ran after you and watched you put the gatehouse book on the ground and cover it with dirt."

"Then what?"

"I'm not sure. I was upset, naturally, and tried to shout at you, but I suddenly found it terribly difficult to breathe—don't tell Nils—then everything went dark. When things became clear—clearer—I was on the ground, and there were fires everywhere! Do I look presentable? Nils always wants me to look quite grand."

"You look fine, Madame Alvarado, but I have to ask you a question—quickly. Mr. Van told me to call one of the limousines. It's an emergency. How do I do that?"

"Oh, it's quite simple. . . . When I saw the lights over here, I had to find out just who—" The aristocratic old secretary could not go on; she went into convulsions, so severe the thick entry log fell away from her arm as she brought her hands to her chest. Her face appeared swollen, her eyes bulging.

"Easy!" shouted Tyrell, unable to reach the woman through the window. "Lean against the side—but you've got to tell me! How do I call the limousines? You say it's simple—what do I do?"

"It . . . was . . . simple." She struggled with the words, gasping for air. "Not now. Nils had me . . . delete everything in . . . the phone system."

"What are the numbers?"

"I . . . don't know—it's been years." Suddenly, the old woman let out a strangled cry. She was holding her throat, her swollen face turning blue under the wash of Tye's flashlight.

Hawthorne leapt through the window, crouching on the grass as he hit the ground, the flashlight flying out of his hand. He got up and ran to Alvarado as Catherine Neilsen appeared above in the shattered frame. "The wet bar inside," shouted Tyrell. "Turn on a lamp and get some water!"

Hawthorne had started to massage the old woman's

throat when the lights went on in the library, throwing a glow over the outside. Tye froze, the sight of the face beneath him sickening. It was grotesque, the contorted flesh a dark grayish-blue, the eyes red, the pupils dilated, the perfectly coiffed white hair a wig, halfway up her bald head. Madame Gretchen Alvarado was dead.

"Here!" Cathy was at the window, holding out a crystal pitcher filled with water. Then she saw the face below at Hawthorne's side. "Oh, my God," she whispered, turning away, as if she might vomit, instantly forcing herself to turn back. "What happened to her?" she asked, more of a plea than a question.

"You'd know if you smelled the odor down here— or maybe you wouldn't. The more macho chemists call it crash gas; you inhale it for a moment or two and it spreads like a lethal fungus in your lungs, choking off all exhalation. Unless it's washed out instantly—literally *washed* out—a person will die within an hour, usually less."

"And unless an experienced doctor handles the flushing process," said Poole, emerging out of the shadows, "the patient drowns. I've read about that stuff; it was a max-priority in Desert Storm. . . . Who is she?"

"Mars and Neptune's loyal factotum and once-celebrated hostess," answered Tyrell. "She just got her pension while praying for them all at their chapel. A cylinder in the air ducts is my guess."

"Nice fellas."

"Top drawer, Jackson. Come on, give me a hand. Let's put her in the library next to her beloved employer and get out of here."

"Get out?" Catherine Neilsen was stunned. "I thought you wanted to tear this place apart."

"It'd be a waste of time, Cathy." Hawthorne reached down for the bloodied gatehouse entry log and shoved it awkwardly under his belt. "This lady may not have been playing with a full deck, but she was a damned efficient robot for Van Nostrand. If she said the place was cleaned out, it was. . . . Get that shipping receipt, I want to take it with us."

The chauffeur was still naked, bound, and unconscious, and for convenience would stay where he was, so Poole drove the limousine, in deference, he said, to the extreme physical stress placed upon an aging former naval officer. "All that runnin' and leapin' in and out of windows—mah word!"

"Your execution is not yet out of the question," said Tyrell, alone in the back seat, stretching out his unacknowledged painful legs. "Major, check the telephone up there," he ordered Neilsen, who was in front with her lieutenant. "See if there are any instructions or numbers to reach the other limo. Look in the glove compartment too."

"There's nothing," said Cathy as Poole raced down the entrance road after raising the gate under Hawthorne's instructions. "Maybe I can call the operator, ask her to trace it."

"You'd have to have the number, or at least a license plate," said Jackson. "Otherwise they won't give it to you."

"Are you sure?"

"More than sure, it's FCC regulations."

"Shit!"

"What about Captain Stevens?"

"I'll try anything!" exclaimed Hawthorne, reaching for the back seat phone attached to the strip between the doors. He pressed the numbers rapidly, telling a navy subordinate that he was in a car nearby and his call was urgent. "Four-zero emergency, sailor!"

"What are you doing up here?" shouted the head of naval intelligence. "You're in Puerto Rico, goddamn it!"

"No time, Henry! There's a limousine owned by a

Nils Van Nostrand, Virginia license plate, but I don't know the number—"

"*The* Van Nostrand?" an astonished Stevens interrupted.

"That's who. I've got to have the telephone number of that limo."

"Do you know how many limousines there are in the state of Virginia, especially this close to Washington?"

"How many are carrying Bajaratt?"

"*What?*"

"Do it, Captain!" shouted Tye, trying to read the jiggling digits on the phone. "Call me back—here's the number." Hawthorne gave it to him and hung up the phone, twice missing the cradle in his anxiety.

"Where to, Commander?" asked Poole.

"Drive around for a while, I don't want to stop any where until he calls back."

"If it'll make you feel a bit relieved," continued the air force lieutenant, "that Gulfstream is headed straight through to Charlotte. It'll land in an hour and a half, plus or minus for a few thunder-bumpers."

"I can't wait to hear who cleared that bastard. Five'll get you twenty it's someone in this gatehouse log."

"Are you feeling all right, Tye?" Neilsen turned, looking over the partition at Hawthorne's stretched-out legs and the hands that were massaging them.

"What does that mean? I'm perfectly fine, except I'm a charter, not a commando."

"I can stop and get some ice," said Poole.

The telephone rang; Tyrell grabbed it. "Yes?"

"This is the cellular operator, sir. Is this number—"

"Never mind, operator, I'd know that bark anywhere," said the overriding voice of Henry Stevens. "We've got the wrong limo."

"We're very sorry, sir, please excuse the inconvenience—"

Hawthorne hung up. "At least he's moving fast," said Tyrell.

They drove around the Virginia countryside, seeing little because of the darkness, and passing the large estates of the hunt-country millionaires, only innocuous comments filling the void of pertinent conversation. The tension was driving the three of them to the point of babbling. Then exactly eighteen minutes later, the limousine phone rang again.

"What have you walked into," asked an ice-cold Captain Henry Stevens.

"What have you got for me?"

"Something neither one of us wants to hear. We traced the cellular number of Van Nostrand's limousine—his other limo—and had the operator verify for line interference. All we heard on the override was the usual, recorded 'driver has left the vehicle.' "

"So? Keep trying!"

"No reason to. Our crossover computers picked up a state police report with the identical license plate and registration—"

"They were stopped? *Hold* them—"

"They weren't stopped," Stevens broke in, his cool manner becoming frigid. "Have you any idea who Van Nostrand is?"

"Enough to know he went around you to reach me, Henry." As an astonished Stevens started to reply, Tyrell cut him off. "You were out of the loop, Captain, and you'd better bless your stars you weren't in it. If you had been, I'd have cut your throat with your eyes wide open."

"What the hell are you talking about?"

"I was summoned to my own execution—fortunately, I survived."

"I don't believe this!"

"Believe me, I don't lie where my life's concerned. We've got to find that other limo, find Bajaratt. Now, where is it?"

"At the bottom of a ravine off a back-country road

in Fairfax," said the stunned chief of naval intelligence in a quiet monotone. "The driver's dead."

"Where are the others? There were two, one of them Little Girl Blood!"

"You say—"

"I *know*! Where are they?"

"There was no one else, just the driver—shot in the head. . . . I ask you again, Tye, do you know who this Van Nostrand is? The police are on their way to his place right now!"

"They'll find him in the library, stone-cold deep. Good-bye, Henry." Hawthorne hung up the phone and leaned back in the seat, his legs and arms in pain, his head throbbing from the anxiety and the tension. "Forget the limousine," he said, bringing his hand to his leaded eyes. "It's totaled, the driver's dead."

"Bajaratt?" Neilsen whipped her head around. "Where is she?"

"Who knows? Somewhere within a hundred-mile radius is as good a bet as any, but we're not going to find her tonight. Maybe we'll learn something from the gatehouse log, maybe more from the Charlotte airport . . . or perhaps even more from a combination of both. Let's find a place where we can rest and get something to eat. As an old trainer once told me, both are weapons."

"We passed a pretty nice-lookin' place a while back," said Poole. "Actually, I don't know where we'd find another; it's the only motel I've seen, and we've been drivin' all over the area. As a matter of fact, Cath and I were supposed to be registered there, courtesy of Van Nostrand. Of course, we weren't—never meant to be."

"The Shenandoah Lodge, wasn't it?" asked the major.

"That's it," replied the lieutenant.

"Turn around," said Tyrell.

20

Nicolo Montavi of Portici paced rapidly back and forth, trembling from fear and exhaustion, rivulets of sweat rolling down his face, his eyes wide and darting this way and that at nothing, betraying his panic. Less than an hour before he had committed not only a terrible crime but a mortal sin in the eyes of God! He had assisted in the taking of a human life—not the killing itself, thanks be to Christ—but he had not stopped it in that swift second or two when he saw Cabrini take the gun from her purse. He had been confused, still appalled, horrified by the gunfire that accompanied their escape from the huge estate. The signora had ordered the chauffeur to stop the limousine, that was all! Then she withdrew her gun and shot him in the back of his head as coldly as if—as if she were swatting a fly, that was it! Moments later she had commanded her dock boy to push the car off the side of the road, where it plunged down the embankment into a ravine. He could not disobey, for the weapon was in her hand, and he knew in his heart—for it was in her eyes—that she would kill him if he refused. *Madonna della tristezza!*

Amaya Bajaratt sat on the couch in the minisuite at the Shenandoah Lodge, facing a hysterical Nicolo. "Is there anything else you wish to say, my dear? If so, please lower your voice."

"You are a madwoman, completely insane! You shot that man for no reason at all—you will send us both to *hell*!"

"I'm glad you understand that you're included on the journey."

"You shot him just as you shot that black servant on the island, and he was only a driver!" interrupted the young Italian feverishly. "The lies, the clothes, this *juego* we play with such important people . . . ah, *bueno, che cosa?* games for the rich who pay money, it is not so different on the docks in Portici . . . but not killing two such people. My God, a simple driver!"

"He was not a simple driver. When I told you to search his pockets, what did you find?"

"A gun," the dock boy replied quietly, reluctantly.

"Do simple drivers carry weapons?"

"In Italy, many do to protect their employers."

"Possibly, but not here in the United States. Here there are laws we don't have."

"I know nothing of such laws."

"I do, and I tell you that man was a criminal, an *agente segreto* sworn to destroy our great cause."

"You *have* such a great cause?"

"The greatest, Nicolo. There is none like it in the world today, a cause the Church itself silently blesses us for dedicating our lives to it."

"*Il Vaticano?* But you are not of my church! You *have* no faith!"

"In this area I do, I give you my solemn word, and that's all I'm permitted to tell you. So you see, your concerns are not that important. Now do you understand?"

"No, I do not, signora."

"You don't have to," Bajaratt broke in firmly. "Think how rich you are in Napoli, and of the great family that welcomes you as its own in Ravello. While you're doing so, go into the bedroom and unpack us."

"You are a very difficult woman," said Nicolo in a monotone, his eyes unblinking.

"Ever so. Quickly now, I have calls to make." The young Italian retreated into the bedroom as the Baj reached for the telephone on the side table. She dialed the number of their hotel and asked for the concierge. She identified herself, giving instructions for the luggage she had left behind, and inquired as to her messages, for which she had handsomely tipped the concierge.

"Thank you for your generosity, madame," said an unctuous voice at the hotel in Washington, "and be assured that your needs are being looked after with utmost care. We're sorry you had to leave so abruptly, but hope to have you back when you're again in the nation's capital."

"The messages, please." There were five, the most important one from Senator Nesbitt of Michigan; several others were in varying degrees helpful but not vital, and the last enigmatic. It was from the red-haired young political consultant they had met in Palm Beach, the op-ed contributor to *The New York Times* who had steered them to the dangerously inquisitive reporter from *The Miami Herald*—so dangerous Bajaratt had had to eliminate him quickly, with a jab of her lethal bracelet. She called the senator first.

"I have promising if unconfirmed news for you, Countess. My colleague in the Senate has tentatively set a meeting with the President in three days. Of course, it will be pursuant to our understanding—"

"*Naturalmente!*" interrupted the Baj. "The *barone* will be so pleased, and you will not be forgotten, Senator, believe me."

"That's most kind of you. . . . Your appearance will be off the books, that is, not listed on the President's schedule. There'll be only one photographer, approved by the White House Chief of Staff, and you will sign a release specifically stating that the photo session is for personal use and not for the press, either here or abroad. Extreme personal embarrassment would follow if the release is violated."

"Completely private!" Bajaratt agreed. "You have the word of a great Italian family."

"And that's completely acceptable," said Nesbitt, his

tone of voice lighthearted, allowing a chuckle. "However, should the baron's financial interests prove politically favorable, especially in regionally depressed areas, I guarantee that the Chief of Staff will have the photo of the President and the baron's son published all over the place. To counter that conceivable eventuality, my colleague from Michigan and I will have separate photographs taken flanking your nephew—*without* the President."

"How interesting," observed the Baj, laughing softly.

"You don't know the Chief of Staff," said Nesbitt. "If that Oval Office picture has mileage, no one else climbs on the trolley. . . . Where may I call you? The hotel said it was taking your messages—"

"We're traveling so much, you see." The Baj, sensing a problem, broke in quickly. "I trust one day soon we'll be going to your state of Michigan, but everything is happening so rapidly. Dante Paolo has the energy of six young bulls."

"It's none of my business, Countess, but I'd think it would be far easier on you, and perhaps more efficient, if you had an office and a staff—at least a secretary who knew where to find you. I'm sure through the baron's many friends here, dozens would be available to you. And I certainly could help you there, perhaps my own office."

"The answer to our prayers, but, alas, it cannot be. My brother is above reproach in all things, but he prizes confidentiality as thoroughly as he does ethics, no doubt because there are so many unethical men in world finance. The staff and the secretaries are in Ravello, nowhere else. We call every day, frequently twice or three times. They've been with him for years."

"He's a cautious fella," said the senator, "and damned right to be so. The BCCI fiasco, along with Watergate and Iran-contra, has taught us all that. I just hope your telephones are secure."

"We travel with point-of-origin scramblers calibrated

to reception frequencies, signore. What could be more secure?"

"My, that *is* sophisticated. The Defense Department tells us that terrorists have homed in on that technology. Pretty damned impressive."

"We would know nothing about such people, Senator, but for us it provides a measure of safety. . . . I will, of course, check with the hotel's concierge every hour or so."

"Please do, Countess. In the Washington circus, three days could become tomorrow or yesterday."

"I understand completely."

"You received the additional materials my office sent you, didn't you?"

"At this moment, Dante Paolo is talking to his father most enthusiastically on the other telephone about your proposals."

"You know, it's really remarkable, Countess. A young man that bright, that intuitive. The baron must be terribly proud. And you, Countess, a knowledgeable, lovely sister he can confide in, a woman of such charm, such diplomacy. Have you ever thought of politics?"

"I think of them all the time," the Baj replied, a smile in her voice. "And how I wish they'd all disappear— they destroy me so."

"Please, some of us need the work. I'll leave a message for you with the specifics of your visit to the White House. . . . And, of course, you know how to reach me if you have news from Ravello."

"Not if, Signor Nesbitt, merely when. *Arrivederci*." Bajaratt replaced the phone, her eyes on the Shenandoah stationery on which she had written the numbers and the names she had been given by the hotel in Washington. Three of them could wait, so could the last, but sheer curiosity forced her to lift the receiver and dial the red-haired young political consultant from Palm Beach.

"Reilly's Plumbers," said the cheerful voice on the

answering machine. "If your message relates to payment for my services, press one. If it doesn't, get the hell off the line and let someone worthwhile call me. You may, however, leave your name and even your number, but I make no promises." A long beep followed and the Baj spoke.

"We met in Palm Beach, Mr. Reilly, and I'm returning your call—"

"Glad you did, Countess," the political consultant interrupted, breaking into the line. "You're not an easy lady to track down."

"How did you, Mr. Reilly?"

"Sorry, that'll cost you," answered the young man, laughing. "On the other hand, since you didn't press one, I'll tell you for nothing."

"How kind of you."

"It was simple. I remembered a few of the Washington bears who were sniffing around your campfire and called their secretaries. Two out of three told me where you were."

"They were so free with the information?"

"They sure were after I explained that I just flew in from Rome with a confidential message for you from the big-shot baron—and how grateful he'd be to know the name of anyone who helped me. Also, I happened to mention that diamond bracelets spelling out the name Ravello weren't out of the question. You know how expansive these rich Italians are."

"You are a rogue, Mr. Reilly."

"I keep trying, Countess. This town is filled with pros."

"Why did you wish to reach me?"

"I'm afraid that *will* cost you, lady."

"What service could you possibly render to me that I would pay for?"

"Information."

"Of what nature, what value?"

"That's two different things, and to be perfectly honest, I can answer the first but I can't put a price on the second. Only you can."

"Then answer the first."

"Okay. Someone's looking in the sewers for a couple of people who may or may not be you and the kid, emphasis on the *not,* because it would be too farfetched. But then, I've got a wild imagination."

"I see." Bajaratt froze. *So near, so close!* "We are who we are, Mr. Reilly," she said, her control at maximum. "Who might the others be?"

"Like I said, sewer rats. Hustlers, maybe Mafia drug missionaries looking for better markets, or just plain scam artists from Sicily who know who to hold up."

"We could be mistaken for such people?"

"Hell, not on the surface. The woman's a lot younger than you, and the kid's described as an illiterate, muscle-bound thug."

"It's all preposterous!"

"Yeah, that's what I kept thinking, but as I say, I've got a crazy imagination. Do you want to meet?"

"Certainly, if only to put this insanity to rest."

"Where?"

"In a city or town called Fairfax, there's an inn or a hotel of sorts called the Shenandoah Lodge."

"I know it. So do most of the wandering husbands in Washington—surprised you could get in. I'll be there in an hour."

"I'll be in the parking lot," the Baj said. "I don't care to upset Dante Paolo, *barone-cadetto di Ravello.*"

Ashkelon!

Forever. What news?

We're about to enter phase one. Prepare for countdown.

Allah be loved; Allah be praised.

Praise an American senator.

Are you joking?

Not for an instant. He's come through for us. The strategy was successful!

Details?

You don't need them. Still, in case I don't survive, his name is Nesbitt. You may have need of him after I'm gone. And your Allah knows, he'll be vulnerable.

The limousine, driven by Poole, pulled into the entrance of the Shenandoah Lodge. The Van Nostrand name secured two adjoining double rooms despite the lateness of the hour and the disheveled appearance of the three travelers.

"What do we do now, Tye?" said Cathy, walking into the room Tyrell and Poole were sharing.

"Order some food, get some rest, and start making calls—oh, my God!"

"What is it?"

"*Stevens!*" cried Hawthorne, rushing to the telephone. "The *police* . . . they could cripple Charlotte, take the pilots into custody, the whole scenario could be blown away!"

"Can you stop them?" Neilsen asked as Tyrell dialed furiously.

"It depends when they got there. . . . Captain Stevens, four-zero emergency! . . . Henry, it's me. Whatever's happening at Van Nostrand's, you have to push every button you've got to keep it quiet!" Hawthorne fell silent, listening intently for nearly a minute. "I have to take back a few of the things I've laid on you, Captain," he said finally, less excitedly, relief in his tone. "I'll call you in a couple of hours with some names. Put each one under a microscope, twenty-four-hour details, telephone logs, scumbag material, the whole bag of dirty tricks. . . . Good thinking, Henry. By the way, I've been doing some thinking too, reevaluating maybe, on another subject. This may sound crazy at a time like this, but how well did you know Ingrid?" A sad smile creased Tyrell's face, his eyes briefly closing. "That's what I thought. Speak to you around midnight. Will you be at the office or at home? . . . Right, I shouldn't have asked." Hawthorne hung up the phone, his hand still on it as he raised his head and spoke. "Stevens anticipated the scenario. He's pulled a black drape over the Van Nostrand estate."

"But the man's dead!" exclaimed Poole. "What about all those *dead* bodies? How the hell are they going to keep all that quiet?"

"Fortunately, only one patrol car went out there, and Stevens reached police headquarters a few minutes before the two patrolmen called in. He put the clamps on all communications relative to Van Nostrand's death, backing it up with something called an 'alternating data-based security code' forwarded by naval intelligence."

"Just like that?"

"*That*, Lieutenant, is apparently the way things are done these days. You don't say 'keep it quiet' anymore, computers do that. You can't be in the spook business unless you're a walking manual of high technology. No wonder I'm history."

"You've done pretty well so far," said Cathy. "Better than anyone else."

"I'd like to, I'd *really* like to. If only somehow to give something back to Cooke and Ardisonne, two other 'has-beens.' . . . God damn that bitch and everyone she deals with! I *want* those bastards!"

"You're gettin' closer, Tye, close even."

Close, thought Hawthorne, taking off his cotton bush jacket now stained with sweat and dirt. *Close . . . ?* Oh, yes, he had been close, so close he had held her in his arms, making love as if the fragments of a shattered dream had been pieced together, dark night turned into a glorious dawn, the sun bursting over the horizon permitting a new and wonderful day. God damn you, Dominique! Liar, liar, *liar*. All you ever said to me were lies. But I'll find you, bitch, and blind you as you blinded me, make you feel the pain I feel. *God damn* you, Dominique, I spoke of love and felt love; you spoke of love and there was only deceit. Worse—far worse—at the roots there had to be hatred, the essential loathing the user has for the used.

"But where is she, Jackson?" Tyrell asked out loud. "That's the real question, isn't it?"

"I think you're overlooking something that's terribly important," Neilsen interrupted. "You've established that she's here, this close to Washington, so the President's security measures will be raised to the zenith. How can she possibly penetrate that shield?"

"Because the man can't stop doing his job."

"I thought you said all appearances, even local trips, were called off. He's isolated, quarantined, a prisoner in his own house."

"I know all that. What bothers me is that she knows it too, but it's not stopping her."

"I see what you mean. The leaks, the killings—Charlie, Miami; even you on Saba and here with Van Nostrand. Who are these people who support her? For God's sake, why?"

"I wish I knew the answer—the answers to both questions." Hawthorne sat down on the bed, then lay back on the pillow, his hands behind his head. "I have to go back, back to Amsterdam and all the goddamned stupid games that were played, the casualties that were never made public, no body counts there, pal. . . . *A* leans on *B* for one reason; *B* on *C* for another, seemingly unrelated; *C* on *D* for something off-the-wall with rearranged words, and finally *D* reaches *E*, who penetrates because he or she can, and it's what *A* wanted in the first place. The chain is so convoluted, you can't follow it."

"Apparently, you did," said Neilsen, a touch of admiration in her voice. "Your service record made it quite clear: You were outstanding."

"Sometimes, not always, and mostly by accident."

Poole was sitting at the desk, running his hand

through his light brown hair. "I wrote down what you just said about *A, B, C, D* and *E*, and since I was pretty alert in math, includin' geometry, trigonometry, calculus, and a touch of nuclear physics, were you sayin' that these people in Amsterdam were programmed in differently calibrated spheres? Like in disassociated quadrants?"

"I haven't the vaguest idea what you mean."

"But you just said it."

"Then I'll stand by it. What did I say?"

"That none of the letters knew exactly what was goin' on except the first and the last."

"It's oversimplified but essentially correct. It's called using blinds, contacts who might sense something but have no specifics to reveal, and usually don't suspect anything."

"What makes them do it?"

"Greed, Lieutenant, ultimately money. Either up front or with information they can use for extortion and even more money."

"You think that's who's behind this Bajaratt?" asked Cathy.

"Not really, the core's too organized, too powerful. But that core—the nucleus—has to use others for loose and not so loose ends; for things they don't want traced, always careful so that if they *are* traced, those being used can't lead back to the major players."

"Like a certain Alfred Simon in Puerto Rico?" suggested Poole.

"And an air controller who was always there but whose name Simon didn't know?" said Neilsen.

"Both up to their necks in Little Girl Blood and her suppliers," agreed Tyrell. "Each controlled, each expendable; and if Simon was an example, neither could offer anything of substance."

"But he did," objected Cathy. "He gave you a name, two names."

"One a washout, a highly respected D.C. attorney

who should put a psychiatrist on retainer, but other than that, zip . . . and the second was an accident, Major. I wasn't kidding before; my 'outstanding' service record is filled with accidents, just like the majority of my more successful former colleagues. A word, a phrase, a casual remark that somehow stays with you, and somewhere down the road an image fits. There's a click in your head—another accident—because the odds against your remembering are loaded dice not in your favor."

"That was Neptune, wasn't it?" said Andrew Jackson Poole.

"Yes, it was. Simon mentioned something to the effect that his manipulator, Mr. Neptune, looked like he stepped out of an ad in *Gentleman's Quarterly*, or a magazine like that. By God, he was right. Van Nostrand, even when he was about to have someone killed in front of his eyes, was a fashion plate."

"I wouldn't call your remembering an accident," said Neilsen. "I'd call it training."

"I didn't say I was an idiot, I was merely pointing out the odds. A short, garbled statement by a blindsided owner of a whorehouse so hung over he weaved like a spinnaker in half-dead air. It's not the sort of thing you write home about. As I said, just chance."

Hawthorne lay down on the bed and closed his eyes. He was dead tired, his legs still fired with pain, his arms aching, his head throbbing. He was vaguely aware of Cathy and Poole's good-natured squabbling over the room-service menu, but his thoughts were still focused on accidents. The accidents of his life, so many accidents, beginning with the one that had brought him into the navy. He was a college graduate who had switched majors so frequently he invariably forgot which one it was if questioned, finally ending up with astronomy. "Why not try single-stitch rug weaving?" his father, the professor, had asked. "Just stay away from my classes, son. Your mother would never understand my refusing to pass you."

Actually, the astronomy course wasn't that stupid; he'd been sailing since he could climb aboard a boat, and came to refine celestial navigation to the point where a quick glance without a sextant could put him reasonably on course. He had been a relatively talented athlete, his size and build leading to varsity status, but his lack of commitment, as well as the company, precluded a suggested career in sports; he had no desire either to stay in training or have his body assaulted. After the University of Oregon (no tuition for offspring of tenured professors), he was at a loss; he had managed a respectable 3.2 average since the courses he chose were interesting to him, but few were interesting to the corporate employers who looked for business administration, economics, engineering, or computer science. Then came accident number one.

On the streets of Eugene, two months after his mother had framed his essentially useless degree, he passed a navy recruiting office. Whether it was the attractive posters showing ships at sea, or because he was restless to do *something,* or a combination of both, was a question he never analyzed, but he walked inside and enlisted.

His mother had been appalled. "You're not remotely the military type!" she had said.

His younger brother, who was already a straight-A student in high school, as well as president of the honor society, added, "Tye, do you understand that you'll have to follow orders?"

His bemused father offered him a drink and was more trenchant than the other two. "Scratch a drifter with half a mind and you'll usually find someone who wants a little structure in his life. Anchors aweigh, son, and as the proctors of Salem said when they unearthed a warlock, 'God have mercy on your soul.' "

Fortunately, the navy had practiced a certain self-serving mercy. After reviewing Hawthorne's accomplishments as a young sailor, which were considerable, including the skippering of large sails and several dozen blue ribbons, he emerged from the San Diego training base as an ensign assigned to destroyer duty, which led to the second major accident.

After two years he was afflicted with battleship-gray claustrophobia. He looked around for something more expansive. A few land-based assignments opened up, but they were logistic jobs—desk work, which he wasn't interested in, but there was one that sounded like fun, if he could get it: protocol officer in The Hague.

He got it, as well as another stripe, a lieutenant (j.g.), and he hadn't the slightest idea that protocol was an observation ground for potential naval intelligence personnel. All the fun and games and embassy receptions and tours for the fat cats, civilian and military, were part of the course. Then one morning, after six months, he was called in to the chargé d'affaires' office, praised beyond his minor contributions, and told he was elevated to lieutenant, senior grade.

"And by the way, Lieutenant," the embassy executive had said. "We'd like you to do a little favor for us." Accident number three. He said yes.

Tyrell's counterpart at the French embassy was suspected of passing Franco-American intelligence to the Soviets. On the pretext of an upcoming dinner party, would Lieutenant Hawthorne take the man out for some heavy sympathetic drinking, pump him, and learn what he could? "Incidentally," the chargé d'affaires had said, handing him a tiny plastic bottle of Murine eye drops. "Two dabs of this in a drink will loosen the tongue of a mute."

Accident number four. Hawthorne never had a chance to use the ersatz eye drops. Unlucky Pierre was at the end of his rope and, filled with wine, spelled out his terrible confession, claiming to be both heavily in debt and having an affair with a Soviet mole who could expose their relationship and destroy him.

Accident number five. Probably due to several bourbons, Tyrell suggested that if the distraught Frenchman gave him the names of his KGB contacts, he could say that his patriotic counterpart was actually working for NATO because he suspected that there were leaks in his own embassy. Hawthorne's cheeks were sore for a week from the Frenchman's kisses of gratitude. The man became a valuable double agent, his turning credited to the protocol officer. Which led to accident six.

The commanding general of NATO summoned him, a man Hawthorne truly respected because he wasn't a debutant brass ass, but a straight-talking boss in shirt-sleeves. "I want to send you on, Lieutenant, because you not only have the qualifications, but, more important, you don't advertise them. I'm sick to death of the egos around here. Things get done with quiet people, observing people. Okay with you?"

Okay what? Certainly, General, whatever you say, *sir.* Tyrell was so much in awe of the man that certain specifics were either glossed over or delivered in such subtle militarese that the flattered Hawthorne enthusiastically agreed to his new horizons. Accident six had him flying back to Georgia for an exhausting twelve-week stay, an officer officially assigned to naval intelligence.

Upon his return to The Hague, presumably to resume his duties, the accidents came one after the other, some more accidental than others. He was becoming good at his real job. Fueled by the widespread hypocrisy and corruption that were rampant throughout NATO, Amsterdam had become the hub of the underground networks where money took the place of commitments, major and minor. He ran assets throughout the Netherlands, with side trips all over Europe, tracking down the despicable who brokered death along with payoffs. It was the mounting deaths, the useless killings, that finally caused him to break in his own way.

Suddenly, Tyrell was aware that Cathy was standing at the foot of the bed, looking down at him. He raised his head. "Where's our lieutenant?" he asked.

"He's using the phone in my room. He remembered he had a date tonight—four hours ago."

"I'd like to hear how he explains that away."

"You probably wouldn't. He's no doubt telling her he's been testing an experimental aircraft, very hush-hush, and sustained a neck injury during a thirty-eight-thousand-foot dive."

"He's a piece of work, that kid."

"He certainly is. . . . What were you doing? Having one of your eyes-open naps?"

"Hardly. Just one of those brief spells when you ask yourself why you're where you are—even why you're who you are, maybe."

"I know the answer to the first. You're here hunting down this Bajaratt woman because you were one of the finest intelligence officers in the navy."

"That's not true," said Hawthorne, sitting up against a pillow as Neilsen sat down in a chair several feet from the side of the bed.

"Stevens allowed that you were, even if he may have done so reluctantly."

"He was trying to calm your fears, that's all."

"I don't think so. I've watched you in action, Commander. Why deny it?"

"Because, Major, I may have been passably effective for a few years, but then something happened and whether my superiors realized it or not, I became the worst man in the field. You see, I didn't care anymore who won or lost the stupid games. I cared about something else."

"Do you want to tell me about it?"

"I don't think you'd want to hear it. Besides, it's pretty personal—I've never told anyone."

"I'll trade off with you, Tye. I have something personal, too, that I've never told anybody, not even Jackson, much less my parents. I'd like to tell somebody. Maybe we can help each other, since we'll probably never see each other when all this is over. Do you want to hear it?"

"Yes," said Tyrell, studying her somewhat anxious, perhaps slightly pleading, expression. "What is it, Cathy?"

"Poole and my folks think I was born to be military, born to be a top-gun air force pilot and all that goes with it."

"If you'll forgive me," said Hawthorne, smiling gently. "I think Jackson believes you were issued, not merely born to it."

"Wrong on every count," countered Major Catherine Neilsen. "Until I was accepted to the Point and a free education, all I ever wanted to be was an anthropologist. Someone like Margaret Mead, traveling all over the world, studying cultures no one knew about, discovering things about primitive people who in so many ways are better off than we are. Sometimes that dream still comes back to me. . . . I sound foolish, don't I?"

"Not at all. Why don't you go for it? . . . I always wanted my own sloop, to make a living sailing under my own flag, as it were. So I got sidetracked for a decade, so what?"

"The circumstances are vastly different, Tye. You started being trained for what you're doing now when you were practically a kid. I'd have to go back to school for God knows how long."

"What, a couple of years? It's not brain surgery. Then you can learn on the job."

"What?"

"You can do what ninety percent of all anthropologists can't do. You're a pilot; you can fly them wherever they want to go."

"This is crazy talk," said Cathy quietly, pensively. Then she sat upright and cleared her throat. "I've told you my secret, Tye. What's yours? Fair's fair."

"We sound like a couple of kids, but all right. . . . Every now and then it comes back to me, and I suppose it's my crutch, my rationalization. . . . One night I went to meet a Soviet, a KGB man pretty much like me, a sailor from the Black Sea. We both knew things were getting out of hand, the corpses in the canals insane. For *what*? The summits couldn't care less about us, and he and I were going to cool down the craziness. When I found him, he was still alive, but his face was carved up by a razor, no less than a hamburger. I understood what he wanted me to do, so I . . . relieved him of his misery, his excruciating pain. It was then that I knew what I really had to do. It wasn't simply to go after the corrupt who made fortunes out of nothing, or the misguided moles or bureaucrats who were brought up to oppose us ideologically, it was to go after the fanatics, the *maniacs* who could do this to one of their own. All in the name of some unwavering, unblemished loyalty that didn't mean a goddamn thing in the changing super bowls of history."

"That's heavy, Commander," said Cathy softly. "Was that when you met Stevens, Captain Stevens?"

"Henry the Horrible?"

"Was he . . . *is* he?"

"Sometimes. Let's say he's aggressively dedicated. Actually, I knew his wife better than I knew him. They had no children, so she worked for the embassy. She was in the transport division, coordinating all personnel travel arrangements, and I had my share of bouncing around. Nice lady, and I suspect she curbed his excesses more than she'd ever admit."

"A few minutes ago you asked him about your wife " Tyrell snapped his head to his left, his eyes locked with the major's. "Sorry," she said, looking away.

"I knew the answer, but it was a question that had to be asked," he said calmly. "Van Nostrand made a crude remark—to provoke me, throw me off guard."

"And Stevens put the lie to it," completed Cathy. "You believed him, of course."

"Without the slightest doubt." Hawthorne grinned,

not so much in humor but in remembrance, his eyes again on the ceiling. "Aggressiveness aside, Henry Stevens is very bright, very analytical, but the main reason he was taken out of the field and shoved upstairs is that he's a totally inept liar. To begin with, you think he's about to sweat, whether you see him or merely hear his voice. It's why I'm convinced he knows more about my wife's death—her murder—than he's telling me. . . . You know what I asked him, so you can assume the implication. His answer was so flat and unequivocal, his reaction so quick, instantaneous, I knew it was the truth. He said he'd met Ingrid only once, at the small wedding reception the embassy gave us—when he accompanied his wife."

"So much for the lie," said Cathy.

"I never had a doubt. Neither would you if you'd known Ingrid."

"I wish I had."

"She would have liked you." Tyrell moved his head slowly, again looking at the major, no hostility in his eyes. "You're about the same age she was, and with that same sense of independence, even authority, but you assert it more—she never had to."

"Thanks a whole hell of a lot, Commander."

"Hey, come on, you're a military officer; you have to. She was a quadrilingual translator; it wasn't called for. I wasn't insulting you."

"By God, she bought it!" shouted Poole, bursting through the door of Neilsen's room.

"Bought what?" asked Hawthorne.

"The fact that I volunteered for an underwater gravity-free bathysphere that sprung an oxygen leak in my lungs! Hot *damn*!"

"Let's eat," Cathy said.

Room service arrived forty-five minutes later, the interim spent with Hawthorne studying the gatehouse entry log,

Poole reading the newspapers he had purchased at the stand in the lobby, and Catherine taking a warm bath, hoping to "wash away a dozen or so anxiety attacks." They kept the television set on, the volume low but sufficient to hear any sudden news bulletins that might concern Van Nostrand. Thankfully, there were none. Their meals finished, Tyrell phoned Henry Stevens at the office.

"Can you plug up any intercepts with a scrambler?"

"You still think we've got leaks here?"

"I'm damn sure of it."

"Well, if you have some new evidence, let me know, because you and I have been on reverse scrambler for the last three days. Which would mean the leaks are on your end."

"Absolutely impossible."

"Christ, I'm sick of your know-it-all attitude."

"Not know-it-all, Henry, just generally knowing more than you."

"I'm sick of that too."

"Then it's simple. Fire me."

"We didn't hire you!"

"If you cut off the funds we need, it's the same thing. Do you want to do that?"

"Oh, shut up. . . . What have you got? Any word on Little Girl Blood?"

"No more than you have," answered Tyrell. "She's here, within a few miles of her strike, and no one knows where."

"There'll be no strike. The President's as good as locked in a vault. Time's on our side."

"I love your confidence, but he can't keep that up too long. An invisible President is no President at all."

"I don't love your attitude. What else? You said you were going to give me some names."

"Here they are, and put every one of them under the sharpest micros you've got." Hawthorne read off the names he had selected from the gatehouse log, having eliminated the usual estate personnel—a plumber, a veterinarian for the horses, and a quartet of Spanish dancers who had been hired for an outside barbecue, Argentine style.

"You're talking about some of the biggest guns in the administration!" Stevens exploded. "You are now *certifiable!*"

"Every one of them was there during the last eighteen days. And since Little Girl Blood is indelibly linked with Van Nostrand, it's entirely possible that one, or more than one, is part of that bastard's agenda—knowingly or unknowingly."

"Do you realize what you're asking me to do? The secretary of defense, the director of the CIA, that crazy chief of clandestine G-2, the goddamned secretary of *state?* You're nuts!"

"They were there, Henry. So was Bajaratt."

"Do you have proof? For God's sake, I could be fried by every one of the President's men!"

"I'm holding the proof in my hand, Captain. The only people on this list who would fry you are working with Bajaratt, again knowingly or unknowingly. Now, damn you, go to work! . . . Incidentally, within the next twenty minutes or so, I'm going to give you a traceable asset that could make you an admiral if you're not killed first."

"That's nice. What the hell is it, and where will the trace take us?"

"To the person behind Van Nostrand's getting out of the country."

"Van Nostrand's dead!"

"They don't know that at his point of departure. I repeat, go to work, Henry." Tyrell hung up the phone and alternately looked at Neilsen and Poole, who stared at him, mouths agape. "Is something bothering you?" he asked.

"You sure play hardball, Commander," said the lieutenant.

"There's no other way to play it, Jackson."

"Suppose you're wrong?" said Cathy. "Suppose no one on that list has anything to do with Bajaratt?"

"I won't accept that. And if Stevens can't come up with anything, I'll see that this list goes public with the larger story and so many innuendos, lies, and half-truths that the power structure will have mass cardiac arrests coming up with explanations. There won't be any safety nets even for the real saints in Washington."

"That's cynical to the point of complete irresponsibility," Neilsen said curtly.

"It certainly is, Major, because to find Little Girl Blood, the core of her support group has to panic. We know they're out there, and we know they've penetrated our closed circles here and in London and Paris. Just one mistake, one person trying to cover his ass, and the experts go to work with their magic serums."

"You make it sound so simple."

"Basically, it's not that complicated. We start with the gatehouse list, men known to have been in close contact with Van Nostrand, then the list expands with the individual microscopes. Who are their friends, their associates; who works in their offices with access to classified materials? Who among them have life-styles seemingly beyond their means? Are there weaknesses that could make them marks for extortion? Everything progresses at top speed, fear and panic the ammunition." The telephone rang and Tyrell pounced on it. "Stevens?" Hawthorne frowned; he covered the mouthpiece and gestured to Poole. "It's for you."

The lieutenant picked up the phone on the desk. "Did it happen, Mac? . . . Ten minutes ago? Okay, thanks. . . . How the hell do I know? Sell the damn thing! If they had any brains, they'd have flown it to Cuba." Poole hung up and looked at Tye. "Van Nostrand's jet landed and apparently there was a lot of confusion. The Washington escort had a blowup with the Jones boys, who left the plane at General Aviation, saying they'd been dismissed by the owner and then got outta there."

"It's time for St. Thomas," said Tyrell, reaching for the phone and dialing the Caribbean. His face creased with anticipation, he waited, then pressed the two-digit ICM code and listened to his messages. . . . *My darling, it's Dominique! I'm calling from a boring cruise off the coast of Portofino.* . . . Hawthorne blanched, his eyes wide, the muscles of his face taut. It was false, as everything about Dominique was false, the mendacity of a killer whose whole life was a lie. And Pauline in Paris was part of that lie, a fragment that could bring them one step closer to Bajaratt.

"What is it?" said Cathy, reading the anxiety on his face.

"Nothing," replied Tyrell quietly. "I just heard from someone who made a mistake." Another message followed; his tension returned.

Suddenly, from outside the hotel window, there was an ear-shattering scream. It continued, growing louder, then hysterical. Neilsen and Poole ran to the window. "Down in the parking lot!" cried the lieutenant. "Look!"

Below, where the huge black surface of the parking area was illuminated by bordering floodlights, stood a blond woman and a middle-aged man. The woman was shrieking in horror, clutching her companion as he tried desperately to quiet her and pull her away. Poole opened the window; the gray-haired man's pleas were now audible.

"Shut up! We've got to get out of here. Will you be quiet, you idiot, people will hear you!"

"He's dead, Myron! Jesus, look at his head—it's half blown away! Holy Christ!"

"Shut up, you goddamned tramp!"

Several white-jacketed waiters came running from a rear door, one of them holding a flashlight, its beam wavering back and forth, finally settling on the figure of a man, his body angled out of the open door of a Porsche convertible, half on the seat, half on the pavement. The dark area around the man's head glistened under the flashlight's beam; the skull was shattered, bleeding.

"Tye, come over here!" cried Neilsen, the shouts below covering the urgency of her voice.

"Shhh!" Hawthorne held the palm of his left hand over his ear, concentrating on the words he was hearing on the line from St. Thomas.

"Someone was just killed down there!" Cathy continued. "A man in a sports car. They're sending for the police!"

"Be quiet, Major, I've got to get this right." Tyrell wrote on the room-service menu.

Outside the room, in the Shenandoah Lodge's corridor, Amaya Bajaratt hurried past Hawthorne's door, removing a pair of surgical gloves.

21

"**G**ood God, it's the secretary of state," said Tyrell quietly to himself. Stunned, he slowly replaced the telephone as the sound of sirens filled the parking lot below. "I don't want to believe it!" he whispered, albeit loud enough to be heard.

"Believe what?" asked Cathy, turning away from the window. "It's a mess down there."

"It's a mess up here too."

"Someone was killed, Tye."

"I understand that, but it has nothing to do with us. We are, however, very involved with something else that'd give the country mass cardiac arrest."

"I beg your pardon?"

"Van Nostrand's military escort at the airport in Charlotte was by direct order of the secretary of state."

"Oh, m'gawd," said Poole softly, his gaze on Hawthorne, his hands closing the window. "And I thought you were hangin' ten on a skateboard when you talked about people like that."

"There's got to be an explanation," Neilsen interrupted, "because you're right, there can't be a connection between him and Bajaratt."

"He had a pretty solid connection with Van Nostrand, strong enough to get him out of the country under damned strange circumstances, and Van Nostrand—Mr. Neptune—had Little Girl Blood hidden in a guest house a few hundred yards away from that library. To go back to the alphabet, if *A* equals *B*, and *B* equals *C*, then there's a specific relationship between *A* and *C*."

"But you said you saw two *men* gettin' into that limo, Tye. One with a hat—"

"Which is standard for covering a bald head," broke in Hawthorne. "I said that too, Jackson, and I was wrong on one count and too limited with the other. They weren't two men; one was a woman, and a hat doesn't cover just a bald head; it also hides a woman's hair."

"It really *was* Bajaratt," Cathy whispered. "We were so close!"

"So close," agreed Tyrell quietly, frowning intensely. "We don't have a choice—I don't have a choice—and there's no time to waste." He reached down for the telephone while there was a knocking at the door. "See who it is, will you, Poole?"

Standing in the hallway were two uniformed police officers. "Are these the rooms of a Major Neilsen, a Lieutenant Poole, and a relative, an uncle, from Florida?" asked the man on the right, reading from a clipboard.

"Yes, sir," answered the lieutenant.

"Your registration is incomplete, sir," said the second policeman, peering inside the room. "The laws of Virginia require additional information."

"Sorry, fellas," said Poole. "I wrote that out myself and we were in an awful hurry."

"May we see your identification?" The man with the clipboard pushed past the lieutenant into the room, his colleague following several steps behind, blocking the door. "And please account for your whereabouts during the past two hours."

"We haven't left these rooms since we arrived well over two hours ago," said Hawthorne, replacing the phone. "And as we're consenting adults, you've no right to interfere with our pursuits no matter how offensive they might appear to you."

"*What?*" Major Neilsen blanched, muffling her throated protest.

"Maybe you don't understand, sir," said the clipboard holder. "A man was shot down there, murdered. We're questioning everyone on the premises, and, if you want it straight, especially anyone with a fishy registration, which yours seems to fit. There's no name for Uncle Joe here and no address in Florida except a town, and no credit card number."

"Ah told you, we were in a hurry and we paid cash."

"At these prices, you must carry a lot of cash, then. Maybe more than a lot."

"That's none of your business," said Tyrell sharply.

"Listen, mister, the victim down in that parking lot was set up," said the clipboard. "He brought a box of fancy chocolates for whomever he was going to meet. The card read, 'To my generous friend.' "

"Oh, that's terrific!" exclaimed Hawthorne. "We shot him, stayed around for the parade, and didn't even take the chocolates!"

"Stranger things have happened."

"Definitely," agreed the officer at the door, reaching under his tunic and pulling out a police radio as he unsnapped the flap of his holster. "Sergeant, we've got three weirdos up here, all possibles, rooms five-oh-five and five-oh-six. Send a detail as fast as you can. . . . Guess what I just spotted? Hurry up!"

Following the gaze of the patrolman, four heads whipped around to the other side of the room. On the top of the bureau were Poole's Walther P.K. automatic and Hawthorne's .38-caliber revolver.

Bajaratt looked out the window at the crowds below. She was not interested in the mayhem or the proceedings, she knew both only too well—the morbidly jostling onlookers beside themselves to catch a glimpse of a bloodied corpse, and the police trying to maintain a semblance of order until higher authority arrived to tell them what to do. Until then, the mutilated body had to stay in place; it was meat for the frenzied bystanders, a bloody sheet covering the corpse in no way diminishing their appetites.

The Baj was not concerned with the infantile activities of the useless; she was desperately trying to find Nicolo, whom she had sent downstairs the instant she returned to the suite, his instructions explicit. *Something terrible happened and we must leave. Find a car even if you have to subdue the owner! Take the suitcases and use the fire stairs!* There he *was!* In the shadows of a pole supporting a floodlight, raising his right hand, holding something in it, and nodding his head. He had done it!

Bajaratt checked the mirror, adjusting the wig of thin white hair. The liquid adhesive on her face held the accentuated lines together; the pale powder, the dark gray half-moons under her lidded eyes, and the thin, white-drawn lips produced the countenance of an old woman, an eccentric old woman who wore a man's brown hat over her head.

Bajaratt opened the corridor door, instantly astonished by the noise and the stream of running police who were converging on a room down the hall, their guns drawn. She proceeded toward the elevator, skirting the uniforms, a bent-over figure fighting the advancing years.

"You sons of bitches, let go of me!"

"Don't get near me, you hogs, or yer all gonna be a lot fuckin' sorrier than me!"

"Don't you dare touch me!"

The Baj was suddenly paralyzed, her every muscle, tendon, and joint inoperative. *You sons of bitches, let go of me.* Only one voice, only one man. *Hawthorne!* Instinctively, she spun her bent-over body to the right, the chaos inside commanding her attention.

Between the bodies and the outstretched arms pinning Tyrell against the wall, their eyes met, hers narrowed in shock, his wide, bewildered, disbelief joining panic.

* * *

Howard Davenport, acknowledged powerbroker and giant of industry, yet withal a frustrated, defeated head of the insatiable Department of Defense, poured himself a second Courvoisier from the brass dry bar in his study and walked slowly back to his desk. He was a relieved man, the relief having come roughly two hours before when the D.O.D. security car had radioed the night watch, confirming that Van Nostrand's limousine had left the estate with a passenger or passengers in the back seat.

If Hawthorne is driven away by my limousine, you'll know my information was wrong, and you must never mention that I brought it up.

Davenport had no intention of ever doing so. There was more than enough muted hysteria over the hunt for Little Girl Blood. To burden the hunters further with blatantly false rumors would only add to the panic— some intelligence zealot would factor them into an esoteric computer, thus spreading more confusion as some other zealot picked them up. Van Nostrand understood that only too well; it was the reason he gave his final instructions should it turn out that former Lieutenant Commander Hawthorne was *not* a member of the infamous Alpha market. . . . Good God, what kind of Defense secretary was he? considered Davenport. He had never heard of the Alpha, whatever it was!

No, the time had come, he thought. He wished his wife were home rather than in Colorado, visiting their daughter, who had just delivered her third child, but there was no separating mothers and daughters and emerging grandchildren; it was a given. He really did want her with him, because he had finally typed out his resignation on the old Remington his parents had given him a lifetime ago. The newspapers frequently made a point of the old typewriter; the scion of Short Hills wealth pecking away, making notes at the antique machine when he could have the finest computerized equipment, to say nothing of an army of secretaries. But the "old Rem" was an old friend, a friend he could think with, so Davenport saw no reason to change.

He sat down, swiveling his chair to the right, facing the typewriter stand, rereading his short letter to the President. Yes, his wife should have been with him, for she loathed Washington, longing for their horse farm in New Jersey's hunt country, and delighted in their joint conspiracy. She especially enjoyed it as the doctors at the Mayo Clinic, where they both went for their annual summer checkups, had pronounced her in excellent health. Davenport sipped his brandy, smiling.

> *Dear Mr. President:*
>
> *It is with enormous regret that I must submit my resignation, effective immediately, due to the recent discovery of a severe health problem within my immediate family.*
>
> *May I say it has been an honor to serve under your superb leadership, secure in the knowledge that following your precepts, the Department of Defense stands tall and committed. Finally, may I thank you for the privilege of being part of "the team."*
>
> *My wife, Elizabeth, may the good Lord comfort her, sends you her affectionate best wishes as, of course, do I.*
>
> *Sincerely,*
> *Howard W. Davenport*

The secretary again sipped his cognac, chuckling at the sight of the phrase that caught his eye and for a few seconds lingered there. He wondered, to be consistent with his image of integrity, whether it wouldn't be more honest to add the words "should be." The passage would then read, ". . . following your precepts, the Department of Defense stands tall and *should be* committed." . . . No, there would be no recriminations, no telltale books placing the blame of excess on others. Perhaps a series of articles might be helpful to those who would succeed him—they would certainly garner attention—but in the final analysis it was up to the man who took the job. If he was the right man, he'd see the flaws of the procurement system and correct them with a steel fist. If he was not the right man, his hands barren of steel, no amount of extraneous warning would help him. And Howard Wadsworth Davenport understood that he fell in the latter category; in fact, he had fallen in office.

He put the brandy glass on the desk, only to have it slip off the edge and crash on the parquet floor. Odd, Davenport thought, he had placed it on the blotter—or had he? His eyesight was becoming blurred, his breathing suddenly audible, difficult—where was the *air*? Unsteadily, he got to his feet, thinking the central air-conditioning had malfunctioned and the night was hot, humid, increasingly suffocating. Then there *was* no air! Instead, a sharp pain formed in his chest and spread rapidly through his whole upper body. His hands trembled; his arms in seconds became uncontrollable, then his legs could no longer bear his weight. He fell facedown on the hard floor, his nose smashed, bleeding, and with an agonizing effort pushed himself up, spastically twisting, finally collapsing again, his eyes wide, focused on the ceiling, yet he saw nothing.

Darkness. Howard W. Davenport was dead.

The study door opened, revealing the figure of a man dressed in black, a filtered mask covering his face, black silk gloves on his hands. He turned and crouched beside a metal cylinder of deadly gas, roughly two feet in height with a rubber tube attached to the petcock and extending to the base of the door, its nozzle narrow and flat. He turned the knob on top, twice checking the closure with strong twists. He rose to his feet, crossed to a pair of French doors leading to a patio, and opened them. The summer night's damp, warm air slowly filled the room with the scents of a garden. The man walked to the typewriter stand and read Davenport's letter of resignation. He yanked it out of the platen, crumpled it, and stuffed it into a trouser pocket. He then inserted a blank page of Davenport's stationery and typed the following:

Dear Mr. President:

It is with the utmost regret that I submit my resignation, effective immediately, for reasons of personal health that I have assiduously kept from my dear wife. Quite simply, I can no longer function, a fact to which a number of my colleagues will no doubt attest.

I have been under the care of a doctor in Switzerland whom I have sworn to secrecy, and he informs me it's now only a question of days—

The letter ended abruptly, and Scorpio 24, under orders given him the previous morning by the original Scorpio One, gathered his lethal equipment, leaving by way of the French doors and the patio.

The Fairfax, Virginia, police had left the adjoining rooms at the Shenandoah Lodge, and in their place stood the uniformed Captain Henry Stevens.

"For Christ's sake, Tye, get with it!"

"I will, Henry, I will," said a still-pale Hawthorne sitting on the edge of the bed, Neilsen and Poole anxiously leaning forward in chairs across the room. "It's just so *crazy*! I knew her, knew those eyes, and she knew me! But she was an old woman, barely able to stand up, but I *knew* her!"

"I repeat," Stevens said, standing over Tyrell. "The woman you saw is an Italian countess named Cabarini or something, and very vain, according to the front desk.

She wouldn't even sign the register downstairs because—catch this—she wasn't 'properly dressed'; she had them bring it up to her. I checked her credentials with Immigration. She's golden, right to the top, her millions and all."

"She left—why did she leave?"

"So did twenty-two other guests, and the place holds only thirty-five. A man was killed in the parking lot, Tye, and these tourists aren't exactly a Delta Force."

"All right, all right . . . I'll 'get with it.' I just can't get that face out of my mind!" Hawthorne repeated, shaking his head slowly. "The age, she was so *old,* but I knew the eyes—I *knew* them."

"Geneticists say there are exactly one hundred thirty-two variations of eye shape and eye color, no more and no less," Poole announced. "That's one hell of a small equation when you figure the number of people in this world. 'Don't I know you?' is one of the more common questions people ask."

"Thanks for nothing." Hawthorne turned back to Henry Stevens. "Before all this craziness began, I was calling you. I don't know how you're going to do it, but you've got to."

"Got to what?"

"First, and tell me the truth, does anybody—*could* anybody—know that Van Nostrand's dead?"

"No, the information's capped, the house sanitized and guarded. The Fairfax dispatcher and the two patrolmen are professionals and understand. So they can't be tracked down in case of a leak; all three are out of the area."

"Okay. Then you use every button you've got and get me an appointment with the secretary of state. Tonight—this morning, now. We can't waste five minutes."

"You're a lunatic. It's almost midnight!"

"Yes, I know, and I also know that Van Nostrand

was getting out of the country secretly because the secretary of state cleared the way for him. Very officially."

"I don't believe you!"

"*Believe*. The elegant pinstriper, Bruce Palisser, made the arrangements, including a military escort and a maximum security passage out of Charlotte, North Carolina. I want to know why."

"Jesus, so do I!"

"It won't be that difficult. Tell him the truth—he probably knows it anyway—that I was recruited by MI-6, not by you or anybody else in Washington, because there aren't too many people inside the Beltway whom I trust. Tell him I claim to have information about Little Girl Blood that I'll give only to him, insofar as my British recruiter was killed. He won't refuse; he's close to the U.K. . . . You might even exaggerate and also tell him that despite the fact that we don't get along, I was once pretty good at my job and may really have something. . . . There's the phone, Henry. *Do* it."

The chief of naval intelligence did so, his words to the secretary of state containing the proper mixture of alarm, urgency, and respect. When he had finished, Hawthorne pulled him aside, handing him a piece of paper. "This is a telephone number in Paris," said Tyrell quietly. "Contact the Deuxième and tell them to put it under surveillance—total."

"Who is it?"

"A number Bajaratt has called, that's all you have to know. It's all I'll tell you."

The taxi pulled up to the curb in Georgetown, that select acreage of Washington that houses the capital's elite. The imposing four-story brownstone stood atop a three-tiered rolling lawn, punctuated by a brightly lighted brick entrance, the black-enameled door polished, the brass hardware glistening. The steep concrete steps were whitewashed, the bordering wrought-iron railings enameled white, all obviously to aid a climber's sight at night. Hawthorne paid the fare and got out of the cab.

"You want me to wait, mister?" asked the driver, glancing at Tyrell's informal open-collared safari jacket and obviously aware of the late hour, if not the home of the secretary of state.

"I don't know how long I'll be," replied Hawthorne, frowning, "but you've got a point. If you're free, why not come back in, say, forty-five minutes, that should do it." Tyrell reached into his pocket, withdrew a ten-dollar bill, and dropped it through the open front window. "Give it a shot; if I'm not out here, take off."

"It's a slow night, I'll give you some time."

"Thanks."

Hawthorne started up the steps, briefly wondering why anybody over fifty would live in a place where one had to be part mountain goat to reach the front door. Then his silent question was answered, for above, on the brick porch, was a large electric escalator chair, and below the right railing a second, wide metal strip that carried the current. Secretary Palisser was no fool where creature comforts were concerned; he was no fool in a lot of ways. Tyrell was not a fan of the Washington establishment, but Bruce Palisser seemed to be a cut above most of the crowd. Hawthorne did not know much about him, but from what he had read in the newspapers and had seen on his televised press conferences, the secretary had a quick mind and a pleasant wit, even a sense of humor. Tyrell held suspect anyone in political power who lacked those qualities. Anywhere. In any country. Yet at the moment he was very wary, suspicious in the extreme, of the secretary of state. Why had he done what he had for Nils Van Nostrand, friend and accommodator of the terrorist Bajaratt?

The shiny brass knocker was more an ornament than a practical instrument, so Hawthorne rang the brightly lighted doorbell. In seconds the heavy door was opened by a shirt-sleeved Palisser, his familiar features creased but distinguished below a crown of wavy gray hair; his trousers, however, were the antithesis of his sartorial reputation—he wore faded blue denims cut off at the knees.

"You've got brass balls, Commander, I'll say that for you," the secretary announced. "Come on in, and as we walk into the kitchen, start telling me why you didn't go to the director of Central Intelligence, *or* the DIA, *or* G-2, *or* your own goddamned superior, Captain Stevens of naval intelligence?"

"He's not my superior, Mr. Secretary."

"Oh, yes," said Palisser, stopping in a foyer and eyeing Tyrell. "He mentioned something about the Brits, MI-6 I believe. So why the hell didn't you reach them?"

"I don't trust Tower Street."

"You don't *trust*—"

"I also don't trust N.I., or CIA, or DIA, *or*—hell, you name it, Mr. Secretary, they're penetrated."

"My God, you're serious."

"I'm not here to make points, Palisser."

"*Palisser* now? . . . Well, I suppose that's refreshing. Come along, I'm brewing some coffee." They walked through a swinging oak door into a large white kitchen with a butcher-block table in the center, an old-fashioned electric percolator at the end, plugged into a side receptacle; it was bubbling away. "Everyone has those plastic things that drip and tell time and how many cups you've got and God knows what else, but none of 'em fills the room with the good old aroma of real coffee. How do you like it?"

"Black, sir."

"First decent thing you've said." The secretary poured; the cups filled, Palisser spoke. "Now, you tell me why you're here, young man. I'll accept the penetrations, but you could have gone back to London, to the top as I understand it. You can't have any problem with that man."

"I have problems with any communications that can be internally tapped."

"I see. So what have you got about the Little Girl that you can tell only me—personally?"

"She's here—"

"I know that, we all know it. The President couldn't be more secure."

"But that's not why I insisted on seeing you—personally."

"You're a presumptuous bastard, Commander, annoying too. Tell me."

"Why did you arrange for Nils Van Nostrand to leave the country in a way that can be described only as highly secretive?"

"You're out of order, Hawthorne!" The secretary slammed his free hand down on the table. "How dare you interfere with confidential State Department business?"

"Van Nostrand tried to kill me less than seven hours ago. I think that gives me a lot of 'dare.' "

"What are you *saying*?"

"I've only just begun. Do you know where Van Nostrand is now?"

Palisser stared at Tyrell, concern turning rapidly into fear, fear close to panic. He sprang to his feet, spilling his coffee, and walked rapidly to a telephone on the wall, a phone with numerous buttons on its panel. He pressed one repeatedly, angrily. "Janet!" he cried. "Did I get any calls tonight? . . . Why the hell didn't you tell me? All right, all right, I didn't look. . . . He what? Good Christ . . . !" The secretary slowly hung up the telephone, his frightened eyes locked with Hawthorne's. "He never got to Charlotte," he whispered as if asking a question. "I was out . . . at my club . . . Pentagon security called—what happened?"

"I'll answer your question if you'll answer mine."

"You have no right!"

"Then I'll leave." Tyrell got to his feet.

"Sit down!" Palisser walked back to the table and grabbed his chair, brushing the spilled coffee to the floor with the back of his hand. "Answer me!" he ordered, sitting down.

"Answer *me*," said Hawthorne, still standing.

"All right—sit down . . . please." Tye did so, noting the sudden painful expression on the secretary's face. "I took advantage of my position for personal reasons that in no way compromised the State Department."

"You can't know that, Mr. Secretary."

"I *do* know it! What *you* don't know is what that man has been through and what he's done for this country!"

"If that's your explanation of why you did what you did, I think you'd better tell me."

"Who the hell are you?"

"If nothing else, someone who can answer your question. . . . Wouldn't you like to know what happened? Why he never got to Charlotte?"

"I damn well better," said Palisser. "There's an angry army brigadier in G-2 who'd love to call me an intelligence screwup. . . . All right, Commander, I'll give it to you, but unless you can give me overriding security reasons to the contrary, it remains confidential information. I won't sacrifice a fine man and the woman he loves for unsupported intelligence garbage. Is that clear?"

"Go ahead."

"Years ago, in Europe, Nils was in a marriage that was falling apart—it doesn't matter whose fault, it was finished. He met and fell in love with a nationally known political figure's wife—an abused wife, I might add— and they had a child, a girl who now, twenty-odd years later, is dying. . . ."

Hawthorne sat back in his chair and listened, his expression neutral until the secretary had finished his tale of love, betrayal, and vengeance. Then he smiled. "My brother, Marc, would probably call it pure nineteenth-century Russian, as in Tolstoy or Chekov. I call it bullshit. Did you ever check on that European marriage?"

"Good Lord, of course not. Van Nostrand's one of the most respected—even revered—men I've ever known. He's been an adviser to agencies, departments, and even to presidents!"

"If there was a marriage, it was solely for the books; and if there was ever a child, he had to work like hell for it. Van Nostrand wasn't the marrying kind. He lied to you, Mr. Secretary, and right now I'm wondering how many others he flimflammed."

"Explain yourself! You haven't explained anything!"

"That'll all come later, but right now you deserve my answer to your question. . . . Van Nostrand's dead, Mr. Secretary, shot while ordering my execution."

"I don't believe you!"

"You might as well, because it's true . . . and Little Girl Blood was across the road in one of his guest cottages."

"What happened, signora? Why was that man in the parking area killed?" The dock boy paused, his question angry as he briefly took his eyes off the Virginia road and stared at Bajaratt. "Oh, my God, was it *you*?"

"Have you lost your *mind*? I was writing letters while you watched television in the bedroom, the volume so loud I could barely think! . . . I heard the police say it was a jealous husband; the dead man was having an affair with his wife."

"You have too many words, too many explanations, *Contessa* Cabrini. Which should I accept?"

"You accept what I tell you or you go back to Portici and be killed on the docks, along with your mother, your brother, and your sisters! *Capisci?*"

Nicolo was silent, his face, unseen in the racing shadows, flushed. "What do we do now?" he asked finally.

"Drive into the woods somewhere, where it's dark, and we will not be seen. We'll rest for a few hours, then early in the morning you will pick up the rest of our luggage at the hotel. We will then resume our roles as Dante Paolo and his aunt, the *contessa*. . . . Look! There's a field with tall summer grass, like the high grass at the foot of the Pyrenees. Drive into it."

Nicolo turned the wheel so sharply that Bajaratt was thrown against the door. Frowning, she studied him.

Secretary of State Bruce Palisser leapt to his feet above the butcher-block table, sending his chair crashing to the floor. "Nils *can't* be dead!"

"Captain Stevens is still in his office over at naval intelligence. Call your night watch and have it connect you; he'll confirm it."

"Oh, my God, you wouldn't make such an outrageous, unbelievable statement . . . unless you could back it up."

"It'd be a waste of time, Mr. Secretary, and in my judgment, there's no time to waste."

"I—I don't know what to say." Like a far older man than he was, Palisser awkwardly leaned over and righted his chair. "It's all so incredible."

"That's why it's real," said Hawthorne. "Because *they're* all so incredible. Here and in London, Paris, and Jerusalem. They're not going for the big bomb, a nuclear weapon or anything like that; they don't have to, it's counterproductive. They're out to vent their rage with instability, with chaos. And whether we want to accept it or not, they can do it."

"They can't, *she* can't!"

"Time's on her side, Mr. Secretary. The President can't live in a deep freeze. Sometime, somewhere, he'll show up where she can get to him, kill him, and while the waiting begins, London, Paris, and Jerusalem are building their assaults against the others. They're not stupid, get that through your head!"

"Nor am I, Commander. What is it? What have you left out?"

"Van Nostrand alone couldn't have done what he tried to do with you. There had to be others."

"What do you mean?"

"You said he was leaving the country and wasn't coming back."

"That's true. It's what he said."

"And everything had happened so fast, in a matter of a couple of days, you implied."

"*He* implied, and it was damn near hours, *was* hours. He had to get to Europe immediately, before that son-of-a-bitch husband knew he was there. That was the story he gave me! He had to reach his child before she died and take the mother of that child away, to be with the woman he loved at all cost."

"That's part of what bothers me," said Hawthorne. "The cost. Let's start with that not-so-minor San Simeon of Van Nostrand's—it's worth millions."

"I think he said he sold it—"

"In a couple of days, forget hours?"

"He wasn't terribly clear, nor did I expect him to be."

"And the assets he must have had all over the place, more millions, multi-millions. A man like Van Nostrand doesn't leave all that behind him without making arrangements, and those arrangements take time, a hell of a lot more than a couple of hours."

"You're out of your depth, Commander. These are the days of computers and legalized memoranda of intent sent across the world instantly. Lawyers and financial institutions take care of such matters every day, funds cross and recross the oceans in increments of millions every minute."

"Aren't they all traceable?"

"The vast majority, yes. Governments are loathe to forgo the taxes due them."

"But you said Van Nostrand was going to disappear, *had* to disappear. Traceability sort of louses that up for him, doesn't it?"

"Goddamn it, I imagine it does. So . . . ?"

"So he needed someone to bury whatever transactions could lead to him and his whereabouts. . . . In my former life, Mr. Secretary, I learned that the smart ones avoided making deals with criminals who could easily expedite their needs, not from any moral postures, simply to avoid future extortion. Instead, they went after the highly respectable, either convincing them or corrupting them to do their bidding."

"You unmitigated bastard!" Palisser uttered contemptuously as he moved back his chair, his eyes glaring. "Are you for a second suggesting that I was corrupted—"

"Oh, hell, no, you were convinced," Tyrell interrupted. "You're not lying, you bought the whole barnyard, manure and all. What I'm saying is that someone else as legitimate as you made it possible for him to disappear, *really* disappear, the paper trail eliminated."

"Who the devil could do that, would do that?"

"Another Secretary Palisser, perhaps, convinced he was doing the right thing. . . . By the way, did you issue him a false passport?"

"Good heavens, no! Why would I? He never asked for one."

"I did—in my former life—dozens of times. False names, false occupations, false backgrounds, false photographs. I needed them because the real me had to disappear."

"Yes, Captain Stevens said you were an exceptional undercover intelligence officer."

"It must have turned his stomach to say it, but do you know why I needed all those fake documents?"

"You answered that yourself. Commander Hawthorne had to disappear, another in his place." Palisser nodded in recognition. "Van Nostrand needed another passport," he said. "Because to disappear he had to have one."

"Two points for the secretary of state."

"You are an insolent young man."

"I intend to be. I'm being very well paid and I do the best I can when people pay me well."

"I won't try to comprehend your malodorous justifications, Mr. Hawthorne, but I think I've got you on this one. No one but the State Department can issue a legitimate passport, and since you rule out illegitimacy where Van Nostrand's concerned, where would he get one?"

"To answer your question, a high-level parallel government agency or department who can access your technology sufficiently to override it."

"That is corruption!"

"Or conviction, sir. *You* weren't corrupted." Tyrell paused. "A last question, Mr. Secretary, and maybe one I shouldn't ask, but I will, I have to. Have you any idea how I landed in Van Nostrand's private plane from Puerto Rico, walking into, as I said a few minutes ago, my own execution?"

"I haven't even considered it. I assume Captain Stevens was involved; he's apparently your liaison, if not your superior, here in the States."

"Henry Stevens was in shock when I told him I was here because he couldn't understand how it happened. Every move I've made has been monitored, when I wanted it to be monitored, by the closed circle of Little Girl Blood hunters. But this *should* have been known because it was expedited by one of your major players. He went around you and the entire intelligence community to have Van Nostrand reach me with a letter I had to follow up. I grabbed the bait, and if it weren't for two extraordinary people, I'd be a corpse in Fairfax and *your* Saint Van Nostrand would be landing in Brussels, leaving Bajaratt to operate from his compound."

"Who did it? Who reached you?"

"Howard Davenport, secretary of defense."

"I can't believe it!" Palisser shouted. "He's one of the most honorable men I've ever known! You're *lying*. You've gone too far. Get out of my house!"

Hawthorne reached into a pocket of his safari jacket and pulled out Van Nostrand's letter, the cracked blue tape on the sealed side apparent. "You're the secretary of state, Mr. Palisser. You can call anybody anywhere in the world. Why not reach the chief of naval intelligence at the base in Puerto Rico? Ask him how this letter got to me and to whom he had to report that it did."

"Oh, my God . . . !" exclaimed Bruce Palisser, his gray-haired head arched back over the chair, his eyes pressed tight. "We're a government of opportunists or benign reformers, of inconsequential minds, too often predators who have no right to govern. But that isn't Davenport! Howard could never have done what he did for personal gain, he just didn't *know*!"

"Neither did you, *sir*."

"Thank you for that, Commander." The secretary of state drew himself up and looked penetratingly at Tyrell. "I accept what you've told me—"

"I want it on the record," Hawthorne cut in.

"Why?"

"Because Van Nostrand's our only link to Bajaratt, and on the assumption that she doesn't know he's dead, she'll try to reach him."

"That doesn't answer my question, not that I won't agree to call Captain Stevens to verify everything you've told me, but again, why?"

"Because I want to use your name around this town to climb down a ladder to Little Girl Blood, and I don't relish thirty years in Leavenworth for illegal impersonation."

"Then I believe we should discuss your proposed agenda, Commander."

The telephone rang, startling both men. The secretary rose from the chair, his eyes on the walled console as he crossed rapidly to the instrument. "Palisser here, what is it? . . . He *what*?" The color drained from the secretary of state's face. "It doesn't make sense!" Palisser turned to Hawthorne. "Howard Davenport just committed suicide! The maid found him—"

"Suicide?" broke in Tyrell softly. "Want to make a bet on that?"

22

Bajaratt, her face veiled in dark lace, sat alone at a desk in the room of a cheap, out-of-the-way country motel, hastily chosen. She had reached the senator from Michigan, pleading exhaustion from the onslaught of calls and callers at the previous hotel, adding that her one-day move to an acquaintance's estate was, if possible, more trying, as her friend proved to be the monarch of social butterflies.

"I believe I mentioned that you'd be swamped," Nesbitt had said. "It's why I suggested an office and a staff."

"And I believe I told you why that was impossible."

"Yes, you did, and I can't blame the baron. This city's a whirlpool, perhaps a cesspool, of intruders, intruding where they shouldn't."

"Then perhaps you might help Dante Paolo and myself."

"In any way I can, Countess, you know that."

"Is there a hotel you could recommend that's, shall we say, not in the center of activity but has the appointments we require?"

"One comes to mind immediately," replied the legislator from Michigan. "The Carillon. It's usually fully booked, but these are the summer months and tourists can hardly afford it. I'll make the arrangements if you like."

"The baron will be apprised of your kindness and cooperation."

"I'd appreciate it. In your own name or would you prefer to be incognito?"

"Oh, I shouldn't care to do anything illegal—"

"It's not illegal, Countess, it's your right. Our hotels are interested only in payment; they're not concerned with why you choose anonymity. My office will guarantee your reliability; what name would you like to use?"

"I feel so—how do you say it?—unclean doing such a thing."

"Don't, you're not. What name?"

"I suppose it should be Italian . . . I shall use my sister's. Balzini, Senator. Madame Balzini and her nephew."

"It's done. Where can I call you back?"

"It's . . . it's better if I call you."

"Give me fifteen minutes."

"Oh, you are *wonderful!*"

"I won't press the point, but I'd be grateful if you'd tell the baron that."

"Certo, signore!"

The new, elegant hotel was perfect, confirmed by the Baj's recognizing four minor members of the Saudi royal family in Savile Row clothes. In the early days she would have shot them on sight and raced away, but now the stakes were so high, the rewards so magnificent, she nodded politely as the quartet of the blood-stained Saudi inheritors passed her in the lobby.

"Nicolo!" she called, getting up from the desk in the suite's sitting room, suddenly noticing the lighted button on the telephone. "What are you *doing?"*

"I'm calling Angel, Cabi!" replied the voice from the bedroom. "She gave me her number at the studio."

"Please hang up, my darling." Bajaratt rushed to the bedroom door and opened it. "I'm afraid you must do as I say."

The young man did so angrily, his bewilderment obvious. "She did not answer. She told me to let the telephone ring five times and then to leave a message."

"You left a message?"

"No, there were only three rings when you shouted at me."

"*Bene*. I'm sorry I spoke so harshly, but you must never use the telephone unless you tell me first and I say it's all right."

"Use the telephone . . . ? Who else would I call? Are you so jealous—"

"Really, Nico, you can sleep with a princess or a whore or a donkey and it makes no difference to me, but you may not place calls that can lead back to us."

"You told me to call her when we were at the other hotel—"

"There we were registered under the names we are using, here we are not."

"I don't understand—"

"You don't have to; it's not part of our contract."

"But I promised to call her!"

"You promised . . . ?" The Baj reflected while glaring at the dock boy from Portici. Nicolo had been acting strangely contrary, given to brief outbursts of temper like a young caged animal increasingly annoyed by his confinement. That was it; the restrictions had to be loosened. At this point, so near to her magnificent kill, it would be foolish to have an even more resentful dock boy on her hands. Besides, there was a call she had to make, and, as others might follow, forming a "pattern," as Van Nostrand had warned, it should not be made from the hotel phone. "You're right, Nico, I'm being far too strict. I'll tell you what we'll do. I need a few things from the *farmacia* across the street, so I'll go downstairs and you'll have privacy. Call your *bella ragazza*, but do not give her the number here or the name of the hotel. Tell her the truth, Nico, for you should not lie to your lovely friend. If you have to leave a message, say we're moving within the hour and you'll reach her later."

"We just got here."

"Something happened; our plans have changed."

"*Madre di Dio,* what now? . . . I know, I know, it is not part of our contract. If we ever get back to Portici, I should bring you to *Ennio Il Coltello.* He frightens everyone, for they say he kills; he shaves men below the beard with his knife when he is displeased, and one never knows where he'll be next or what he will do. I think, Cabi, that you would frighten *him.*"

"I did, Nico," Bajaratt said simply, a slow smile on her face. "He helped me find you, but no one on the docks should fear him any longer."

"*Che?*"

"He's dead. . . . Make your call to your beautiful actress, Nicolo. I'll return in fifteen minutes." The Baj picked up her purse from a chair, walked to the door adjusting her veil, and let herself out.

Alone in the elevator, she silently repeated the telephone number Van Nostrand had given her, the number now programmed to reach the new Scorpio One. The order she was about to issue had to be obeyed without question and within twenty-four hours, preferably far sooner. If there was the slightest hesitation, the wrath of the Baaka Valley, especially the Ashkelon Brigade, would descend on all the Scorpio leadership. *Death* to those who would interfere with Ashkelon!

The doors opened and Bajaratt stepped out into the small, tasteful lobby, crossing directly to the gold-filigreed entrance. On the pavement outside she nodded to the uniformed doorman.

"May I get you a cab, Madame Balzini?"

"No, *grazie,* but how gracious of you to know my name." The Baj studied the man from beneath her veil.

"It's the Carillon's policy to know our guests, madame."

"Very impressive. . . . It's such a lovely afternoon, I thought I'd get a bit of air."

"A fine day for a walk, madame."

Bajaratt nodded again and strolled down the sidewalk, stopping at several storefronts, ostensibly to admire the expensive merchandise but in reality to further appraise the courteous doorman with casual glances as she touched her hair or her veil. She did not trust such polite employees who could relay the comings and goings of hotel guests; she had bribed too many in the past. Her concerns vanished rapidly, however, as the doorman aimlessly glanced at pedestrians but never once in her direction. That would not be the case, she considered, had she dressed normally, without the matronly padding Nicolo so detested. She continued down the pavement, seeing what she hoped to find: a public telephone near the corner across the street. She hurried to it, once more repeating the number that was now so vital to Ashkelon. So vital!

"*Scorpione Uno?*" said the Baj softly but sharply enough to be heard over the occasional automobile horn on the quiet street.

"I assume you're speaking Italian," replied the flat, hesitant voice on the line.

"And I assume that the numerous odd sounds that followed my dialing this number have led me to the man I must speak with—in total confidentiality, without fear of being overheard."

"You may be assured of that. Who is this?"

"I am Bajaratt—"

"I've been waiting for your call! Where are you? We must meet as quickly as possible."

"Why is that?"

"Our mutual friend, who is now somewhere in Europe, left you a package he said was crucial to your . . . enterprise."

"What is it?"

"I gave my word I would not open it. He told me it was for my own benefit not to know the contents. He said you'd understand."

"Of course. You could be interrogated with chemicals, with drugs. . . . So Van Nostrand survived, then?"

"Survived . . . ?"

"There were gunshots—"

"Gunshots? I don't—"

"Never mind," Bajaratt instantly interrupted herself. Van Nostrand's security had saved him from his would-be assassin, Hawthorne. At the last, the retired intelligence agent was no match for the serpentine Neptune. Van Nostrand had Hawthorne followed, then arrested at the Shenandoah Lodge, no doubt leaving a corpse or two at the estate directly implicating the troublemaker from naval intelligence. *Arrested!* She had seen it for herself! How delicious, how exquisitely devious. "Then our previous Scorpion is safely in another country, no longer to be heard from?" she added.

"Oh, yes, that's been confirmed," said the new Scorpio One. "Where are you now? I'll send a car for you—and the boy too, of course."

"As eager as I am to have the package," the Baj broke in, "there's another matter that must be attended to immediately, *immediately.* I met with a young man, a red-haired political consultant you'll read about in the papers. His name was Reilly and he's dead, but the information he thought he was selling is devastating to our mission and must be cut off at the source."

"My God, what is it?"

"An attorney named Ingersol, David Ingersol, has put out an alarm among the lower elements in your ghettos to look for a woman and a young man, foreigners probably traveling together, and whoever finds them will receive a hundred thousand dollars. The scum of the world will murder their mothers and brothers for such an amount! The search must be stopped, *aborted,* this lawyer *killed*! . . . I don't care how it's done, but it must be done in time to appear in the morning papers. It *must* be!"

"Jesus Christ!" whispered the voice on the phone.

"It's two-thirty in the afternoon," continued Bajaratt. "This Ingersol must be dead by nine o'clock tonight, or all the blades of the Baaka Valley will cut the throats of the Scorpions. . . . I'll call you for my package when I hear the news on the radio or the television. *Ciao, Scorpione Uno.*"

David Ingersol, attorney-at-law, and newly elevated Scorpio One, if in name only, hung up the black secure phone that resided in a steel cabinet hidden in the paneled wall behind his office desk. He stared out the window at the clear blue Washington sky. It was incredible. He had just received the order for his own death! It wasn't happening to him, it *couldn't* be happening to him! He had always been above the violence, above the filth; he was the catalyst, a coordinator, a general orchestrating events through influence and position, not in the trenches with the "scum of the world," as this Bajaratt so accurately described the lower Scorpios.

The *Scorpios*. Oh, God, why? Why had he done it, why had he been so easily recruited? . . . The answer was all too simple, all too pathetic. His father, Richard Ingersol, prominent attorney, celebrated judge, a giant associate justice of the Supreme Court—and a man on the take.

"Dickie" Ingersol had been born into riches that were diminishing at an alarming rate. The thirties were not kind to the warlords of Wall Street, by and large the products of inherited wealth who were unable to discard the memories of their great estates of the twenties, with platoons of servants they gradually realized they could no longer afford any more than they could their limousines or their cotillions or their summer tours of Europe. It was an unfair world they were entering, unfair and untenable, and then the war came at the end of the decade, and for many it was a proper Armageddon for an era, for a way of life few could abandon. They would lead charges or go down in flames or fill the battleships with an aristocracy of an officer corps. Many did not wait for the draft, much less Pearl Harbor; more than a few of "their crowd" joined the ranks of Britain's services, romantics all, above the hoi polloi in tailored uniforms and with clean-cut features. As one of the Roosevelts phrased it—the Roosevelts of San Juan Hill and Oyster Bay, not that traitor to his class from Hyde Park—"My God, it's better than driving a Ford!"

Richard "Dickie" Ingersol was among the first to enlist in the United States Army, the Air Corps his promised objective, the wings on his tunic guaranteed. However, the army learned that Richard Abercrombie Ingersol had recently passed the New York State bar exam. So much for the wild blue yonder; he was assigned to the army's legal division, for there was a lack of bona fide attorneys, certainly few who had passed bar exams above the "barely qualified" classification, and none who had weathered the stiff New York bar.

Dickie Ingersol spent the war prosecuting and defending courts-martial from North Africa to the South Pacific, loathing every minute of his toils. Finally, America won the war on both sides of the globe, and Dickie found himself in the Far East; it was the occupation of Japan, and war crimes trials were under way in abundance. Many of the enemy were tried and hanged under Ingersol's aggressive prosecutions. Then, on a Saturday morning he received a telephone call from New York at his B.O.Q. in Tokyo. His family fortunes had collapsed; there was nothing left but bankruptcy, ignominy; a way of life had disappeared.

But the army *owed* him, Dickie believed, the nation itself owed him, owed his entire class which had led the country since its inception. So deals were made, dozens of "war criminals" were exonerated or their sentences reduced in exchange for Japanese money funneled to secret accounts in Switzerland from the great industrial families in Tokyo, Osaka, and Kyoto. Along with these payments were documents of "participation" in the projected corporations that would rise like phoenixes out of the rubble that was the defeated Japan.

Back in the United States, and once more secure in his wealth, Ingersol jettisoned the "Dickie," became Richard, and started his own firm with more capital than any other lawyer his age in the city of New York. He rose rapidly, the upper firmaments welcoming back one of their own, applauding when the Second Court of Appeals named him a judge, exulting when the Senate confirmed him to the Supreme Court. One of "their crowd" had made it, reaffirming their rightful place in the celestial legal heavens.

And then one day years later, now years ago, on another Saturday morning a man who called himself only "Mr. Neptune" arrived at the home of Associate Justice Ingersol's son, David, in McLean, Virginia. By now Ingersol *fils,* his background impressive and the legal furrows plowed for him, was the sought-after partner of Ingersol and White, a highly respected firm in Washington, although it was a given that the son would never argue a case before the highest court in the land. (The majority of clients did not really think it was necessary; their petitions would reach the proper ears.) The unexpected visitor to the house in McLean had been admitted pleasantly by David's wife, his elegance overriding his unannounced appearance.

Mr. Neptune courteously asked the brilliant young attorney to grant him a few minutes of his time for an urgent matter; there had been no minutes to waste seeking out Ingersol's unpublished telephone number. It was an emergency that concerned his father.

Alone in David's study, the stranger produced a sheaf of financial statements that had evaded the sanctity of one of the oldest banks in Bern, Switzerland. The portfolio contained not only the history of original Japanese deposits dating back to 1946, but also current and ongoing payments to the account of "Zero, zero, five, seven, two thousand," revealed and documented to be that of

Associate Justice Richard A. Ingersol of the United States Supreme Court. These payments were from many of Japan's highly successful companies as well as several worldwide conglomerates controlled by Japanese interests. Finally, attached to the portfolio was a record of the decisions rendered by Justice Ingersol that favored those companies and conglomerates with respect to their operations in the United States.

Neptune's "solution" was as clear as it was concise. Either David joined their highly selective and restricted organization, or "those above" would be forced to make public the entire story of Richard Ingersol's postwar wealth as well as his actions on the Supreme Court, thus destroying both father and son. There had been no alternative; the son had confronted the father, who resigned from the Court, claiming weariness and intellectual stagnation, a burnout that required a more active life after a period of rest. So universal did his explanation appear that Justice Ingersol was hailed for his courage and forthrightness, raising similar questions about several other members of the aging contentious Court. In reality, Ingersol *père* moved to the Costa del Sol, in southern Spain, his "active life" centering around golf, horse racing, croquet, and deep-sea fishing, along with formal dinner parties and colony dances. Behaviorally, if not geographically, Dickie had come home. And David Ingersol, the son, became Scorpio Three.

Now, as Scorpio One, he had been given his own death sentence. *Insanity!* David reached for the intercom on his desk. "Jacqueline, hold all calls and cancel whatever appointments I have for the rest of the day. Phone the clients and say there's been an emergency that I must attend to."

"Certainly, Mr. I. . . . Is there anything I can do to help?"

"I'm afraid not—yes, there is. Call the rental agency and have them bring a car around right away. I'll meet them downstairs at the side entrance in fifteen minutes."

"Your limousine's in the garage, sir, and your driver's in the mailroom—"

"This is personal, Jackie. I'll be using the freight elevator."

"I understand, David."

The lawyer swung around to the hidden telephone in the open wood-paneled wall. He picked it up and dialed; following a series of signals, Ingersol pressed five additional digits and spoke clearly. "I assume you'll get this within the next few minutes. To use your language, this is a four-zero problem. Meet me along the river, as we discussed. *Hurry!*"

Across the Potomac, at his office in the Central Intelligence Agency, Patrick O'Ryan—Scorpio Two ... in name only—felt the slight vibration from the electronic device beneath his jacket in his shirt pocket. He counted the tiny jolts and understood: There was an emergency that concerned the Providers. It was also awkward, as there was an L.B.G. conference with the director in forty-five minutes, and Little Girl Blood was the Agency's very top priority. *Goddamn it!* Yet there was nothing else to do; the Providers came first, always first. He picked up his phone and dialed the DCI's office.

"Yes, Pat, what is it?"

"It's about the conference, sir—"

"Oh, yes," the director interrupted. "I understand you've got a new slant you want to present. I can't wait to hear it; in my opinion, you're the best analyst we've got."

"Thank you, sir, but it's not quite complete. I need an extra couple of hours to pull it together."

"That's disappointing, Patrick."

"More to me than anyone else. There's an Arab, a blind I think, who could fill in a couple of gaps that need filling. I just got word from him; he's agreed to meet me, but it's got to be in an hour—in Baltimore."

"Hell, go to it! I'll postpone the conference, give you as long as you like. Call me from Baltimore."

"Thank you, sir, I will."

The Riverwalk Bridge did not span the river at all, but a minor offshoot of the Potomac, deep in the Virginia countryside. On the east bank was a rustic restaurant of limited quality that catered to the young in search of hoagies, hot dogs, burgers, and beer, and on the west side various paths into the woods, where it was said more boys and girls became men and women than in the days of Sodom and Gomorrah. It was a public relations exaggeration; the paths were too narrow and the ground was filled with rocks.

Patrick O'Ryan swung into the parking lot, relieved to see that only three other cars were there; the restaurant saw little action until dark. Scorpio Two got out, checked his pocket for his portable telephone, and started toward the bridge while lighting a cigar. David Ingersol had sounded panicked on Patrick's untraceable answering machine and that was not a good sign. The WASP quasi-fag was a bright legal, but he had never been tested when the mud was slinging and a little blood was in the offing. Davey-boyo was a weak son of a bitch despite his lawyer smarts; the Providers would learn that sooner or later. Maybe sooner than later.

"Hey, mister!" A drunken young man came reeling out of the restaurant's door. "Those pricks cut me off, the bastards! Lend me five and I'm yours for life, man! I mean I'm coming down off a high, *man!*"

An analyst's instincts, which were always projections of the possible and the impossible, came into play. "Suppose I gave you ten, say maybe twenty, will you do what I tell you to do?"

"Hey, man, I'll climb all over you naked if that's what you want. I need *bread,* man!"

"That's not what I want. And you may not have to do anything."

"I'm on your side, man!"

"Follow me after I cross over the bridge, but keep out of sight when I go into the woods. If I whistle for you, you run like hell and reach me. Got it?"

"Hell, yes, *man*!"

"Maybe I'll even give you fifty."

"Heaven, man, pure heaven! Fifty would set me free, y'know what I *mean*?"

"I'm counting on it . . . man." O'Ryan approached the sturdy, thick bridge that spanned the rushing waters below, crossed it, and entered the second path on the right. Stepping on the dirt and the rocks, he had progressed roughly thirty feet when the figure of David Ingersol suddenly emerged from behind a tree.

"Patrick, it's crazy," cried the attorney.

"You heard from Bajaratt?"

"It's *insane*. She demanded that I be killed! That David Ingersol be killed. Me, Scorpio One!"

"She doesn't know you, boyo! Why would she make such a demand?"

"I sent the word out on the streets, the worst elements, of course, to look for them——"

"Oh, did you now, Davey? That wasn't too smart a move. You didn't clear it with me."

"For God's sake, O'Ryan, we both agreed this madness had to stop!"

"Yes, we did, boyo, but not that way. That was just dumb, Davey, you should have used a cover. Jesus, Mary, and Joseph, they traced the word back to you? You'd last twelve minutes in the field, y'ninny!"

"No, you're wrong, I thought it out completely; the angles were covered. The raison d'être had all the appearance of legitimacy and thus immensely tempting——"

"The raison d'être, is it?" the CIA analyst interrupted. "That sounds grand, I'll give you that. And just how was all this legitimacy so tempting while it covered the angles, whatever the hell that means?"

"The firm was looking for these people, not an individual, not *me*! I was merely the one who should be contacted for the reward. I even backed up the search with a notarized affidavit clearly stating that the woman and the young man were the inheritors of a great deal of money, the implication being seven figures. A finder's fee of ten percent is perfectly normal."

"Oh, that's splendid, Davey, only I think you forgot that the searching parties you were appealing to wouldn't be able to spell *affidavit* and couldn't give a shit about legitimacy. However, they can smell out a rogue hunt faster than a spraying skunk in a jail cell. . . . No, boyo, you wouldn't last five minutes in the field."

"What are we going to do—what am *I* going to do? She said my death had to appear in the papers tomorrow, or the Baaka Valley—oh, Christ, it's all getting out of control!"

"Calm down, Scorpio *One*," said O'Ryan sardonically, looking at his watch. "I suspect that if your 'disappearance' is in the papers, that'll suffice for a day or so."

"Oh?"

"It's only a diversion, Davey, I know what I'm talking about. For starters, you've got to get out of Washington right away—you're kind of a minor celebrity, Counselor, and for a few days you don't want to be seen. I'll drive you to the airport; we'll stop and get you sunglasses—"

"I have a pair in my pocket."

"Good. Then buy a ticket to wherever you like, in cash, not a credit card. Do you have enough?"

"Always."

"Good again. . . . There's only one problem, and it could be a toughie, boyo. For the next day or so we've got to program your S-One number to me. If Bajaratt calls and doesn't get an answer or isn't contacted after leaving a message, the Baaka could explode, especially her hotheaded tribe of lunatics. The *padrone* guaranteed as much to me."

"I'd have to go back to the office—"

"You shouldn't do that," the analyst broke in. "Take my word for it, Davey, I know how these things are done. Who did you last speak to?"

"My secretary . . . no, it was the man from the rental agency who brought me a car. I drove out here alone; I didn't want to use my limousine."

"Very good. When that car's found here, they'll start looking. What did you tell your secretary?"

"That there was an emergency, a personal problem. She understood; she's been with me for years."

"I'll bet she did."

"That's hardly called for."

"Neither was Puerto Rico. . . . Did you have any plans tonight?"

"Oh, my *Lord*," exclaimed Ingersol. "I forgot! Midgie and I are going to the Heflins' place for their annual anniversary dinner."

"No, you're not." Patrick Timothy O'Ryan smiled benignly at the panicked attorney. "It's all falling into place, Davey. Your disappearance for a couple of days, I mean. . . . Let's go back to the S-One telephone in your office; where is it?"

"In the wall behind my desk. The panel opens by a switch in my lower right-hand drawer."

"Good. I'll program the phone to my number after I drop you off at the airport."

"It does it automatically if I don't respond after five hours."

"With this Bajaratt, we need it done right away, boyo."

"Jacqueline, my secretary, would never let you in. She'd call security."

"She will if you tell her to, won't she?"

"Well, of course."

"Do it now, David," said O'Ryan, yanking the portable telephone out of his jacket pocket. "This thing doesn't work too well in a car—all that steel and no ground—and we won't have time at the airport. I'll just drop you off and get out of there."

"You really mean it, don't you? You think I should take a plane out of Washington right away, this afternoon. What will my wife think?"

"Call her tomorrow, wherever you are. It's better she spend one miserable night worrying than the rest of her life without you. Remember the Baaka Valley."

"Give me the phone!" Ingersol called his office and spoke to his secretary. "Jackie, I'm sending a Mr. . . . Johnson over to pick up some papers in my office for me. It's extremely confidential, and I'd appreciate it if, when the reception desk announces him, you'd leave our doors unlocked and go out for coffee. Would you please do that, Jackie?"

"Of course, David. I understand completely."

"All right, Patrick, let's go!"

"Just a minute, I gotta take a leak, as I'll be doin' a lot of driving for the next hour or so. Keep your eyes on the bridge; we sure as hell don't want anyone seeing us together." O'Ryan took several steps into the woods, glancing at the attorney as he did so. However, instead of relieving himself, he bent down and picked up a large jagged rock the size of a softball. He walked silently back on the path, approached the excited lawyer, who was staring through the foliage at the bridge, and smashed the heavy rock with all his considerable strength into David Ingersol's skull.

O'Ryan shoved the body off the path and whistled for the drunken young man he had temporarily employed; the response was immediate.

"I'm right here, man!" The hopped-up recruit came careening around the path. "I can smell the bread!"

It was the last thing he would ever smell, for he was greeted with a thick, jagged rock crashing into his face. Patrick O'Ryan again looked at his watch; there was plenty of time to move both corpses to the waters below. And to remove a few articles from the clothes of one body, placing them in the other. After that it was merely a question of timing the logistics. First, the visit to Ingersol's office; second, an angry, humiliating apology to the director of the CIA—the Arab blind never showed up in Baltimore; third, several anonymous phone calls, perhaps one from an unidentified source who had spotted two bodies on the west bank below the Riverwalk Bridge.

It was 10:15 at night and Bajaratt paced the sitting room of the suite in the Carillon hotel while Nicolo was in the bedroom, watching television and gorging himself on room-service fare. He had accepted her explanation that they would be moving in the morning, not that night.

The Baj, too, had the television on, but it was the local ten o'clock news. She kept staring at it, with every look growing angrier. Then abruptly her anger subsided, a smile creased her lips as the anchorwoman suddenly stopped in midsentence, the fortunes of some baseball team interrupted as a paper was shoved before her on the desk.

"We've just been handed a bulletin. The prominent Washington attorney David Ingersol was found dead roughly an hour ago beneath the Riverwalk Bridge in Falls Fork, Virginia. At his side was the corpse of a man in soiled clothes, identified as Steven Cannock, a man the nearby restaurant claimed was intoxicated and ejected for drunkenness and inability to pay his bill. Both bodies were bloodied, giving rise to police speculation that Attorney Ingersol put up a violent struggle when the drunken Cannock tried to mug him. . . . David Ingersol, considered one of the capital's most influential lawyers, was the son of Richard Abercrombie Ingersol, who startled the nation eight years ago when he retired from the Supreme Court, claiming 'intellectual stagnation,' bringing up the question of life tenure for Supreme Court justices. . . ."

Bajaratt snapped off the television. Ashkelon had another victory. The finest was yet to come, but come it would!

It was close to two o'clock in the morning when Jackson Poole burst into the bedroom he shared with Hawthorne. "Tye, wake up!" he cried.

"What . . . ? I just fell asleep, damn it!" Hawthorne blinked his eyes and raised his head. "For God's sake, what is it? There's nothing we can do until morning. Davenport's dead and Stevens is on top of—is it *Davenport*? A breakthrough?"

"Try Ingersol, Commander."

"Ingersol . . . ? The lawyer, the cipher?"

"The corpse, Tye. He was killed in someplace called Falls Fork. Maybe our pilot, Alfred Simon, gave you more than a cipher."

"How do you know he was killed?"

"Frankly, I was watchin' a rerun of *Gone With the Wind*—that's a hell of a movie—and when it was over they put on the news."

"Where's the telephone?"

"Right by your head."

Hawthorne whipped his legs from under the sheet and off the bed and grabbed the phone as Poole switched on the lights. He dialed naval intelligence, unnerved to find Stevens himself answering the phone. "Henry . . . *Ingersol*!"

"Yes, I know." Stevens's voice was weary. "I've known for damn near four hours. I've been expecting your call, but between an apoplectic Secretary of State Palisser, who's activated his own channels over Davenport's death, and the White House, where Ingersol was on the *A* list for invitations, and that killing in your parking lot that's got the fucking *New York Times* on my ass—our asses—I haven't had a hell of a lot of time to call you."

"Ingersol, goddamn it! Impound his law office."

"Done, Tye-Boy—you were called Tye-Boy in the islands, weren't you?"

"You did?"

"No, *I* didn't. I had the FBI do it. That's the way it works."

"Christ, what the hell now?"

"The sun will come up and everything will be messier."

"Don't you see what she's doing, Henry? It's the bottom line. Everybody's running for and against the clock, colliding with one another. *Destabilization.* Who's suspect, who isn't? That bitch has got us racing around in circles, and the faster we run, the more collisions take place, and she'll jump through one of the cracks!"

"Words, Tyrell. The President's still in isolation."

"You think. We don't know who else she's manipulated."

"We're running micros on everybody on your list."

"Suppose it's someone not on the list?"

"What can I tell you? I'm not psychic."

"I'm beginning to think Bajaratt is—"

"That doesn't help us, it only confirms the worst we've heard about her."

"She's got a group here, a cadre high up that's beholden to her . . . or her resources."

"That's logical. Would you do us a favor and find it?"

"I'll do my damnedest, Captain, because now it's between her and me. I want Little Girl Blood, and I want her *dead.*" Hawthorne slammed down the phone.

But it wasn't only Bajaratt he wanted, it was a living lie named Dominique who had ripped him apart in a way no human being should ever do to another. Taking love and mocking it, trading the innermost secrets of the manipulated for lies from the manipulator. For so long, so lovingly, so deviously. How often had the killer laughed at the fool who truly believed he had found the person he loved?

The *killer*.

She forgot something. He was a killer too.

23

Patrick O'Ryan sat in the deck chair, wishing to hell and back that summer was over and the brats were in school—*away* at school, thanks to the Providers. Not that he didn't enjoy the kids, he did, especially since they kept his wife occupied and he and she had less time to fight. Not that he didn't love his wife; in a way, he guessed he did, but they had grown too far apart, basically because of him, he understood that. The average guy could go home and bitch about his job or his boss or the fact that he didn't make enough money, but he couldn't do any of those things. Especially not the money, once the Providers had come into his life.

Patrick Timothy O'Ryan was a product of a large Irish family in the borough of Queens, New York. Thanks to the nuns and a few priests in the parochial school system, he was urged to forgo the traditional police academy that three of his older brothers had entered, following in the footsteps of their father and grandfather, and his father before him. Instead, the assumption was made that Patrick Timothy had an exceptional mind, so far above the average that he was encouraged to seek a scholarship to Fordham University; it was a foregone conclusion that he would receive one. Then, having impressed the Fordham professors, he had received another to pursue his master's degree at Syracuse University, Foreign Service Department, one of the prime recruiting pools for the Central Intelligence Agency.

He had joined "the Company" three weeks after re-

419

ceiving his degree. Within a month he had been apprised by several superiors that there was a certain dress code he should abide by; unpressed polyester trousers and an orange tie over a blue shirt beneath an ill-fitting jacket from a Macy's sale simply would not *do*. He had done his best to comply, aided by his bride, an Italian girl from the Bronx, who thought her husband looked fine, but nevertheless cut out newspaper ads that showed how the proper Washingtonian male should be clothed.

The years progressed and, as those early nuns and priests had perceived, the higher echelons of the Agency came to understand that they had an extraordinary brain in Patrick Timothy O'Ryan. He was not the sort of fellow one ever sent up to testify on the Hill; his wardrobe had marginally improved, but his speech was blunt to the point of being crass, discourteous, and peppered with vulgarities. Yet withal, his analyses, like the man, were curt, sharp, and went directly to the issues without indulging in self-serving reservations or obfuscation. In 1987 he had projected the collapse of the Soviet Union within three years. This outrageous judgment was not only buried, but O'Ryan was called into a deputy director's office and told to "shut the goddamned hell up." The next day he was upgraded with an increase in pay, as if to emphasize the axiom that good boys got rewarded.

In the early days the O'Ryans had five children in eight years, a stressful economic situation for a low-ranking employee of the CIA. But Patrick Timothy could tolerate those circumstances because his working at the Agency made bank loans both available and relatively cheap. What O'Ryan could *not* tolerate was the fact that the results of his labors frequently were in the spotlight but no glare ever fell upon him. His words were repeated in congressional hearings by hotshot button-downs who spoke as though they should have been born in England, as well as by selected senators, representatives, and Cabinet personnel on the most-watched television shows. He had busted his ass over those analyses, but everyone *except* him was being given the credit for them. He was totally pissed off, and to further infuriate him, when he complained directly to the DCI after two weeks of waiting for an appointment, he was succinctly dismissed with the following words.

"You do your work, we'll do ours. We know what's best for the Agency, you don't."

Bullshit!

Then one Sunday morning, fifteen years ago, a danfancy who called himself Mr. Neptune came to his house in Vienna, Virginia, and brought with him an attaché case filled with many of O'Ryan's ultraclassified analytical reports.

"Where the hell did you get this shit?" O'Ryan had demanded, alone with the man in his kitchen.

"That's our business. Your business, as well as your concern, is fairly obvious. How far do you really think you can go at Langley? Oh, you might rise to a G-12, but that's just money and not actually a great deal. Others, however, using what you provided, could well write books making hundreds of thousands, claiming to be experts when in reality they've relied on your expertise. . . ."

"What are you drivin' at?"

"To begin with, you owe an aggregate of thirty-three thousand dollars to one bank in Washington and two in Virginia, Arlington and McLean—"

"How the *hell*—"

"I know, I know," Neptune interrupted. "It's confidential information but far less difficult to obtain. Beyond this, you have a substantial mortgage, and the parochial schools have raised their tuitions. . . . I don't envy your position, Mr. O'Ryan."

"Neither the fuck do I! You think I should quit and write my own book?"

"You can't legally. You signed a document stating you wouldn't—at least not without being vetted by the CIA. If you wrote three hundred pages, you'd probably

end up with fifty when they got through with it. . . .
However, there's another solution, one that would eliminate your financial difficulties and allow your life-style
to expand considerably."

"What's that?"

"Our organization is very small, very well financed,
and has only the country's interests at its core. You must
believe that, for it's true, and I will personally vouch for
it. I also have an envelope that contains a check made
out to you from the Irish Bank of Dublin in the amount
of two hundred thousand dollars from the estate of your
great-uncle, Sean Cafferty O'Ryan, of County Kilkenny,
who died two months ago, leaving a rather strange but
court-certified will. You are the only surviving relative
he acknowledged."

"I don't remember any uncle by that name."

"I shouldn't bother myself with introspection if I were
you, Mr. O'Ryan. The check is here and it's certified.
He was a successful breeder of Thoroughbreds, that's all
you have to remember."

"Is it now?"

"Here's the check, sir." Neptune had reached into the
attaché case and pulled out an envelope. "May we discuss our organization and its benevolent intentions regarding this nation?"

"Why the hell not?" answered Patrick Timothy
O'Ryan, accepting the envelope.

All that was fifteen years earlier, and Christ almighty,
had the following years gone *whacko!* Every month the
Irish Bank of Dublin sent him a record of deposit in
his name at the Banque Crédit Suisse in Geneva. The
O'Ryans were rich by their lights, and the legend of a
horse-breeding great-uncle became a truth, if only due
to repetition. The brats went on to fancy boarding
schools and the older ones to fancier universities, while
his wife went gaga in the department stores and ultimately with Realtors. They moved to a larger house in

Woodbridge and bought a substantial summer cottage on Chesapeake Beach.

Life was good, really good, and it bothered Patrick less and less when others took credit for his work because it was the *work* he basically enjoyed. This tolerance generally disappeared when some fatuous clown postured thoughtfully in a congressional hearing or on a Sunday morning television show and delivered one of Patrick's painstaking conclusions.

And the Providers? He simply gave them all the intelligence information they wanted, from the routine to the top secret to the maximum classified. Always, of course, through Scorpio One or the *padrone*. Holy Mary, some of the stuff was so hot, the Oval Office hadn't a clue, forget the Senate and the House; those people were either too politically harebrained or too dumb or just plain irresponsible. . . . In any event, the Providers were none of those. Whoever they were, they undoubtedly had motives below the level of sainthood, but O'Ryan had long since determined that the Providers' driving force was primarily economic. They sure as hell weren't Communists, and surer than that they had every reason to protect and defend the country they found so financially rewarding. Probably more effective than leaving it in the hands of politicians who were sworn companions of the polls and whose spines could be bent by a generous contributor's fart. So if the Providers made a buck and a half with advance information, it was probably a good thing in the long run; they'd make damn sure the goose who produced so many golden eggs remained a healthy bird. . . . There was a last consideration, and the analyst from Queens, New York, would never forget it.

One afternoon in Langley, twelve years ago, three years after he became the silent Scorpio Two, he was emerging from a procedural conference with a group of other analysts, when a tall, well-dressed—elegantly dressed—man walked down the corridor directly to-

ward the door of the DCI's office. Jesus, Mary, and
Joseph, it was Neptune! Without thinking, the younger
O'Ryan approached him.

"Hey, remember me . . . ?"

"I beg your pardon," replied the man coldly, quietly,
his eyes two orbs of ice. "I have an appointment with
the director, and if you ever approach me in public again,
your family will be penniless and you'll be dead."

It was not a greeting one forgot.

But now, right *now*, today, *tonight*, thought O'Ryan,
looking out at the water from the deck of their house on
Chesapeake Beach, something had gone terribly wrong
with the Providers. The late, unlamented Davey Ingersol
had been right; the whole Bajaratt business was madness. Some group, or network, had inserted itself into
the decision process—had the *power* to insert itself. Or
was it simply one deranged, dying old man on a blown-
up island in the Caribbean whose orders still had to be
obeyed? The answer did not really matter; a solution
had to be found that maintained the status quo without
damaging the Scorpios. It was why six hours ago he
understood that he had to become Scorpio One, with all
the rights and privileges thereof. The realization came
with Ingersol's words: "She demanded that I be killed,
that David Ingersol be killed!"

So be it. The Scorpios could not be damaged. Sometime, somewhere, a call would come to him and he
would have a unique explanation: the truth. Now, right
now, he had to bring into play all his reputed analytical
prowess; he had to think and outthink not only Bajaratt
and those behind her, but also the United States government. The Scorpios could not be damaged.

There was laughter on the beach; the brats and their
friends and his wife were around a pit fire in the sand.
It was a late evening clambake on the shores of the
Chesapeake. Oh, Christ almighty, it was a good life! . . .
No, the Scorpios could not be damaged, nothing could
change.

A telephone erupted softly; it was a muted ring that everyone in the household understood could be answered only by the father. The whole family referred to it as the "spook-tune," the kids frequently making fun of the single gray phone in their father's small den. O'Ryan good-naturedly took the ribbing, knowing it reenforced the assumption that Langley was calling him, sometimes inventing melodramatic nonsense that had the younger children wide-eyed until the older boys would puncture the story. "They want Dad to deliver a pizza, right, Double-O?"

It was all fun, macabre but fun; it was also necessary. The gray telephone had nothing to do with the Agency. Patrick Timothy pushed himself out of the deck chair and walked across the short living room to his den. He picked up the secure phone, pressed the digits required, and spoke.

"Who's this?" he asked quietly.

"Who are *you*?" The female voice on the line was accented. "You are not the same man."

"Temporary backup, nothing unusual."

"I don't like changes."

O'Ryan thought quickly. "He'd rather keep his gallbladder too, so what? Even we get sick, you know, and if you think I'm going to give you his name and the hospital he's at, forget it, lady. You have your results; Ingersol's dead."

"Yes, yes, I acknowledge that and I commend your efficiency."

"We try to oblige. . . . The *padrone* told me we were to accommodate you in any way we could, and I think we've done so."

"There is one other man who must be taken out," Bajaratt said.

O'Ryan's voice went cold. "We're not in the killing business. It's far too dangerous."

"This must be," Amaya Bajaratt whispered intensely. "I demand it!"

"The *padrone*'s gone, so perhaps there are limits to your demands."

"*Never!* I will send out teams from the Baaka to find you through our routes in Athens, Palermo, and Paris! Do not joke with me, signore!"

The analyst was cautious; he was all too aware of the terrorist mentality, the proclivity for rash and violent behavior. "Okay, okay, cool down. What do you want?"

"Do you know of a man named Hawthorne, a former naval officer?"

"We know all about him. He was pulled in by MI-6, London, because of the Caribbean connection. The last we heard he was in Puerto Rico, sizzling his ass in San Juan."

"He's here, I saw him!"

"Where?"

"At a place called the Shenandoah Lodge in Virginia—"

"I know it," O'Ryan interrupted. "He followed you?"

"Kill him. Send the *animales*!"

"You got it, lady," said O'Ryan, his impulse to promise the fanatic anything. "He's dead."

"Now, as to the package—"

"What package?"

"The hospitalized *Scorpione Uno* said his predecessor left a package for me. I'll send the boy for it. Where?"

O'Ryan pulled the phone away from his ear, thinking rapidly. *What the hell had Ingersol done? What package?* . . . Still, "the boy" could be had. Whatever his purpose, or wherever he fitted into Bajaratt's agenda, he could be eliminated. "Tell him to drive south to Route 4 until it meets 260, then head for a place called Chesapeake Beach; there are signs along the way. When he gets here, have him call me from a diner down the road with a telephone outside. I'll meet him ten minutes later on the rocks of a jetty on the first public beach."

"Very well, I'm writing this down. . . . I trust you have not opened the package."

"No way, it's not my business."

"*Bene.*"

"I think so too. And don't concern yourself about this Hawthorne. He's *finito.*"

"Your Italian improves, signore."

Nicolo Montavi stood in the rain on the rocks of the jetty, watching the taillights of the taxi that had brought him to this deserted spot recede. The taxi was literally commanded by the hotel's stern doorman to take the young man where he wished to go or not to bother coming back for fares. The nearly two-hour trip had angered the driver; he left quickly. Nico trusted that Cabrini's associate would find him a way back. The darkness was now complete, and the stevedore from the docks of Portici watched as the figure came into view in the wet, gray-black night. The nearer the man came, the more uneasy Nicolo felt, for there was no package in his hands; instead, they were in the pockets of his raincoat, and a person meeting another person at night in a heavy rain did not walk so slowly—it was not natural. The figure climbed up the irregular rocks of the man-made seawall; he slipped, both hands yanked out of his pockets to break his fall. In his right hand was a *gun*!

Nicolo spun around and plunged over the rocks into the dark waters as gunshots filled the night and the rain, a bullet grazing his left arm, another exploding above his head. He swam underwater for as long as he could, silently in panic thanking the docks of Portici for giving him the skill to do so. He surfaced less than thirty meters from the beach, spinning again until he could concentrate on the barrier of rocks. His would-be murderer now held a flashlight, its beam crisscrossing the water as he walked out to the end of the jetty, apparently satisfied that the killing had taken place. Nico stayed in the water, slowly making his way back to the wall of stone. He took off his shirt, raising his hands in the darkness and wringing out the cloth as best he could; it would float for a minute or two before sinking. Perhaps it would be enough, if he could place it correctly; he sidestroked along the jetty as the figure headed back toward the beach. Only moments now; then it *was* the moment! He lobbed the shirt ahead of him as the flashlight beam waved back and forth over the water.

The gunfire was thunderous, the punctured cloth erupting under the impact of the bullets before it sank. And then Nicolo heard what he wanted to hear: the repeated clicks of an empty magazine. He lunged up, his hands scraped and bleeding from the jagged rocks, then dived forward, gripping the ankles of the stunned figure with the empty automatic. The heavyset man roared in defiance, but his bulk was no match for the lean, strong swimmer from Portici. The young Italian leapt up, crashing his fists into the man's stomach, then his face, finally clutching his throat and hurling him down over the rocks. The body lay still, the head shattered, the eyes wide. Slowly in the night rain, the dead man slipped into the water.

Nicolo felt the panic spreading through him, paralyzing him, causing the sweat to break out on his face and his neck despite the cold rain and his drenched clothing—what was left of it. What had he done—yet what else could he *do*? He had killed a man, but only because that man had tried to kill him! Still, he was in a strange country, a foreigner in a foreign land, where they executed men for killing other men because people who were not there decided that those who killed should die, believing their judgments replaced the eyes of God.

What should he do now? Not only were his trousers soaking wet but his bare chest was scraped and bleeding, the wound in his shoulder open, although not deep. He had been cut worse by the ancient stones and anchors while diving for the ocean scientists; it was not an explanation he could offer the *polizia* in America. They would say it was not *pertinente;* he had killed an American; perhaps he was a *capo-subalterno* in the hated Sicilian Mafia. Mother of Christ, he had never been to Sicily!

He had to get hold of himself, Nicolo understood that. He had to think, not waste time imagining useless possibilities. He had to reach Cabrini—Cabrini the bitch! Had she sent him out to die for a "package" that was not there? ... No, he was too important to the grand *contessa;* the *barone-cadetto* was too important. Something had gone wrong for his *signora salvatora puttana;* a man she thought she could trust wanted only to destroy her—by killing one Nicolo Montavi, dock boy from Portici.

He rushed along the slippery jetty in the downpour, deciding that he could make better and safer time in the shallow water. He jumped down and raced to the beach, then up across the sand to the parking area; there was only one other automobile, without doubt his would-be killer's. He wondered if he could yank the ignition wires, cross them, and start the engine as he had done so many times before with others.

He could not. The car was an expensive *macchina da corsa,* a sports car for the rich, who protected their investment. One never touched them in Napoli or Portici; even if one could open the hood, an alarm was heard for three hundred meters, the battery neutralized, the steering wheel incapable of being turned.

The roadside restaurant with the enclosed glass booth that had a telephone! He had coins in his pocket, several thrown at him by the angry taxi driver, until he apologized when Nico gave him a twenty-dollar *mancia,* telling the man he knew how important tips were. He started down the road in the rain, staying on the side and constantly turning his head, dashing into the bordering woods whenever he saw headlights or taillights.

Thirty-five minutes later he reached the restaurant, its

glaring red neon sign spelling out ROOSTER'S NEST. He crouched in the shadows at the edge of the building as automobiles and trucks came and went, only a few stopping in front of the telephone booth. The outside phone was a familiar sight in the Italian cafés; a convenience that more often than not led callers inside for food and wine. ... Suddenly, a furious woman inside the booth screamed so loudly she could be heard through the downpour. She then smashed the receiver with such force against the folding glass door that it shattered, then she walked unsteadily outside and vomited in the nearby bushes of the front parking lot. Several newcomers dashed around her in the rain, and Nicolo knew the time was right; the light was still on in the booth, the broken glass menacingly reflected in its wash. He raced across the pavement, the coins in his hand.

"*Informazioni*—information, if you please? The number for the Carillon hotel in Washington?" The operator gave it to him as he scratched it with the rim of another coin on the ledge. Without warning a large truck stopped in front of the booth, the driver a heavyset man with a full, unkempt beard, his fleshed eyes squinting. He shouted, seeing Nicolo's bleeding upper torso.

"Who the fuck are you, *Speedo*?"

Instinct propelling him, the large, muscular dock boy crashed open the shattered door and yelled. "I have been shot, signor! I am Italian and there are *mafiosi* surrounding this place. Will you *help* me?"

"In your fuckin' dreams, Eyetal!" The truck burst forward and Nicolo completed his call.

"You *what*?" said Bajaratt harshly.

"Do not show anger with me, signora!" replied a furious Nicolo over the telephone from Chesapeake Beach. "That terrible man came to kill me, not to give me a package."

"I cannot believe it!"

"You did not hear the gunfire or nearly have your left arm shot off, which mine was, and is swollen and still bleeding a little."

"*Il traditore! Bastardo!* . . . Something has happened, Nico, something very wrong, very horrible. The man was not only to guard your safety with his life, but to deliver a package for me."

"There was no package. You cannot do this to me, and do not tell me it is part of our contract! I will not *die* for you, not for all the money in Napoli!"

"Never, my boy-man, never! You are my young love, have I not proven it to you?"

"I've seen you kill two people, a maid and a driver—"

"I explained both to you. Would you rather they killed *us?*"

"We run from one place to another—"

"As we did in Napoli, in Portici . . . to save your life."

"There is too much I cannot understand, Signora Cabrini! Perhaps tonight is the last!"

"You must not think that way, never think that way! There is too much at stake! . . . Stay where you are and I will come to you—where are you?"

"At a restaurant called Rooster's Nest in this Cheez-a-peake Beach."

"Stay where you are, I'll be there as soon as I can. Remember Napoli, Nicolo; think of your future. Stay there!"

The Baj slammed down the phone, furious, shaken, uncertain where to turn. The Scorpios would die, *all* die, but to whom could she give the order? The *padrone* was gone, Van Nostrand incommunicado somewhere in Europe, a man claiming to be Scorpio Two had been killed by Nicolo on an obscure American beach, and the unknown Scorpio One was unreachable in a hospital under a name she did not know. The primitive dock boy was right; it was all insane. Yet where could she turn? The Baaka's network extended everywhere, all over the globe, but *she* had relied on the *padrone*'s connections in America. The Scorpios. Oh, God, had the Scorpion leadership turned against her, her one extraordinary asset now a terrible liability?

It could not happen! The final statement of her life of pain, the only reason she had left to survive the agony of the Pyrenees—*Muerte a toda autoridad!* She could not be stopped by men in dark suits and grand estates and large limousines that carried them from one place of power to another like the killer pharaohs of Egypt in their chariots. It could not be! What did they know of earthbound brutality, of the horror of being forced to watch as their mothers and fathers were beheaded in front of their eyes by the *authorities*? . . . It was like that in so many places; whole Basque villages in flames because they wanted something of their own; her beloved husband's people slaughtered, their homes bulldozed out of the ground because *they* wanted their own, stolen from them by a people armed by the giants of the world because they carried the guilt of not stopping the killers of Jews, which her husband's people had *nothing* to do with! Where was the justice, where the humanity? . . . No, the "authorities" everywhere had to be taught a lesson. They had to be *hurt,* had to learn that they were as vulnerable as those they destroyed with their false agendas.

Bajaratt picked up the phone and dialed the numbers given her by Nils Van Nostrand. There was no answer. She remembered the *padrone*'s words.

All my connections have devices, like pacemakers, that tell them they must answer the calls immediately, no matter their situations. And if their situations deny them access for an excessive length of time, another descending number is programmed. Wait twenty minutes, then try again.

But what if there still is no answer, my only father?

Don't trust anyone. Electronic codes can be broken in these days of extraordinary technology. Be conservative, my child, assume the worst and leave wherever you are.

What then?

The Baj is on her own, my only daughter. Use others.

Bajaratt waited twenty minutes and called once more. *Nothing.* As instructed by the *padrone,* she assumed the worst. Scorpio Two had tried to kill Nicolo and had been killed in the attempt.

Why?

It was 4:36 A.M. when the shrill ring of the telephone assaulted Hawthorne's ears in the room he shared with Poole at the Shenandoah Lodge.

"You got it, Tye?" asked the far more alert lieutenant in the other bed.

"I'm *getting* it, Jackson." Tyrell fumbled the phone off the hook and pulled it to his ear at the side of the pillow. "Yes?" he asked.

"Is this Lieutenant Commander Hawthorne?"

"*Was,* yes. Who are you?"

"Lieutenant Allen, John Allen, naval intelligence, temporarily standing in for Captain Stevens, who has relieved himself from duty to get some much needed rest, sir."

"What is it, Lieutenant?"

"I've been briefed on a restricted need-to-know basis, Commander, but I wanted to get a quick analysis from your point of view on a recent development that conceivably might influence my disturbing Captain Stevens—"

"For Christ's sake, speak English!"

"Do you know, or have you ever known, or recently been in contact with, or been apprised of a Central Intelligence analyst by the name of Patrick Timothy O'Ryan?"

Tyrell paused, then answered quietly. "Never heard of him. So?"

"His body was found by a Chesapeake oyster boat, entangled in one of its nets, I'm told, about an hour ago. I thought I'd call you first before disturbing the captain."

"Where did you get the report from?"

"The Chesapeake C.G.—that's the coast guard, sir."

"Are the local police informed?"

"Not as yet, sir. When this kind of thing happens, like when that navy commander was shot in a rowboat ten or twelve years ago, we try to restrict it temporarily just to us, with nothing touched—"

"That's enough, Lieutenant, I understand. Keep it all secure until I get there. Where are you?"

"At the River Bend Marina, about two miles south of Chesapeake Beach. I'm heading out there now, sir. Should I call Captain Stevens?"

"No way, Lieutenant. Let the man sleep. We'll take it from here."

"Thank you, sir. He can get real mad."

Hawthorne swung out of the bed as Poole, already on his feet and across the room, turned on the lights. "Here we go, Jackson," said Tyrell. "This is a breakthrough, a real one."

"How do you figure?"

"I said I didn't know a dead man named O'Ryan, and I don't personally, but I know he's just about the best son-of-a-bitch analyst the Agency ever had. . . . He also floated through Amsterdam six or seven years ago on one of those silent CIA evaluation exercises, looking to find fault with military input. Fellows like me avoided him as though he had the plague."

"So what's the relevance?"

"He was the best, and Bajaratt uses only the best until he or she doesn't serve her any longer. Then she discards them, kills them to cut off any connection."

"That's wild, Tye. You're really reachin'."

"Maybe, Jackson, but I feel it, I sense it—he must have been the primary leak. It's all I have to go by."

"That's pretty awesome, Commander. You're talkin' the top of our secret intelligence charts."

"I know, Lieutenant. Wake up the major."

*   *   *

On a tree-lined street in upper-class Montgomery County, Maryland, a low hum persisted on the telephone beside Senator Paul Seebank's bed. It was so muted, it could not be heard by his wife, who slept beside him, a cellolike sound that awoke only the person next to the instrument. Seebank opened his eyes, reached over, and pressed the redial button, terminating the hum, then quietly, slowly, got out of bed and went downstairs to his book-lined study. He repressed the lighted redial button, inserted the code for reception, and heard the following words in a flat British monotone.

There is a problem with our associates as our lines are no longer operative. You will receive all calls. Assume all authority.

Senator Paul Seebank, one of the leaders of that august legislative body, with trembling fingers pressed the appropriate numbers that gave him access to the Providers' clandestine personnel. He was Scorpio Four, now for all intents and purposes, the first of the Scorpions.

The senator froze in his chair, his face chalk-white, the blood drained. He could not ever remember when he had been more terrified.

24

The corpse tangled in the fishing net was chalk-white and rigid, the flesh swollen, blown up by the intake of water, the face a balloon version of its former features. On the dock, under the glare of the single floodlight, were the personal effects that had been removed by the coast guard patrol from the deceased's pockets.

"That's all there was, Commander," John Allen, the naval intelligence officer, said. "Nothing else was disturbed, and prongs were used to extract the materials. As you can see, he's CIA, top security, maximum clearance, and very dead. The doctor here, who's done only a preliminary forensic, says he believes death occurred when O'Ryan's head was smashed by a solid object or came in contact with multiple solid objects. He tells us that an autopsy might reveal more, but he doubts it."

"Good work, Lieutenant," said Hawthorne. Poole and Catherine Neilsen were at his side, both mesmerized by the ugly sight below them. "Remove the body and proceed with the autopsy."

"Could I ask a question?" said Poole.

"I'm amazed you've been silent so long," replied Tyrell. "What is it?"

"Well, ah'm jest a country boy—"

"Cut the bullshit," interrupted Cathy quietly, looking away from the dead, swollen body. "Ask."

"Well, in Loo'siana we got offshoots from the Pont-chartrain goin' all over the place—backwaters, we call

436

'em. Does this here Chesapeake flow like normal, north to south?"

"I assume so," said Allen.

"Sure does," added a bearded fisherman, overhearing the conversation while disentangling the dead body. "What the hell else is there?"

"Well, the river Nile doesn't subscribe to that, sir. She goes—"

"*Forget* it," broke in Hawthorne. "What's your question?"

"Well, assumin' that the flow is north to south, and 'solid objects' were involved, are there any backwater dams north of here?"

"What do you mean, Jackson?" asked Cathy, turning around, aware that her subordinate officer did not pose foolish questions.

"Take a look, Major—"

"I'd rather not, Lieutenant."

"What's your point, Poole?" said Tyrell.

"That man's head has been bashed in more than one location—I mean, take a look, the swellin' and all. That ain't *one* 'solid object,' but a whole bunch of 'em. That old boy got smashed in all directions. You got backwater stoppages here?"

"Breakwalls," said the bearded fisherman, his hands on the net, his eyes on Poole. "Up and down the 'Peake,' so's the rich people can swim in front of their houses."

"Where's the nearest, sir?"

"This ain't prime real estate down here, buddy," answered the fisherman. "I suppose you could figure the jetty north of Chesapeake Beach. The kids hang out there a lot, y'know."

"It's my turn to say it, Tye. Let's *go*."

Bajaratt controlled her impatience. "Can't you drive faster?" she coolly asked the chauffeur of her hotel-appropriated limousine.

"If I do, ma'am, we'll be stopped by the police and it will take longer."

"Just hurry, please."

"I'm doing the best I can, ma'am."

The Baj sat back in the seat, detonations going off in her mind. She could not lose Nicolo, he was the *key*! She had planned it all so carefully, so brilliantly, every step orchestrated, every move and nuance calculated—she was only days away from the ultimate kill of her life, prelude to chaos across the world. *Muerte a toda autoridad!*

She had to be gentle, concerned, convincing. Once the dock boy got her into the White House, into the President's office itself, then *out,* she could dispose of the *barone-cadetto* at will. He certainly could not be permitted to live more than a few minutes after the news of the President's assassination was heard around the globe.

Until then, she would feign near hysteria over Nico's well-being, swear on the graves of the saints to force those responsible to pay for their hideous crime, make love to the young Adonis in ways he had never dreamed of—oh, God, *anything*! He had to become once more her marionette as quickly as possible. The appointment in the Oval Office was too close. This ride was taking forever!

"We're in Chesapeake Beach, ma'am, the diner's over there on the left," the uniformed chauffeur announced. "May I escort you inside?"

"You go inside, please," said the Baj. "My friend will come to me privately. I may need a blanket; do you have one?"

"Right behind you, madam, between the lamps. There are two lap rugs."

"Thank you. Now leave me."

* * *

"Yes, Captain Stevens, I did, sir," said a subdued Lieutenant Allen over the car telephone in the naval intelligence vehicle. "The commander was explicit, sir. He
ordered me not to disturb you—honest."

"He's *not* a commander and he can't give you orders!" Stevens shouted over his bedside telephone.
"Where the hell is he?"

"They mentioned something about a jetty in Chesapeake Beach—"

"The same place where O'Ryan lives?"

"I believe so, sir."

"Have the O'Ryans been notified?"

"Absolutely *not,* sir. The commander—"

"He's not a *commander*!"

"Well, his instructions were to keep everything secure, and that's consistent with our policy in these matters. We agreed upon that. On a temporary basis, of
course."

"Of course," sighed the resigned Henry Stevens. "I'll
inform the DCI right away; he can handle that part. And
then you go find that son of a bitch and make damn sure
he calls me immediately!"

"Excuse me, sir, but if Hawthorne isn't an intelligence
officer, just who is he?"

"A remnant, Mr. Allen. A rogue has-been we'd all
like to forget."

"Then why is he here, Captain? Why is he in the loop?"

Silence. Then finally Stevens answered quietly. "Because he was the best there was, Lieutenant. We came
to understand that. *Find* him!"

While the chauffeur was inside the diner, the bare-
chested, bleeding Nicolo came up to the rain-swept window of the limousine. Bajaratt flung open the door and
pulled him into the back seat, holding him fiercely and
throwing the lap rug around him.

"Stop it, signora," he shouted. "You have gone too far with me. I was nearly killed!"

"You don't understand, Nico. He was another *agente segreto,* a man who opposed us, opposed me, opposed the wishes of your Holy Church!"

"Then why is everything so secret? Why do you and the people with you and my holy priests not speak out about this terrible thing, whatever in God's name it is?"

"Things are not done that way, my glorious child. You tried it, you tried to openly expose a corrupt man on the piers and what did it get you? Everyone on the Portici docks wants you dead; your own beloved family cannot acknowledge you, for they'd be killed. Don't you see?"

"I see that you are using me, signora, using your invention, the *barone-cadetto,* for your own purposes."

"*Naturalmente!* I chose you because you had a native intelligence far above anyone else; I've told you that, haven't I?"

"Sometimes. When you don't call me a fool and a dock boy."

"Explosions of frustration. What can I tell you? . . . Believe in me, Nico. In later years, when I am gone, and you are a *studioso,* thanks to your money in Napoli, you will look back and understand. You will be proud of the silent part you played in this great cause."

"Then in the name of Mary, Mother of Christ, tell me what it *is*!"

"In the broadest sense, it's not much different from what you did before they wanted to hang you off that pier in Portici. Expose the corruptors, not on a deserted dock on the waterfront but all over the world."

Nico shook his head, trembling under the limousine blanket, his teeth chattering. "Again, so many words, so many things I cannot understand."

"You will, my darling. In time. . . . You're in pain! What can I do for you?"

"This is a restaurant, no? Perhaps coffee or some wine. I'm so cold."

The Baj yanked down the handle of the door and dashed outside in the oppressive rain toward the steps of the diner. Suddenly, two automobiles careened into the front parking lot, skidding on the wet concrete, screeching to a stop beside each other as Bajaratt reached the door. Then she heard the words through the wind and the downpour.

"Commander, you must do as I say! It's an *order*!"

"Fuck off, pissant!"

"Tye, for Christ's sake, *listen* to him!" yelled a woman as the parade of arguing voices approached the steps of the diner.

"*No!* They've screwed up enough! I'm going down and dirty, using everything that I can get from the O'Ryans and the Ingersols. That's *it*!"

It was *Hawthorne*! Bajaratt, dressed in her matronly fashionable clothes from the Via Condotti, rushed into the diner and saw the chauffeur eating a large slice of pie in a nearby booth. "*Out!*" she whispered. "*Now!*"

"Who the hell are—oh, my *God*! Yes, of course, madam!" The chauffeur threw down three dollars and got up quickly as five people, angry people, walked through the door of the diner, at least three or four arguing vociferously.

"Stay *down*!" commanded the Baj, clasping the chauffeur's shoulder and pushing him beneath the top of the booth. The five intruders took a large table across the entrance aisle against the wall, their angry debate now muted, but, as Amaya Bajaratt saw, her once and former lover would not be moved. She had seen it too often: The intelligence officer from Amsterdam knew when his instincts were right—right on the mark. The dead man was another key to Little Girl Blood. *Well done, Tye-Boy,* she mused to herself as she and her driver stayed below the banquette in the aisle. *I rarely, if ever,*

*made love to an inferior. Oh, you, so like my husband,
Tyrell, a gentle animal who wanted only the best, and I
gave it to him as I gave it to you, my darling. Why, in
all that's so insane in this world, could you not have
been on my side? I'm right, you know, my darling. There
is no God! For if there were, children would not starve
to death with pain and swollen bellies—what has that
God have against them? I hate your God, Tyrell! If it
ever was your God; I never knew that, really; you never
said so, one way or another. And now I must kill you,
Tye-Boy. I don't want to; I couldn't in St. Barts, although I should have—I think the* padrone *understood.
I think he sensed how much I really loved you, and was
wise enough not to probe, for he loved another he could
not kill, yet knew he should. If the truth were told, my
darling Tye-Boy, the Scorpios have collapsed because
my only father could not do what he should have done
years ago. Neptune should have been cut down. He was
far too emotional where love was concerned.*

That is not me, Commander!

"*Now,*" said Bajaratt to the chauffeur beside her.
"Get up slowly, walk to the door, go outside, and run
to the car. Don't be alarmed—an injured young man is
in the back. He is my nephew, a good boy who was
attacked by men who robbed him. Bring the car to the
front steps. Touch the horn twice when you are there."

"Madam, I've never been asked to behave this way!"

"You are now, and you will be a thousand dollars
richer for it. *Go!*"

The limousine driver, in his anxiety walking to the
entrance far more rapidly than instructed, pushed the
door open with such force that the occupants of several
tables glanced up at the sharp noise, among them, Tyrell
Hawthorne in the corner seat. The Baj could not see his
face, the questioning frown on that face, but another
could. "What is it, Tye?" asked Catherine Neilsen.

"What's an angry chauffeur doing in here?"

"You heard that fisherman on the dock. He said rich people lived out here, up and down the 'Peake,' I think he called it. Why shouldn't they have chauffeurs?"

"Maybe."

Neither could Bajaratt hear that brief exchange of conversation; she had ears only for the signal that would tell her the limousine was out front. It came, two short bursts of a horn.

"A chauffeur?" said Hawthorne more to himself than anyone else. "*Van Nostrand's!*" he exclaimed out loud. "Let me *out* of here," he cried, shoving Poole, and in turn Cathy, along the soiled green plastic banquette.

Simultaneously, Bajaratt rose from the booth and started for the door, her chin locked into her neck. There were now two figures rushing toward the diner's entrance, each intent on racing outside.

"*Sorry!*" said Tyrell curtly as he dashed past the woman, grazing her, shoving his right shoulder against the brass-plated latch cover, propelling the heavy door out into the rain, once more a downpour. "*You!*" he roared at the unseen driver of the limousine as he ran down the steps toward the huge automobile. He stopped, spinning around in the rain, the lightning bolts of his mind crashing down, then up at the diner's entrance and the woman he had just shoved aside. The Shenandoah Lodge, the old woman—the eyes! *Dominique! Bajaratt!*

The gunshots echoed in the rain; bullets pierced the limousine's metal and ricocheted off the pavement as Hawthorne raced to his left, suddenly feeling an ice-cold sensation in his upper thigh. He had been *hit*! He dived, rolling under the cover of a parked pickup truck as another woman burst through the diner's door, screaming for him. Bajaratt fired the remaining shells in her direction while pulling the door open and jumping into the automobile. Catherine Neilsen plummeted down the steps as the limousine bolted forward into the darkness of the highway.

*   *   *

It was five o'clock in the morning and Henry Stevens recognized an affliction that went with his job. He was at that point beyond exhaustion where sleep would not come, not after his initial rest had been shattered by a startling interruption. The mind would not stop, could not stop, the questions geometrically building until his head was filled with so many possibles and probables that they crowded out all thoughts of immobility. To stay in bed meant only turning constantly, eyes open and glazed, concerned that his wife in the twin bed next to his would hear his movements and, as usual, wake up and try to calm him down. She was good at that; she had always been good at that. He could not admit it, but deep in his silent reflections he knew that he would not be where he was without Phyllis. She was irritatingly rational, always calm, the strong helmsman who kept their own ship on a steady course, never dictatorial, but making damn sure her husband rode out a heavy sea without capsizing.

It was funny in a way, he mused as he sat on the couch in their glassed-in sun porch, that he should think in nautical terms. The only time he had been on the water was during his final year at Annapolis, when all the graduating midshipmen had to endure ten hellish days on some huge sailing ship, pretending to be sea-men from the goddamn nineteenth century. He could barely remember those ten days for, in truth, he'd spent most of the time throwing up in the toilet—the head, the *head*.

Seamanship notwithstanding, the navy came to recognize his other talents, organizational talents, bureau-cratic talents. He was one hell of a desk sailor, spotting mediocrities and incompetents, dismissing them out of hand without suffering their feeble explanations. If there was a job to be done, *get* it done; if there was a problem he or she could not solve, come to *him*, do not wallow in the shallows of indecision. He had been right—most of the time.

And once—just once—he had been wrong. Fatally. In Amsterdam he had told Phyllis about Hawthorne's wife, Ingrid, and she had said simply, quietly: *You're wrong, Hank, you're wrong on this one. I know Tyrell and I know Ingrid, and you're missing something.*

And when Ingrid Hawthorne's dead body was pulled out of the Amsterdam canal, his wife had come to his office from the embassy.

Did you have anything to do with this, Hank?

Good God, no, Phyll! It was the Soviets, the markings were all there!

I hope so, Henry, because you're about to lose the finest intelligence officer the navy has ever had.

Phyllis never called him Henry unless she was furious with him.

Goddamn it! How could he have known? Logged out of the system! What kind of crap was *that*?

"Hank?"

Stevens snapped his head around to the door of the sun porch. "Oh, sorry, Phyll, I was just sitting here thinking, that's all."

"You haven't slept since that phone call. Do you want to talk about it—can you talk about it, or am I out of the loop?"

"It concerns your old friend Hawthorne."

"Is he back in the system? If so, that's a real stunner, Hank. He's not very fond of you."

"He always liked you."

"Why not? I programmed his travels, not his life."

"Are you saying I did?"

"I don't really know. You told me you didn't."

"I didn't."

"Then the chapter is closed, isn't it?"

"It's closed."

"What's Tyrell doing for you, or can't you tell me?" There was no resentment in Phyllis Stevens's remark, for it was understood that wives and husbands of high-level intelligence personnel were vulnerable; what they did not know could not be extracted from them. "You've been working around the clock several times over, so I assume it's a red alert."

"I can give you a couple of brush strokes, the leaks probably go beyond them anyway. . . . There's a terrorist out of the Baaka Valley, a woman who's sworn to assassinate the President."

"That's *cartoon* time, Hank!" interrupted the wife, suddenly stopping, her head tilted in thought. "Or maybe it isn't. In fairness to my gender, there are an awful lot of things we can do and places we can go that men can't."

"She already has, leaving a number of very strange deaths and 'fatal accidents' in her wake."

"I won't ask you to amplify that."

"I wouldn't."

"And Tyrell? Where does he fit in?"

"For a while the woman operated from the Caribbean, from the islands—"

"And Hawthorne has his charter business down there."

"Exactly."

"But how did you ever get him back? I wouldn't have thought it possible."

"We didn't, MI-6 did. We're just paying his plus per diems; he got his contract from London."

"Good old Tye. Third class never appealed to him unless it was necessary for his cover."

"You really liked him, didn't you?"

"You would have, too, if you'd ever given him a chance, Hank," said Phyllis, sitting down in a rattan armchair opposite her husband. "Tye was smart—covert smart, street smart—but not in your class, not a MENSA candidate with an IQ of a hundred and ninety, or whatever, but he had the instincts and the strength to follow them, even when upstairs thought he was wrong. He was a risktaker."

"You sound like you were in love with him."

"All the youngsters were, hardly me. Like him, yes; fascinated by what he did, of course, but 'love' in any sense of the word, no. He was like a talented, off-the-wall nephew, not even close enough to be a brother, but someone you watched with interest because he broke the rules and every now and then brought in the borscht. You yourself said that."

"Yes, I did. And he did get results. But he upset a lot of networks which took considerable work to put back together. I never told him about those assets who temporarily fled from us because they said there was a maniac loose in our underground. They were frightened; he was trying to make deals with our enemies—no more *killings,* that's what they told us he was saying to them. But we weren't doing the killings, others were!"

"And then Ingrid was killed."

"She was killed. By the Soviets, not by us."

Phyllis Stevens crossed and recrossed her legs under her silk nightgown, studying her husband of twenty-seven years. "Hank," she said softly, "something's eating the hell out of you, and I know by now when not to intrude, but you've got to tell somebody. You're living with something you can't handle, but I have to tell you, dear, no one in the navy could have done what you did in Amsterdam. You held the whole organization intact, from the embassy to The Hague to NATO. You were the brains behind all our accomplishments in a time when one superior intellect was required to guide clandestine operations. You did that, Hank, rotten temper included, but you *did* it, dear. I don't think anybody else could have, Tye Hawthorne, least of all."

"Thanks for that, Phyll," Henry said. Suddenly, he sat forward on the couch, bringing both hands to his pallid face, his fingers spread, covering the tears that began to fall from his eyes. "But we were *wrong* in Amsterdam, *I* was wrong. I killed Tye's *wife!*"

Phyllis leapt out of the chair and sprang to the couch beside her husband, cradling him in her arms. "Come on, Hank, the Soviets killed her, not you. You said it yourself, and I saw the reports. The markings were there!"

"I led them to her. . . . And now he's here, and because I've been wrong and wrong and wrong again, he may be killed too."

"*Stop* it!" shouted Henry Stevens's wife. "That's *enough,* Hank. You're exhausted, but you're better than this, stronger than this. If that's what's eating your insides away, bring Tyrell in; you can do it easily."

"He'll fight me; you don't know how he feels. Friends of his were killed, too many friends."

"Send a unit and force him in." And then a telephone rang, its bell deep-toned, unnatural. Phyllis rose from the couch and crossed to a small alcove on the sun porch, where, behind a short, louvered panel, three phones stood side by side; they were beige, red, and dark blue. "The Stevens's residence," she said, picking up the red phone, its light pulsating.

"Captain Stevens, please."

"May I ask who's calling? The captain's been up for nearly seventy-two hours and really needs his sleep."

"Okay, I guess it doesn't matter at this hour," said the youthful voice on the line. "I'm Lieutenant Allen, N.I., and the captain should know that Commander— former Commander—Hawthorne was shot outside a diner in Chesapeake Beach, Maryland. As near as we can determine, the wounds may not be life-threatening, but until the ambulance and the paramedics get here, we can't be sure. However, the woman air force officer—"

"*Henry!*"

25

H awthorne and a tear-stained Poole sat opposite
each other in the corridor outside the hospital
operating room, Tyrell in a chair, crutches by
his side, the lieutenant on a bench, leaning forward, his
head in his hands. Neither spoke; there was nothing to
say. Hawthorne's thigh wound had required extraction
of the bullet and seven stitches, which he barely lay still
for on the table, demanding to be brought to the waiting
area where, inside, Major Catherine Neilsen was fighting
for her life.

"If she dies," said Poole, breaking the silence, his
voice strained, barely audible, "I'm gettin' out of this
goddamned outfit, and if I have to, I'll spend the rest of
my life trackin' down the fuckers who killed her."

"I understand, Jackson," said Tyrell, looking over at
the distraught lieutenant.

"Maybe you don't, Commander. One of 'em may be
you."

"I can even understand that, as misdirected as I believe it to be."

" *Misdirected*'? You son of a bitch." Poole removed
his hands and raised his head, glaring at Tye. "In my
vocabulary, which is a hell of a lot superior to yours,
that's as exculpatory as you can get. You're not blame-
less, Mr. Hawthorne. You didn't even tell Cath and me
what this whole thing was about until I forced you to
on that lousy island after Charlie was killed."

"Would it have made any difference—after Charlie
was killed?"

"How do *I* know?" exclaimed the lieutenant. "How do I know anything? I just figure you weren't straight with us."

"I was as straight as I could be without unnecessarily jeopardizing your lives with information you shouldn't have."

"That's spook bullshit!"

"It certainly is, but then, I was once a spook, and I saw men and women killed because they knew things—even fragments of things—that sealed their death warrants. I've been away a long time, but those people still haunt me."

The door to the operating room opened, and a white-jacketed doctor emerged, his loose-fitting hospital outfit splotched with blood. "I've been up here a long time," he said wearily. "Which one of you is Poole?"

"That's me," replied Jackson from the bench, his breath suspended.

"She told me to tell you to cool it—that's what she said."

"How is she?"

"I'll get to that." The surgeon turned to Tyrell. "You're Hawthorne, then, the other patient?"

"Yes."

"She wants to see you—"

"What the hogdamned hell are you talkin' about?" Poole leapt to his feet. "If she's gonna see anyone, it's me!"

"I gave her a choice, Mr. Poole. I didn't even want to do that, but she's a very stubborn lady. One visitor, two minutes maximum, and less is medically advisable."

"How *is* she, Doctor?" said Tye, repeating Jackson's question but with an authority that required an answer.

"I assume you're replacing her immediate family?"

"Assume whatever you like," Hawthorne continued quietly. "We were brought here together and you're certainly aware of the government's concern."

"I certainly am. Two admissions off the books, no

police reports, any and all inquiries turned aside by our having no knowledge of the events suggested . . . and the patients involved were shot. Highly irregular, but I can't question the authority. I never spoke to anyone with such credentials in the intelligence community."

"Then answer my question, please."

"The next twenty-four hours or so will tell."

"Tell *what*?" Poole exploded. "Whether she'll die or not?"

"Frankly, I can't promise you she won't die, but I think we've eliminated the probability. What I also can't promise is that she'll be a whole person, with full mobility."

Poole sank down on the bench, his head again in his hands. "Cath, oh Cath . . ." he sobbed.

"Spinal?" asked Tyrell coldly.

"Then you know about such wounds?"

"Let's say I've been here before. The nerve endings after trauma . . . ?"

"If they respond," nodded the surgeon, "she could be in normal convalescence in a couple of days. If they don't, what can I say?"

"You've said enough, Doctor. May I see her now?"

"Of course. . . . Here, let me help you up, I understand you had a bit of an invasive procedure yourself." Hawthorne got to his feet, precariously balancing himself, and started for the door. "Your crutches," said the surgeon, holding them out.

"I've just de-requisitioned them, Doctor," replied Tyrell. "Thanks very much anyway."

He was escorted into Catherine's room by a nurse who said kindly but firmly that his visit would be timed. Hawthorne stared at the figure on the bed; strands of her blond hair fell in the back of her operation net, the precise, lovely features of her pallid face caught in the soft light of a bedside lamp. She heard footsteps and opened her eyes, turning her head, and, seeing Hawthorne, gestured with her hand for him to come closer, indicating the chair by her side. He did so, limping across the room and sitting down. Then slowly, hesitantly, their two hands drew nearer each other, finally clasping.

"They told me you're okay," said Cathy, her voice weak, her wan smile approving.

"So will you be," said Tye. "Hang in there, Major."

"Come on, Tye, you can do better than that."

"I'm trying. . . . Jackson's a little upset that you didn't ask for him."

"I love him dearly, but it's not the time for a brilliant child, and I'm not up to his predictable behavior." Neilsen spoke in soft bursts of breath, with effort, but clearly, shaking her head when Hawthorne raised his left hand to slow her down. "Isn't that the kind of decision we officers are trained to make? I think you tried to tell me something like that when Charlie was killed."

"I may have said it, Cathy, but I'm not the best teacher. This officer fell apart in Amsterdam, remember?"

"You won't now, will you?"

"That's an odd thing for you to say, but I would hope not. I'm an angry man, Cathy, as angry as I was in Amsterdam—and you're part of it now. . . . Why did you say that?"

"I've put a couple of things together, Tye, and I'm frightened—"

"We're all frightened," Tyrell interrupted gently.

"Frightened for you, for what I think you're carrying around. . . . When you and Jackson came back from Old San Juan, from Simon's place, you'd changed. I couldn't put a name on it, I'm not sure I want to know, but it's something deep, something terrible—"

"I'd lost two friends," Hawthorne broke in nervously, "just as you lost Charlie."

"Then later," the major went on quietly, disregarding his interruption, "you had a message over the phone at the Shenandoah. I never saw a face change so much, it was suddenly pale white, then almost blue, and your eyes were on fire. All you said was that you'd heard from someone who made a mistake. Still later—I know you didn't realize I could hear you—you gave Henry Stevens a telephone number in Paris."

"*That* was—"

"Please. . . . Then tonight you raced out of that diner like a maniac, as though you wanted to kill the chauffeur. . . . I ran after you, and when I got to the door which was closing, just before the shots, you shouted—no, Tye, you screamed, *you*! And then the woman opened fire."

"Yes, she did," said Tyrell, his eyes locked with Cathy's.

"Bajaratt, of course."

"Yes."

"You know who she is, don't you? I mean, you knew her."

"Yes."

"She's someone you knew very well, isn't she?"

"I thought I did. I didn't."

"I'm so sorry, Tye. . . . You haven't told anyone, have you?"

"There's no point. She's not who she was, there's no connection whatsoever."

"You have no doubts about that?"

"None. Her world is in the Baaka Valley. I knew her in another world that had nothing to do with the Baaka."

"In that good world, the good life, where your boat cuts through the water from island to island and the sundowns are peaceful?"

"Yes."

"Will the number in Paris help?"

"It could. I hope so. I want it to."

Catherine studied his tired face, the eyes that held such pain and such anger. "Oh, God, you poor, unhappy man. I feel so for you, Tye . . . and we'll say no more about this."

"I appreciate that, Cathy. . . . Lying there, with what you've been through, you can think about me?"

"Sure," she whispered, growing weak but smiling. "It's better than thinking about myself, isn't it?"

Tyrell leaned forward in the chair, removing his hand from hers and cupping her face. They drew closer until their lips met. "You're lovely, Cathy, so very lovely."

"Hey, that's better than 'outstanding,' Commander."

The door opened, the nurse in the frame; she cleared her throat softly. "Time's up," she said. "The best-looking patient in this hospital has to rest."

"I'll bet you say that to everyone who's been operated on," offered Neilsen.

"If I do, I lie a lot. But not here, not now."

"Tye?"

"Yes?" said Hawthorne, standing up.

"Use Jackson, make him a full partner. He can do everything I can do, and do it better."

"Of course I will, but you're saying something else."

"It'll take his mind off me."

Phyllis Stevens pounced on the telephone. It was nearly ten o'clock in the morning, but it had taken until six-fifteen when she finally got her exhausted, guilt-ridden husband to bed. The woman air force officer had been operated on, the prognosis unknown, but Tye Hawthorne had not been seriously wounded, a fact that relieved Henry Stevens's current concerns but did nothing to relieve his deeper anxiety—*only inches and he might have been killed*!

"Yes, what is it?" said Phyllis quietly into the phone, pulling the cord to the far side of her bed.

"FBI, Mrs. Stevens. May I speak with the captain, please."

"Frankly, I'd rather you didn't. He's had no sleep for

nearly three days, and he's finally getting some. Can't you give me the message?"

"Only part of it, ma'am."

"I understand completely."

"Phyll, what is it?" Henry Stevens bolted upright in the bed next to hers. "I heard the phone, I know I heard the phone!"

"He's all yours, federal man." Phyllis sighed, handing the receiver to her husband, who had already swung his feet to the floor.

"This is Stevens, what is it?"

"FBI, sir, Field Agent Becker, on the Ingersol office detail."

"Anything?"

"It's hard to explain, sir. We found a telephone in a steel cabinet camouflaged by wood paneling as though it were part of the wall. We had to torch it open—"

"Is it a regular phone, and if it is, why was it concealed?"

"That's what's crazy, Captain. The tech men have been working on it most of the night and all this morning and have only gotten so far."

"How far is that?"

"They found a satellite dish on the roof which accesses the hidden phone, but all they've been able to figure is that it beams up and beams down to the state of Utah."

"Utah? Where the hell is Utah?"

"There could be a couple of hundred laser frequencies to a thousand receiving dishes out there, sir. Maybe more of both."

"That's nuts!"

"That's the new technology, Captain."

"Then put your high-priced computers to work, those same magic machines that cost the taxpayers so goddamn much money, and come up with something."

"We're working on it, sir."

"Work harder!" Stevens slammed down the phone,

falling back on his pillows. "They have their own satellites up there in space," he whispered. "It's unreal!"

"I don't know what you're talking about, Hank, but if you're saying what I think you're saying, all of us everywhere made it possible. All it takes is money."

"Progress," said Stevens, "isn't it wonderful?"

"Depends on who controls it, I imagine," said his wife. "We all thought we would—the best and the brightest. Apparently we don't."

It was late morning and the hospital had nothing new to report on Catherine Neilsen other than she was resting, her vital signs stable. Hawthorne, in shorts, tested his leg in the bedroom of the Shenandoah Lodge under Poole's scrutiny. "It hurts, doesn't it?" said the lieutenant. "You're hurtin'."

"Not so bad," replied Tyrell. "I slept halfway decently, which I didn't expect to. The main thing is to keep the weight off the left side."

"It'd be better if you stayed off it completely for a couple of days," said Poole. "Let the sutures set."

"We don't have a couple of days. Get more of that tape and bind it tighter." The telephone rang. "It's probably Stevens. Phyllis promised she'd have him call me when he woke up."

"I'll check it out," said Jackson, going to the desk. "Hello? . . . Yes, yes, he's here. Just a moment." The lieutenant turned to Hawthorne. "It's someone who says he's your brother and I figure he is. He even sounds like you, except kinda nicer."

"He isn't really; it's an act he learned while teaching." Tyrell limped to the bed, slowly sitting down. "I called St. Thomas from the hospital last night." Tye picked up the bedside phone. "Hello, Marc, I figured you'd be mooring sometime today."

"About an hour ago, and it's very kind of you to let me know you're still around," said Marc Anthony

Hawthorne sarcastically. "You *are* still around, aren't you?"

"Cut it out, bro, I've been busy, and don't be curious because that phone is off limits."

"Not to a couple of others—"

"What others? I didn't check for messages."

"The first is from a B. Jones. He called yesterday at 4:12 in the afternoon, leaving you a number in Mexico City and strongly advising you to reach him within the next twenty-four hours."

"Give it to me." The brother did and Tyrell wrote it down on yet another menu. "Who's the other?"

"A woman named Dominique, who said she was calling from Monte Carlo. The timer says the call came in at 5:02 this morning."

"The *message!*"

"I'll switch it on for you. It's not the sort of thing an innocent younger brother should repeat to his role model. . . . Oh, you're a real island man, *mon*."

"Let me hear it, and stay on the line and drop the comments."

"Aye, *aye*, sir."

"*Tyrell, my darling, my love, it's Domie! I'm calling from L'Hermitage in Monte Carlo. I know it's very late, but my husband is at the casino and I have wonderful news! I performed extremely well during these past few days, but frankly I'm sick of it all and I do miss you so—as I, indeed, feel it's my duty to be with my uncle during his last days. I broached the latter consideration to my husband, and you cannot believe what he said! He said, 'Go back to your uncle, for he needs you, as I'm equally sure you need your lover.' I tell you, I was astonished. I asked him if he was furious and his reply was a gift from God. 'No, my dear wife, for I have my own plans for the next several weeks. To the contrary, I'm very happy for you.' . . . Isn't it wonderful—I told you he was kind, if lacking in some male qualities. At any rate, I'm driving to the airport in Nice now to catch*

*the first plane. I'll be in Paris tomorrow, dashing around
everywhere, of course, for there are so many things to
do before leaving on an extended vacation, but if you
need me, call Paris. If I'm not in, speak only to Pauline.
I will reach you. . . . I can feel your arms around me, my
body pressed against yours. Oh God, I sound like a
lovesick young girl, and so young I am not! I'll be in the
islands in a day, perhaps two, certainly no later than
three, and I'll call you instantly. . . . My love, my darling.*"

A primeval roar of fury was forming in Hawthorne's
throat; he controlled it, but not the violence of his outrage. Words of love so viciously, so unfeelingly used to
propel a lethal myth. The call had been placed within an
hour after the caller had tried to kill him! Not from a
yacht in the Mediterranean but from the steps of a diner
in Maryland. . . . How easy to tell an answering machine
that one was wherever he cared to say he was. Remem-
brances of the games in Amsterdam: Hold on to your
cover at all cost, it may be all you have left. Little Girl
Blood was playing out her false cards, believing he would
accept them on the table. He would make sure she did
with his own call to Paris, to the ubiquitous "Pauline,"
alerting the Deuxième beforehand.

"Okay, Tye" came his brother's words over the telephone. "I've rewound the tape, and we're starting from
scratch at this end. Aren't you happy I'm not making
any comments?"

"None are called for, Marc."

"Well, something must be, because you wanted me
to stay on the line—"

"Oh, Christ, I'm sorry, bro," Hawthorne interrupted,
bringing his focus back. "Practical matters. . . . I assume
the money came through and you're looking for a couple
of class A's."

"Hey, come on, Tye, I just sailed into Red Hook an
hour ago! But, yes, I did contact Cyril at the Chase in

Charlotte Amalie, and he told me we got an unbelievable transfer from London. He was pressing me for any connections to the old *Noriega* crowd!"

"He'll trace and find it's as clean as the queen's lingerie. Get to work on the boats."

"Without you?"

"I said get to work, don't make a deal. If you find something promising, put a binder on it."

"Oh, yes, I remember now, a binder. When do you think you'll be back?"

"It can't be too much longer—one way or another."

"What do you mean, one way or another?"

"I can't tell you. I'll call you in a day or so."

"Tye . . . ?"

"Yes?"

"For God's sake, be careful, will you?"

"Of course, bro. You know my dictum, I despise foolhardy people."

"You say."

Hawthorne replaced the telephone, wincing as he leaned to his left. "Where are the notes that were in my trousers?" he asked Poole.

"Right here," replied Jackson, going to the bureau and picking up several pages scrunched together.

Hawthorne took the scraps of paper, rustling through them, extracting one and flattening it out on the bed. He picked up the phone, again wincing as he turned, reading the figures on the paper, and dialed. "Secretary Palisser, please," he said courteously. "T. N. Hawthorne calling."

"Yes, sir," said the secretary. "I'm to put you right through."

"Thank you."

"*Commander?*" Palisser's voice was like the man—authoritative, not aggressive. "What have you learned, if anything?"

"Another killing, and I almost made it one after that."

"Good *Lord,* are you all right?"

"A couple of stitches, that's all; I walked—ran—right into it."

"What happened?"

"Later, Mr. Secretary, there's something else. Do you know a CIA analyst named O'Ryan?"

"Yes, I believe I do. He was the DCI's senior aide at our last briefing. As I recall, he's been around for quite a while and is considered one of those back-room whizzes. I could be wrong, but I think it was Ryan or O'Ryan."

"You're not wrong and he's dead, courtesy of Little Girl Blood."

"Oh, my *God!*"

"If I read it correctly, he was the primary intelligence leak to Bajaratt and her crowd."

"Aren't you contradicting yourself?" interrupted an astonished yet thinking Palisser. "If he was of such value to her—them—why would they kill him?"

"Only a guess, but he may have made a mistake that could lead us to her, or, even more likely, he'd fulfilled his function and had to be eliminated because of what and who he knew."

"Which leads back to your thesis that the Baaka penetration in Washington reaches into dangerously high places."

"Knowingly or unknowingly, Mr. Secretary," Hawthorne broke in quickly. "For example, your helping Van Nostrand was an act of compassion, not complicity. You were conned."

"It's so hard to believe—"

"Further, if Howard Davenport's death is related, and I'm convinced it is, even the most avid conspiracy freak would back away from calling him a friend of Bajaratt's, any more than you. You're just not logical candidates."

"Good heavens, never!"

"But O'Ryan was—"

"How can you be certain?"

"She was within a mile of where he was killed."

"How do you know that?"

"I told you, she tried to add me to the list."

"You *saw* her?"

"Let's put it this way, I was trying like hell to get out of her line of sight.... Please, Mr. Secretary, we're wasting time. Have you got the papers I asked for?"

"I'll have them all in a half hour, although I still have misgivings."

"Do you have a choice—do we have a choice?"

"Not if your service record is accurate and wasn't written by your mother. Incidentally, we took your photograph from your last navy ID, which was six years ago. It appears you haven't aged perceptibly."

"I look better, because I have a better job. Ask my mother."

"Thank you, but I shouldn't care to have another Hawthorne in my life, no matter how charming she may be. Have the lieutenant come around and pick everything up. He should ask to see the undersecretary for Caribbean affairs. He'll have the envelope with your credentials—Special Agent, Consular Operations. It will be logged, sealed, and marked Geological Survey, North Coast: Montserrat."

"As in Bajaratt?"

"One should always anticipate the esoterica of future congressional hearings, Commander. Also, the mentalities of the inquisitors. Such an obvious code mitigates the specter of criminal secrecy."

"It *does*?"

"Certainly.... A senator asks, 'Montserrat and *Bajaratt*? Isn't that kind of obvious, Mr. Secretary?' ... 'Why, Senator, you're very astute. Therefore, as you've so brilliantly perceived, we did not engage in duplicity when we enlisted former Commander Hawthorne. If we had, we surely would not have been—as you've pointed out—so obvious.' "

"In short, you're covering the State Department's ass."

"Most assuredly," agreed the secretary. "As well as yours, Commander. And, Hawthorne?"

"Yes, sir?"

"What's your approach with the families?"

"Down and dirty."

"Right now, since I've prepared your credentials, be a little more specific, please."

"Direct confrontation. I'll claim there's a State Department crisis of extreme sensitivity that could well involve the deceased. There's no time for the usual period of mourning prior to interrogation."

"You'll be resented, perhaps stopped by family members or the religious."

"I hope I am, because I can summon up a few resentments of my own. . . . Let's say I'm very personally motivated. In addition to everything that's happened, there's a friend of mine in the hospital who may never walk again." Tyrell hung up the phone and turned to a pensive Poole, who was staring out the window. "You're elected, Jackson," he said. "You're to see the undersecretary for Caribbean affairs; he's got a large padded manila envelope for me. . . . What's the matter?"

"Things are happening awful fast, Tye," replied the lieutenant, stepping back from the window, his eyes on Hawthorne. "The body count is risin' quicker than we can keep up with it. . . . Van Nostrand and his head of security, plus a gatehouse guard, then the old woman, a chauffeur, and a red-haired guy right down in that parking lot, then Davenport, Ingersol, and now this O'Ryan."

"You're forgetting a few, aren't you, Lieutenant?" asked Hawthorne. "If I recall, they were close friends of mine, and one was a very close friend of yours. I don't think this is the time for evangelical pacifism."

"You're not hearing me, Commander."

"What did I miss?"

"We're not a thousand miles away in the Caribbean, where you and I can sorta control the things we can control. The geography's narrowed down a whole hell of a lot, and there's a lot of people involved we don't know."

"That's logical. We don't have a schedule, but we know this is ground zero, and Bajaratt's systematically eliminating every conceivable link to her."

"We know where she's comin' from, but who's on our side? Who's on those controls?"

"It'll be San Juan again," Hawthorne replied. "You'll take Cathy's place and handle the base camp here. You'll coordinate my moves as the additional information comes in."

"With what and from whom?"

"With the high technology that's supposedly replaced men like me—what we used to be. I imagine it was there, but we didn't have much use for it, or the laboratory boys didn't think we could learn."

"What's the equipment?"

"First, there's a device called a transponder—"

"It's a tracing module on UHF," Poole explained sharply. "Within given distances it can relay your position to a map grid."

"That's what I gathered. It'll be embedded in a belt that's in the envelope. Then there's a paging mechanism that emits small electrical charges telling me whoever's at the other end wants to reach me, two shots repeated twice meaning as soon as it's convenient, three shots repeated a number of times signaling emergency. It's fiber-optic and implanted in a plastic cigarette lighter so it can bypass a metal detector."

"Who controls it?" asked the lieutenant.

"You. I'll set it up that way."

"Set it up so I know by alternatin' codes whoever it is at the Agency or the State Department who's delivering information for you. The number should be restricted to the required personnel on four-hour shifts, all sequestered under guard and with no access to telephones."

"Were you in my former business, Poole?"

"No, Commander, I'm a senior computer operator of an AWAC. False information—deliberately false—is a nightmare we gotta live with."

"I wonder where Sal Mancini is? . . . Sorry."

"Don't be. If I ever see him, you'll know it when you read the papers. He's a dead snake, 'cause he's as much responsible for Charlie's death as any of the others! And make damn sure the people forwarding you information are the same ones on the grids."

"What grids?"

"The screen printouts that pinpoint your whereabouts relayed by the transponder. One team can handle both; separate teams leave everything too loose."

"Aren't we getting a little paranoid? Palisser made it clear to me that only the most experienced and trusted people at Central Intelligence would be working with us."

"In other words," said the lieutenant, "it might have been someone like the late Mr. O'Ryan?"

"I'll tell Palisser and make it clear that's the way it's got to be," said Hawthorne, nodding slowly. "All right, let's get started." Tyrell rose unsteadily from the bed and pointed to his hip. "I meant what I said, Jackson. Tape this thing up firmer."

"What about your clothes?" Poole grabbed the adhesive gauze from the desk as Hawthorne stood up, pulled down his shorts, and watched the lieutenant expertly crisscross the tape across his wound. "You can't head out to the O'Ryans and the Ingersols in skivvies."

"I gave my measurements to Palisser's secretary. Within an hour everything will be delivered here. Suit, shirt, tie, and shoes—the whole fish and fancy chips. A State Department employee can't violate a dress code."

The telephone rang and Hawthorne bounced down on the bed, once again wincing. "Yes?" he said curtly.

"It's Henry, Tye. Did you get any sleep?"

"More than I thought."

"How are you feeling? How's the wound?"

"I'm anxious and the stitches are holding. Phyllis said you finally hit the sack with a loud thump yourself. You'll never learn to be subtle, will you, Hank?"

"Thanks for that—the Hank."

"You're welcome. You're not off my personal hook, and maybe someday you'll fill in the missing pages that were lost in Amsterdam, but right now we're working together. Speaking of which, do you have anything new? What about the telephone in Paris?"

"It's a mansion in Parc Monceau belonging to a family, a dynasty, I guess, named Couvier, very old, very large French fortune. According to the Deuxième, the owner is the last of the great boulevardiers; he's close to eighty with a fifth wife who, until last year, was a beach hostess in Saint-Tropez."

"Any phone records, international, I mean?"

"Four from that side of the pond. Two from the Caribbean and two from the mainland during the past ten days. They've got it tapped; from now on they'll get specific locations by area codes and numbers."

"Are the Couviers in residence?"

"Not according to the head housekeeper; they're in Hong Kong."

"Then the housekeeper takes the calls?"

"The Deuxième figured that out," Stevens cut in. "Her name's Pauline, and she's under tight surveillance, electronic and physical. The moment anything breaks, they'll reach us."

"That's the best we can ask for."

"May I ask how you knew about the Couviers?"

"Sorry, Henry, maybe later, much later. . . . Anything else?"

"Definitely. We have proof of sorts that Ingersol was up to his ass in the Bajaratt circle." The navy captain described the concealed telephone in the dead attorney's office as well as the rooftop satellite relay. "It was obviously networked with the yacht in Miami Beach and that crazy old man's island."

"*Crazy*'s the operative word, Henry. I can understand Van Nostrand, but why men like O'Ryan and Ingersol? Why would they be a part of it? It doesn't make sense."

"Sure it does," replied the chief of naval intelligence. "Look at that pilot of yours from Puerto Rico, Albert Simon. He thought they had something on him that called for forty years in Leavenworth. Same kind of thing with O'Ryan and Ingersol, maybe. Incidentally, the Agency's sending over whatever information it has on both of them."

"Where is Simon, by the way? What's happened to him?"

"He's got his tail in a tub of warm molasses, living it up in a suite at the Watergate, courtesy of an adoring Pentagon. A private ceremony was held—in the Oval Office, no less—where he was presented with a couple of medals and a sizable back paycheck."

"I thought the President was keeping a low profile these days—"

"You weren't listening. It was a very private ceremony, no photo ops, no press, over in five minutes."

"How the hell did Simon explain away his—to say the least, his prolonged absence? *Christ*, all those years!"

"Very smart, I'm told. Just obscure enough for people who don't really want explanations. His long-ago discharge was mailed to him in the Australian outback and subsequently lost. He's been moving around for years, a real expatriate, from one flying job to another, one country to another. Nobody cared to learn anymore."

"That's the washed-out Simon," said Hawthorne. "Not an influential lawyer on the White House's A list, or a highly respected analyst at the Central Intelligence

Agency. Ingersol and O'Ryan weren't cut from the same cloth as Al Simon."

"I didn't say they were, just a variation in a better quality of fabric." There was the sound of chimes over the naval officer's phone. "Hold on, Tye, there's someone at the front door and Phyll's taking a shower."

Silence.

Captain Henry Stevens did not return to the telephone.

26

"**W**e're leaving now!" said Bajaratt loudly, opening the door of the bedroom, awakening Nicolo from a deep sleep. "Get up and pack us, quickly!"

The young man raised himself from the pillows and rubbed his eyes in the bright afternoon sunlight streaming through the windows. "I faced my God last night and I am fortunate to be alive. Let me sleep."

"Get up, and please do as I say. I've ordered a limousine; it will be here in ten minutes."

"Why? I'm so tired and I ache so."

"To be frank, our chauffeur may have a bigger mouth than a thousand dollars will keep shut, although I've promised him more."

"Where are we going?"

"I've made arrangements; don't concern yourself. *Hurry!* I've another phone call to make." The Baj rushed back into the suite's sitting room and dialed the number she had so well committed to memory.

"Identify yourself," said the strange voice on the line, "and state your business."

"You are not the man I spoke to before," replied Bajaratt.

"Changes have been made—"

"There have been entirely too many changes," said the Baj quietly, ominously.

"They were made for the better," interrupted the man on the Scorpio phone, "and if you're who I think you are, you're better off for them."

"How can I be sure—how can I be sure of *anything*? This chaos would not be permitted in Europe, and in the Baaka you'd all be executed."

"Scorpios Two and Three aren't around any longer, are they? Weren't they executed, Little Girl Blood?"

"Don't play your childish games with me, signore," said Bajaratt, her voice now ice cold.

"Nor you with me, lady. . . . You want proof, okay, I'll buy that. I'm in the circle here and know every move that's being made to find you. Among the men involved is a Captain H. R. Stevens, chief of naval intelligence. He's been working with a retired N.I. lieutenant commander named Hawthorne—"

"Hawthorne? You know this—"

"That's right, and they've traced you to a place called Chesapeake Beach. Each of us in the circle has been alerted over our secure faxes. However, Captain Stevens won't be doing any more tracing. He's dead, and sooner or later they'll find his body in a thick row of hedges behind his garage. If they do, you'll read about it in the afternoon papers. It may even be on the evening news, if they haven't blacked it out."

"I'm satisfied, signore," said Bajaratt softly, quickly.

"So fast?" asked the elite Scorpion. "From what I've read and heard, that doesn't sound like you."

"I have my proof."

"My word?"

"No, a name."

"Stevens?"

"No."

"Hawthorne?"

"That will be enough, *Scorpione Uno*. I need equipment. The time will come any day now."

"If it's smaller than a tank, you've got it."

"It's not large but quite sophisticated. I can have one flown overnight from the Baaka via London or Paris, but I don't trust our technicians. In two out of five occasions the equipment malfunctioned. I can't afford the risk."

"Neither can the men who think like I do, and we're all over this city. Remember Dallas thirty years ago—we do. How do you want to proceed?"

"I have with me a detailed blueprint—"

"Get it to me," interrupted the Scorpio.

"How?"

"I suppose you won't tell me where you are."

"Of course not," the Baj broke in. "I will leave a copy for you at the concierge's desk in the hotel of my choice. I will call you within minutes of depositing it."

"What name?"

"Choose it."

"Racklin."

"You chose so quickly."

"He was a lieutenant, a prisoner of war who bought it in Vietnam. He thought the way I do; he hated our running out of Saigon, hated the goddamned pansies in Washington who wouldn't give us the firepower."

"Very well, Racklin it shall be. Where do I call you, this number?"

"I'll be here for a couple of hours, that's all. After that I have to return to the office for a meeting. . . . The conference is about you, Little Girl Blood."

"Such a charming sobriquet, so diminutive yet so lethal," the Baj said. "I will call you . . . say within the next thirty minutes." Bajaratt hung up the telephone. "*Nicolo!*" she shouted.

"*Henry!*" Tyrell yelled into the phone. "Where the hell *are* you?"

"Is anything wrong?" asked Poole.

"I don't know," Hawthorne answered, squinting and shaking his head. "Henry was always easily distracted if something new came up, intruding on his personal tunnel vision. Maybe he got a security report from the inner circle; he'd read it first, forgetting he was on the phone. I'll call him later; he didn't have anything new anyway." Hawthorne replaced the telephone and looked up at the air force lieutenant. "Come on, strap this meat up and haul your tail over to the State Department. I want to get started. I can't wait to meet the mourning O'Ryans and the Ingersols."

"You're not going anywhere until you've got your papers and your clothes. May I respectfully suggest that until then you lie down and rest, sir? I've taken medical courses in combat *triage* and wound-stress relationships, and I truly believe that the commander—"

"Shut up, Jackson, and tape the damn thing!"

Having called the Scorpion with the name of the hotel, Bajaratt left the envelope containing the deadly blueprints with the Carillon's concierge; it was clearly marked: *Racklin, Esq. To be picked up by courier, seals intact.*

"*Sono desolato!*" whispered Nicolo as their luggage was being put in the limousine. "My head is not yet on straight. I promised Angel I would call her from our new hotel and I am late!"

"I have no patience for such nonsense," said Bajaratt, walking toward the huge white vehicle.

"But you must!" cried the dock boy, grabbing her by the shoulders and stopping her. "There must be respect for me in this matter, respect for *her*!"

"How dare you talk to me this way?"

"Listen to me, signora, I have lived through terrible things with you and killed a man who would kill me— but you brought me into this mad world of yours and to this young woman I have great affection for. You will not stand in my way. I know I am young, and I have had many women for all the reasons you say about me, but *this* girl is different."

"You sound better in Italian than you do in English. . . . Certainly, call your friend from the limousine, if you must."

Inside the car, the elderly black driver started the engine and turned in the front seat as Nicolo grabbed the telephone off its receptacle. "The dispatcher said you'd have an address for me, ma'am."

"A moment, please." Bajaratt touched Nico's cheek. "Keep your voice down," said the Baj in Italian. "I must be clear with our chauffeur."

"Then I'll wait until you're finished, for I might yell with happiness."

"If you'd wait a bit longer, say a half hour or so, you may shout for joy as loud as you wish."

"Oh?"

"Before we go to our next lodgings, we must make a stop—*I* must make a stop. There's no reason for you to accompany me, so you'll be alone in the car for at least twenty minutes."

"I shall wait, then. Do you think the driver would be offended if I asked him to raise the partition between us?"

"Why should he?" Bajaratt stopped, her eyes squinting, cold. "I'm sure he does not speak Italian. You *do* speak only Italian with your actress, do you not?"

"Please, signora, she saw through me before she left for California. She knows I understand English. She told me she saw it in my eyes when we were with other people—how I laughed with my eyes when something funny was said."

"You admitted you spoke *English?*"

"We speak it all the time on the telephone, where is the harm?"

"Everyone thinks you do *not* speak English!"

"You're wrong, Cabi. That journalist in Palm Beach knew otherwise."

"He doesn't matter, he's—"

"He's what?"

"Never mind."

"The address, ma'am?" interrupted the chauffeur, hearing the break in the Italian conversation.

"Yes, here it is." The Baj opened her purse and pulled out a scrap of wrinkled brown paper on which were written Arabic characters, in themselves coded words and digits. Decoding them from memory, she read aloud a number and a street in Silver Spring, Maryland. "Do you know where it is?" she asked.

"I'll find it, ma'am," replied the driver. "It won't be a problem."

"Raise the partition, please."

"A pleasure, ma'am."

"Does this 'Angel' of yours speak to others about you?" asked Bajaratt angrily, unpleasantly, her head snapping around to Nico.

"I don't know, Cabi."

"Actresses are cheap, they're exhibitionists, and always seek publicity!"

"Angelina is not like that."

"You saw all those pictures in the newspapers, all that gossip—"

"It was terrible what they said."

"How do you think it got there?"

"Because she is a famous person, the three of us understood that."

"She engineered it all! What she wants from you is publicity, that is all."

"I don't believe you."

"You are a stupid dock boy from the waterfront, what do you know about anything? If she knew who and what you really are, do you truly believe she'd look at you twice?"

Nicolo fell silent. Finally, he spoke, his head arched back in the seat. "You're right, Cabi, I'm nothing, a nobody. I have gone beyond myself, believing things I should not believe because of all the attention and the fancy clothes I wear for this grand game of yours."

"You have the rest of your life ahead of you, my darling boy. Consider all this as an experience that will help you grow into a man. . . . Now, be quiet, for I must think."

"What must you think about?"

"About the woman I'm about to meet in this Silver Spring."

"I must think also," said the dock boy from Portici.

Hawthorne dressed in his new clothes with the help of Poole, who tied his tie, stood back, and rendered judgment. "You know, you're not a bad-lookin' civilian, as civilians go."

"I feel like a starched cornstalk," said Tyrell, stretching his neck inside the shirt collar.

"When was the last time you wore a tie?"

"When I took off my uniform, and that's the truth." The telephone rang, and Hawthorne pivoted in pain toward it.

"Stay where you are," said Poole. "I'll get it." He crossed to the desk and picked up the telephone. "Yes? . . . This is the commander's military aide. Please hold on." He covered the phone and turned back to Tyrell. "Wooly muleshit, it's the office of the director of Central Intelligence. The man wants to talk to you."

"Who am I to object?" said Hawthorne, lowering himself awkwardly on the bed and reaching for the phone. "This is Hawthorne," said Tye.

"The director wishes to speak with you, sir. Please hold on."

"Good afternoon, Commander."

"Good afternoon, Mr. Director. I assume you know my rank is in retirement."

"I know a great deal more than that, young man, and it's all to my regret."

"What do you mean?"

"I've been talking to Secretary Palisser. Like him, I was part of Van Nostrand's extraordinary scam. My God, that man was brilliant."

"He was in a position to be brilliant, sir. He's also dead."

"He knew which buttons to push; if things had turned out otherwise, we all would have falsely exonerated one another in light of his so-called contributions. He was the consummate actor, and I, like my colleagues, believed him completely."

"What did you do for him?"

"Money, Commander, over eight hundred million dollars transferred to various European accounts."

"Who gets it now?"

"With sums like that, I imagine it will go to international litigation. First, when the time is right, we'll have to disclose the illegal transfers. I'll resign, of course, and whatever grand illusions I had in taking this job are down the tube."

"Did you make a profit from the transfers?"

"Good Lord, no."

"Then why take the fall?"

"Because regardless of my good intentions, what I did was illegal. I used my office to benefit an individual by disregarding the law and concealing my action."

"So you were guilty of poor judgment; you weren't the only one. The fact that you're willing to admit what you did and why you did it would seem to me to let you off the hook."

"For a man with the baggage you carry, that's a remarkable statement. Can you imagine the pressure on the President? An appointment of his to an extremely sensitive and influential position expediting illegal transfers of eight hundred million dollars? The opposition would scream corruption at the highest levels, as in Iranscam, and I didn't even get a security fence."

"Forget that crap, Mr. Director," said Hawthorne,

his eyes above the telephone wide, glazed, filled with an admixture of anger and fear. "What *baggage* do I carry?"

"Well, I . . . I assumed you understood."

"Amsterdam?"

"Yes. Why do you sound so surprised?"

"What do you know about Amsterdam?" Tyrell interrupted, his voice hoarse.

"That's a difficult question, Commander."

"Answer it!"

"I can only tell you that Captain Stevens was not responsible for your wife's death. The system was at fault, not the individual."

"That's the coldest goddamn statement I've heard since 'I was just following orders.' "

"It happens to be the truth, Hawthorne."

"Whose? Yours, his, the system's? No one's accountable for anything, right?"

"To cure that disease was one of the illusions I had when I took this job. I was doing pretty well until you and Bajaratt came along."

"Get off my case, you son of a bitch!"

"You're upset, Commander, but I might say the same to you. Let me tell you something. I don't like trained U.S. personnel—superbly trained as you were at the tax-payers' expense—selling out to a foreign government for money! Do I make myself clear?"

"What you say or think doesn't interest me. You and your *system* killed my wife, and you know it. I don't owe you bastards a thing!"

"Then get out of our nest. I've got a dozen deep-cover agents better than you, and I can insert them without missing you for a minute. Do me a favor, get out."

"In your dreams! Friends of mine were killed—good friends—and one who survived may never walk again! You and your hotshots have been about as inadequate as you've ever been. I'm going down and deep, and I'd advise you to keep track of me because I'm going to lead you to Little Girl Blood."

"You know, Commander, I believe that's possible, for as I mentioned, you were well trained. As to monitoring you, you can take that to the bank, insofar as your equipment is frequencied into our macrocomputers. Let's get down to business, Commander. As your people requested, and relayed through Palisser, the communications and transponder units will be combined with no access to outside telephones. Frankly, I think it's overkill, and our personnel will be individually and collectively upset—they're among the finest we have."

"So was O'Ryan. Have you told them about him?"

"I see your point." The director was silent for a moment or two, not finished, merely pausing. "Perhaps I will, although we have no concrete proof of his having turned."

"Since when are we in a court of law, Mr. Intelligence Man? He was there and she was there. One survived and one didn't. Have our rules of engagement changed?"

"No, no, they haven't. Coincidence is rarely, if ever, a factor. Perhaps I'll explain that there's evidence that this operation has been penetrated; that could be enough. Sequestration is very bad for internal morale, and these people are all outstanding. I'll have to think about it."

"Don't think. Tell them about O'Ryan! What the hell else do you need? Why, when there's a hundred thousand square miles of coastline, was he within a couple of hundred yards of Bajaratt when he was taken out?"

"It's not conclusive, Mr. Hawthorne—"

"Neither was my wife, Mr. Director. But you know and I know what killed her! We don't have to think, we *know*. Haven't you made that leap? Because if you haven't, you don't belong in that chair."

"I made it years ago, young man, but where I am now

demands that I make another leap—not so much of faith, but one of practicality. There are a lot of things I'd like to change around here, and I can't do it being imperious. There's been too much of that. Regardless, you and I are working on the same side now."

"No, Mr. Director, I'm working for *my* side and some degree of sanity, if it's any comfort to you. But not yours. To repeat, I don't owe you bastards anything—you owe me what you can never pay." The blood rushing to his head in fury, Hawthorne slammed down the telephone, the strength of the impact cracking the tan plastic shell.

Raymond Gillette, director of the Central Intelligence Agency, leaned over his desk, his fingers massaging the terrible ache in his forehead. Bewilderingly, the memory of Command Saigon had come back to him, filling him with anger and sorrow, and he did not know why. Then suddenly it was clear—it was Tyrell Hawthorne ... what he was *doing* to the retired naval officer. The similarity to Saigon was acutely painful.

Back in Vietnam, a young air force officer, an Air Force Academy graduate, had been shot down with his crew, parachuting out of a burning plane near the border of Cambodia, less than five miles from the camouflaged, crisscrossing Ho Chi Minh supply routes. How that man survived the jungles and the swamps while evading the Cong and the North Vietnamese, only God knew, but he had done so. He had made his way south through the rivers and the forests, living on berries and bark and rodents until he reached friendly territory. And the story he brought back to his intelligence debriefing was incredible.

There was a hidden complex the size of twenty football stadiums carved out of the side of the mountain, into which hundreds of trucks and tanks, gasoline haulers and armored vehicles disappeared regularly during the daylight hours, only to proceed south again at night. According to the young officer, it was also an ammunition depot, as he had seen webbed ammo vehicles enter and leave empty.

Visions of the World War II German rocket base, Peenemünde, fueled the imagination of the interrogating intelligence officer, who now sat at his desk as director of Central Intelligence. To bomb out, to utterly destroy and close up such a massive complex, would not only be an immense strategic victory but also a much needed psychological boost to a military machine that was being worn down by the sheer perseverance of an enemy who had neither the use nor the need of false body counts.

Where was this enormous mountain sanctuary large enough to house an entire division and all its firepower? *Where?*

The young air force officer could not accurately pinpoint it on the aerial maps; he had been hiding and running for his life on the ground. However, he knew the coordinates where he had been shot out of the sky, and he believed that if he was chuted down in the area, he could retrace his escape route. In retracing it he was sure he would reach the ascending hills opposite the armed mountain retreat from which he had observed the activity. Not only sure, but *positive;* there was only one such group of hills, "like scoops of green ice cream piled on top of each other," but not defined in the aerial photographs.

"I can't ask you to do that, Lieutenant," Gillette had said. "You've lost over twenty-five pounds and your physical condition is marginal."

"I think you can and you should, sir," replied the pilot. "The longer we wait, the more screwed up my memory gets."

"For Christ's sake, it's just another depot—"

"Correction, sir, it's *the* depot. I've never seen anything like it anywhere, and neither have you. It's like turning part of the Grand Canyon sideways and driving into it! Let me go, Captain, please."

"I sense a wrinkle here, Lieutenant. Why are you so eager? You're a rational man; you're not after extraneous medals, and this could be a very dangerous operation."

"I've got all the reason I need, Captain. My two crewmen bailed out with me; they landed near each other in a field while I bounced through some trees, maybe a quarter of a mile away. I threw my chute under some branches and ran toward that field as fast as I could. I reached the edge of it at the same time as a group of soldiers came out from the other side—soldiers in *uniforms*, not kids in pajamas—and I knelt in the grass and watched those bastards hack my crew to death with bayonets! They weren't only my friends, Captain, one of them was my cousin. *Soldiers*, Captain! Soldiers don't bayonet prisoners in a field! . . . You see, I have to go back there. Now. Before it all becomes too much of a blur."

"You'll have all the protection we can give you. You'll be wired with the most sophisticated communications equipment we have and monitored every step of the way. The Cobra choppers will never be more than three miles from your position, prepared to swing down at your signal and take you out."

"What more can I ask, sir?"

A great deal more, young man, for you didn't understand any more than I did. Covert Operations doesn't work that way. There's another morality, another ethic, the credo of which is "get the job done, whatever the cost."

The young officer was flown northeast with a Cong defector who had lived on the Cambodian border. Both were parachuted at night over the vicinity where the pilot's plane had gone down, and together they started the retrace. Gillette, the intelligence captain responsible for the mission, flew north, just south of Han Minh, joining the Cov-Op unit monitoring the two-man insurgency team.

Where are the Cobras? asked the intelligence officer from Command Saigon.

Don't worry, Captain, they're on their way was a colonel's reply.

They should be there now. Our pilot and the Cong defect are closing in. Listen to them!

We're listening, said a major who hovered over a radio. *Relax. They're reaching Zero target and we've got a perfect fix on their position.*

If they give the signal, they're roughly a thousand meters west of Zero, added the Colonel.

Then send in the Cobras! roared the captain from Saigon. *It's all we asked them to do!*

When they do it, said the colonel.

Suddenly, there was an eruption of static accompanied by an erratic staccato of gunfire. Then silence—a dreadful silence.

That's it! yelled the major. *They've been cut down. Contact the bombers to move in and unload everything they've got! Here are the coordinates!*

What do you mean, they've been cut down? Gillette shouted.

They were obviously found and killed by North Viet patrols, Captain. They gave their lives for an outstanding operation.

Where the hell were the Cobras, the choppers that were to take them out?

What Cobras? said the major from Cov-Op sarcastically. *You think we were going to blow the whole show with Cobras in the air only miles from Zero? They'd be picked up by radar and that's a goddamned mountain!*

That wasn't my understanding! yelled the captain. *I gave that pilot my word!*

Your word, said the colonel, *not ours. We're trying to win a war that we're losing.*

You bastards! I gave that pilot a promise—

Your promise, not ours. By the way, what's your name, Captain?

Gillette, the intelligence officer replied, perplexed. *Raymond Gillette.*

I can see it now: Gillette's Razor Cuts Off Major Supply Route! We're also pretty big in the Press-Op department.

Raymond Gillette, director of the Central Intelligence Agency, raised his head, arched his neck, and again pressed his fingers against his temples. *Gillette's Razor* had opened the corporate world for him at the expense of a young pilot's life as well as that of his Vietnamese companion. Was he doing it again? With Hawthorne? Was it possible that there was another O'Ryan in the upper echelons of the CIA?

Anything was possible, concluded Raymond Gillette as he got out of his chair and walked to his office door. He was going to talk personally to every man and woman in the transmission unit, staring into their eyes and using the expertise of a lifetime to find a flaw in any of them. He owed that much to a dead air force officer and his Vietnamese scout from many years ago. He owed that much to Tyrell Hawthorne, to whom he had given his word only minutes before. He had to do better than that; he had to study each man and each woman in whose hands Hawthorne's life would rest. He opened the door and spoke to his secretary.

"Helen, I want you to alert the Little Girl unit. All personnel are to meet me in Operations, room five, in twenty minutes."

"Yes, sir," said the gray-haired, middle-aged woman, rising from her chair and walking around her desk. "But first, I promised Mrs. Gillette that I'd make sure you had your afternoon pill." The secretary extracted a tablet from a small plastic box, poured water from a Thermos into a paper cup, and handed both to the impatient director of the Central Intelligence Agency. "Mrs. Gillette insists you use the bottled water, sir. It's salt-free."

"Mrs. Gillette can be damned annoying, Helen," said the DCI, throwing the pill in his mouth and drinking the water.

"She wants to keep you around, sir. She also insists, as you well know, that you sit down for a minute or two until the medication is digested. Please, sit down, Mr. Director."

"You two are in cahoots, Helen, and I won't have it," said Gillette, smiling and sitting down in a straight-backed chair in front of his secretary's desk. "I hate these damn things; they make me feel like I've had three bourbons without the pleasure of drinking them."

Suddenly, without any indication of being in discomfort, Raymond Gillette lurched out of the chair, grimaced, and choked as he spread his fingers over his face and fell forward on the floor, his head angled into the front of his secretary's desk, his mouth agape, his eyes wide. He was dead.

The secretary rushed to the office door, locked it, and returned to the corpse. She pulled the body away from the desk, dragged it into the director's office, and placed it in front of the couch beneath the north window. She returned to the anteroom, closing her employer's door behind her, and slowly, breathing steadily, picked up her secure telephone. She pressed the interagency extension for the officer heading up Task Force, Communications, Little Girl Blood.

"Yes?" said the male voice on the line.

"This is Helen in the DCI's office. He asked that I call you and tell you to start testing your unit's equipment as soon as you hear from Commander Hawthorne that he's in place."

"We know that; we all agreed fifteen minutes ago."

"I imagine he didn't want you to think you had to wait for him. He'll be tied up in conferences most of the afternoon."

"No problem. It's a go as soon as we get the word."

"Thank you," said Scorpio 17, hanging up the phone.

27

I t was 4:35 in the afternoon and Andrew Jackson Poole V was impressed as he sat at the desk in the Shenandoah Lodge in front of the equipment supplied by the Central Intelligence Agency. He had received the two components he had insisted upon: a reverse noninterceptor line to Hawthorne that bypassed the CIA traffic, a single yellow X on his screen indicating invasion; and a second miniature screen whose movable blip confirmed Hawthorne's operating transponder. The personnel at Langley were outraged, believing their integrity was being challenged, but as Tye had made clear to the DCI, there could be another O'Ryan, whether Gillette wanted to consider it or not.

"You read me, Tye?" said Poole, flipping the switch on the small console to the isolated line that connected him to Hawthorne's frequency.

"Yes, I do," replied Tyrell in the car, his voice echoing over the speaker. "Are we alone?"

"Totally dedicated," replied the lieutenant. "I can read these scans like findin' honey in a biscuit. We're one on one, no intercepts."

"Anything from the hospital?"

"Nothing one way or another. All they'll say is that Cath is stable, whatever the goddamn hell *that* means."

"It's better than the alternative, Jackson."

"Man, you're one cold prick."

"I'm sorry you think that. . . . Where do the grids put me?"

"Oh, yeah, I've got you in operation and Langley

has you southeast on Route 270, approaching a local intersection that branches off into 301. The girl on the map-screen says she knows it. There's a run-down, third-rate amusement park on your left, where the Ferris wheel gets stuck, and you can't win anything at the shooting gallery because the sights are fixed."

"I just passed it. We're in good shape."

The console telephone erupted, its ring continuous. "Hold it, Tye, my emergency Langley connection's blowin' smoke. I'll get back to you."

Inside the car with the State Department plates, Hawthorne kept his eye on the road and the late afternoon traffic, but his mind was elsewhere. What could have happened at CIA headquarters that caused the emergency? Any and all emergencies should be coming from him, not from anything at Langley. He was within perhaps forty-five minutes of Chesapeake Beach and the O'Ryans' summer house; if there was going to be an emergency, it would happen there. Tyrell felt the plastic lighter in his shirt pocket that emitted electrical impulses when he was out of the car and was being called. Poole had tested it; it worked, but it was weak, perhaps too weak. Had Langley found the malfunction? That could be an emergency.

"Good Lord, it's terrible!" came Jackson's excited voice, "but nothing's changed. We go on!"

"For Christ's sake, what's terrible?"

"Director Gillette was found dead in his office. It was his heart; he had a history of cardiac problems and was on medication."

"Who says so?" demanded Hawthorne.

"His doctor, Tye," replied Poole. "He told the CIA medics that one day it was inevitable, but he didn't expect it so soon."

"You listen to me, Lieutenant, and listen hard. I want an immediate—and I mean *immediate*—independent autopsy on Gillette, concentrating on substances from the trachea to the bronchi and into the stomach. It's got to be done within a couple of hours. Have it done now!"

"What are you talkin' about . . . ?" stammered Poole. "I told you what his own doctor said."

"And I'll tell you what Gillette told me barely three hours ago! 'Coincidence is rarely, if ever, a factor.' And the death of the director of Central Intelligence, who's ultimately responsible for this operation, is just too god-damned *coincidental*! Tell them to look for evidence of digitalis!" he went on. "It's as old as scopolamine before the Amytals, and every bit as effective. You don't need a heart condition to blow a person into arrhythmia, and even with a mild dysfunction, a short dose will do it. It also disappears in the blood quickly."

"How do you know that . . . ?"

"Son of a *bitch*," Hawthorne swore, "because I just *know* it! Now, *move*, and until you have an outside analysis with a lab that will go on record that he was clean, these communications are shut down. If and when you get such a report, give me five shocks on your trans-mitter. I won't answer otherwise, and I don't care if it takes all night!"

"Tye, you don't understand. Gillette was found roughly two and a half hours ago. His body was taken to Walter Reed emergency—"

"A government-operated hospital!" exploded Haw-thorne. "We're shut down."

"That's just plain dumb," Poole broke in. "I know this equipment, and Langley knows I know it. There's no one tapping into us. I ran two invasives and both showed up. We're one on one, nobody else here."

"I've got a long litany of Washington double-crosses, Jackson. I say we *could* be."

"Okay, let's go bayou and say you're right, which is impossible, and there are other nasty people in Langley like Mr. O'Ryan, who figure to follow you and treat you poorly. We cut the *grids* off, not communications."

"I take off my belt with the transponder in the buckle and throw it out the window," said Tyrell, no question in his words.

"May I suggest, sir, that you take the next U-turn, go back to that amusement park, and leave the goldarned thing near the fun house? Or maybe that Ferris wheel?"

"Poole, you really *do* have possibilities. I'm heading back to the fun house. I can't wait till I hear about a team of deep-cover CIA agents assaulting the tunnel of love."

"Or maybe, with luck, stuck on top of that Ferris wheel."

The flagstone path led to the colonnaded entrance, the home a huge replica of a pre–Civil War plantation's great house. Bajaratt walked up the steps to the thick, carved double doors, the bas-reliefs depicting the journeys of Mohammed as he came to understand the teachings of the Koran as shown to him by the mountain prophets. *"Rubbish!"* she whispered to herself. There were no exalted mountains, no Mohammed, and the prophets were ignorant goatherds! There was no Christ either. He was a radical Jew troublemaker manufactured by the semiliterate Essenes, who hadn't the ability to cultivate their land. There was no God but the voice within the aroused individual, the inner commands that made a man or woman do what he or she had to do to fight for justice—for all who were oppressed. What else *was* there? The Baj spat on the flagstone porch, then composed herself, raised a ladylike hand, and pressed the bell.

Moments later the door was opened by a caftanned Arab, his robes gliding over the parquet floor. "You are expected, madame, and you are late."

"If I were later still, would you have denied me entrance?"

"It is possible—"

"Then I shall leave—now," said Bajaratt. "How dare you?"

A female voice came from within. "Please permit the lady to come inside, Ahmet Ashad, and do put away your weapon, it's most discourteous."

"It is not in evidence, madame," the servant called out.

"That is even more discourteous. Show our visitor in."

The room was a perfectly normal suburban living room in terms of its windows, curtains, and wallpaper, but that was where the ordinariness ended. There were no chairs, only enormous cushions placed around the floor with miniature tables in front of each. And reclining on one such hill of scarlet satin was a dark-skinned woman of extraordinary beauty and indeterminate age, her face a supple mask of classic features, yet warm, somehow not rigid or masklike at all. When she smiled, her eyes lit up like opals, communicating interest and genuine curiosity.

"Sit down, Amaya Aquirre," she said in a soft, mellifluous voice that belonged to the emerald-green silk pantsuit she wore. "You see, I know your name and something more than that about you. As you can also see, I subscribe to the Arabic custom that we be on the same level—for us, the floor, as it is with the Bedouin sand—so that no individual has a symbolic position over the other. I find it one of the more attractive Arab concessions; we treat even our inferiors with equal eye contact."

"Are you saying that I'm inferior?"

"No, not at all, but you are not an Arab."

"I have fought for your cause—my husband died for your cause!"

"In a foolish expedition that served neither the Jew nor the Arab."

"The Baaka permitted it, gave us its blessing!"

"The Baaka conceded because your husband was a

firebrand, a hero of the people, and his death—which was a foregone conclusion—would make him a symbol, a battle cry. *Remember Ashkelon!* I think you've heard the phrase. It was all nonsense, except for the emotional appeal."

"What are you saying to me? My life, my husband, we are *nothing*?" The Baj sprang off the cushion as the robed Ahmet appeared in the doorway. "I'm willing to die for the greatest cause in history! Death to the pigs of authority!"

"That's what we must talk about, Amaya. . . . Leave us, Ahmet, she has no weapon. . . . Your willingness to die is not terribly important, my dear. There are men and women all over the world willing to die for what they believe in, and the vast majority are never heard of, either before or after the act. . . . No, I want more than that for you, for us."

"What *do* you want from me?" asked Bajaratt, slowly lowering herself to the cushion, her eyes locked with the beautiful, aging, yet ageless woman across the room.

"You've come this far brilliantly, with certain assistance, of course, but basically because of your own extraordinary talents. In a matter of mere days you've become an influential force, a behind-the-scenes power whom powerful men seek out for what they believe you can deliver. None of us could have done that for you; it had to spring from the idea, the concept you created, and it was absolutely brilliant. The young man, a baron in training, no less, and a family in Ravello with millions to invest. Even the child actress—such an appealing sideshow, so genuinely touching. You deserve 'the Baj's' reputation."

"I do what I do, and let others judge. Their judgments, frankly, are insignificant to me. I ask again, what do you want from me? I was told by the Baaka Councils to reach you prior to my last days here—quite possibly my last days alive. Either way, they are approaching."

"You understand that we—I—have no authority over you. That is reserved for the High Councils alone."

"I understand that. However, I am to render you the respect due a true friend, an ally of our cause, and listen to your words. . . . I'm listening."

"Friend, yes, Amaya, but an ally only up to a point, my dear. We are no part of Van Nostrand's Scorpions, that group of underground opportunists whose only aim is to profitably serve the Providers, whose only cause is wealth and power. I— we—have enough of both over here."

"Who are you, then? You know a great deal."

"It's our job to know."

"But who are you?"

"The Germans had an applicable term during the Second World War. *Der Nachrichtendienst.* An elite intelligence unit that even the Third Reich's High Command knew little or nothing about. It was comprised of fewer than a dozen elderly members, Prussians mainly, aristocrats all, who collectively brought nearly eight hundred years of expertise and influence to the table. They were German to the core, but they operated above the fray, above the passions of war, seeking only what was best for the Fatherland, realizing the disadvantages of their nation being led by Adolf Hitler and his thugs. . . . As we recognize the disadvantages we face with terrorists murdering women and children in Israel. It's simply counterproductive."

"I think this conversation has gone far enough!" said the Baj, rising to her feet. "Have you and your elitists considered the displacement of an entire people? Have you been to the refugee camps? Have you watched the Israeli bulldozers plow down your own homes on mere suspicions? Have you forgotten the bloodbaths of Shatila and Sabra?"

"We're told your appointment with the President is tomorrow night, approximately eight o'clock," said the woman quietly, resting farther back on the satin pillows.

"It *is* tomorrow, then? Eight o'clock?"

"It was originally scheduled for three o'clock in the afternoon, but considering the nature of the '*contessa*'s' American visit, which is to further foreign investment—a delicate subject these days for a proud country—it was suggested to the White House that perhaps a later hour, an evening hour, might be more appropriate. There'd be less chance of the press learning that the President was giving preferential treatment to an ambitious foreign aristocrat taking advantage of the economy here."

"Their reaction . . . ?" asked a bewildered Bajaratt.

"The Chief of Staff instantly and enthusiastically approved. He hates accommodating senators and congressmen, but the President equally loathes offending anyone politically. Also, you'll have a far better chance to escape—escape and fight again—if you strike at eight o'clock. The White House guard details change then, which means there's a degree of relaxation at their posts as up-to-the-minute records and instructions are given to the relief contingents. You will be aided by three men, one in a chauffeur's uniform, who will guide you, under the pretense of protecting you from the press, through backstairs corridors that lead to another limousine. Ours. They will use a name to identify themselves. *Ashkelon.* I trust you approve."

"I don't understand," said Bajaratt. "Why would you do this? You just led me to believe that you disapproved—"

"Of your *other* intentions," the Arab woman interrupted sharply. "However, for your life, we have something to ask of you, demand of you if you wish. You see, we have no objective disagreement, geopolitically or specifically, with the assassination of the American President; he's ruled by polls, not principle, and therefore expendable. The people sense it; he arouses no passion. Oh, there'll be outrage and endless investigations, but it will all dwindle. The Vice President is extremely popular. And although we think it's melodramatic, we can even accept the killings in England and France if you insist. They are sophisticated governments—European governments—who don't make idols of their political leaders. Instead, they face harsh realities and negotiate. Frankly, with the chaos of an American power vacuum, we can further escalate our influence here, but more to the point, a message will be sent to this President's successors and their Cabinets. We may not have the Jewish vote or its money, but we have something else, something worthy of the celebrated Mossad. We are not a myth or a fantasy of the lunatic fringe. We are real. As you said only minutes ago, we have men and women who will die to cut off the head of a snake. That's visceral, my child, and as you have proved with your brilliant strategy, they'll never know where we're coming from or when, and in the back corridors of power they'll think twice before constantly kissing the Israeli boot. Then in a word, America, too, will become sophisticated."

"What do you ask of me, demand of me, for my life, which is of no great consequence?"

"Don't kill the Jew. Call off your people in Jerusalem and Tel Aviv."

"How can you *say* that? It's our final statement, the vengeance of Ashkelon!"

"And the death of thousands upon thousands of our people, Amaya. Israel acts unilaterally, personally if you like. She really doesn't care what happens beyond her borders, unless it threatens her; and if any other small country had gone through the German Holocaust, that country wouldn't either. I told you, we are coldly objective. You assassinate a Jewish leader, sorties of Jewish planes day and night will fly over and bomb our camps and settlements for weeks on end until they're utterly destroyed, reduced to rubble and burning flesh. Consider recent history—the Jews released twelve *hundred* prisoners for *six* Israeli soldiers, and later exiled more than four hundred Palestinians over the death of one soldier. Their leader is the equivalent of ten thousand Jewish soldiers, for he is more than a man, he is the living symbol of their nation."

"You ask a terrible price of me," said Bajaratt barely above a whisper. "One I'm not prepared to pay. I've waited all my life for this moment, this one magnificent moment that will justify so much of my having lived at all."

"My child—" the woman began.

"*No!* I am not your child or anyone's child," said Bajaratt, her voice distant, frozen. "I was never a child. *Muerte a toda autoridad.*"

"I don't understand you—"

"It is not your business to understand me. As you yourself said, you have no authority over me."

"Certainly not, I agree. I'm only trying to reason with you, protect you."

"*Reason?*" whispered the Baj. "Where has reason gotten your people, or *my* people? Yours are at least in camps, no matter how filthy, but mine are hunted like animals in the mountains, executed, slaughtered on sight—*beheaded. Muerte a toda autoridad!* Everywhere they must *die.*"

"Please, my dear," said the ageless dark-skinned woman, her expression conveying her alarm at the sight of the mesmerizing figure in front of her. "*Please,* I am not your enemy, Amaya."

"I see it now," Bajaratt said. "You're trying to stop me, aren't you? You have an armed servant who can easily kill me."

"And have the wrath of the Baaka descend on all our necks? You are their adopted, most-favored daughter, wife of the dead hero of Ashkelon, a woman so revered, the Councils seek your advice and forever give you their blessings. For all I know, the Baaka had you followed to this house."

"Never! I act on my own, never to be interfered with!"

"I'm sure that's your understanding, but I have no such assurance, therefore no harm would ever come to you here. Please, you're overwrought, and I say again, I'm not your enemy, I'm your friend."

"Yet you're saying you want me to eliminate the Jerusalem agenda, how *can* you?"

"For the reasons I just gave you—among them the slaughter of perhaps a million Palestinians. There would be no Palestinian cause, then, for the heart of a people would be ripped out."

"They've taken our lands, our children, our future, why not our hearts?"

"Words, Amaya, foolish declarations—"

"They will never take our souls!"

"Even more foolish words. Souls can't fight without bodies. One must survive to fight, you of all women must know that. You are the supreme strategist."

"And you? Who are you, living in all this, to lecture me?" Bajaratt's hand swept the opulent room.

"Ah, this," the ageless beauty said, laughing softly. "The image of wealth and self-indulgence, a combination that denotes power and influence, for one follows the other in this materialistic world. We all show off. It's always the images that are important, isn't it? I don't have to tell you that, you are an *imagiste extraordinaire*. . . . We're not so different, Amaya Aquirre. You create diversions from the outside, aimed at penetrating the exterior; I, on the other hand, bore my way into the interior, and when the time is right, blow apart the shell with the ammunition at hand. . . . *You* are that ammunition, that nitroglycerin, my child—and don't tell me you are *not* my child in this cause, this holy cause—because you are now my daughter."

"I am no one's daughter any longer! I sprang from death, watching death!"

"You are *mine*. Whatever you watched, whatever you

observed, is nothing compared to what I went through. You spoke of Shatila and Sabra, but you weren't there. I was! You think you want vengeance, my non-Arab child? I want it far more than you can ever imagine."

"Then how can you stop me from killing the Jew?"

"Because you will unleash a thousand air strikes against my people—*my* people, not yours."

"I am one with you, and you know it! I've proved it. I gave you my husband and I'm willing to give you my life."

"It's not terribly difficult to give away something one despises, Amaya."

"And if I refuse your request, your misplaced demand?"

"Then you will not reach the White House, much less the Oval Office."

"*Ridiculous!* My access to the White House is guaranteed! The man who accommodates me is committed to the Ravello millions, and he's not a fool."

"And this man, this Senator Nesbitt from the state of Michigan who accommodates you, what do you know about him?"

"You know who he is, then?"

The woman shrugged. "The appointment was changed, Amaya."

"Yes, of course. . . . He appears to be the usual American politician, and I've done considerable research. He must be reelected in a state that has widespread unemployment, therefore he has to convince the voters that he deserves his office. What better way than to bring hundreds of millions into a depressed workplace?"

"Yes, you've done your research, my dear. But what of the man himself? Would you say he's a good man, an honest man?"

"I have no idea, nor do I care. I was told he was a lawyer or a judge, if it means anything."

"Not much, there are judges and then there are judges. . . . Had you ever considered that he might be a

Scorpio? That he might be accommodating you because he was ordered to do so?"

"No, that never occurred to me—"

"We know there is a Scorpio in the Senate."

"He would have revealed himself," said Bajaratt defensively. "Why not? Van Nostrand did; he gave me the telephone codes to reach the Scorpios."

"Untraceable satellite transmissions. We know all about them."

"I find that hard to believe—"

"It took us nearly three years, but we finally found and bought our own Scorpion. As a matter of fact, you met her in Florida. Your hostess in Palm Beach. It is a very pleasant estate, is it not? Sylvia and her husband could not possibly afford it without enormous assistance. The husband's one unique talent was going through an inheritance of over seventy million dollars in less than thirty years. She's the Social Register Scorpio, unearthed by Van Nostrand. Very useful. Quite simply, we traced her through Van Nostrand, offered more than the Providers, and enlisted an ally."

"She introduced me to Nesbitt—they're *both* Scorpions!"

"She is, yes, the senator, absolutely not. It was my idea to fly him down to Palm Beach for what he believes are perfectly legitimate political reasons. He hasn't the slightest idea who you really are or why you're here. He knows only the Countess Cabrini with an immensely wealthy brother in Ravello."

"Then you confirm my judgment. You cannot stop me unless you kill me, and you yourself have accurately described the consequences from the Baaka. I think this conference is at an end. I've fulfilled my obligation to the Councils, for I've listened to you!"

"Listen a bit further, Amaya. It will do you no harm and might be instructive." The Arab woman got to her feet slowly, with the grace of a cat, startling Bajaratt with her size. She was short, barely five feet tall, an elegant doll-like figure contrarily projecting immense authority. "We knew you were working with the Scorpions—our Palm Beach ally was apprised of it through Fort Lauderdale immigration—and since we learned of your imminent appearance at the White House, I had to make certain you came here first."

"You knew I would," interrupted the Baj. "Our meeting was scheduled weeks ago in the Baaka, the pertinent information coded in Arabic. Address, day, date, and hour."

"I had every confidence in you, but then I didn't *know* you; surely you can understand my apprehension. If you had not arrived tonight, a Madame Balzini would have been picked up at the Carillon hotel in the early hours of the morning."

"Balzini . . . the Carillon? You *knew* all that?"

"Certainly not through the Scorpios," the woman replied as she walked across the room to a gold-plated intercom in the wall, "for they didn't know either," she continued, turning back to Bajaratt. "Our friend in Palm Beach called and said even she was having trouble reaching her superiors through the Scorpio telephone codes. In point of fact, she stopped trying for fear of exposure."

"There have been several problems," the Baj offered without further comment.

"Apparently. . . . However, we had no need of the Scorpions, as you will see." The sleek, diminutive woman reached up without looking and pressed a silver button on the intercom. "Now, Ahmet," she said, her eyes still on Bajaratt. "What you are about to observe, dear Amaya, is a man with two distinctly different personalities, even identities, if you like. The one you already know is as real as the one you are about to observe. The first is a dedicated public servant, an honest man, a good man. The other is someone who has endured the pain of an unfortunate life, no matter his trappings of power. . . . Unfortunate is inadequate; unbearable is far more appropriate."

Stunned, Bajaratt watched as a man she barely recognized walked down the wide staircase, flanked by the robed servant Ahmet and a striking blond-haired woman dressed in a sheer negligee that revealed the flesh beneath, clearly emphasizing the swell of her breasts and the sinuous movement of her hips. The man was Nesbitt! Each held the senator from Michigan, steadying him down the steps. His face was pale, nearly death-white, his eyes two ceramic balls devoid of movement, his expression frozen as if in a trance. He wore a bathrobe of blue velveteen; his feet were bare, the veins apparent.

"He's had his injection," said the Baj's hostess softly. "He won't recognize you."

"He's drugged?"

"Medically prescribed by an excellent physician. He's a dual."

"Dual?"

"Dual personality, Amaya. A Jekyll and Hyde without the evil, only with unfulfilled hungers. . . . Shortly after his marriage more than forty years ago, a tragic event took place, an assault that left his wife physically and psychologically impaired, in a word, permanently frigid. The act of intercourse was repugnant to her, the mere thought of it sending her into hysterics, and for good reason. She had been raped by a psychopath, a burglar who broke into their apartment, bound the young lawyer, and forced him to watch the rape. From that night on, his wife could not fulfill her marital obligations. Yet he was a devoted husband, and far worse, a religious man; he sought no release from his perfectly natural sexuality. Finally, after she died three years ago, the burden destroyed him, or, I should say, destroyed a part of him."

"How did you find him?"

"There are a hundred senators, and we knew that one of them was a Scorpio. We studied them all, starting alphabetically—every shred of their lives. . . . Alas, we never found the Scorpion, but we discovered an obviously deeply disturbed man whose frequent and mysterious absences were covered up by the only close friend he had, his housekeeper of twenty-eight years, a woman in her seventies.''

Nesbitt and his two guardians reached the bottom of the staircase and walked past the door to the living room. "He sees nothing!" whispered the Baj.

"No, he doesn't," Bajaratt's hostess agreed. "In an hour or so he will, although he will not remember the specific events of tonight. He will only realize that he's been satisfied, that inner recognition that produces peace."

"He does this often?"

"Once or twice a month, and usually in the late evenings. At first it started with his humming a strange melody from long ago in his past. Then, like a sleepwalker, he would change his clothes, an entirely different wardrobe he kept in his deceased wife's closet. They were hardly the clothes of a powerful senator, instead the trappings of a well-to-do roué out slumming for the night. A suede or leather jacket, frequently a wig or a beret, always dark glasses, but never any identification. Those were terrible days for the housekeeper. When it happens now, she calls us and we pick him up."

"She cooperates with you?"

"She has no choice. She is well paid, as is his driver-bodyguard."

"And so you control him."

"We're very special friends. We're there when he needs us, and there are times such as now when we need him, need the power of his office."

"I can see that," said Bajaratt icily.

"Of course, the optimum would be to learn who in the Senate is the highest-placed Scorpio, for as the Providers control *him*, so can we. However, it's only a matter of time before a pattern is established, no matter how subtle. Your own actions will help us, as every member of that body will be studied anew, and in their reactions to the chaos will be found the weakness that attracted Van Nostrand."

"Is it so important to you?"

"Make no mistake, dear Amaya, it's of vital importance. I repeat what I said before, we have great sympathy as well as close ties to the Baaka, but these do not extend to the mercenary Scorpions. They are the creation of Van Nostrand and his mad companion in the Caribbean, recruited by blackmail and kept on their tethers with money—money that pales into insignificance compared to the money they make for the Providers, who, in reality, have always been the *padrone* and Van Nostrand, no one else. The Scorpios have no cause but fear of exposure and, of course, the money they receive. Such people have no calling beyond themselves, beyond their petty little lives, driven by greed and anxiety. They must be destroyed, or rendered impotent . . . or recruited by us."

"I remind you," interrupted the Baj. "The Scorpios have served me well, and by doing so have served the Baaka through me."

"Ordered to do so by the all-powerful Van Nostrand. He can cut off their funds with a telephone call, to say nothing of revealing their crimes—past and present—to the authorities. Do you think they give a damn about us, about the things we hold so dear? If you do, you're not the woman I was led to believe you are."

"Van Nostrand has retired. He's somewhere in Europe, or he is dead. He's no longer Scorpio One."

". . . Palm Beach's trouble with the telephone codes," said the diminutive, catlike Arab, barely audible. "That's astonishing news—are you sure?"

"Whether he's alive or dead, I can't be certain. Another survived, a former intelligence officer named Hawthorne, who I thought had been taken into custody; he hadn't. But Nils Van Nostrand is gone; he told me himself he was going to disappear."

"Not only astonishing, but extremely disturbing. As

long as Van Nostrand was in place, we could monitor him; we had people at his estate, at the gate, informers loyal to us. . . . Who are you dealing with now? You must tell me!"

"I don't know—"

"The White House, Amaya!"

"I'm not lying to you. You say you have the codes, dial them yourself. Whoever answers certainly will not volunteer his identity."

"You're right, of course—"

"I *can* tell you that the Scorpio I last spoke with is a man so privileged as to be given the most secret information. He had details about the government's progress in its search for me; they were accurate details. He called it the inner circle."

"The inner circle . . . ?" The Palestinian beauty frowned, producing few lines on her dark, classic features. "The inner circle," she repeated as she walked across the immense room in thought, her small, lacquer-tipped fingers brought to her dainty chin. "If it's the senator we're looking for, there's only one committee that's accorded such classified information. Senate Intelligence. Of course, it's so natural, so brilliantly simple! Since the scandals of Watergate and Iran-contra, every agency in Washington makes sure it reports the details of its covert operations to Senate Intelligence. They can't afford not to; none cares to be left facing accusations of illegality in front of the entire Congress. . . . You see, dear Amaya, already you've been of *immense* help."

"Further, he is a man who kills, at least that's what he told me. He said he killed a man named Stevens, the head of naval intelligence, because this Stevens had come close to finding me. For that I owe him."

"You owe him nothing! He was following orders, that's all he was doing. . . . Whether he told you the truth, or lied to you so you would be beholden to him, is immaterial. There's only one man in the Senate who would speak in such crude, bravado terms, and we've studied them all. . . . Seebank, the intolerable, ill-tempered General Seebank. Thank you, Baj."

"If it is he, I should also tell you I gave him a test of his commitment to me. As you may know, in certain military situations where it's imperative to eliminate an obstacle, even a command post, a man is chosen to walk into a compound, knowing he will not walk out. It is in his footwear."

"The Allah Boot," the Palestinian said. "Explosives packed into the sole and the heel, set off by kicking the toe into a solid object. Death to the wearer and everyone in the vicinity."

"Yes, I even provided him with a blueprint." The Baj nodded slowly. "If he sends back the authentic article, I will know I can trust him. If not, I will break off all communication. Should he be true, I shall use him . . . and you will have your Scorpio."

"Is there no end to your skills, Amaya?"

"*Muerte a toda autoridad,* that's all you have to know."

28

S enator Paul Seebank walked down the country road on the outskirts of Rockville, Maryland, the afternoon dark, the sky heavy with clouds. He carried a flashlight which he continuously, nervously snapped on and off. His brush-cut gray hair was covered by a walking cap, his chiseled features concealed by the upturned lapels of a lightweight summer raincoat. In truth, the lean, tough, former Brigadier General Seebank, now the lean, tough, outspoken Senator Seebank, was in panic, close to losing his equilibrium. He could not stop the trembling in his hands, or halt the progressively obvious tic that drew down his lower right lip in short, abrupt spasms.

He had to keep his thoughts focused; he could not lose control. Yet he could not contain his dread at becoming Scorpio One.

The madness had started eight years before on this very road—where it led to a dilapidated shell of a long-deserted barn in the long-abandoned fields of a long-forgotten farm, now merely the unused, infertile acres of some estate, more interested in gardens than in crops.

It had been initiated by a frighteningly obtuse telephone call on his private office line, the sacrosanct line of a newly elected senator that rang only at his desk, a standard privilege for family and very close friends. However, the caller had not been a member of his family or a friend at all; he was a stranger who introduced himself as Neptune.

"We watched your campaign for the Senate with great interest, General."

"Who the hell are you and how did you get this number?"

"That's irrelevant, our business is not. I suggest we meet as soon as possible, for my superiors are most anxious that we make contact."

"And I suggest you pound sand!"

"Then I must further suggest that you examine the basis, the essence, of your campaign for your office. The heroic prisoner of war in Vietnam who kept his men together under intolerable conditions through sheer leadership and his own personal courage. We have friends in Hanoi, Senator. Need I say more?"

"What the *hell* . . . ?"

"There's an old barn on a road outside the town of Rockville—"

Goddamn it! What did they know?

Seebank had gone to that barn on that road eight years earlier, as he was going to it now because of another phone call from another stranger. But eight years ago, under the glow of an old lantern, in the presence of the shadowed, elegant Neptune, he had read the affidavits of the commandants of the five prison camps in which he and his men had been interned.

"*Colonel Seebank was most cooperative and frequently dined with us . . .*"

"*The colonel would describe for us the escape procedures his other officers created . . .*"

"*A number of times we pretended to subject him to physical abuse while he screamed in earshot of his comrades . . .*"

"*We used a mild acid to discolor his flesh—usually while he was quite happily drunk—and sent him back later to his quarters in torn clothing . . .*"

"*He was cooperative, but we did not admire him . . .*"

Everything was there. Brigadier General Paul Seebank was no hero. He was something else.

And he was valuable to the Providers, so valuable, he was given an elite position: Scorpio Four. All future elections were guaranteed, for no opponent could ever match his political war chest. He had won his second term by burying the contender in an avalanche of money. The senator, a military expert, had merely to steer defense contracts to the coffers of those selected by the Providers.

The old barn was in sight, a ramshackle silhouette against the gray sky, on the rise of a hill of wild grass. Seebank left the road and climbed toward the rendezvous, the beam of his flashlight now steady. Six minutes later he reached the broken-down doors, half doors, slats really, and called out, "I'm here. Where are you?"

His answer was the brief illumination of a second flashlight. "Come inside," said the voice in the darkness. "It's a pleasure to meet my superior officer—in a different army, of course. . . . Turn off your light."

Seebank did so. "Did we serve together? Do I know you?"

"We've never met personally. You might, however, remember a unit number and a rank, even a barracks location—the 'south compound.' "

"A prisoner, you were a prisoner! We were prisoners together!"

"It was a long time ago, Senator," interrupted the unseen figure. "Or do you prefer General?"

"I prefer to know why you called me and why you chose this place."

"Isn't this where you were recruited? This very barn? *I* was. I merely thought it would convey how very urgent the emergency is."

"Recruited . . . ? You? Then you are—"

"Of course I am. Why else would you be here? Let me introduce myself, General. I am Scorpio Five, the last of the elite Scorpions, the remaining twenty every bit as vital but without our authority."

"I can't say I'm not relieved." Seebank's hands were

still trembling, the tic in his lower lip now constant. "Of course, this location had an immediate impact on me. Frankly, I thought I'd be meeting with one of our . . . our—"

"Say it, Senator, one of our Providers, right?"

"Yes . . . a Provider."

"In light of the extraordinary events of the past two days, I'm surprised that you haven't—also somewhat relieved."

"What do you mean?"

"Well, according to the telephone codes, Scorpio Four is now, for all intents and purposes, Scorpio One, isn't that so?"

"Yes, yes, I suppose it is." Seebank's tic accelerated. "Do you know why?"

"No, not actually." The senator clasped his hands around the extinguished flashlight to control the trembling.

"No, you probably wouldn't. You don't have access to the information. Fortunately, I do, and I've acted upon it."

"You're talking in circles, soldier. I don't like that!"

"What you *like* doesn't matter. Scorpios Two and Three were taken out. They chickened; they couldn't live with the current scenario, so Little Girl Blood had them eliminated, and that's good enough for me."

"I don't understand. Who the hell is Little Girl Blood?"

"I wondered if you knew; you don't. You work for the Providers in a different area, very profitable but very different, and this isn't your thing. Considering what you are—what we *know* you are—you couldn't hack it. It's called no guts. You're a fraud, Scorpio Four, and I was told years ago to watch you. . . . Now you're a liability."

"How dare you!" roared the panicked Seebank. "You are my subordinate!"

"Sorry, I couldn't wait for that to change—couldn't

wait for the electronics to untangle the signals and replace you. If you could call your wife right now, she'd tell you that a telephone serviceman came to your house at eight-ten this morning, twelve minutes after you left for your Senate office. He did his work on the phone in your den. . . . You see, we're too close, General, too close to putting this country back where it belongs. We've been stripped bare, our military budgets cut disastrously across the board, our personnel decimated, our armed might reduced to chickenshit. There are twenty thousand nuclear warheads all over Europe and Asia pointed at us and we pretend they don't exist! . . . Well, that'll change when Little Girl Blood carries out her operation. We'll be in charge again, the nation ours to govern the way it should be governed! The country will be paralyzed, and, naturally, as always, it will turn to us for guidance and protection."

"I'm not against you, soldier," the trembling senator managed to say. "Those could be my very words; surely you must know that."

"Hell, General, I certainly do, but they're only words. You're all words, no action. Your cowardice is a deficiency we can't afford. You couldn't hack it."

"Hack *what*?"

"The killing of the President. How does that grab you?"

"My God, you're *insane*!" whispered Paul Seebank, his hands suddenly steady, his tic diminished in sheer terror. "I can't believe what you're *saying*. Who are you?"

"Yes, I guess it's time." From behind the brick wall a one-armed figure, his right sleeve folded into his shoulder, emerged. "Do you recognize me, General?"

Seebank stared, uncomprehending, at a face he knew all too well. "*You* . . . ?"

"Does the absence of my arm bring back any memories? Certainly, you were told about it."

"No! . . . No memories! I don't know what you're talking about."

"Sure you do, General, although you never saw my face back then—I was simply Captain X, as far as you were concerned—a very particular Captain X."

"No . . . no! You're fantasizing—I never knew you!"

"As I said, not personally, no, you didn't. Have you any idea how amused I was sitting at a table in front of your interminable Senate hearings, listening to your so-called military expertise, which was pure bullshit, fed to you by our mutual benefactors through Scorpio One? The army graciously provided me with a prosthesis, a false right arm that filled the uniform, for the Pentagon recognized that my talents did not require an arm, only a brain and a certain minor eloquence which is allowed the military."

"I swear to Christ, I know you only as you *are*, nothing before!"

"Then let me prod your temporary amnesia. Do you remember the south compound? Do you remember hearing that an obscure captain had engineered a foolproof escape? An escape that would have worked. . . . But it didn't—because an American officer had tipped off the compound's prisoner council. The gooks came into our hut, held out my right arm, and cut it off with one of their fucking swords. And in near perfect English the camp translator said, 'Now you try escape.' "

"I had nothing to do with that—with you!"

"Move off it, General, I have you dead to rights. When I was recruited, Neptune showed me the depositions from Hanoi, including a paragraph you never saw. He was the one who told me to watch you. How to alter your telephone if it was ever necessary."

"That's all in the past! It doesn't *matter* anymore!"

"Would you believe it does to me? I've waited twenty-five years to pay you back."

Two shots were fired as a drizzle caressed the old

dilapidated barn in a barren field in Rockville, Maryland.

And the chairman of the Joint Chiefs of Staff walked through the high grass toward his concealed civilian Buick. If everything remained on schedule, Little Girl Blood was one step nearer Ground Zero.

A perplexed, frustrated Hawthorne drove the State Department vehicle toward McLean, Virginia, trying to understand the enigma of the family O'Ryan. They were either the dumbest, most gullible bunch of human beings he had ever encountered, or they were taught so well by O'Ryan they could all pass a polygraph claiming they weren't even on the premises while robbing a bank!

He had arrived at the beach house shortly past 5:30, and by 7:00 o'clock Hawthorne had begun to think that Patrick Timothy O'Ryan was the most close-mouthed Irishman in the history of that Gaelic race. From O'Ryan's Agency file, delivered to him an hour before he had left the Shenandoah Lodge, Tyrell's antennae had been assaulted by a gaping omission in the analyst's background check. The family's sudden reversal of fortune, from a modest house on a median CIA salary to a much larger residence, as well as a substantial summer home on the beach, was just too pat to be explained by an inheritance from a horse-breeding uncle in Ireland. The Agency had settled for the legal paperwork; they hadn't gone any deeper. In Hawthorne's judgment, they should have, much deeper. For starters, O'Ryan had older brothers in the New York City police department. Where were they and why had they been bypassed by a wealthy relative who, according to Mrs. O'Ryan, had never met any of the boys?

"Uncle Finead was a *saint*!" Maria Santoni O'Ryan had shouted through her tears. "The Lord God told him my Paddy was the most beloved of Jesus Christ! In my hour of sorrow and torment, you've got to come here with such questions?"

Not good enough, Mrs. O'Ryan, Tyrell thought. *But then, you don't have any answers.* Neither had the three sons and two daughters in varying degrees of innocent anger. Something was rotten, the smell overpowering, but Hawthorne could not locate the source of the odor.

It was close to nine-thirty when he swung into the McLean, Virginia, private road that led to the large colonial house belonging to the Ingersols. The long double-lined circular drive was filled with dark limousines and expensive cars—Jaguars, Mercedes, and a smattering of Cadillacs and Lincolns; a separate lawn to the left of the house was also a parking area, served by attendants who parked the visiting mourners' automobiles.

He was greeted at the door by David Ingersol's son, a pleasant young man, sincere, courteous, and with a pool of sadness in his eyes, Tyrell thought as he showed him his credentials.

"I think I'd better get my father's partner," said the dead man's son. "I wouldn't be of any help to you— whatever you're here for."

Edward White, of Ingersol and White, was a compact, medium-size man with a balding head and piercing brown eyes. "I'll take care of this!" he said curtly after studying Hawthorne's identification. "Stay by the door, Todd. This gentleman and I will go into the corridor." Once in a narrow hallway, White continued. "To say that I'm appalled at your appearance here tonight would be an understatement. A State Department investigation, when the poor soul hasn't even been . . . finished at the funeral home? How can you?"

"Very easily and very quickly, Mr. White," replied Tyrell. "Immediacy is vital to us."

"For God's sake, why?"

"Because David Ingersol may have been the prime mover in a massive money-laundering operation involving both the old Medellín and the new Cali drug cartels. Both were brokered out of Puerto Rico."

"That's utterly preposterous! We have clients in Puerto Rico, David's clients mainly, but there's never been a scintilla of wrongdoing. I was his partner, I ought to know."

"Perhaps you know less than you think. Suppose I were to tell you that through State Department intercession we've learned that David Ingersol has accounts in Zurich and Bern in excess of eight figures, American. Those sums didn't come from your law firm. You're rich, but not that rich."

"You're either a liar or a paranoiac. . . . Let's go into David's study; this is nowhere to talk. Come this way." The two men bypassed the crowd inside the large living room and walked down another hallway, where Edward White opened a door. Inside was a book-lined study; it was wood-paneled with dark brown leather everywhere—chairs, tables, two couches, even the tall back of a turned-around desk chair behind the huge surface that held David Ingersol's papers. "I don't believe you for an instant," White said as he closed the door.

"This isn't an arrest, Counselor, merely one arm of an investigation. If you doubt me, call the State Department. I'm sure you know the right people to reach."

"You callous son of a bitch! Think of David's family!"

"I'm thinking of several foreign accounts that could have been designed by the BCCI and an American citizen who used his considerable influence to keep the drug mobs in business."

"Are you all things to this highly suspect investigation, Mr. Hawthorne? Police, judge, and jury? Have you ever considered how simple it is to establish 'foreign accounts' in any name you like simply by writing out a scan-proof signature?"

"No, I don't, but you apparently do."

"Yes, I do, because I've made a minor study of them,

and any client of our firm has to have a damn good reason for possessing one, especially if we're paid from such an account."

"That's a world I don't know anything about," lied Tyrell, "but if what you say is true, all we have to do is fax David Ingersol's signature to Zurich and Bern."

"Machine facsimiles are not acceptable to spectrograph scans. I'm surprised you don't know that."

"You're the expert, not me. But I'll tell you what I am an expert in—I'm a terrific observer. I watch you limousine cowboys drive around this city, bathed in respectability, while you peddle your influence to the highest bidders. And when you cross over the line, I'm there to nail you."

"That's hardly State Department language; you sound like a paranoid comic-book avenger, and you're way out of line. I think I will make that phone call you suggested—"

"Don't bother, Edward." A third voice in the room startled both men. Suddenly, the high-backed leather chair behind the desk swiveled around, revealing an old man, slender, obviously quite tall, and dressed so perfectly, so fashionably that Tyrell gasped, believing for a moment in the dim light that he was staring at Nils Van Nostrand.

"My name is Richard Ingersol, Mr. Hawthorne, formerly associate justice of the Supreme Court. I believe we should talk—by ourselves, Edward, but not in this room. Not in any room in this house."

"I don't understand, sir," said the astonished partner of Ingersol and White.

"There's no way you could, dear fellow. Please keep my daughter-in-law and grandson occupied with all those . . . limousine sycophants. Mr. Hawthorne and I will slip outside through the kitchen."

"But Justice Ingersol—"

"My son is dead, Edward, and I don't think he cares what the society pages of *The Washington Post* write about his well-heeled mourners, a number of whom in the legal fraternity have undoubtedly sought out his personal clients." The old man struggled out of the chair and walked around the desk. "Come along, Hawthorne, there's no one here who can tell you anything. Besides, it's a lovely night for a stroll."

A frustrated White held the door as Tyrell followed the elder Ingersol down the hallway, through the hectic kitchen, and out into the fenced back lawn complete with a lighted swimming pool and what appeared to be an immense garden fronting a row of twenty-foot-high hedges. The former associate justice stepped onto the brick deck of the pool and spoke.

"Why are you really here, Mr. Hawthorne, and what do you know?"

"You heard what I told your son's partner."

"Money laundering? Drug cartels? . . . Come, sir, David had neither the inclination nor the audacity even to consider such activities. However, your reference to Swiss accounts is not without merit."

"Then maybe I should ask you what you know, Justice Ingersol."

"It's a macabre story with elements of triumph and anguish and a fair degree of tragedy—Athenian to the core but without the majesty of Greek drama."

"That's very eloquent, but it doesn't tell me anything."

"You looked at me strangely inside," said Ingersol, disregarding Tyrell's remark. "It wasn't merely the surprise of finding me there; it was something else, wasn't it?"

"You reminded me of someone."

"I thought so. Your crude appearance here smacked of a shock strategy—throw the subjects off balance, perhaps into panic. Your reaction to *me* confirmed it."

"I don't know what you're talking about."

"Certainly you do. Nils Van Nostrand—Mr. Neptune, if you prefer. . . . The similarity of our appearance struck you instantly; it was in your expression, although I assure you the similarity is surface only. Given certain characteristics—height, figure, and coloring—men of our advanced age and station tend to look alike. In our case it's basically sartorial. You know Van Nostrand, and the last place on earth you expected to find him was in this house. That told me a great deal."

"Considering what it told you, I'm surprised you admit you know Neptune."

"Oh, that's part of the story," continued Ingersol, entering a latticed arch to a garden profuse with flowers, an isolated arbor away from the house and the crowds. "Once all the pieces were in place, Nils came to the Costa del Sol a number of times. I didn't know who he was, of course, but we became friendly. He seemed like so many of us—elderly drifters with enough money to jet from place to place in search of shallow amusement. I even sent him to my personal tailor in London."

"When did you learn he was Neptune?"

"Five years ago. I'd begun to suspect that there was something off kilter about him, about his sudden brief appearances and abrupt departures, also his family background when he'd discuss it, even his wealth, which seemed elusive at its sources."

"That's an odd thing to say," interrupted Tyrell. "I don't know too many people from your part of town who open their portfolios for their neighbors."

"Of course not, but fundamental origins are generally known. A man invents something or provides something the marketplace doesn't have, filling a gap; or he starts a bank at the right time, or develops real estate; these are the springboards to the portfolios you speak of. In my case, before my ascension to the Court, I was the founder and senior partner of an immensely lucrative law firm with offices both in Washington and New York. I could easily afford the honor of the Court."

"Yes, you could," Hawthorne said, recalling the dossier on David Ingersol which included copious data on the father. The one missing piece was the real reason Richard Ingersol had resigned. Suddenly, Hawthorne knew he was about to hold the missing piece in his hands.

"Neptune," Ingersol said as if reading Tye's thoughts. He sat down on a white wrought-iron bench at the far end of the isolated garden. "It's part of the story, a rather seedy part and unnecessarily brutal. One night on the yacht club veranda, overlooking a moonlit Mediterranean, Van Nostrand, ever observant, said, 'You find something strange about me, don't you, Mr. Justice?' I replied that I assumed he was a homosexual, but that was nothing new. The international set was rife with them. Then, with the most diabolical thin smile I've ever seen, he said to me, 'I'm the man who ruined you, the man who rules the future of your son. I'm Neptune.'"

"Jesus Christ! He came right out with it?"

"I was shocked, of course, and asked him why he wanted me to know at this late date. What cruel and perverse satisfaction could he derive? I was eighty-one years of age and hardly in a position to challenge him, much less kill him. My wife had died and I was alone, frankly wondering each night when I went to bed whether I'd wake up in the morning. 'Why, Nils?' I asked him again. 'Why did you do it, and why tell me now?'"

"Did he have an answer?"

"Yes, Mr. Hawthorne, he had an answer. It's why I came back. . . . My son was not killed by an itinerant drug addict; he was methodically murdered by the people who 'ruined' me and 'ruled' him, to use Van Nostrand's words. I'm eighty-six now, and the way I live means I'm living on stolen time, utterly confusing my doctors. But one day soon I won't wake up to greet the sun, I accept that. What I cannot accept is that I'll carry to that ostentatious grave of mine the secret that turned a dishonorable life into one of utter disgrace, and in the doing killed my son."

"Neptune's answer?" Tyrell pressed.

"Delivered with that same malicious smile and the ice-cold eyes that held such fire behind them. I remember the words precisely, they're burned into my mind. . . . 'Because we proved we could do it, *Dickie* old sport—over two generations. Given time, we can run the United States government—Mars and Neptune. I wanted you to see it, know it, and realize that you can do nothing.' . . . That was his satisfaction, throwing it in my face, in the face of a helpless old man whose reborn wealth was built on corruption. But when they killed my son, I knew it was time to come out from the luxurious heaven of my hell and find someone to whom I could tell the truth. I wasn't sure where to begin, for there are some things that can never be told. I have a fine grandson to protect—potentially far better than his father and grandfather—but the rest must be told. Then I heard you in the study, Mr. Hawthorne, and turned the chair around and studied you. You're elected, young man; there's something about you that gives rise to cautious confidence." Ingersol's eyes bored into Hawthorne's. "You're not simply doing a job," he said. "You're committed to it; that probably accounts for your excessively forceful appearance on our stage here."

"I'm not an actor, Ingersol."

"We're all actors, Hawthorne, we who move in and out of other people's lives, either for self-preservation, self-enhancement, or settling scores."

"Who does that leave out?"

"As I said, we're all actors. . . . Now, to my unwritten contract—"

"*What* contract?"

"I'm prepared to give you certain information as long as it's understood that my identity is never revealed. I'm your unknown 'source,' our communications must be private, beyond scrutiny."

"That's out of bounds. I need confirmation."

"Then after the funeral I shall return to the Costa del Sol; and if Van Nostrand shows up, my last act will be to take a small revolver from my pocket, shoot him in the head, and throw myself at the mercy of the Spanish court. An act of personal honor without elaboration; it's not unknown."

"Van Nostrand won't show up. He's dead."

The old man stared at Tyrell. "There's been no news, no reports of his death—"

"You're one of the privileged few. It's been silenced."

"For what purpose?"

"To confuse the enemy is as good an answer as any."

"The 'enemy'? Then you know there's a structured organization."

"We do."

"Recruited, as my son was recruited. Extortion, blackmail, and guaranteed destruction if the candidates don't comply; guaranteed compensation if they do."

"Except for the few we found or think we found— all dead—we don't know who they are or where they are. Can you help us?"

"I think you mean can I help *you*."

"Friends of mine were killed, one probably crippled for life, let's leave it at that."

"Again, I accept your reply. . . . They're called the Scorpios, One through Twenty-five, the first five above the rest insofar as they transmit the orders from, shall we say, the board of directors."

"What board of directors?"

"They're known, aptly enough, as the Providers."

"Who are they?"

"Is my contract accepted? With *you*?"

"How can you ask me to keep my mouth shut? You have no idea what's involved."

"I know that I will not involve my grandson. Todd has his whole lifetime in front of him, and I refuse to have him stigmatized as the offspring of corrupt men."

"You realize I could lie to you."

"You'll think about it, but I don't believe you will,

not if you give me your word. It's a risk I'll take. . . . Your word?"

Tyrell took several angry steps to Ingersol's right, gazed briefly at the pale moon, then turned back and looked down into the old man's sad but steady eyes. "You're asking me to relay information based on an unknown source? It's crazy!"

"I don't think so. There was a Deep Throat, remember, and the integrity of a newspaper that followed his leads."

"Can you furnish me with concrete information?"

"I can furnish you with leads I believe are substantial; the rest is for you to establish."

"Then you have my word," said Hawthorne finally, softly. "And I'm not lying. . . . Go ahead."

"Van Nostrand had one of those small but very expensive villas, the sort designed for single people who don't care to have overnight guests, except for lovers, of course. After he told me who he was and what he had done, I had that villa under what the intelligence branches call a microscope. I bribed his help, as well as the local telephone office and the switchboards at our clubs. I knew I couldn't kill the man without facing consequences I didn't care to face, but if I could learn everything there was to learn about the bastard, perhaps I might reverse the hold he had on my son and me."

"By using his own technique?" interrupted Tyrell. "Extortion? Threatening to expose what you learned?"

"Precisely . . . in conjunction with what my son told me. We had to be extraordinarily cautious, you understand. No letters, no telephone calls, nothing like that. . . . David traveled a great deal, oddly enough at times reporting to the Central Intelligence Agency on matters they asked him to look into—"

"I was told that," Hawthorne broke in again. "When I first broached his name, the head of naval intelligence said I was an idiot. Your son was so clean he was a CIA asset when they wanted him."

"It's all so ironic, isn't it? . . . Nevertheless, we would meet secretly, taking every precaution not to be seen together. In the crowds of Trafalgar Square, or in boisterous cafés on the Rive Gauche, or in out-of-the-way country inns. David gave me the telephone codes— they're satellite transmissions, incidentally—"

"We know that—"

"You've made progress."

"Not enough. Go on."

"He knew Van Nostrand socially, that was unavoidable within the Washington circles they traveled, although they rarely spoke to each other in public. Then, due to an emergency that required immediate action— an urgent analytical revision at the CIA—Van Nostrand instructed my son to carry the revised information to Scorpio Two."

"Scorpio Two . . . ? O'Ryan?"

"Yes. You see, David was Scorpio Three."

"He was one of the top five, then."

"With the utmost reluctance, I assure you. As to why, that is not part of the information I will give you."

"Who are the other two? Of the five highest Scorpios, I mean."

"He never specifically learned, but he assumed that one was a senator because Van Nostrand once told him that the Senate Intelligence Committee was an excellent source of information. As to the fifth man, David said O'Ryan had traced him, but would say only that S-Five was 'a heavyweight—the heaviest at the Pentagon.' "

"It's a big place with a lot of heavyweights," observed Tyrell.

"I agree. Nevertheless it confirmed what I learned on the Costa del Sol. Van Nostrand made scores of calls to Washington whenever he was in residence, many of them to the Pentagon. However, as David pointed out, the list is useless. If Neptune wanted to reach a Scorpio, he'd use the satellite codes."

"Unless he was using blinds to send a message," Hawthorne said. "Your son was right. It's a useless avenue. . . . Did you learn anything else from that villa outside of the telephone calls?"

"Yes, I found correspondence from a real estate firm in Lausanne. Apparently Van Nostrand owned property on the lake in another name, a Spanish name. He himself was listed as custodian."

"Nothing there, and even if there were, it would take too long to unscramble. Anything else?"

"Again, yes." Ingersol smiled thinly. "A list of twenty names and addresses on the stationery of the Gemeinschaft Bank in Zurich. Eighteen months ago it was in Van Nostrand's wall safe. I paid ten thousand dollars to have the alarms neutralized and the safe opened by a delightful rogue currently incarcerated in Estepona. Twenty names, Mr. Hawthorne. *Twenty*."

"The mother lode!" whispered Tyrell. "The rest of the Scorpios. Did your son know?"

"I'm an experienced jurist, Hawthorne. I know when to deliver sealed evidence and when not to, especially if that evidence could bring great harm to counsel."

"What does that mean?"

"To put it bluntly, David was neither raised nor prepared for the position he was forced into. He was a fine attorney, a good corporate lawyer, but he was no street lawyer, no legal knife for the underworld. He put on a good act as Scorpio Three, but it was just that, an act. He was constantly frightened, prone to periods of depression and moments of panic. If I had given him the list, he very well might have used it in an attempt to extricate himself during one of his anxiety attacks."

"Could he have?"

"Good Lord, use your head, young man! Van Nostrand, an intimate of presidents with connections all over

Washington; O'Ryan, a top-flight analyst, privy to the deepest secrets; and a list of unknown names delivered by a panicked man who can't substantiate who or what they are?"

"What about the satellite codes?"

"Instantly shut down by any number of Scorpios in a position to send out the alarm. . . . If I were a conspiratorialist where the John Kennedy assassination was concerned, I could detail how a cover-up was easily managed, totally eluding the Warren Commission. The Scorpios are proof of how it can be done."

"Why was your son killed?"

"He panicked. Over what, I have no idea, but it must have been recent. As I told you, we never allowed ourselves written or wired communication. He was convinced his house and his office were monitored by the Providers."

"Are they tapped?"

"The house isn't; the office, I don't know. It's a large firm with a complicated telephone system. Intercepts might raise suspicions."

"Are you certain about the house?"

"I have my own people check it out once a month, but I could never convince David. He kept saying 'You don't know what they can do.' I agreed I didn't; I merely insisted that his house was clean. Bugs are easily discovered in residences, as you well know."

"Who are the Providers?"

"I'm not sure, I can only give you leads. People flew in on private aircraft to see Van Nostrand, and naturally, I spread some money around at the airport in Marbella and among its customs officials. Oh, yes, Mr. Hawthorne, I have the names and points of origin of everyone he saw, among them certainly several of the Providers, but to my regret nothing made sense. Lies are normal on such documents, but there was no core, no center that I could unearth. . . . But there was a man and a woman, he from Milan, she from Bahrain, who appeared much more frequently than the others. At first I thought they were *raisons de coeur*—lovers accepting Van Nostrand's private hospitality. Then I realized my foolish naiveté. They were both quite elderly, gross, enormous. If they were lovers, neither could mount the other without the help of grooms. . . . No, Hawthorne, they were not lovers. In my opinion, they were intrinsic to the Providers, possibly their leaders, at least their brokers."

"Milan, the northern conduit for Palermo, for the Mafia," said Tyrell softly. "Bahrain, with all the money in the world, often a major source for the Baaka Valley. Can you identify them, tell me who they are?"

"*Shh!*" Ingersol abruptly raised his right hand, palm forward. "Someone's coming through the archway."

Hawthorne started to turn; he was too late. A loud spit cracked through the air, a silenced gunshot. The bullet shattered the old man's forehead. Tyrell lunged to his right, diving into a cluster of rosebushes, his hand plunging under his belt for his weapon, but not in time. A silhouetted figure swooped down on him like a giant bird, filling his vision with darkness. A heavy metal object crashed down on his skull, and there was nothing.

29

H awthorne felt the sharp, agonizing pain first,
then the rivulets of blood rolling down his face.
Gasping for breath, he tried raising his head,
only to have his hair and his flesh caught and scraped
by thorns. He was deeply entangled in a rosebush, the
needled branches enveloping him, pressed into his clothing everywhere as if someone had used his feet to crush
the pain-inducing stems into his body. Someone had;
a silhouetted killer who had ended the life of Richard
Ingersol, father of Scorpio Three.

Slowly, unsteadily, and wincing through the web of
thorns, Tyrell got to his feet, suddenly realizing that
there was a gun in his hand but it was too large, too
heavy to be his own. He looked down through the wash
of light from the nearby pool. The weapon was a .38-
caliber Magnum with a perforated silencer attached to
the barrel, the same gun used to kill the elder Ingersol.
A setup! thought Hawthorne, only then realizing that
there was a pulsating irritation inside his jacket—*one,
two, three . . . one, two, three*—Poole was trying to
reach him on the emergency signal. For how long, he
had no way to tell.

He lurched up from the soft earth of the garden, trying
with all his concentration to orient himself while pulling
out his shirt and blotting the blood on his face with the
ends. There was no one else there, only Ingersol's corpse,
his entire skull drenched in blood, his face a shining
scarlet mask. Tye rushed forward, instinct telling him
what to do, as long as it was done quickly. He lowered

Ingersol's body off the white wrought-iron bench, placed it on the ground, and dragged it under the base of the tall hedges beyond the garden. He searched the old man's pockets; there was nothing but a billfold filled with money and credit cards; he left it there and took the unsoiled handkerchief from Ingersol's breast pocket. The light from the swimming pool—*water*!

Hawthorne raced to the latticed trellis, carefully peering around the corner as he shoved the Magnum under his belt. Again no one. The muted sounds of quiet voices confirmed the presence of several dozen figures moving slowly beyond the tinted sliding glass doors of the living room. He soaked the handkerchief in the pool, moving the wet surface over his face and head. If he could just get through the crowded, overworked kitchen without notice, he could reach the hallway only steps away from the younger Ingersol's office. He had to! He had to reach Jackson, had to learn what the emergency was, had to tell him what had happened. There was a limp bath towel hanging over a deck chair; he grabbed it, not sure what he would do with it other than to somehow cover his soiled clothes. But suddenly he was sure what had brought him out of his unconscious state. The weak but incessant pulsating electric charges from the plastic lighter against his chest. Without that electronic interference he would have been found within feet of Richard Ingersol's blood-drenched body and held by the police for murder. Thus would be eliminated two men, perhaps the only two people outside of the terrorist Bajaratt, who knew about the underground Scorpios. Move, *now*!

Tyrell held the towel against his face and rushed up the flagstone path to the kitchen door. He entered the white-aproned melee as though he were an overcome mourner or one who, in sorrow, had drunk too much in this house of death. Those who noticed his pitiful presence turned away; they had their work to do. In the narrow hallway he hurried to the study, grateful to see that the door was still closed. He slipped inside, locked the door behind him, and went to each window, pulling the drapes shut. The wound in his head had opened again, but thank God the stitches on his hip had held. There was blood above, but none below; Poole's extra taping had done its work. There was a bathroom in Ingersol's study, the door open. He would take care of the gash in his skull as soon as he could, but first there was A. J. Poole V, Lieutenant, United States Air Force.

"Where have you *been*?" an anxious Poole shouted. "I've been trying to reach you for the past forty-five minutes."

"Later, Jackson. Your news first. Is it *Cathy*?"

"No. The hospital says there's no change."

"Then what is it?"

"I'd rather not tell you, Tye, but you'd better hear it. . . . Henry Stevens was killed, a huge knife wound in the chest. His body was found by the police behind his garage." The lieutenant paused, then said, "I thought you'd want to know, Mrs. Stevens beat down Secretary Palisser until he gave her this number. She has a message for you and wouldn't take no. I wrote it down and swore on my honor to tell you. It goes as follows: 'First Ingrid, now Henry, Tye. How long can it go on? Get out for all our sanities.' . . . What does it mean, Commander?"

"She's associating one thing with another when there's no linkage." Tyrell could not allow himself to think about Phyllis Stevens's pain. There wasn't time! "Do the police have anything on Henry's killing?" he asked.

"Only that very unusual wound so far. Everything's being kept silent. The police are under orders to issue nothing to the press or anyone else."

"What about the wound?"

"It was a big blade and also thick, extremely rare, they say."

"Who are they? Who told you that?"

"Secretary Palisser. Since Director Gillette's heart attack, or whatever it was, Palisser's inserted himself insofar as you're working on behalf of the State Department. He's running the show."

"Then you talk directly to him?" asked Tyrell.

"It's a little scary for a silver bar, but yes, I do. He gave me his private numbers, both at home and at the Department."

"Listen carefully, Jackson, and take notes, and stop me if there's anything you don't understand." Hawthorne told Poole in detail everything that had happened at the Ingersol home in McLean, Virginia, specifically detailing his discussion with Richard Ingersol and the former justice's violent death in the garden.

"How badly are you hurt?" asked the lieutenant.

"I'll survive with a couple more stitches and a hell of a headache. Now reach Palisser and tell him everything I've told you. I want him to arrange for me to have immediate access to the Central Intelligence files of every senator on the intelligence committees and all the upper-level officers in the Pentagon, anyone high enough to be a decision-maker."

"I'm writin' as fast as I can," said Poole. "Jeezuss, what a scenario!"

"Have you got it all?"

"I don't make too many mistakes, Commander. I happen to have what's called an aural memory. What you told me, he'll get. . . . Incidentally, your brother Marc called again. He was upset."

"He's usually upset. What is it now?"

"Those pilots from Van Nostrand's place, the Jones boys. You've got twelve hours to get back to them or they'll go public."

"To hell with them. Let them go public. It'll panic the whole Scorpio network, and one of them is right here in this house! Whoever it is saw me go outside with the old man, Scorpio Three's father. Three's gone, so are O'Ryan and Van Nostrand. That leaves two of the upper five. The panic's just begun."

"Tye, how bad is your head?"

"A little messy and it hurts like hell." ·

"Find some tape somewhere and crisscross it over your hair. Make it tight and steal a hat."

"The check's in the mail, Doctor. . . . I have to get out of here. Tell Palisser I'm on my way to Langley. It'll take me at least twenty minutes, so he has enough time to get me admitted and have the first of those CIA files spewing out of the computers in one of their secret rooms with no windows. Tell him to move his ass, and make it clear I ordered you to say it."

"You love spittin' in the face of authority, don't you?"

"It's one of the few joys left."

In the secure off-limits forensic laboratory at Walter Reed Hospital, the two doctors working over the corpse of Captain Henry Stevens, U.S.N., looked at each other, astonished. On the sterile stainless-steel table at the foot of the operating table was an assortment of blades, some thirty-seven, from a medium vegetable knife to the largest cutlery available.

"My God, it was a bayonet," said the doctor on the right.

"Some psycho was sending a message," agreed the doctor on the left.

Bajaratt proceeded through the crowds to the platform's electronic doors. Inside the El Al terminal she veered to the right, away from the counters, toward a bank of storage lockers. She unzipped the side of her purse, took out a small key that had been given to her in Marseilles, and began studying the numbers of the locked panels. Finding the one marked 116, she opened it, reached her hand inside, and, fingers stretched, probed the unseen upper part, where there was an envelope taped to the surface. The Baj ripped it off, tore it open, and shook out a claim check which she quickly dropped into the side pocket of her purse, replacing the key that remained in the now-empty locker.

She walked back into the crowds and over to the El Al checkroom, where she casually removed the claim check and gave it to the girl behind the counter. "I believe one of our pilots left a package for me," she said, smiling sweetly. "The older we get, the more we need perfume from Paris, no?"

The clerk took the check. Several minutes passed while Bajaratt's anxiety mounted. It was taking far too long. As the Baj's eyes darted around like a potentially ensnarled animal nearing a trap, the woman returned.

"I'm sorry, but your pilot friend got his countries mixed up," explained the clerk, handing Bajaratt a heavily taped package, roughly a square foot in bulk. "This isn't out of Paris, it's straight from Tel Aviv. . . . Between you and me, we store the homeland packages in a separate area. People are so anxious when they come here to get things, y'know what I mean?"

"Not entirely, but thank you." The Baj took the package; it was light; she shook it. "That naughty pilot must have flown home first and given half my share to another woman."

"Men," the clerk agreed. "Who can trust 'em, especially pilots?"

Bajaratt carried the package back through the milling bodies to the entrance. She was elated, the procedure had worked. If the neutralized plastic explosive material had passed through Israeli security, it would pass through anything the White House could produce! Less than twenty-four hours! *Ashkelon!*

She walked through the electronic doors out to the platform area only to see that the limousine was not there; it was obviously circling the no-parking area. She was irritated but not angry; the success of her package's arrival filled her with purpose. It had gone *undetected* not only through the airport equipment but through the checkroom scans, which were constant since the explosions in the Tel Aviv terminal in the seventies. Little did anyone know that in the lower seam of the detonating purse was a single strand of black steel thread, no more than a half inch in length, that when pulled out activated the tiny lithium batteries, producing a bomb equivalent to several tons of dynamite, set off by merely moving the hands of an enclosed diamond wristwatch to twelve noon and pressing the crown three times. She felt like a girl of ten again, when she had plunged a hunting knife into the Spanish soldier who was hungrily, furiously breaking her virginity. *Muerte a toda autoridad!*

"If it isn't the sabra from the kibbutz Bar-Shoen." The words came like a bolt of lightning, firing her brain, fragmenting her thoughts. She looked up to see a stranger who was not a stranger at all! It was the once-dark-haired Mossad agent, now bleached blond, whom she had slept with years before, the man she had seen at the Carillon hotel's front desk. "Except I don't think the name is Rachela," he continued. "I believe it starts with the letter B, as in Bajaratt. We knew you had colleagues in Jerusalem and Tel Aviv, so where better to receive messages or parcels but in the one place no one would think you'd appear. It was only a hunch, but then, we're rather good at hunches—"

"It's been so *long,* my darling!" shouted the Baj. "*Hold* me, *kiss* me, my dearest, *dearest* love!" Bajaratt flung her arms around the Mossad intelligence officer under the smiling, sympathetic glances of the crowds on the platform. "Not since the kibbutz *Bar-Shoen!* Come inside, to the café. We must talk and talk and *talk!*"

The Baj gripped his arm, pulling the agent through the willing, parting crowds back into the terminal, all the while singing his praises in Hebrew. Once they were beyond the doors, she led the embarrassed Israeli toward the nearest and fullest lines in front of the ticket counters. Suddenly she screamed, her screams rooted in sheer terror.

"It's *he*!" Bajaratt shouted hysterically at no one and

everyone, her eyes wide in fright, the veins in her neck pronounced. "It is *Ahmet Soud,* of the *Hezbollah!* Look at his hair, it's bleached, but it is *he*! He murdered my children and *raped* me in the border war. How can he *be* here? Call the police, call our officials! *Stop* him!"

Men broke from the lines and converged on the Mossad officer as the Baj raced through the platform doors and ran against the stream of one-way traffic.

"Get *out* of here!" she roared, stopping the slowly approaching limousine by banging on the window and leaping into the rear seat beside a startled Nicolo.

"Where to, ma'am?" asked the driver.

"The nearest hotel, as decent as possible," answered the Baj breathlessly.

"There are several right here at the airport."

"Then the best will do."

"*Basta,* signora!" said Nicolo, his large dark eyes riveted on Bajaratt and continuing in Italian as he closed the glass partition between the chauffeur and the rear of the limousine. "For the last two hours I have tried to talk to you but you will not listen. You will listen now."

"I have a great deal on my mind, Nico. I have no time—"

"You will make time now, or I will stop the car and get out."

"You'll *what*? How dare you?"

"It is not such a dare, signora. I simply tell the driver to stop, and if he does not, I will force him to."

"You are an insolent child. . . . Very well, I will listen to you."

"I told you, I spoke to Angelina—"

"Yes, yes, I heard you. The actors are on strike in California and she is flying home tomorrow."

"She's flying into Washington first, and we shall meet at two o'clock in the afternoon at National Airport."

"It's out of the question," said Bajaratt firmly. "I have plans for tomorrow."

"Then make them without me, *Aunt* Cabrini."

"You cannot—you *must* not!"

"You don't own me, signora. You tell me you have a great cause and people die because you say they will stop this great cause of yours . . . although I cannot see how an island servant and a driver can be so important—"

"They would have betrayed me, *killed* me!"

"So you have told me, but you tell me nothing else. You give me too many orders that I do not understand. If this great cause of yours is so good and so virtuous, so cherished by the Church, why must we pretend to be people we are not? . . . No, I think perhaps I will not touch the lire in Napoli, and you will not give me orders any longer, or tell me I cannot see Angelina. I am strong and I am not stupid. I will find work—perhaps Papa Capelli will help after I tell him the truth, and I *will* tell him the truth."

"He'll throw you out of his house!"

"I will have a priest accompany me, with the blessings and absolution of my confession. He will know I'm sincere, that I am truly repentant for my sins of falsehood . . . however, I will not speak of the man who tried to kill me. He has paid his debt, and I will not be punished for what I had to do."

"You would speak of *me*?"

"I will tell them that you are not the countess, but a wealthy woman of high birth who enjoys the games among the rich that we on the docks know are very fashionable. How many times have we prepared yachts in Portici and Napoli for the grand signores and signoras, who in truth are pimps and whores from Rome?"

"You cannot do that, Nicolo!"

"I will not speak of the bad things—I know nothing of them, and you deserve my silence for bringing Angelina Capelli into this poor young man's life."

"Nico, listen to me. Only *one* more day and you are rich and free!"

"What are you saying . . . ?"

"Tomorrow—only tomorrow. In the evening, just the

evening, for a short while! That's all I ask of you, and I shall be gone—"

"Gone . . . ?"

"Yes, my adorable boy, and then the money in Napoli is yours, a great family in Ravello ready to accept you as their own—it's all for *you*, Nicolo! The dream of a thousand children on the piers; don't throw it away!"

"Tomorrow evening?"

"Yes, yes, barely an hour of your time. . . . And certainly you may meet Angel in the afternoon—I was preoccupied and not listening. I myself will go with you to the airport. It's settled, then?"

"No more lies or fast stories, Signora Cabrini. Remember, I am a dock boy from the streets. I think I hear the truth quicker than you do. It is much less complicated."

Hawthorne hung up the phone in Ingersol's study and looked around. He walked inside the private bathroom and opened the medicine cabinet. There were various medications, including Valium tablets, antacid pills, two styptic pencils, shaving cream, a bottle of shaving lotion, a small can of Band-Aids, and a roll of adhesive tape. On the counter was a marbled box containing facial tissues. He pulled out five or six layers, angled his head into the mirror, pressed the gash in his skull together, and placed the tissues over the wound. Frantically manipulating his fingers, he tore off strips of tape and stretched them over the tissues, locking his hair and the wound together as best he could. He went back into the study, found a Burberry checkered hat in the dead attorney's closet, and clamped it on his head. The rough dressing would absorb the blood until he reached Langley—he sincerely hoped.

He walked out into the hallway, suddenly wondering if he could find a way to steal the guest book, so obviously placed and signed by the mourners who were so eager to be noted. The gatehouse log at Van Nostrand's had been selectively helpful—and someone in *this* house was a Scorpio. The death of an old man was proof, the unfamiliar weapon in Tyrell's belt further evidence. However, all thoughts of the theft were voided when he reached the front door.

"Are you leaving, sir?" asked young Todd Ingersol, joining Hawthorne in the foyer.

"I'm afraid I have to," answered Tyrell, sensing a quiet anger in the boy-man's voice. "My business was official because I have a job to do, but your family has my sympathies."

"I think we've had enough of them, sir. This place is beginning to look like a dull, half-smashed fraternity party, so I'd like to find my grandfather."

"Oh?"

"He's as sick of this crap as I am. After a short sentence about my father, everyone in there is talking about himself. For starters, look at that Cro-Magnon, General Meyers, he's really holding forth. Dad hated his guts; he just pretended to tolerate him."

"I'm sorry. This *is* Washington." Suddenly a burly man with close-cropped hair and wearing a plain blue suit rushed through the front door, passing Hawthorne and Ingersol's son. He walked rapidly up to Meyers and spoke intently into his ear, almost as though he were giving orders to the general. "Who's that?" asked Tyrell.

"Maximum Mike's aide. He's been trying to get him out of here for the last half hour. I actually saw him grab the general's arm a little while ago. . . . Where's my grandfather? Mr. White said he was talking to you. He can throw these ball-breakers out nicely—I can't, because I wouldn't be nice and my mother would be mad as hell."

"I see." Hawthorne had studied the young man's face briefly. "Listen to me, Todd—your name *is* Todd, isn't it?"

"Yes, sir."

"This won't make sense to you right now, but your grandfather loves you very much. I don't know a great deal about him, but the few minutes I spent with him told me that he's a very superior man."

"We all know that—"

"Cling to it, Todd, believe it. . . . At least as far as you're concerned."

"What the hell does that mean?"

"I'm not sure. I just want you to know that I'm leaving this house with clean hands."

"Your face, sir. Look at your *face*!"

Tyrell felt the rivulets of blood rolling down his cheeks. He turned and ran out the door.

Hawthorne was halfway toward Langley when he slammed on the brakes, propelling the State Department car into the shoulder of the road. Meyers! *Maximum Mike* Meyers, chairman of the Joint Chiefs of Staff. A "heavyweight" at the Pentagon—O'Ryan's description—was it possible? The name at first had meant nothing to Tyrell; he was not a follower of military structure, in fact, he avoided most articles pertaining to the services. But the nickname Maximum Mike had stuck in his memory, if for no other reason than he loathed it, loathed everything the sobriquet stood for. And the last name was *Meyers*. The heaviest of the heavyweights!

Tyrell yanked out the dedicated line to Poole and pressed the button.

"Here I am," replied the lieutenant's voice instantly.

"What's the word on Cathy?"

"She moved her left leg, that's supposed to be a maybe, not conclusive. How about you?"

"Scratch Langley. Call Palisser and tell him I'm on my way to his house. We've got a new tornado."

30

"**K**eep going!" Bajaratt ordered as the driver of the limousine swung into an entrance of an airport hotel. "I'd prefer something farther away."

"They're all pretty much the same, ma'am," said the chauffeur.

"Try another, please." The Baj kept her eyes on the window, on the receding circular drive outside, watching for any sign of a following automobile, a hesitant car, wavering headlights—anything. She could sense her pulse racing as she gripped the package on her lap and felt the perspiration rolling down her neck. The Mossad had found her, *found* her despite every tunnel she had buried! Jerusalem was now in the equation, sending over the one man they knew might identify her more quickly than anyone else, a one-time lover who knew her walk, her body, the small gestures indelibly printed on the memory of an intelligence officer who beds a suspicious target.

How did the Mossad fit in? *How?* What was its connection to Washington's Little Girl Blood circle? . . . The newest leader of the Scorpions, would he know? He had as much as admitted that he not only knew but *approved* of her mission. *Remember Dallas thirty years ago? We do,* he had said enthusiastically. He had also mentioned that *he hated the goddamned pansies in Washington who wouldn't give us the firepower in 'Nam.* It was worth a try; he was worth a try.

"Driver," Bajaratt called out. "Take us into one of the parking areas, if you please."

"What, ma'am?"

"I realize it's inconvenient, but there are several items I'd like to get from my luggage."

"Whatever you say, ma'am."

"And please make sure there are convenient public telephones."

"There's a real convenient one right here."

"I'd prefer the other—"

"Yeah, folks are doing that more and more, I saw it on television. People can listen in on these cellphone things."

"Hardly my concern." But something else was, considered the Baj. An outside parking lot was an enclosed area; cars coming and going were easily spotted. If they were being followed, she'd know it in a matter of moments, and vast shadowed areas at night were familiar places to Amaya Aquirre . . . Bajaratt. She fondled her purse, feeling the hard steel of her automatic. It was fully loaded.

The only automobile that arrived within minutes of their entry was a brightly painted Jeep, the driver and her passengers boisterous young people. The exit was several hundred meters across the lot, beyond the rows of parked cars. They were safe; there was no surveillance. There was, however, a telephone booth.

"It is I," said the Baj. "May we speak?"

"I'm in my Pentagon chariot, give me ten seconds to put us on scrambler and I'll be back on the line." Eight seconds later, the chairman of the Joint Chiefs returned. "You're anxious, lady. I gave the blueprint to a G-2 specialist on my payroll who knew all about it; he's worked the Middle East. It'll be delivered tomorrow morning, no later than seven A.M."

"You're very professional, Scorpio One, but that's not what I called about. May we talk freely, or are you monitored?"

"You could spell out the nuclear codes and no one could intercept."

"But you're in an automobile—"

"A very special vehicle. I just came from paying my respects to a yellowbelly you did me the courtesy of getting rid of. The son of a bitch would have blown the whistle on all of us."

"Perhaps he did."

"No way, lady, I'd know about it."

"Yes, you said you were privileged—"

"All the way to the max," Meyers cut in, "which is kind of funny, considering my nickname."

"I beg your pardon?"

"Nothing, just a little inside humor."

"What I must ask you is not remotely humorous. The Mossad has shown up. What do you know about it?"

"Over *here*?"

"Precisely."

"I'll be goddamned. It's not in any of our circulations and I'd pick it up if it were. I have a couple of special friends over there, the right ones, not the lefties."

"That hardly gives me confidence."

"I separate and distinguish, lady. Mine comes first, everybody else gets in line."

"Including me?"

"You're the top of my priorities right now. You're going to bring us back to where we should be, so there's nothing I wouldn't do for you. I can smell the fires, hear the shouting of the scared-shitless mobs, see the columns as we continue the march. We'll be in charge again."

"*Muerte a toda autoridad.*"

"What did you say?"

"It matters not to you. Only to me."

Bajaratt hung up the parking lot phone, frowning in thought. The man was a zealot; she liked that, if it was true and not a charade. Was he genuine, or was he an accomplished plant inserted by the same inner circle he disavowed? She would know in the morning when she disassembled the Allah's Boot, verifying its structure and components as only a skilled activist knew how to do. A technician could build an authentic-looking facsimile, but there were three contact points that could not be duplicated without lethal consequences. Friend or enemy, it didn't really matter. She had told him nothing.

The Baj inserted another coin and called the Carillon to get her messages from the concierge. They were numerous, supplicants all but one. That message was from the office of Michigan's Senator Nesbitt, and the words were magnificently precise. *The countess's appointment at the White House is scheduled for eight o'clock tomorrow evening. The senator will call her in the morning.*

Bajaratt walked back to the limousine, instinctively searching the parking lot for new arrivals and the dark sky for hovering aircraft.

"Take us back to the first hotel," she said to the driver. "I was too hasty."

Hawthorne stood over the butcher-block table in the secretary of state's kitchen; his angry, reluctant host sat beside the ever-present coffeepot. Their exchange was heated.

"You sound like a jackass with a commensurate IQ, Commander! Have you lost all skepticism?"

"You're the jackass if you're not listening to me, Palisser!"

"May I remind you, young man, that I'm the secretary of state."

"Right now, you're the secretary of guacamole!"

"You're not at all amusing—"

"You said that the last time, about Van Nostrand. You were wrong then and you're wrong now. Will you please *think*, and follow me?"

"I listened to everything your aide, what's his name, told me, and my head's still spinning."

"His name is Poole, and he's a first lieutenant in the

air force, and he's a hell of a lot brighter than you or me, and everything he told you is true. I was there, you weren't."

"Let's get this straight, Hawthorne," said Palisser. "What makes you think that under the circumstances old Ingersol has any of his marbles left? He's damned near ninety, his son was brutally murdered, and he's been flying all day against six or seven time zones. Considering his age and the stress he's under, a bereaved old man like Ingersol might well fantasize, conjure up an army of demons marching out of hell to wreak havoc, including the murder of his son. . . . Good God! A network of *Scorpions* with elite leaders who carry out the demands of a mystical order of the Providers? It's all out of some outrageously implausible novel!"

"So was the *Schutzstaffel*."

"The early Nazis?"

"The same thugs who had uniforms and several thousand pairs of leather boots when a wheelbarrow full of deutsche marks couldn't buy a loaf of bread. Certainly not during the Weimar economic collapse."

"What the hell are you talking about?"

"A very relevant pattern, Mr. Secretary. Somebody supplied all those uniforms and boots; they didn't just materialize out of thin air—they were bought and paid for by very special interests who wanted a country! The Providers here aren't much different. They intend to gain control of this government and one way they can do it is with the assassination of the President and the chaos that would follow. They're in place in the Senate and the Pentagon, that much we know, and probably in the courts and communications, ready to jump into the power vacuum."

"What do you mean, we know?"

"The Ingersols, father and son, put it together, from what the son knew as a reluctant Scorpio, and from what Van Nostrand told the old man on the Costa del Sol."

"Van Nostrand . . . ?"

"You heard me. That piss-elegant son of a bitch was at the heart of the whole thing. He laid it on the line to our former justice of the Supreme Court—made it clear that he and his crowd were going to run Washington and there was nothing Ingersol or his son could do about it. Those two were the proof—from generation to generation."

"Absurd!"

"And as sure as you and our late secretary of defense, Howard Davenport, are clean, the chairman of the Joint Chiefs isn't. He's one of them."

"You're stark raving mad. . . ."

"I'm mad as hell, Palisser, but I'm as sane as I've ever been, and I've got a gash in my skull to prove it." Hawthorne yanked off the Burberry hat he had stolen from the younger Ingersol's closet, bent over, and revealed the bloody tape on his head.

"That happened at Ingersol's place?"

"Roughly two hours ago, and Maximum Mike Meyers, the almighty chairman of the Joint Chiefs, was there. One of the Scorpios was described as 'a heavyweight at the Pentagon, the *heaviest*.' Do you need a roadmap to get from Ingersol's house to the Pentagon, Mr. Secretary?"

"We'll bring in the old man and question him with the appropriate doctors," said Palisser gruffly, pensively.

"Forgive me for using an old technique." Hawthorne lowered his voice and braced himself wearily on the butcher-block table, beads of sweat forming on his hairline. "It's something I refined in Amsterdam. I used to call it the clincher, in case an asset was wavering. . . . You can't bring in Justice Ingersol because he's dead. A bullet from a .357 Magnum blew his forehead apart, and I was set up to take the kill as my own."

Palisser's chair screeched as he involuntarily scraped it backward across the stone floor of the kitchen. "What are you—"

"It's true, Mr. Secretary."

"It would be all over the news! I would have been reached!"

"Not by the Pentagon, and it's entirely possible that no one at Ingersol's house has walked back into an outside garden beyond the swimming pool. They may not find him until morning; tonight's occasion at that house didn't call for skinny-dipping in the pool, unless I've grossly underestimated my distaste for Washington get-togethers."

"Who shot him and *why*?" Palisser's face was white, his lips parted in shock.

"I can only guess, but it's based on what I saw, what I was told when I was beat up and getting out of there. I watched as Meyers's extremely agitated aide rushed up to him and damn near forced his boss to leave, not exactly the behavior of an underling to the chairman of the Joint Chiefs. Then old Ingersol's grandson said the aide had been trying to get the general out of there for the past half hour. That would correspond to the time when Ingersol was killed and I took the fall."

"Nothing makes sense. Why would anyone want to kill the old man?"

"Because the Scorpios exist, they're real. I don't know what the killer heard, but Ingersol was about to tell me the identities of two people who frequently visited Van Nostrand on the Costa del Sol. He felt that they were keys to the Scorpios—that was uppermost in his mind. He would do anything to break the hold they had on his son."

"So you're saying Meyers's aide shot Ingersol?"

"It's the only assumption that makes sense."

"But if you saw him when you were leaving, why didn't he see you—a man he bludgeoned half to death—and if he did, why didn't he react accordingly?"

"The foyer was dark, I was wearing this hat, and the place was crowded. Besides, he raced past the kid and me like a man possessed. He had only one thought on his mind, and that was to get the hell out of there."

"And on those disjointed suppositions you want me to impugn the integrity and the patriotism of the chairman of the Joint Chiefs, a man who endured four years as a prisoner of war in North Vietnam, and have him taken into custody?"

"That's the last thing I want you to do!" Tyrell said emphatically. "I want you to help me do what I started to do, go down and dirty, and insinuate myself into the core of these people just as fast as I can. . . . He's part of the 'circle,' isn't he, one of the few people who are apprised daily, even hourly, of the Little Girl Blood progress, right?"

"Naturally, he's the—"

"I know who he is," Hawthorne interrupted. "But he doesn't know that *I* know he's a Scorpio."

"So?"

"Bring us together. Tonight. I'm the expert where Bajaratt is concerned, and I was almost killed at the Ingersols'."

"For God's sake, if you're right, *he* tried to have you killed!"

"*I* don't know that, I don't even suspect it," said Tyrell disingenuously. "I believe it was someone else at the house, and since he was there, I'm joining *him* to find out who it was." Hawthorne suddenly turned and approached the dark glass of an upper oven, his voice becoming harsh, inquisitorial. "*Think*, General! Go back over every name, every face you can remember! It's vital, General, someone in that crowd is working for Little Girl Blood!" Again Tyrell spun around, his eyes on Palisser. "You see how it's done, Mr. Secretary?"

"He'll see through you."

"Not if I do it right. Incidentally, I'll need one of those small tape recorders, the kind you can put in your shirt pocket. I want to record every word that son of a bitch says."

"I don't have to tell you, Hawthorne, that if you're right and Meyers even suspects he's being recorded, he'll kill you."

"If he tries, he won't have much of a future."

General Michael Meyers, chairman of the Joint Chiefs of Staff, stood impatiently in his trousers, bare to the waist, as his aide removed the prosthetic right arm that had filled out the sleeve of his civilian suit. Once the straps were off, the general shook the flesh-encased stump protruding from his shoulder, annoyed to see that the skin was reddish; it was time for a new harness.

"I'll get the salve," said the aide, following his superior's eyes and noting the resulting frown.

"Get me a drink first, and make a note to call the Walter Reed doctors in the morning. Tell them to get the damn thing right this time, okay?"

"That's what we told them last time," replied the middle-aged master sergeant, "and that was over a year ago. If I've told you once, I've told you a hundred times, these things stretch, and when they're loose they scratch. But no, you don't listen."

"You're a pain in the ass—"

"Don't insult me, you prick. You owe me big for tonight."

"I *hear* you," said the general, laughing. "But be careful or I'll take away that fancy Porsche you've got stashed in Easton."

"*Take* it. I'll use the Ferrari you keep in Annapolis; that's in my name too."

"You are one unholy grunt, Johnny."

"I know," said the master sergeant, pouring two drinks at the bar and looking at Meyers. "We go back a long time, Michael. It's been a good life, give or take a couple of interludes in gookville."

"It's going to get even better," added the general, sitting down in an easy chair, his feet on a hassock. "We're on our way back to where we should be."

"Is that what tonight was all about?"

"You better believe it," answered Meyers reflectively, quietly, staring at a wall. "The Ingersols, both of them, were greaseball shyster cowards. They connect with that bastard Hawthorne—either one of them—it's bad news, the worst."

"Hawthorne . . . ? He's the fall guy you wanted, the one with the old man? Don't tell me if you don't want to. I'm not curious, I just follow the leader."

"Ed White told me he was with him outside. White wanted to know if I knew anything about a State Department investigation of his partner. It was a smoke screen. Hawthorne's in another ballpark. Bad news."

"There isn't any news now, M.M. They're both history." The phone rang, diverting the master sergeant named Johnny from the drinks to the telephone. "General Meyers's residence," he said. "Yes, sir!" he exclaimed several seconds later, turning his head quickly to the general, his expression one of astonishment. "The chairman is in the shower, Mr. Secretary, but I'll have him return your call the moment he's out." The master sergeant picked up a pencil and wrote on a notepad. "Yes, sir, I've got it. He'll get back to you in a few minutes." The middle-aged noncom hung up the phone, his eyes still on the general; he swallowed as he spoke. "It was the secretary of state! They must have found the bodies. . . . Christ, and you wanted to stick around longer!"

"You're sure you weren't recognized outside the place?"

"No way! I'm too good, and you know it. How many times did I do this kind of thing to the yellow crud snitches in Hon Chow? Nine kills and not a spit leading to me."

"I believe you. What did Palisser say?"

"Only that something terrible happened and they—he said 'they'—needed your help. . . . I don't want anything to do with this, Max. I don't want to drive you, I don't want to be seen with you, not tonight!"

"You've got a point. Call your relief, Everett, from the car, tell him to get into a dark suit, and go over and pick him up. On the way back, fill him in on everything you did inside the house, including everyone you remember seeing, especially nodding at."

"I'm on my way," said Johnny, bringing Meyers his drink and heading for the door. "Don't take too long calling Palisser. He's really uptight."

"You forget, Sergeant, you've got lousy handwriting. I'll have to decipher it."

"For Christ's sake, Michael, he'll call you back and it won't look good!"

"No sweat. Your *sevens* look like *twos*, and your *threes* look like *eights*—"

"Asshole! You could ask *me*!"

"Not likely—and this part is true. I sent you out on an errand in the event the secretary's conversation should be confidential. No one who isn't cleared from on high can be privy to any information concerning a certain bloody girl."

"What the *hell* are you *talking* about?"

"See what I mean? Get going, Johnny." The aide shook his head and left, muttering vulgarities.

Maximum Mike Meyers sipped his Canadian rye whiskey, his eyes on the bar telephone, thinking. Bruce Palisser was smart, brave in war, and probably the most honest man in the administration, as the media frequently suggested. He called the shots as he saw them, frequently at the expense of fellow Cabinet officials, and amid rumors—always gracefully denied—that he had admonished the President over certain issues. He was this administration's George Shultz, as the press often suggested, and a man like that did not play the Washington games, it was not in him. So if he called asking for help, he wanted it; he was too honest to fake the request. Meyers did not basically like the secretary of state—he had little use for academicians in government; they were prone to endlessly debate too many sides of an issue without a firm commitment to one—but he respected the bastard.

The general got up slowly, his left hand propelling the weight of his body from the arm of the leather chair and, reaching down for his drink, he walked over to the bar. He placed the glass down on the black marble surface and turned his wrist to check the time. Seven minutes had passed since Johnny had left; he picked up the phone and pressed the numbers clearly written on the notepad by his aide.

"This is Palisser," said the secretary of state on the line.

"Bruce, forgive me," apologized Meyers firmly. "The sergeant's a worthy adjutant, but his handwriting's lousy. I called three other numbers until I deciphered this one. I sent him out before I started, of course, and we're phone secure."

"I was about to call you back, Michael. Something terrible has happened—terrible and grotesque, but may very well be tied in with the Bajaratt woman."

"My God, what is it?"

"You were at the Ingersols' tonight, is that right?"

"Yes, my office agreed that I should show up. David was a friend to the Pentagon; we frequently called on him for pro bono advice in our dealings with the defense contractors."

"That may have been misguided, but you'd have no way of knowing it."

"I don't follow you."

"You've kept up with the Little Girl Blood progress reports, haven't you?"

"Naturally."

"Then you're aware of the fact that it's been determined she has an organization behind her—loose or tight, we have no idea—but there are influential people working on her behalf."

"It's a given," said the general, smiling grimly for the benefit of no one but himself. "She couldn't have eluded all the dragnets if she didn't."

"A new development came today. It hasn't been sufficiently documented to be circulated, but it's legitimate. Tonight proves it."

"Proves what?"

"Ingersol was part of the Bajaratt group."

"*David?*" exclaimed Meyers in mock astonishment. "That's the last thing on earth I ever expected to hear."

"There's more. So was his father, the former justice of the Court."

"That's very hard to believe. Who's advanced this?"

"Commander Hawthorne put it together."

"*Who?* . . . Oh, the retired N.I. deep cover recruited by the Brits, I remember now."

"He's lucky to be alive. He was at the Ingersols' too."

"Alive . . . ?" Startled, Meyers quickly recovered. "What happened?"

"He was out in the garden, behind the pool, talking to the old man and learning a number of shocking details about both father and son. Apparently, they were followed, and someone shot Richard Ingersol in the head, killing him instantly. Before Hawthorne could adjust, that same someone assaulted him, rendering him unconscious and leaving the murder weapon in his hand."

"This is incredible!" said the general in a harsh monotone.

"Incidentally, a CIA salvage unit was sent out to remove the body, taking it through the adjacent woods. Mrs. Ingersol and her son were told that the old man was tired of the whole affair and was driven to a hotel."

"Did they buy it?"

"The son did. He said if he had known, he would have joined his grandfather. Since this is tied to Little

Girl Blood, we've got to keep it quiet and figure out what to say later."

"I agree, but Jesus, Bruce, I didn't hear any gunfire and I'd recognize it a half mile away!"

"You wouldn't have. The commander has the weapon, it's a .357 Magnum with a silencer. He regained consciousness before anything was discovered—thorns from a rosebush awakening him, he says—and got out of there. . . . Here, let me put him on the phone, he wants to talk to you."

Before the startled chairman of the Joint Chiefs could assimilate the news, Hawthorne was on the line.

"General Meyers?"

"Yes . . . ?"

"By the way, sir, I'm an enormous admirer of yours."

"Thank you."

"We've got to talk right away, sir, and not on the phone. We've got to go over everything you and I witnessed tonight, every person you saw or spoke to, because I didn't know anybody. I know only this, General. Someone who was there is working for Bajaratt!"

"Where do you want to meet?"

"I can come to your place."

"I'll be waiting, Commander." General Michael Meyers hung up the phone, briefly staring at the stump of flesh that protruded from his shoulder. He had not come this far to be stopped by a turncoat sailor.

31

MOSSAD HEADQUARTERS, TEL AVIV

The shirt-sleeved Colonel Daniel Abrams of the antiterrorist unit assigned to the Bajaratt enterprise sat at the head of the conference table. On his right was a woman in her late thirties with sharp features, her skin tanned by the Israeli sun, her dark hair swept back and woven into a bun at the nape of her neck. On his left was a boyish-looking man with thinning blond hair, bright blue eyes, and a reconstructed nose that had been smashed during his capture by the Hezbollah Party of God in south Lebanon. They were, respectively, a major and a captain in the Mossad, both experienced in undercover operations.

"Our man Yakov was outflanked by Bajaratt," said the colonel. "He found her in the El Al terminal at Dulles Airport, but she reversed the trap. She nearly created a riot by screaming that he was a disguised Palestinian terrorist and got away. Yakov was damned near killed by enraged travelers, mostly American, until our people listened to him and pulled out his papers."

"He never should have approached her alone," said the woman major. "She couldn't help but recognize him; he had cultivated her in the Bar-Shoen kibbutz. She had an immediate advantage."

"Or it could have been the other way around," suggested the young captain. "Yakov never knew she was Bajaratt when she was at the kibbutz. We established that later, after Ashkelon, from our agents in the Baaka.

He was simply suspicious; he speculated that she might be someone, or something, else."

"She certainly turned out to be," said Abrams. "Why did Yakov let her go?"

"He didn't. He took her out a few times, very unofficial, very low key, to see if he could learn more about her. She must have had her own ideas, and learned more about him than he did about her. One morning she didn't show up for the kibbutz breakfast; she'd disappeared."

"Then it was stupid of him to be in the vicinity by himself, much less confront her alone."

"Look, Major," said the captain, "would you rather have had a circle of agents closing in on her, no doubt resulting in indiscriminate gunfire, perhaps killing a number of people, mostly Americans? We decided to send him and let him act alone because he might recognize her despite her well-known talents for disguise. In addition, Yakov changed his own appearance; his black hair was made blonder than mine, what's left of it, and his eyebrows were bleached, shaped far differently from their natural curve. It wasn't perfect, only surgery could do that, but it was sufficient for even short distances."

"Men glance at a face, then study the body. Women appraise a body, then study the face."

"Please," interrupted Colonel Abrams, "let's not descend into sexist psychospeculation."

"It's proven, sir," insisted the major.

"I'm sure it is, but something else came out of this misadventure and we must determine how to use it. . . . We broke the Palestinian we had in custody, the singer of songs that so entertained our ever alert officers, the idiots. A guard reported an attempted bribe to free him, so we moved our prisoner to the Negev and sent the guard to another outfit."

"I thought Bajaratt's Ashkelons had sworn to be tortured to death before revealing anything," said the female officer scornfully. "So much for Arab courage."

"That's a stupid remark, Major," rebuked the colonel. "In all likelihood, no amount of torture—which we do not employ in the accepted sense—would have produced a thing. When will we learn that these people are as committed as we are? Only when we accept that will there be peace. We used chemicals."

"I stand corrected, Colonel Abrams. What did we learn?"

"We walked him through Bajaratt's various phone calls from the United States, probing each for a word, a name, a phrase—anything that might lead to something. About two hours ago we found it." The Mossad officer took a notebook from his shirt pocket and opened it. "Here are the words. '—an American senator . . . strategy successful . . . he's come through for us . . . name is Nesbitt.' "

"Who?"

"A senator from the state of Michigan named Nesbitt. He's the key. We'll forward it to Washington, of course, but not by the usual channels. To be frank, I don't trust the traffic; too many things have gone wrong."

"We would have caught her by now," agreed the boyish-looking Mossad officer. "It's ridiculous."

"Arrogance doesn't become us, Captain. We're not there, and she's an accomplished adversary. She's also as dedicated as anyone I've ever studied. It all goes back to her childhood, and perhaps that's the only way her fanaticism can be explained."

"The channel you wish to use, sir?" The female major was impatient.

"You two," replied the colonel. "We're flying you over tonight; you'll be there in the morning, Washington time. You're to go directly to Secretary of State Palisser, no one else—you'll be cleared for an immediate audience."

"Why *him*?" the captain half protested. "I'd think you'd choose an intelligence branch or the Secret Service."

"I know Palisser. I trust him. I don't really think I

know anybody else I *can* trust. That sounds paranoid, I guess."

"Yes, it does, sir," said the major.

"So be it," said the colonel.

Bajaratt stood by the airport hotel's thick window that muted the sounds of the arriving and departing jets. The early sun was breaking through the mists, announcing the most important day of her life. The exhilaration she felt was not unlike the excitement she had experienced spreading through her so many years before when she led a Spanish soldier into the forest, a long-bladed knife strapped to her thigh under her dress. The similarity was there, for the brutish army pig was her first kill and filled her with purpose, but today was far beyond that child's raw emotions. Today was the triumph of the woman, a thinking adult who had outthought the Praetorian guard of the most powerful nation on earth. She would go down in history, for she would *change* history, her life at last justified. *Muerte a toda autoridad!*

The child that was smiled up at her, at the giant who was the woman, and in that smile was love and gratitude, vengeance for all that had been done to both of them. *We walk together, my young self, into the bloodred glory of revenge. Be not afraid, my child who was me. You weren't afraid then, be not afraid now. Death is a peaceful sleep, and perhaps the cruelest thing for us would be to survive. But if we do, you angry youngster, keep the fire in your eyes, the fury in your breast.*

"Signora!" exclaimed Nicolo from the bed. "What time is it?"

"Too early for you to be awake," replied the Baj. "Your Angel hasn't even boarded her plane in California."

"At least it's morning," said the dock boy, yawning audibly and stretching. "I kept waking up, hoping to see sunlight."

"Call room service for one of your gargantuan breakfasts, and when you're finished I have a chore for you. I want you to dress and take a taxi to the Carillon. Pick up the rest of our luggage, along with a package addressed to me at the concierge's desk, and bring everything here."

"Good, it will pass the time. . . . Can I order something for you?"

"Just coffee, Nico. After a cup, I'm going for a walk, a very long walk in the very bright sun that is climbing gloriously in the sky."

"Is that poetry, signora?"

"If it is, it's not very good, but for me it's superb. The day is superb."

"Why do you stare out the window and speak so quietly?"

The Baj turned and looked down at the dock boy from Portici on the bed. "Because the end is near, Nicolo, the end of a long and very difficult journey."

"Oh, that's right, you said that after tonight I was free to do what I wished. To go back to Napoli and all the money you have left for me, and even to the great family in Ravello you say would welcome me as their own."

"You must do what you must do."

"I was wondering, Cabi. Of course I will return to Italy, and surely I will at least meet this fine noble family and thank them most graciously whether or not I stay with them, but can't it wait a few days?"

"For what?"

"Need you ask, *bella signora*? I should like to spend some time with Angelina."

"Do as you wish."

"But you said you would leave me after tonight—"

"I said that," agreed Bajaratt.

"Then I will need a great deal of money, for I am the *barone-cadetto di Ravello* and must afford my station."

"Nicolo, what are you saying to me?"

"Just what you heard, *mia bella signora*." The young Italian threw off the sheet and stood up naked, facing his benefactress. "A part of the dock boy does not change, Cabi, although I hope one day he disappears. I've studied the *fari al casos,* the bills you order me to get for you from the hotels and the *ristorantes,* and I've watched you. . . . You make a telephone call and money is delivered to you, usually at night and always sent in a very thick envelope. Palm Beach, New York, Washington; it's always the same."

"How do you think we live?" asked Bajaratt calmly, smiling sweetly. "With credit cards?"

"How will I live after you're gone? Here, where I wish to stay for a while. I do not think you've thought about that, and it concerns me that you have not. Dock boys stay close to their passengers for fear that they will vanish and the tips vanish with them."

"Are you telling me you want *money?*"

"Yes, I am, and I think I should have it this morning, before tonight."

"Tonight . . . ?"

"Long before tonight. In one of those heavy envelopes that I will give to Angel when I see her this afternoon in the airport. I have even figured out an amount, based on the bills I bring to you," continued Nicolo, overlooking the anger on Bajaratt's face. "It is so expensive, the way we live. . . . Twenty-five thousand American dollars will be enough. *Naturalmente,* you may deduct it from the money in Napoli, and I will sign a paper saying that I agree."

"You are an *insect,* a nothing! How dare you talk to me this way? Make such outrageous demands on *me* when I've opened your life for you? I refuse to continue this obscene conversation!"

"Then I refuse to get our luggage or be here when you return from your walk. . . . As to this evening, which you've been so secretive about, you may go yourself. A great lady like you does not need an insect like me."

"Nicolo, you will meet the most powerful man in the world, I once promised you that! You are going to meet the President of the United States!"

"I have no interest in him. Does he have an interest in me? Or in the *barone-cadetto di Ravello,* who I am not?"

"Don't *do* this to me!" screamed the Baj. "Everything I've worked for, lived for! You cannot understand!"

"I can understand an envelope which I know Angelina will not open until I see her in Brooklyn. In my heart I know she will help me get rid of your dock boy." Nicolo stood erect, his eyes locked furiously with those of Bajaratt. "*Do* it, Cabi. Do it or I am gone."

"You *bastard!*"

"You taught me that too, *bella signora.* When we reached that strange island after those terrible storms, I called you a monster. . . . You are worse than a monster, you are something evil that I cannot understand. Go to the telephone and call one of your *subalterni.* Have the money here by noontime, or I am gone."

MI-6 HEADQUARTERS, LONDON

It had been past midnight when the Afro-haired black man rushed into the strategy room, closed the door, and walked rapidly to the first seat on the left side of the circular conference table. He was dressed in a sleeve-fringed brown suede jacket and flared rust-colored trousers. There were three other men present: at the north end of the table was the chairman, Sir John Howell; counterclockwise, a man in a dark pinstripe suit; and nearest the newcomer a figure draped in a caftan, his *ghotra* headdress next to the file folder in front of him. His skin was dark, neither white nor black. An Arab.

"I think we've got an opening," said the recent arrival, trying to smooth down his wild hair; his accent was upper-class English. "It came originally from the motor pool."

"How do you mean, originally?" asked the pinstriper.

"One of Downing Street's senior mechanics. On several occasions he noted that the bonnets of two diplomatic cars had been lifted, ostensibly to check the engines while the vehicles were away from the garage."

"So?" asked Sir John. "If there's a problem with a bloody motor, how else does one find out what it is if not by raising the bonnet?"

"These are diplomatic automobiles, sir," said the Middle Eastern MI-6 officer. "Tampering cannot be permitted."

"And every driver is checked, double-checked, and damn near given an encephalograph."

"That's the point, Mr. Chairman," interrupted the black with the Oxford speech. "All engine difficulties are to be reported to the dispatchers regardless of how minor. Furthermore, each vehicle has an automatic inner seal on the bonnet's release mechanism; if it's been broken before routine inspection, a yellow dye appears on the tape. Neither of the cars in question had been reported as having problems, and each was driven by the same driver."

"You're saying that perhaps an encephalograph malfunctioned?" observed the man in the pinstripe suit, permitting himself a weak smile as he glanced at the chairman.

"Or the subject is extremely talented and terribly well trained," answered the black officer. "Enough so as to get a job in the motor pool."

"Let's get on with it. You obviously have the name of this driver and no doubt far more."

"A great deal more, sir. He's passing himself off as a naturalized Egyptian, a former chauffeur for Anwar Sadat's household, but his papers are meaningless; they're obviously fakes, although superb ones."

"Why was he permitted naturalized status?" asked the pinstriper. "That is, according to those papers."

"The army officers' coup against Sadat included the killing of his entire staff. He was granted asylum."

"Damned clever," interjected Howell. "Sadat was a special friend to the Foreign Office. Those chaps bent over backwards for his associates, far more than we would have liked for just this reason; too many rotten fish in the rescue nets. Go on."

"He goes by the name of Barudi, and I've been following him for a good part of the evening. He went into Soho, to the most disreputable places, I might add, and met with four different people at four separate bars. . . . I really must pause here, sir, and give credit where it's due."

"I beg your pardon?"

"The training course at the estate in Sussex. It was truly outstanding, sir. I refer to the relieving of personal articles from our subjects when we desire further information that's not readily available."

"Oh?"

"I believe James is referring to the craft of pickpocketing," said the man in the pinstripe suit. "He's apparently raised it to an art form."

"I managed to cop billfolds from two of the gentlemen; the woman's purse was heavily clasped, and the other fellow didn't seem to have pockets. I took the billfolds into a stall in the loo, scanned all the materials with my hand copier, and returned the property to our subjects, one, to my dismay, in a different pocket, but it was unavoidable."

"I'd say it was remarkable," said the chairman. "What did you learn about our driver's rather odd associates?"

"Again, the usual items such as driver's licenses and bank cards appeared authentic, and probably are except for the names. However, in each billfold, squared together so tightly they were barely larger than two postal stamps, and recessed into the bottom of the leather, were these." The MI-6 officer reached into the pocket of his suede jacket, pulled out four small packets of rolled-up copy paper, and with flicks of his wrist spread them out across the table like tentacles. "I ran my duplicator down the columns on the two sheets of paper and these are the results."

"What are they?" asked the pinstriper as he and the other two men picked up the strips of paper.

"The typed lines are classical Arabic," said the Middle Easterner. "The handwritten inserts are translations."

"Arabic?" Howell had interrupted. "Bajaratt!"

"As you can see, they're lists of dates, times, and locations—"

"They're ruddy *good* translations," broke in the Arab MI-Sixer, "and some of these places are damned near untranslatable. Who did this?"

"I called our head Arabist in Chelsea and went over there around nine o'clock. It didn't take him long."

"I'd think not," said the robed officer. "He was familiar with the locations, and after the first several, saw the key and used phonetics. Good man."

"What do they mean?" persisted the chairman. "Are they drops?"

"That's what caused my delay, sir. For the past three hours I drove from one location to another—there are twelve on each list—and to begin with, I was totally bewildered. Then I reached the fifth place and it became clear. I rechecked the first four and was convinced. They're not drops, sir, they're public telephones."

"Our subjects are receiving calls, obviously not placing them," offered the Middle Easterner.

"Why do you say that?" asked the Englishman on his left.

"It would be simple to write out the numbers to be reached in Arabic, no doubt using a differential plus or minus, to eliminate memory error. There're none here, but then there would have to be a minimum of ninety-six and a maximum of a hundred eighty digits to memorize."

"Suppose there's just one number?" said James.

"It's possible," replied the Arab, "but that presupposes the receiving party remains in one place, which would exclude Bajaratt. Furthermore, it's too dangerous to use a single number in any operation such as this, and lastly, every profile we've all worked up on Bajaratt indicates her manic obsession with secrecy, which means that wherever possible, she refuses to use intermediaries. She talks directly with her associates."

"I'm convinced," said Sir John. "When and where is the next contact?" he asked, scanning the tape nearest him.

"Noon, tomorrow, Brompton Road, Knightsbridge, outside Harrods," answered the black intelligence officer. "Seven in the morning, Washington time."

"The lunchtime crowd of shoppers here," the pinstriper observed. "It sounds like an IRA strategy."

"The next after that?" pressed the head of MI-6.

"Twenty minutes later at the corner of Oxford Circus and Regent."

"More crowds," suggested the olive-skinned officer. "Heavy traffic."

"I shouldn't have to tell you what to do, James," said the chairman. "A communications van at each location, open lines to both Washington and the underground telephone computers with the two public numbers. We'll need instant traceability, and I mean *instant*."

"Yes, sir. I took the liberty of alerting our communications division, but I'm afraid you'll have to reach the telephone people; they'd never accept it from me. I think it takes a High Court order to activate traceability."

"High Court order, my ass!" exploded the head of MI-6, suddenly slashing his damaged right hand across the table, instantly aware that it was not what it once was. "God help me, I sent Geoffrey Cooke to his death from this room. The maps were right here on this table, and he had to turn the pages for me, tell me what I didn't know! . . . I want that maniacal bitch dead! Do it for me; do it for Officer Cooke!"

"We'll be up to speed, sir, I promise you." James rose from his chair.

"Wait!" Sir John Howell paused, his intense eyes suddenly unfocused, his head angled down, his mind obviously racing. "I said open lines to Washington—that's too broad, too damned inclusive. Bajaratt has her own moles lined up over there. We have to restrict. One line only."

"To whom?" asked the pinstriper.

"Who's taken over for Gillette at the CIA?"

"His first deputy, temporarily. Handpicked and considered a fine chap by our fellows there," answered James.

"That's good enough for me, I'll reach him on scrambler. Also that fellow who's running Hawthorne. What's his name?"

"Stevens, sir. Captain Henry Stevens, naval intelligence."

"Whatever comes out of this remains in-house, and I mean totally secret until the three of us decide where to take it."

The midnight conference had taken place ten hours and thirty minutes earlier. The vans were now in place in Knightsbridge and Oxford Circus. It was approaching seven o'clock in the morning at Dulles Airport.

32

Bajaratt walked up the airport hotel's cement path, then strolled across the bordering grass, and slipped around the corner of the building, her head at the edge, her eyes on the entrance. She glanced at her diamond-encrusted watch; it was 6:32. She had stayed in the hotel room watching Nicolo dress and devour a breakfast fit for a wolf pack, urging him to hurry, but not so harshly as to alarm him further.

The Baj watched the hotel's entrance as the dock boy, resplendent in his expensive navy blue blazer and gray flannel slacks, hurried to the curb and a waiting taxi. He was, without doubt, the perfect male Galatea, sculpted by the mistress of all Pygmalions—quite simply, a magnificent-looking human being, young, beautiful, and vibrant. It was only just that such a creation should die in pursuit of a magnificent kill.

It was 6:47. She could walk calmly back onto the path and return to the hotel. She had five calls to make—two to London, one to Paris, one to Jerusalem, and the last to a bank that held the unlimited Baaka Valley reserves. It did not matter that she used the hotel phone, nothing mattered any longer. She would be out of there within the hour and leave the address of another hotel in Washington where Nicolo should bring their belongings, the only address where he would receive his money. Insignificant funds that he would never use.

* * *

KNIGHTSBRIDGE, LONDON

On Brompton Road, directly across from the entrance to Harrods, three men waited in a van, elaborately marked with the name The Scotch House. The electronic equipment inside was far beyond the ken of mortals who could barely read their television manuals. The walls of the soundproof vehicle had three tinted windows above the equipment on both sides. Those looking outside could see clearly, those outside looking in saw nothing. The man currently by the curbside window was the black MI-6 officer named James. His eyes roamed the area around the public telephone booth while his two companions kept checking their dials and the sonic grids with the weaving green lines, their headsets in place.

"There he is," James said, sharply but calmly.

"Which one?" A middle-aged technician in shirt-sleeves raised his eyes to the window.

"The chap in the gray suit and the regimental tie, with a newspaper under his arm."

"He doesn't look like either of the two you described in the Soho joints," commented the third, a slender, bespectacled man, swiveling in the street-side chair and partially rising from his electronic panel. "More like a tight-assed loan officer in a bank on The Strand."

"He very well may be, but right now he's glancing at his watch and moving toward the booth. . . . Look! He's just spotted a woman hell-bent on getting there first!"

"Good lad," said the shirt-sleeved man, grinning. "He's probably a rugby player; he damned near body-checked the old girl."

"She's pissed, all right," noted the slender colleague operating the street-side equipment. "She's looking daggers at him, she is."

"She's also in too much of a hurry to stand there making a scene," said James, concentrating on the disagreement between strangers outside. "She's heading for the booth down the street."

"*Ninety seconds to program scan,*" erupted a voice from a speaker on the curbside panel.

"Recheck your Washington line," ordered the MI-Sixer.

"D.C. Special Force, are you there, old chap?"

"Ready and waiting, London."

"Is our frequency still confirmed as being free of all intercepts?"

"Right down to the last static pebble; revolving astronauts couldn't pick us up. But we'd like to wing whatever we get to the police in the surrounding areas so we can dispatch personnel to the trace faster. We'll simply call it Priority Red, no mention of the particulars beyond the descriptions of the subjects."

"We have no problem with that, D.C. Go ahead."

"Thanks, London."

"All channels switch to activate," said the black MI-6 officer. "The program scan's begun."

Silence.

Eighty-seven seconds passed and only the quiet breathing of the three intelligence personnel could be heard. Suddenly a woman's voice, amplified by the speakers, pierced through the accompanying undercurrent of static.

"*Ashkelon, it is I!*"

"You sound tense, our beloved daughter of Allah," said the bemused voice thirty feet from the van in Knightsbridge.

"It is tonight—early tonight, my devoted one!"

"So soon? We have much to be thankful for and we're ready! You've worked with amazing speed."

"Does that surprise you?"

"Where you're concerned, nothing surprises me. I have only astonishment at your capabilities. Are there any particulars we should be aware of?"

"None. Just stay by your radios. When you hear the news, be prepared to act. Governments everywhere will be called into immediate session. There will be chaos throughout the capitals, massive disorder. Need I tell you more?"

"I trust not, for darkness there still means darkness here. Darkness and disorder are searchlights for those desirous of a kill. Quite simply, protection is in disarray; it can't be otherwise, for nothing and everything is expected. Disarray."

"You were always one of the wiser men—"

"*Wait!*" The man in the glass telephone booth suddenly focused his eyes to his left.

"Jesus Christ!" cried James of MI-6 inside the van, binoculars held to his face. "He's staring at us!"

"Get out of wherever you are!" roared the voice thirty feet away over the speakers. "The windows, they're opaque, black! Get out, they're *tracing* you!" The man in the dark business suit dropped the telephone, raced out of the booth, dodged the heavy traffic on Brompton Road, and disappeared into the crowds entering Harrods.

"*Goddamn it!*" shouted the agent named James. "We've lost him!"

"D.C., *D.C.!*" repeated the curbside technician. "*London* calling, come in, please, we've got an upset at our end."

"We know all about it, London," said the American voice over the speakers. "We hear what you hear, remember?"

"And?"

"We've got a lock, it just came in. It's a hotel at Dulles Airport!"

"Excellent, old chap. You're moving in, then?"

"Not so excellent and not so easy, but we're moving."

"Please explain that!" cried the MI-6 officer, leaning over the panel.

"To begin with," replied the American, "the hotel's got two hundred and seventy-five rooms, which means two hundred and seventy-five telephones that don't have to go through a switchboard to dial London or anywhere else in the world."

"You can't be *serious*!" roared James. "Scan the fucking *board*!"

"Be realistic, London, it's a hotel, not Langley. However, don't blow your gaskets, Dulles security is on its way and will be there as soon as they can."

" 'As soon as they *can*'? Why aren't they there *already*?"

"Because Dulles covers some ten thousand acres, and we happen to be in a recession, and a lot of services have been pretty severely cut, like security police in public areas."

"I don't *believe* this! This is the zenith of emergencies!"

The manager of the hotel at Dulles Airport shot up from his desk, telephone in hand. He had been berating a linen-supply service when the conversation was abruptly terminated by an operator, stating that there was an emergency and he should stay on the line for the police. A firm, cold voice followed, the man identifying himself as chief of airport security. His demands were short and curt. The hotel's computers and all elevators were to be shut down immediately, the guests told there was a massive electric failure, or whatever was deemed appropriate, but all departures were to be delayed as long as possible, bellhop service suspended. Frantically, the manager reached his secretary and carried out the orders.

Two blocks away, its siren parting the traffic, the first of three patrol cars raced toward the hotel. "What the hell are we looking for?" asked the driver. "I can't hear a damned thing!"

"A woman between thirty and forty traveling with a

big foreign kid who can't speak English," replied the
police officer's partner, his head bent down to hear
the dispatcher's voice over the speaker and through the
clamor of the sirens and surrounding horns.

"That's it?"

"It's all we've got."

"If they're running, they'll separate, for Christ's
sake!"

"So we look for the kid, then an anxious female. . . .
Hold it!" The partner shouted into his microphone. "Repeat that, please. I want to make sure I got it right. . . .
Ten-four." The police officer hung up his microphone.
"Here's one for you," he said to the driver. "The subjects
are armed and considered extremely dangerous, like in
instantly fatal. We're going into the front, our buddies
covering the grounds, like in fire escapes and windows."

"So?"

"The boys are carrying shotguns, and if we or they
can isolate either one, we don't bother with Miranda.
We just blow 'em away."

The white telephone rang in the office of the temporary
director of the Central Intelligence Agency. It was the
secure line from the Little Girl Blood unit; the head
of the electronic operation was icily professional. He
insisted on being put through to the new DCI immediately, which, according to the private secretary, was impossible. The man was on an international conference
call with the heads of security of three foreign governments, a conference set up by the President himself to
show how cooperative the new chief of U.S. Intelligence
would be with the country's allies. It was no time to
break into such a call.

"Give your information to me and I'll rush it in to
him."

"Make sure you do, it's urgent plus-plus."

"Please, I've been here for eighteen years, young man."

"Okay, hear this. The word is tonight, the Little Girl strikes early tonight. Alert the White House!"

"So we're both covered, send an in-house fax up here—immediately."

"On its way, as we speak. Secure, no copy at this end except in computer."

The copy of the Little Girl Blood unit's information erupted from the secretary's machine.

Scorpio Seventeen lit a match and burned the paper over an empty wastebasket.

Bajaratt slammed the two suitcases shut, shoving whatever clothes remained under the bed. She then raced into the bathroom, soaking a towel and rubbing it rapidly, harshly, over her face, removing all makeup, and picked out a tube of light Cover Girl Base from the toilet articles on the shelf. As quickly as she had removed the makeup, she spread the pale cream over her cheeks, forehead, and eyelids, raced back into the room, and grabbed her veiled hat off the bureau; she placed it on her head, pulled the lace veil over her face, retrieved her shoulder bag from the desk, and picked up the suitcases. She crossed to the door and went out into the corridor, looking up and down the hallway. She saw the obvious near an exit sign.

Ice. Beverages.

She dragged the suitcase from the doorway, pulled the door shut, retrieved the luggage, and ran to the small, neon-lit enclave that housed the ice and the vending machines. She threw the two suitcases into a corner; both would be stolen within the hour, she thought as she stood erect, adjusted her dress and her veil, and walked to the exit staircase.

Four stories below, the lobby was chaotic. The lines were growing longer at the cashiers' counters, and the exiting luggage was piling up at the doors and the pavement outside. The Baj understood instantly: Orders had been given. Obfuscate, procrastinate, claim confusion, even a computer shutdown—*delay*!

Cries were raised about airline departures, countered by others claiming that they should have used express checkouts; a number swore, bolting to the doors, their keys thrown to the floor, yelling phrases like "Sue me!" and "Talk to my lawyer, you incompetent morons!" and "I'll be damned if I miss my plane!" and "Fix your goddamned elevators!"

All was perfect, thought Bajaratt as she stooped over and limped outside to the taxi stand, a frail, delicate, elderly lady needing assistance. Suddenly a police car, its siren screaming, its lights flashing, swung into the curb, cutting off the first cab; two patrolmen leapt out, glanced into the head taxi, and raced across the crowded pavement toward the entrance, jostling the bodies in their path. Angry roars filled the area; abused and frustrated travelers were at the end of their patience. Then two other police cars arrived, their combined sirens and revolving lights abruptly quieting the mob, replacing the cries of protest with hushed observations of disaster.

The police from the additional patrol cars raced in all directions, across the east and west lawns, each man carrying a shotgun. *Perfect*, considered Bajaratt as she limped toward the end of the taxi line.

"Please take me to the nearest telephone booth," said the Baj, dropping a twenty-dollar bill through the slot in the driver's bulletproof partition. "After I make a call, I'll tell you where to drive me."

"I'm with you, lady," replied the long-haired cabbie, snatching the twenty dollars from the slot.

Less than two minutes later the taxi pulled to the curb in front of a dozen plastic-encased public phones. Bajaratt climbed out and ran to the nearest unoccupied one. From memory, her extraordinary memory, she thought in satisfaction, she dialed the Carillon hotel and asked for the concierge. "This is Madame Balzini," she said. "Has my nephew arrived?"

"Not yet, madame," said the unctuous voice on the line. "But a package was delivered for you less than an hour ago."

"Yes, I'm aware of it. When my nephew arrives, tell him to stay there. I'll join him."

Bajaratt hung up the phone and returned to the taxi, her mind racing. How had London found the telephone schedules? Who had failed or—worse, the worst—who had been discovered and broken?

No! She could not dwell on unanswerable speculations. Only today, only *tonight*! The signal would be sent across the world like a monstrous, shattering bolt of lightning! Nothing else mattered, only to get through the day.

It had been 2:48 in the morning when Hawthorne left General Michael Meyers's condominium complex in Arlington, Virginia. As he started out the exit drive, he pulled the recorder from his inside jacket pocket, relieved to see that the tiny red light was still on; he rewound the tape for several seconds, pressed the replay button, and heard their voices. His foot automatically bore down heavily on the accelerator; it was at once a gesture of exhilaration as well as of genuine desire to reach the Shenandoah Lodge as quickly as possible. Everything had worked; he had nearly two hours' worth of taped conversation between himself and the chairman of the Joint Chiefs of Staff—between himself and the last elite Scorpio.

Meyers had studied him when he first arrived, his gaze a mixture of grudging respect and fury, as a powerful man might observe the corpse of an adversary who could prove more dangerous dead than alive. Tyrell knew the type only too well; they were in abundance in Amsterdam, forever jockeying for the strategic kill, none without immense egos. And Hawthorne had appealed to Maximum Mike's ego, relentlessly playing to it, until, finally, Meyers's gargantuan sense of self could not be denied. The obsequious admirer asking him questions was a worshiping idiot; he could say whatever he liked with impunity, the reverent interrogator his first line of defense, should a defense ever be needed.

The general needed that defense more than he realized, thought Tyrell, turning into the highway. Hawthorne knew that the moment the general's aide opened the door to admit him. On first glance, the heavy subordinate was not unlike the military aide Tyrell had seen from the dark foyer of the Ingersols' house, but he was not the same man. He was someone else. A killer had been excused.

Hawthorne drove into the Shenandoah Lodge's parking lot at 3:30. Two minutes later he walked into the room where Poole sat wide awake at the desk, the miniaturized electronic equipment in front of him.

"Any word on Cathy?" asked Tyrell.

"Not since we spoke a few hours ago, and I've called a half dozen times."

"You said she moved a leg. That meant something, didn't it?"

"That's what they said at first, now they're not saying anythin' except to tell me not to call again, that they'll call me. So to stop from thinkin', I've been messing around with Langley."

"What do you mean, messing around?"

"Someone picked up your transponder, and it's drivin' the grid-kids crazy. They keep calling me, asking if we're in touch, and I say sure, every now and then, and they want to know why you stopped at Wilmington, Delaware, and then drove to New Jersey?"

"What did you tell them?"

"That the air force obviously has far more accurate equipment than they do, that I thought you were on your way to Georgia."

"Don't mess anymore; and if they call again, tell them the truth—I'm here and we have work to do. Which we do."

"The tape?" Poole's eyes widened.

"Get us both some paper so we can take notes." Hawthorne had rewound the tape in the car; he placed the recorder on the bureau. "Here we go," he added as the lieutenant brought them both a legal pad from the supplies on the coffee table, and Tyrell walked to the bed, cautiously lowering himself against the pillows.

"How's your head?" Poole broke in, stopping the recorder and taking it to the desk.

"Palisser's maid threw a box of gauze and a roll of tape over it. Now turn that damn thing back on, and I'll keep my hat where it is." The two men listened in silence to the taped conversation; it lasted an hour and twenty-three minutes. Each took notes, and when it was over, each had specific sections he wished to re-hear.

"You're very good at what you do, Commander," said Poole admiringly. "For a couple of minutes I thought you were real partial to Attila the Hun."

"Some of it's coming back, Lieutenant. Not enough, but some. . . . Come on, let's keep going."

"Okay, we'll take the segments in sequence from the beginning. I'll skip from one to another, 'cause I sketched out the areas of discovery and know where they are."

"What the hell are you now, a lawyer?"

"Oh, the pity. My daddy wanted me to be, just like him, but—"

"Spare me," Tyrell interrupted. "Just turn it on."

(HAWTHORNE) *Was there anyone at the Ingersols' tonight who you didn't expect to see, sir, someone who perhaps surprised you?*

(MEYERS) *That's difficult to answer, Mr. Hawthorne. For starters, it was damn crowded and*

*the lights weren't that bright—those candles on
the buffet tables were the only source actually, but
then, I restrict eating between meals, so I wasn't
there. A soldier may travel on his belly, but not if
it's too full, right?*

(HAWTHORNE) *Absolutely, sir. But was there
anyone who stood out in your mind as you think
back? I'm told you have an incredible memory.
Your tactics against the Cong, I've been told, were
based on aerial photographs no one else remembered.*

(MEYERS) *Quite true, quite true, but then, I
always had my aides, I won't short them. . . . Yes,
come to think of it, there were several members of
the Senate whose presence did astonish me. Politically quite far to the left, if you read me, and it
was common knowledge that David Ingersol was
a friend to the Pentagon.*

(HAWTHORNE) *Could you be more specific,
General?*

(MEYERS) *Yes, I can. That senator from Iowa,
the one who keeps whining that the farmers are
sacrificed for defense allocations, when who has
more subsidies than the farm belts? He was, as
usual, pontificating in that Midwest-deacon's pose
of his. Also a couple of other lefties whose names
I can't recall, but I'll go over the congressional
albums and I'll call you.*

(HAWTHORNE) *That'd be a great help, sir.*

(MEYERS) *I'm not sure how.*

(HAWTHORNE) *Anything unexpected is a plus,
General. Such people could be throwing off suspicion by their presence. We've heard there's dissension in the ranks of the Bajaratt conspiracy.*

(MEYERS, interrupting)   *There . . . is?*

(HAWTHORNE)   *It's spreading. Within days, perhaps hours, we'll have names.*

(MEYERS)   *That sounds incredible, Commander. . . . God knows I hope you're right.*

"Okay, that's the first one," said Poole, shutting off the recorder. "Any comment? I didn't choose it, you did, Tye."

"Because I was inside, watching from a corner in the hallway, and saw Meyers eating up a storm at the buffet table. There was no light problem for him; those candles were very bright, and there were sconces on the walls. As to whom he saw, I didn't care, I just wanted to see the types he put down so I could agree with him."

"And throw a little scare into him about dissension in Bajaratt's ranks?" said Poole, grinning.

"These days they call it psych-imbalance, Lieutenant. I call it shoving a small poker up his ass. Let's hear the second."

"It's short, but I think it's hog-wild, and you did too."

(HAWTHORNE)   *Did David Ingersol, who we now know was a traitor and dealing with Little Girl Blood, ever give you bad advice in your dealings with contractors?*

(MEYERS)   *By Christ, I certainly questioned a number of his legal decisions! Of course I'm not an attorney, but something smelled, I can tell you that!*

(HAWTHORNE)   *Did you follow up on your objections, sir?*

(MEYERS)   *I certainly did! Orally, if not in reports. Good God, he was a golfing partner of the President!*

"Perfect obfuscation," said Poole. "Nobody can establish nuthin' 'orally.' "

"Agreed," agreed Tye. "Next, please."

"Also short, and we both caught it."

(HAWTHORNE) *Edward White, Ingersol's partner, told us that he asked you if you knew anything about a State Department investigation into David Ingersol's affairs. Certainly you must have, General, because you constantly monitor the Little Girl Blood progress reports on the confidential equipment—*

(MEYERS) *What's your question?*

(HAWTHORNE) *It's not a question, sir, merely a thank-you for handling a deep-cover situation so well. Lesser men would have fallen into the trap.*

(MEYERS) *Of revealing max-security information? Not on any staff of mine, I'd have the bastard shot. Of course I knew about it, but no one would hear it from me.*

"That's a bingo," Tyrell said. "I was off the books, so it was never sent out. Palisser got me the papers but kept everything quiet."

"That's why I picked it up." Poole nodded. "Let's go on to the next one, okay?"

(MEYERS) *What do you think really happened here, Commander?*

(HAWTHORNE) *I can show you what happened to me, sir. You can see the top of my head, General. It's not pretty, but here it is.*

(MEYERS) *Terrible, simply terrible—of course I've seen a lot worse, but that was combat-oriented, not at a suburban wake, for God's sake!*

(HAWTHORNE)   *You were the finest combat officer in the army.*

(MEYERS)   *No, son, my boys were the finest—*

(HAWTHORNE)   *Your modesty is exceptional for a man with your record.*

(MEYERS)   *One shouldn't blow one's horn, especially when others blow it for you, right?*

(HAWTHORNE)   *Again, so right, sir. . . . But someone shot Richard Ingersol and attacked me in the garden before I could see who it was, and we've got to find out who!*

(MEYERS, interrupting)   *You should have had Ranger training, Commander. Except for the SEALs, I don't imagine you get much of that in the navy. On the other hand, I heard you had a pretty close call down in the islands, running down the Little Girl. I gather two former spook colleagues of yours were killed, a Brit and a Frenchman, but you got out of it. You must be pretty talented yourself, Commander—*

"Hold it, Jackson," said Tyrell, leaning forward in his chair as Poole stopped the recorder. "I wanted to make sure I heard it right. I did and it's another bingo. At no time did London or Paris acknowledge that Cooke or Ardisonne was attached to MI-6 or the Deuxième. Meyers got that information from the Scorpio network. Washington never mentioned it in the Bajaratt progress reports; we don't talk about allied intelligence personnel and they don't talk about ours."

"One more nail in the Maximum's pine box," noted Poole. "Now, let's peel away a couple of layers of the general's psyche. We both chose this one 'cause it makes for one scary psychological profile. You did a hell of a job here, Tye. . . . Here we go."

(HAWTHORNE) *Your service record, sir, is the top of the military, the envy and the glory of every soldier who's ever served this nation—*

(MEYERS, interrupting) *That's very kind of you, but, as I have said, I was never alone. Even in the torture crates and tiger holes of the Viet Cong, I knew I had the American people supporting me. I never lost that faith.*

(HAWTHORNE) *Then, General—and this is a personal question, having nothing to do with tonight—how can you accept the stripping of the military down to the bare bones? I ask you this as a great admirer of yours.*

(MEYERS) *It won't happen! It can't happen! There are intercontinental ballistic missiles pointed at our shores from all points of the globe! We must arm and rearm! The Soviets may be finished, but others have taken their place. Rearm, for the love of God, rearm! Take us back to where we were!*

(HAWTHORNE) *I agree, of course, sir, but how can it be done? The politicians in both parties are demanding cuts, promising the country a "peace-dividend," mainly from defense.*

(MEYERS, voice lowered) *How can it be done? Let me tell you, Commander, and now we're talking just between ourselves—okay, okay?*

(HAWTHORNE) *On my oath as a naval officer—under God and you, General.*

(MEYERS, voice barely audible) *We must first destabilize, Hawthorne, alarm the nation, let it know there are enemies everywhere! And once alarmed, we resume our rightful place as the guardians of the country.*

(HAWTHORNE)   *What kind of alarm, sir? Against what?*

(MEYERS)   *Against the inevitable in a torn society ravaged by undesirables and malcontents. We must be strong and fill the void with leadership.*

"He'd be a joke," said Poole, turning off the recorder. "A real comedian if he had a sense of humor. Instead, he's one grotesque son of a bitch."

"He's paranoid," Tyrell added quietly. "The perfect, dedicated Scorpio for the Providers. Not only are his bank accounts filled—though he probably doesn't give much of a damn about that—but he really believes his dreams of right-through-might are within reach. What's so frightening is that it could happen in seconds, with a single bullet or a grenade, fired or thrown by someone we can't find, someone who's dedicated her entire life to this one kill. *Where . . . where is she?*"

33

It was 8:12 A.M. when the Carillon hotel welcomed back Madame Balzini and her nephew, all formalities confidentially taken care of by an accommodating concierge who was far richer for his labors. At 8:58 Bajaratt phoned the Baaka Valley's bank of choice in the Cayman Islands, used her pass code, and was assured that the sum of fifty thousand American dollars would be delivered to the hotel within the hour, no mechanism of transfer sought nor one offered. The money arrived in a document envelope.

"Should I take it?" asked Nicolo when the bank executive left.

"You'll take what I give you. I trust the noble dock boy understands that I may have made some provisions for myself. You shall have your twenty-five thousand, but the rest is for me, for my endeavors. Why are you looking at me so strangely?"

"What's going to happen to you, signora? Where will you go, what will you do?"

"Everything will be answered for you tonight, my child lover, whom I adore."

"If you adore me so, why don't you tell me? You say you will leave me tonight—you are vanished, gone, I am alone. . . . Can't you understand me, Cabi? You've made me a part of you. I was nobody and now I am somebody *because* of you. I will think of you for the rest of my life. You cannot just disappear and leave me with confusion, a nothingness."

"There'll be no confusion, and as for your being alone, you have your Angel, don't you?"

"It is a faraway hope only."

"Enough talk," said Bajaratt, crossing to the desk and opening the envelope by breaking the three seals and ripping the tab of the striped tape. She removed twenty-six thousand dollars, handing Nicolo a thousand, placing twenty-five on the table, and leaving twenty-four thousand in the envelope. The Baj pressed the seals together and gave it to the dock boy from Portici, along with the thousand dollars. "That should be enough for your expenses to New York," she said. "Can I be fairer or more honest with you than this?"

"*Grazie*," said Nicolo. "I will give the envelope to Angelina this afternoon."

"Can you trust her, dock boy?"

"Yes. She's not of your world, and not of the waterfront. I spoke to her a few minutes ago, she was on her way to the airport. She'll be here at two twenty-five, gate seventeen. I cannot *wait*."

"What will you say to your famous lady?"

"Whatever comes from my heart, signora, not from my head."

Bruce Palisser, secretary of state, had been awakened by the White House at 5:46 A.M. and was in his limousine, heading toward the Oval Office, by ten past six. Syria and Israel were at an impasse; hostilities—conceivably nuclear—were about to break out unless the combined efforts of the United States, England, France, and Germany could cool off the hard-liners of both countries. At six-thirteen Palisser's wife took the call from Lieutenant Commander Hawthorne, asking to speak with the secretary right away. It was urgent.

"Apparently something else is also," Janet Palisser replied. "He's at the White House."

*   *   *

"I'm sorry, sir, but we've been ordered not to interrupt the Security Council meeting under any circumstances—"

"Suppose," interrupted a frustrated Tyrell, "just suppose a ballistic missile was in the air, headed directly at the White House! Could I get through then?"

"Are you saying there is such a ballistic missile—"

"No, I'm not saying that! I'm saying that I've got to reach the secretary of state on an extremely urgent matter!"

"Call the State Department."

"I can't call the State Department! . . . He made it clear that I was to speak only to *him*."

"Then call his emergency beeper—"

"I don't know how to—"

"If you don't have the number, you can't be very important."

"Please, I've got to get a message to Secretary Palisser!"

"Wait a sec—what did you say your last name was?"

"Hawthorne."

"Jeez, I'm sorry, sir. Your name was added at the end of the list in the computer. The letters are so small, you know what I mean? The message, please."

"Have him call me immediately. He knows where, and I'll be waiting. He'll get it right away?"

"I'm sending it down, sir." There was a click and the line went dead.

Hawthorne turned to Poole, who sat forward in an armchair, listening. "There's an emergency meeting at the White House, and the switchboard has to read the small print to get me through to Palisser to tell him that a maniac general who's probably in that room is aiding and abetting the assassination of the President."

"What do we do now?"

"We wait," said Tyrell. "It's the worst part."

* * *

The couple walked out of U.S. Customs and into the main terminal of Dulles International Airport. Their manner was casual, their presence in the United States was not. They were agents of the Mossad and their assignment was as vital as any in recent memory. They carried the identity of the man who was the key figure in the Bajaratt enterprise, a senator named Nesbitt, who, beyond reasons of sanity, was leading the terrorist to her kill, a kill that would take place any day, any hour.

They had arrived on El Al, Flight 8002, from Tel Aviv, and, as they had explained to the customs official, their stay would be brief. They were engineers employed by the Israeli government, in Washington to attend a fund-raising conference relative to further irrigation projects in the Negev desert. The uninterested clerk wielded his stamp, wished them a good day, and raised his head for the next applicant.

The Mossad officers continued rapidly into the terminal, the woman dressed in a severe black business outfit, her male companion in a similarly somber gray suit. Each carried a fabric-covered flight bag and identical attaché cases. Together, they approached a row of public telephones; the dark-haired woman spoke.

"I'll telephone his private number at the State Department, the one Colonel Abrams gave us."

"Quickly," said her colleague, a blond man whose hair had thinned perceptibly, the strands matching the flesh of his scalp. "But remember, if there's no answer after the fifth ring, hang up."

"I understand." After five rings the major replaced the telephone. "There's no answer."

"Then we're to call his house. We are to avoid all switchboards."

"I've got the number right here." The major retrieved the quarter from the slot, inserted it, and dialed.

"Hello?" A woman spoke.

"The secretary of state, please. It's most urgent."

"There's a lot of that going around," replied the irritated voice. "If you've got something urgent to tell the secretary, get in line and call the White House. *I'm* going to our beach house in St. Michaels."

"A rather angry woman hung up," said the bewildered Mossad officer, turning to the captain. "She said to call the White House—"

"Which we're prohibited from doing," broke in the subordinate. "We are to speak only to the secretary of state."

"He's obviously at the White House."

"We can't go through that switchboard—no one is to be trusted, only Palisser. Abrams sent word through diplomatic channels that he was to expect two visitors. The colonel and the secretary are friends, and coming from Abrams, Palisser will assume our urgency."

"Then I disagree with our instructions. Since Palisser's at the White House, I see no reason why we don't call the switchboard and get a message to him. Abrams said every hour was vital."

"What kind of message? We're not to identify ourselves."

"We'll leave word that the cousins of his friend Colonel David have arrived, and will call him as often as possible on his private line or his house, or even his office if we have to—"

"His office?" the captain interrupted, frowning.

"Every hour is vital," said the major. "We're not identifying ourselves, and he can instruct an aide or a secretary or a servant how and where we can reach him. We must get Nesbitt's name to him. . . . Let's find a limousine—with a telephone."

The seemingly oblivious customs official waited several minutes until he was sure the couple would not return to watch him. Convinced they had left, he placed the red delay sign on his counter and picked up his telephone. He pressed three numbers, instantly reaching the head of immigration security in an upper office, the room itself having two rows of mounted television monitors on the wall slightly above the myriad electronic consoles.

"The two Israeli possibles," said the clerk. "Male and female, ages and descriptions roughly similar."

"Occupations?"

"Engineers, verbal and written. It's on their cards."

"Purpose of visit?"

"Fund-raiser for projects in the Negev desert. They should be in the terminal by now. The female's slightly taller and dressed in black, he's in a gray suit, both carrying flight bags and attaché cases."

"We'll pick them up on a monitor and check them out. Thank you."

The head of immigration security, an obese middle-aged man with a puffed face and neutral eyes, rose from his desk behind a large glass partition and walked into the outer room, where five people sat in chairs in front of their consoles and television monitors.

"Look for a couple," he ordered. "The woman's taller and dressed in black, the guy's in a gray suit."

"I've got 'em," said a woman in the fourth chair barely thirty seconds later. "They're talking by a telephone."

"Good work." The security chief crossed to the female operator. "Give me a closer look." The woman turned a dial on her console, which in turn activated a telescopic lens on a terminal camera. The figures came into larger focus, the sight only to be greeted with disgust by the chief. "Christ, they don't look anything like the photographs. Forget it, kiddo. We got a trigger-happy stamper down there."

"Whaddya looking for, Stosh?" asked one of the men.

"A couple who may be bringing in diamonds."

"May I go down and escort them to my personal jeweler?"

The superior laughed with his crew and headed for the outer door. "For that you cover my phone. I gotta take a leakeroonie." The security official went out into the narrow corridor, turned left, and hurried to the end, where there was a railing and an even narrower balcony that overlooked much of the terminal. He reached into his pocket, pulled out a hand-held radio, and switched to another frequency. He then held it to his lips and spoke while squinting down at the crowds until he saw what he had seen on the television monitor. "Rattler, it's Catbird. Come in."

"Rattler on. What is it?"

"Targets are confirmed."

"The M couple? Where?"

"They're heading for the limo platform. He's in a gray suit; she's taller and dressed in black. *Move!*"

"I see them!" whispered a third voice over the radio. "I'm not fifty feet away. Jesus, they're picking up speed; they're in a hurry."

"So are we, Copperhead," said the chief of immigration security, listed among the Scorpios as number fourteen.

The two Mossad officers sat in the back of the limousine, their attaché cases on top of their flight bags on the jump seats; the captain's case was open. In his left hand, the blond undercover agent held a laminated card, four by six inches in size, that listed every nonsecure telephone number he might possibly need in the United States, from major addresses to embassies and consulates, from allied and enemy intelligence agencies to favorite restaurants, bars, and several women he felt might welcome his attention.

"Where did you get that?" asked the major.

"I made it myself," answered the captain. "I hate

looking things up in telephone books. Remember, I was posted here for eighteen months." He slid a credit card through the telephone slot, waiting for the word *dial* to appear on the thin panel. "Be quiet now," he continued as he pressed the numbers on his index. "This is the White House switchboard, and they don't care to ask questions; they only take messages."

"You've done this before . . . ?"

"Frequently. There was a sweet thing, a maid in the third floor private quarters— . . . *Shhh!* I've got an operator."

"The White House," said a tired female voice on the line.

"Forgive me, miss, but I've just spoken with the secretary of state's wife, Mrs. Bruce Palisser, who informed me that her husband was with the President. I should like to leave a message for Mr. Palisser, please."

"Are you cleared, sir? Otherwise, the Security Council can't be interrupted."

"I would not presume to interrupt, madam, I simply wish to leave a message."

"Yes, sir."

"Just tell him that the cousins of his old friend, Colonel David, are in town and will be in touch with his residence and his office as frequently as we can. He may leave word where we can reach him at his convenience."

"You want to give me a number?"

"That would be presumptuous on our part, and I wouldn't care to put you to any more trouble."

"He'll get your message as soon as the meeting's over."

The Mossad captain replaced the phone and leaned back in the seat. "We'll take turns calling his office and his residence every five minutes. As you say, we've got to get Nesbitt's name to him even if we have to give it over the phone," he said. The captain had leaned forward to put his laminated telephone index back into his briefcase, when he suddenly looked to his left outside the closed window. A second limousine was crowding them off the highway! Its rear windows were open . . . and in those dark spaces were weapons!

"Get *down*!" he screamed, throwing himself over the major as an unending fusillade of gunfire exploded, sending full-jacket bullets through glass and metal, penetrating the bodies inside. During the murderous attack, a grenade was lobbed through the shattered window. The limousine spun off the highway, rolling over and over on the shoulder of the road until it crashed into a metal sound wall and exploded in fire.

34

The highway from Dulles Airport was in shambles. Thirty-seven vehicles had piled up, smashing into one another as the fires from the explosion spread across the road, the result of the multi-punctured fuel tank of the destroyed limousine. Within minutes the sound of sirens and the deafening roars of helicopter rotors filled the morning air, joined shortly by the two-note screeching *nah-noahs* of the medical emergency units skirting both shoulders of the road to reach the casualties.

It was not only the death of the messengers from Tel Aviv, it was the end of their lives for twenty-two innocent men and women who wanted only to get home and to their families after arduous journeys. It was an obscenity born of a far more obscene conspiracy, born yet again years before by a child forced to witness the beheading of her mother and father in the mountains of the Pyrenees. Madness at 10:52 A.M. on a bright summer's day.

11:35 A.M.

Bajaratt was close to losing her temper, if not her sanity. She could not get through to Senator Nesbitt! Instead, it was first a receptionist, then a subordinate secretary, followed by the personal secretary, and finally an aide to the senator himself.

"This is the Countess Cabrini," said the Baj firmly. "I truly believe the senator wishes to speak with me."

"He does, indeed, Countess, but unfortunately he's out of the office. You must remember, Countess, the Senate's in summer recess, and our schedules are not as rigid as when we're in session."

"Are you saying you cannot find him?"

"We're trying, Countess. He might well be on the golf course, or visiting friends—"

"He has a housekeeper and a driver, young man. Certainly they know where he is."

"The housekeeper knows only that the senator went out in the car, and the car's telephone merely repeats that the owner has left the vehicle."

"I find this quite intolerable. I wish to speak to the senator himself."

"And I'm sure he would wish to speak with you, Countess, but if you're inquiring about your appointment at the White House, let me assure you that it's on the firm schedule. I have it here in front of me. You'll be picked up at the Carillon hotel at seven-fifteen sharp this evening. It's somewhat early, but just in case there's heavy traffic."

"You do reassure me. Thank you very much."

12:17 P.M.

Hawthorne pounced on the Shenandoah Lodge's desk telephone. "Yes?" he said.

"It's Palisser. I'm surprised I haven't heard from you."

"Haven't *heard*? I've left a half-dozen messages!"

"You did? . . . That's odd, you were cleared to reach me."

"I know that; the operators said that. They told me each time they were sending my name down to you."

"I never got it. On the other hand, the whole day so far has been a basket case. There was a foreign policy crisis, but with luck and a few threats we may have diffused it. . . . What happened with General Meyers?

Frankly, he behaved like an idiot during the conference. His answer to everything was 'sweet bombs'!"

"What's that?"

"Missiles that blow up selected targets housing the leaders on both sides—he was serious."

"He's more than that, he's a confirmed Scorpio. We've got him on tape. He had information that could have come only from the Scorpio network. He's one of them, there's no doubt any longer. Trust me, I know. Take him, isolate him, put him under chemicals!"

"We've got something else too. A friend of mine in Israel, a colonel in the Mossad who thinks we're riddled with so many leaks we're a sieve, sent two of his people here with what must be vital information. He wouldn't take such drastic measures otherwise. Let's wait until they reach me, then we'll move on all fronts."

"That works for me. We'll pull them all in and blow this bitch out of the sky."

"What's the bromide, Commander? 'From your mouth to God's ear'? Let us hope."

As Hawthorne hung up the phone, the hotel television set was showing the carnage on the Dulles access road from a helicopter in the sky on the outskirts of the airport. Cameras transmitted pictures of burning vehicles, some suddenly exploding, charred bodies on the pavement, a tragedy beyond words.

The obese chief of immigration security felt the short, sharp impulses of his Scorpio monitor, excused himself once again from his quarters, and walked rapidly to the nearest public phone in the outside corridor.

"Number Fourteen," he said, after pressing the digit litany.

"Number One here" came the harsh voice on the line. "Outstanding, Fourteen, well done. It's all over the news."

"I hope to hell it was the right couple," said Scorpio

Fourteen. "I figured the fund-raiser for the Negev desert was the key."

"It was. My source in Jerusalem gave it to me, and he's a tough old bastard. If he could pop-gun this whole administration, he'd do it himself. I'll reach him and give him the news. He wants what I want and we're going to get the whole *enchilada*!"

"Don't tell me, Number One, I don't want to know."

"You can count on it."

Eight thousand miles away, on Jerusalem's Ben Yehuda Street, a heavyset, barrel chested man in his early seventies sat hunched over his desk, studying the contents of a file folder. His face was like leather, the creases deep, the eyes small and hostile. His constantly swept private telephone rang; if the caller was a member of his family, he would cut him off quickly, for that line had to stay clear, it *had* to.

"Yes?" said the old Israeli curtly.

"*Shalom*, Mustang," said the voice on the other end.

"Goddamn you, Stallion, what took you so long?"

"Are we secure?"

"Don't start the foolish questions. *Talk*."

"The messengers have been rerouted—"

"For Christ's sake, you're not in a wired bunker, speak English!"

"The couple's limousine was shot to pieces, then blown up—"

"Documents?" asked the Israeli sharply. "Instructions, identifications?"

"Nothing could have survived the explosions, and even if anything did, it would take the forensic laboratories days to piece it together. It'd be too late."

"Ah-hah! You have something *else* to tell me?"

"Word from our person at the Agency is that it will happen tonight. London intercepted the call."

"My god, then the White House will be alerted!"

"No, they won't. Our person short-circuited the in-channel information, and *nothing* goes outside that channel. As far as anyone here in Washington is concerned, the MI-6 operation never took place, or was aborted. Tonight is just another night."

"Bravo, Stallion! Everything we wanted, no?"

"Thanks to you, Mustang."

"A terror will spread across the world like a gargantuan brushfire! And if London and Paris are successful—may God in His wisdom permit it—the fires will become a global conflagration, and we, the *soldiers,* will again be supreme."

"I said as much a short while ago. But it could not happen without your call to me, old friend."

"Friend?" the Israeli broke in. "No, we are not friends, General; you're as big an anti-Semite as I've ever known. We simply need each other, you for your reasons, me for mine. You want your massive toys back, and I want Israel to maintain its strength, which we cannot do without America's largess. When this is over and we trace the horrors to the Arabs in the Baaka, your administration and your Congress will open their coffers to us—for those who would destroy *us* have done this terrible thing to you, this horrible, *demeaning* thing!"

"We see alike, Mustang, and you'll never know how grateful I am that you did call me."

"Do you know *why*?"

"I think you just explained it."

"No, no, not *that* why, the *how* before the why?"

"I don't understand you."

"That compromising intellectual Abrams, Colonel Abrams of the almighty Mossad, *confided* in me. Can you imagine, that so-called organizational genius thinks I'm on his side, that I want peace with the filthy Arab savages, simply because I was the greatest fighter in our country's history, who now gives lip service to the government idiots so as to keep my position and stay in the public eye. . . . He said to me, he said—and I swear on the Torah—'The leaks are too deep, too copious, I can no longer trust our channels.' . . . So I said, 'Who *can* you trust?' and he said, 'Only Palisser. When I was the military chargé d'affaires at the embassy, we spoke frequently, and I spent a weekend at his house on the seashore. We see alike.' . . . Then I told him, 'Send couriers, two, not one, in case there is trouble, but only to see him. Make them engineers—*everybody's* an engineer—and I have projects in the Negev, I'll back you up.' . . . Like a hungry puppy, he yapped how marvelous it was, how creative I was. I *was*. Now his Senator Nesbitt from the state of Michigan is a nonissue!"

"Then you called me," said the voice quietly.

"Yes, I called you," agreed the heavyset old man. "We met twice, my *friend*, and I saw a man filled with hate, with a hatred that matched my own for not dissimilar reasons. It was an intuitive risk that I felt was worth taking. I spelled out the facts but drew no conclusions, you did that by yourself."

"Your intuition was right."

"Outstanding soldiers, especially battle-tested leaders, have a way of seeing into each other's souls, don't we?"

"You're wrong about one thing. I'm not an anti-Semite."

"Certainly you are, and so am *I*! I want fighters first and Jews second, just as you want fighters first and gentiles second! The temples and the churches are too often impediments."

"Come to think about it, you're right."

"What will you do—tonight over there?"

"Stay close to, or perhaps even in the White House. After all, I'll have to take charge very quickly, very firmly."

"Is that where it's going to happen?"

"Where else? . . . I doubt that we'll talk again."

"I should think not. Have a good day, Stallion."

"*Shalom*, Mustang." General Meyers, chairman of the Joint Chiefs of Staff, hung up the phone.

35

2:38 P.M.

Angel Capell walked through gate seventeen of National Airport, passengers and paparazzi crowding her, shouting questions. She spotted the *barone-cadetto* and his aunt; they were taken by an airline official into a private office.

"I'm so sorry, Paolo! All this nonsense must make you very uncomfortable."

"Everyone loves you! How can that make me uncomfortable?"

"It does me. My only consolation is that a month after the series is over, I'll be a has-been and I'll hear things like 'Didn't she used to be Angel Capell?' "

"Never!"

Bajaratt interrupted, giving Angel the sealed document envelope. "Dante Paolo's father does not want him to see the instructions until tomorrow."

"Why not?"

"I cannot say, for I don't know, Angelina. My brother has his brilliant ways and I do not question them. All I know is that I have business elsewhere, and Dante Paolo tells me he wishes to go to New York tomorrow morning to see you and your family."

"If you will permit it, Angel," said Nicolo questioningly, his eyebrows together in fear.

"Permit it? Holy moly, that's terrific! I got my folks a place on a lake in Connecticut. We can all go up there

for the weekend, and I'll show you an actress who can cook, noble guy!"

The airline official who had escorted them into the room suddenly opened the door. "Miss Capell, we've been in touch with your studio and they agree. We have a private jet that will fly you to New York; it will be much simpler and you won't be bothered."

"It doesn't bother me being bothered. Those people are my audience, mister."

"Well, they also keep leaving their seats and fill up the aisles while in flight."

"Oh, I see. Then you're the ones who are bothered."

"Safety is the issue, Miss Capell."

"Oh! Well, I can't fault you there, sir."

"Thank you so much. If you don't mind, we'd like to depart right away. Gate seventeen is a mess."

Angel turned to Nicolo. "Hey, noble guy, you can kiss me good-bye if you want to. There're no photographers here, or my father."

"Thank you, Angel." They embraced, kissed sweetly, and the young television star left the room with the airline official, carrying twenty-four thousand dollars in a thick brown envelope.

3:42 P.M.

"Have you *got* him?" asked Hawthorne over the phone. "It's been damned near three hours and we haven't heard a word from you! That's shit-kicking unfair!"

"And I haven't heard from the two Israelis who are bringing me crucial information, and that's even more unfair, Commander," said Secretary of State Palisser, doing his best to control his anger.

"What about Meyers?"

"He's under close surveillance, that's all the President would agree to until there's more substantive evidence.

He made it abundantly clear that it would be a very unpopular move for his administration to arrest a hero of Meyers's stature. He suggested that we go to the Senate with your information and let *it* take the heat."

"He's all balls, isn't he?"

"He vacillates, I'll go that far."

"Well, where *is* Meyers?"

"Currently in his office, doing whatever he does."

"Is his telephone tapped?"

"He'd know it instantly. Don't even think about it."

"Anything from the CIA?"

"Not a thing. I spoke with the interim director himself and he's heard nothing. Obviously London was a bust, otherwise MI-6 and our own unit would light up all the panels. Also, there appear to be so many leaks over there that I don't dare make further inquiries even through our supposedly secure channels."

"There's an old adage, Mr. Secretary. When an exercise fails, let it die fast and silently; and if anyone mentions it, you don't know what the hell he's talking about."

"What should we do now, Hawthorne? Or, more precisely, what can *you* do?"

"Something I'd rather not but damn well should. I'm going over to see Phyllis Stevens."

"You think she might know something, be able to tell you something?"

"She could and not even know it herself. She was always overly protective where Henry was concerned. She was the concrete wall around him, nobody got past her. It's an area we haven't explored."

"The police have kept everything quiet, but they haven't a clue—"

"The people we're dealing with don't leave clues," Tyrell interrupted. "At least not the kind the police would find. What happened to Henry Stevens had something to do with me."

"You're certain of that?"

"No, not really, but the odds are fair."

"Why?"

"Because Hank made a mistake, the same mistake he made in Amsterdam. Despite his normal professional reticence, he talked too much when he shouldn't have. He did just that in Amsterdam."

"Would you explain, please?"

"At this point, why not? Your director, Gillette, knew there was bad blood between us; he told me himself. Infinitely more dangerous, he knew the root cause of the problem, which was intensely personal. Bad move on Henry's part."

"I fail to see the significance. As I recall, you made no secret of your hostility where Captain Stevens was concerned. It was common knowledge that he failed to recruit you; that was left to the British."

"Hostility, yes, but I never elaborated on it to you or anyone else. I simply made it clear that he wasn't my superior."

"I think you're splitting hairs."

"I am. That's what this business is all about. . . . There's another axiom that goes back to when the pharaohs sent spies up into Macedonia. The abused can make all the accusations he likes, but the abuser keeps his mouth shut. Why would Henry tell anyone of consequence about the trouble between us? It would raise questions about his own conduct. The salient point here is, who else might he have told? Someone who would immediately see the advantage of taking him out, cutting off my control since I couldn't be reached."

"I really don't see the connection," protested the secretary of state. "*What* control?"

"He was my inside man until I found you, Mr. Palisser."

"I still don't understand—"

"Neither do I," said Tyrell, interrupting. "Maybe Phyllis can help us out."

4:29 P.M.

The vapor was so dense that the figure in the corner of the steam room could barely be seen. The hissing came to a stop, the door opened, and a second person came inside, propping the door open and carrying a large towel to the sole naked inhabitant on the tile seat. The steam rushed out in billows and streaks, revealing the sweat-drenched body of Senator Nesbitt. His eyes were in that phase between glazed and focused, his mouth open, sucking in the remaining vapors.

"I blacked out again, didn't I, Eugene?" he said hoarsely as he rose unsteadily to his feet, accepting the towel that was draped over his shoulders by his driver-bodyguard.

"Yes, sir. Margaret spotted the signs just after lunch—"

"My God, it's *afternoon*?" broke in the senator, close to panic.

"You haven't done that in a long time, sir," said the bodyguard, leading his disturbed employer out of the steam room toward a shower several feet away. "Only one or two slips," he added.

"Thank heavens it's summer and the Senate's in recess. . . . Did you take me to . . . Maryland?"

"We couldn't, there wasn't time. The doctor came down here instead. He gave you a couple of shots and told us what to do."

"There wasn't time . . . ?"

"You have an appointment at the White House, Senator. We have to pick up the countess and her nephew at seven-fifteen."

"Oh, *Jesus*, I'm a wreck!"

"You'll be fine, sir. After your shower Maggie will give you a massage and a B1 shot, then you rest for an hour before dressing. You'll be in top shape, boss."

"Top shape, Eugene?" Nesbitt's expression was pathetic. "I'm afraid not, my friend, that's a luxury I may never know. I live with a horrible nightmare, *in* that nightmare. It strikes without warning and I have no control over it. I sometimes think almighty God tests me to the edge of my endurance, to see if I will commit the mortal sin of taking my own life to remove the pain."

"Not while we're around, sir," said the bodyguard-keeper, gently placing his naked charge on a white plastic stool beneath the shower head and slowly turning on the lukewarm water, gradually making it colder and colder until icelike sprays pounded the politician's body. "Your head's a little messed up at certain times, sir, but like the doctor says, you can function otherwise better than the best of them. . . . We're getting a little cooler now, sir. Stay here, please."

"*Aughh!*" cried Nesbitt as the cold spray assaulted him. "That's enough, Eugene!"

"Not yet, sir, just a few moments longer."

"I'm freezing!"

"I'll shut it off in about fifteen seconds, that's what the doctor said."

"I can't stand it!"

"Four, three, two, one—*off*, sir." Once again the nurse-cum-guard threw the heavy towel over his patient and helped him to his feet. "How's that, Senator? You're back in the land of the living, sir."

"They say there's no cure, Eugene," replied the senator softly, his eyes clear, his facial muscles in place as he stepped out of the shower with his driver's assistance. "They say it either goes away with time and therapy, or you take massive drugs to contain it. Naturally, they diminish the assaulted brain to the point of dysfunction."

"There's none of that crap while we're around, sir."

"Yes, I understand, Eugene, and my gratitude is such that you and Margaret will be well compensated after I'm gone. But, good God, man, I'm two people! And I never know when one takes over the other. It's pure *hell!*"

"We kinda know, sir, and so do your friends in Maryland. We'll all take care of you."

"Do you realize, Eugene, that I haven't the vaguest idea where those friends of mine in Maryland ever came from?"

"Sure you do, sir. Their doctor came down to see us after we had that little problem in the adult movie place in Bethesda. You didn't do anything wrong; it was just that a couple of people thought they recognized you."

"I have no memory of that."

"That's what the doctor figured. . . . Hey, it's all gone, right, boss? You're back on track, and you got a big night, right? The *President,* sir! You're gonna make a lot of points with the voters with this rich countess and her richer kid nephew, right?"

"Yes, I guess I will, Eugene. Let's have Margaret's massage and a short nap."

5:07 P.M.

The permanent secretary to the interim director of the Central Intelligence Agency had for the third time taken the call from London, finally making it clear that the newly installed temporary DCI, having "gotten the word from the Little Girl Blood unit," was up to his neck in emergency meetings all over Washington, currently with the President's Cabinet at the White House, and would get back to the chairman of MI-6, Special Branch, as soon as the crisis passed. She had been as firm as her position allowed, perhaps dangerously firm, but there was no alternative. With Dulles airport successfully executed, she was the final checkpoint; the news from London could not get past her. She looked at the crystal clock on her desk; it was her last few minutes in that office.

Scorpio Seventeen gathered up the materials in front of her, rose from the desk, and approached her employer's door; she knocked. "Come in," said the voice inside.

"It's that time of day, sir." The secretary opened the door and walked through, carrying the papers and a stack of messages. "Here are the notes you wanted, as well as the calls that've piled up while you were on the phone. My Lord, it's like the *Who's Who* in Washington; everyone's trying to reach you." She placed the papers on the director's desk.

"Everybody's got advice and wants me to know how much they think of me. Naturally, it'll all disappear once the President nominates his permanent choice for this job."

"I thought you knew—"

"Knew what?"

"The Beltway rumor is that he likes you, respects your record here, and knows that the Agency upper levels want you to take over rather than some amateur from the political hat box."

"I've heard it, but I wouldn't bank my mortgage on it. The Man's got a lot of political debts, and a deputy director isn't one of them."

"Well, if that's all, I'll head for home and hearth, sir."

"Nothing from the Little Girl unit? I was to be informed immediately."

"The message's in the pile. You were on the phone with the Vice President."

"*Damn* it, you should have broken in!"

"There was nothing to break in with, sir. I don't know all the circumstances, but I assumed that 'no dice in London' meant what it usually means. The operation didn't pan out."

"*Goddamn!*" exploded the temporary DCI. "If I could have delivered on this one, I might have had a chance! . . . Where's what's-his-name, the fellow that headed up the unit?"

"He and the others have been here since three this

morning, over fifteen hours with very little sleep before that. The way he put it was that he was closing up shop and hopes for a better day tomorrow—after they got the red out of their eyes."

"All right, I'll speak to him tomorrow. You, too, of course."

"I'll stay if you like."

"What for? To watch me lick my wounds and start my good-byes to this pretty damned impressive office? Go home, Helen."

"Good night, Mr. Director."

"It has a nice sound, doesn't it?"

The secretary drove into the nearest shopping center in Langley, Virginia, locked her car, and walked to a pay phone on the pavement next to a supermarket. She inserted a coin, dialed a number long committed to memory, and waited for the usual series of beeps. She then dialed five additional digits and in moments, a voice was there. "Utah, I presume?"

"Number Seventeen. . . . As it must eventually happen with most of us, my time has come. I can't go back in the morning."

"I kind of figured that. I'll get you out of the country tonight. Take as little as possible with you."

"There's basically nothing. Everything I want is already in Europe, has been for several years."

"Where?"

"That I won't tell even you."

"Fair enough. When do you want to leave?"

"As soon as I can. There's nothing I need from my apartment except my passport and some jewelry. I'll get there in a taxi. Everything should remain the way it is, as if I'd never returned. I live near here, so I can be ready in fifteen or twenty minutes."

"Then take the cab to Andrews and go to security.

You'll be cleared for the next diplo-military shuttle to Paris."

"Good choice. When is it?"

"In about an hour and a half. Have a good life, Seventeen."

"I intend to. I've earned it."

36

Having instructed Poole to stay by the phone at the Shenandoah Lodge, basically for news about Catherine Neilsen, Hawthorne drove down the tree lined suburban street, swinging into the curb in front of the house of Captain Henry Stevens, murdered head of naval intelligence. In the driveway was a gray Navy Department vehicle, a security patrol car. An armed and uniformed chief petty officer admitted Tyrell; the man nodded toward the living room, where a woman dressed in black stood looking out a window at the far end.

The meeting between Phyllis and Tye was at first the awkward reunion of two former friends grown apart by the distance born of a deep personal loss, now seeing each other again under circumstances that painfully, inevitably, recalled the earlier tragedy in Amsterdam. More was said in silence, and in their eyes, until Hawthorne approached her and she rushed into his arms, the tears rolling down her cheeks. "It's all so rotten, so goddamned *rotten!*" she cried.

"I know, Phyll, I know."

"Of course you do!"

They held each other, the unspoken words understood, two decent people who had lost a part of their lives, the folly of those deaths essentially incomprehensible. The long moment passed and Hawthorne slowly released Henry Stevens's wife.

"May I get you something, Tye? Tea, coffee, a drink?"

"No, thanks," said Hawthorne, "but a rain check's accepted."

"Then it's offered. Sit down, please. I'm sure you didn't come out here simply to be kind; you're far too busy for that."

"How much do you know, Phyll?"

"I'm an intelligence officer's wife, not necessarily a highly intelligent one, but I've pieced together perhaps more than Henry suspected. My *God,* that man went nearly four days without sleep . . . and he was worried sick about *you,* Tye. You must be exhausted."

"You know we're hunting someone, then?"

"Obviously. Someone extremely dangerous, with equally dangerous people behind her—"

"*Her?* You know it's a woman?"

"Hank told me that much, a female terrorist from the Baaka Valley. If he hadn't been so tired, I doubt he would have."

"Phyllis," said Hawthorne, leaning forward in a chair next to the widow, looking hard at his old friend from the embassy in Amsterdam. "I've got to ask you some questions about the days before Hank was killed. I know it's not the time, but we don't have any other—"

"I understand. I've been around this scene for years, remember?"

"You're alone here?"

"Not now. My sister flew down from Connecticut to be with me; she's out now."

"I mean you and Hank lived here alone—"

"Oh, yes, with all the usual trappings. Armed navy vehicles cruising around the clock, limousines to pick him up and bring him back from the office, and an alarm system that would frighten rocket scientists. We were secure, if that's your question."

"Forgive me, but obviously you weren't. Someone came in and killed Henry while he was on the phone with me."

"I didn't know it was you, but I discussed that with

both the navy and the police; the regular kitchen phone was off the hook. But in one area you're right—obviously. We have the usual deliveries and repairmen; you can't stop them all, we'd be stigmatized, and probably couldn't order a pizza. Hank generally called the patrols when we expected guests, but over the months he frequently forgot; it was so unnatural here, not like Amsterdam. He called it paranoid."

"In other words, a guy in overalls with a toolbox, or a man in a business suit carrying a briefcase, or a military in uniform might not be challenged," said Tyrell, not asking a question.

"Probably not," agreed the widow, "but to anticipate you, both the navy and the police have this information, the patrol on duty at the time was interrogated at length. The two S.P.'s said that except for a newspaper boy, no one came near the house."

"And they were parked outside the whole time?"

"Not actually, not like the security outside now, but I'd have to say it's not terribly relevant. As I mentioned, they cruised. Hank insisted on that for both practical purposes and neighborly relations."

"Cruised . . . ?"

"Around the block, a distance that takes less than a minute and ten seconds to drive."

"And Hank's 'practical purpose' was just that," said Hawthorne, nodding. "A stationary patrol, marked or not, is a target."

"Unmarked," Phyllis interrupted. "And our neighbors would certainly not appreciate a series of unfamiliar cars parked in front of the house for long periods of time. It's not the turf for it, although it might spice up the street. If I weren't so old, they might think I was running my own cat house."

"You're not old, Phyll, you're a very beautiful woman."

"Ah, the charmer returns. I missed that when you left the embassy."

"So anybody who had access to the security routine here could be Henry's killer. A minute and ten seconds is an hour and ten minutes in tactical, nonchronological time."

"You mean someone in the navy?"

"Or high enough in the military to have access."

"Please be clearer," said Phyllis sternly.

"I can't, not now."

"He was my husband!"

"Then I'll tell you what your husband would have told you, and I'll be as honest as I can. There are things I can't log you into yet."

"That's pure shit, Tyrell! I have a *right* to know! Twenty-seven years' worth of privilege, sir!"

"Come on, Phyll." Hawthorne grabbed Phyllis's hands, holding them in his grip. "I'm doing exactly what Henry would do if he were me right now. Contrary to what I often told him, he was a terrific analyst—maybe not the best in the field, that wasn't his bag—but in the foreseeables department there weren't many in his league. I respected him for that . . . even more for having you as his wife."

"Oh, stop it, you snake-oil salesman," said Phyllis Stevens, smiling briefly, sadly, as she squeezed his hands and withdrew hers. "Get on with your questions."

"It really comes down to three. When and how often and to whom did he mention my name?"

"When you were shot at that beach resort in Maryland—he went out of his mind, thinking he was responsible again—"

"Again?"

"Later, I beg you, Tye," said the widow softly.

"*Ingrid?*"

"It's complicated. Later, please."

"All right." Hawthorne swallowed, his face flushed with the rush of blood to his head. "Go on."

"He said your name, maybe three or four times, demanding that you be given the finest treatment available, and that he'd hang whoever gave you less."

"To whom, Phyll?"

"Hell, *I* don't know. Someone who was tight with whatever you're doing. Hank told him he wanted a full report circulated—no room for error."

"Which means the entire Little Girl Blood circle got it, including the heavyweight."

"What are you talking about?"

"Forget it—"

"I wish you'd stop saying that. In Amsterdam, whenever people who cared about you and saw you come back with an arm in a sling or a swollen face and asked you what happened, all you ever said was '*forget* it.' "

"I'm sorry, really I am." Tyrell frowned, slowly shaking his head.

"Is there anything else, old friend?" asked the widow.

"I can't think of anything. I've got a pattern. As Henry always said, 'There's got to be a pattern, that's what you look for,' when I usually looked for the small pieces."

"But when you found them, that's when Hank put together the patterns. He never stopped giving you credit for that, if not to your face."

"Never to my face. . . . Okay, at least we've got another clamp in the trap for a pathological general, unless there's anything, *anything*, no matter how seemingly inconsequential that you haven't told me, Phyll."

"I suppose there are the calls from London—"

"*London?*"

"They started about seven or eight o'clock this morning, my sister took them, I refused."

"Why?"

"Because, old friend, I've had it! Henry gave his life for this rotten, *rotten* business, and I don't want calls from London, or Paris, or stations in Istanbul, or Kurdistan, or Mediterranean fleet intelligence. For God's sake, the man is dead! Leave him—and me—in peace!"

"Phyll, those people don't *know* he's dead!"

"So what? I told my sister to tell them to call the Navy Department. Let those bastards make up the lies, *I* can't do it any longer."

"Where's the phone?"

"Henry never allowed one in the living room. It's on the sun porch—*they're* on the sun porch—three of them in different colors."

Hawthorne got to his feet and raced through the open French doors to the glass-enclosed sun porch. On a table in the left corner were three phones: beige, red, and dark blue, all partially concealed by a louvered panel that had been spread halfway open. He picked up the red telephone, pressed the O button, and spoke to an operator. "This is Commander Hawthorne, acting attaché for Captain Henry Stevens. Connect me to the senior officer on the N.I. watch."

"Right away, sir."

"Captain Ogilvie, red line," said the voice at naval intelligence headquarters. "Your name's Hawthorne? I'm entering it."

"The same, Captain, and I have to ask you a question."

"On this line I'll answer whatever I can."

"Have there been any messages from London to Captain Stevens's office?"

"None that I'm aware of, Commander."

"I don't want an 'aware of,' Captain, I need—repeat *need*—a confirmation one way or another."

"Hold on." There was silence for roughly ten seconds, then Ogilvie returned. "Nothing from London, Commander. No messages at all."

"Thank you, Captain." Tyrell hung up the phone and walked back into the living room. "There was nothing from London for Henry at his office," said Hawthorne.

"That's crazy," said Phyllis, her head snapped up at Tyrell. "They must have called a half-dozen times."

"I wonder if it's back channel," said Hawthorne. "Do you know which phone the calls came in on?"

"No. I told you, my sister answered. All she said to me was that each time it sounded like the same very official, very agitated Englishman. And each time she told him to call the Department of the Navy."

"But he never did," said Hawthorne. "He kept calling *here*. Why? . . . What else did your sister say?"

"Not much, I wasn't really listening."

"Where is she?"

"Down at the supermarket, getting some things. She'll be back any minute; actually, when you arrived I thought it was she." There was a short burst of a horn from outside. "There she is. The chief will go and help with the packages."

The introductions were brief and rapid, the urgency apparent to the sister. The chief petty officer carried her grocery bags as she was escorted into the living room by Tyrell.

"Mrs. Talbot," he began.

"Joan's fine; Phyll's told me a lot about you. Good Lord, what's happened?"

"That's what we have to find out from you. . . . The calls from London, who were they from?"

"They were simply dreadful, I never felt so uncomfortable in my life!" cried Joan Talbot, the words rushing out. "That horrible man kept asking for Henry, saying it was urgent, and how could he reach him immediately. And *I* had to say we were trying to locate him, and had his office checked with the Navy Department, and he kept telling me the navy said he was unavailable—unavailable, my God, the man's *dead* and the navy won't admit it and I can't say it! It's all sickening."

"There are good reasons, Joan, very good reasons—"

"For putting my sister through this *hell*? Why do you think she doesn't want to, and I won't let her, answer the phone? Either I do or the 'admiral' in the hallway does. Let me tell you. All this time people have been calling for Henry, and she had to say, 'Oh, he's in the shower,' or 'Oh, he's playing golf,' or 'Oh, he's in a meeting somewhere' . . . as if she expected him to walk through the door and ask what's for dinner! What kind of ghouls *are* you people?"

"Joannie, stop it," said Henry Stevens's wife. "Tye is simply doing his job, a distasteful job he has to do. Now, answer his question. Who were the calls from?"

"It was like mumbo-jumbo talk, made worse by that bastard's 'veddy Eenglish' accent, damn near sinister, in fact."

"Who was he, Joan?"

"He didn't give a name, just M something or other, and Special something."

"MI-6?" asked Hawthorne. "Special *Branch*?"

"Yes, that sounds right."

"Christ, *why*?" whispered Tyrell, as if to himself, his mouth stretched, his eyes wandering, seeing nothing but clouds of confusion. "It's got to be deep back channel."

"More mumbo jumbo?" said the sister from Connecticut.

"It may be," admitted Hawthorne. "Only you can tell me. Which phone did the calls come in on?"

"The blue one, always the blue one."

"That's it, the 'blue boy.' Direct, dedicated lines constantly swept for intercepts."

"I'm beginning to understand," added Phyllis. "Whenever Hank wanted to talk to someone in his position in Europe or the Middle East, he always used that phone."

"Makes sense. It's a global network designed for the head honchos of allied intelligence and their counterparts in the military. You can't get any more internationally secure than with a blue boy, except you have to have a number to call, and I don't have one. I'll reach Palisser, he'll get it for me."

"You mean the number in London?" asked Joan Talbot. "If you do, it's on a pad next to the phone."

"He gave it to you?"

"Only after he repeated twice that it would be . . . 'altered in the morning, madam,' each word pronounced as though he were giving a satanic benediction."

"It may not have to be." Hawthorne walked rapidly back into the sun porch, found the pad, and started dialing the fourteen numbers for London. As he did so, he felt a sharp pain in his chest, sharp but hollow, a warning he had experienced too often to count, a warning that had nothing to do with his physical health, instead a state of mind born of instinct. In questioning Phyllis he had hoped to find a gap, a word, a scrap that led to a linkage between himself and the killing of Henry Stevens. He knew he had found it with Henry's having demanded a full circulated report on his condition after Chesapeake Beach, a report demanded as a threat to ensure his proper care, but one that inevitably reached every member of the Little Girl Blood circle, including a Scorpio named Meyers, Maximum Mike Meyers, scourge of civilian thought, who could easily access the routine of a military patrol car guarding Stevens's house. That information was the linkage he had been looking for, but the deep back-channel calls from MI-6, London, outflanking naval intelligence to Stevens's home blue line, was a totally unexpected occurrence, a tactic that engendered panic, thus accounting for the sharp pain in Tyrell's chest. *Axiom:* Beware the outrageously unexpected when it comes from user-friendly territory. Something was off-the-charts, as Poole might say.

"Yes?" fairly shouted the voice from London.

"This is Stevens," lied Hawthorne, hoping the rapidly spoken words would be accepted in the event the man from London knew Henry Stevens.

"For God's sake, Captain, what are you people *doing*

over there? I can't get through to your DCI, and I've been trying to reach you for damn near ten hours!"

"It's been a difficult day—"

"I should hope to kiss a pig, it has! Since we've never met, my name is Howell, John Howell—there's a Sir in front of it in case you're checking a computer, but it's very droppable, I assure you."

"MI-6, Special Branch?"

"Well, I'm hardly the queen's equerry, old man. I assume you're taking all maximum precautions, God knows we are, and so is Paris. We haven't heard from Jerusalem, but those chaps are usually way ahead of us. They've probably got their blighter in a tunnel beneath Mount Sinai."

"So we're in sync, John, and since I've been confined to a crisis meeting most of the day and may be out of the loop, bring me up to speed, will you?"

"You've got to be *joking*!" yelled Howell. "You *are* the running control of Commander Hawthorne over there, aren't you?"

"Yes, of course," answered Tyrell, thinking quickly, desperately trying to find logic within the illogical. "Incidentally, thanks for recruiting him—"

"Geoffrey Cooke did that, rest his soul, not I."

"Yes, I know, but as I say, I just got your message here at the house, there was nothing from you at my office."

"Damn it, Captain, I certainly wasn't going to leave my name or who I was. Your new director at the Agency and I agreed to keep this whole thing so bloody secret, it was to be restricted to the three of us; you were included because you're Hawthorne's control. What the hell *happened*? Didn't your DCI contact you? His secretary, a damned arrogant bitch if I may say so, told me her chap got word from the unit and was on top of things, but how could he be without reaching you?"

"There was a Syrian-Israeli problem," said Tyrell lamely. "It's all over the radio and television now."

"Utter nonsense!" interrupted the chairman of MI-6, Special Branch. "They're simply posturing, both of them. As far as I'm concerned, they can blow each other to smithereens. What we're facing makes their goddamned theatrics insignificant."

"Wait a minute, Howell," said Tyrell quietly, his face growing pale with the panic he had known was on his own personal horizon. "You mentioned a unit . . . are you referring to the coordinated telephone surveillance operation between you fellows and the Agency?"

"This is preposterous! Do you mean you don't know?"

"Know what, John?" Hawthorne's breath was suspended.

"It's *tonight*! Bajaratt claims she'll strike tonight! *Your* time!"

"Oh, my God . . ." said Tyrell, barely audible, exhaling slowly, his face white. "And you say the Agency unit relayed this to the director?"

"Of course."

"You're *sure*?"

"My dear man, I spoke with that bitch secretary myself. She said your DCI was in meetings all over Washington, and specifically, when I called the last time, with the President's Cabinet at the White House."

"The Cabinet? . . . What the hell for?"

"It's *your* country, old chap, not mine. Of course, if it were *our* Prime Minister, he'd be under the protection of Scotland Yard—which he is—not meeting with his Cabinet at 10 Downing Street; too many of those fellows might just care to blow him away."

"It's a possibility here too."

"I beg your pardon?"

"Forget it. . . . You're telling me that the director of the Central Intelligence Agency was aware of this information, and by extension, since he was in meetings, he had spread the word to all those in Washington who should *know*?"

"Look, old boy, he's new and he obviously panicked, don't be too harsh on him. Perhaps I should have been more circumspect. I took the word of our people who said he was an experienced hand, a splendid fellow."

"They're probably right, but there's a small omission."

"What's that?"

"I don't think he ever got the information."

"*What?*"

"You don't have to alter this number, Sir John. I'll burn it and get back to you on normal channels."

"For the love of God, will you please tell me what's going on over there!"

"I don't have time. I'll talk to you later." Tyrell instantly hung up the blue telephone, picked up the red one, and pressed the O button; it was answered quickly. "This is Commander Hawthorne—"

"Yes, Commander, we spoke before," said the operator. "I trust you reached the senior officer of the watch at naval intelligence?"

"Yes, I did, thank you. Now I need Secretary of State Palisser, preferably on this line, if you can manage a secure patch."

"We can, and we'll find him, sir."

"I'll stay on. It's an emergency." As he waited, Tyrell tried to formulate the words he could use to deliver the incredible news to the secretary of state, a revelation Palisser might well find impossible to believe. The coordinated telephone surveillance between London and Washington had *not* been a failure, it had *worked*! Bajaratt had been intercepted, her words recorded: She would strike sometime *tonight*! The insanity was that no one knew about it! . . . That was incorrect, mused Hawthorne, *someone* knew, and that someone had short-circuited the information. Where the hell was *Palisser*?

"Commander . . . ?"

"I'm right here. Where's the secretary?"

"We're having a little difficulty tracing him, sir. We have your red line code, so when we locate him we can patch him directly through to you if you wish."

"I don't wish, I'll stay on."

"Very well, sir."

Again the line was silent, the further delay aggravating the hollow pain that refused to leave his chest. It was past six o'clock, thought Hawthorne, turning his wrist to look at his watch—well past, it was nearing six-thirty. Daylight savings or no, the night had begun. *Goddamn it,* Palisser, where *are* you?

"Commander—"

"Yes?"

"I'm not sure how to put this, sir, but we simply can't locate the secretary of state."

"You've got to be joking!" shouted Tyrell, unconsciously echoing Sir John Howell.

"We reached Mrs. Palisser in St. Michaels, Maryland, and she said the secretary called her, saying that he was stopping at the Israeli embassy and would join her within an hour or so."

"And?"

"We spoke to the ambassador's first attaché—the ambassador is temporarily in Jerusalem—and he said Secretary Palisser was there for roughly twenty-five minutes. They discussed, as he phrased it, 'State Department business,' and then Secretary Palisser left."

"*What* business?"

"We could hardly ask that question, sir."

"Since when does the American secretary of state lapdog over to the Israeli embassy rather than the other way around?"

"I can't answer that, sir."

"Maybe I can. . . . Connect me to the Israeli attaché, and make sure you tell him this is an emergency call. If he's not on the premises, find him."

"Yes, sir."

Thirty-nine seconds later a deep voice came on the line. "This is Asher Ardis of the embassy of Israel. I'm told this is an emergency call from a ranking officer of U.S. Naval Intelligence. This is so?"

"My name's Hawthorne, and I've been working closely with Secretary of State Bruce Palisser."

"A lovely man. How may I be of service to you?"

"Are you aware of an operation called Little Girl Blood? We're on red line, so you can talk."

"I could talk, Mr. Hawthorne, but I know nothing of such an operation. May I assume it is coordinated with my government?"

"It is, Mr. Ardis. With the Mossad. Did Palisser talk to you about two Mossad agents who were flying over to deliver him a package? It's very important, sir."

"A package means so many things, doesn't it, Mr. Hawthorne? It could be a slip of paper, or blueprints, or a case of our outstanding fruit, no?"

"I don't have time for Twenty Questions, Mr. Ardis."

"Neither do I, but I *am* curious. We extended the courtesy of putting your secretary of state in a private room with a secure telephone to Israel so he could reach Colonel Abrams, who is naturally with the Mossad. You'll grant it was a most unusual request and an equally unusual courtesy, do you not?"

"I'm not a diplomat, I wouldn't know."

"The Mossad frequently operates outside normal channels, which is often irritating, but we try to understand its penchant for living up to its image of the clandestine octopus, a mollusk with far-reaching secret tentacles—"

"You're not its biggest fan, I gather," Tyrell interrupted.

"I give you Jonathan Pollard, currently in your prison system for an indeterminate number of years. Need you ask more?"

"Again, I'm not concerned with your interdepartmental rivalries, sir, I'm interested only in Secretary Palisser's visit to your embassy. Did he reach Colonel Abrams, and if he did, what did he say? And since I'm on a red line, you can assume I'm entitled to privileged information—we're working *together,* for God's sake! If you want confirmation, press whatever your code numbers are and get it!"

"You're very excitable, Mr. Hawthorne."

"I'm sick of your *bullshit!*"

"That makes sense to me. An intelligent man's outrage reveals truth."

"I don't need a fucking Talmudic parable! What happened when Palisser reached *Abrams?*"

"In fact, he didn't. The elusive Mossad colonel was unavailable, but when he returns to his office, he has an emergency message to reach your secretary of state, for which we have six telephone numbers, half secure, half not. Does that answer your question?"

In disgust, Tyrell slammed down the phone and walked back into the Stevenses' living room. Phyllis greeted him just beyond the French doors. "A Lieutenant Poole called on the regular line, I took it in the kitchen—"

"*Cathy?* A Major Neilsen? Was it about her?"

"No, it concerned General Michael Meyers, chairman of the Joint Chiefs of Staff. He phoned you. He wants to meet with you right away. He said it's urgent."

"I'll bet it is. He's looking for ducks in his own personal shooting gallery."

6:47 P.M.

The limousine with the license plate DOS1 sped along Route 50, heading south on the eastern shore of Maryland toward the village of St. Michaels. In the back seat, the secretary of state kept pressing the buttons on his secure mobile telephone with increasing irritation. Finally, in exasperation, he lowered the glass partition and spoke to his driver.

"Nicholas, what the hell is wrong with this phone? I can't get anything on it!"

"I don't know, Mr. Secretary," replied the chauffeur provided by the Secret Service. "I've been having trouble with my base radio too. I haven't been able to raise dispatch."

"Wait a minute. You're not Nicholas. Where is he?"

"He had to be replaced, sir."

"Replaced? What for? Where did he go? He was in that seat when we reached the Israeli embassy."

"Perhaps a family emergency. I was called to replace him, that's all I know, sir."

"That's also highly irregular. My office should have informed me, that's absolutely standard."

"Your office didn't know where you were, sir."

"They have this number."

"The phone isn't working, Mr. Secretary."

"*Hold* it, mister! If my office didn't know where I was, how did *you* know?"

"We have our ways, sir. We're behind-the-lines oriented."

"Answer me!"

"I'm only required to give my name, rank, and serial number. That's what we do with the enemy."

"*What* did you say?"

"You set up the general last night, set him up so high the White House put him under surveillance. That's a disgraceful thing to do to a great man like General Meyers."

"Your name, soldier?"

" 'Johnny' will do, sir." The driver suddenly swerved to the left, entering a barely discernible dirt road. He instantly accelerated, racing over the rough, bumpy surface to a small clearing where the first object that struck the eye was a Cobra helicopter. "You can get out now, Mr. Secretary."

The shaken Palisser fumbled for the handle; the door swung open and he lurched outside into the harsh, leveled grass. Ten feet away stood the uniformed chairman of the Joint Chiefs, his right sleeve creased and folded neatly into his shoulder.

"You were a pretty fair soldier in World War Two, Bruce, but you forgot the lessons of combat incursion," said the general. "When you walk into hostile territory, make damn sure which of the occupied can be trusted. You missed one in the White House. If he had interrupted the Security meeting to bring you your messages, he would have been shot."

"Good Lord," Palisser spoke quietly. "You're everything Hawthorne said you were. You're not only willing to stand by and permit the President to be assassinated, you're actually helping the assassin."

"He's only a man, Bruce, a misguided politician on whose watch the armed might of the United States is being decimated. All that will change tonight, the world will change tonight."

"*Tonight?*"

"In a little more than an hour."

"What the hell are you saying?"

"That's right, you wouldn't have any way of knowing, would you? The messengers from the Mossad never reached you, did they?"

"Abrams," said Palisser. "Colonel Abrams!"

"A dangerous man." Meyers nodded. "Because of his warped morality, he can't see the advantages. Incidentally, he rightly trusted no one, so he sent his two people to give you a name, the name of a nondescript little senator who's going to make everything possible—in an hour or so."

"How do you know this?"

"Through someone I'm sure you never noticed—a small, again nondescript, aide to the Security Council, the same man who intercepted the messages for you this morning from that turncoat Hawthorne. Our White House mole's a true yes-man; the President likes him a lot and they talk together. He's also a former adjutant of mine, a lieutenant colonel—I got him the job. We talk too." The general looked at his watch in the light of the descending summer sun. "In a little over an hour, the President, to accommodate this innocuous little senator, will hold a private, off-the-books audience with—guess who, Bruce? I see you just figured it out, and you're right. Little Girl Blood. . . . Then *poof*! The explosion that'll be heard around the world."

"You sick son of a *bitch*!" roared Palisser, stiffening his aged body and rushing forward, his hands outstretched.

The chairman of the Joint Chiefs swung his left arm behind his tunic and whipped a carbine bayonet out of his belt. As the elderly secretary of state grasped the general's throat, Meyers plunged the heavy knife into Palisser's stomach, and with a furious motion yanked the blade up through his chest cavity.

"Dispatch the body," he ordered his master sergeant, "and deep-six the limo off the barge out of Taylor's Island."

"Right on, Maximum."

"Where's the driver?"

"Where no one'll ever find him. Guaranteed."

"Good. This is one of those blanks in history, that's all it is. In an hour it won't matter, nothing will matter. I'm chopping to the White House. I'll be in the second-floor courtesy lounge."

"Hell, you'd better. Someone's got to take charge."

On a dark back street in Jerusalem, in the pounding rain, a figure lay in an alley, his clothes drenched, the blood from his body mingling with the water from the sky and flowing down the cobblestones to the curb. Colonel Daniel Abrams, leader of the Bajaratt enterprise, had been shot six times by a silenced pistol. And an old, heavyset man walked down the Sharafat, secure in the knowledge that he had done the right thing.

37

6:55 P.M.

Bajaratt checked her dress for the most important moment of her life, the justification for a lifetime. As she studied herself in the full-length mirror, she saw the image of a ten-year-old child, looking up at her in wonderment and adoration.

We have done it, you dearest thing to me who was myself! No one can stop us now, for we will change history. The pain from the mountains will vanish as the blood flows across the world, and you and I will be fulfilled, avenged for the horror that was inflicted on us. . . . *Do you remember when the heads of Mama and Papa rolled into the rocks, severed from their bodies, their eyes wide open, pleading with their obscene God who would permit such a thing to happen—pleading perhaps for you and me, who would live with that memory for the rest of our lives? Muerte a toda autoridad!* . . . *We will do it, you and I, for we are one, and we are invincible!*

The image faded as the Baj drew closer to the mirror, now examining the silver streaks in her hair and the coordinated lighter makeup with hints of shadow below her eyes, all designed to produce a face older than her own, but only subtly so. Her outfit was as expensively chic as it was tastefully subdued: a below-the-knees navy blue silk dress with sewn-in padding that filled the space between her breasts and her hips, again subtly, gracefully tailored to create the appearance of a woman in her

624

middle years, doing battle against a fuller figure. A double strand of costly, matching pearls, the pale blue hose, and dark blue Ferragamo shoes completed the look. The total picture was that of a wealthy Italian aristocrat whose presence was a familiar sight on the Via Condotti, Rome's answer to Paris's Saint-Honoré. And to perfectly accessorize the final product, there was a small slate-blue evening purse with a pearl clasp; no one could doubt that these two pearls were as genuine as those above.

On the wrist of this doyenne of haute couture was a delicate diamond-encrusted watch, at first glance the finest of the Piagets. It was not; it was a superbly designed counterfeit, capable of withstanding the battering of a hurricane at sea, with a mechanism so simple yet so strong that it could send a powerful electronic impulse to a receiver fifty yards away, penetrating glass, hard wood, and thick plaster by three abrupt presses on its crown. The receiver of that electric impulse was within the silk lining of the slate-blue purse: a tiny circular module attached to a thin wall of plastique that when detonated set off a second wall in the opposite lining. The total destructive potential was equal to that of twenty-six ounces of nitroglycerin, or the power of a two-hundred-pound bomb. *Muerte a toda autoridad!* Death to the leaders everywhere who ordered death, either by commission or omission.

"*Cabi!*" Nicolo called from the bedroom, startling Bajaratt, who turned away from the mirror and rushed to the door.

"What is it?"

"These foolish gold things will not go through my sleeve! The left one, yes, not my right—"

"Because you're right-handed, Nico," interrupted the Baj, walking inside. "You always have trouble with your right cuff link, don't you remember?"

"I can remember nothing, I can think only of tomorrow."

"Not *tonight*? The President of the United States?"

"Forgive me, signora, but he is a prize for you, not for me. Mine is in New York, and I am so excited! Did you hear her at the airport? Angel said we might spend a 'week . . . end'—a *fine di settimana*—on a *lago* somewhere with her family."

"You'll get to know her better, Nico." Bajaratt inserted the cuff link and stood back, appraising her creation. "You are magnificent, my beautiful dock boy."

"But still a dock boy, signora?" Nicolo broke in, his eyes locked with his creator's. "You never let me forget. You bring me so high, so far, but you never let me forget. Does it give you pleasure?"

"I've brought you to the point where you can be whatever God wants you to be."

"That's very strange coming from you. You have no God, you've made that clear to me. You have a *visione* that I cannot understand, and I am very sorry for you. I cry for you, for you do so much that I truly believe is wrong in spite of this great cause of yours which you do not explain."

"Do not weep for me, Nico. I accept my destiny."

"*Destino?* Such a full word, signora. It is beyond me."

"Let it stay there. . . . Put on your jacket with the brass buttons." The young man did so, and his creator stepped farther back, enamored of what was, in essence, her work of human art. "You are incomparable. Your height, the breadth of your shoulders, the slim, tapered waist, your perfect face crowned by your dark wavy hair. *Splendido!*"

"Stop it, you embarrass me. I have a brother taller than me—he is four inches above six feet, I am only three, if that."

"I met him, of course; he is an *animale*. His face is flat, and his eyes are dull, and he thinks slowly."

"He's a *good* boy, signora, and far stronger than I! If anyone is improper with our sisters, he throws him into a wall ten feet away—I can manage only four or five."

"Tell me, Nico, do you look up to him?"

"I must, for he is older and very protective of our family since our papa died."

"But do you look up to him, respect him?"

"My sisters, all three, adore him. He is now the *padrone*, and he takes care of us all with his strength."

"But you, Nico, *you*? Do *you* adore him?"

"Oh, stop it, signora, it is *non importante*."

"It is for me, my darling boy, for I want you to know why you were chosen!"

"For what?"

"Another question that I will not answer. Tell me! What is your older brother to you?"

"*Aaugh*," shrugged Nicolo, shaking his head. "If you must know, he mistakes his strength for his brains. All he cares to do is run the docks with his muscles. He will do that until another *lupo* comes along and he is replaced with his death. *Stupido!*"

"So now you see! I looked for perfection, and I found it."

"And I think you're *pazzo*. Can I call Angelina—Angel—in Brooklyn, New York? She must have arrived by now."

"By all means. Have your loving conversation, but no longer than ten minutes. We're being picked up by the senator in *twenty* minutes."

"I would like to speak with her alone."

"*Naturalmente*," said the Baj, walking out of the bedroom and closing the door.

7:09 P.M.

Hawthorne was about to explode! Every contact he and Phyllis Stevens could recall in all the intelligence agencies in Washington were either "gone for the day," "unavailable," or "did not care to talk to a commander they never heard of." The usage of the term *Little Girl Blood* meant nothing; the security had been so tight, the circle so closed, there was no one who could take responsibility because no one had been given any access to authority. It was the ultimate circus of nonaccountability; nobody was in a position to transmit the emergency, for none had the authority to reach those in higher authority because he—she—they—were not authorized to do so! The White House switchboard was the worst.

"We get these calls a dozen times a day, sir. If you've got any substance, call the Secret Service or the Pentagon."

The Secret Service was succinct. "Your call is duly noted, sir, and we can assure you the President is fully protected. Now we have work to do, Commander, as I'm sure you do. Good-bye."

Tyrell could not call the Pentagon. Maximum Mike Meyers would be alerted; the head of the Scorpios would cut off all communications.

Bruce Palisser, the secretary of state, was nowhere to be found, nor was his contact in Israel, Colonel Daniel Abrams of the Mossad. What was *happening*?

A phone rang in the sun porch and Phyllis Stevens, who was nearest, raced to it. *"Tye!"* she shouted. "It's Israel. The red telephone!" *Breakthrough?*

Hawthorne lunged out of his chair and ran through the French doors, grabbing the phone from Phyllis. "I'm your contact," he said. "Who's this?"

"Let's be clear with each other," said the voice in Jerusalem. "Who are you?"

"Former Lieutenant Commander Tyrell Hawthorne, temporary attaché to Secretary of State Palisser and the runner to Captain Henry Stevens, U.S. Naval Intelligence. If I have to explain the latter, you shouldn't be on this phone."

"You don't, and I am, Commander."

"What have you got, Jerusalem?"

"Terrible news, but you have to know. . . . Colonel

Abrams was taken out on the Sharafat. The police found his body only minutes ago—"

"I'm sorry, really sorry, but Abrams was flying over two Mossad agents to reach Palisser!"

"I know, I processed their documents. I am—I *was*—Colonel Abrams's personal aide. Your Secretary Palisser left six numbers for the colonel to reach in the United States when he returned. Among them was a red line to you on Captain Stevens's phone."

"Can you tell me anything?"

"Yes, I can, and I hope it can help you. The key is a Senator Nesbitt from your state of Michigan, that was the information our agents were carrying to Mr. Palisser."

"A senator from Michigan? What the hell does it mean?"

"I don't know, Commander, but it's what our intelligence officers were to convey to Mr. Palisser. According to Colonel Abrams, it was of such maximum-classified value, he couldn't trust even diplomatic channels."

"Thank you, Jerusalem."

"You're welcome, Commander, and if you learn what happened to our agents, we'd appreciate your getting in touch as soon as possible."

"If I find out, you'll know." Tyrell hung up the phone; he was a man in total confusion.

7:32 P.M.

Something had gone wrong! Nesbitt's limousine was *late*, nearly *twenty minutes* late! It was not the behavior of an insecure politician who, in one brief appearance at the Oval Office, could bring hundreds of millions into his state, thus guaranteeing his reelection to the Senate. . . . *You'll be picked up at seven-fifteen sharp. It's somewhat early, but in case there's heavy traffic.* The words of

Nesbitt's senior staff aide. Seven-fifteen *sharp*. . . . Oh, *God*! Had Nesbitt been struck by one of his *seizures*? Had he suddenly reverted to a pathetic old man wearing strange clothes and an ill-shapen wig, eluding his keepers and prowling the seedy, sex-ridden streets of the city? Had his demented other self surfaced at this, the most glorious, the most important moment of a life that began in hell in the Pyrenees? She could not accept it, she *would* not accept it!

"Nicolo, my darling," said Bajaratt, her frozen monotone denying the endearment. "Stay here and watch for the senator's car. I'll be inside at the nearest public telephone."

"Per certo," replied the tall dock boy, standing under the canopy, so striking in appearance that strollers' eyes were drawn to him as though he were a celebrity they did not quite recognize, or a motion picture star whose name escaped them.

At a pay phone across from the hotel's front desk, the Baj dialed collect the number in Silver Spring. "It is I," she said, "we have an emergency."

"You may speak, Amaya, we are secure," the voice of the diminutive Arab from the northern suburb quickly broke in.

"Nesbitt's limousine is late, too late to be normal. Is *he* normal?"

"He had a relapse this afternoon, but the doctor saw him—"

"It cannot be!" whispered the Baj gutturally. "Then I shall go there myself. My appointment is scheduled!"

"I'm afraid it's not. It's off the books and you'd never get through the gate without him."

"I will, I must. The Scorpios have turned against me! They're trying to *stop* me. They've got Nesbitt!"

"That's entirely possible, my dear, for they enjoy the status quo and you now threaten it. But don't do anything rash; stay on the phone. I'll call the senator's car on another line."

Bajaratt stood by the phone, her body rigid, her expression as though it were set in concrete. Suddenly, she was aware of a figure standing behind her; she turned around. Without betraying her shock, she stared at the expensively dressed woman from Palm Beach, the middle-aged hostess with bluish hair and teeth too large for her mouth. In her left hand she held a large green purse; it was partially open. Her right hand gripped the handle of an automatic, flesh and steel apparent. "This is as far as you go," said the Scorpio.

"What do you think you'll gain other than a thousand knives across your throat by your action?" asked the Baj icily.

"What do we *lose* if you fuck up what we've got?" said the leader of Palm Beach society.

"Good heavens, such language from a matron of the social rich?"

"And that's the way it's going to stay, Miss Baaka Valley," answered the woman of fine breeding.

"You are so *wrong*," insisted Bajaratt calmly. "The Baaka is *with* you, has *always* been with you. Our mutual *padrone* proved it—"

"He's dead," interrupted the socialite. "The island's gone, we all know that; now we can't reach any of the upper five. Everyone's cut off, and the only reason can be *you*!"

"Let us talk, but not here," said the Baj as she hung up the pay phone. "This call is immaterial, and you certainly cannot shoot me here in the lobby, I believe the word is counterproductive. You'd be taken or shot yourself. . . . Come, there is a side entrance—for deliveries and diplomatic cars—we can talk there. And I assure you, I'm very aware of your weapon. I shall be most obedient, for I'm not armed." As they crossed the lobby toward the brass-bordered side doors, Bajaratt continued. "Tell me, and I ask it only as a compliment to you, how did you find me?"

"I'm sure it won't come as a surprise that I'm quite

well known in Washington," said the woman, walking on the Baj's right, her purse angled into Bajaratt's side, the concealed gun episodically jamming the Baj's hip.

"Nothing surprises me where you are concerned—"

"The fact that I'm a Scorpio, naturally."

"For starters, as you Americans say. . . . How *did* you find me?"

"I knew you and the boy had gone under, obviously using different names, but you couldn't change your appearances, at least not his. I had my secretary check all the elegant hotels with your descriptions, claiming that my poor husband had forgotten your names and where you were staying—a not-uncommon and also well-known habit of his. The rest was simple—Madame Balzini."

"How positively ingenious!" said Bajaratt, opening the door to a loud, exhaust-filled tunnellike area where there was a platform fronting the incessant traffic. "No wonder you were chosen to be a Scorpio."

"Where I'm going to *remain*," interrupted the Palm Beach hostess vehemently. "Where we're all going to remain! We know what you intend to do, and you're not going any further!"

"Do *what*, for heaven's sake?"

"Don't lie to me, Miss Baaka!" exclaimed the social-ite. "Another of our crowd is—was—the personal secretary of the DCI in Langley. Helen's in Europe now, gone and forgotten, but she called me and told me what was happening. She was stunned, frightened to death, but the new Scorpio One demanded that she follow orders, leaving her no choice if she wanted to live and get away. . . . Well, we haven't been given any orders and we *like* what we've got, and nobody's going to change it. You think you're going to be picked up by my old friend Nesbitt tonight? . . . Oh, cut the bulge in your eyes, sweetie, he calls me Sylvia and I introduced you two, remember? With what Helen told me and a call to his house, I put one and one together and came up with 'This is *it*!' I'm afraid his limousine was just in an accident, sorry about that. And now you're going to have another one, a stray bullet during one of our nightly D.C. robberies—and what better place than this howling cavern, where you can barely see, much less hear beyond five feet." The woman named Sylvia glanced around, and then started to remove the automatic from her purse.

"I shouldn't do that if I were you," said the Baj, noting the approach of a huge, mechanized garbage truck stopping for admittance at the street gate.

"You're not me. I'm me."

"My life means nothing," went on Bajaratt, "but I'm told you treasure yours, even to the betrayal of your Scorpios."

"What are you talking about . . . ?"

"Silver Spring, Maryland. Just yesterday I visited the royal house of the diminutive Arab queen bee—you're on her payroll. You sold out the Scorpions for additional money. For money alone, as if you weren't being paid enough."

"That's *absurd*!"

"Then explain it to Scorpio One. You cannot reach him, but I can. I have. If I don't get to the White House tonight, a lengthy note detailing your betrayal will be on his desk in the morning. . . . You forget. I am the Baj. I never stop looking, searching, and when I find weakness, I do my best to convert it to a strength I might not have had." Bajaratt moved slowly to her right as the hostess from Palm Beach, her mascaraed eyes wide, her upper teeth protruding between her gaping lips, stood immobile. "Now, tell me, signora, do you really wish to kill me?"

The answer never came, for the Baj stepped back, as if tripping on the pavement, then fell forward, crashing her shoulder against the Scorpio, sending her into the path of the mammoth garbage truck racing toward the platform. The screeching brakes did nothing to abort the tragedy. The celebrated hostess from Palm Beach was crushed under the front wheels.

"I'll call an *ambulance*!" screamed Bajaratt, racing through the side doors. Instead, she instantly slowed down and walked rapidly, under total control, to the nearest pay phone. She inserted a coin and again dialed collect.

"Yes?" said the Arabian cat from Silver Spring.

"They *found* me," said the Baj coldly in a monotone. "Nesbitt's car was in an accident."

"We know. I have a limousine on its way, it will be there in a matter of minutes."

"The *Scorpios*, they've turned against me!"

"It was to be expected, my child, we both agreed to that."

"Your bitch from Palm Beach, she was the one!"

"It makes sense. She's well connected in the city; she's especially close to the Scorpios' intelligence network."

"She made a point of that, but she'll make no further points. She's dead, under the wheels of a garbage truck, where she belongs."

"Thank you for saving us the trouble. As the Scorpions go down, and they will, we shall rise. . . . Now, to return the favor. The limousines will be switched, you'll be picked up and proceed to the White House where everything's in place. At eight o'clock, two agents of the Federal Bureau of Investigation, their White House security clearances attached to their jacket pockets, will come down from the second-floor courtesy lounge. They will be joined by a liveried chauffeur, also cleared, who will be given a weapon inside in case there is trouble. The three will head down the Oval Office corridor, where they will wait for you to emerge. As I told you before, the code word is 'Ashkelon.' Follow them quickly."

"Agents from the Federal *Bureau* . . . ?"

"Where we penetrate, we penetrate deeply, Amaya Aquirre. It's all you have to know. Now, proceed, child of Allah."

"I am *no* child of Allah, or anybody else's child," said the Baj. "I am only myself."

"Then go yourself, fulfill your mission."

Bajaratt and Dante Paolo, *barone-cadetto di Ravello,* climbed into the limousine, sitting beside the senator from Michigan in the spacious back seat. "I'm so sorry we were delayed," exclaimed Nesbitt, "but can you imagine, we had an accident, our front end smashed to pieces, and the driver of the other car ran from the scene. However, my office is so efficient, they sent another car."

"Your staff is to be complimented, *Signor Senatore.*"

"They're fine people, and let me tell you, the President is so eager to meet you both. He told me personally that he believes he met the baron and his father—your father—when he landed at Anzio in the Second World War. He mentioned that many of the great landowners were very helpful. He was a young lieutenant then."

"Entirely possible," said the *contessa* enthusiastically. "The family was against the *fascisti* from the beginning. While feigning loyalty to that pig, Il Duce, they worked with the partisans, making it possible for scores of downed pilots to escape."

"Then you'll have something in common to talk about."

"Forgive me, Senator, but I was born after the war—"

"Well, naturally, of *course.*"

"My brother is quite a bit older than I."

"I never meant to imply that you were there, Countess."

"*Non importa,*" said Bajaratt, glancing at Nicolo and smiling. "I wasn't so far behind."

The limousine cruised east in Washington's twilight.

Depending on the traffic, they would reach the White House in fifteen minutes or less.

7:33 P.M.

The red-line operator had given Hawthorne the number of Senator Nesbitt's residence; the phone was answered by a woman who either did not know anything or refused to say what she knew. "I'm only the housekeeper, sir. The senator doesn't tell me where he goes and I wouldn't expect him to. I just make sure his meals are ready when he wants 'em."

"*Damn!*" roared Tyrell, slamming down the beige telephone.

"You tried his office?" asked Phyllis, walking into the sun porch.

"Of course. There's an answering machine that spews out banalities for his constituents. . . . 'The senator or a member of his staff will be in touch with you by phone or mail if you will leave your name, address, and number. The senator is always available'—et cetera, *et cetera!*"

"What *about* his staff?" pressed the widow. "When Hank wanted information, he frequently managed to get it from a senior member of someone's staff, quicker than the person he couldn't reach."

"There's a not-so-minor problem. I haven't a clue about Nesbitt's staff."

"Hank did," said Phyllis, rushing to a solid piece of furniture roughly thirty inches high and two feet wide, its dark wood filled with ornate Oriental carvings, a lamp on the top. "This is a file cabinet," she continued, bending down, her fingers roaming along the right side. "Good God, he *locked* it and I never had the combination; he said I shouldn't have it."

"What are you talking about, Phyll?"

"It's a huge Chinese puzzle box, we picked it up years

ago on his Hong Kong tour. If the side release doesn't
open it, you have to press various carved figurines in
sequence."

"What I mean is, what's *in* it?"

"Henry kept up-to-date lists of everyone in Washington, as well as the senior staffs of anyone he might have
to reach in an emergency, including all the senators and
congressmen. He was a—"

"I know," Hawthorne interrupted. "He was a stickler
about things like that. How do we open it?"

"We smash it." Phyllis Stevens reached for a heavy-
based floor lamp, pulling the cord out of its socket.
"Smash away, Tye!"

Hawthorne crashed the thick, leaden base of the lamp
repeatedly against the top of the chest. On the seventh
assault it fell apart, and Tyrell and Phyllis crouched in
front of the destroyed Chinese box, removing the debris,
their hands plunging into the racks of folders.

"Here it is," exclaimed Henry Stevens's widow, pulling out a thick file. " *'House and Senate.'* Everything's
in there!"

The first person Hawthorne reached without an answering machine was not on the top of the senator's staff
list; he was a middle-level aide with a name that began
with the letter A.

"There were rumors that he was going to the White
House tonight, Commander, but I wasn't privy to the
circumstances. I just joined the office, but I have a master's degree in political science—"

"Stay well," said Tyrell, hanging up and turning to
Phyllis. "Next, and look for someone with rank," he
added.

"Here's a better choice," said Phyllis. "She takes dic-
tation."

The second call reached Nesbitt's personal secretary.
Her words caused Tyrell to freeze and the sharp pain
in his chest to explode, spreading to all points of his
body.

"It's really quite wonderful, Commander. The senator has a private meeting with the President this evening. He's escorting the Countess Cabrini and her nephew, the son of a very wealthy Italian baron who's investing heavily—"

"A countess and her nephew?" Tyrell broke in. "A woman and a *young man*?"

"Yes, sir. I suppose I shouldn't say this, but it's quite a coup for my boss. All those millions into our state—"

"When is this meeting?"

"Around eight o'clock; between eight and eight-fifteen, I believe. The White House is always a little flexible about these private, off-the-record things."

"They're meeting in the private quarters?"

"Oh, no, sir, the First Lady was very specific about that, especially since their grandchildren are around. It's in the Oval Office—"

Hawthorne, his face the pallor of death, hung up the phone. "Bajaratt's on her way to the White House!" he whispered. Then he yelled, "The kid's *with* her! Christ, she snaked through every security fence they mounted! . . . That patrol outside, Phyll, are they good?"

"They're not allowed to leave the premises, Tye."

"And I don't have time to set them loose. But I know the way, I passed 1600 to get to the highway, and I've got a State Department patrol car with a button that reads *siren*."

"You're going *alone*?"

"I don't have a choice. I can't reach Palisser, the CIA's either out of the loop, or, worse, in collusion, the Pentagon's off limits, the Secret Service won't listen to me, and the police would put me into a straitjacket!"

"What can I do?"

"Reach every debt Henry had coming to him, every son of a bitch in naval intelligence, or any other spook department he ever worked with, and get me through the White House gate!"

"I've got several in mind, including an admiral Hank got off the hook for giving advice to a defense contractor. He plays poker with the chief of 1600 security."

"*Do* it, Phyll!"

7:51 P.M.

The senator's limousine stopped at the South Gate of the White House; his name was checked off on a list, and he was smartly saluted by the marine guard. In seconds, as prearranged, the driver sped right toward the main entrance rather than left toward the West Wing, where the Oval Office was located. Once at the curb, in front of the short flight of steps, Nesbitt ushered the countess and her nephew out, had short, polite words with the guards flanking the door, and brought them inside.

"This is my colleague from Michigan," he said rapidly. "The other senator from our state." Handshakes were exchanged, names lost in the obvious haste as a photographer emerged from a doorway, his camera at the ready. "As I mentioned to you, Countess, my colleague is from the President's party and was extremely influential in arranging this meeting."

"Yes, I recall," said Bajaratt. "You wished a photograph with yourself, your colleague, and Dante Paolo, all together."

"You too, of course, if you'd like."

"No, signore, my nephew is your catalyst, not I. But please hurry."

Four successive photographs were taken as another figure appeared walking swiftly down the corridor. "I *apologize!*" cried the man in a dark suit as he approached them. "The instructions were somehow off the track. You were to come to the *West* Wing entrance."

"Off the track, my ass," whispered the junior senator

from Michigan to his legislative associate. "Can you imagine the Chief of Staff allowing us in a picture?"

"*Shh!*" mumbled Nesbitt. "Accept the mistake, Josh."

"Sure. . . . Of course."

"If the guard hadn't radioed us, you'd be standing here for quite some time," said the escort, making light of yet another White House error. "Come along now, I'll bring you to the West Wing."

Forty-six seconds later, the short journey traversed quickly through the hallways, the quartet reached the Oval Office and all were introduced—two reintroduced—to the President's Chief of Staff. He was a slender man, not large, and with a pale face, perpetually creased, as if he expected a sudden assault from an area his eyes could not see. Yet, withal, his demeanor was pleasant, nonthreatening, and he spoke in the frank, weary voice of a man overworked.

"It's a pleasure to meet you both," he said, shaking hands with the Baj and Nicolo. "The President's on his way down now, but I hope you will understand, Countess, the meeting will necessarily be brief."

"We asked no more, signore. Only a photograph for my brother, the *barone di Ravello.*"

"Well, the President wanted you to know—he'll probably tell you himself—he wishes that grave matters of state caused the brevity, but the truth is that his very large family, including eleven grandchildren, are visiting him this week, and the First Lady has a very definite schedule."

"What mother, or especially a *grandmother,* doesn't? We Italians are not famous for small families or the chaos that results."

"That's very kind of you. Come, sit down."

"What a magnificent room, is it not, Dante Paolo?"

"*Non ho capito.*"

"*La stanza. Magnifica!*"

"*Ah, si, zietta.*"

"It houses the power of the universe . . . we are so honored!"

"I don't know about the universe, Countess, but certainly a large part of the world. . . . Senators, would you care to sit down?"

"Thanks, Fred, I don't think so," replied the younger senator. "We're all sort of in a hurry, aren't we?"

"Young man . . . ? Mr. Baron . . . ?"

"My nephew is too nervous to sit, signore."

"*Ah, bene*," said Nicolo as if he had only vaguely understood his aunt's words.

Suddenly, from the corridor outside the Oval Office came a booming voice, the figure speaking blocked by the two senators. "*Jesus*, if one more kid punches me in the stomach, or slathers my face, or puts me in a hammerlock, I'll make commercials for birth control!"

President Donald Bartlett briefly, automatically, shook hands with the senators and walked into the room. He was a man in his late sixties, short of six feet, with straight gray hair and the lined, clean-cut features of an aging actor holding on to the enthusiasms of years past. In essence an accomplished politician capable of summoning the required energy and humor for a host of situations. He was a presence that would not be denied.

"The Countess Cabrini and her nephew, the baron of . . . the *baron*, Mr. President," choked the Chief of Staff.

"Good Lord, I'm *terribly* sorry!" exclaimed Bartlett sincerely. "I thought I was early. . . . *Scusi, Contessa. Non l'ho vista! Mi perdoni.*"

"*Parlare Italiano, Signor Presidente?*" asked the astonished Bajaratt, rising from her chair.

"Not all that well," said the President, shaking her hand. "*Per favore, si sieda.*" The Baj sat down. "I had to learn some in the war. I was a supply officer in the invasion of Italy, and let me tell you, we had a lot of help from some of your great families. You know, people who weren't too fond of Mussolini."

"*Il Duce,* the pig!"

"Heard a lot of that, Countess. Before the landings we flew in drops of supplies at night in case things went screwy—*pazzo*—and our troops were cut off heading north. We called 'em distribution points. In fact, I mentioned to the judge here—the senator—that I think I met your brother in Ravello."

"I believe it was our father, Mr. President. A man of honor who could not tolerate the *fascisti.*"

"You're probably right. *Scuzzi di nuovo.* I'm getting so old that decades seem like years! Of course it was your father. You were a mere child, if you were around at all."

"In many ways I am still a child, sir, a child who remembers many things."

"Oh?"

"*Non importa.* May I present my nephew, the *barone-cadetto di Ravello.*" Bajaratt again rose to her feet as Bartlett turned and shook hands with Nicolo, who was appropriately dignified as well as awed. "My brother, who is ready to make substantial commitments to American industry, asks only for a photograph with you and his son."

"It's no problem, Countess. However, I've got to tell you, this young fella may be the next baron, but from where I stand, he could be a wide receiver for the Washington Redskins. . . . Hey, boys, maybe I should stand on a box, this kid dwarfs me!"

"I did my homework, Mr. President," said the White House photographer. "I suggest you both be seated in two chairs behind your desk. Shaking hands, naturally."

As the photographer and the Chief of Staff arranged the chairs, Bajaratt slid her small pearl-beaded evening purse into the cushions of the chair, and as the flashes of the camera erupted, she pressed it farther, completely out of sight.

"That is *wonderful,* Mr. President! My brother will be so enthusiastic, so *grateful*!"

"I'll be grateful if Ravello Industries sees fit to—shall we say—seek an industrial base or two in this country."

"Be assured, sir. Why not discuss the specifics with your two senators? I've made my brother's position clear, and it will not disappoint you, Mr. President."

"I intend to, Countess," said Bartlett, smiling and nodding pleasantly as he and Nicolo got out of their chairs. "At least as long as it takes to have a cool drink and stay away from those hooligans upstairs for a few peaceful minutes."

"You are a *brigante,* signore!" said Bajaratt, laughing, accepting the President's hand. "But I know you love your family."

"I do indeed. Give my regards to your brother."

"*Ma guardi,*" said the Baj, looking at her diamond-encrusted wrist watch; it was shortly past eight o'clock. "My brother. I really should call him on our special telephone in less than a half hour."

"My car will take you back to the hotel," said Nesbitt.

"I'll show you to the portico, Countess," added the White House escort. "I've already arranged for the senator's limousine to be there."

"We've taken up enough of your time, Mr. President. And the baron will be so disappointed if I don't reach him."

"Special phones, special times, special frequencies, even satellites now," said the President. "I don't think I'll ever get used to all that electronic stuff."

"You beat the *fascisti, Tenente* Bartlett! You won on *human* terms, what greater triumph is there?"

"You know, Countess, I've been called a lot of things, good and bad, and it goes with the office. But that's one of the nicest things anyone's ever said about someone like me."

"Ponder it, Mr. President. On this earth we must *all* win on human terms. Otherwise, there is nothing. . . . Come, Paolo, we must think of your father."

8:02 P.M.

Hawthorne drove the State Department car through the South Gate of the White House, having been cleared by red line highest authority, no identifications asked for, the car noted by instant radar the moment it turned into the drive. Phyllis Stevens had done her job, and then some. Tyrell swung right toward the West Wing entrance, screeching to a stop in front of the steps. He got out and raced up the marble stairs to a marine captain who stood in front of a four-man unit of White House security guards. "The Oval Office," said Hawthorne, no equivocation in his order.

"I hope to *hell* you have credentials, Commander," said the marine officer, his hand on his unlatched holster. "They *say* you do, but nothing like this has ever happened, and it's my ass if you're a freak!"

"Freaks don't get through that gate, Captain. Let's go."

"*Hold* it! Why the Oval?"

"I'm going to interrupt a meeting. Which way?"

"*No* way!" shouted the marine, stepping back, slapping his .45 Colt out of his holster and nodding at his unit, all of whom did the same.

"What the hell are you *doing*?" yelled Hawthorne, furious, as five weapons were leveled at him. "You have your orders!"

"They're voided when you deliver an outright lie."

"*What?*"

"There is no meeting!" said the marine officer menacingly. "We got that call fifteen minutes ago, and we checked it out—*I* personally checked it out."

"What call?"

"The same one that cleared you with the emergency watch codes. I'll be damned if I know how you did it, but this is as far as you go—"

"For Christ's sake, what are you *talking* about?"

" 'Locate Zeus,' the man-on-high says. 'Get him out of his meeting and secure him in the cellars—' "

"So far you've got it right—"

"Wrong! There *is* no meeting! We high-tailed it down the hallway here to the O.O., and who do we find but the Chief of Staff. He told us—me to my face—that we should check our logs, that the President hadn't scheduled *anything* for tonight; and if we wanted to take him anywhere, we'd have to go up to the private quarters and convince the First Lady, because the whole family was there, including a passel of grandchildren!"

"That's not the information I have, Captain."

"Well, you can add this to whatever you've got, Commander. Since we're a roving patrol, the Chief of Staff made it clear that if the press had screwed around with us for a little snooping, tabloid style, we could kiss good-bye to the sweetest jobs we'd ever see in the Corps."

"That's *stupid*—"

"I put it a different way, but he got the point in respectful military terms. Now *you're* going to get the point too, freak. You're lockstepping it over to security—"

"Get *off* it, you idiot!" roared Tyrell. "I don't know what games are being played around here, but I know what the *stakes* are! Now, I'm running as fast as I can down that hallway, Captain, and you can open fire if you want to, but all I'm trying to do is prevent someone from killing the *President*!"

"*What* did you say?" The stunned marine officer was suddenly frozen in place, his words barely heard.

"The part you got right, Captain. Get him out of that meeting."

"There is no meeting! The Chief of Staff said—"

"Maybe he doesn't want you to know about it, maybe that's why it isn't on the schedule—maybe, since I'm cleared to get in here—you ought to find *out*! . . . Let's *go*!"

Hawthorne raced ahead, down the long, wide hallway as the leader of the roving guard unit looked at his men and nodded. In seconds the four marines were flanking Tyrell, the captain beside him.

"What are we *looking* for?" the marine officer whispered breathlessly.

"A woman and a kid—"

"A kid . . . a little *kid*?"

"A big kid, a young guy in his late teens."

"What do they look like?"

"It doesn't matter, we'll know them. . . . How much farther?"

"Right around the corner, a large door on the left," answered the captain, gesturing toward a T-shaped cul-de-sac twenty feet ahead.

Tyrell held up his hand, instructing the others to stop and walk slowly as they approached the end of the hallway. Suddenly, there were voices, a cacophony of *"adios," "arrivedércis,"* and *"good-byes,"* followed by the appearance of three men in the opposite east corridor; two were dressed in dark business suits, the third in a chauffeur's gray uniform and visored cap, all with plastic clearance tags attached to their lapels.

"Ashkelon!" cried the chauffeur, addressing someone on the other side.

"Who the hell are *you*?" asked the stunned marine captain.

"FBI, assigned to the State Department for diplomatic security," said the startled man next to the chauffeur, his eyes switching back and forth between the officer and the unseen figures emerging from the Oval Office. "We're escorting the countess to her hotel. Didn't the dispatcher alert you?"

"*What* dispatcher? Bureau or no Bureau, where the Oval is concerned, *our* security calls me with a minimum P.M. lead time of an hour, it's standard!"

"He's lying!" mumbled Hawthorne, moving himself partially behind the marine as he pulled the automatic from his belt. "They used the name Ashkelon, and that means only one thing. . . . *Bajaratt!*" yelled Tyrell suddenly, whipping around and firing into the ceiling, instantly realizing how foolish the warning shot was.

Staccato gunfire erupted, the marine captain hit first, the blood spilling out of his stomach as the other marines spun into the hallway walls. The Ashkelons lunged backward, shooting wildly and shouting, intent only on pulling someone to them for cover while they minimized the crossfire. A marine pivoted around the east corner and shot five rounds, felling the two men who claimed to be federal agents, one of whom kept firing from the fetal position as a woman dashed across the T-shaped cul-de-sac, screaming.

"*Kill* him, kill the *boy*!" she shrieked. "He must not *live*!"

"Cabi . . . *Cabi*!" came the screams from the unseen teenager beyond the corner of the wall. "What are you *saying*? . . . *Auhh!*"

A second marine guard lunged forward, firing two rounds, blowing apart the head of the chauffeur, who fell in Bajaratt's path. Tyrell grabbed the second marine. "Get the President *out* of there!" he shouted. "Get *everybody* out!"

"*What*, sir?"

"Just *do* it!"

Bajaratt shoved the falling dead body of the chauffeur out of her way, grabbed his gun, and ran down the corridor as the marine, joined by his colleagues, raced into the Oval Office. Hawthorne, his weapon extended, crouched and spun around, looking for the woman he once thought he loved but now hated, a serpent with glass eyes and a mouth filled with poison. She was nearing the end of the hallway! Tyrell sprang forward with such force, the wound in his thigh split open, the blood spreading throughout his trousers as he raced after her.

When he was halfway down the corridor, there was a massive explosion from the Oval Office. Horrified, Hawthorne whipped around, stunned by the smoke and the flying debris, then instantly relieved by the sight of blurred, excited figures on a lawn beyond an open side door at the far end of the hall. The marines had done the job; the President and several others were running around in panic, but they were out of the White House, out of harm's way. Spinning again, Tyrell was paralyzed—where was *Bajaratt*? She had disappeared! He ran, reaching a large circular room with three hallways beyond a wide staircase; she had chosen one of them—which *one*? Suddenly, sirens and ear-shattering bells echoed throughout the hollow caverns of the executive mansion. Then there were voices—screams, commands, mass hysteria—seemingly from everywhere and nowhere. And through the chaos a tall figure walked slowly down the staircase, a figure with one arm, his face taut, his eyes wide and bright, as a cruel man looks observing an act of brutality that excites him profoundly.

"It's *done*, isn't it, General?" shouted Hawthorne. "You really *did* it, didn't you?"

"*You!*" yelled the chairman of the Joint Chiefs as streams of marines and civilians raced out of the hallways, crossing the large circular room toward the Oval Office corridor, oblivious of the celebrated general and the bleeding man who limped to the staircase below the soldier. "And you were too late, weren't you, *mister*?" Meyers moved his arm behind him as he stared at the gun in Tyrell's hand. "I've faced a thousand weapons and none have ever frightened me."

"You don't have to worry about this one, General. I may blow both your kneecaps off, but I want you alive. I want the rest of your wriggling carcass for all the world to see—because I wasn't too late. You *lose*."

Without warning, without the slightest body movement, Meyers arced his arm from behind him, and in a single motion brought the blade of his bayonet slashing down across Hawthorne's chest. Tyrell leapt backward, firing his gun as rivulets of blood spread throughout the shirt under his jacket. And General Maximum Mike Meyers fell forward down the staircase, most of his neck obliterated, a mass of white tissue and soaked, bright red flesh, his head more off the rest of his body than on.

Bajaratt! *Where?*

A gunshot—a scream! From the far right hallway. Dominique had killed again—no, *Bajaratt!*

Bunching his shirt together to absorb the blood, Hawthorne limped to the corridor where the shot and the scream had come from; the walls were soft yellow, the light from crystal chandeliers, not neon tubes. It was a short hallway with anterooms, probably for social functions, where invited guests primped for state occasions, two doors on the right, two on the left. There was no corpse in evidence, but there were blotched streaks of red, as if a body had been dragged into the second door on the right. A killer setting a trap had made a mistake that only another killer would recognize. In such a situation, one did not follow the blood, one looked in another direction. Tyrell sidestepped down the hallway, his back against the left wall, the wound in his thigh now draining profusely. He reached the first door and, summoning what strength he could, spun around, crashing his shoulder into it while twisting the knob with his left hand. The ornate room was empty, several full-length mirrors reflecting Hawthorne's image; he limped quickly back into the hall, into the pandemonium of screaming sirens and deafening bells. He proceeded to the second door in the left wall; it was the assassin's illogically logical sanctuary, he knew it, he felt it.

Once again, finding what was left of his reserves, he turned the knob and propelled his body against the door, sending it crashing back into the inside wall. *Nothing!* . . . Then, in a microsecond flash of understanding, he whipped around and lunged to the right—for knowing her pursuer, Bajaratt had *reversed* the trap! She came flying through the open door from the room across the hallway, half her clothes torn to shreds, her face the face of the demonically possessed, her eyes wild, her features stretched in fury. She fired twice, the first bullet creasing Tyrell's left temple as he swung his head away, the second shattering a mirror on a dressing table, the third attempted shot . . . a *click*. The gun she had taken from her fallen colleague was out of bullets.

"*Shoot!*" screamed Bajaratt. "*Kill* me!"

Thunder cracked across Hawthorne's mind, bolts of lightning searing his inner eyes, blinding his thoughts yet leaving him the torture of outer sight. Opposing wind shears of loathing and remembered love collided as he stared at the contorted features of the hellhound who had slept in his arms in another time, in another life. "Whom would I be killing?" he asked weakly, taking long gasps of breath. "Dominique or the terrorist they call Bajaratt?"

"What does it *matter*? Neither of us can live any longer, can't you understand that?"

"Part of me does, another part isn't quite sure."

"You're *weak*! You were always weak and filled with sickening self-pity! You're *pathetic*! Go on, *do* it! Haven't you the courage?"

"I don't think courage has anything to do with it. It doesn't take bravery to kill a quartered mad dog. But maybe it takes a little more courage to capture it, dissect it, and learn what makes it diseased. Also, to learn what other mad dogs travel in the pack."

"*Never!*" shrieked Bajaratt, flicking the gold bracelet on her wrist and lunging at Hawthorne. His thigh crippling him, Tyrell fell back under her attack, his strength sapped; he was almost no match for the maniacal strength of the fanatic. Then, as the gold bracelet came nearer his throat, blocked only by his grip on her wrist, he saw the open hole of a jagged gold point. It was dripping fluid meant for him. He fired. Into her chest.

Bajaratt gasped and rolled over, trembling in the rattle of death. "*Muerte a toda—*" The head of Amaya Aquirre fell to the right, into the comfort of her shoulder. Somehow, her face became younger, the lines of hatred diminished, a ten-year-old child at peace.

— EPILOGUE —

The International Herald Tribune
Paris Edition—(Page 3)

ESTEPONA, Spain, Aug. 31—It was reported yesterday that police, accompanied by the American ambassador, sealed off the villa belonging to retired former justice of the United States Supreme Court Richard A. Ingersol, who suffered a fatal heart attack while attending his son's funeral in Virginia. Justice Ingersol was a prominent member of the exclusive community Playa Cervantes, on the Costa del Sol. The American ambassador's presence was deemed proper pursuant to instructions from Ingersol's survivors that his personal papers be removed and returned to the United States, including those that contained confidential information and advice sought by U.S. government officials.

The Washington Post
(Front page, lower right)

General Meyers Found Dead; Termed a Suicide

WASHINGTON, D.C., Sept. 5—The body of Gen. Michael Meyers, chairman of the Joint Chiefs of Staff, was discovered early this morning in the bushes several hundred yards from the Vietnam Memorial. His death was attributed to a massive

651

bullet wound to his neck, the weapon fired at close range, said weapon found gripped in the general's hand. The motive for suicide is best described in Meyers's own words delivered in a speech last May to the Forever America convention. "Should the time come when my infirmities determine that I cannot fulfill my commitments to the best of my ability, I shall quietly take my own life rather than become a burden to the country I love. If I had my wishes, it would be among the troops who served me and the nation so magnificently." The general, a former prisoner of war, sustained multiple wounds in the Vietnam action.

Highlights of Meyers's life and military career appear in the obituary section of this paper. A Pentagon spokesman said its flags would be lowered to half mast for a week, and that there would be a minute of silent prayer at noon today.

The New York Times
(Page 2)

Is There a Purge?

WASHINGTON, D.C., Sept. 7—Sources close to the CIA, Naval Intelligence, and the Immigration Service say that a massive reevaluation of numerous employees, as well as stringer personnel under loose contracts to the three departments, is under way. No one will go on record as to what prompted this action, but it has been confirmed that several dozen arrests have been made.

The Los Angeles Times
(Page 47)

MEXICO CITY—Two American pilots, Ezekiel and Benjamin Jones, appeared at the offices of *La Ciudad,* a Mexican tabloid, claiming to have information about the "disappearance" of Nils Van Nostrand, the multimillionaire international financier and adviser to the past three administrations, as well as select committees of the Congress. A spokesman for Mr. Van Nostrand said he had never heard of the two brothers and was amused to learn that Van Nostrand had "disappeared," as he was merely taking a three-month world cruise, a trip he had promised himself for years. The charter service in Nashville, Tennessee, where the pilots claimed to have been hired, said it had no record of their employment. This morning it was reported that two men fitting the description of the Joneses stole a Rockwell jet, and under false aircraft identification flew south, presumably to Latin America.

"Now you know the truth, *famiglia Capelli*," said Nicolo, sitting nervously forward in a chair, his chest strapped under his jacket, his left arm in a sling. They were in the spacious living quarters above the delicatessen-restaurant. "I am only a dock boy from Portici, although I'm told there is a great family in Ravello who will accept me as their own, for they lost a son not unlike myself. . . . I cannot do that, for I have been false to myself long enough, lied to people long enough."

"Don't be so hard on yourself, Paolo—*Nico*," said Angel Capell from a chair across the room, a tactic devised by her doubting father. "My attorney spoke with the government people—"

"Her 'attorney,' Papa!" cried the actress's younger brother, laughing. "Angelina has an *attorney*!"

"*Basta!*" said the father. "Perhaps if you work hard enough, *you* may be your sister's *avvocato*. . . . What did this lawyer say, Angelina?"

"It's a government thing, Papa, everything is *silenzio*. Nicolo has spent the last four days in isolation, being questioned by dozens of officials, telling them everything he knew. There were those who wanted to put him in prison for years, but our laws require a trial. Everyone accused of a crime is guaranteed an attorney for his defense—and frankly, Papa, I guaranteed the best lawyers my attorney could find to defend him." Angel Capell, née Angelina Capelli, paused, blushing slightly as she smiled at Nico. "Naturally, there'd be a lot of publicity and, I'm told, a great deal of embarrassment for lots of people all over the place, in and out of the government, helped that terrorist because they thought they could get money from her."

"*So?*" thundered Capelli. "This is all *incredibile!*"

"No, Papa. Among the classified statements made by the marines and the naval officer in charge, each clearly heard the woman order Nicolo killed—*killed*, Papa!"

"*Madre di Dio*," whispered Mrs. Capelli, staring at Nico. "He's such a good boy, maybe not so perfect, but not *cattivo*."

"No, he's not, Mama. He comes from the streets, as so many of our young people do who roam in gangs and act stupidly, but he wants to better himself. How many dock boys in Italy have gone to high school? Nico has."

"Then he won't go to prison?" asked the Capelli brother.

"No," replied Angel. "As long as he swears to say nothing, they accept the fact that he was a puppet—*un fantoccio*, Papa—for that terrible person. The attorney has arranged the papers, and Nico will sign them this afternoon."

"*Scusa*," said the elder Capelli, his eyes wide in bewilderment. "Your friend here—the *barone-cadetto* . . . this Paolo, or this *Nicolo*—spoke of a great deal of money in Napoli, say nothing of the envelope filled with so much *denaro* I should work six months to see such a profit—"

"It's all *there*, Papa," answered Angel. "My attorney checked with the bank in Naples. . . . The instructions are clear. If Nicolo Montavi of Portici, with proper identification, claims it, it is his. In the event of his death, it reverts to the depositor who does business with the bank; and if neither claims it within six months, the funds are to be transferred to a confidential account in Zurich."

"All that is true, Signor Capelli," said Nicolo. "I knew nothing about my employment other than that it would be a *sciarada,* a game for money, which, to be honest, the docks of Portici play many times."

"And this money is still available to you?"

"It wasn't meant to be," acknowledged the dock boy, a flash of anger crossing his face as he briefly closed his eyes. "As Angelina has told you, she ordered me to be killed," he added in a quiet monotone.

"But now it *is,*" exclaimed Angel. "My attorney said that all we have to do is fly to Naples, to the bank, and it's all *Nico's!*"

"*We* fly . . . ? You both together?"

"He is an *innocente,* Papa. He'd get on the wrong plane."

"How much money is there?"

"A million American dollars."

"Take your *avvocato* with you, Angelina," said Angelo Capelli, fanning his face with a menu. "You must have a proper chaperone, but if your attorney is anything like your *agente,* the worm who changes your name, I put a *maledizione* on him too!"

Dear Cath:

It was great seeing you yesterday, and even better to know you're going to be okay after a stretch. You looked terrific, by the way, but then, you always do to me. I'm writing this letter so you won't have a chance to pull that superior-officer stuff with me, or talk to me like I was your nerd kid brother who always gets lost in a shopping mall, okay? I appreciate this here leave they gave me, but the truth of the matter is that I don't care to take it. I know I talked some about my daddy, and your saying you didn't even know he was a big lawyer and all, but I guess I didn't mention that Daddy retired last year. He wasn't that young, Cath. You might say my little sister and I were late babies on account of they were both in their forties. As a fact, Daddy claimed that's how Sis and I got our brains, because his and Momma's were fully developed, which, of course, wouldn't stand up in any biological study of heredity. But there isn't any overpowering reason for me to go home because they're not there much. They're traipsing all over Europe like a couple of kids, and when they wear out Europe, they'll head elsewhere—last time I heard it was someplace called Adelaide in Australia on account of there's a great casino—Momma loves to gamble, and Daddy likes to have a few bourbons with the foreign folks and has a hell of a time. I thought about going out to see my little sister, she and I pretty much always got along, but she's heavy dating a guy who's got his own company and wants to steal her away from where she's at, like with a senior vice presidency, and when I called her, she said, "Don't you dare come out now, big brother, because he'll offer you the job!" I guess she's got a point, Cath. The kid's good, very inventive, but I taught her most of what she knows. Gosh, I'm a hell of a prize for anyone in the private sector! Okay, okay, so maybe I'm exaggerating a bit, but I know enough to stay away.

What'll I do? I'm going back to the only home I've got right now, to the base, and I hope you don't have a problem with that—my leaving without saying good-bye in person, I mean. Now may I say something as it pertains to you, Major? I believe you've got a fair amount of thinking to do, if you'll pardon me. I know you, Cath, and I've watched you for almost five years now, and I don't

*have to tell you that I truly love you, sometimes in
my thoughts profanely, but I know when not to
continue the march. Also, you're at least maybe
seven or eight years older than I am, and I don't
care to take advantage—just kidding, Major! All
I'm saying is that you've got a couple of options
that I don't have and one of them is with a guy I
truly respect, a man who's a real man because
among other things, he doesn't go around thinking
he's got to prove it. He just is. I first learned that
when Charlie was killed, and I was way out of line.
But you know what happened then, and, as I recall,
he had a talk with you too. Times like that tell you
a lot about a guy, you know what I mean? Tye
may have jumped ship, as they say, but in my
lexicon he's just about everything that's implied in
the bullshit phrase "an officer and a gentleman."
Like I said, he just is, although he'd probably never
talk to me again if I told him to his face.*

*I know I've always said you were born to run
the air force and things like that, and you probably
could, but that was before Tye told me what you
said you might have done if you could have afforded college. Maybe you could do it now, like
the commander suggested. I sure hope you think
about it, then maybe I'll run the air force.*

*The hospital told me you got the uniform.
Frankly, I think you look terrific in a dress.*

*I love you, Cath, I always will. Please think
about what I said. Incidentally, I'd make a hell of
an uncle for your kids. How many families have
a real genius to help with the homework? Just
kidding—not!*

Jackson

In her blue air force uniform, Major Catherine Neilsen
sat in a wheelchair alone at a table in the hospital's

outdoor restaurant lounge overlooking the Potomac. In front of her was a tall glass of iced coffee; across the table in a metal ice bucket a half-bottle of white wine was chilling. It was early evening, the orange sun settling in the western sky, casting long shadows over the rippling waters below. Movement at the glass doors caused her to look over as the figure of Tyrell Hawthorne limped, weaving through the seated visitors and patients, toward their table at the railing. She quickly shoved Poole's letter into her shoulder bag.

"Hi," said Tyrell, sitting down. "You soften a uniform considerably."

"I was sick of the hospital attire, and since I couldn't go shopping, Jackson had this flown up from the base. . . . I ordered you some Chardonnay, I hope that's all right; they don't serve the hard stuff."

"It's probably too good; my stomach may revolt."

"Speaking of which, or close to it . . . ?"

"The new stitches are holding nicely, thanks, but then, they're bound in cloth cement. The marine captain's better off; the bullet went right through his side, messy but clean."

"How did the meeting go?"

"Try to imagine a cage full of ocelots racing around in the mud. . . . They really don't know what hit them, or how it all got through their impenetrable security."

"Come on, admit it, Tye, the whole strategy was ingenious."

"That doesn't wash, Cathy. It was ingenious because we were so flawed internally, a Mack truck could have driven through the gaps. *Christ,* the kid was all over the papers, the ersatz countess way in the background, I do admit, but still she was there. Where were the super counterintelligence yuppies who employ all those marvelous computers that check and cross-check and triple-check?"

"You didn't join up early enough and Poole wasn't operating the computers."

"I'd like to believe that about me, but, as usual, there were too many accidents . . . Poole, I'll buy—you too, lady. You were outstanding. . . . Anyway, Howell—Sir John Howell—of MI-6, was on the speakers in the White House Situation Room. London's rounded up four of—Bajaratt's—accomplices; the rest, if there are any more, they figure have flown back to the Baaka. Paris was *really* good. The Deuxième sent out a signal that the Baaka Valley unit had to figure was the one it was waiting for. At two o'clock in the morning it was announced over all the radio and television stations that an emergency meeting of the Chamber of Deputies was called into immediate session. Nothing short of a global catastrophe, a terrible event that was temporarily being kept quiet could produce such an action. They caught five terrorists getting the hell out of there through a single exit."

"What about Jerusalem?"

"They're beautiful. They won't say—just that everything is under control. Also, Van Nostrand's death will be covered. Somewhere down the road, or maybe an ocean, it'll be announced that he had a heart attack or an accident, and be eulogized in absentia."

"The White House?"

"They're holding to the story of Oval Office renovation, which has supposedly been going on at the White House for a couple of weeks, thus eliminating the tours. If they need it, they've got a mocked-up schedule from the Army Corps of Engineers as well as one from an outside construction company."

"Will that wash?"

"Who's going to contradict it? The timing was right; the President was upstairs with his family, and the explosion was a lot louder inside than outside."

"People were *killed,* Tye, and that was all damned messy!"

"The Secret Service moves quickly and they knew exactly what to do." A waitress approached; amenities were exchanged as the aproned woman opened the bottle of wine. "Thanks," said Tyrell. "We'll order later."

"So that's that," said the major, watching Hawthorne drink most of his wine in several swallows, the lines of weary exhaustion all too apparent on his face.

"That's that," agreed Tyrell. "It's not the end of it, you know, it's only the beginning. Before long the leaks will begin and the news will spread to the crazies everywhere. 'How close they came, how she nearly pulled it off!' The cry of 'Ashkelon' will probably be replaced by 'Bajaratt—remember *Bajaratt*' . . . otherwise known as Dominique—Dominique Montaigne." Hawthorne's voice trailed off as he refilled his glass. "I hope we've learned something," he added, barely above a whisper.

"What would that be?"

"Know every goddamned link in your secret chain of command, everyone who's accountable, or throw the whole thing out. Go public."

"Wouldn't that create confusion, even hysteria?"

"I don't think so, and I've thought about it. In war, an imminent bombing raid is announced by sirens and searchlights, and by and large the citizens calmly go to the shelters, knowing that those trained for the event will do their best to protect them, protect the interests of the country. It's not that much different, but it could be a hell of a deterrent. . . . Suppose the FBI, in conjunction with the CIA, had held a nationally televised press conference—an alert, actually—declaring that a woman and a young man, entering the country illegally, were on a mission from the Baaka Valley . . . et cetera, et cetera. Do you think Dominique"—Hawthorne paused, breathing deeply while gripping his glass—"*Bajaratt* could have gotten away with Palm Beach or New York? I doubt it; somewhere an enterprising reporter would have made the connection, at least asked questions that went beyond a carefully constructed background. It's possible one or two did; a man from *The Miami Herald*, and a red-headed specialist in dirt named Reilly."